NATIONAL
GEOGRAPHIC

GUIDE TO THE
National Parks
of Canada

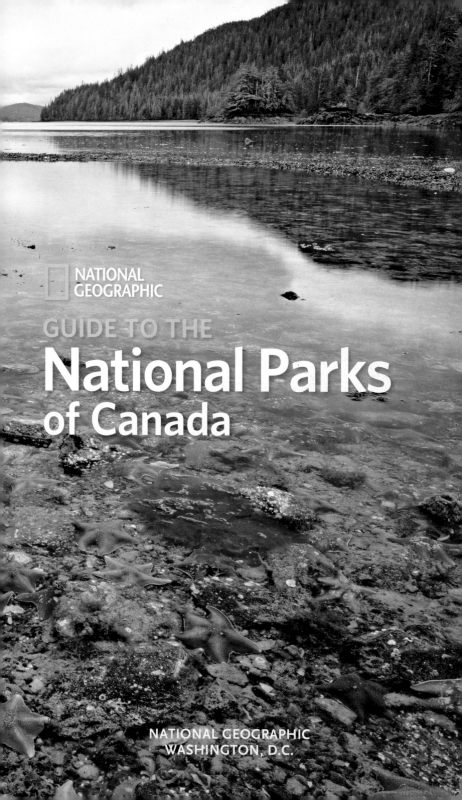

NATIONAL
GEOGRAPHIC

GUIDE TO THE

National Parks
of Canada

NATIONAL GEOGRAPHIC
WASHINGTON, D.C.

CONTENTS

Cover: Cavell Lake, Jasper National Park, Alberta.
Pages 2-3: Bat Star *(Asterina miniata)* group, Gwaii Haanas National Park Reserve, British Columbia.
Opposite: Winter sunrise on Waskesiu Lake, Prince Albert National Park, Saskatchewan.

Plains bison, Riding Mountain National Park, Manitoba

CANADA'S GIFT TO THE EARTH

Since humans first walked this planet, our footsteps have touched nearly every part of the globe. Marked by these travels, we have developed an incredible diversity of cultures, adapted to the various climates and landscapes that the world has presented. To understand a culture, one must examine the land that shaped it. To understand the Aboriginal peoples of Canada, and the many who subsequently settled and adapted here, one needs to understand Canada's landscapes—their climates, forests, plants, wildlife, and spiritual places. The goal of Canada's national parks system is to protect and present outstanding examples of each of

Canada's 39 natural regions. With 28 natural regions so far represented by national parks, and a total national park area greater than all of Germany, Canadians proudly offer travellers one of the world's greatest opportunities to connect to the grandeur and the intimacy of nature and to experience unforgettable moments of personal discovery.

I will never forget the rain forest of Pacific Rim National Park Reserve, where I gained an insight into the culture of the Nuu-chah-nulth First Nations, or the challenging hikes in the mountains of Banff and Yoho, which reminded me of the courage of the early explorers. The mixed prairie

terrain of Grasslands National Park inspired me to reflect on the massive bison herds that once supported native peoples. Discovering Forillon National Park aboard a kayak, one can be rendered speechless by the dramatic landscapes, where people have lived in harmony with nature for thousands of years.

Such voyages of external discovery inevitably become voyages of internal discovery. Through them, we understand more about who we are, and the essential connections that humans must have with the environment that nurtures us. Canada's Aboriginal peoples certainly understand this. Many of these places remain sacred to them, and one of Parks Canada's great achievements in the past decade has been the manner in which we have protected these areas in partnership with first peoples.

Generation by generation, Parks Canada has put together one of the world's largest networks of protected places—some 42 national parks, 167 national historic sites, and 4 marine conservation areas. One of the early visionaries of the world conservation movement, James B. Harkin, the first leader of what is now Parks Canada, wrote, "National Parks are maintained for all the people—for the ill, that they may be restored, for the well that they may be fortified and inspired by the sunshine, the fresh air, the beauty. . ."

Canada was the first country in the world to establish a dedicated national park service, and has since protected a network of wilderness areas of truly global significance. As Parks Canada's passionate and expert team journeys into its second century, we are inspired by the importance of what we do and strengthened by the knowledge that, as the World Wildlife Fund has recognized, our work is truly a "Gift to the Earth."

I am proud to be a member of an extraordinary team of exceptional Canadians. We look forward to offering you a warm, cheerful, and knowledgeable welcome to some of the greatest places on Earth. If you have already discovered some of the wonders of Canada's vast network of protected wilderness, this book will encourage you to explore further. If you are thinking about visiting us for the first time, I can promise you good memories that will last a lifetime. Come discover. Be inspired.

— ALAN LATOURELLE
Chief Executive Officer
Parks Canada

Dawn, Ingonish Beach, Cape Breton Highlands National Park, Nova Scotia

USING THE GUIDE

Each of Canada's 42 scenic parks offers you fun, adventure, and splendour. Exploring the parks can be done on your own, with a guide if you choose, or perhaps only with a mandatory guide or outfitter, depending on the accessibility, terrain, and safety of the environment.

Our coverage of each park begins with a portrait of its natural wonders; ecological setting; history; and, sometimes, its struggles on behalf of endangered species and its means of protecting its fragile environment from human intrusion. These parks were established not only for people to enjoy but also for preservation of whole ecosystems. Nine of the parks have been designated UNESCO World Heritage sites for their outstanding natural or cultural values; and eight parks form the core protected area of Canada's 15 International Biosphere Reserves.

Before starting off on your own, use this guide to preview the parks. You'll notice that each park introduction is followed by the following three how-and-when sections:

How to Get There

Many of the national parks are not in close proximity to one another, so you may need to plan several trips to make the most of what they have to offer. Allow enough time in your travel schedule to get from place to place, as roads may be rugged or crowded, and base your itineraries on time rather than on mileage. When visiting the more remote destinations, contact the park staff for guidance on how and when to go.

When to Go

All parks have a lot to offer at different times of the year. To avoid crowds, visit a popular park during the off-peak months (April, May, or late August), and time your arrival for early on a weekday. In many parks, fall is glorious, and autumn vistas coincide with a relative scarcity of visitors. Summer brings wildflowers, and with winter comes snow-swept beauty that beckons backpackers, campers, cross-country skiers, and snowshoers. Most parks are open year-round, but off-season visitor facilities may be limited or nonexistent. Consult the Information & Activities section for each park.

How to Visit

Don't rush through a park. Give yourself time to savour your surroundings. No matter how long you decide to stay, the How to Visit section recommends specific itineraries and suggests the amount of time to allot. In the parks of the Far North, the visitor must allow extra time for contingencies related to travel schedules and weather. Although this guide offers specific plans, don't be afraid to explore on your own or, if necessary, with a guide. And don't neglect the Excursions at the end of many park entries. They generally include national historic sites within 100 km (60 mi) of the parks.

OTHER FEATURES OF THE GUIDE:

Maps

The park maps were prepared as an aid in planning your trip. For more detail on trails and other facilities inside a park, call the park, or visit the Parks Canada website at www.parkscanada.gc.ca.

Always use park maps or detailed topographic maps when traveling within park borders. Park maps indicate specially designated wilderness areas that are managed to retain their primeval beauty. They also include hiking trails, which are marked for safety or protection of environmental species, and which you should not stray from.

For a list of map abbreviations, see p. 351.

Information & Activities

This section, which follows each park entry, offers detailed visitor information. Call, write, or visit the park's website *(www.parkscanada.gc.ca)* for further details.

Regional brochures for the parks can be downloaded online at www.parkscanada.gc.ca/eng/voyage-travel/index/pdf.aspx.

Entrance Fees. The prices listed in Canadian dollars throughout the book are average prices. The daily entrance fees at the time of printing range from $5.80 to $9.80 for adults; $4.90 to $8.30 for seniors (65 and older); $2.90 to $4.90 for youth (ages 6–16); and $14.70 to $19.60 for a family or group (up to seven people in a single vehicle). You can purchase daily entry passes at the park. Check the Parks Canada website *(www.parkscanada.gc.ca)* for all current prices.

Visitors can purchase online an annual Parks Canada Discovery Pass for entry into national parks, national marine conservation areas, and national historic sites. The pass provides unlimited access to 100 park properties. The current cost for the annual Discovery Pass is $67.70 for an adult, $57.90 for seniors, $33.30 for youth, and $136.40 for a family/group. The passes are available at www.parkscanada.gc.ca/pass or by phone at (888) 773-8888, and at information or visitor centres within individual parks.

Pets. Although you might want to bring your pet along, pets can attract and antagonize wildlife. If they are permitted on hiking trails, they must be leashed. Refer to specific park information or inquire ahead for restrictions.

Accessible Services. This section of the guide lists places within the parks, including visitor centres and trails, that are accessible to visitors with disabilities.

Special Advisories
• Take care when visiting parks; accidents do occur. Most of them are caused by recklessness or failure to heed warnings.

• Stay away from wild animals no matter how harmless they may appear. Do not feed them or touch them—not even the smallest animals.
• Try not to surprise a bear. Wear bear bells, whose jingle will alert them to your presence. If one approaches, scare it off by yelling, clapping your hands, or banging pots. Store all food in bearproof containers; keep food out of sight in your vehicle, with windows closed and

Quttinirpaaq

Aulavik

Ivvavik

Vuntut

YUKON

NUNA

NORTHWEST TERRITORIES

Tuktut Nogait

Kluane

Nahanni

Ukkusiksalik

C   A   N   A

Wood Buffalo

BRITISH COLUMBIA

Gwaii Haanas
(both national park reserve and national marine conservation area)

Wapusk

ALBERTA

Jasper

Elk Island

Prince Albert

MANITOBA

Yoho
Glacier

Banff

Pacific Rim
Mount Revelstoke

Gulf Islands

Kootenay

Waterton Lakes

SASKATCHEWAN

Grasslands

Riding Mountain

ONT

Map Key

■ National Park or National Park Reserve
□ National Marine Conservation Area

0   400 miles
0   400 kilometers

doors locked, or suspend it at least 4.5 m (15 ft) aboveground and 3 m (10 ft) out from a post or tree trunk.
• Know your limitations. If you are not fit, don't overexert yourself.
• Boil or chemically treat water that doesn't come from a park's drinking-water tap.
• Heed all park warnings—they are posted for your protection.
• Always plan for delays: passes closed by snow; scheduled pickups delayed because of weather conditions; road blockages resulting from construction, fallen rocks, landslides, or smoke. Check road regulations as you enter a park. Along some roads you will not be able to manoeuvre large campers or RVs.

Campgrounds. The Campground Reservation Service (877-RESERVE, *www.pccamping.ca*) handles reservations for 20 parks: Banff, Bruce Peninsula, Cape Breton Highlands, Elk Island, Forillon, Fundy, Georgian Bay Islands, Gros Morne, Gulf Islands, Jasper, Kejimkujik, Kootenay, Kouchibouguac, La Mauricie, Pacific Rim, Prince Albert, Prince Edward Island, Riding Mountain, Terra Nova, and Waterton Lakes. Check early for availability.

Hotels, Motels, & Inns. This guide lists a sampling of accommodations as a service to readers. The lists are by no means comprehensive, and listing does not imply endorsement by the National Geographic Society or Parks Canada. The information can change without notice. Many parks keep lists of the lodgings in their areas, which they will provide on request. You should also contact local visitor centres and provincial tourism offices for suggestions.

Sirmilik

Auyuittuq

V U T

Torngat Mountains

D A

NEWFOUNDLAND AND LABRADOR

QUEBEC

Terra Nova

Gros Morne

Mingan Archipelago

Forillon

Saguenay-St. Lawrence

Cape Breton Highlands

Prince Edward Island

PRINCE EDWARD ISLAND

A R I O

Lake Superior

Pukaskwa

Kouchibouguac

NEW BRUNSWICK

Fundy

NOVA SCOTIA

La Mauricie

Kejimkujik

Fathom Five

Georgian Bay Islands

Bruce Peninsula

St. Lawrence Islands

Point Pelee

ATLANTIC PROVINCES

Page 12: top, Autumn foliage, Cape Breton Highlands; middle, Atlantic puffin; bottom, Canoeing in Kejimkujik. Page 13: Grazing sheep in Gros Morne. Above: Mill Falls on the Mersey River, Kejimkujik.

ATLANTIC PROVINCES

Sprinkled from Labrador to Nova Scotia, these eight parks show off the beauty of mountain building, erosion, and glaciation and a shoreline nearly 9,656 km (6,000 mi) long. At Terra Nova, visitors can hike and bike in a boreal forest. Gros Morne amazes visitors with expansive views of mountains, valleys, and a freshwater fjord. At Torngat Mountains, local Inuit guides share their intimate knowledge of flora and fauna. The "Hiking Capital of Canada," Cape

Breton Highlands includes part of the scenic Cabot Trail. Kejimkujik boasts old-growth forests, hills called drumlins, and one of the world's largest collection of petroglyphs. Prince Edward Island looks just like the rolling landscape described in *Anne of Green Gables,* the beloved novel by island resident L. M. Montgomery. Kouchibouguac is considered the best biking destination among these parks, while Fundy ties for the highest tidal range in the world.

Torngat
Mountains

NEWFOUNDLAND
AND LABRADOR

Gros Morne

Terra Nova

PRINCE
EDWARD Cape Breton
Kouchibouguac ISLAND Highlands
NEW BRUNSWICK

Fundy Prince Edward Island

Kejimkujik NOVA SCOTIA

A double rainbow arches over Terra Nova.

▶ TERRA NOVA

NEWFOUNDLAND & LABRADOR
ESTABLISHED 1957
400 sq km/99,000 acres

On the northeast coast of Canada's most easterly province, a boreal forest dares embrace the forbidding North Atlantic. Terra Nova National Park, whose name derives from the Latin for Newfoundland, is about a two-hour drive from Bonavista, where early European explorer Giovanni Caboto (John Cabot) "discovered" North America. Fittingly, the park's rocky extremities continue to stretch into the sea—an ageless geological invitation to explorers far and wide.

Terra Nova, the oldest national park in Newfoundland and Labrador, protects an interesting collection of diverse habitats: woodlands, ponds, marshes, and bogs, as well as the occasional granite promontory and a significant stretch of coastline.

This Eastern Island boreal forest represents what is historically a traditional Newfoundland landscape. History, however, is changing.

The area's once vibrant evergreen and deciduous forest is fading as moose—browsing on balsam fir, birch, maple, and other species—have been literally eating away at the forest understorey.

Moose are the second largest land animal in North America (bison are the largest). An adult male will grow up to 2 m (7 ft) in height at the shoulder, weigh anywhere from

380 to 720 kg (840–1,600 lbs), and consume almost 10,000 calories per day. They are not native to Newfoundland. They were introduced to the island in 1904, at a time when the Newfoundland wolf still existed. Today the Newfoundland wolf is extinct, and moose have no natural enemies aside from black bears and human hunters. Unchecked, they will decimate Terra Nova's forest.

It's an important forest to maintain: Terra Nova is one of the few remaining homes of the threatened Newfoundland marten, a subspecies unique to the island and one of only 14 mammals native to it. There are thought to be only 300 of these animals left in existence. Other animals evident throughout the park include black bears, ospreys, lynx, Atlantic salmon, and bald eagles.

How to Get There

Because Terra Nova is located on the island of Newfoundland, travel there must include some element of air or sea transportation.

The closest airport is Gander International, which will put you approximately 90 km (56 mi) west of the park. The next closest airport, albeit larger and with a more frequent flight schedule (which often translates to cheaper rates), is 200 km (124 mi) to the east in the province's capital city, St. John's. Deer Lake, home to the smallest of the three airports, is 390 km (242 mi) west of Terra Nova. If you fly to Newfoundland, you'll have to rent a vehicle upon arrival.

It is possible for you to drive to Newfoundland provided you're prepared to travel by ferry from North Sydney, Nova Scotia, to either Argentia (126 km/78 mi east of the park) or Port aux Basques (655 km/407 mi west). The 14-hour Argentia crossing operates seasonally from mid-June to September, while the 4.5- to 8-hour Port aux Basques run operates year-round.

The park is also accessible via personal watercraft (GPS coordinates 48 34 45.35 N; 53 56 51.31 W). Docking and launch facilities can be found at Salton's Brook.

Once you're on the island, finding the park is simple. Trans-Canada 1 runs through the park for 40 km (25 mi). Along the way, you'll find clearly marked signage indicating campgrounds, swimming areas, hiking trails, and other park attractions.

When to Go

As Newfoundland rarely experiences the extreme highs and lows of other locales with comparable latitude, Terra Nova is open for year-round enjoyment. On average, the coldest temperatures during the winter are around minus 15°C (5°F), while the warmest summer temperatures are around 22°C (72°F). Note, however, that electrically serviced campsites are only available during the summer season.

Endangered Newfoundland marten

Pitcher plant

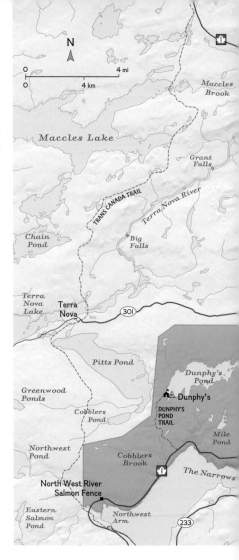

How to Visit

With few exceptions, the park's broad offering of activities and habitats is readily accessible. Of Terra Nova's 15 hiking trails, ranging in length from 1 to 29 km (0.6–18 mi), you'll find nature walks that are friendly to young children and people who enjoy a slower pace (some are even negotiable by wheelchair), as well as hikes to test the most resilient individuals.

There's freshwater swimming, mountain biking, kayaking, and canoeing in the warmer months, as well as cross-country skiing and snowshoeing during the winter. Camping and hiking are year-round activities in the park.

Reservations are highly recommended, particularly for campsites with electrical service. For primitive camping (i.e., wilderness camping without services or facilities). On-site information kiosks about specific campgrounds are open seasonally.

Of particular note are the on-site shower and laundry facilities (yes, there is hot water). Although you may want to bring provisions with you, there is a convenience store in Newman Sound Campground, which carries all the essentials and a small selection of prepared food items.

Deciding what you'd like to do depends on the type of adventure you're looking for. Regardless of the specific activity, however, always remember to follow the golden rule: Other than footprints, leave behind no evidence of your presence.

SANDY POND & MARINE EXHIBIT AT THE VISITOR CENTRE
a full day

Though Terra Nova's camping facilities are superb, even a day visit is

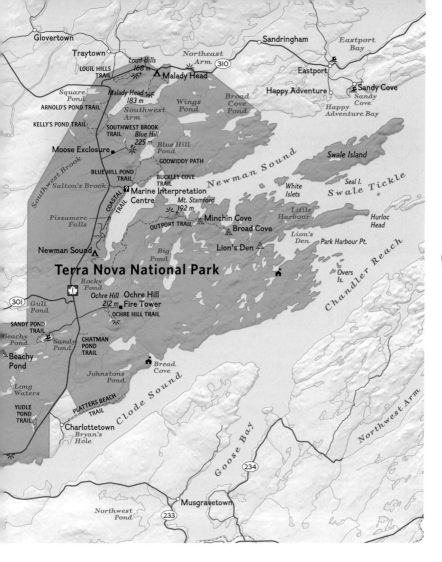

time well spent. Plan to arrive early in the morning and head directly to **Sandy Pond.** While waiting for the sun to warm the day, ease into the park with a leisurely 3-km (2 mi) stroll around the pond.

Along the route, be on the alert for beavers, ducks, and assorted local flora such as the provincial flower, the pitcher plant. Most often found in marshy areas, the pitcher plant is easily recognizable due to its inverted red-wine flower and hollow cone-like leaves. These "cones" capture water, which in turn traps insects—a fact you will come to appreciate once you've been properly introduced to Terra Nova's prodigious population of blackflies and mosquitoes.

Walk complete, stake your claim to a portion of Sandy Pond's sand beach, notable because most beaches in this province are comprised of less hospitable gravel and rock. The water here is always warmer than most Newfoundland ponds, due to the shallow water depths.

Sandy Pond

When you've tired of swimming, have lunch at one of the many picnic tables conveniently spaced nearby. If you didn't bring lunch with you, purchase a snack at the concession stand. While there, rent a canoe for an enjoyable paddle and a new perspective of Sandy Pond.

Time does have a way of slipping away from you at Terra Nova, but if you aren't too tired and want to experience the oceanic side of the park, head to the **Marine Exhibit** at the Visitor Centre at Salton's Brook. Here, you'll find interactive displays about the North Atlantic marine life around the park. Children of all ages will especially enjoy the touch tanks and the opportunity to hold a live crab or sea star in their hands.

If you weren't hungry at Sandy Pond but are feeling peckish now, step into the on-site Starfish Eatery for soup and a sandwich. Finish what's been a very full day by exploring the seaweed- and shell-strewn shore around the visitor centre.

OTHER HIKES & ACTIVITIES

If the setting sun finds you at the ocean's edge with the wind tickling your hair and the scent of salt water tingling in your nose, pause for a moment to slowly inhale. Should that breath of North Atlantic air leave you wistful for more, remember that life is too short for regrets. Plan your next trip to include at least a week in the park, and create an itinerary that encompasses the award-winning **Coastal Connections ecotour** (departing Salton's Brook twice daily, mid-May– early Oct.), introduce your children to Terra Nova's junior naturalist programs, or take part in the weekly campfire singalong.

You might even tread the paths of the Beothuk. Sadly, Newfoundland's original native inhabitants became extinct in 1829, their demise blamed on confrontations with Europeans, disease, and increased competition for food. Though they lived throughout the island, they were particularly populous along the northeast coast. Hiking along the **Ochre Hill Trail** (named for the red dye with which the Beothuk coloured themselves on ceremonial occasions), it isn't difficult to imagine you're sharing the path with quiet moccasin-clad feet. It's a gentle reminder that, though the park itself is a youthful 54 years, the land it protects is ageless.

TERRA NOVA NATIONAL PARK
(Parc national Terra-Nova)

INFORMATION & ACTIVITIES

VISITOR & INFORMATION CENTRE
Visitor Centre located at Salton's Brook. Phone (709) 533-2942. Open from May to October.

SEASONS & ACCESSIBILITY
Park open year-round.

HEADQUARTERS
Glovertown, NL A0G 2L0. Phone (709) 533-2801. www.parkscanada.gc.ca/terranova.

FRIENDS OF TERRA NOVA
Heritage Foundation for Terra Nova National Park Glovertown, NL A0G 2L0. hftnnp@gmail.com.

ENTRANCE FEES
$6 per person, $15 per group per day; $30 per person, $75 per group per year ($37 if purchased Jan.–May).

PETS
Dogs must be on a leash. Pets permitted at the beaches but must be kept off the beach and boardwalk at Sandy Pond. In winter, keep dogs on the ungroomed side of skiing trails.

ACCESSIBLE SERVICES
The Visitor Centre, Heritage Trail, and boardwalk at Sandy Pond are all accessible to wheelchairs.

THINGS TO DO
Swimming at Sandy Pond (freshwater) and at Eastport and Sandy Cove beaches (saltwater). Fishing for trout and salmon from May to August; ice fishing at Dunphy's Pond in February and March (permit $10 per day, $34 per season). Call (709) 533-2801 for the status of closed waters and for catch-and-possession limits.

Cross-country skiing in Newman Sound and Sandy Pond from January to March; call **Airport Nordic Ski Club,** (709) 651-3169, or **Clarenville Nordic Ski Club,** (709) 466-1066. Call the Visitor Centre for recommended snowshoeing trails.

Hiking and bicycling are also available, as well as beach volleyball at Eastport Beach. Canoes and paddleboats are available for rent at Sandy Pond concessions. Call (709) 533-9797.

SPECIAL ADVISORIES
- Watch for wildlife when driving with poor visibility.
- Keep campsites clean and tidy to avoid attracting wildlife.
- Report fires or suspicious smoke to park staff or call (709) 533-6090.
- No open fires or charcoal barbecues permitted in Newman Sound Campground.

OVERNIGHT BACKPACKING
Primitive campgrounds on Outport Trail and Dunphy's Pond Trail. Canoe route through Sandy Pond, Beachy Pond, and Dunphy's Pond. Call (709) 533-2801.

CAMPGROUNDS
Electrical sites $29 per night, nonelectrical sites $26 ($24 and $19 respectively with Early Bird Pass). **Newman Sound,** 343 sites (100 with electricity), open year-round with The Nature House Activity Centre, grocery store, and laundromat. Call (877) 737-3783 or visit www.pccamping.ca. **Malady Head,** available June to September. Unserviced campsites with washrooms, kitchen shelters, playground, fire pits, a filling and dumping station, and a day-use area. $22 per night; $17 with Early Bird Pass. Call (709) 533-6774.

HOTELS, MOTELS, & INNS
(unless otherwise noted, rates are for a 2-person double, high season, in Canadian dollars)

Outside the park:
Port Blanford, NL A0C 2G0:
By d'Bay Cabins (709) 543-2637. info@bydbay.com; www.bydbay.com. $95–$140 for two nights.
Terra Nova Resort & Golf Community (709) 543-2525. info@terranovagolf.com; www.terranovagolf.com. $109–$350.

View from the Long Range Mountains down to Western Brook Pond

▶GROS MORNE

NEWFOUNDLAND & LABRADOR
ESTABLISHED 1973
1,805 sq km/446,000 acres

Surrounded by silent granite guardians whose tips stretch into endless sky to regularly converse with clouds, you might feel the natural
and unavoidable impulse to look up. Succumb to the temptation. But
don't forget—an equally impressive and revealing story lies patiently
beneath your feet.

That the literal French translation of
gros is "big" seems a criminal under-
statement when applied to Gros
Morne National Park. Even words
like "immense," "majestic," and
"momentous" fail to do it justice.

This, the second largest of
Atlantic Canada's national parks
(more than four times the size of its
east coast boreal cousin, Terra Nova),
is host to a gargantuan panorama
of natural wonder: Newfoundland's
second highest peak (standing

806 m/2,622 ft), a freshwater fjord
sheltered by towering cliffs, the
highest waterfall in eastern North
America, sandy beaches, sea stacks,
and sea caves.

All of this natural beauty helps
account for the park's standing as a
UNESCO World Heritage site. The
scenery, however, is a by-product of
Gros Morne's greatest gift: a highly
visible example of plate tectonics.
Here, on the isolated and uninhab-
ited mountaintops of western

Newfoundland, you will find one of the world's best examples of continental drift and the physical remnants of those millennia-old collisions and separation. Here, deep ocean crust and rocks from the Earth's mantle lie exposed for all to see. Glaciation has added a coastal lowland, alpine plateau, fjords, glacial valleys, waterfalls, and lakes to this breathtaking landscape.

How to Get There

Of the four commercial airports in Newfoundland, Deer Lake is the smallest and the closest—a mere 32 km (20 mi) from the park entrance. It has direct flights from Toronto, Montreal, and Halifax.

If you're driving or cycling to Gros Morne, you'll have to catch the ferry from North Sydney in Nova Scotia (http://marine-atlantic.ca). A six-hour ferry ride will land you in Port aux Basques, 300 km (186 mi) from the park entrance. If you take the 14-hour North Sydney–Argentia crossing (which operates mid-June–Sept.), it's a 570 km (354 m) trip to the park. A word of warning: Both ferries regularly feature weather and mechanical delays; reservations are a must.

When you've landed in Newfoundland, take Trans-Canada 1 to Deer Lake. Then leave the highway and head 32 km (20 mi) north along Rte. 430 (also known as the Viking Trail) to the park entrance in Wiltondale.

When to Go

Precipitation is a given in Gros Morne, with some form of it falling every two days on average. Summer can bring rain and fog, which sometimes creates an otherworldly atmosphere for summit seekers. For winter visitors, the rain, drizzle, and fog give way to thick falls of the white stuff that ski, snowshoe, and snowmobile enthusiasts adore.

Given the extreme differences in elevation throughout the park, temperatures and wind speed can quickly fluctuate. As long as visitors are of the non-complaining sort and come prepared with multiple layers and water-resistant clothing, Gros Morne is a park to be adored year-round. That said, you should check with park officials prior to setting out. The Gros Morne Mountain and Long Range Traverse highland trails are closed in spring to minimize soil erosion and human interference with animal habitats and breeding. They are also closed for hiker safety during periods when snow conceals the trails. For local weather updates, visit www.weatheroffice.gc.ca.

How to Visit

Truly appreciating the natural wonder of Gros Morne requires extended excursions along challenging uphill trails. However, the park is prepared to play host to many different age levels, with shorter, easy walks on level ground, lots of coastal access, and great sandy and pebble beaches.

If you are visiting with children, there are five frontcountry camping locations in Gros Morne, most of which have playground facilities (though none offer serviced sites). Combined, the five frontcountry locations have a total of 235 campsites between them. Each of the five sites has something different to offer, from wide-open grassy areas to beachside locales to glorious mountain vistas. The **Berry Hill** location offers the broadest range of services; **Green Point**'s 31 beachside sites are the only frontcountry campsites without showers and flush toilets.

If you aren't a camper, a number of alternative accommodations are available in communities adjacent to and inside the park.

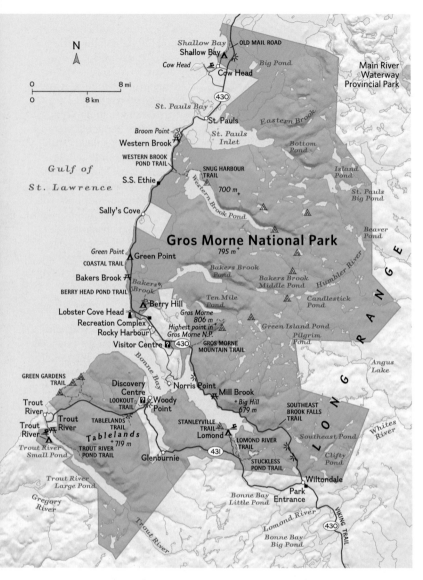

N

| 0 | 8 mi |
| 0 | 8 km |

Shallow Bay
Shallow Bay
OLD MAIL ROAD

Cow Head
Cow Head

Big Pond

Main River
Waterway
Provincial Park

430

St. Pauls Bay

St. Pauls

Eastern Brook

Broom Point
Western Brook

St. Pauls
Inlet

Bottom
Pond

WESTERN BROOK
POND TRAIL

S.S. Ethie

SNUG HARBOUR
TRAIL

Island
Pond

Gulf of
St. Lawrence

700 m

St. Pauls
Big Pond

Sally's Cove

Western Brook Pond

Beaver
Pond

Gros Morne National Park

795 m

Green Point
COASTAL TRAIL
Green Point

Bakers Brook
Pond

Bakers Brook
Middle Pond

Humber River

Bakers Brook
BERRY HEAD POND TRAIL
Bakers
Brook

Ten Mile
Pond

Candlestick
Pond

Lobster Cove Head
Recreation Complex
Rocky Harbour
Visitor Centre

Berry Hill

Green Island Pond

Gros Morne
806 m
Highest point in
Gros Morne N.P.

Pilgrim
Pond

430
GROS MORNE
MOUNTAIN TRAIL

Angus
Lake

Bonne Bay

GREEN GARDENS
TRAIL

Norris Point

Mill Brook

Trout
River

Discovery
Centre
LOOKOUT
TRAIL
Woody
Point

Big Hill
679 m

SOUTHEAST
BROOK FALLS
TRAIL

Whites
River

Trout
River

Trout
River

TABLELANDS
TRAIL
Tablelands
719 m
TROUT RIVER
POND TRAIL

STANLEYVILLE
TRAIL
Lomond

Southeast Pond

Clifty
Pond

Trout River
Small Pond

Glenburnie

431

LOMOND RIVER
TRAIL

STUCKLESS
POND TRAIL

Wiltondale

Trout River
Large Pond

Gregory
River

Trout River

Bonne Bay
Little Pond

Park
Entrance

Lomond River

430

VIKING TRAIL

Bonne Bay
Big Pond

TABLELANDS

a full day

Though you've already travelled a significant distance to get to the park, your arrival is just the beginning of your adventure. In order to get from the southernmost end of the park and around Bonne Bay to continue northward to the park's uppermost boundary will take two hours of non-stop driving. In fact, to fully appreciate Gros Morne will require a minimum stay of several days, as well as vehicular transportation. If, however, all you can spare is one day, use it to travel to the **Tablelands.**

Start your morning at the **Discovery Centre** in the south end of the park (there's no mistaking its vibrant

Camping, Lomond Campground

rare opportunity to get up close and personal with peridotite, a type of rock usually found 12 km (7.5 mi) or more below ground but which has been pushed to the surface thanks to continental collisions more than 470 million years ago. Rich in iron, chromium, and nickel but lacking in nitrogen, potassium, phosphorus, and calcium, peridotite inherently discourages plant growth. Don't be deceived by the plants you see here; that 5-cm-high (2 in) greenery may be decades in age.

Though two hours is ample time for the actual hike and return to the parking lot, you'll want to allow yourself at least another hour to assimilate the avalanche of sensory information. The seeming isolation atop this ancient seabed, with the wind whispering in your ears. The feeling of the sun's rays as they warm you and this ageless rock into a golden mood. The sight of a neighbouring verdant mountain with cottony clouds as its crowning glory. The jaw-dropping descent to your starting point and the realization that you really did climb that high. This is Gros Morne at its best.

yellow hue and impressive circular facade). Spend a comfortable hour or two enjoying its modern comforts and informative displays about the area's geology, and rare plant and animal life. You might even catch a presentation from the artist in residence if you're there at the right time.

Once you're ready to head back outside, you'll find the **Tablelands Trail** parking lot 4 km (2.5 mi) west of the Discovery Centre along Rte. 431. Before setting out, make sure you're carrying a couple of bottles of water and wearing sensible footwear (preferably hiking boots, but sneakers will suffice if you're careful). Following an easy to moderately difficult uphill hike along an old gravel road, passing the occasional pitcher plant (a carnivorous flower with a thirst for insects) and delicate purple flora, you'll find yourself stepping out on the rust-tinted lunarlike landscape of the Tablelands. The final climb is challenging, but the view from the top is well worth it.

In addition to the picturesque vistas from every angle, this is a

OTHER ATTRACTIONS

The smart explorer knows better than to slight this most singular of parks with a mere day's excursion. There are freshwater ponds to swim in and fjords to explore, wildlife to see and kayaks to paddle, communities to visit and trails to hike—not the least of which is the strenuously rewarding 16-km (10 mi) round-trip expedition to the top of **Gros Morne mountain** itself.

You may well find, as have many adventurers before you, that the more of Gros Morne you see, the more there is to discover.

GROS MORNE NATIONAL PARK
(Parc national du Gros-Morne)

INFORMATION & ACTIVITIES

VISITOR & INFORMATION CENTRES

Gros Morne Visitor Centre Hwy. 430, 3 km (2 mi) east of Rocky Harbour. Open May to October. **Discovery Centre** Hwy. 431 at Woody Point. Open late May to early October.

SEASONS & ACCESSIBILITY

Park open year-round.

HEADQUARTERS

Rocky Harbour, NL A0K 4N0. Phone (709) 458-2417. www.parkscanada.gc.ca/gros morne.

FRIENDS OF GROS MORNE

Gros Morne Co-operating Association Rocky Harbour, NL A0K 4N0. Phone (709) 458-3610. info@grosmornetravel.com; www.grosmornetravel.com.

ENTRANCE FEES

$10 per person, $20 per group per day (winter, $8 per person, $16 per group per day); $49 per person, $100 per group per year.

PETS

Pets permitted but must be leashed at all times. Dogs not permitted on boat tours.

ACCESSIBLE SERVICES

The visitor centres, Lobster Cove Lighthouse, campground service buildings, and boardwalk section of the Berry Head Pond Trail are wheelchair accessible. An all-terrain wheelchair is available at the visitor centre; call in advance for booking.

THINGS TO DO

Wilderness hiking (July–mid-Oct.) on **Long Range Traverse** ($85 per person, $25 reservation fee) and **North Rim Traverse** ($70 per person), both unmarked. Reservations required. Maximum nine people and three tents per site. Backcountry permit required.

Fishing permits free but provincial licence and tags required for salmon fishing (for a fee). Kayaking in **Trout River Pond** and **Bonne Bay.** Boat ramps at Trout River Pond, Mill Brook, and Lomond day-use areas. Powerboats permitted on Trout River Pond and Bonne Bay.

Tours on **Western Brook Pond** (July–Sept.); call (709) 458-2016 or (888) 458-2016 for reservations. Cruises available on Bonne Bay.

Indoor swimming at Recreation Complex (late June–early Sept.); unsupervised outdoor swimming at **Shallow Bay, Lomond** (saltwater), and **Trout River Pond** (freshwater). Cross-country skiing, snowmobiling, self-guided tour of **Lobster Cove**

EXCURSIONS

L'ANSE AUX MEADOWS NATIONAL HISTORIC SITE
L'ANSE AUX MEADOWS, NL

This living history site at the northernmost tip of the Great Northern Peninsula has been identified as the original landing place for Vikings in North America around 1000 AD. Here you'll discover the excavated remains of the base camp used by Leif Eriksson. Open June to early October. Located north of St. Anthony, but to get there, you must turn off Hwy. 430 onto Hwy. 436, about 10 km (6.2 mi) south of St. Anthony. (709) 623-2608 (in season only); (709) 458-2417 (rest of the year).

Lighthouse (late May–early Oct.), **Broom Point;** and guided tour of inshore fishing at Gros Morne also available.

SPECIAL ADVISORIES

- Strong winds common from mid-morning to mid-afternoon. Boaters should check the forecast before setting out.
- The ocean at the mouth of Western Brook is too dangerous for swimming due to an undertow. Elsewhere, use caution in choosing where to swim.
- If hiking in the backcountry, call (709) 458-2417 to obtain topographic maps.
- Prevent avalanche; do not highmark or hammerhead when snowmobiling.

OVERNIGHT BACKPACKING

Primitive/backcountry campsites at **Green Gardens, Stanleyville Trail, Ferry Gulch,** and **Snug Harbour** equipped with picnic tables, pit toilets, and tent pads (where necessary). Open fires not permitted, so bring camp stove. Permit required; first-come, first-served basis. Visit www .pccamping.ca or call (877) 737-3783. Fees: $10 overnight, $70 per season.

CAMPGROUNDS

All campgrounds unserviced with toilets and showers, $26 per night. Annual entry and off-season $20. **Trout River Pond,** 44 sites, boat launch. **Lomond,** 29 sites, ideal for fishing and boating. First come, first served. **Berry Hill,** 69 sites and 2 group

sites, has toilets, showers, and a kitchen shelter. Make reservations in advance. Group campgrounds available from mid-June to September. Call (709) 458-2066. **Green Point,** 31 sites, near fishing area. Self-registration. Primitive campgrounds $16 per night. Group camping $6 per person. **Shallow Bay,** 52 drive-in sites, near sand beach and outdoor theatre. **Trout River Pond** and **Lomond,** 4 walk-in sites each. Trout River Pond, Lomond, Green Point, and Shallow Bay suitable for camping with a kayak. For Berry Hill, Shallow Bay, and Trout River Pond, make reservations online at www.pccamping.ca.

HOTELS, MOTELS, & INNS

(unless otherwise noted, rates are for a 2-person double, high season, in Canadian dollars)

Outside the park:
Fisherman's Landing Inn Rocky Harbour, NL A0K 4N0. (709) 458-2711. www.fishermanslandinginn.com. $139–$169.
Red Mantle Lodge Shoal Brook, NL A0K 1P0. (709) 453-7204 or (888) 453-7204. info@redmantlelodge.ca; www.redmantlelodge.ca. $99–$225.
Sugar Hill Inn Norris Point, NL A0K 3V0. (888) 299-2147. www.sugarhillinn.nf.ca. $148–$165 for standard rooms, $195–$245 for king suites.

For more accommodations visit www.new foundlandandlabrador.com.

PORT AU CHOIX NATIONAL HISTORIC SITE
PORT AU CHOIX, NL

The limestone bedrock throughout the Port au Choix area has preserved evidence of 5,500 years of aboriginal history, including a 4,000-year-old slate bayonet and the antler harpoon used by a Groswater Paleo-Eskimo. Open June to early October. Drive 110 km (68 mi) north of Gros Morne. Turn off the Viking Trail at Port Saunders and drive through to Port au Choix. Take Point Riche Road to the visitor centre. (709) 861-3522 (in season only); (709) 458-2417 (rest of the year).

Small glacier near Mount Caubvick/Mont D'Iberville

▶ TORNGAT MOUNTAINS

NEWFOUNDLAND & LABRADOR
ESTABLISHED 2005
9,700 sq km/2,400,000 acres

The region of Torngait, or "a place of spirits," was named after Torngarsoak, the most powerful spirit in Inuit mythology. Like the spirits, the land tends to be harsh. But the stark beauty of the region is tempered by the hospitality of the people and the unique opportunity to participate in traditional practices firsthand.

Coming to a sharp point at the northeasternmost edge of continental Canada, Torngat Mountains National Park covers a wedge of land between northern Quebec and the Labrador Sea. Rising from a rugged and barren coastline, this mountain range at the tip of Labrador is home to the highest peaks on mainland Canada east of the Rockies (the highest being Mount Caubvick at 1,652 m/5,420 ft). Massive, glacier-carved fjords, some more than 1 km (0.6 mi) high, saw-tooth the coast. Vast, exposed mountainsides put their underlying geologic formations on swirling display.

As you travel through this country, a couple of the most striking elements against the green velvet landscape are the surreal, luminescent blue icebergs that stud the dark waters and *nanuk*—the polar bears that wander the shores.

Torngat Mountains is the first national park in Labrador and the newest national park in Canada. The park is on the migratory path of the George River caribou herd, once the world's largest, but now numbering fewer than 100,000. The mountains are also home to wolves, arctic foxes, peregrine falcons, and the world's only tundra-dwelling black bears.

The park is above 55 degrees latitude and the tree line. Although Inuit no longer live here year-round, they still use the region for traditional food gathering. An all-Inuit cooperative management board, the first in the Parks Canada system, provides advice and guidance for the management of the park.

How to Get There

There are no roads to the Torngat Mountains. Access is through charter air flight or boat. Charter flights to Saglek Bay in Labrador may be arranged through Air Inuit *(www.airinuit.com)*, usually departing from Kuujjuaq in Nunavik (northern Quebec); Air Labrador *(www.airlabrador.com)*; or Innu Mikun *(www.provincialairlines.ca)*, departing from Goose Bay, Labrador.

Charter flights land on an airstrip near a military radar station, just south of where Torngat Mountains Base Camp and Research Station is located. The final leg from the airstrip to base camp requires a boat trip or a helicopter ride. The Labrador Inuit Development Corporation (709-922-2143) has a weekly return charter flight from Goose Bay to Saglek, departing every Saturday during the summer operating season.

Expedition Cruise ships travel to the park and into some of the fjords. For an updated list of cruise companies, check the Cruise Newfoundland and Labrador website *(www.cruisetheedge.com)*.

Those who seek to arrange their own travel into the park should contact Parks Canada to secure permits

and arrange orientation sessions (888-922-1290).

When to Go

The summer season is short and the mildest weather occurs from mid-July to mid-August. For spring conditions, March and April can be good times to travel.

Mean average temperatures in the park range from 4°C (39°F) in the summer to minus 16.5°C (2°F) in the winter.

Climatic conditions, influenced heavily by latitude, altitude, and coastal currents, can change rapidly. Heavy wind, fog, and strong rain can sweep in, grounding planes and boats.

How to Visit

Last year about 450 visitors set foot in the Torngats, about one-third of whom travelled through on cruise ships, zipping ashore on zodiacs for day excursions. The number of visitors who came for a more immersive stay in base camp—including scientific researchers—numbered fewer than a hundred. Seven self-supported groups made their way into the park last year.

Because of its remote location, it's time-consuming and expensive to travel to the Torngats. A trip of at least four days makes sense to get a meaningful visit of the park.

TORNGAT EXPERIENCE

Torngat Safaris, officially launched in 2010, is a joint cooperation between the Labrador Inuit Development Corporation, Parks Canada, and Inuit-owned Cruise North Expeditions *(www.cruisenorthexpeditions.com)*. They offer four-night and seven-night stays.

The base for these organized expeditions is kANGIDLUASUk (St.

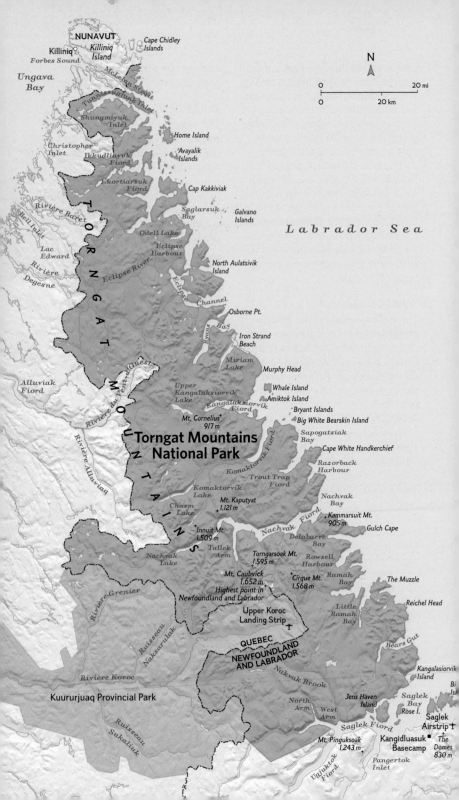

John's Harbour) in Sallik (Saglek) Bay, just outside the southern end of Torngat Mountains National Park. The base camp is an assembly of semipermanent wall tents, housing kitchen and mess areas, parks offices, and supply depots. Among them are rows of tents for short-term guests and staff. Torngat Safari guests stay in heated wall tents and sleep on cots. There is plenty of opportunity for interaction with the base camp Inuit staff and visiting researchers over meals in the mess tent and during evening presentations.

Fresh drinking and washing water comes straight from the stream beside the camp, but they also just recently installed flush toilets and hot showers. More permanent structures have been constructed to support the work of visiting research scientists. The other notable physical feature of the camp is the 10,000-volt electric fence that surrounds it, keeping out nearby polar bears.

Polar bear safety is of paramount concern in the park. Parks Canada recommends that visitors hiking in the park, especially those on overnight trips, engage the services of experienced Inuit polar bear guards. In the event this is not possible, visitors should have portable electric fences, appropriate bear deterrents, and/or a trained bear dog.

After settling into camp on your first day, part of the orientation will be a bear safety talk followed by a video—the first of its kind—that accumulates polar bear knowledge from Inuit elders. Inuit bear guards (allowed to carry firearms in the park) will accompany any foray outside the base camp and they soon become fixtures of the landscape, often distant figures in high-visibility vests or silhouettes on the horizon. It's common practice for Inuit to periodically turn around and survey the land behind them to

make sure they're not being stalked. Along with the awe-inspiring scale of the Torngats, being in the midst of an apex predator is part of the experience, putting humans into their proper perspective.

INUIT GIFT

Torngat Mountains isn't just about grand landscapes. In fact, the park itself was a gift from the Inuit people to Canada, and interaction with the Inuit guides—most of whom have lived off this land for generations—can easily be the richest part of your visit here.

This isn't just their homeland in the conceptual sense. As you glide

Artifact from a Thule sod house, Nachvak Fjord

along the banks of a fjord, your Inuit guide might point to the spot where his mother was born. Or he may spot wildlife off in the distance, a polar bear perhaps or caribou, that would otherwise have gone unnoticed. He might even kneel down by evidence of habitation by the Inuit, or by their predecessors the Dorset and Thule, such as a Ramah chert shard tool nestled in the tundra or the faint remains of a tent ring.

As seminomadic subsistence hunters, the Inuit were inextricably tied to the land, and an intimate

Southwest Arm, Saglek Fjord

Arctic hare

knowledge of the habits of wildlife is still of great importance. Experiencing traditional Inuit harvesting practices can be as hands-on as rolling up sleeves and helping to dress and skin a caribou or just simply observing. Others may prefer to fish for arctic char, wander in the tidal zone picking mussels, or pluck berries. It's also possible to join the guides on their hunt for caribou and seal.

Excursions from base camp are usually made on working longliners with all-Inuit crew. A typical outing might be to **Sallikuluk** (Rose Island), where there are more than a dozen archaeological sites, dating back 5,000 years. You can stand on the edge of sod-house excavations, in some cases numbering as many as 14 dwellings in one place. Besides traditional stone burial sites scattered over the island, one mass burial site houses repatriated ancestral remains.

Helicopters are best for hitting remote points north including **Nachvak Fjord,** 70 km (43 mi) as the crow flies from base camp, with its archaeological sites and broad inland valleys.

Another outing could be to the north arm of **Sallik (Saglek) Fjord,** about three hours by boat from base camp. Along the way, crumbling cliffs of gneiss—shot through with striations—tower along the shore. Some of the rock in this area is 3.9 billion years old, putting it among the oldest on the planet. At the end of the inlet, you can go ashore for a meal of freshly caught arctic char and *panitsiaks* (bannock) baked over a beach fire. This is a good place for overnight excursions in the park.

NORTHERN LIGHTS

Wherever one stays in the park, there's the opportunity to view *atsanik*—the **northern lights.** On a good night, swaths of green light might arc across the night sky before seemingly turning to liquid and dripping down in molten tendrils. If you haven't already felt that spirits inhabit the park, that sight alone will convince you otherwise.

TORNGAT MOUNTAINS NATIONAL PARK
(Parc national des Monts-Torngat)

INFORMATION & ACTIVITIES

VISITOR & INFORMATION CENTRE
Parks Canada has a visitor reception and orientation tent at the **Torngat Mountains Base Camp and Research Station** in St. John's Harbour in Saglek Bay. Available from late July to the end of August. For information call (709) 922-1290 or (888) 922-1290.

SEASONS & ACCESSIBILITY
Park open year-round; visits recommended in March and April and from early July to September. No road access or facilities. Landing permits required for aircraft or helicopters. Access to Inuit lands on the coast at Iron Strand Beach requires permission from the Nunatsiavut Government; call (709) 922-2942.

HEADQUARTERS
Box 471, Nain, NL A0P 1L0. Phone (709) 922-1290 or (888) 922-1290. torngats .info@pc.gc.ca; www.parkscanada.gc.ca/ torngat.

FRIENDS OF TORNGAT MOUNTAINS
Torngat Arts and Crafts, P.O. Box 269, Nain, NL A0P 1L0. Phone (709) 922-1659. torngatartscrafts@gmail.com.

ENTRANCE FEE
No entry fee.

PETS
Pets must be under control at all times.

ACCESSIBLE SERVICES
None.

THINGS TO DO
Hiking, mountain climbing, backcountry skiing, sailing or motorboat tours along the coast, and fishing in the park can be arranged.

Tour company licensed to operate in Torngat National Park: **Cruise North Expeditions** 111 Peter St., #200, Toronto, ON M5V 2H1. (416) 789-3725 or (888) 263-3220. www.cruisenorth expeditions.ca.

SPECIAL ADVISORIES
- All visitors must register before entering and leaving Torngat Mountains National Park either by phone, fax, or in person at the administration office in Nain.
- Travel with experienced Inuit polar bear guards is recommended.
- The weather is highly variable. In summer, temperatures can drop from mild during the day to below freezing at night. Dress appropriately.
- Do not plan on using wood for cooking. Build only small fires in emergencies, and ensure they are extinguished when you are done.
- Do not remove artifacts or disturb features at archaeological sites.

CAMPGROUNDS
No designated campsites or facilities. Visitors may camp anywhere in the park except at archaeological sites.

HOTELS, MOTELS, & INNS
(unless otherwise noted, rates are for a 2-person double, high season, in Canadian dollars)

Outside the park:
Atsanik Lodge Sand Banks Rd., Nain, NL A0P 1L0. (709) 922-2910. $150–$165.
Auberge Kuujjuaq Inn Kuujjuaq, QC J0M 1C0. (819) 964-2903. reservations kuujjuaqinn@tamaani.ca. $275.

For more accommodations contact the Fédération des coopératives du Nouveau-Québec (FCNQ), (514) 457-3249 or (866) 336-2667, www.fcnq.ca.

Freshwater Lake Trail

▶ CAPE BRETON HIGHLANDS

NOVA SCOTIA
ESTABLISHED 1936
948 sq km/235,000 acres

Cape Breton Highlands National Park was the first national park designated in Atlantic Canada. The Cabot Trail, a world-famous scenic highway, runs along parts of the coastal borders on both sides of the park and crosses the highlands. Renowned for its hiking trails, the park is home to a diverse mix of boreal and temperate species not found elsewhere in Canada.

The human history of northern Cape Breton reaches back 10,000 years. The Mi'kmaq have lived here about 4,000 years. Portuguese, French, Scottish, Irish, and Dutch immigrants settled here from the 1400s onward, and there continues to be a rich cultural history in the region that is active and engaging.

The park is often referred to as the place "where the mountains meet the sea." The dominant feature of this region is the elevated plateau, divided by steep-walled river canyons; northern species and habitats on the plateaus coexist with the more temperate habitats and species of the lowlands. Consequently, there is much diversity.

Approximately 88 percent of the park is forested. The plateau or upper reaches is dominated by both boreal and taiga vegetation and is part of the worn-down Appalachian mountain chain that stretches from Georgia to Newfoundland. The boreal land region part of this plateau features large swaths of coniferous trees, sprinkled with barrens and wetlands. Most of the entire population of Nova Scotia's endangered Canada lynx live here, as well as moose, hare, grouse, and marten. The taiga land region of the plateau features a tundra-like landscape characterized by scrub forest, barrens, and bogs.

In the lowlands, the Acadian forest includes a mix of northern and temperate plants and animals. Most worthy of note are the old-growth stands—more than 350 years old—as well as some pure sugar-maple stands found only in the northern part of this species' range.

The park and its treasures have been shaped by the Gulf of St. Lawrence, which flanks it on the westward side, and the Atlantic Ocean to the east. The shorelines range from rocky shores and dramatic headlands to cobbled and sandy beaches. A healthy marine food chain includes krill, lobster, and salmon. Minke whales, pilot whales, and harbour seals are frequently seen along the coast. Around 230 species of birds frequent various sections of the park, the most noticeable being bald eagles.

The park has six campgrounds, 26 hiking trails, several beaches, and a world-class golf course. Bordering communities have seasonal amenities, recreational programs, and cultural activities.

How to Get There

Airports are located in Sydney, in Cape Breton, and Halifax, in mainland Nova Scotia. From Sydney, take Rte. 125 to Hwy. 105, then take the Cabot Trail at the Englishtown ferry or at St. Ann's to Ingonish Beach. Driving time is two hours.

If driving from Halifax, take Hwy. 102 to Truro, then Hwy. 104 to the Canso Causeway that links mainland Nova Scotia to Cape Breton Island. Allow 3 hours to reach Cape Breton. At this point you need to decide which park entrance/visitor centre you want to check into: Ingonish Beach or Chéticamp.

For the Ingonish Beach entrance, take Hwy. 105 to exit 11 at Southaven. Follow the Cabot Trail north to the visitor centre. Driving time is 2 hours. Approaching the park from the west side, once you've crossed the Canso Causeway, follow Rte. 19 (the Ceilidh Trail) along the coast to Margaree Forks, then follow the Cabot Trail to Chéticamp. Allow 2 hours. The park entrance is ten minutes from Chéticamp.

When to Go

The park is open year-round. The best time to go will depend on your interests. Bird-watchers may prefer spring and early summer as there is less foliage and chances are better for spotting birds, although peak breeding activity is June through July.

Hiking is great from May to November, when the ground is usually snow free. Some people prefer to hike in the fall as there are no flies and fall foliage is spectacular. It's also when the Celtic Colours International Festival takes place, which is a bonus.

The best time for cycling is summer and fall. Ocean temperatures warm up by July and start to cool off in September, so beach activities are best during the summer. Although there is limited infrastructure during the winter, snowshoeing and skiing in the park can be a once-in-a-lifetime experience; valleys and plateaus become veritable winter wonderlands.

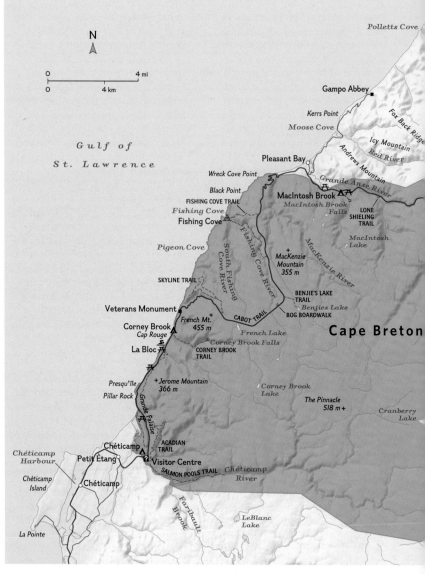

N

| 0 | | | 4 mi |

| 0 | | 4 km |

Gulf of
St. Lawrence

Polletts Cove

Gampo Abbey

Kerrs Point

Moose Cove

Fox Back Ridge

Icy Mountain
Red River

Andrews Mountain

Pleasant Bay

Wreck Cove Point

Grande Anse River

Black Point

MacIntosh Brook

MacIntosh Brook Falls

LONE SHIELING TRAIL

FISHING COVE TRAIL

Fishing Cove

Fishing Cove

Pigeon Cove

MacIntosh Lake

MacKenzie River

South Fishing Cove River

Fishing Cove River

MacKenzie Mountain
355 m

SKYLINE TRAIL

BENJIE'S LAKE TRAIL

Benjies Lake

BOG BOARDWALK

Veterans Monument

Corney Brook

Cap Rouge

La Bloc

French Mt.
455 m

CABOT TRAIL

French Lake

Cape Breton

Corney Brook Falls

CORNEY BROOK TRAIL

Presqu'île

Pillar Rock

Jerome Mountain
366 m

Corney Brook Lake

The Pinnacle
518 m

Cranberry Lake

Grande Falaise

Chéticamp

ACADIAN TRAIL

Chéticamp Harbour

Petit Étang

Visitor Centre

Chéticamp Island

Chéticamp

SALMON POOLS TRAIL

Chéticamp River

La Pointe

Faribault Brook

LeBlanc Lake

How to Visit

The possibilities at Cape Breton
Highlands are endless. You can be
as busy or as laid-back as you please.
The best place to start is at one of the
visitor information centres located
at either end of the park. The views
and vistas are spectacular no matter
where you enter the park.

INGONISH BEACH TO SOUTH HARBOUR

a full day

Beginning at **Ingonish Beach,** pack
a lunch and head for the stunning
view at **Lakies Head** (20 mins.),
where you can learn about bird
migrations, whales, and sea turtles.

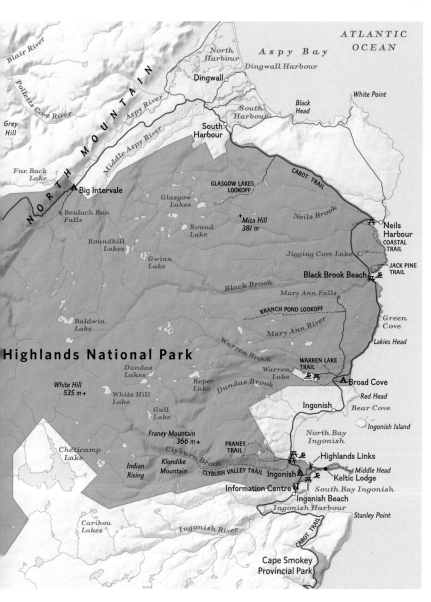

Map labels:
Blair River, Polletts Cove River, Grey Hill, NORTH MOUNTAIN, Aspy River, Middle Aspy River, Fox Back Lake, Big Intervale, Beulach Ban Falls, Glasgow Lakes, Roundhill Lakes, Gwinn Lake, Baldwin Lake, Highlands National Park, White Hill 535 m +, White Hill Lake, Dundas Lakes, Roper Lake, Gull Lake, Franey Mountain 366 m +, Cheticamp Lake, Indian Rising, Klondike Mountain, Caribou Lakes, North Harbour, Dingwall Harbour, Dingwall, Aspy Bay, South Harbour, Black Head, ATLANTIC OCEAN, White Point, South Harbour, GLASGOW LAKES LOOKOFF, CABOT TRAIL, Mica Hill 381 m, Round Lake, Neils Brook, Neils Harbour, COASTAL TRAIL, Jigging Cove Lake, JACK PINE TRAIL, Black Brook, Black Brook Beach, Mary Ann Falls, BRANCH POND LOOKOFF, Mary Ann River, Green Cove, Lakies Head, Warren Brook, WARREN LAKE TRAIL, Warren Lake, Dundas Brook, Broad Cove, Ingonish, Red Head, Bear Cove, Ingonish Island, North Bay Ingonish, Clyburn Brook, FRANEY TRAIL, CLYBURN VALLEY TRAIL, Highlands Links, Keltic Lodge, Middle Head, Ingonish, Information Centre, Ingonish Beach, South Bay Ingonish, Ingonish Harbour, Stanley Point, Ingonish River, CABOT TRAIL, Cape Smokey Provincial Park

A few minutes later, you'll arrive at **Green Cove** rocky ocean headland for a look at the 375-million-year-old granite formations along the shore. Next head to **Black Brook Beach**, a small beach divided by Black Brook. A little farther on is **Jigging Cove Lake.**

For lunch, stop at the picnic area near **Neils Harbour**, or carry on another 20 minutes to **South Harbour.** Not listed on most maps, the stunning yet rather secluded beach here draws few visitors. Drive north to see the gypsum cliffs—a relic of when Cape Breton Island lay in the tropics. A short excursion leads to **Dingwall**, a tiny fishing village on a scenic harbour.

You can do the entire loop—a two-hour drive from one visitor centre to the other—in one day, selecting a few activities en route. Or, return to Neils Harbour taking the alternate route along the coast. Carry on to Ingonish Beach, enjoying the view from a different perspective.

CHÉTICAMP TO NORTH MOUNTAIN & BACK

a full day

From Chéticamp head toward Pleasant Bay, where the Cabot Trail turns inland. Your first destination is just past Pleasant Bay at **MacIntosh Brook,** where a short hike of 15 to 20 minutes will take you through an old-growth forest to a lovely waterfall. Next is **Lone Shieling,** a 15-minute loop through a 350-year-old maple stand, where you'll see a reproduction of a Scottish crofter's hut.

Ascending **North Mountain,** you'll see the oldest rocks in Nova Scotia—more than one-billion-year-old Grenville gneiss and anthracite, once part of the Canadian Shield. At the top look down on **Aspy River,** whose slopes are especially resplendent in the fall, when vibrant yellows and reds paint the maples.

As you descend on the return trip toward **Pleasant Bay,** look for the sparkling waters of the Gulf of St. Lawrence in the V of the mountains ahead. If it's time for lunch, drive to the picnic area at MacIntosh Brook. After lunch, ask one of the locals for directions to **Gampo Abbey,** a Buddhist monastery perched on the coastline, or the Whale Interpretation Centre. Guided tours are available in summer.

On your way back to Chéticamp, stop at the look-off where the road narrows to a ridge called the **Boar's Back.** About 305 m (1,000 ft) below you is **Fishing Cove,** once a tiny Scottish settlement reached only by footpath or boat, and now a wilderness campsite.

Your next stop is **the Bog.** A 15-minute walk on a boardwalk will take you through some fascinating terrain with several interpretive panels. The treasures here include frog eggs, orchids, and carnivorous plants.

If you want to see a moose, head for the **Skyline Trail.** You'll need two to three hours; it's worth keeping to the right and walking the entire loop. Part of the trail leads to a dramatic headland overlooking the **Gulf of St. Lawrence,** where you're likely to catch sight of bald eagles and pilot whales.

As you travel back down North Mountain to meet the Gulf, there are two more places to pull over and enjoy the view: **Veterans Monument** and **Cap Rouge.** The latter has an excellent geology exhibit. You may also see gannets here plummeting 20 to 30 m (66–98 ft) in a nearly vertical dive for food. Next, pull over at **La Bloc,** a picnic area with a great beach—the perfect place for a swim, stroll, or rest. Close off your day with a visit to **Pillar Rock** at Presqu'ile. If there's been a wind, the waves hitting the rock will be mesmerizing.

KAYAKING

The shore along the western side of the park just above Chéticamp up to Corney Brook is accessible in several places. If you paddle north along the coast, you'll pass by **Jumping Brook** and find yourself beneath some towering cliffs. A little farther on you'll find a large sea cave with a high, vaulted ceiling. If the tide is up, you'll be able to paddle all the way in.

Experienced kayakers can launch at Pleasant Bay and paddle to **Pollets Cove.** Pack a few apples for the horses that may greet you when you arrive. If the winds rise and the seas become agitated, you will need extra

A tranquil view of a Cape Breton sunset

time to wait for calmer waters to paddle out. Bring extra food.

On the Atlantic Coast, the best launching and takeout points are the beaches at Neils Harbour, Black Brook, Broad Cove, and Ingonish. On both coasts there are outfitters where you can rent gear or hire guides for paddling excursions.

HIKING, BIKING, & MORE

Up for a challenge? Hike to **Franey,** a two- to three-hour loop from the Information Centre. At the top, follow the narrow gravel trail near the look-off for a breathtaking view of the **Clyburn Brook canyon** and the Atlantic.

For a more relaxed pace, spend the afternoon playing golf at the world-famous **Highlands Links,** voted the best public course in Canada. Or head to **Ingonish Beach,** named one of the top 25 Canadian beaches by *Canadian Geographic Traveller.*

Or consider the **Slacker's Guide:** Sample ten short trails in one day in a variety of habitats. If you have two or more days, you could explore all the trails that lead to a waterfall including **Mary Ann Falls, Beulach Ban Falls,** or **MacIntosh Brook Waterfalls,** and **Corney Brook trails.**

Or go geocaching; 14 caches are strategically placed throughout the park including an Eco-Cache, Cultural Cache, Earth Cache, and the Boomer's Kid Cache. Learn more at the visitor centres.

Cycling can be hugely rewarding along the **Cabot Trail.** A number of private companies offer personalized tours, and many provide shuttle service to get up the steep hills.

Lively and informative interpretive events take place throughout the park during July and August. Programs focus on everything from moose and mountains to whales and local history. Sunset hikes, lake safaris, and Acadian-Scottish concerts are just a few popular programs, along with a star party in August. Schedules are available at the visitor centres, campgrounds, and online.

As well, the local communities host dozens of suppers, ceilidhs, cultural events, and festivals throughout the region. Check local papers and community bulletin boards or ask park staff for more information.

CAPE BRETON HIGHLANDS NATIONAL PARK
(Parc national des Hautes-Terres-du-Cap-Breton)

INFORMATION & ACTIVITIES

VISITOR & INFORMATION CENTRES
Chéticamp Visitor Centre Western entrance near Chéticamp. Phone (902) 224-2306. Features interpretive exhibits, a nature bookshop, and a family corner with games for children ages 3–12. **Ingonish Visitor Centre** Eastern entrance in Ingonish Beach. Phone (902) 285-2691.

SEASONS & ACCESSIBILITY
Park open year-round; full services from late May to early October.

HEADQUARTERS
Ingonish Beach, NS B0C 1L0. Phone (902) 224-2306. www.parkscanada.gc.ca/cape breton.

ENTRANCE FEES
$8 per person, $20 per group per day; $40 per person, $100 per group per year. (A group is up to 7 people in one vehicle.)

PETS
Pets must be in physical control at all times. Owners must control noise levels.

ACCESSIBLE SERVICES
Many of the washrooms and look-offs are accessible, as is the Chéticamp Visitor Centre, some campsites, and the Bog and Freshwater Lake Trails.

THINGS TO DO
Interpretive events in July and August. Interpretive exhibits at 14 look-offs including **La Bloc, Cap Rouge,** the **Veteran's Monument,** and **Fishing Cove,** as well as 7 short trails.

The park also offers 26 hiking trails, geocaching, and swimming at **Ingonish, North Bay, Black Brook, Warren Lake,** and **La Bloc.** Fishing permits $10 per day, $35 per year.

Golfing at Highlands Links *(www .highlandslinksgolf.com);* permit $105 per day. For tee time, call (800) 441-1118. Cross-country skiing in winter. Call (902) 285-2549 for snow and trail conditions.

SPECIAL ADVISORIES
• Be aware of wildlife encounters, especially with coyotes, black bears, or moose. To report incidents, call (877) 852-3100.
• Rogue waves and riptides can be a concern during and after storms.
• Blackflies and mosquitoes are common in the summer; bring insect repellent.

OVERNIGHT BACKPACKING
Permit required for backcountry trekking. Wilderness camping at **Fishing Cove**

EXCURSIONS

ALEXANDER GRAHAM BELL NATIONAL HISTORIC SITE
BADDECK, NS

Teacher, inventor, and humanitarian Alexander Graham Bell accomplished wonders. Located in Baddeck, this site celebrates the life of the man who not only invented the telephone but also produced important inventions and discoveries in medicine, aeronautics, and electrical science. Bell even developed teaching methods to help deaf people better communicate. This site has fascinating exhibits and activities for all ages. (902) 295-2069. 95 km (60 mi) southeast of Cape Breton Highlands on Hwy 105.

campground, accessible only on foot, with tent pads, food cache, and pit privy. Beach nearby. For information and reservations for backcountry camping, call (902) 224-2306.

CAMPGROUNDS

Open year-round; full services available from late May to early October. Unlimited length of stay; for information on camping for longer than 7 nights, visit park website. Maximum four people per site. For reservations call (877) 737-3783 or visit www .pccamping.ca. For information on winter camping, call (902) 285-2691.

Chéticamp, open year-round, has hot showers, kitchen shelters with wood stoves, group fireplaces, playgrounds, and an outdoor theatre. Full services available from late May to early October; flush toilets and kitchen shelters available from October to mid-May. Serviced campsites with electricity, water, and sewer $35 per night. Serviced campsites with electricity $29 per night; unserviced campsites with washroom building (toilets and showers) $26 per night. Winter camping available.

Ingonish, unserviced campsites with washroom building (toilets and showers) $26 per night. Winter camping available. **Broad Cove,** open late June to early September. Serviced campsites with electricity, water, and sewer $35 per night; unserviced campsites with washroom building (toilets and showers) $26 per

night. **MacIntosh Brook** and overflow unserviced campsites with washroom building (toilets only) $22 per night. **Corney Brook,** unserviced campsites with washroom building (toilets only) $24 per night. **Big Intervale,** primitive campground with pit privies $18 per night. Winter camping available at **Black Brook.**

HOTELS, MOTELS, & INNS
(unless otherwise noted, rates are for a 2-person double, high season, in Canadian dollars)

Outside the park:
Inverary Resort 368 Shore Rd., Box 190, Baddeck, NS B0E 1B0. (902) 295-3500 or (800) 565-5660. www.capebretonresorts .com. Packages $99–$229.
Inverness Beach Village Ceilidh Trail, Inverness, NS B0E 1N0. (902) 258-2653 or (902) 463-1663 (Feb.–April). www .macleods.com. $140–$160.
Keltic Lodge 313 Keltic Inn Rd., Ingonish Beach, NS B0C 1L0. (902) 285-2880. www.kelticlodge.ca. Packages $140–$409.
The Normaway Inn & Cabins 691 Egypt Rd., Margaree Valley, NS B0E 2C0. (902) 248-2987 or (800) 565-9463. www.the normawayinn.com. $159–$259.

FORTRESS OF LOUISBOURG NATIONAL HISTORIC SITE
LOUISBOURG, NS

Founded by the French in 1713, later fortified and twice besieged, Louisbourg was demolished and abandoned in the 1760s. In 1961, the Government of Canada invested in what would become the largest reconstruction project in North America. Interpreters in period clothing reenact life as it was before the first siege. There are a multitude of programs and activities. (902) 733-2280. 140 km (87 mi) from park on south side of Cape Breton Island.

Twilight, Kejimkujik seaside

▶KEJIMKUJIK

NOVA SCOTIA
ESTABLISHED 1974
403 sq km/100,000 acres

Referred to by staff and locals as "Keji," Kejimkujik National Park and National Historic Site (see p. 47) teems with wildlife and boasts the greatest diversity of reptiles and amphibians in Atlantic Canada. The park is also home to ancient petroglyphs. Here, the Mi'kmaq cultural landscape dates back centuries. Spanning waterways and forests, the park includes Kejimkujik Seaside, a 22-sq-km (8 sq mi) coastal area replete with a lagoon system and an abundance of beaches, bogs, wildflowers, and coastal wildlife.

In 1995, the inland portion of Kejimkujik was designated a national historic site because of its significant Mi'kmaq heritage. It is the only national park in Canada that has this dual designation. In 2001, UNESCO designated the five counties of southwest Nova Scotia as a biosphere reserve. Kejimkujik inland—which is situated next to the Tobeatic Reserve and the historic Shelburne River, a Canadian Heritage River—is part of this important biosphere.

The park has numerous lakes, many of them dotted with islands, and several still waters. Features also include fascinating barrens, old-growth forests, and elongated hills known as drumlins. Many of the physical features of the park were sculpted in the last ice age.

Keji also has a large concentration of rare plant, insect, and animal species, many of them at risk of extinction. Great care and attention is paid to the preservation and propagation of these species, and the park has a number of educational programs in which visitors can take part.

How to Get There

Kejimkujik inland is accessible from both major highways on either side of the province. From Hwy. 101 take exit 22 close to Annapolis Royal and head inland on Hwy. 8. Allow approximately 30 minutes from the exit. From Hwy. 103, take exit 13 at Bridgewater and follow the signs to Kejimkujik. Allow approximately 50 minutes from the exit.

To visit Kejimkujik Seaside, drive toward Liverpool. Continue west on Hwy. 103. Approximately 7 km (4 mi) past exit 21, turn left onto St. Catherine River Road; it's 6 km (3.5 mi) to the park entrance.

When to Go

Keji is open year-round. Although spring, summer, and fall are the most popular times to visit, many people visit the park during the winter to hike, snowshoe, ski, or experience winter camping. Spring and fall temperatures range from 10° to 15°C (50°–59°F); summer temperatures reach upwards of 24°C (75°F) and in winter they drop between minus 2° and minus 10°C (14°–28°F).

How to Visit

With more than 80 percent of the park accessible only by foot or canoe, Kejimkujik National Park offers backcountry experiences to suit every taste, from relaxing on a secluded island to traversing the park's ancient canoe routes. In fact, one of the best

ways to experience the park is by canoe—the vehicle of choice here for thousands of years.

It's easy to see why Albert Bigelow Payne was so eager to recount his journey here by penning *The Tent Dwellers* more than a hundred years ago. The famous author took a historic fishing trip with his friend Eddie Breck and two guides, Charles "the strong" Charleston and Del "the stout" Thomas. The book is hilarious, poignant, insightful—and for sale in the visitor centre.

Boats and bikes can be rented hourly or for up to a week; fishing permits can also be purchased. Consider renting a canoe or kayak at Jake's Landing and paddling around Lake Kejimkujik, or drive to Merrymakedge for a picnic and swim.

Camping is hugely popular in Kejimkujik, which includes full-service sites along with places for group tenting and backcountry wilderness camping. With 46 backcountry campsites scattered along hiking trails and canoe routes and plenty of space between each site, you'll feel as if you are the only person in the park. Each site is equipped with two tent pads, a fire box, a picnic table, a privy, firewood, and a pulley device to hoist and safely store your food supply.

PETROGLYPH TOUR
a full day

For a one-day visit, sign up at the Visitor Centre for the **Petroglyph Tour** with a Mi'kmaq interpreter. There are more than 500 petroglyphs in the park—the largest collection in North America. These images give a glimpse into the lives of the Mi'kmaq and how they changed when the Europeans arrived. You'll hear stories of how these images came to be and why they are protected.

HIKES

A hiker's haven, Keji features 17 trails ranging from the 0.2-km (0.1 mi) **Mersey Meadow** boardwalk loop to the challenging 19.5-km (12 mi) **Fire Tower Road** hike. Mill Falls (2 km/1 mi return) is an easy hike with a surprise ending, while the **Hemlocks and Hardwoods** 5-km (3 mi) loop will take your breath away when you see 400-year-old hemlocks. Six trails are also suitable for biking.

BIRD-WATCHING

Bird-watchers will have plenty to do at both the inland and seaside locations of the park. You can take part in a variety of monitoring programs like the Piping Plover Guardian Program or become a LoonWatcher, tracking pairs of loons in June or their chicks in August on one of 16 lakes in the park.

Keji lies within the Acadian forest zone, a transition between southern deciduous trees (hardwoods) and northern evergreen trees (softwoods). Pockets of original, ancient forests still stand tall in the park. Most impressive are the towering groves of old-growth eastern hemlocks: nature's cathedrals. If you look up, you may see the northern goshawk, a swift and powerful hunting hawk that likes to nest in the hemlock stands.

KEJI AT NIGHT

Kejimkujik has been designated a Dark Sky Preserve by the Royal Astronomical Society of Canada (see pp. 58–59). This means that Keji

is an area in which active measures are taken to educate and promote the reduction of light pollution.

Join park staff for an evening astronomy program. Bring a blanket and get ready to experience something special as Keji is one of the best places for night sky observation on the eastern seaboard. Kejimkujik dark sky programming is unique as staff combine scientific data with Mi'kmaq legends in a spellbinding presentation.

OTHER ACTIVITIES

When visiting the park with children, consider enrolling them in the Kejimkujik Explorers Club. Sponsored and promoted by a group of volunteers called The Friends of Keji, the Explorers Club is a series of indoor and outdoor educational activities that score high on the fun scale. Each child receives an Explorers Club Passport (available at the outdoor theatre or visitor centre), and every evening the explorers are recognized at a special ceremony.

The park also offers plenty of volunteer opportunities. You can join a core of scientists and trained volunteers and take part in a variety of projects ranging from searching for eastern ribbon snakes and examining their movement patterns to working on loon surveys or protecting Blanding's turtle eggs and tracking their hatchlings.

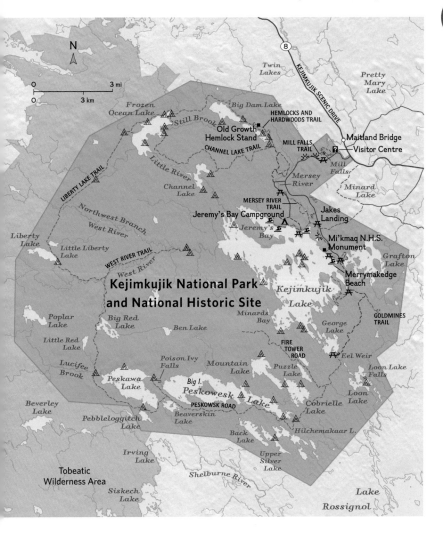

KEJIMKUJIK NATIONAL PARK
(Parc national Kejimkujik)

INFORMATION & ACTIVITIES

VISITOR CENTRE
Kejimkujik and National Historic Site Visitor Centre 3005 Main Parkway, Rte. 8, Maitland Bridge, NS B0T 1B0. Phone (902) 682-2772. Open mid-June to early September (limited hrs. late Sept.–early June).

SEASONS & ACCESSIBILITY
Park open year-round.

HEADQUARTERS
Kejimkujik and National Historic Site Visitor Centre. Phone (902) 682-2772. www.parkscanada.gc.ca/kejimkujik.

FRIENDS OF KEJIMKUJIK
Friends of Keji Cooperating Association 50 Pinetree Crescent, Hammonds Plains, NS B3Z 1K4. info@friendsofkeji.ns.ca; www.friendsofkeji.ns.ca.

ENTRANCE FEES
$6 per person, $15 per group per day; $30 per person, $75 per group per season.

PETS
Owners must leash pets, pick up waste.

ACCESSIBLE SERVICES
The following are wheelchair accessible: visitor centre; boardwalk and viewing platform at **Mersey Meadow Trail;** picnic shelter, deck, and washrooms on **Mill Falls Trail;** six sites and one washroom at **Jeremy's Bay Campground;** washrooms and picnic sites at **Jake's Landing;** playground and picnic area at **Merrymakedge Beach.**

THINGS TO DO
Guided canoe outings, hiking, cycling, swimming, fishing (April–Aug.; permit $10 per day, $34 per year), skiing, and snowshoeing. Rent canoes and bicycles at Jake's Landing.

SPECIAL ADVISORIES
- Bring portable camp stoves for backcountry camping. Open fires may be banned in dry conditions.
- Do not leave food unattended. Pack coolers in vehicles.
- Check with staff before going into backcountry to learn about avoiding wildlife.

OVERNIGHT BACKPACKING
Backcountry camping registration mandatory. 46 backcountry campsites, each with two tent pads, a firebox, a picnic table, a pit privy, and firewood. Backcountry guide and map available for purchase at the visitor centre. For reservations, call (902) 682-2772 or stop by visitor centre.

CAMPGROUNDS
Campgrounds open mid-May to mid-October; 60 sites open for winter camping. **Jeremy's Bay,** 358 sites (91 with electricity), near Kejimkujik Lake. Hot showers, washrooms, outdoor sinks, playgrounds, picnic tables, fireplaces, tent pads, dumping station, and outdoor theatre. For reservations call (877) 737-3783 or visit www.pccamping.ca. Serviced sites with electricity $29 per night; unserviced sites with washroom building (toilets and showers) $26 per night. Primitive sites $26. Group camping at **Jim Charles Point** for up to 80 people, $5 per person.

HOTELS, MOTELS, & INNS
(unless otherwise noted, rates are for a 2-person double, high season, in Canadian dollars)

Outside the park:
Milford House Rte. 8, South Milford, RR#4 Annapolis Royal, NS B0S 1A0. (877) 532-5751. www.milfordhouse.ca. $155–$265. **White Point Beach Resort** Queens County, NS B0T 1G0. (902) 354-2711. www.whitepoint.com. $145. Packages $178–$198. **The Whitman Inn** 12389 Hwy. 8, Kempt, NS B0T 1B0. (902) 682-2226. www.whitmaninn.com. $69–$125. **Caledonia Country Hostel** Caledonia, NS. (902) 682-3266. $60. www.caledoniacountryhostel.com.

EXCURSIONS

FORT ANNE NATIONAL HISTORIC SITE
ANNAPOLIS ROYAL, NS

Canada's oldest national historic site and most attacked fort is full of wonder and intrigue. Its story reaches back more than 3,000 years to the Mi'kmaq. In the 1600s and 1700s, the French and the British set up forts and vied for supremacy. Fort Anne houses an impressive 2.4-by-5.5-m (8 by 18 ft) heritage tapestry, crafted by more than a hundred volunteers using some three million stitches. (902) 532-2397 or (902) 532-2321. 50 km (30 mi) north of park via Hwy. 8.

KEJIMKUJIK NATIONAL HISTORIC SITE
MAITLAND BRIDGE, NS

The entire landscape of Kejimkujik is designated as a national historic site and commemorates Mi'kmaq culture dating back thousands of years. Visitors can join a tour led by a Mi'kmaq interpreter and visit ancient rock carvings known as petroglyphs. The park has a rich history of aboriginal campgrounds and traditional canoe routes. Discover more in the park's visitor centre. (902) 682-2772.

MELANSON SETTLEMENT NATIONAL HISTORIC SITE
ANNAPOLIS ROYAL, NS

Starting in the 1660s and for almost a century, the Melanson Settlement was home to Charles Melanson, Marie Dugas, and their descendants. This site was discovered during a survey for Acadian sites in 1984. Archaeologists eventually located the ruins of several cellars, and the site is now well documented. A short interpretive trail tells the story of this historic Acadian homestead. (902) 532-2321. 75 km (47.5 mi) north of park via Hwy. 8.

Lighthouse at Dalvay in Cavendish, on the north side of Prince Edward Island

▶ PRINCE EDWARD ISLAND

PRINCE EDWARD ISLAND
ESTABLISHED 1937
22 sq km/5,440 acres

Prince Edward Island National Park spans a spectacular stretch of land encompassing sand dunes, salt marshes, remnants of an Acadian forest, coastal headlands, beaches, and sandstone cliffs. This is the land that inspired Lucy Maud Montgomery's *Anne of Green Gables* and prompted an oil tycoon to build an elegant Victorian home. Both Green Gables and Dalvay-by-the Sea are national treasures and showcased within the park.

Approximately 285 million years ago, a mountain chain existed in this region. Over time, its rivers deposited gravel, silt, and sand into a low-lying basin forming sandstone bedrock. As the glaciers retreated, Prince Edward Island gradually took shape.

Situated on the central north shore of Prince Edward Island, the park faces the Gulf of St. Lawrence, where sunsets are storybook perfect. Although one of the smallest parks in Canada, it's a popular destination, with famous beaches and outstanding coastal landscapes. The other attraction is the lure of Lucy Maud Montgomery through her beloved 1908 novel, *Anne of Green Gables*.

The park's ecosystems support a variety of animal species and 400 different species of plants. Although there are no deer or moose on the island, coyotes, red foxes, raccoons, beavers, mink, and weasels are common. With more than 300 species of birds, including the endangered piping plover, the park plays a significant role in shorebird migration in spring and fall.

In 1998, the park expanded to include 4 sq km (990 acres) on the Greenwich Peninsula where rare, U-shaped dunes known as parabolic dunes are located. This is also the region where archaeological digs revealed that Paleo-Indians lived here 10,000 years ago. Evidence indicates that Mi'kmaq, French, Acadian, Scottish, Irish, and English were also early settlers here.

The park is bordered by a number of traditional farming and fishing communities, which adds to the cultural fabric of the island and enhances the visitor's experience.

How to Get There

A number of airlines fly into Charlottetown, the island's capital. Direct service is available from Halifax, Montreal, Toronto, and Ottawa with seasonal direct service from Boston, Detroit, and New York. Connecting service is available every day from Halifax International Airport.

If you are driving, there are two ways to approach the island. One is to take the 12.9-km-long (8 mi) bridge—the longest bridge over ice-covered water in the world—from Cape Jourimain in New Brunswick to Borden-Carleton on Prince Edward Island. The other is to board Northumberland Ferries *(www.peiferry.com)* for a 75-minute sail from Caribou, Nova Scotia, over to Wood Islands.

When to Go

Beach lovers and families will want to visit during July and August, when daytime temperatures range from 18° to 24°C (64°–75°F) and nights are warm. Park activities run full tilt during the operational season (late June–Sept.).

If you prefer solitude, spring and fall are the best seasons for hiking, kayaking, cycling, and bird-watching. Average daytime temperatures in both spring and fall range from 9° to 18°C (48°–64°F) during the day and 5° to 10°C (41°–50°F) at night. The fall tends to be balmy and quite warm until mid-October.

Birders have lots to observe in the park year-round; highlights include migration and nesting seasons. Seasonal dates determined by the migratory habits of most birds are: mid-March to late May (northerly migration), early June to mid-August (nesting season), and mid-August to mid-December (southerly migration).

If you are interested in adding culinary travel to your park experience, the island hops with a special food festival called Fall Flavours during the month of September. The annual Fall Frolic hosted by the Parks and People Association features pumpkin carving and is fun for all ages.

During the winter, many trails are kept open and maintained. A pair of skis or snowshoes is all you will need to disappear into a unique wonderland. Access to facilities such as washrooms and visitor services may be limited outside the summer season.

How to Visit

There are three distinct segments of the park: **Cavendish, Brackley-Dalvay,** and **Greenwich,** each with its own unique characteristics. You'll need a vehicle to get from one to another. Once you have arrived, however, the best way to enjoy the park is by foot or bike.

Visitors to the Cavendish and Brackley-Dalvay sectors of the park will find supervised beaches, camp-grounds, and a number of trails of easy to moderate difficulty adapted to both hiking and cycling.

Both Cavendish and Stanhope have full-service campgrounds; organized groups can contact the park to arrange for group camping at a unique campsite and day-use area. There is no camping offered at Greenwich, but private accommodations are located close by and it's only a 30- to 40-minute drive to Stanhope or Brackley. Natural and cultural history really come alive at evening campfire activities held at **Cavendish** and **Stanhope Campgrounds,** where interpreters present the park's heritage through storytelling and skits with the aid of costumes and music.

Along with your camp gear, consider bringing a kite. With all the wide-open spaces and gentle breezes, kite flying is a snap. Field glasses are also a good thing to have along as there's always something that you'll want to see up close and personal. Tracking animals is especially fun.

In-park interpretive activities such as guided walks, geocaching programs, and evening campfire presentations are listed in the visitor guide and posted throughout the park during the summer peak season. All activities are presented in both French and English and are delivered by experienced and engaging interpreters. Programs and activities change on a daily basis.

The key is to talk with park personnel. Find one of the many uniformed staff persons and ask for suggestions of things to do and places to go. They always have great ideas. Don't be surprised if one of the staff invites you to come along and see a hidden treasure or shares with you a favourite place. Known to be friendly, islanders are also a good source of information.

Guided walks along trails in Cavendish and Greenwich are always a big hit. The focus is usually on wildlife, ecology, and other natural features of protected coastal areas,

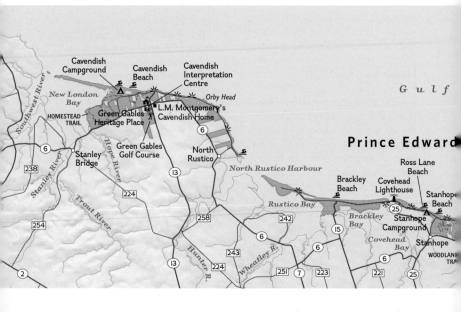

as well as the rich cultural history of Prince Edward Island's north shore.

Interpretive signage throughout the park enhances self-guided hikes and provides insights into the natural and cultural significance of each area.

CAVENDISH
a full day

If you are approaching from Confederation Bridge, head to Cavendish to experience **Green Gables Heritage Place** (separate fee applies). Kids love the puppet show and old-fashioned games and races. You'll also want to visit the home of Lucy Maud Montgomery (1874–1942). The bucolic setting has not changed since the author lived here.

Top up your day with a stroll or swim at the beach, famous worldwide for its sweeping shores and endless vistas. Golfers can enjoy a round at **Green Gables Golf Course,** designed in 1939 by Stanley Thompson, one of the world's most celebrated golf

course architects. Or, if you like to run, walk, hike, or bike, select one of six unique trails to explore, such as the 8.8-km (5.5 mi) **Homestead Trail** and the wooded trail network at **Cavendish Grove.**

BRACKLEY TO DALVAY
a full day

Bird-watchers will want to start the day at **Brackley,** where **Covehead Wharf** offers the best place for shorebird-watching, especially at low tide, when exposed mudflats become popular feeding and resting grounds for dozens of species.

This is also one of the nesting grounds of the endangered piping plover, which is monitored and protected by Parks Canada resource conservation staff in closed-off sections. These sections offer excellent vantage points to observe the bird without posing a threat; if they are not present, many other species will equally delight. Check with park staff about

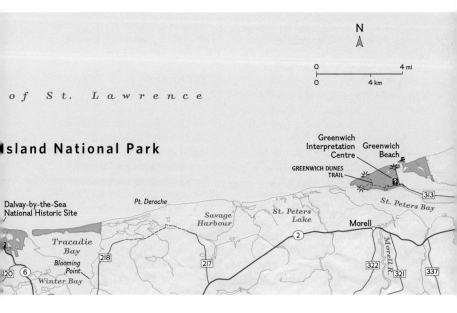

Greenwich Dunes Trail

weekly bird-watching activities led by experienced interpreters. Checklists are available at visitor centres, campgrounds, and entrance kiosks.

Covehead Lighthouse and the surrounding shoreline make for an interesting stop between Stanhope and Dalvay-by-the-Sea. Look for the plaque on the lighthouse commemorating the infamous Yankee Gale storm of 1851, which wrecked close to one hundred ships and claimed the lives of more than 150 sailors. On the **Bubbling Springs** and **Farmlands Trails,** look for the unmarked gravestones that mark the resting place of the sailors who perished in that storm.

In the afternoon, picnic or swim at **Ross Lane Beach.** Or drive over to **Dalvay-by-the-Sea** for high tea. Enjoy the famous sticky date pudding at this national historic site while admiring the building's exquisite late Victorian–style architecture.

Hikers will find eight trails in this part of the park including **Gulf Shore Way,** which spans 10 km (6 mi) from Brackley to Dalvay-by-the-Sea and is also suitable for in-line skating. Walking or biking even part of this trail provides excellent views of the park's coastal ecosystems, and there are several stopping points and observation posts along the way. Bike rentals are available at Dalvay-by-the-Sea.

The **Reeds & Rushes Trail** is also hugely popular. Hike the trail early in the morning or around dusk and you may see some beavers. Just about any time of day you'll see hundreds of dragonflies including sedge sprites, wandering gliders, and ruby meadowhawks.

GREENWICH

a full day

If you enter the island from Nova Scotia and have only one day to spend in the park, head for Greenwich. Although Greenwich is part of the park system, it is one of the island's best kept secrets, and it can be far less crowded than Cavendish or Brackley-Dalvay. Nevertheless, it has a full range of services including beach supervision, washrooms, change rooms, and showers as well as an indoor resting and picnic area.

Increasingly, outdoor-activity lovers are including the Greenwich portion of the park into their itinerary. Start your visit at the **Greenwich Interpretation Centre,** where you'll find a variety of interactive exhibits geared toward all ages—such as the **Salt Water Touch Tank,** with walkover three-dimensional floor map and coastal environmental exhibit—that showcase the natural features and ecology of the park. Moreover, these exhibits highlight the rich cultural history of the Greenwich area, which has been inhabited by different cultural groups over the past 10,000 years. Along with the exhibit there's a Mi'kmaq People interpretive program and an informative 12-minute multimedia presentation that will catapult you back in time. Kids can also sign up for the new Parks Canada Xplorer Program.

Your visit to Greenwich won't be complete until you go for a hike on the **Greenwich Dunes Trail.** The longest and most popular of the three trails in this part of the park, the Greenwich Dunes Trail is a 4.5-km (3 mi) return trail of moderate difficulty that features an interesting floating boardwalk. Along the trail you'll discover different ecosystems including field, forest, wetlands, and coastal systems while enjoying breathtaking views of Greenwich's parabolic dune system and associated counter ridges, or Gegenwälle—all rare dune formations.

The Greenwich Dunes Trail also leads to one of Prince Edward Island's most spectacular beaches. While unsupervised and not recommended for swimming, it boasts breathtaking views of the parabolic dune system. Upon your return, you will still have time for a stroll or swim on the supervised main beach at **Greenwich.**

The short, 1.25-km (0.8 mi) **Havre St. Pierre Trail** leads you to interpretive signage on an observation deck that explains the history of St. Peter's Bay and the rope-cultured mussel harvest that is part of the economic fabric of the island. The trail is wheelchair accessible.

The third trail, **Tlaqatik,** runs an easy 4.5 km (2.8 mi) through the dunes with terrific views of the bay.

A summer sunset on the island's beach

Great blue herons, Tracadie Bay

KAYAKING

One of the more interesting ways to take in the natural beauty of Prince Edward Island National Park is to kayak segments of the coastline. Consider paddling between **Tracadie Bay** and **Blooming Point. Covehead Bay** and **Brackley Bay** are also great spots, as is **New London Harbour.** Although not as well-known, **St. Peter's Bay** and the rivers that flow into the bay, such as the **Morell, St. Mary's,** and **St. Peter's,** offer many kayaking pleasures.

Park staff can advise you about where to launch your boat and can also make suggestions on how to navigate the waters safely. Although you can't rent a kayak in the park, there are reputable outfitters in the nearby communities who have excellent gear for rent; some even offer day trips.

LONGER STAYS

3 days

For an extended visit, consider any combination of the above scenarios. For example, you may want to spend one full day in the Cavendish area, checking out Green Gables Heritage

Place, relaxing on the beach, and hiking or cycling along the Homestead or Gulf Shore Way. Finish the day by taking part in an interpretive walk or enjoying an evening campfire.

A second day would give you a chance to explore the Brackley-Dalvay area and uncover its natural and cultural history, perhaps by taking in a popular bird-watching activity at Covehead Wharf or a guided pond walk in nearby Dalvay. Check the interpretive activity schedule, or visit these areas on your own if you've brought along binoculars and an appropriate bird or field guide.

Another full day can easily be spent exploring Greenwich, especially if the weather is fine.

VISITING IN WINTER

During the winter season, ice along the north shore gives the impression that the beach extends forever into the Gulf of St. Lawrence. Snowshoeing to the **Greenwich Dunes** is a breathtaking hike as is skiing on the groomed trails in Cavendish or Brackley-Dalvay. Skating on **Dalvay Lake** on a crisp winter day is also a great family activity.

PRINCE EDWARD ISLAND NATIONAL PARK
(Parc national de l'Île-du-Prince-Édouard)

INFORMATION & ACTIVITIES

VISITOR & INFORMATION CENTRES
Cavendish Destination Centre Open May to September. **Greenwich Interpretation Centre** Open June to September.

SEASONS & ACCESSIBILITY
Park open year-round. Full services available in July and August.

HEADQUARTERS
2 Palmers Lane, Charlottetown, PE C1A 5V8. Phone (902) 672-6350. www.parks canada.gc.ca/pei.

FRIENDS OF PRINCE EDWARD ISLAND
Parks & People Association P.O. Box 1506, Charlottetown, PE C1A 7N3. Phone (902) 894-4246. parksandpeople@pei. aibn.com; http://parksandpeople.ca.

ENTRANCE FEES
$8 per person, $20 per group per day; $39 per person, $98 per group per season.

PETS
Pets must be leashed and attended at all times. Dogs are not permitted on the beaches from April to mid-October.

ACCESSIBLE SERVICES
Brackley Beach is wheelchair accessible, and a beach wheelchair is available free of charge for wheelchair users who wish to explore the shoreline.

THINGS TO DO
Public interpretive activities are available throughout the park and **Green Gables Heritage Place** in the summer. Green Gables Heritage Tour ($8 per person, $20 per group per day; $4 per person, $10 per group Nov.–April).

The park also offers seven beaches for swimming; surfguards are on duty from late June to late August. Canoeing and kayaking are available on the ponds and in the Gulf of St. Lawrence; motorized watercraft are not permitted.

In winter, cross-country skiing is available on the **Woodlands** and **Bubbling Springs Trails** and on the **Cavendish Grove Ski Trail;** warm-up shelters and washrooms are located nearby. Skating is available on **Dalvay Lake.** Call (902) 672-6350 for snow and ice conditions.

The private 18-hole **Green Gables** Golf Course is located within the park boundaries. Call (902) 963-4653 or (888) 870-5454 or visit www.ander sonscreek.com.

SPECIAL ADVISORIES
- When swimming, watch for heavy surf, deep channels, currents, rocks, shallow sandbars, and rip currents.
- Do not get too close to the edges of the cliffs, as the rocks are eroding quickly.
- Arctic red jellyfish in the Gulf of St. Lawrence may sting. If you are stung while swimming, rub wet sand over the irritated area.
- Watch for poison ivy in some parts of the park.

CAMPGROUNDS
Campgrounds open June to October. Maximum number of persons per site is six. For reservations call (877) 737-3783 or visit www.pccamping.ca. $35 for serviced campsites with electricity, water, and sewer; $32 for serviced campsites with electricity and water; $26 for unserviced campsites with washroom building (toilets and showers); and $27 for unserviced high-occupancy sites at Stanhope and Cavendish campgrounds.

Stanhope, fire pits at some sites; showers; playground, laundromat, and kitchen shelters. On-site interpretive programs in July and August. **Cavendish,** more than 200 sites, beach on-site, fire pits at some sites, showers, playground, and laundromat. On-site interpretive programs in July and August. Group camping is available for organized groups. Contact the park for reservations and rates.

HOTELS, MOTELS, & INNS
(unless otherwise noted, rates are for a 2-person double, high season, in Canadian dollars)

Outside the park:
Greenwich Gate Lodge (877) 961-3496. www.greenwichgate.com. $119–$169. Weekly cottage rental $1,180.
Johnson Shore Inn 9984 Rte. 16, Hermanville, PE C0A 2B0. (902) 687-1340 or (877) 510-9669. http://johnsonshore inn.com. $175–$350 breakfast included.
Rodd Crowbush Golf & Beach Resort

632 Rte. 350, Morell, PE C0A 1S0. (902) 961-5600. www.roddhotelsandresorts .com. 49 hotel units, $130–$315; 32 cottages, $195–$590 for one to four occupants. Open mid-May to mid-October.
Shaw's Hotel 99 Apple Tree Rd., Brackley Beach, PE C1E 1Z3. (902) 672-2022. info@ shawhotel.ca; http://shawhotel.ca. $145–$350 for rooms, suites, and cottages.

For additional visitor information:
Prince Edward Island Tourism (902) 368-4444 or (800) 463-4734, www .tourismpei.com.

EXCURSIONS

ARDGOWAN NATIONAL HISTORIC SITE
CHARLOTTETOWN, PE

This site was the home of William Henry Pope, one of the Fathers of Confederation. It was also the scene of lavish entertaining during the historic Charlottetown Conference. Pope was an avid gardener and the property reflects his passion. Visitors are encouraged to stroll around the grounds and have a picnic. Parks Canada administrative offices are located inside. (902) 566-7050.

PORT-LA-JOYE—FORT AMHERST NATIONAL HISTORIC SITE
ROCKY POINT, PE

Established in 1720, this site was originally a French outpost. Later it served as a British fort and also as the administrative capital of the island until 1768, when the capital was moved to Charlottetown. Located in Rocky Point on Rte. 19, the grassy ruins of the fort are still visible. Enjoy guided walks, interpretive events, animated theatre skits, and a great view of Charlottetown harbour. (902) 566-7626. 26 km (16 mi) south of Charlottetown via Capital Drive/Hwy. 1.

DALVAY-BY-THE-SEA NATIONAL HISTORIC SITE
PRINCE EDWARD ISLAND NP, PE

Located on Rte. 6 in Prince Edward Island National Park, this Queen Anne Revival–style home was built in 1896 as a summer residence for Alexander McDonald, a Scottish-American oil tycoon. Dalvay-by-the-Sea now operates as a resort inn. Learn about the fascinating features of this home, how it was constructed, and the extravagant lifestyle of the original owner. (902) 566-7626. 35 km (21.9 mi) east of Cavendish via Hwy. 13.

L. M. MONTGOMERY'S CAVENDISH NATIONAL HISTORIC SITE
CHARLOTTETOWN, PE

This site includes Lucy Maud Montgomery's Cavendish Home and Green Gables Heritage Place, where the world-renowned author drew the inspiration to write *Anne of Green Gables*—the first of 23 novels. View a film and exhibits at the visitor centre, enjoy guided activities, and stroll to Montgomery's gravesite. Close by are the Haunted Wood Trail and Lovers Lane, featured in her books. (902) 963-7874. Palmers Lane, Cavendish.

PROVINCE HOUSE NATIONAL HISTORIC SITE
CHARLOTTETOWN, PE

Although July 1, 1867, marks the birth of Canada, delegates met for the first time in Province House in September 1864 to discuss the future of the British colonies in North America. No formal records of the Charlottetown Conference exist—only letters. But, guided tours, displays, and an audiovisual presentation help visitors imagine the deliberations in the original library setting. (902) 566-7626. 2.5 km (1.5 mi) south park headquarters corner of Richmond & Great George.

Preserving Starry Skies

Diamond dust. It looks as if the mighty hands of the gods spread a broad arc of diamond dust across the heavens. The sharp, cold glitter of thousands of distant stars encircles the sky with a ghostly embrace of ancient light. This is the Milky Way, our home galaxy. But only if you are lucky enough to be somewhere free of light pollution will you see its majestic splendour.

Comet Lulin as it passed near Saturn, in the early hours of February 24, 2009

When was the last time a view of the night sky sent shivers up your spine? Most North Americans live in urban areas where there is so much artificial light at night that the stars are only a faint memory. From cities and towns we see only a handful of the brightest stars. The rest are lost in an expanding glow of artificial light that is enveloping the world. Globally, more than 1.3 billion people—one fifth of the world's population—can no longer see the Milky Way with unaided eyes.

In the face of swelling populations and spreading urbanization, what can be done to save some of the night? The Royal Astronomical Society of Canada has initiated a Dark Sky Preserve (DSP) program *(www.rasc.ca/lpa/darksky.shtml)*. Working with partners like Parks Canada, the program has been remarkably successful in establishing areas where nature's night environment is protected and preserved for the benefit of all species, including humans.

"Parks Canada supports the DSP program," says Jonathan Sheppard, of Kejimkujik National Park and National Historic Site, "because it fits our mandate of protection, education, outreach, and visitor experience: protecting nocturnal ecology, implementing an energy-saving dark-sky-compliant lighting strategy for our facilities, teaching about astronomy and light control, working with astronomy partners, and creating new, engaging programs for visitors."

DSPs protect the night sky by controlling the number, placement, and design of lighting fixtures. No excess light spills over where it is not needed. Eliminating light pollution ensures visitors can appreciate the night while also providing plants and animals with the most natural habitat possible.

Every species on Earth is connected and interdependent. Can we afford to ignore half of the systems that sustain us? Life's systems have evolved, and continue to need, to experience the day-night cycle. It is necessary for our health and well-being.

Light pollution affects humans and wildlife, interfering with the growth, behaviour, and survival of nocturnal species everywhere. Many species need the day-night cycle to synchronize their biological rhythms. Some adapt behaviour in response to changing nighttime light levels from the lunar cycle. But light levels at night in urban and suburban areas are brighter than full moonlight.

Parks Canada is charged with protecting and presenting Canada's natural and cultural heritage, and fostering understanding, appreciation, and enjoyment of that heritage into the future. People come to Canada's national parks for recreation and to reconnect with nature. DSPs enable us to fully experience nature's diurnal cycle. We can see the stars and feel night's whispering magic. DSPs will become increasingly important as society becomes more urbanized with more people living in a 24-hour artificial day.

By lighting up the night we have divorced ourselves from our evolutionary history and cultural heritage. We have disconnected ourselves from Earth's life-sustaining natural systems. We are losing touch with our place in the universe.

We must dim the lights!

Parks Canada's Dark Sky Preserves are leading the way, becoming "dark beacons" of hope for the future of our natural environment. Come see the stars!

— MARY LOU WHITEHORNE, *President*
The Royal Astronomical Society of Canada

RASC Dark Sky Reserves/Preserves

The Royal Astronomical Society of Canada has certified 11 Dark Sky Preserves in Canada to date. Seven* of these are part of the Parks Canada system. More are planned.

- Torrance Barrens Dark Sky Reserve, ON—1999
- Cypress Hills National Park Dark Sky Preserve, AB—2005*
- Beaver Hills Dark Sky Preserve, AB—2006
- Point Pelee National Park Dark Sky Preserve, ON—2006*
- Gordon's Park Dark Sky Preserve, Manitoulin Island, ON—2008
- Kouchibouguac National Park Dark Sky Preserve, NB—2009*
- Bruce Peninsula National Park and Five Fathoms National Marine Park Dark Sky Preserve, ON—2009*
- Mount Carleton Provincial Park Dark Sky Preserve, NB—2009
- Grasslands National Park Dark Sky Preserve, SK—2009*
- Kejimkujik National Park and National Historic Site Dark Sky Preserve, NS—2010*
- Jasper National Park Dark Sky Preserve, AB—2011*

View of Kellys Beach from the boardwalk

▶ KOUCHIBOUGUAC

NEW BRUNSWICK
ESTABLISHED 1969
239 sq km/59,000 acres

Kouchibouguac National Park covers an area of protected land on the eastern shore of New Brunswick. Representative of the maritime plain natural region and the Atlantic–Gulf of St. Lawrence marine region, it features a number of fascinating ecosystems including the Acadian forest, bogs, salt marshes, tidal rivers, lagoons, open fields, and approximately 25 km (15 mi) of fragile white-sand dunes.

Pronounced ᴋᴏᴏ-she-boo-gwack, Kouchibouguac is a Mi'kmaq word meaning "river of long tides." There are 26 known aboriginal archaeological sites in the park—a testimony to the park's rich cultural history. Acadian, Irish, and English settlers also lived and worked here, and their legacy lives on.

More than half of the park is occupied by forests, including significant stands of rare forest vegetation that are part of the Acadian forest. Peat bogs cover another 21 percent of the park. These bogs are about 5,000 years old and measure up to 6 m (20 ft) deep at the domed centres of the bogs. Although salt marshes are not a large part of the park, 72 plant species have been identified. As well, several species of waterfowl breed here.

The Barrier Islands—a unique feature that includes a series of dune systems—span a small but significant portion of the park. Stretching 25 km (15 mi), these dune systems shelter estuaries, lagoons, and salt marshes in an intensely dynamic coastal environment. Influenced by the presence of the Gulf of St. Lawrence, the dunes are ever changing due to the influence of tides, storms, and shifting sands.

The diverse wildlife and flora in the park includes salmon, eel, piping plovers, common terns, ospreys, mussels, crabs, and oysters along with widgeon grass and eelgrass. There are nine rare plants including the rayless aster and southern twayblade. Recreational clam harvesting is encouraged and enjoyed.

How to Get There

The park is located in Kent County on New Brunswick's central eastern shore in an area known as the Acadian Coastal Drive. It is a one-hour drive north from Moncton, a four-hour drive from the Quebec border, or a four-hour drive northeast of Maine. Take Hwy. 15 to Shediac and then either Hwy. 11 heading north or the more scenic Rte. 134.

When to Go

The park is open year-round. Although the warmer months (May–Oct.) are the most popular, people are discovering the joy of winter activities. There are three trails specifically designated for winter walking, three for snowshoeing, and a 22-km (14 mi) groomed trail system for cross-country skiing. Cozy warm-up huts with wood stoves are strategically placed along the trails, and winterized camping shelters are accessible by ski or snowshoe. Skis, snowshoes, and sleds for transporting young children or gear are available for rent.

How to Visit

Start at the visitor reception centre and plan to spend time at the new interpretive centre. Here you will get an overview of the natural aspects of the park, learn how it was created, and experience the four seasons through a lively audiovisual presentation. At the visitor centre you will also find detailed information about park activities.

If you have two or more days to spend, Kouchibouguac has 311 campsites (both serviced and unserviced) as well as semiprimitive campsites for those who want to rough it—but not too much. Primitive campsites, accessible only by foot, bike, kayak, or canoe, are available for those who *really* want to rough it. Dune camping, referred to as "no impact camping," is also an option but special conditions apply. For example, no open fires are allowed, walking paths are restricted, and tents must be placed on sand and 5 m (16 ft) away from any vegetation.

The park offers Step-on-Guide Services for motorcoach tours, organized groups, or families. Simply request that a park interpreter accompany you on a specific trail or for a particular activity and this will be arranged (service available in spring,

Bicycling along a summer path

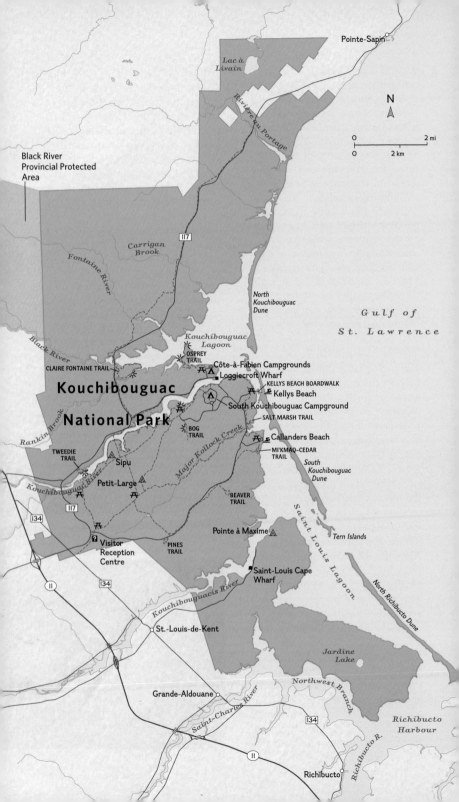

Pointe-Sapin

Lac à Livain

Rivière au Portage

Black River Provincial Protected Area

117

Carrigan Brook

Fontaine River

North Kouchibouguac Dune

G u l f   o f
S t.   L a w r e n c e

Kouchibouguac Lagoon

OSPREY TRAIL

Black River

CLAIRE FONTAINE TRAIL

Côte-à-Fabien Campgrounds
Loggiecroft Wharf

KELLYS BEACH BOARDWALK
Kellys Beach

South Kouchibouguac Campground

Kouchibouguac

National Park

SALT MARSH TRAIL

BOG TRAIL

Rankin Brook

Major Kollock Creek

Callanders Beach

MI'KMAQ–CEDAR TRAIL

South Kouchibouguac Dune

TWEEDIE TRAIL

Sipu

Petit-Large

Kouchibouguac River

117

134

BEAVER TRAIL

Saint Louis Lagoon

Tern Islands

Visitor Reception Centre

PINES TRAIL

Pointe à Maxime

11

134

Saint-Louis Cape Wharf

North Richibucto Dune

Kouchibouguacis River

St.-Louis-de-Kent

Jardine Lake

Northwest Branch

Grande-Aldouane

Saint-Charles River

134

11

Richibucto

Richibucto R.

Richibucto Harbour

N

0   2 mi
0   2 km

summer, and fall seasons only; advance notice is required).

HIKING & KAYAKING

With 60 km (37 mi) of bikeways, Kouchibouguac is recognized as one of the best biking destinations in Atlantic Canada. The trails are wide, relatively flat, and topped with fine gravel. If you plan to spend one day, rent a bike and choose one of the flat cycling loops. They range from 14 to 27 km (9–17 mi) and boast spectacular scenery.

If paddling is your style, rent a canoe or kayak and explore the lagoons or paddle along the **Kouchibouguac River** and see the **Great Leaning Red Pine Tree** growing out of a sandstone outcropping. The tree stretches horizontally over the river, and you can actually paddle underneath it. With eight Class I (flat-water) rivers flowing into the park, canoeing and kayaking are ideal and safe activities.

VOYAGEUR CANOE MARINE ADVENTURE
3 hours

For a unique adventure, book a three-hour excursion with a park interpreter and join a few others in the "grand canoe" for a trek to the **Barrier Islands,** where you'll see hundreds of grey seals. There are approximately 700 in the colony. Along the way you'll also likely see ospreys, bald eagles, and other bird species including the second largest tern colony in North America. Paddling experience is not necessary; age limit is six years and up. Reservations are highly recommended as the canoe can only accommodate eight people at a time. (506) 876-2443. Cost $30 per person. 186 Rte 117, Kouchibouguac, NB E4X 2P1.

VISITING WITH KIDS

If you are visiting with children, consider going to **Kellys Beach,** where you can enjoy a swim, take part in the Puppet Theatre presentation, or join a park interpreter for a hands-on activity to see what's lurking in a salt-water lagoon. Through the Lagoon Life Program, children learn all about crabs, sticklebacks, and moonsnails.

Another option is to buy a picnic lunch at Kellys Beach Canteen then head to **Callanders Beach** (day-use area), a great place for young children as the water is warm and shallow. If you have time, check out the self-guided **Mi'kmaq Cedar Trail.** Chances are you'll be able to join a First Nation interpreter for a Mi'kmaq cultural experience in a wigwam.

Kids aged six to ten love the Young Naturalist Club, which exposes them

Relaxing at a winter shelter

KOUCHIBOUGUAC NATIONAL PARK
(Parc national Kouchibouguac)

INFORMATION & ACTIVITIES

VISITOR CENTRE
Visitor Reception Centre Phone (506) 876-2443. Open mid-May to mid-October. Park attendants available from December to March.

SEASONS & ACCESSIBILITY
Park open year-round. Administration office open weekdays year-round.

HEADQUARTERS
186 Rte. 117, Kouchibouguac National Park, NB E4X 2P1. Phone (506) 876-2443. www.parkscanada.gc.ca/kouchibouguac.

FRIENDS OF KOUCHIBOUGUAC
Amica, Inc. Kouchibouguac National Park, 186 Rte. 117, Unit 1, Kouchibouguac National Park, NB E4X 2P1. Phone (506) 876-1234. amica@nbnet.nb.ca; www .friendsofkouchibouguac.ca.

ENTRANCE FEES
$8 per person, $20 per group per day; $39 per person, $98 per group per season. Reduced rates April to mid-June and September to end of November.

PETS
Pets must be leashed and attended at all times. Pets are not permitted on the barrier islands or on the boardwalks leading to the barrier islands.

ACCESSIBLE SERVICES
The **Salt Marsh Trail, Mi'kmaq Cedar Trail,** and boardwalk at **Kellys Beach** are wheelchair accessible. All washroom facilities are also wheelchair accessible.

THINGS TO DO
Hiking; biking (helmets mandatory); swimming (warm waters in Kouchibouguac inner bay, cooler waters in the Northumberland Strait); canoeing; and kayaking.

Bicycles and boating equipment available for rent at the Ryans Recreation Equipment Rental Centre (mid-May–mid-Sept.) near South Kouchibouguac Campground. Fishing permits $10 per day, $34 per year.

In winter, cross-country skiing, snowshoeing, and sledding. Cross-country skiing trail use $8 per person, $20 per group per day; $39 per person, $98 per group per season.

---

to new adventures and challenges. Children and adults can also take part in the Citizen Science Program while contributing to the park's ecological integrity. Join a group and participate in a mission to count aquatic species from the estuaries.

DARK-SKY DELIGHTS

In 2009, the Royal Astronomical Society of Canada designated Kouchibouguac a Dark Sky Preserve (see pp. 58–59). This means the park minimizes lighting at night and encourages public awareness of the cultural heritage of the night sky. As a bonus, one of the park's interpreters is an expert astronomer and leads some of the nighttime programs for visitors.

During one of these programs, you may witness the wonders of a meteor shower, glimpse planets, and hear stories, legends, and myths from Mi'kmaq folklore and as portrayed by the stars. Visitors are also introduced to the basics of astronomy and learn why the dark sky is important to the birds, bats, insects, and amphibians that live in Kouchibouguac. You can also observe Saturn's rings, craters on the moon, galaxies, and nebulae by using the park's special light-gathering telescopes.

SPECIAL ADVISORIES
- Wear minimum SPF 15 sunscreen at Kellys Beach; there is no natural shade.
- Contact the visitor centre to inquire about jellyfish conditions in the beaches.

OVERNIGHT BACKPACKING
Fees for backcountry use and camping: $10 per person per night, $69 per person per year. Eight primitive campsites at **Petit-Large** open year-round and accessible by bicycle or on foot. Four canoe campsites at **Pointe-à-Maxime** accessible only by canoe and/or kayak. Four canoe campsites at **Sipu** accessible by canoe or on foot. Parking lot camping, $19 per vehicle per night, available mid-October to April.

CAMPGROUNDS
South Kouchibouguac, open mid-May to mid-October, 311 frontcountry sites for tents and RVs; 127 have electrical hook-ups. Campground has fireplaces, kitchen shelters, picnic tables, playgrounds, washrooms, and showers. Unserviced campsites with washroom building (toilets and showers) $27–$32 per night. $16 per night for primitive and backcountry camping. Rustic shelters available early December to late March; stove and firewood provided; accessible only by

skiing and snowshoeing. **Côte-à-Fabien,** open mid-June to early September, 32 campsites with fireplaces, picnic tables, and pit toilets. Group camping $5 per person per night. For reservations call (506) 876-2443.

HOTELS, MOTELS, & INNS
(unless otherwise noted, rates are for a 2-person double, high season, in Canadian dollars)

<u>Outside the park:</u>
Auberge Le Vieux Presbytère Bouctouche, NB E4S 3B8. (506) 743-5568 or (866) 743-1880. aubergevp@nb.aibn.com; www.vieuxpresbytere.nb.ca. $109–$165.
Kouchibouguac Resort 10983 Rte. 134, St. Louis, NB E4X 1W6. (506) 876-4317 or (888) 524-3200. www.kouch.com. Rooms $170–$180, cottages $115–$135, and condo-chalets $125-145.
Maison Tait House 293 Main St., Shediac, NB E4P 2A8. (506) 532-4233 or (888) 532-4233. Rooms start at $159.

EXCURSION

BOISHÉBERT NATIONAL HISTORIC SITE
MIRAMICHI, NB

During the deportation of 1755, many Acadians followed French-Canadian officer Charles Deschamps de Boishébert, taking refuge on an island of the same name. Now Beaubears Island, it achieved fame for its shipbuilding in the early 19th century. The island contains part of an old-growth Acadian forest and can be reached via a short shuttle ferry (foot passengers only) from Nelson-Miramichi. (506) 876-2443. 52 km (32.1 mi) northwest of Kouchibouguac via Hwy. 134.

Sea kayaking on the Bay of Fundy

▶ FUNDY

NEW BRUNSWICK
ESTABLISHED 1948
206 sq km/50,900 acres

Time and tides wait for no man, the saying goes. And it's most true at Fundy National Park on New Brunswick's east coast, where, twice daily, the most dramatic tides in the world cover the ocean bed with up to 12 m (38 ft) of water—the equivalent of a four-storey building. Over the next six hours, the water then sluices back to reveal the sea bottom: mucky, covered with seaweed, and bursting with intertidal wildlife.

One of Canada's smallest national parks, New Brunswick's first, and now a finalist for one of the seven Natural Wonders of the World, Fundy encompasses about 12 km (8 mi) of famous Fundy shoreline along Chignecto Bay, as well as a large slice of the maritime Acadian Highlands natural region of Canada. This rich natural system of forests, once threatened by human development,

is now recovering nicely; the only human activity here these days is the quiet footfall of hikers travelling its varied network of coastal, forest, and waterfall-destination trails.

The Acadian forest here blends two types of tree populations: the more northern spruce and fir evergreen boreal forests common in northern New Brunswick, and the maple, yellow birch, larch, aspen, beech, and balsam hardwood forests typical of the more southeasterly Great Lakes–St. Lawrence region. This forest, much of it festooned with dangling "old man's beard" lichen, is growing in place of earlier, logged-out softwoods. A century ago, logging came close to destroying vast swatches of woodland. Today the park is home to the world's oldest red spruce tree at 400 years old.

How to Get There

Nearby airports include Moncton, St. John, and Fredericton, New Brunswick, with Moncton the closest to the park and Fredericton the farthest away. All three airports have car rentals available.

Bus terminals operate in Moncton and in the village of Sussex, just off Trans-Canada 2. Sussex is closer to the park than Moncton and also has car rental services. Note that there is no public transportation to and from the park itself.

If you are driving to the park from Fredericton, head east on Trans-Canada 2 toward Moncton, turning south at exit 365 (Coles Island) and onto Provincial Hwy. 10 to Sussex. Then head northeast on Hwy. 1, turning east on Hwy. 114 (at exit 211) to the park. From St. John, drive northeast on Hwy. 1, then turn onto Hwy. 114 at exit 211. From Moncton, drive southwest, all the way on Hwy. 114.

When to Go

Peak season runs from late spring through autumn, with the summer months of June, July, and August offering the best weather and a somewhat lower likelihood of stubborn fog, though morning fogs are common throughout the summer and can be great for viewing. The visitor centre closes at 4:15 p.m. in spring and fall, and stays open until 9:45 p.m. throughout July and August.

Most campgrounds and campsites are seasonal, except for Headquarters Campground, which is open year-round. Ski and snowshoe trails are kept groomed, as is a tobogganing hill. The road to Point Wolfe closes with the first snow and reopens when it's clear in the spring.

How to Visit

If you are interested in seeing the tides, be prepared to spend a full day. Tidal timetables change, so check in advance and plan the timing of your visit around them. The federal Fisheries and Oceans timetable can be found online (www.tides.gc.ca).

In addition to the tides, the park offers a nine-hole golf course designed by Stanley Thompson, heated salt-water swimming pool just off Point Wolfe Road, summer hiking, shore exploration, and camping, as well as winter cross-country skiing, hiking, and snowshoeing. It's also liberally peppered with iconic Canadian imagery for photographers lucky enough to catch sunlight instead of frequent morning fogs (which usually burn off by mid-afternoon) in summer.

TIDAL EXCURSIONS

For most visitors to Fundy, the remarkable tides along the park's coastline are its major magnet. Tides—the regular rise and fall of the height of the sea—are caused by the gravitational pull of the sun and moon. There are two high and two low tides in a 24-hour period, with the time between a high and a low tide about 6 hours and 13 minutes. High tides move about an hour later every day because of the motion of the moon's orbit relative to the Earth.

Spring tides, which happen twice monthly in conjunction with the new moon and the full moon, offer the most dramatic highs and lows. Neap (from the Old English word "nep," or nipped) tides, when the moon is in a quarter phase, are less dramatic.

Spring tides at the full or new moon phase sometimes coincide with the moon's perigee, the point when the moon is closest to the Earth. When this happens, tides in the 150-km-long (93 mi) **Bay of Fundy** can rise to 16 m (53 ft)—higher than anywhere else in the world.

Imagine the bay is a basin of water. Water in a basin will slosh from end to end (called a seiche) in response to a disturbance such as a tremor, big wind, or tidal push from the ocean. Because of the particular length of the Bay of Fundy, the timing or period of that sloshing in the bay coincidentally matches the timing of the tidal push from the Atlantic Ocean. These two separate water movements resonate with and amplify one another, resulting in the giant tides of the Bay of Fundy.

During spring, summer, and fall, park naturalists time daily group Beach Walks for low tide, the perfect time for a stroll along the seabed in rubber boots or aqua socks. Be prepared. Thick brown sea mud cakes the feet and legs of all who wander out onto the mudflats; you will get thoroughly mucky.

When the seafloor is exposed, it reveals what's called the intertidal zone, an array of tenacious organisms able to survive underwater for half the time and in the open air for the other half. Barnacles, periwinkles, little crabs, dog whelks, limpets and other crustaceans, and all sorts of seaweeds become visible. During bird migrations south or north, flocks of tiny shorebirds stop on the mudflats to load up on the tiny sea animals exposed at low tide.

The interpreters here are experts on their subject. They guide people

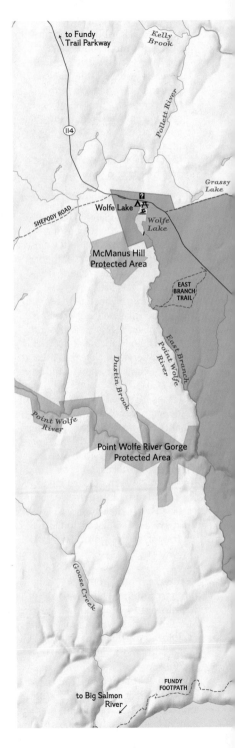

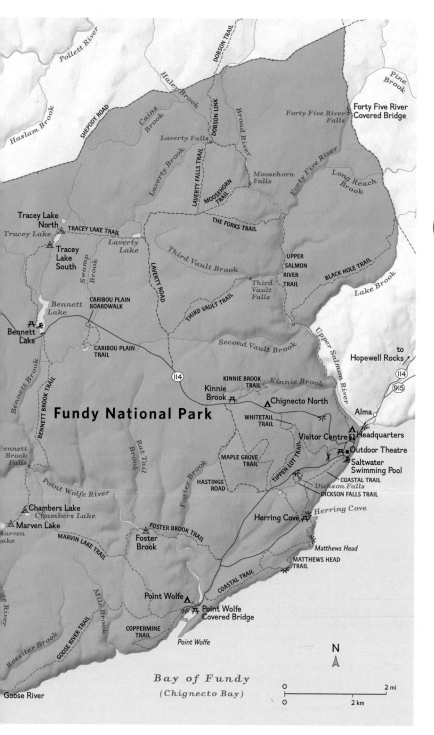

Bay of Fundy
(Chignecto Bay)

N

0   2 mi
0   2 km

Hopewell Rocks

Covered bridge at Point Wolfe

on how the tides work and what happens to the area's ecosystem when tides are high and low.

The Crab Nab is a citizen science project where volunteers help count the non-native green crabs to track their population growth.

HIKES & WATERFALLS

Hiking trails here cover more than 100 km (62 mi), ranging from short jaunts, like the **Point Wolfe Beach Trail,** to the **Fundy Circuit,** which runs almost 50 km (31 mi) around the park. Requiring three to five days to complete, the Fundy Circuit comprises seven trails linked together, with two wilderness campsites along the way (pre-registration required) and a couple of campgrounds.

The 0.5-km (0.3 mi) **Caribou Plain Trail** boardwalk is accessible to wheelchairs and leads through the forest to a beaver pond with interpretive signs and an occasional moose wandering through the terrain. Beyond the wheelchair-accessible portion, another 2 km (1.2 mi) worth of wooded trail leads to a wetland bog with plenty more wildlife.

The short **Shiphaven Trail** starts beside Point Wolfe Bridge at the gorge of the Point Wolfe River and leads about 1 km (0.6 mi) along a glacial ridge. Find interpretive panels marking an early logging dam and the remains of a sawmill that are slowly crumbling back into the river.

Originally built in 1908, the old covered bridge was accidentally destroyed in 1990 by a rock blasting crew whose purpose was to blast away some rock that would enable shoring up and stabilization of one side of the bridge. But the best-laid dynamite can oft go awry, and in this case, though the rockwork imploded nicely, the bridge also collapsed. It was rebuilt in 1992.

There are more than two dozen waterfalls in the park. The most popular, **Dickson Falls,** is relatively easy to reach on a 1.5-km (1 mi) trail loop, most of it boardwalk, with some stairs to climb and a number of interpretive signs along the way.

At the end of Laverty Road, the **Laverty Falls Trail,** another much loved trek, runs 5 km (3 mi) in total, out and back. A sweet little all-natural wading pool at the foot of the falls makes a handy midpoint cooling-off spot, but watch for slippery rocks. An alternate but more challenging route to Laverty Falls that involves fording the river starts at the intersection of Shepody Road and the **Dobson Trail** link trailhead. Track south on the Dobson Trail for 2.6 km (1.6 mi) to the Laverty River ford. The falls lie just 300 m (984 ft) to the left once you've crossed the river.

FUNDY TRAIL

A 16-km (10 mi) paved parkway that edges the cliffs along the Bay from the village of St. Martins to Cranberry Brook Lookout, this scenic drive can be reached by taking Shepody Road west out of the park onto Hwy. 114 to St. Martins. The parkway entrance gate is about 10 km (6.2 mi) from the village. It's also less than an hour's drive from St. John, taking Trans-Canada 1 east to exit 137A, then following Hwy. 114.

The attractions here are legion: coastal scenery, hiking and cycling trails, the **Big Salmon River Interpretive Centre,** and a suspension footbridge. The **Fundy Footpath** stretches from the Big Salmon River all the way to the park (41 km/24 mi; about four days' worth of travel time for hardy hikers).

Once a hunting retreat for newspaper baron William Randolph Hearst and his friends, the wilderness **Hearst Lodge** now welcomes overnight visitors in little, early 20th-century lodge bedrooms or separate cabins. For hikers in a hurry, a four-hour guided hike to and from the lodge includes lunch there.

HOPEWELL ROCKS
a full day

Perhaps the most photographed site in New Brunswick, the **Hopewell Rocks**—a half-hour drive north of the national park via Hwy. 114—are iconic conglomerate stone and red sandstone "flowerpot" rocks that tower up to 15 m (49 ft) or more in height at low tide.

Once part of the sedimentary rock cliffs formed here millions of years ago, they are slowly eroding. In fact, in the centuries to come, the surging tides will completely wash the rocks away. New ones will form behind them, however, and geologists think there's enough conglomerate rock—that's the top layer of stone that wears away less rapidly than the underlying sandstone—to make more flowerpot rocks for about another hundred thousand years.

Begin the day exploring the ocean floor around the rocks at low tide, then poke around some of the caves gouged into the cliffs over the centuries. Take a lunch break at the park's restaurant while you wait for the tide to turn. Once the ocean begins moving toward high tide, meet up with one of the local kayaking outfitters and paddle around the tops of the very rocks whose bases you explored just hours earlier.

Independent kayakers can go it on their own, but you must stop at the visitor information desk first in order to sign a waiver and get permission to drive to the kayak launch area. The best timing is during the two hours prior to or following high tide, when beach access is easier. Outside that time window, water

FUNDY

FUNDY NATIONAL PARK *(Parc national Fundy)*

INFORMATION & ACTIVITIES

VISITOR CENTRE
Phone (506) 887-6000.

SEASONS & ACCESSIBILITY
Park open year-round. Road from the Headquarters area to Point Wolfe closed from first snowfall until spring. Call Headquarters (see below) for weather and road conditions.

HEADQUARTERS
P.O. Box 1001, Alma, NB E4H 1B4. Phone (506) 887-6000. www.parks canada.gc.ca/fundy.

FRIENDS OF FUNDY
Fundy Guild Inc. 8642 Unit 2, Rte. 114, Fundy National Park, NB E4H 4V2. Phone (506) 887-6094. info@fundyguild.ca; www.fundyguild.ca.

ENTRANCE FEES
$8 per person, $20 per group per day; $39 per person, $98 per group per year.

PETS
Pets must be on a leash at all times.

ACCESSIBLE SERVICES
The visitor centre, **Caribou Plain board-walk,** and **Point Wolfe Look-out** are all accessible to wheelchairs. Chignecto North Campground has wheelchair accessible washroom facilities. Two yurts are wheelchair accessible.

THINGS TO DO
Interpretive programs in July and August. Activity schedules posted throughout the park; call the visitor centre for details. Evening outdoor theatre events and campfire programs. Guided events. Swimming in the heated saltwater pool off Point Wolfe Road (late June–early Sept., lifeguards on duty).Unsupervised beaches at **Bennett Lake** and **Wolfe Lake.** Fishing at Bennett Lake; permits ($10 per day, $34 per year) available at boat concession at Bennett Lake and visitor centre. Mountain biking on **Goose River, Marven Lake, Black Hole, Bennett Brook, East Branch,** and **Maple Grove.** Tennis and lawn bowling in Headquarters area (rent equipment at the Pro Shop, mid-May–early Oct.). Golfing from mid-May to early October ($33 per day, $19 for 9 holes); for reservations, call the Pro Shop at (506) 887-2970.

Also available, hiking, skiing, snow-shoeing, and tobogganing; ski trails and tobogganing hill groomed regularly after storms or snowfalls. Nonmotorized watercraft not permitted on **Wolfe Lake.**

levels sink fast and you may have to drag your kayak across the sensitive mudflat ecosystem.

Though you can kayak in Fundy National Park at high tide as well, viewing the oddly comical formations of the Hopewell Rocks from two completely different dramatic angles is a treat you can get nowhere else in the world.

ALMA

Located on the southeastern edge of the park, the fishing village of **Alma** makes a good base for exploring everything that Fundy has to offer. At **Alma Beach,** low tides reveal more than 1 km (0.6 mi) of mudflats. Fishing boats are propped up in wobbly positions, held by cradles placed there to keep them vertical.

In lobster season, usually lasting about three months from late spring to early summer, Alma's the place to find seafood restaurants serving up traditional lobster suppers with crustaceans just plucked from the sea or from lobster "pounds," where the creatures are sized as canners (170–454 g/0.4–1 lb in weight), markets (454 g/1 lb and up), or jumbos (more than 1,135 g/2.5 lbs).

Canoe, rowboat, and kayak rentals at **Bennett Lake.**

SPECIAL ADVISORIES
• The weather is variable. Wear layers and footwear with good traction and support.
• Watch for the rising tide; be aware of tide times posted on boards along trails. Call the visitor centre for information.

OVERNIGHT BACKPACKING
13 backcountry sites at **Goose River, Marven Lake**, **Tracey Lake,** and **Foster Brook.** Tent pads, fireplaces with wood, pit privies, and picnic tables. Backpacking stoves and drinking water recommended. Reserve at visitor centre or call headquarters. Goose River and Tracey Lake sites open year-round.

CAMPGROUNDS
Campsites available on a first-come, first-served basis. For reservations call (877) 737-3783 or visit www.pccamping.ca. **Wolfe Lake,** primitive campsite with pit privies $16 per night. **Chignecto North,** serviced with electricity, water, and sewer $35; serviced with electricity and water only $32; unserviced with washroom (toilets and showers) $26. **Chignecto South** group campground, $5 per person.

Headquarters open mid-October to mid-May; serviced campground with electricity (mid-Oct.–mid-May) $24; unserviced with washroom (toilets and showers) $26; unserviced campground with washroom (toilets and showers) $16. Seasonal camping with full service $2,000 per site per season. Yurts with picnic table and two deck chairs $90 per night. **Point Wolfe** unserviced campground with washroom (toilets and showers) $26.

HOTELS, MOTELS, & INNS
(unless otherwise noted, rates are for a 2-person double, high season, in Canadian dollars)

Inside the park:
Fundy Highlands Chalets 8714 Rte. 114. (506) 887-2930. info@fundyhighland chalets.com; www.fundyhighlandchalets.com. $94–$109.

Outside the park:
In Alma, NB E4H 1N6
Captains Inn 8602 Main St. (506) 887-2017. captinn@nb.sympatico.ca; www.captainsinn.ca. $80–100.
Parkland Village Inn 8601 Main St. (506) 887-2313. www.parklandvillage inn.com. $95–$150.

FUNDY

EXCURSION

MONUMENT LEFEBVRE NATIONAL HISTORIC SITE
MEMRAMCOOK, NB

Named for Father Camille Lefebvre, founder of the first French-language degree-granting college in Atlantic Canada, Monument Lefebvre has long been a centre of Acadian pride. In the mid-19th century, Lefebvre helped educate many leaders of the Acadian renaissance, a movement to reawaken and preserve Acadian culture. Today the building houses an exhibit chronicling the Acadians' history in Atlantic Canada. Guided tours are available. (506) 758-9808. 118 km (73 mi) northeast of park via Hwy. 114.

QUEBEC & ONTARIO

Page 74: top, Visitors at Lake Bouchard, La Mauricie; middle, Northern saw-whet owl; bottom, Dwarf lake iris.
Page 75: Sunset in Georgian Bay Islands National Park. Above: Brébeuf Island, Georgian Bay Islands National Park.

QUEBEC & ONTARIO

From Mingan Archipelago in Quebec to Pukaskwa in Ontario, these parks represent Canada's wonderful inland waters. Mingan's islands are known for strange monoliths that trim the shore. Boaters paddle by, spotting seals, dolphins, and nesting birds. At the tip of the Gaspé Peninsula, Forillon marks one end of the Appalachians. Hikers at La Mauricie spot moose and black bear, while campers sleep, listening to loons singing on a lake. More than

20 islands dot St. Lawrence Islands, home to endangered plants like the eastern prairie fringed orchid. At Georgian Bay Islands, 63 islands pepper the shore, and visitors hike and camp in settings accessible only by boat. Visitors at Bruce Peninsula hike along the Bruce Trail, Canada's longest hiking trail, while Point Pelee draws serious bird-watchers. Hikers in Pukaskwa can follow a trail on the last undeveloped shoreline on the Great Lakes.

Detail of granitic islets and reefs, Mingan Archipelago National Park

▶MINGAN ARCHIPELAGO

QUEBEC
ESTABLISHED 1984
100 sq km/24,711 acres

Famous for the largest concentration of erosion monoliths in Canada, the Mingan Archipelago National Park Reserve encompasses close to a thousand islands and islets sprinkled along 150 km (93 mi) from east to west. Although the park is restricted to the islands themselves, the sea shapes everything here—rocks, plants, wildlife, climate . . . even the visitor's experience itself.

The Mingan Archipelago tells a fascinating geological story. Difficult to imagine today, the sedimentary rock formations date back almost 500 million years to a time when a warm, shallow tropical sea covered today's St. Lawrence Lowlands region. Saturated with calcium carbonate and teeming with a diversity of marine organisms, the bottom of this ancient sea received a steady deposit of fine marine sediments and animal shells. Over tens of millions of years, they accumulated to form a blanket several kilometres thick that gradually turned to rock under its own weight.

With passing time, continents shifted, the sea receded, and this vast plateau of relatively soft and partly soluble rock found itself under the aggressive attack of erosion. Among other factors, rivers carved up the land, carrying away most of the material, but fortunately left behind several "hard to do" rocky mounds. After several other episodes of sea level fluctuation, these mounds became today's islands.

As if to decorate them still further, the sea continued to carve their shores, creating a mesmerizing array of monoliths, festooned cliffs, arches, and grottoes. At the same time, a surprising diversity of plant and animal species managed to establish itself on the islands. Due to the particular combination of geology and climate, many rare plants are found nowhere else in the region. In springtime, marine birds—such as puffins, razorbills, guillemots, terns, and kittiwakes—congregate on certain islands to form important nesting colonies, taking advantage of both island safety and a bountiful supply of food in surrounding waters. All of these and much more make the archipelago a unique part of our natural heritage.

How to Get There

Take Hwy. 138, driving about two hours east of Sept-Îles. The Mingan Archipelago stretches along the north shore of the Gulf of St. Lawrence between the towns of Longue-Pointe-de-Mingan and Aguanish. There are information and interpretation centres located in Longue-Pointe-de-Mingan and Havre-St.-Pierre, as well as information kiosks in Baie-Johan-Beetz and Aguanish.

When to Go

The best time to visit is from June to early September. The park is only accessible by boat, so unless you have your own kayak or boat, you will require the services of registered marine transportation companies, most of which operate only from mid-June to early September. It is recommended that you contact them ahead of time to obtain information and make reservations.

How to Visit

The most popular way to visit the Mingan Archipelago is to take one or several of the boat tours offered by commercial marine transportation companies departing from Longue-Pointe-de-Mingan and Havre-St.-Pierre. Boat capacities vary from 8 to 58 passengers. Tours usually last three to five hours and allow a visit to several different islands, often including one or two guided visits led by Parks Canada interpreters. Enjoy the cool ocean breeze and unbounded horizons. If you are lucky, you may see whales or seals along the way. Admire the spectacle of giant monoliths and festooned cliffs sculpted by the sea. Keep your eyes peeled and search for fossils embedded in the rock and dating back to a time so ancient that fish and other vertebrates had not yet evolved.

Once in the area, chances are you will want to spend a few more days exploring these unique islands at a more leisurely pace. Take a taxi boat and spend a couple of nights camping in the archipelago. Experience genuine island seclusion. Wake up to the rhythm of waves. Inhale the rich smells of the sea. Observe passing seabirds and whales. Relax and soak in the solitude. You will be smitten.

If camping is not your style, the taxi boats also offer numerous possibilities for day or half-day trips. There are relatively easy hiking trails on several different islands, varying in length from 300 m (0.2 mi) to about 10 km (6.2 mi), either in the interior or along the shoreline. Explore "your" island at your own pace. Relax and picnic along the way. Walk on a pebble or sandy beach. Marvel at the unique and hardy sea-

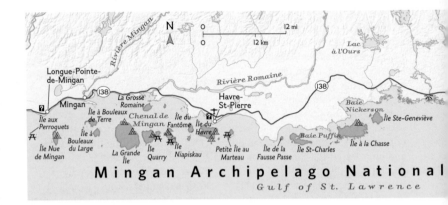

M i n g a n   A r c h i p e l a g o   N a t i o n a l
G u l f   o f   S t.   L a w r e n c e

shore flora. Venture onto the rocky flats at low tide. Discover the diversity of marine organisms that make their home in the tidal pools. Hike into the interior of an island and discover a diverse mosaic of unique ecosystems, each with its specific flora and fauna.

If you feel adventurous, try kayaking in the archipelago. Possibilities for day and multiday trips are endless, and kayak rentals and guided excursions are available. Whichever itinerary you choose, you are bound for an unforgettable experience of discovery and awe.

Whether you embark on a short three-hour boat tour or a ten-day kayak journey, be sure to begin your stay by stopping at either of the two Parks Canada visitor information and interpretation centres located in Longue-Pointe-de-Mingan or Havre-St.-Pierre. Visit the exhibits on show. Talk to Parks Canada employees to discuss the different excursions that are offered. Obtain all necessary maps, information, and permits. And while you are there, take a tour of the Mingan Islands Cetacean Studies Centre adjacent to the Parks Canada information centre in Longue-Pointe-de-Mingan. It provides a fabulous opportunity for visitors to dive deep into the fascinating underwater world of whales.

Fog envelops Île aux Perroquets Lighthouse at dawn.

Mingan Archipelago National Park Reserve
includes all offshore islands between
Île aux Perroquets and Aguanish

Park Reserve

THE WESTERN ISLANDS

If you drive east from Sept-Îles along Hwy. 138, stop in Longue-Pointe-de-Mingan and take a boat tour or taxi boat to visit Île aux Perroquets and Île Nue de Mingan. Standing proud and strong on **Île aux Perroquets,** at the western end of the archipelago, the old **lighthouse buildings** beckon the visitor back to a time when there was no road and the sea provided the backbone of the local economy and transportation system. For almost a century, six different light keepers, often accompanied by a helper and some by their families, made their home on this tiny isolated island during most of the year to ensure mariners steered clear of the forbidding islands and shoals of the archipelago. The light keepers are long gone, but the island and surrounding islets are still home to the many seabirds—eiders, terns, guillemots, razorbills, and puffins—that congregate here during the nesting period.

Just east of Île aux Perroquets lies **Île Nue de Mingan,** a treeless island with fascinating Arctic and subarctic vegetation, home to the southernmost patches of permafrost along Canada's eastern coastline. This peculiarity is likely due in part to a microclimate caused by cold water

upwelling in the area, which at the same time enriches the surrounding waters, attracting several species of seals and whales, a regular sight on the water.

You can visit both islands during the same three-hour tour, but if you have the whole day, it is worthwhile to make arrangements with the tour operator and spend the rest of the day hiking around Île Nue de Mingan, a loop of about 8 km (5 mi) along the shoreline. Note, however, that this trail does not open until mid-July in order to avoid disturbing nesting seabirds.

Roseroot (*Sedum rosea*)

Another alternative for a full-day activity is to take a longer tour which also includes **Grande Île** and its impressive monoliths. Camping is also possible on either **Île Nue de Mingan** or **Grande Île,** a unique experience as each campground is limited to just two or four tents.

THE CENTRAL ISLANDS

The central part of the archipelago, accessible from Havre-St.-Pierre, is home to some of the largest islands of the archipelago, as well as some of the park's most stunning monoliths and rock formations. As a result of their size and relative proximity, these islands are less susceptible to the cooling effect of the sea and boast a diversity of ecosystems such as coniferous forests, bogs, barrens, small lakes, salt marshes, seashores, and cliff habitats.

To see the most imposing and famous monoliths, be sure to visit **Île Niapiskau** and **Île Quarry.** Short excursions with interpretive stops on each island are available. Day and multiday trips are also possible as both islands have campgrounds and hiking trails. Just across Île Niapiskau, you will find **Île du Fantôme** with its fascinating check-ered reef flats and its trail across rocky barrens, home to a peculiar and hardy flora.

Less than a kilometre across from Havre-St.-Pierre, **Île du Havre** is a quickly accessible island offer-ing seashore hiking possibilities, as well as two campgrounds. Just east of it is easily accessible **Petite Île au Marteau,** which is sure to captivate

with its old **lighthouse buildings.** Go for a picnic, relax, and discover local culture and history. Still farther east, you will find **Île de la Fausse Passe** with its incredible festooned cliffs that you can admire directly from the water. And if seclusion is what you are looking for, spend a night or two camping on **Île à la Chasse,** a rarely visited island due to its remoteness.

THE FAR EAST

Besides protecting the sedimentary rock islands which make it famous, the national park reserve also encompasses a maze of a thousand small rose-coloured and often tree-less Precambrian rock islands and islets sprinkled along some 70 km (43 mi) of coastline in the vicinity of Baie-Johan-Beetz and Aguanish. Home to the largest migratory bird sanctuary in Quebec, this area offers no tourist infrastructure for the time being. It can, however, be admired from two roadside viewpoints at **Baie Pontbriand** and **Rivière Corneille.**

A hiker walks along the boardwalk at Niapiskau Island.

MINGAN ARCHIPELAGO NATIONAL PARK RESERVE
(Réserve de parc national de l'Archipel-de-Mingan)

INFORMATION & ACTIVITIES

VISITOR & INFORMATION CENTRES
Havre-St.-Pierre Reception and Interpretation Centre 1010 Promenade des Anciens, Havre-St.-Pierre, QC G0G 1P0. Phone (418) 538-3285 or (888) 773-8888.
Longue-Pointe-de-Mingan Reception and Interpretation Centre 625 Du Centre St., Longue-Pointe-de-Mingan, QC G0G 1V0. Phone (418) 949-2126.

SEASONS & ACCESSIBILITY
Park open from mid-June to early September.

HEADQUARTERS
Mingan Field Unit, 1340 de la Digue St., Havre-St.-Pierre, QC G0G 1P0. Phone (418) 538-3331. www.parkscanada.gc.ca/mingan.

ENTRANCE FEES
$6 per person, $15 per group per day; $29 per person, $74 per group per season.

PETS
None permitted.

ACCESSIBLE SERVICES
Universal access at Havre-St.-Pierre, Longue-Pointe-de-Mingan Reception and Interpretation Centre. The film *The Mingan Islands* subtitled in English and French for visitors with hearing disabilities. Petite île au Marteau has wheelchair accessible wharf, picnic area, washrooms, and look-out point.

THINGS TO DO
Hiking along 24 km (15 mi) of trails on four islands. More than 97 km (60 mi) of navigable waters for sea kayaking. For boating, contact **Club nautique de Havre-St.-Pierre** (418-538-1679). For scuba diving, contact local businesses such as **Plongée Boréale** (418-538-3202, *www.plongeeboreale.com*) to rent equipment.

SPECIAL ADVISORIES
- Sea conditions may delay return to mainland. If camping, bring a small axe for kindling and food for an extra two days.
- Some areas along the shoreline may present difficult or hazardous falling conditions. Avoid walking beneath over-hanging rocks and do not stop next to the base of overhanging cliffs to avoid falling rocks.
- Rocks can be slippery at low tide. At high tide, water may block the trail.
- Do not climb on the monoliths.
- Check with the park office about sites that are off-limits during seabird nesting season (May–Aug.).
- For water activities, ensure one of the party can interpret marine and tide charts, navigate in fog, and perform first aid. Wear wet suits to avoid hypothermia. In case of emergency, call (888) 762-1422.

OVERNIGHT BACKPACKING
No backcountry camping.

CAMPGROUNDS
Campgrounds are open mid-June to early September. Primitive campgrounds $16–$18. Group camping $5–$6 per person. $6 per reservation. For opening dates, call (418) 538-3331. 42 campgrounds on 6 islands. Camping permits can be obtained at the visitor centres or at the Park Reserve administrative office in off-season. Maximum stay is 6 nights on the same island or 12 nights within the park. Reservations accepted up to 6 months in advance. Call (418) 538-3285.

HOTELS, MOTELS, & INNS
(unless otherwise noted, rates are for a 2-person double, high season, in Canadian dollars)

Outside the park:
Hôtel Motel du Havre 970 boulevard de l'Escale, Havre-St.-Pierre, QC G0G 1P0. (418) 538-2800. info@hotelduhavre.ca; www.hotelduhavre.ca. $82–$140.

For more accommodations visit www.tourisme duplessis.com.

Twilight on Cap-des-Rosiers, Forillon National Park

▶ FORILLON

QUEBEC
ESTABLISHED 1970
240 sq km/59,305 acres

Depending on your perspective, Forillon marks either the beginning or the end of the Canadian portion of the International Appalachian Trail. Much of the park is pure mountain wilderness, with remarkable hiking trails that skirt seaside cliff edges. It also boasts a cluster of traditional Gaspé fishing villages, pebble beaches in quiet coves, and rugged cliffs looming along a coastline that wraps around two of the triangular park's three sides. At its northeastern tip, the park pokes into the Gulf of St. Lawrence via a peninsula topped by a lighthouse.

Forillon National Park protects a range of varied little ecosystems: natural prairies and farm fields, seaside cliffs, rivers, lakes, marshes, the seashore itself, and forest. Virtually all the park is covered with forests that shelter a peculiar combination of some 700 kinds of local flora along with plants normally found in Arctic or alpine environments, such as purple mountain saxifrage, tufted saxifrage, and white dryad.

Historically, this resource-rich area of Quebec was also exploited for its supply of wood. People living off the coast in the village of L'Anse-au-Griffon, on the park's northwest side, were involved in the early lumber industry here. Sawmills turned out planks, beams, cedar shingles, barrel staves, even timbers to build wharves and bridges.

Wildlife spotters on the prowl in the park can look for moose, black bears, lynx, red foxes, beavers, porcupines, coyotes, snowshoe hares, mink, and ermine. Bird-watchers are drawn by 225 known species. Along the cliffs, perfect for breeding, seabirds such as black-legged kittiwakes, double-crested cormorants, black guillemots, and razorbills are plentiful. Great blue herons, terns, gulls, and sandpipers inhabit shorelines, and more than two dozen inland raptor species include northern harriers, American kestrel, bald eagles, peregrine falcons, and great horned owls.

How to Get There

Fly into Quebec City from any major North American city, then make the ten-hour drive on Trans-Canada 20 from Quebec City to the park. The magnificent route follows the south side of the vast mouth of the St. Lawrence River, skirting the northern edges of the Gaspé Peninsula and passing through its small towns and villages. Stop in the city of Rimouski about halfway to the park, or shorten the drive by flying from Quebec City into Rimouski and renting a car there.

A quicker alternative is to fly from Quebec City or Montreal to the town of Gaspé. From there, the park lies just 30 km (18.6 mi) away on Hwy. 132, an extremely pretty coastal drive. You can also reach the park by train. The Montreal–Gaspé Chaleur route operated by VIA Rail (www.viarail.ca) runs along the Bay of Chaleur on the south side of the Gaspé Peninsula.

When to Go

Summer's the season that really shines in Forillon. The coastal scenery is at its finest, wildflowers bloom almost frantically, beaches are easily accessible, and trails are at their peak of natural beauty. But there is plenty to do in winter, too. There are a half dozen cross-country ski trails (trailheads start at the Le Portage parking area near Penouille, La Vallée parking area at L'Anse-au-Griffon, and Le Castor parking area near Cap-des-Rosiers), three off-trail ski areas, and a half dozen snowshoeing trails with equipment for rent at the Penouille Visitor Centre.

How to Visit

As the Québécois would say, the de rigueur exploration of this varied landscape involves rambling the coast by car, exploring a few beaches on foot, and doing a little sea kayaking or whale-watching on the first day. On the second day, check out the Hyman & Sons General Store, populated by character actors, and the restored homestead and farm of Anse-Blanchette, which are virtually all that remains of the old fishing village of Grande-Grave. Take the late

American porcupine

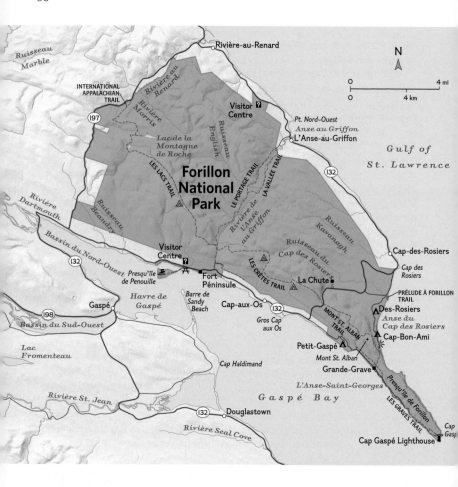

afternoon and evening to spend time in nearby Gaspé, where more than three dozen small hotels and B&Bs can provide cozy, lacy Québécois-style beds. Explore the restaurants in town, which also has a few interesting local museums.

If there's time for a third day, fill up the backpack with the day's necessities and squeeze in some wilderness hiking. Or do like the locals do and go for a picnic along the rugged cliffs. Spend some time ranging along the round-pebble beaches, or climb the Cap Gaspé lighthouse for the towering sea view. The lighthouse is just 13 m (43 ft) high, but it

squats on the edge of an impressive 95-m (312 ft) cliff.

WATER ACTIVITIES

Six different kinds of whales and porpoises can be seen in the park's protected marine environment. Whale-watchers flock to Forillon all summer to see whales from the only vessel licensed to ply these waters. From early June until the beginning of October, the 48-passenger, open-deck **Narval III** (866-617-5500, www .baleines-forillon.com) sails from the park's Grande-Grave harbour on 2.5-hour cruises throughout the day. Onboard guides are very good at spotting blue, fin, humpback, and minke whales, as well as white-sided dolphins and harbour porpoises.

For more hands-on water sports and the chance to watch seals up close, the recreation centre on the coast in the south section of the park offers guided sea kayaking tours from mid-June until the end of August. Tours range from two hours to half-day trips. It's also possible to paddle independently from Grande-Grave all the way up the coastline to Cap Gaspé, provided you register your trip at the recreation centre.

For scuba diving, push off from **Petit-Gaspé, Grande-Grave,** and **Anse-St.-Georges** to explore the ocean floor and check out marine Atlantic sealife. Fishing is permitted off the wharves at Grande-Grave and **Cap-des-Rosiers** on the north side of the peninsula.

Almost a half dozen pebbled beaches around the cape make for great strolls, and the sand beach at **Penouille,** just down a long spit of land not far from the park's south side visitor reception centre, is a good, sheltered wading and swimming spot, equipped with picnic areas, playgrounds, washrooms, and showers. Near Penouille beach, you will find the remains of a **World War II fortification,** built to protect the Bay of Gaspé in the unlikely event that Germany managed to invade North America. You can also explore the underground tunnel here, home to unused cannon.

The south side recreation centre has a heated outdoor swimming pool, as well as a wading pool.

HIKING & CAMPING

Remote Forillon is a hiker's heaven, with nine mostly interconnecting trails cutting through the park. For a challenge and some great sea views, the **International Appalachian Trail** continues along the **Les Graves Trail.** Beginning at Anse-aux-Amérindiens, this 15-km (9 mi) trek along the coast

FORILLON

Cap Bon Ami, Forillon National Park

A northern gannet fishes off the coast of Bonaventure Island

Forest rapids

Lobster traps on Grande-Grave Wharf

will take you past sea coves and beaches all the way to Cap Gaspé, where you may well see whales and seals around. (Hikers can pick up the International Appalachian Trail again by getting to Sackville, New Brunswick, via bus, train, or car, then hiking over the Confederation Bridge to Prince Edward Island and points north.) For a shorter trek, an 8-km (5 mi) portion of the Les Graves Trail starts at Grande-Grave.

There's a wilderness camping area on the **Les Lacs Trail** for overnighters. Other long trails that require carrying camping gear are the 18-km (11 mi) **Les Crêtes Trail,** mountainous and forested, with periodic lookout points and two unserviced camping areas (registration is required before heading out on this one), and the 10-km (6.2 mi) **Le Portage Trail** in the park's southern area. Used by cyclists and horseback riders as well as hikers, the trail is especially good for wildlife-watching (use bear bells).

The Les Graves Trail short version, **Mont St. Alban Trail,** and **La Vallée Trail** all run about 8 km (5 mi), and each can be done in a day. The first two concentrate on cliffside views (the first few kilometres of the Mont St. Alban Trail are steep and sometimes a bit tricky to navigate), and La Vallée follows the Anse-au-Griffon River in the woods.

For much shorter excursions, **Prélude à Forillon,** which starts near the visitor centre, runs just over 0.5 km (0.3 mi), is wheelchair accessible, and offers interpretive material along the way. The 3-km (1.8 mi) **Une tournée dans les parages** ("a walk around the area") is less a hike than a short stroll around local history, passing by **Fruing Beach,** the historic **Hyman & Sons General Store** and **Anse-Blanchette,** and the remains of old houses and barns, once part of the now gone cod-fishing and drying village of Grande-Grave (see below). Exhibits along the way explain the area's history. The short, all-natural **La Chute Trail** blends a charming little waterfall, a maple grove, and a small river cascade into an easy and serene 1-km (0.6 mi) ramble through the woods.

The little village of **L'Anse-au-Griffon** still exists just outside the park boundaries on the northwest side, on its traditional fishing harbour. The village can be reached along Hwy. 132, which loops all the way around and through the park. Dedicated hikers can reach L'Anse-au-Griffon at the northwest end of the hiking/cycling Le Portage Trail. Pick up the trailhead just off Hwy. 132 on the southeast side of the park. Two restored buildings in the village, the **Centre Culturel Le Griffon** and the **Manoir Le Boutillier** (a national historic site), both house local history. The cultural centre has a small café, and there is also a small motel here, the Motel Le Noroît.

THE GHOST FISHING VILLAGE

Forillon's rich fishing has attracted settlement for 9,000 years, the most recent being the village of **Grande-Grave** ("Grave" refers to a pebble beach where cod was dried) in the late 19th and early 20th centuries. Here, hundreds of workers for two large fishing companies caught cod, and dried and salted it for sale to Europe and the West Indies. Families fleshed out their earnings, and their groceries, with a little farming. Today, visitors can prowl the remains of many buildings that mark the location of the village. Two of the buildings have been restored and are populated by character actors in summer.

The ground floor of the two-storey **Hyman & Sons General Store,** built in 1864 as a home, was turned into a business in 1918. Today it has been refurbished and refurnished with all the dry goods a period fishing and farming family might have needed. Upstairs, a small permanent exhibition documents life in Grande-Grave, and a projection room adjacent to the main floor store offers a documentary video. At Anse-Blanchette, the **Blanchette homestead** has been restored, complete with its barn, fish house, and woodshed. In the barn, you can watch a video, "We Always Looked to the Sea."

FORILLON

FORILLON NATIONAL PARK *(Parc national Forillon)*

INFORMATION & ACTIVITIES

VISITOR & INFORMATION CENTRES

L'Anse-au-Griffon Visitor Centre. Penouille Visitor Centre open June to September.

SEASONS & ACCESSIBILITY

Park open year-round; most services available June to October.

HEADQUARTERS

122 Gaspé Blvd., Gaspé, QC G4X 1A9. Phone (418) 368-5505. www.parks canada.gc.ca/forillon.

ENTRANCE FEES

$8 per person per day; $39 per year.

PETS

Pets must be leashed at all times.

ACCESSIBLE SERVICES

The following are wheelchair accessible: visitor centres, interpretive exhibits at Fort Peninsula, interpretive programs at Grande-Grave, and Prélude à Forillon interpretive trail.

THINGS TO DO

Sea kayaking service available June to September. Reservations recommended (418-892-5056); register at the recreation centre. Whale-watching services available from June to October. Reservations recommended (418-892-5500). Scuba diving and snorkelling. Reservations recommended (418-892-5888).

Hiking on the **International Appalachian Trail.** To hike with an interpreter, call (418) 368-5505. Cycling, in-line skating, and horseback riding. For bike rentals call (418) 892-5058.

Swimming, tennis, volleyball, shuffleboard, and a playground are available at the recreation centre. Also fishing, scuba diving, and snorkelling. Beaches at **Cap-Bon-Ami, Petit-Gaspé, Grande-Grave,** and **Des-Rosiers Campgrounds.** In winter, cross-country skiing, off-trail skiing, snowshoeing, kicksledding, and dogsledding. Call (418) 892-5873 for rentals.

SPECIAL ADVISORIES

• Remain on designated trails. Do not leave waste; there are no trash cans.
• Open fires forbidden in backcountry.
• Snowmobiling is forbidden everywhere in the park except for boundary corridors.
• For water sports, use a buddy system and check the weather and tides before setting out.
• Do not harass, trap, or feed wildlife. No fishing permitted in fresh water.

OVERNIGHT BACKPACKING

Backcountry camping available only at **Les Lacs** and **Les Crêtes** campsites along the International Appalachian Trail; registration mandatory.

CAMPGROUNDS

Camping fees $26 for unserviced campgrounds; $29 for serviced campgrounds; $6 per person for group camping ($5 for winter camping). 367 semiserviced campsites, 1 group campground, and 3 unserviced campgrounds in the backcountry. **Petit-Gaspé** 167 sites (32 with electricity); **Des-Rosiers** 151 sites (38 with electricity); **Cap-Bon-Ami** 41 sites; **Petit-Gaspé Group Campground** 41 sites. For reservations, call (877) 737-3783; (866) 787-6221 for the hearing impaired; www.pccamping .ca. Winter camping in **Petit-Gaspé Group Campground** and Loop C of the **Petit-Gaspé Campground.** Registration required. Call (418) 368-5505.

HOTELS, MOTELS, & INNS

(unless otherwise noted, rates are for a 2-person double, high season, in Canadian dollars)

Outside the park:
Gîte des Trois Ruisseaux 896 boulevard Griffon, L'Anse-au-Griffon, QC G4X 6B2. (418) 892-5528. www.gites-classifies .qc.ca. $67.
La Maison de la Demoiselle 1796 boulevard Forillon, Cap-aux-Os, QC G4X 6L2. (418) 892-5449. www.gaspesie .net /maison_de_la_demoiselle. $1,150 per week.
Motel le Noroît 589 boulevard Griffon, L'Anse-au-Griffon, QC G4X 6A5. (418) 892-5531. www.motellenoroit.com. $60–$70.

▶ NATIONAL MARINE CONSERVATION AREA

SAGUENAY-ST. LAWRENCE
QUEBEC

This 1,245 sq km (481 sq mi) marine park near the village of Tadoussac at the confluence of the Saguenay and St. Lawrence Rivers offers jaw-dropping scenery and whale-watching opportunities from land, boat, and kayak. It was created in 1998 to protect and showcase part of the St. Lawrence Estuary and the Saguenay Fjord.

SAGUENAY-ST. LAWRENCE

Kayaking along the Saguenay River

Jointly managed by the provincial and federal governments, this stunning park features one of the southernmost fjords in the world. Measuring 276 m (905 ft) deep in some places, the fjord is home to more than ten species of marine mammals including seals, seabirds, blue whales, and about a thousand endangered St. Lawrence belugas.

The marine park's headquarters (418-235-4703, *www.parcmarin .qc.ca*) are located in the pretty village of **Tadoussac** (*www.tadoussac .com*), a few hours north of Quebec City along Hwy. 138 and a ferry ride from Baie-Sainte-Catherine. French explorer Jacques Cartier came here in 1535. Pierre Chauvin built the first trading post in 1599, and explorer Samuel de Champlain arrived in 1603. Fur traders and the area's First Nations people traded at Tadoussac. Visitors can find accommodations in local hotels and B&Bs, as well as at Camping Tadoussac and Camping du Domaine des Dunes (*www.domaine desdunes.com*).

From Tadoussac, go to the **Marine Environment Discovery Centre** in Les Escoumins, about 30 km (19 mi) from Tadoussac, to participate in a dive without getting wet. Sit in a theatre and watch a giant screen as biologist-divers equipped with a camera go live beneath the St. Lawrence River. You may see sea stars and other marine life. Visitors can talk to divers underwater through a real-time two-way video link and follow along on the dive. The centre also has a permanent exhibit about the rich marine life that makes the St. Lawrence so attractive for whales.

WHALE-WATCHING: One of the highlights for visitors to the park is being able to see whales. The sociable and highly vocal beluga is often called "sea canary" because its calls are reminiscent of singing. It also emits ultrasonic sounds for echolocation. The returning echo allows

A child examines the living treasure at a tide pool.

it to locate prey, find holes in the ice, and avoid obstacles. Whale-watching boats and Zodiacs operate from May to October, departing from Tadoussac or Baie-Sainte-Catherine. It can get chilly on the water, so wear long pants and bring a hooded windbreaker, sweater, gloves, and a hat.

Whale-watching companies include: Croisières Otis *(www.otis excursions.com)*, Croisières Groupe Dufour *(www.dufour.ca)*, Croisières 2001 *(www.quebecweb.com/croisieres 2001)*, and Croisières AML *(www .croisieresaml.com)*. Some of these

companies also offer tours of the Saguenay Fjord.

Regulations adopted in 2002 require that motorized boats and kayaks stay at least 400 m (1,312 ft) from beluga and blue whales and impose speed limits and flyover height restrictions.

The marine park covers a portion of the St. Lawrence Estuary and Saguenay Fjord, but visitors can whale-watch and experience the park from interpretation and observation points set up on dry land along the park's boundary. Each site focuses on a particular theme related to the marine environment.

MARINE OBSERVATION: At **Cap de Bon-Désir,** 25 km (15.5 mi) east of Tadoussac, fresh water from the St. Lawrence River mixes with salt water from the Gulf of St. Lawrence. This makes the St. Lawrence Estuary a rich environment for marine life and Cap de Bon-Désir a good spot to learn about the evolution of navigation on the St. Lawrence and the diversity of marine life. Visitors can whale-watch from land at the end of a 500-m (1,640 ft) trail and also participate in interpretive activities.

Pointe-Noire sits across from Tadoussac, at the confluence of the Saguenay Fjord and the St. Lawrence Estuary. An exhibit at this interpretation and observation centre explains riptide zones and the formation of plumes. A panoramic trail leads to a lookout. The site also has alignment beacons that guard the mouth of the Saguenay River.

Baie Sainte-Marguerite, 30 km (19 mi) from Tadoussac, is another good spot for beluga-watching. The whales sometimes stay there for hours. An interactive exhibit at the

Sea anemones

Beluga Discovery Centre shares information with visitors about the habitat in which belugas live.

These and a number of other sites link together to form the Saguenay-St. Lawrence Discovery Network (call 888-773-8888 for a brochure). Other sites focus on the area's history. The **Centre d'interprétation Archéo Topo** *(www.archeotopo.com)* in Bergeronnes, for example, looks at the park's archaeology and paleohistory. At **Saint-Fulgence,** the fjord's rocky cliffs disappear, only to be

replaced by large marshes. There is a 605-m (1,985 ft) spit. The spit and marsh are a unique feature of the fjord. The **Centre d'interprétation sur les battures et de réhabilitation des oiseaux** looks at the plants and birds that make their home in the Saguenay's tidal flats.

KAYAKING: Novice kayakers can try half-day excursions in the sheltered waters of **Baie Éternité,** on the south side of the Saguenay River. More experienced paddlers could opt for the 72-km (45 mi) scenic route from **Sainte-Rose-du-Nord** to Tadoussac at the mouth of the St. Lawrence River. Mer & Monde Écotours *(www.mer-et-monde.qc.ca)* in Tadoussac and Azimut Aventure *(www.azimutaventure)* in Baie-Sainte-Catherine offer guided sea-kayaking tours in the Saguenay Fjord and out onto the St. Lawrence Estuary. **Saguenay-St. Lawrence Marine Park,** 182, rue de l'Église, Tadoussac, phone (418) 235-4703.

Beluga whale

Lac Wapizagonke, La Mauricie National Park, in autumn

▶ LA MAURICIE

QUEBEC
ESTABLISHED 1970
536 sq km/132,500 acres

Nestled in the Laurentian foothills, La Mauricie National Park presents an untamed yet homelike environment. It is bordered by two wildlife refuges, the Mastigouche, and the Saint-Maurice, and the Saint-Maurice and Matawin Rivers. A sprawling network of valleys and a multitude of lakes, streams, and falls all bear witness to its history. Conifers and hardwoods intermingle to form a gigantic forest mosaic. Visitors will be awestruck by the park's strings of lakes, flowering coves, natural beaches, rock cliffs, speckled trouts, loons, and moose.

The view from the top of the Laurentian foothills embraces a huge plateau rising from east to west and undulating as far as the eye can see. Formed from rock dating to the first billion years of the Earth's existence, the land is split among three main valleys running in a northwest direction. Here and there, glaciers have

left their traces on the landscape in the form of eskers, erratic boulders, and sand beaches. Tectonic forces in combination with glaciations have, with time, given birth to a multitude of lakes in all shapes and sizes. As the glaciers melted and receded, the Champlain Sea inundated the lowlands, leaving its imprint in the form of clay marine terraces along the Saint-Maurice River.

Following the disappearance of the glaciers, forests slowly returned to the area and today cover 93 percent of the park. The diversity of stands is apparent at a glance: Maple, which is dominant in the southern portion, is gradually overtaken by balsam fir to the north. The park numbers more than a hundred different stands, some of which—including pine, hemlock, and oak—are of exceptional quality.

Owing to the richness and diversity of these forests, moose and black bears are frequently sighted. The eastern wolf, designated a species of special concern, and the wood turtle, a threatened species, are present but more discreet. Lakes and streams sporting picturesque names evoke the age-old presence of the aboriginal peoples and the more recent passage of loggers and fish and game club members.

How to Get There

Nestled in the heart of Quebec, the park is located midway between Montreal and Québec City, less than an hour's drive from Trois-Rivières. To get there, first take Rte. 40 in the direction of Trois-Rivières, and then Rte. 55 N. Turn off Rte. 55 at exit 226 and follow the directions to Saint-Jean-des-Piles, the only entrance open year-round. If you wish to enter the park via the other entrance, take exit 217 and follow the directions to Saint-Mathieu-du-Parc.

When to Go

The Mauricie region is canoeing country par excellence. But no matter the season, it is also a great place for getting out and about in any number of ways—hiking, biking, skiing, and kayaking. In the summertime, dally about Lac Wapizagonke or take off into the backcountry until you reach Waber Falls. Spring and fall put on a show of colour and offer excellent opportunities for viewing wildlife up close. From January to March, an extensive network of cross-country ski and snowshoe trails is bound to make your outings memorable.

How to Visit

If you have only one day to spend in the park, travel the length of the parkway and stop off at any of the numerous lookouts, where exhibits tell the story of the surrounding landscape. Stroll along an interpretation trail and get acquainted with the local wildlife. Cool off in a falls or on a natural beach.

Extend your getaway at one of the park's three semiserviced campgrounds or in the comfort of a heritage lodge; interpretation activities are presented by naturalists nearby. Embark on a canoe adventure, paddling in pace with the movements of the sun and the wind. You can choose from a range of itineraries throughout the park lasting one to three days, with stops at primitive campsites. Hiking and mountain-biking trails will afford you both access and insight into the landscapes around you.

CANOEING ON LAC WAPIZAGONKE
a half to full day

At **Lac Wapizagonke,** all the charm, beauty, and richness of the park is on display, making for a 16-km-long (10 mi) natural spectacle. Resembling a river, this lake can be easily reached from the south (4 km/2.5 mi) or the north (25 km/15.5 mi) via the parkway starting from

the St.-Mathieu entrance. A broad range of services and activities is available on location: campground, picnic area, snack bar, canoe and kayak rental outfit, as well as swimming, canoeing, hiking, fishing, and nature interpretation. The entire area is pervaded by a particular spirit.

Serving as point of departure, the **Shewenegan picnic area** boasts an interpretation module offering insights into little-known aspects of the lake. A footbridge crossing over the lake provides access to the easy 2-km (1.2 mi) **Les Cascades Trail**—so named for the gushing waterfalls that create a continuously cool, calming environment. Spring

and fall colours make for a spellbinding experience along the trail.

Once you've completed your walk, you're ready to take off and canoe or kayak for two hours in the direction of the Esker, following in the path of the first aboriginal peoples. Sightings of wildlife are frequent mornings and evenings and include such species as the beaver, moose, loon, and, more rarely, wood turtle. **Esker** is where you stop for lunch, a dip in the lake, or a bit of aural and visual contemplation. Your ears will tickle to the sound of nearby waterfalls and your eyes are sure to delight at the sight of the majestic white pines rising on the Esker point. Close by, a

250-m (820 ft) boardwalk leads to a bog featuring wild orchids and carnivorous plants.

More adventuresome canoers will enjoy paddling out to the **Vide-Bouteille**. The diversity of landscapes along this 9-km (5.5 mi) return route is nothing short of amazing, including sandy beaches, marshy coves, and stream outlets. This outing will take you over a route travelled by the aboriginal peoples. Logging companies later dammed the route and used it to carry timber, while wealthy Americans and Canadians belonging to the Shawinigan Club canoed along it in quest of prize catches.

There is quite a mixture of forests to be seen along the way, including stands of pine, balsam fir, spruce, maple, and cedar. **Île aux Pins** is only to be admired, as no stopping is allowed on it. A little marshy cove harbours a number of aquatic plants—water lily, pickerelweed, pond lily—whose names are as evocative as their flowers are lovely to behold. American black duck, mallard, and common merganser can be seen swimming, diving, and dabbling, while the peregrine falcon silently wheels and turns above its hunting territory. Le Vide-Bouteille, the stopping point, is home to a large sandy beach and sheer cliff faces that lend themselves well to relaxation and daydreaming. As you paddle your way back, you are likely to be rocked gently by the wind and the current.

If you're keen to add to your experience of Lac Wapizagonke, a series of three roadside lookouts show off the surrounding valley in its full grandeur. The fall colours make for spectacular viewing. Perched at an altitude of 150 m (492 ft), **Le Passage lookout** (km 35) tells the story of the formation of the valley. The **Vide-Bouteille lookout** (km 46) reveals the origin of its peculiar name. **Île-aux-Pins lookout** (km 52) recalls both the presence of an aboriginal camping site and the impact of the great fire of 1923.

WABER FALLS
1 to 2 days

The trip to **Waber Falls** combines canoeing (8 km/5 mi), hiking (9 km/ 5.5 mi), and swimming, all in a spectacular environment unlike any other. Depart from the Wapizagonke picnic area, located at km 38 on the parkway. A convenience store and a canoe rental outfit are also on site. It is recommended that you get an early start.

The outing begins with an hour of canoeing through the islands of

White-tailed deer

Lac Wapizagonke until you reach the Lac Waber portage. Moose and beaver are frequently sighted along the way. Then, during the climb by foot, be sure to stop at **Le Portageur lookout** and take in the view out over Lac Wapizagonke and its islands. A series of ponds lines the trail until you reach Lac Waber. The sound of a low roar means the falls are not

LA MAURICIE

Top: A group of visitors takes a voyage of discovery aboard Rabaska canoes. Bottom left: Aboriginal petroglyphs dating back centuries. Bottom right: Arrowhead flowers.

far off. And what a pleasure it is to cool off in the prettiest and, at 30 m (98 ft), the tallest falls in the park.

On your way back, follow the portage trail in the direction of Lac Anticagamac for 2 km (1.2 mi). Midway, a lookout offers a panoramic view out over the lake, famous for its majestic cliffs, vast aquatic grass beds, unique forest, and richly diverse fauna. **Lac Anticagamac** and **Lac Wapizagonke** are linked by a

3-km-long (1.8 mi) portage. In 1997 and 1998, prescribed burning was carried out in this area as part of efforts to restore the white pine.

In order to camp, you'll need to portage your canoe and camping gear. Lac Anticagamac offers a primitive campsite at the foot of some daunting, 100-m (328 ft) cliffs. The evening's program of events includes a sunset, black sky, and a concert of loon song and eastern wolf howls.

The next day, take the opportunity to meander through a most unusual aquatic garden, where pickerelweed, watershield, and water lilies can all be seen blooming on a midsummer's day. A diversity of wildlife also wends its way through these teeming grass beds. The northern pike and yellow walleye, species that are absent from the park's other lakes, are attracted by the abundance of food that flows in with the flood waters of the Matawin River. All in all, it is an ideal place for fishing, nature-watching, and photography.

ALONG RIVIÈRE À LA PÊCHE
a half to full day

After a stop at the **Saint-Jean-des-Piles Reception Centre** for some useful information and advice, continue along the parkway for another 5 km (3 mi) until you reach the **Rivière à la Pêche Service Centre.** Recently upgraded, the centre is a meeting point for seasoned hikers, skiers, and cyclists and offers an array of services, including restrooms and showers, a dining room, and exhibits. It is also the head of a major network of trails, such as the 17-km (10.5 mi) **Deux-Criques Trail,** the 11-km (6.8 mi) **Mekinac Trail,** the 5.7-km (3.5 mi) **Lac-Solitaire Trail,** and several others that vary in terms of distance and level of difficulty.

Rivière à la Pêche is the longest watercourse in La Mauricie National Park. It originates in Lac Édouard, flows into Lac à la Pêche and Lac Isaïe, and then empties into the Saint-Maurice River. **Trail No. 3,** a former logging road, runs alongside the river, Lac Isaïe, and Lac à la Pêche over a distance of 15 km (9 mi). It is easily accessible by foot or by mountain bike. The route bears the unmistakable stamp of past logging and log-driving activities. The point of departure is located within view of the oldest white spruce plantations in Canada (1930–1932).

At km 2, the trail crosses over Rivière à la Pêche, the site of some magnificent waterfalls. It then hugs **Lac Isaïe** until it reaches a lovely log

LA MAURICIE

Hikers stop to admire the view.

LA MAURICIE NATIONAL PARK
(Parc national de la Mauricie)

INFORMATION & ACTIVITIES

VISITOR & INFORMATION CENTRES
Saint-Jean-des-Piles Visitor Reception and Interpretation Centre Hwy. 55, exit 226. **Saint-Mathieu Reception Centre** Hwy. 55, exit 217. Phone (819) 538-3232. Open mid-May to October.

SEASONS & ACCESSIBILITY
Park open year-round. Contact park office for information on snow cover in winter and snowmelt in spring.

HEADQUARTERS
702 Fifth St., P.O. Box 160 Main Station, Shawinigan, QC G9N 6T9. Phone (819) 538-3232. www.parkscanada.gc.ca/mauricie.

FRIENDS OF LA MAURICIE
Info-Nature Mauricie 702, Fifth St., Box 174 Main Station, Shawinigan, QC G9N 6T9. Phone (819) 537-4555. info-nature@cgocable.ca; www.info-nature.ca.

ENTRANCE FEES
$8 per person, $20 per group per day.

PETS
Pets not permitted on beaches, trails, boats, or in the backcountry.

ACCESSIBLE SERVICES
Accessible displays at Saint-Jean-des-Piles Visitor Reception and Interpretation Centre. Dock is wheelchair accessible. **Lac Étienne Trail** is a universal-access interpretive trail with observatories and interpretation panels, tactile exhibitions, and braille text. Campgrounds, beaches, picnic areas, and some hiking trails are also accessible.

THINGS TO DO
Hiking, mountain biking, canoeing, and fishing ($10 permit). Boat rentals, snack bar, beaches, picnic tables and barbecues, launching ramps, and interpretive activities at **Shewenegan** and **Lac-Édouard** picnic areas. Tables and barbecues available at **Wapizagonke, Esker,** and **Lac-Bouchard** picnic areas. In winter, cross-country skiing ($10 per day) and snowshoeing ($8 per day).

SPECIAL ADVISORIES
• Glass containers not allowed on beaches or Les Cascades Trail.
• Motorboats are prohibited on all lakes.
• Cutting down trees or branches to start or maintain a fire is forbidden.

---

shelter (km 3.5). Lac Isaïe recently underwent a bit of rejuvenation. Upward of 13,000 sunken logs littering its floor were retrieved as part of efforts to return the lake to full health. These wood fossils offer proof that some impressive hemlock forests were growing here at the time of Jacques Cartier's arrival in Canada in 1534. Today, the richest maple stands in the park are located here. Such species as the great-horned owl and the pileated woodpecker attest to the maturity of this forest. In addition, rare plants such as yellow lady's slipper and maidenhair fern exemplify all the grace and richness of the hardwood forests lining the Rivière à la Pêche route.

A bit farther along the way lies **Lac à la Pêche** (km 6). There is a pretty little shelter at the junction with **Trail No. 7** (km 8), followed by the **Wabenaki** and **Andrew Lodges,** the last living reminders of the Laurentian Fish and Game Club (1883–1970). In the immediate vicinity of the lodges, you can make your way up the river some 500 m (1,640 ft) to cool off in **Parker Falls** before heading back (11 km/6.8 mi).

- Strong winds over some lakes; boaters should check weather conditions.
- Campers should store food, garbage, and odour-producing items appropriately. Bear-proof racks are available near backcountry campsites.

OVERNIGHT BACKPACKING
Laurentien Trail open daily mid-May to mid-October. Backcountry camping available year-round. Permit necessary for backcountry camping; reservations on a first-come, first-served basis by phone or in person at the reception centres. $39 per person for four nights; $7 per reservation. Campfires prohibited at primitive campgrounds along the trail.

CAMPGROUNDS
Rivière à la Pêche, Mistagance, and **Wapizagonke** semiserviced campgrounds with 581 campsites total equipped with a fireplace and picnic table. Service buildings have washbasins, toilets, and showers. Unserviced campsites with toilets and showers $26; serviced campsites with electricity $29; group camping with showers $6 per person; primitive campsites for canoe camping $16. **Rivière-à-la-Pêche Campground** open mid-May to mid-October. **Wapizagonke Campground** open late June to early September. **Mistagance Campground** open mid-May to early October. Backcountry

camping available year-round. For reservations call (877) 737-3783 or visit www.pccamping.ca. Cancellation at least 7 days in advance of reservation date for complete refund. **La Clairière** group campground. For reservations call (819) 538-3232.

HOTELS, MOTELS, & INNS
(unless otherwise noted, rates are for a 2-person double, high season, in Canadian dollars)

Outside the park:
St.-Jean-des-Piles, QC G0X 2V0:
Aux Berges du St.-Maurice 2369 rue Principale. (819) 538-2112. www.cdit .qc.ca/absm. $65.
La Maison Cadorette 1701 rue Principale. (819) 538-9883. www.cdit .qc.ca/cadoret. $65–$75.

Shawinigan, QC G9N 6T9:
Wabenaki and Andrew Lodges St.-Gérard-des-Laurentides. (819) 537-4555. www.info-nature.ca. $65–$69 for 2 nights (Fri. & Sat.); $28 per night during the week.

EXCURSION

FORGES DU SAINT-MAURICE NATIONAL HISTORIC SITE
TROIS-RIVIÈRES, QC

Relive the history of Canada's first industrial community at the site where, from 1730 to 1883, resourceful engineers produced bar iron and cast iron objects for military or domestic use. Stop in at the Grande Maison, explore the blast furnace, and engage in some time travel at the Devil's Fountain. An amazing range of experiences are on tap, including guided tours, exhibits, a sound and light show, a history trail, and archaeological vestiges. (819) 378-5116 or (888) 773-8888. 70 km (45 mi) south of park via Hwy. 55.

History of Canada's Parks

The goal of Parks Canada is to protect and present nationally significant examples of Canada's natural and cultural heritage. Over the past 125 years, this effort has resulted in the dedication of 42 national parks and national park reserves as well as related systems of national historic sites and national marine conservation areas.

East entrance to Rocky Mountains Park, later Banff National Park, circa 1920

The achievement has been based on the efforts of individuals interested in the conservation of Canada's wild places, wildlife, and cultural treasures. Promotion of tourism, however, has also played a role. In 1883, shortly after the Canadian Pacific Railway (CPR) penetrated the Canadian Rockies, hot springs were discovered near modern-day Banff, Alberta. Government officials withdrew the surrounding areas from private development and, in 1885, created the Banff Hot Springs Reservation. In 1887, legislation turned the area into Rocky Mountains Park (now Banff National Park), with the government and the CPR aiming to make the park into a spa attracting wealthy railway travellers.

In 1886, the CPR convinced the government to set aside park reserves farther west, forming the basis for Yoho and Glacier National Parks. Other reserves followed, including a small forest park around Waterton Lakes (now Waterton Lakes National Park) in 1895; a major game reserve for elk in northeastern Alberta (now Elk Island National Park) in 1913; and a large forest park at Jasper along the line of two new, more northerly transcontinental railways (now Jasper National Park) in 1907.

By 1911, the unorganized state of the parks led Minister Frank Oliver to create the framework for Canada's park system, the

Dominion Parks Branch. He appointed James B. Harkin commissioner. Known as the "father of Canada's national parks," Harkin saw the necessity of making parks relevant to Canadians. His crowning achievement in mountain park creation came with the formation of Kootenay National Park in 1920 along the route of the Banff–Windermere Highway. He also established parks to protect wildlife, such as wood buffalo at Wood Buffalo National Park in the Northwest Territories in 1922 and migratory birds at Point Pelee, Ontario, on Lake Erie in 1918. He focused on expanding the system eastward, and in the 1910s the first historic parks were created in Nova Scotia and New Brunswick, forming the basis for what today is Parks Canada's extensive system of national historic sites. By the mid-1920s, Harkin had become a proponent of "a park in every province," resulting in the creation of the first prairie parks: Prince Albert, Saskatchewan, in 1927 and Riding Mountain, Manitoba, in 1930. He completed his career by doing the same in the Maritime Provinces, with Cape Breton Highlands, Nova Scotia, in 1936 and Prince Edward Island in 1937.

After Harkin's retirement, Canadian park creation went into eclipse, with only four new parks—Fundy (1948) and Kouchibouguac (1969) in New Brunswick, Terra Nova (1957) in Newfoundland, and Kejimkujik (1968) in Nova Scotia—inaugurated over the next 30 years. In the late 1960s, however, Jean Chrétien, minister for Canada's north and future prime minister, picked up the gauntlet to make the system reflect all of Canada. Chrétien reached agreement for La Mauricie and Forillon in Quebec (1970), Pacific Rim on the Pacific Coast (1970), Gros Morne in Newfoundland (1973), Pukaskwa in Ontario (1978), Kluane in the Yukon (1972), and Nahanni in the Northwest Territories (1972). For his work, he was the first recipient of the J. B. Harkin Medal, awarded to those dedicated to parks protection.

Banff Springs Hotel

Since the 1970s, park authorities have continued to make the system representative, resulting in new parks in the eastern Arctic at Auyuittuq (1972), Ellesmere Island (1986), and Aulavik (1992); in the Yukon at Ivvavik (1984) and Vuntut (1995); in Ontario at Bruce Peninsula (1987); in Quebec at Mingan Archipelago (1984); in Saskatchewan at Grasslands (1981); in Manitoba at Wapusk (1996); and in British Columbia at Gwaii Haanas (1993). Several of Canada's parks, including Banff, Kootenay, Yoho, Jasper, Wood Buffalo, and Kluane, have been awarded UNESCO World Heritage site status, and Waterton Lakes forms an International Peace Park with Glacier National Park in the United States.

— E. J. (TED) HART, *author of* J. B. Harkin: Father of Canada's Parks

International Bridge, St. Lawrence Islands National Park

▶ ST. LAWRENCE ISLANDS

ONTARIO
ESTABLISHED 1904
24 sq km/5,931 acres

Ten thousand years ago, retreating glaciers scraped sediment from the landscape near what is now Kingston, Ontario, leaving behind a granite chain of more than a thousand mountains. Today, these hills are the 1000 Islands—a winding necklace of glittering river jewels. Whispering marshlands, rugged rock outcroppings, and a rich diversity of plant and animal life characterize the 24 islands, 129 islets, and 8 mainland tracts that compose St. Lawrence Islands National Park.

The St. Lawrence Islands have a long history of community connection. Their strategic seaway location (within the Frontenac Axis that connects Ontario's Algonquin Provincial Park to New York's Adirondack State Park) means they've played host to many people over the years.

The islands are part of a corridor that acts as a funnel for the north-to-south movement of wildlife. They're also the traditional territory of the Haudenosaunee and the Mississauga Anishinaabe. During the late 1600s, explorers, fur traders, and missionaries relied on the islands, which also played a role in the wake of the American Revolution, as demonstrated by the amount of man-made heritage within park parameters.

More recent man-made structures, such as cottage estates and rustic cabins, might pepper an even higher percentage of the islands if local influence hadn't established a national park here at the turn of the 20th century. In 1904, the Mallorys, a local family, donated a small slice of waterfront property to the government on the condition that the land be used for park purposes. Though this sentiment has always resonated throughout the region, in 1997, St. Lawrence Islands was named one of four national parks with the highest levels of impairment to ecological integrity.

Today, prescribed burns in the park promote the regeneration of the pitch pine, at risk throughout the province. Studies conducted in partnership by Queen's University and Carleton University examine the road mortality of a range of species including the northern map turtle. The Ministry of Natural Resources monitors the impact of purple loosestrife, an exotic plant that thrives in the park. Local partnerships have proven key to maintaining this small, fragmented site.

How to Get There

From Kingston, take Hwy. 401 E toward Cornwall for 62 km (38.5 mi). Take exit 675 and turn right at Mallorytown Road, which will take you to the Mallorytown Landing Visitor Centre.

When to Go

Services are offered May to mid-Oct. Though the visitor centre closes in early October, the park is open year-round and the islands are popular sites for Thanksgiving picnics. Special events, such as guided snowshoe hikes and geocache tutorials, are offered in the winter and spring. Call ahead for details. Recreational boating slows in fall, making it the best time to visit the islands by canoe or kayak.

How to Visit

If you're only stopping in for a few hours, particularly if you have kids, the Mallorytown Landing Visitor Centre combines play with park history. A short walking trail allows you to stretch your legs while taking in wooded and wetland habitats along the shore.

For a full-day adventure, the park's extensive Jones Creek Trail System consists of 16 km (9.9 mi) of looping paths and gorgeous views. Those wishing to overnight on the islands, where all 68 of the park's campsites are located, can do so by renting kayaks in Gananoque and paddling along one of the dozens of routes through the park. Short, beginner trips from the harbour can be completed in 20 minutes. Experienced paddlers can go as far as Cedar Island off Kingston's Cartwright Point.

MALLORYTOWN LANDING VISITOR CENTRE

1.6 km/1 mi return; 3 hours

Heading east on **Thousand Islands Parkway,** a sweeping waterfront road that offers stunning river views, the **Mallorytown Landing Visitor Centre** is on your right. Before the parkway (or any roads, for that matter) existed in the region, local farmers shipped grain from the docks here. Travellers boarded boats to Kingston and Brockville. Today Mallorytown Landing, the original park site, serves as an interpretive centre.

Aquariums feature local fish, turtles, mudpuppies, and frogs. An indoor theatre shows films like *Voices of Akwesasne,* a Parks

Canada–produced video project that highlights the relationship between the Mohawk people and the park. Roving interpretive programs touch on everything from turtles and the role of prescribed burns to cultural history. You might even see a black rat snake as part of one of the live exhibits. Habitat loss in the 1000 Islands has helped make the snake an endangered species.

The gardens around the centre feature playground equipment and staked placards—part of a program called Leaders of the Landscape—that focus on the environmental stewardship efforts of local residents.

The trailhead for the centre's trio of walking paths lies on the east side of the main building. The 0.8-km (0.4 mi) **Smoky Fire Trail** cuts across the 1000 Islands Parkway and through red pine plantations and rocky lowland forests. You'll also see the former location of the **Andres farm,** a Loyalist settlement cultivated until 1956. Continue along the 1.4-km (0.8 mi) return **Loyalist Trail** and, if you have time, the 2.8-km (1.7 mi) return **Six Nations Trail.** Or return to the visitor centre and enjoy a picnic lunch in its massive granite gazebo (one of three such structures in the park), where you can read the Mohawk Thanksgiving address etched into the nearby rock.

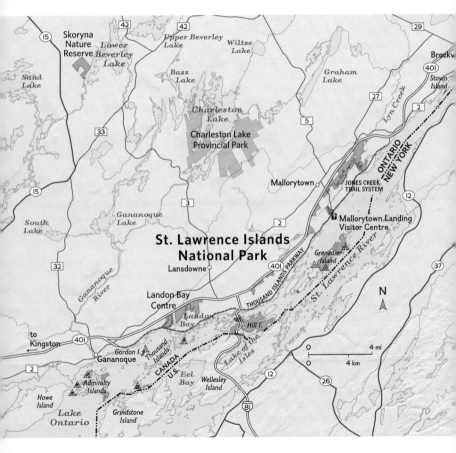

Red fox (*Vulpes vulpes*)

HIKE AT JONES CREEK
16 km/10 mi one way; a full day

Drive east from Mallorytown Landing. As you approach **Brown's Bay Day Use Area** on the right, you'll notice a sign for the **Jones Creek Trail System** on the left. This land here is one of the mainland tracts that were transferred to St. Lawrence Islands in 2005, a move that doubled the size of the park.

Pull into the small parking lot and self-register at the trailhead. Four trails at the front of the system loop into one another and make for 3 km (2 mi) of easy-to-moderate hiking. The five trails at the rear of the system offer 12 km (7.5 mi) of more challenging terrain.

A gravel trail leads from the lot to **Bear Loop** on your left. Forested ridges and rock faces make this the most difficult of the front trail paths. If you'd rather forgo it, take the **Eel Loop** to the right, where you'll pass beneath the canopies of century-old white pine. After Eel merges with **Turtle Loop**, look to a clearing on your left, where beavers have harvested the beech and maple trees.

The **Heron Trail,** the rearmost of the four front trails, features a lookout (complete with rustic wooden bench) over the vast **Mud** and **Jones Creek Wetlands**. To go farther, follow Heron downhill. A floating boardwalk crosses the wetlands to connect with the rear system, where five trails carve a semistraight line southwest. Keep your eyes open for wildlife. Turkey vultures, mink, beavers, and coyotes are regularly spotted on the rear trails.

In the spring, **Wolf Trail** is decorated with wildflowers. Come prepared if you're going to hike the whole 16 km (9.9 mi). **Snipe Trail,** the first loop of the rear system, offers incredible overviews of **Jones** and **Mud Creeks,** but you have to earn them.

Remember to stick to the trails. Black-legged ticks are present in eastern Ontario and are often found in the long grasses of non-established paths.

ADMIRALTY ISLANDS
12 km/7.5 mi loop; 1 to 2 days

Gananoque was founded by Loyalist Colonel Joel Stone, who took possession of a 700-acre (283 ha) land grant from the British crown in 1792. Drive past the town's turreted houses, with their wraparound porches and gingerbread accents, to **Gananoque Municipal Marina** at the west end. In addition to kayak rentals, 1000 Islands Kayaking Company (*www.1000islandskayakingco.com*) offers guided half-day, full-day, and multiday adventures to park visitors. Their guides undergo Parks Canada training in order to deliver a comprehensive interpretive experience.

Picnic area near Mallorytown Landing

Black-capped chickadee

bays, makes this the ideal trip for beginners (though seasoned paddlers can use the launch as a starting point for longer trips). Put in at the harbour and paddle south to the breakwall. Head west, past **Sisters Island** and **Ormisten Island,** and turn to your left. **McDonald Island** lies directly in front of you. Hug McDonald's eastern shore and follow it around to the south side. Just after you pass a stand of cattails you should see the park dock. Eleven campsites, composting toilets, and recycling/garbage collection make this one of the busiest islands in the park. Hike the perimeter and move on, or use McDonald as a base camp while you explore surrounding islands.

Wanderer's Channel slips southwest between **Lindsay** and **Bostwick Islands** on its way to **Aubrey Island,** which offers more secluded camping. Nearby **Beau Rivage Island** has a perimeter hiking path.

From Aubrey, paddle southeast to round **Bostwick** and **Halfmoon Bay.** To the southeast, **Thwartway**

If you do go out alone, maps are provided. There are plenty of options for beginner and experienced paddlers. The **Admiralty Islands** are a cluster situated slightly southwest of the harbour. Their proximity to the mainland (20-min. paddle), combined with the shelter of their many

ST. LAWRENCE ISLANDS NATIONAL PARK
(Parc national des Îles-du-Saint-Laurent)

INFORMATION & ACTIVITIES

VISITOR & INFORMATION CENTRE
Mallorytown Landing Visitor Centre 1121-1000 Islands Parkway.

SEASONS & ACCESSIBILITY
Park office open weekdays year-round.

HEADQUARTERS
2 County Rd. 5, RR3, Mallorytown, ON K0E 1R0. Phone (613) 923-5261. www.parkscanada.gc.ca/stlawrenceislands.

ENTRANCE FEE
Fee to self-register. Docking fee if paddling out to any of the islands.

PETS
Pets not permitted on beaches and must be kept on leash at all times elsewhere in the park.

ACCESSIBLE SERVICES
A 0.6-km (0.4 mi) wheelchair accessible trail from Mallorytown Landing. Visitor centre is wheelchair accessible.

THINGS TO DO
Boat rentals at local marinas. Boat launching $10 per person per day, $98 per season. **Gananoque Boat Lines** (888-717-4837, *www.ganboatline.com*) runs regular tours of the islands. Sea kayaking along the **1000 Islands Water Trail** in the **Frontenac Arch Biosphere Reserve.** Geocaching. Visitor centre with live animals, hands-on exhibits, and children's activities. Hiking available on **Jones Creek trails,** 11-km (7 mi) trail network, and **Landon Bay Centre,** 6.4-km (4 mi) trail network.

SPECIAL ADVISORIES
- Black-legged ticks are abundant. Stay on trails, dress accordingly, and conduct regular tick checks.
- If camping overnight on the islands, pack so animals can't get at the food.

OVERNIGHT BACKPACKING
No mainland overnight camping; campsites on islands are only accessible by boat.

CAMPGROUNDS
Island camping $16 per night; group camping $5 per night. 67 primitive campsites on 12 islands. Reservations for group campsites at Central Grenadier Island. Other services such as day use and overnight docking are on a first-come, first-served basis. Call park office for group camping reservations (see above).

HOTELS, MOTELS, & INNS
(unless otherwise noted, rates are for a 2-person double, high season, in Canadian dollars)

Outside the park:
The Athlone Inn 250 King St. W, Gananoque, ON K7G 2G6. (888) 382-7122. stay@athloneinn.ca; www.athlone inn.ca. $120–$200.
Glen House Resort 409 1000 Islands Pkwy., P.O. Box 10, Gananoque, ON K7G 2T6. (800) 268-4536. www.smugglers glen.com. $125–$309. Smuggler's Glen golf course on-site.
Victoria Rose Inn 279 King St. W, Gananoque, ON K7G 2G7. (613) 382-3368. $135. vr@victoriaroseinn.com; www.victoriaroseinn.com. Up to $265 per night.

Island hugs the **Canadian Middle Channel** and features small sandy beaches, perfect for swimming.

Thanks to the microclimate created by the Great Lakes, this area has one of the highest rates of biodiversity in Canada. Explore the phenomenon by moving from island to island.

To the east, the sandstone surface of **Grenadier Island** features a mix of trees. Slightly west, the thin acidic soil carpeting the granite of **Georgina Island** offers ideal growing conditions for pitch pine. Elsewhere, you'll find a mix of Carolinian, boreal, and mixed deciduous hardwood.

EXCURSIONS

BELLEVUE HOUSE NATIONAL HISTORIC SITE
KINGSTON, ON

The lavish home of Sir John A. Macdonald, Canada's first prime minister, has been restored to its pristine 1840s condition. Visit the sprawling Tuscan-style house and its gardens for tea and live outdoor theatre from the Parks Canada Players—an acting troupe that performs historic stories, legends, and lore. Tours of the house are self-guided, but costumed interpreters are well versed in the history of the house and surrounding area. Open April to October. (613) 545-8666.

FORT HENRY NATIONAL HISTORIC SITE
KINGSTON, ON

Built over five years in the 1830s, Fort Henry replaced a crumbling fort from the War of 1812. Visitors can watch (and sometimes participate in) live dramatizations of significant events from the 19th-century history of the fort. Guided tours, musical performances, and military demonstrations by the Fort Henry Guard (university student recruits trained according to British regulations) are scheduled through the season. Open mid-May to mid-September.

FORT WELLINGTON NATIONAL HISTORIC SITE
PRESCOTT, ON

Constructed between Montreal and Kingston during the War of 1812, Fort Wellington was meant to defend St. Lawrence River shipping routes. It was used for various military purposes until established as a historic site in 1923. The fort offers crafts, games, and costumes for kids. Explore the barracks and take part in a live cannon firing. A handful of special events, including Canada Day celebrations and guided tours, take place throughout the summer. Open mid-May to September. (613) 925-2896.

KINGSTON FORTIFICATIONS NATIONAL HISTORIC SITE
KINGSTON, ON

The Kingston Fortifications encompass a network of sites in and around Kingston Harbour including Fort Frederick, Fort Henry, Cathcart Tower, Murney Tower, and Shoal Tower. Together, these sites form a semicircle around the harbour and were meant to serve as defence against American invasion. In 2007, the Kingston Fortifications, along with the Rideau Canal, were designated Ontario's only UNESCO World Heritage site.

MURNEY TOWER NATIONAL HISTORIC SITE
KINGSTON, ON

Built in 1846 on a raised point southwest of Kingston Harbour, Murney Tower has been in operation as a museum since 1925. Managed by the Kingston Historical Society, it houses war and domestic artifacts from the 1800s. Taken together, Murney Tower, Shoal Tower, Cathcart Tower, and Fort Frederick Tower illustrate Kingston's contributions to the defence of British North America in the 19th century. Open mid-May to September.

SHOAL TOWER NATIONAL HISTORIC SITE
KINGSTON, ON

A squat, round-bellied structure, Shoal Tower lies opposite Kingston's City Hall. Along with Murney Tower, Cathcart Tower, and Fort Frederick Tower, Shoal was one of a quartet of defensive towers erected to protect Kingston Harbour. All four towers are examples of the Martello style—short towers with thick walls and roof-mounted artillery. Built in 1847, Shoal protected Kingston's commercial harbour as well as the entrance to the Rideau Canal. The tower is not open to the public.

The Canadian Shield landscape in Georgian Bay Islands National Park dates to the Precambrian era.

▶ GEORGIAN BAY ISLANDS

ONTARIO
ESTABLISHED 1929
14 sq km/3,459 acres

Windswept white pine, rock faces scraped bare, and wide, wild waters number among the most prominent features of Georgian Bay Islands National Park. These characteristics are what drew a collective of painters—known as the Group of Seven—to the area during the 1920s. Their paintings, done in strong, bold brushstrokes, wove the park into the fabric of the Canadian national identity.

A frontcountry park with backcountry scenery, Georgian Bay's vistas and accessibility make it a popular destination. Beausoleil is the park's largest island, with facilities including docks, 130 campsites, and 8 rustic cabins. It also boasts a network of 11 well-marked and groomed trails ranging from wheelchair-accessible walking paths to more difficult scrambles across the Precambrian rock of the Canadian Shield. Beausoleil's size has made it a popular seasonal stopover for centuries. Natives first used the island as a base for hunting and trading as far back as 7,000 years ago. Early voyageurs marked it as a midpoint on their travels between the Severn River and north Georgian Bay.

The southeast side of Beausoleil hosts evidence of a 19th-century

Ojibway village, abandoned when the poor quality of the island's thin, acidic soil drove the community west to more arable environs.

While Beausoleil's glaciated ridges proved too rugged to work, they were perfect for settling. The Georgian Bay cottage boom that cropped up in the early 1900s surrounds the park on all sides. Thanks to a handful of locals, whose petitions led the government to establish the park in 1929, visitors today can still find pristine beauty among the 63 park islands and islets that pepper the shore between Honey Harbour and Twelve Mile Bay. Though all islands are open to the public, Bone is the only island besides Beausoleil to offer services including docking facilities, outhouses, and picnic tables.

How to Get There

From Toronto, 166 km (103 mi) south of the park, get on Rte. 400 N. Take exit 156 and follow the signs for Honey Harbour Road/Regional Road 5. From Sudbury, which lies 240 km (149 mi) north of the park, take Rte. 69 S to Rte. 400 S. Then take exit 162 toward White's Falls Road. Turn right at South Bay Road and follow it to Honey Harbour Road/Regional Road 5.

The gateway to the park is located at the Parks Canada Operations Base, across from the Honey Harbour Towne Centre. A sign at the left of the road directs you downhill to the docks where you can catch the park's *Day Tripper* to Beausoleil *(www.parkscana da.gc.ca/pn-np/on/georg/index.aspx)*.

When to Go

During summer, Georgian Bay churns with the chop of powerboats. Even experienced paddlers should wait until the end of August, when visitor numbers drop and boating slows down. During fall the water is calm, the campsites quiet, and the trails less travelled. Late September to early October is the best time to see the stunning fall foliage for which southwestern Ontario is so well known. The park's paths are quilted with a patchwork of leaves in shades of scarlet and cinnamon.

In winter, visitors must blaze their own trails across the bay via snowshoe, ski, or snowmobile as services are not maintained. Hiking on Beausoleil's windward west side is a trade-off—much of the snow blows into the woods, but you have to contend with December gales. Winter camping is only offered at Cedar Spring and Chimney Bay.

How to Visit

For an afternoon visit, book a seat on the *Day Tripper* to **Beausoleil** and hike a leisurely 5.5-km (3.4 mi) loop around the south end of the island. If you have a full day, explore the immense diversity of the park. Though small, Georgian Bay Islands is home to more than 600 different plant and animal species. Beausoleil also marks Ontario's north-south transition zone. Cycling or hiking the island's bike-friendly **Huron Trail** highlights the dramatic differences between the two regions.

Despite the rugged appearance, the park's primitive campsites are considered frontcountry camping due to constant activity on the bay. Mimic a backcountry experience with a weekend trip at the end of September, when you're likely to pass days without seeing anyone. Rent a kayak in nearby Waubaushene, establish a base camp on Beausoleil, and hike out to the **Beausoleil Island Light Range.** If you happen to have your own boat, you may wish to explore the surrounding islands as well.

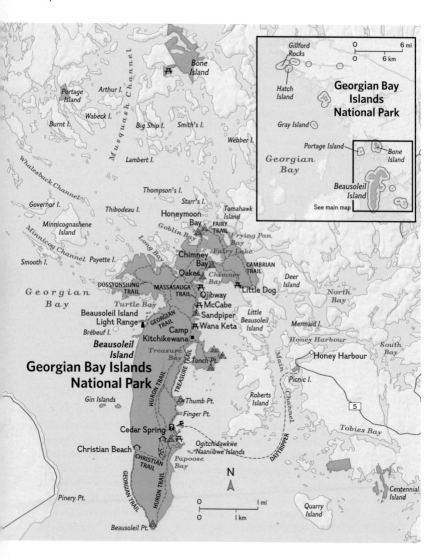

SOUTH END OF BEAUSOLEIL ISLAND

5.5 km/3.4 mi return; 3 to 4 hours

Unless you have your own boat, you'll need to book transportation in advance. Parks Canada runs the *Day Tripper* out of Honey Harbour. This modified, open-air barge-style boat makes a 15-minute trip across the azure waters of Georgian Bay to **Beausoleil Island** an average of four times daily. Water taxis are also available through the Honey Harbour Boat Club Marina northeast of the Delawana Inn.

Disembark at **Cedar Spring** (the main campground and the *Day Tripper's* only drop-off point) on the southeast side of the island where you'll find a picnic area, campsites, and washroom facilities. Behind the visitor kiosk is the trailhead for the 1.5-km (0.9 mi) **Lookout Trail**. Follow it through the open meadows that skirt **Papoose Bay** and into cool forests of beech and maple. Lookouts afford views of the bay and the forest canopy from 210 m (688 ft) above sea level.

When the path forks off to the right, keep straight and follow the **Huron Trail** south toward **Beausoleil Point**. Midland and Penetanguishene, where William Beausoleil, a Métis settler, lived during the 1800s, lie across the water. From there, take **Georgian Trail** north to **Christian Beach,** where a stretch of shore alternates between sand and cobblestones. If you can, time this trek so you're hiking here later in the day, when sunset stains the horizon and sets the bay ablaze.

Once you reach Christian Beach, follow Christian Trail to the right. This leads through stands of balsam fir and hemlock as the path crosses the island and meets back up with the Heritage Trail loop.

END-TO-END HIKE OF BEAUSOLEIL

13 km/8 mi one way; a full day

Take the Honey Harbour water taxi to **Honeymoon Bay** at the north tip of **Beausoleil,** where a handful of trails piggyback off one another as they loop south. To the east, **Fairy Trail** passes **Goblin** and **Fairy Lakes,** both noted hot spots for loon sightings. Jog left to take the **Cambrian Trail** through quintessential Canadian Shield country. Scores of white pine twist up from the rock and cobalt-coloured waves lap the shore as you hike along **Little Dog Channel.**

Cambrian eventually cuts to **Chimney Bay,** where it merges with the Fairy Trail. Walk west for 15 minutes

and take the **Massasauga Trail** to **Huron**—the island's longest trail. You'll pass **Camp Kitchikewana,** a YMCA camp that has operated on the island since 1919. Veer left at the **Treasure Trail.** This easy 3.8-km (2.3 mi) hike moves through forest and along the shoreline below **Treasure Bay,** where Caspian terns, mallards, and kingfishers dip and dabble. Osprey also frequent the area thanks to the conservation efforts of the Georgian Bay Osprey Society. At **Honeymoon Bay,** you can see an example of the platforms this group erects to keep the birds from nesting on power poles.

Farther along the trail is the brush-covered clearing where the Ojibway abandoned their settlement in 1856. Here, gnarled white pine and juniper give way to deciduous species like sugar maple and beech. This is a prime example of "edge effect." Beausoleil Island marks a shift from the hardwood forests of the Great Lakes–St. Lawrence

Calypso (*Calypso bulbosa*)

Rocky shore along Fathom Five National Marine Park

paddlers. Canoes are always best left to the shoulder seasons, when there is less wake.

Put in at Honey Harbour and stay close to the shore as you follow **Main Channel** north. Pass **Little Beausoleil Island** on the left and slip between **Deer Island** and Beausoleil. Continue along **Main Channel**, between **Frying Pan Bay** and **Tomahawk Island**.

A single campsite with 13 tent pads abuts the docks at Honeymoon Bay. Cook dinner on the wood stove in a nearby pavilion and take in spectacular views of the **North Channel**. At night, store food securely in your vessel or hang it. In midsummer, when berries are ripening but not edible, opportunistic black bears visit the islands looking for food. You'll also want to protect your cache from bold, smaller mammals like raccoons, squirrels, and chipmunks.

On day two, hike the windy western shore. Trails at the north end are marked by coloured blazes posted on poles according to sight lines. Follow the Fairy Trail to the **Rockview Trail,** but watch your step. The granite is branded with age-old evidence of retreating glaciers, including smiling chatter lines and thick bands of snow white quartz. The rock also acts as prime sunbathing space for the at-risk eastern Massasauga rattlesnake. Though poisonous, the Massasauga is a timid snake. If you come across one, keep a wide berth and note its location for Parks Canada staff, who monitor the reptiles.

As Rockview heads south, it meets up with the **Dossyonshing Trail**. Stunning views of **Long Bay, Lost Bay,** and **Turtle Bay** make this 2.5-km (1.5 mi) side trip worthwhile. The Georgian Trail, a short rutted route, passes through wetlands on its way to the **Georgian Island Range Light**, established in 1900.

Lowlands to the boreal forests that stretch north toward Hudson Bay.

You'll also notice the granite, so prominent at Honeymoon Bay, disappears as you move south. Twenty thousand to 40,000 years ago, glaciers scoured away the soil and carved depressions into the rock at Beausoleil's north end. The resulting harsh topography is ideal for the island's sphagnum mosses, lichen, and hardy pine. As you follow Huron south to Beausoleil Point, however, you'll find the land (where layers of rich glacial till were dumped) lies in lush contrast.

GEORGIAN BAY

11 km/7 mi one way; 2 days

The eastern shore of Georgian Bay is the world's largest freshwater archipelago. Plentiful islands and shelter from Lake Huron make it a paddler's dream. However, peak season kayaking is only encouraged for confident

GEORGIAN BAY ISLANDS NATIONAL PARK
(Parc national des Îles-de-la-Baie-Georgienne)

INFORMATION & ACTIVITIES

VISITOR & INFORMATION CENTRE
Welcome Centre open daily in summer, weekends only in fall.

SEASONS & ACCESSIBILITY
Park open year-round; services run from mid-May to mid-October. The park consists of 63 islands accessible by boat from Honey Harbour. Private marinas and docking available at Beausoleil and Bone Islands, as well as Honey Harbour. *Day Tripper* boat service and kiosk on Beausoleil Island open daily in summer; boat service available only on weekends in the fall.

HEADQUARTERS
Administrative Office 901 Wye Valley Rd., Box 9, Midland, ON L4R 4K6. Phone (705) 526-9804. www.parkscanada .gc.ca/georgianbay.

ENTRANCE FEES
$6 per person per day; $29 per season.

PETS
Pets must be on a leash and attended at all times.

ACCESSIBLE SERVICES
Full access on Beausoleil Island with a wheelchair accessible dock, washrooms, showers, camping, and trails at Cedar Spring Campground. Two of the campsites are fully accessible.

THINGS TO DO
Sailing, boating, and fishing (Ontario sport angling licence required). Beaches for swimming on Beausoleil Island. Also, hiking and cycling on designated trails.

SPECIAL ADVISORY
• Check weather forecasts before sailing.

OVERNIGHT BACKPACKING
8 primitive campgrounds available on a first-come, first-served basis. All camping must be at designated campgrounds.

CAMPGROUNDS
Tenting only. $10 nonrefundable reservation fee for campsites. Call (877) 737-3783. 11 campgrounds accessible by boat only. Each campground includes a tent pad or platform, picnic table, hibachi, pit privies or composting toilets, and picnic shelter. Maximum capacity per site is 2 sleeping tents and 1 dining tent; some sites can only accommodate 1 tent. **Cedar Spring Campground** on Beausoleil Island offers 61 semiserviced campsites with washrooms (flush toilets, showers, and electricity) and treated water; $25.50 per night. 5 campsites for group camping ($6 per person in **Cedar Spring Campground**). Also on **Beausoleil Island:** 10 primitive campgrounds with 5–13 sites each, some with tent pads, some with platforms; $16 per night. Running water is not available.

HOTELS, MOTELS, & INNS
(unless otherwise noted, rates are for a 2-person double, high season, in Canadian dollars)

Outside the park:
Delawana Inn in Honey Harbour 42 Delawana Rd., Honey Harbour, ON P0E 1E0. (705) 756-2424, (888) 335-2926, or (800) 627-3387. www.delawana.com. $150–$165 room; $205 suite; $225 chalet.

Inn at Christie's Mill 263 Port Severn Rd. N, Port Severn, ON L0K 1S0. (705) 538-2354 or (800) 465-9966. www.christies mill.com. $149–$229 room; $279–$489 suite; $1,995 per week for cottage.

1875 A Charters Inn B&B 290 Second St., Midland, ON L4R 3R1. (705) 527-1572 or (800) 724-2979. www.chartersinn.com. $175, breakfast included. Private charters to Georgian Bay islands available.

EXCURSIONS

BETHUNE MEMORIAL HOUSE NATIONAL HISTORIC SITE
GRAVENHURST, ON

Visit the childhood home of Canadian humanitarian Dr. Norman Bethune, best known for his role as a prominent surgeon during the Spanish Civil War and the Sino-Japanese War of the late 1930s. This picturesque Victorian house offers guided tours, interpretive talks, and large expanses of manicured lawn and garden. Many commemorative gifts from visiting Chinese delegates decorate the house. Open June to October. (705) 687-4261.

MNJIKANING FISH WEIRS NATIONAL HISTORIC SITE
ATHERLEY, ON

Located at Atherley Narrows near Orillia, the Mnjikaning Fish Weirs were used as a fishing site and meeting place by indigenous people more than 5,000 years ago. A system of underwater wooden fences, the weirs were used by the Huron and Anishinaabe until the 20th century. Parks Canada works with the Mnjikaning Fish Fence Circle to preserve and promote the site. No facilities. Open year-round.

▶ **NATIONAL MARINE CONSERVATION AREA**

FATHOM FIVE
TOBERMORY, ONTARIO

Fathom Five plucked its moniker from Shakespeare's *The Tempest*: "Full fathom five thy father lies; Of his bones are coral made; Those are pearls that were his eyes: Nothing of him that doth fade." A fitting namesake considering the purpose of the park is preservation.

A diver explores an historic shipwreck in Fathom Five National Marine Park.

Largely underwater, Fathom Five (114 sq km/28,170 acres) was established in 1972 to protect the many shipwrecks that litter its shoals. In 1987, the park was transferred to the federal government to become Canada's first national marine conservation area. It is also the sister park to Bruce Peninsula National Park (see pp. 122–127).

The water clarity here, caused by a natural absence of silt and algae, makes for first-rate scuba-diving. Visitors can dive the coastal caves or snorkel the skeletal remains of 19th-century schooners that carried supplies between the villages on Georgian Bay. If you prefer to stay dry, book a cruise with the Blue Heron Company or rent a canoe or kayak from a local outfitter.

BOAT CRUISES: The Blue Heron Company (855-596-2999, *www.blue heronco.com*) is open from early May to early October.

There is a ticket kiosk on the east side of **Little Tub Harbour,** but the main parking lot and central ticketing location are at 7425 Hwy. 6 across from the Tobermory Community Centre. You'll find a good range of transportation services, tailored to all schedules. There are five different options for exploring Fathom Five. Departure times are date-dependent, so check the website for current information.

Hop on a Zodiac boat and zip over to **Flowerpot Island.** The 15-minute option goes straight there, while a longer 25-minute tour passes over two shipwrecks—the *Sweepstakes*

▶ NATIONAL MARINE CONSERVATION AREA

Dolomite rock formations on Flowerpot Island

schooner and the *City of Grand Rapids* steamer—before heading to the island. If you'd like more time to observe the wrecks, sign up for a two-hour tour aboard the *Great Blue Heron*. This glass-bottom boat offers eerie, incredible views of the shipwrecks in **Big Tub Harbour** before it completes a circle around the islands.

The *Blue Heron V* allows for the same glass-bottom view of the harbour floor but skips the smaller islands in favour of a long look at Flowerpot Island. You also have the option to disembark at **Beachy Cove** and explore the island's hiking trails and lighthouse, but you must make this decision when you buy your ticket.

During peak season (June–early Sept.), you can sign up for a two-hour

sunset cruise along the northern coast of the Bruce Peninsula all the way to Cave Point. Departure times vary, so be sure to call ahead for information.

(Note that while the larger tour boats accommodate strollers and wheelchairs, the Zodiac boats do not, so plan accordingly.)

DIVING: Some of the most incredible sights (and interesting stories) in Fathom Five lie below the waves. Not only is the park home to submerged cliffs, overhangs, forests, and underwater waterfalls, it also acts as the final resting place for more than 20 different shipwrecks. The frigid freshwater temperature here (even during summer it can drop to a mere 4°C/39°F 30 m/98 ft down) and the absence of marine ecosystems help preserve the remains, another part of the reason Tobermory is known as the scuba-diving capital of Canada.

All divers must register and obtain dive tags at the visitor centre on Chi sin tib dek Rd. before the first dive of each season. Book lessons and rentals in Tobermory. Centrally located in Little Tub Harbour, Divers Den (519-596-2363, *www.diversden.ca*) offers everything from basic open water training to advanced technical certifications including night diving and peak performance buoyancy up to the Divemaster level. It operates from mid-May through October but is open year-round to answer questions and accept bookings.

Walk-on scuba charters make regular departures for popular sites including the *W.L. Wetmore* (a storm-wrecked ship off **Russel Island** that's suitable for divers and snorkellers) and the caves at the **Grotto** along the Georgian Bay shoreline. Phone ahead as schedules vary from spring to fall. If you want to visit a combination of dive sites not included in the standard schedule, ask about tailoring a tour. Dive boats can be booked for full and half days.

Be sure to ask your guide for the history of the wrecks you're diving. The *Avalon,* at the mouth of **Hay Bay,** was a floating restaurant until it was stranded in 1980 and eventually burned by vandals. The *Arabia,* a barque that foundered off **Echo Island** in the 1800s, lay undiscovered for almost a hundred years. It wasn't until the 1970s, when fishermen in the area noticed their catches coming up with bellies full of corn scavenged from the supplies aboard the ship, that people realized the massive wreck sat 34 m (110 ft) down.

G & S Watersports (519-596-2200, *www.gswatersports.net*), located in Little Tub Harbour, also provides diving services.

PADDLING: You can explore the waters of Fathom Five by kayak or canoe. Check Thorncrest Outfitters (888-345-2925, *www.thorncrestout fitters.com*) for reasonably priced rentals from mid-June to mid-September. The Tobermory store is located on Hwy. 6, just across the road from the turnoff to Little Tub Harbour. Note that you must arrange any necessary park permits on your own as they are not included in rental fees.

Kayaking is an ideal way to discover the endless coves of Fathom Five's many islands and inlets. First-timers can book a tour of the Tub. This full-day paddle is the perfect introduction to sea kayaking on Georgian Bay and comes complete with certified guides, safety gear, and lunch. More experienced paddlers can head all the way out to Flowerpot Island for an overnight camping trip. If you intend to do this, be sure to book well in advance (the island's six sites start to fill up as soon as registration opens in early May), and remember to take extra food and water as weather conditions on the bay can delay departures.

Beachy Cove, on the south side of the island, hosts the only docks on Flowerpot. Campsites are a short walk east on the **Loop Trail.** From here, continue northeast along the trail, past the towering sea stacks that give the island its name. Just beyond the second flowerpot is a large cave with an observation deck. Farther along the path is the stunning **Castle Bluff** light station. The light itself is automated now, but volunteers with Friends of Fathom Five offer tours of the original keeper's house.

During the summer, the island is also staffed with Parks Canada employees who can answer your questions about Fathom Five and Bruce Peninsula.

Flowerpot is the only island with trails and camping, although day use is permitted on all the others. Though the marine park is one of the most ecologically healthy places on the Great Lakes, the food web is in a period of change. A long legacy of invasive species and overfishing, compounded with more recent climate change and coastal development stresses, is transforming the ecosystem. Currently, invasive mussel species are depleting many of the nutrients native species rely on, but natural populations (including lake trout, cisco, and sturgeon) are making a slow, steady comeback.

Fathom Five Parks Canada Visitor Centre, Chi sin tib dek Road, Tobermory, phone (519) 596-2233 ext. 0.

The brilliant blue water of Georgian Bay, Bruce Peninsula National Park

▶ BRUCE PENINSULA

ONTARIO
ESTABLISHED 1987
123 sq km/30,394 acres

The Bruce Peninsula is a 100-km (62 mi) finger of land that cleaves the waves between Lake Huron and Georgian Bay. Though water temperatures here are frigid, the shores seem more lagoon than lake. The sheer limestone face of the Niagara Escarpment—the fossilized edge of a 430-million-year-old saltwater sea—rises 40 m (131 ft) from the tropical turquoise of the bay within the park.

When Bruce Peninsula National Park was formed in 1987, it included lands formerly known as Cyprus Lake Provincial Park (est. 1966). The park was created to protect the spectacular shoreline and rock formations of the Niagara Escarpment. In 1990, portions of the peninsula were designated a UNESCO World Biosphere Reserve.

Here, you'll find the northern terminus of the famous Bruce Trail.

At 843 km (524 mi), the Bruce is the oldest and longest hiking trail in Canada. It begins in the town of Tobermory and runs all the way to Niagara, connecting 105 parks and protected areas scattered across the most populated part of Canada. The 35 km (22 mi) of the trail that lie within park boundaries show off what the Bruce is best known for— crystal clear waters, karst formations, cobblestone beaches, and rocky cliffs.

Bayside forests, in jewelled shades of emerald and aqua, look lush as any exotic locale.

Despite its appearance, the thin soil cover (a reminder of the glaciers that scraped the land 15,000 years ago) makes for harsh growing conditions. Regardless, a diversity of plant and animal life thrives in the park. Pine grows in the dry areas; tamarack in the wet. Sugar maple takes root in the deep soil and eastern white cedar grows everywhere. The park is also home to the at-risk eastern Massasauga rattlesnake and Canada's southernmost population of black bears.

How to Get There

The park is located 100 km (62 mi) from Owen Sound. Take Hwy. 6 N through Shallow Lake and Wiarton. The highway ends at the tip of the Bruce Peninsula. Just before Tobermory, turn right on Cyprus Lake Rd., which winds through the woods for 5 km (3 mi) before reaching Cyprus Lake Campground.

When to Go

If you're after scenery and solitude, visit the park during the shoulder seasons. In spring, wildflowers carpet the forest floor and the sky fills with migrating birds. Autumn offers stunning fall colour and ideal hiking weather. If you plan on water-based exploration (swimming, diving, and kayaking), consider braving the crowds. Water temperature remains low year-round but reaches its peak, around 22°C (71°F), in summer.

How to Visit

The visitor centre mixes education with exercise. Indoor exhibits are hands-on and interactive, offering a comprehensive overview of Bruce Peninsula and Fathom Five. Outside, the Burnt Point Loop and Lookout Tower allow you to stretch your legs.

For a full-day adventure, park at Cyprus Lake Campground and hike to the bayfront Grotto and Indian Head Cove. Afterward, cross the highway and try one of the lakeside loops at Singing Sands.

If you're around for a few days, plan to go backcountry camping at Stormhaven and High Dump, catch a sunrise at Halfway Log Dump, and hike a section of the Bruce Trail.

VISITOR CENTRE & AROUND

3.5 km/2 mi; 2.5 to 4 hours

Drive toward Tobermory on Hwy. 6. Turn right at Chi sin tib dek Road and follow it to the visitor centre. Your admission fee here acts as a day-use pass for the centre, the nearby tower and trails, as well as Flowerpot Island in Fathom Five (see p. 119).

The **visitor centre** features a permanent multilevel exhibit that showcases the past and present of the national parks on the Bruce Peninsula. See photographs of each of the 42 species of orchid that grow within the park, catch a screening in the movie theatre, and check out artifacts salvaged from Fathom Five including the original 1897 lantern from the light station at Flowerpot Island.

Outside, at the edge of the parking lot is a **Lookout Tower.** This 20-m (66 ft) wooden structure allows for spectacular views of Tobermory's two harbours and the ribbon of escarpment cliffs that edge the shore. The Fathom Five Islands are also visible from here. According to Anishinaabe tradition, the flood waters from the

BRUCE PENINSULA

Paper birch and maple trees in autumn

Yellow lady slippers

animals, like fishers, that require a great deal of space.

Head back down the tower and follow an 800-m (2,624 ft) trail to a small lookout platform on Little Dunks Bay. This is the trailhead for **Burnt Point Loop**—a 3.3-km (2.1 mi) path dotted with a boulder beach and lookouts where you can see Cove Island, Flowerpot Island, and Bear's Rump Island. Clamber into any one of a dozen nooks in the rocks to take a breather and enjoy the view before looping back through the forest.

NORTH & SOUTH SHORE HIKES

12 km/7.4 mi return; a full day

From Hwy. 6, take Cyprus Lake Rd. to the heart of the park, Cyprus Lake Campground (about 5 km/3 mi into the woods) and register at the office. Follow the road and park in the lot at the trailhead. Take **Georgian Bay Trail** north. The wide, well-worn path snakes between towering trees, passing marshlands and

breaching of giant beaver dams created the islands 9,100 years ago. Before that, they were part of a land bridge that connected the peninsula to Manitoulin Island.

Look inland, to the south, to see the largest contiguous forest in southwestern Ontario. This entire area was logged in the late 1800s, so much of the surrounding forest is new growth. The wide, uninterrupted cover provides the perfect habitat for

Horse Lake en route to a boulder-strewn beach. Turn left and follow the white blazes of the Bruce Trail west along the water. The going is tough here, with many rocks and ridges to scramble over.

The shallow water at Indian Head Cove makes for popular swimming. Two minutes west is the Grotto—a must-see cave, carved into the rock by centuries of pounding waves. You can climb down into the Grotto, but watch your step. There are no handrails or stairs here. Inside, the cave is otherworldly. Algae and lichen decorate the dolomite ceiling. The water glows a brilliant blue-green where sunlight from an underwater tunnel filters through from the bay.

Back on the Bruce Trail, hike a rugged section west past Boulder Beach to Overhanging Point. A wave-cut hollow in the soft shale at the base of the escarpment has created a dense, narrow dolostone point that stretches out over the water.

Take the Bruce Trail back to Boulder Beach and turn right to follow Marr Lake Trail to Cyprus Lake Trail. The 5-km (3 mi) path skirts the perimeter of Cyprus Lake where a day-use area allows for swimming and canoeing on the inland lake.

Once you've returned to the parking lot, drive out of the campground and turn right on Hwy. 6. Take the first left, Dorcas Bay Rd., to Singing Sands. The view from the south side

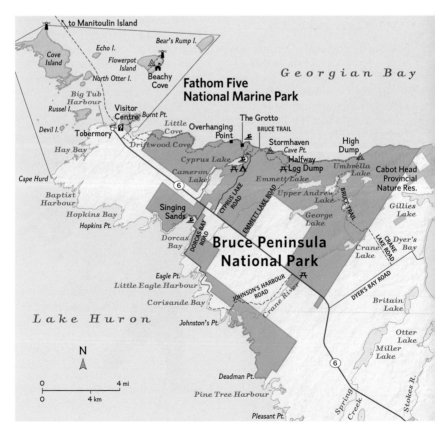

of the peninsula is vastly different from the north. The beaches, dunes, fens, and forests of Singing Sands are spotted with rare species like the dwarf lake iris and Indian plantain.

The 200-m (656 ft) **Boardwalk Loop** is a quick, easy stroll. If you have the time, try the 3-km (1.8 mi) **Forest Beach Loop.** The slight, sandy hills of the woods here host rare and delicate flowers like the purple fringed orchid. The peninsula is also home to more than 165 species of breeding birds, so bird-watchers may spot warblers, thrushes, and shore-birds. Spend the night at Cyprus Lake Campground.

BACKCOUNTRY OVERNIGHT

13 km/8 mi one way; 2 days

From the trailhead at Cyprus Lake Campground, take **Horse Lake Trail.** Pick up the Bruce Trail, and turn right to follow it to the Grotto. Explore the surrounding area including Indian Head Cove and the **Natural Arch.** The Arch has two entrances, both above lake level, making it more of a swiss cheese–style hole in the shorescape than an enclosed cave. Then follow the Bruce Trail east to the cobblestone beaches of **Halfway Rock Point,** with Flowerpot Island and Bear's Rump Island visible to the north.

Stormhaven lies 2 km (1.2 mi) beyond. One of only two backcountry campgrounds in the park, this ter-raced dolostone site offers nine tent pads, bear poles to secure food, and a shared composting toilet. Be sure to book your stay well in advance as these beachfront sites are popular among kayakers.

After dark, look up as well as around. Bruce Peninsula was designat-ed a Dark Sky Preserve (see pp. 58–59) in 2009. The lack of light pollution in the area makes it one of only three places (along with nearby Manitoulin Island and the centre of Algonquin Provincial Park) in southern Ontario where you can see the night sky as it appeared two generations ago.

Wake early to catch a stunning sunrise, then continue 9.5 km (6 mi) east along the Bruce Trail

A visitor enjoys one of the cross-country skiing trails in Bruce Peninsula National Park.

BRUCE PENINSULA NATIONAL PARK
(Parc national de la Péninsule-Bruce)

INFORMATION & ACTIVITIES

VISITOR CENTRE
Visitor centre Chi sin tib dek Rd., Tobermory. Open year-round but closed Sun.–Mon. during winter.

SEASONS & ACCESSIBILITY
Park open year-round but with limited services in off-season.

HEADQUARTERS
P.O. Box 189, Tobermory, ON N0H 2R0. Phone (519) 596-2233. bruce-fathom five@pc.gc.ca; www.parkscanada.gc .ca/bruce.

FRIENDS OF BRUCE PENINSULA
Friends of the Bruce District Parks Association www.castlebluff.com.

ENTRANCE FEES
Contact park for current fees.

PETS
Pets must be kept on a leash of 2 m (6.5 ft) or less at all times.

ACCESSIBLE SERVICES
Wheelchair accessible campsites, an accessible yurt, and trail to Burnt Point Lookout. All-terrain wheelchair available at Cyprus Lake Campground office.

THINGS TO DO
Hiking, swimming, and canoeing and kayaking on Cyprus, Cameron, and Emmett Lakes. In winter, cross-country skiing, snowshoeing, and winter camping. Interpretive programs throughout summer; inquire for other times of the year.

SPECIAL ADVISORIES
- Check with park staff for safety tips if kayaking or canoeing in the park.
- Fires only in designated fire pits.
- Use only locally purchased firewood.
- Campgrounds fill up in July and August. Reservations strongly recommended.
- Water from Georgian Bay should be boiled.

CAMPGROUNDS
Cyprus Lake Campground 242 drive-in sites (about 10 are yurts) with picnic tables, fire pit with grill, firewood, potable water taps, and washroom buildings (toilets), $24; $16 per site for winter camping. 3 drive-in group sites, $5 per person; minimum 12 people. Backcountry camping in **Stormhaven** and **High Dump,** 9 sites each with tent platforms and shared primitive composting toilet. Preregistration required, $10 per person. For reservations, visit www .pccamping.ca or call Cyprus Office: (519) 596-2263 (May–Oct.), (519) 596-2233 (Nov.–April).

HOTELS, MOTELS, & INNS
(unless otherwise noted, rates are for a 2-person double, high season, in Canadian dollars)

Outside the park:
Home to Home Network B&Bs on the Bruce Trail. (888) 301-3224. www.home tohomenetwork.ca. $165–$175, including meals. Minimum 3 days of overnight backpacking.

For more accommodations visit www.tober mory.com.

to **High Dump.** The trail here moves back and forth between cedar forest and cliffside walkways. Frothy turquoise waves wash over the rocks at the base of dramatic drops. The views from these dizzying lookouts are striking in every direction.

The same rules that apply at the campground at Stormhaven also apply at High Dump: Book well in advance, and be sure to bring a camp stove, as fires are prohibited.

For additional information on the Bruce Trail, pick up a copy of the latest edition of the detailed *Bruce Trail Reference,* available from the Bruce Trail Conservancy *(http:// brucetrail.org).*

Explore the secrets of the marshlands by canoe with a park interpreter.

▶ POINT PELEE

ONTARIO
ESTABLISHED 1918
15 sq km/3,707 acres

In May, the skies of Point Pelee National Park fill with feathers. Each year the lush Carolinian forests that stretch between the Mississippi River and the Appalachian Mountains to this, the southernmost tip of mainland Canada, are the stopping point for more than 386 species of migrating birds.

Point Pelee National Park has little of the rugged wilderness that characterizes most Canadian parks. At 42° N latitude, it lies in line with northern California and parts of the Mediterranean. Crickets chirp and hum past dusk, even in October, and the sycamore trees here drip with Virginia creeper. Grape vines twist through the trails, creating an exotic jungle aesthetic. There are very few coniferous trees in Point Pelee, despite the fact that their presence

here first piqued mass interest in the region.

In the late 1700s, British naval reserves logged the point's white pine for shipbuilding. Eventually, Lake Erie's ample supply of trout, whitefish, and herring drew fisheries, which gave way to farming and finally hunting. Oddly enough, the latter is what led to the park's creation.

In 1882, while duck hunting, naturalist W. E. Saunders was so bowled over by the diversity of birds at Point

Pelee that he helped found the Great Lakes Ornithological Club—the same organization that played a major role in establishing Point Pelee National Park in 1918.

Pelee, one of few national sites where sport hunting and private ownership were still allowed, quickly became a recreational hot spot. By the 1960s the park had hosted more than 700,000 visitors. A total of 6,000 parking spots couldn't accommodate daily demand. The natural ecosystem was so destroyed that Point Pelee was nearly removed from Canada's list of national parks.

In 1972, a restoration framework was drafted to govern visitor access to the park. Anything alien, including plants, animals, roads, and cottages, was removed. Today, Point Pelee is home to more at-risk species than any other national park in Canada, and there has been 50 percent land restoration since the 1960s.

How to Get There

From Windsor, 60 km (37 mi) northwest of the park, take Walker Rd. to Rte. 3 W. A right at County Rd. 31 followed by a left at County Rd. 20 leads to County Rd. 33. Turn right and continue to the park gates.

When to Go

Mid-May offers an incredible show of song and colour as birds move through the park. Note that Pelee's popularity can mean that parking lots fill by 7 a.m., even on weekdays. Mid-September is the perfect time to witness the exodus of monarch butterflies, which roost in the hackberry trees, waiting for the winds that will aid them in their journey to Mexico. During winter, the marsh serves as a skating rink and trails are open for hiking, showshoeing, and cross-country skiing.

How to Visit

Point Pelee is one of Canada's smallest national parks, but there's plenty to see. If you have just an afternoon to spend, rent a bike at the Cattail Café at the Marsh Boardwalk and ride the 4-km (2.4 mi) Centennial Bike and Hike Trail. Catch the shuttle to the tip and stand at mainland Canada's southernmost point.

If you have a full day, rent a canoe at the Marsh Boardwalk and paddle through the cattails. Afterward, enjoy a hike along the DeLaurier Homestead Trail—a 1.2-km (0.7 mi) footpath that winds past farm, field, and forest.

Visitors with a second day can easily hike all of the park's eight trails.

CENTENNIAL BIKE & HIKE TRAIL
5 km/3 mi one way; 2 to 3 hours

Enter the park through its north entrance and drive 1 km (0.6 mi) down the straight roadway. The first left turns off to a point overlooking **Sanctuary Pond.** Stop to have a look or carry on to the second left. Here you'll find the **Marsh Boardwalk Trail** and the Cattail Café. Managed by Friends of Point Pelee, a volunteer organization that aids in park programming, the café offers meals, drinks, and rental services.

Park your car and rent a mountain bike. Exit the same way you came in. Directly across the road is the trailhead for the Centennial Bike and Hike Trail, a flat, packed-gravel path that travels 4 km (2.4 mi) to the visitor centre.

Along the way, duck off onto some of the well-marked side trails to get a true sense of the park's diversity. In addition to sand dunes, marshes, and tall-grass prairies,

POINT PELEE

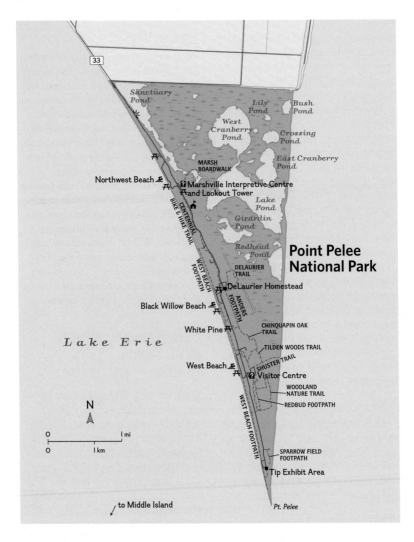

you'll find deciduous forests including hackberry, black walnut, and shagbark hickory. Though classified Carolinian (represented in less than one percent of Canada), Point Pelee is somewhat atypical of this zone in that its southern species mix with midwestern and prairie vegetation like sycamore. White pine grows in nutrient-poor exposed soils. The park is home to Canada's only naturally occurring population of the endangered eastern prickly pear cactus.

Watch for wild turkeys, especially early in the morning when they tend to mill around the trees by the path. Previously extirpated from the park, these birds were reintroduced outside park boundaries. Since 2005, they have reestablished themselves in the park itself.

Once you reach the **Visitor Centre,** park your bike and have a look at the interactive exhibits inside. From here, take one of the free open-air shuttles to the tip that gave the park its name. French explorers christened the area Pointe Pelée for the bald, sandy spit that reaches out into the water.

Though the beaches at Point Pelee are popular for swimming, the tip is off-limits. Here, east and west waves collide, creating dangerous currents and undertows.

PADDLING THE MARSH
6 km/3.7 mi; 3 to 4 hours

Point Pelee represents five separate habitats including beach, cedar savanna, dry forest, and wet forest. The fifth and final—freshwater marsh—accounts for two-thirds of the park's total area. As such, the Marsh Boardwalk Trail is one of the most popular hikes. For a different experience, rent a canoe from the Cattail Café. Pick up a map of the marsh and put in at the docks.

From here, a single canoe route travels 1 km (0.6 mi) east through **Thiessen Channel** to **Lake Pond. West Cranberry Pond** lies directly to the north; **East Cranberry,** which opens up to **Crossing Pond,** is slightly northeast of that. If you are interested in a challenge, paddle southeast on Lake Pond to portage to the south-lying **Redhead Pond.**

Keep your eyes open for wildlife among the swishing reeds and rushes; Point Pelee is home to more than 40 species of fish, reptiles, and amphibians including painted turtles. The water is also a great place for bird-watching. Geese and ducks eat the roots, shoots, and seeds of surrounding plants. Red-winged blackbirds whistle in the grasses. Marsh wrens weave cattail stalks into nests, feathering them with the fluff of catkins, and black terns nest on the vegetation mats near the trail.

HIKING
11.5 km (7 mi); a full day

Entrances for seven of the park's eight main trails are on the north-south road that runs from Pelee's main gates to the visitor centre; the eighth is the Centennial Trail, which parallels the main road. Pick up a map when you pay admission.

Follow the **Centennial Trail** to the short, simple **Marsh Boardwalk Trail.** Ascend the 12-m (40 ft) **observation tower** for a view of the wetlands (equivalent to 2,200 football fields) before strolling the floating boardwalk loop. Look for the small yellow flowers of the carnivorous bladderwort—an aquatic plant

Monarch butterfly

whose roots eat water fleas, roundworms, and mosquito larvae via underwater trapdoors.

From here, get back on the Centennial Trail and follow it 2 km (1.2 mi) down the main road to the entrance of the **DeLaurier Homestead and Trail** on the left-hand side of the road. This 1.2-km (0.7 mi) loop begins near the home of the

POINT PELEE

POINT PELEE NATIONAL PARK
(Parc national de la Pointe-Pelée)

INFORMATION & ACTIVITIES

VISITOR & INFORMATION CENTRE
Visitor Centre open daily April to November, and weekends from November to March.

SEASONS & ACCESSIBILITY
Park open year-round. Shuttle service available April to October.

HEADQUARTERS
407 Monarch Ln., Leamington, ON N8H 3V4. Phone (519) 322-2365. www.parks canada.gc.ca/pointpelee.

FRIENDS OF POINT PELEE
1118 Point Pelee Dr., Leamington, ON N8H 3V4. Phone (519) 326-6173. info@ friendsofpointpelee.com; www.friendsof pointpelee.com.

ENTRANCE FEES
Daily: $8 per person, April to October; $6 per person, November to March. Annual: $39 per person, $98 per family or group.

PETS
Dogs are allowed in all areas including the visitor centre, beaches, and shuttle, but must be leashed at all times.

ACCESSIBLE SERVICES
Call visitor centre to have programs modified to serve people with special needs. Wheelchair accessible washrooms available at **Blue Heron, the Tip,** and visitor centre.

THINGS TO DO
Hiking to Canada's southernmost tip, cycling on designated trails. Tour of **DeLaurier Homestead and Trail.** Freighter canoe tour through the marsh operates July to Labour Day weekend in September; call (519) 322-2365 ext. 200. Fishing permit $10 per day.

SPECIAL ADVISORIES
- Wear life jacket at all times during canoe cruise tours.
- Winds change rapidly. Check forecasts before visiting the park or arranging canoe or kayak tours.

DeLauriers—a French family that came to Point Pelee in the 1830s. The site, small considering it housed a family 17 members strong, is decorated with artifacts and accoutrements of the time, including the tools Charles DeLaurier used to coop barrels for local fisheries.

Heading southwest, the trail passes through the gnarled remnants of a small and stunted apple orchard. An easy hike through open fields and cedar savanna leads to a swamp forest, where an **observation tower** at the edge of the marsh offers views of eagle-nesting platforms.

From the trailhead, follow the **Anders Footpath** south, where it connects with four trails: **Chinquapin, Tilden Woods, Shuster,** and the **Woodland Nature Trail**. Highlights include the Chinquapin oak (a southern tree that grows in the cloud forests of Mexico) and the ridged barrier beach of the eastern shore.

Once you reach the end of the Woodland Nature Trail, cross the main road and follow the **West Beach Footpath** south. **Pelee Island** is visible from the sandy dunes here. Behind it, lying 30 km (18.6 mi) southwest of the mainland, is **Middle Island**—given to the park by the Nature Conservancy of Canada in 2000. Though inaccessible to the public, Middle Island is managed as a Zone 1 Special Preservation Area, where parks staff monitor flora and fauna.

End your day by visiting the exhibit area at the tip and taking a shuttle back.

CAMPGROUNDS

Individual camping is not available in the park. **Campers Cove Campground** family camping resort with 324 campsites on shores of Lake Erie, 239 seasonal, 85 for overnight campers. $39 for water and electricity; $50 for water, electricity, and pull-through site. Cabins available at $67–$75 per night. Wireless internet and general store on-site. Call (519) 825-4632.

White Pine picnic shelter fits 80–100 people, parking capacity for 35 cars, close to beach and trails and enclosed in winter, with electrical outlets, wood-burning stove, and outdoor barbecues (bring charcoal). Firewood must be purchased at the park.

HOTELS, MOTELS, & INNS

(unless otherwise noted, rates are for a 2-person double, high season, in Canadian dollars)

<u>Outside the park:</u>
Comfort Inn 279 Erie St. S, Leamington, ON N8H 3C4. (519) 326-9071. cn276@ whg.com; www.choicehotels.ca/cn276. $113–$128. Breakfast and wireless internet are included.

Leamington Days Inn 566 Bevel Line Rd., Leamington, ON N8H 3V4. (519) 326-8646. www.daysinn.com. $99–$175.

Ramada Limited South Windsor 2225 Division Rd., Windsor, ON N8W 1Z7. (519) 969-7800. www.ramada.com. $99–$140.

Seacliffe Inn 388 Erie St. S, Leamington, ON. (519) 324-9266. info@seacliffeinn .com; www.seacliffeinn.com. $119–$179.

POINT PELEE

EXCURSION

FORT MALDEN NATIONAL HISTORIC SITE
AMHERSTBURG, ON

Built in 1796, where the Detroit River drains into Lake Erie, Fort Malden preserves parts of a garrison erected by the British to defend Canada from American attack in the early 19th century. Orientation and interpretation centres provide context for the surrounding buildings. Watch a live demonstration, join a tour of an 1800s-era earthworks, or explore the barracks on your own. The site offers wheelchair accessible paths and buildings. Parking, washrooms, and a gift shop are also available. (519) 736-5416.

Canada's Boreal Regions

Canada's boreal landscape is home to billions of migratory birds and some of the world's largest populations of wolves, bear, caribou, and moose. Hundreds of First Nations communities exist in these areas that stretch from Labrador in eastern Canada and move across Quebec, Ontario, Manitoba, Saskatchewan, Alberta, and British Columbia. To the north, the boreal taiga and tundra continue until the high Arctic. These taiga and tundra regions continue into Alaska to the Pacific Ocean.

Forested woodland view along the Beach Trail, Pukaskwa National Park

Here megafauna such as grizzly and polar bears, elk, moose, and woodland caribou live alongside small mammals like beaver, wolverine, otter, and fox. Range areas for boreal taiga caribou herds in the tens of thousands cover millions of acres. Woodland boreal caribou face many risks and are now listed as threatened. Recent efforts to make sure we keep secure migratory bird habitat mean increases in bird-watching, citizen bird counts, and celebration of six billion songbirds that migrate through Canada's boreal forest regions each year.

Some of the largest lakes in the world, and rivers that dominate huge continental watersheds, define the Canadian boreal. Tens of thousands of lakes and hundreds of rivers from these regions supply water to most Canadian communities. There is very little private land in these boreal regions; most boreal lands and waters in Canada are publicly owned lands. Most boreal lands are also historic traditional lands for Canada's Aboriginal Peoples.

The last to 30 years have seen dramatic expansion of forestry operations, mineral exploration and new mines, road building, and protected lands in Canada's boreal regions. New national parks and protected areas established by provincial governments are a response to this expansion of resource extraction. Today we are much more aware of what Canada's boreal regions mean to us now and into the future. Canadians have also steadily, over the last twenty years, indicated in national polls their concern for the future of our boreal forests—and preference to keep these regions intact, healthy, and protected.

In the recent past, natural resource extraction permits and licences have been issued without regional, lands planning, or remedial plans. In fact, development of the oil sands in Canada's west-central boreal region is expected to affect an estimated 13.8 million ha (34.1 million acres) of boreal forest. Today, in part due to the dramatic growth of the oil sands, Canadians are demanding planning *before* resource extraction. They want to see the establishment of national parks and protected lands. Canadians also know that stewardship of the boreal regions is a moral and international responsibility for today and for future generations.

In the same 30 years Canada's constitution was repatriated and our Charter of Rights guaranteed aboriginal rights. Certain court rulings defining aboriginal rights arise from boreal regions and communities. The consultations and negotiations between governments that result include maintaining the natural world, stewardship of boreal lands and waters, and establishment of newly protected areas. National parks establishment steps now must include any First Nation or aboriginal community that considers itself affected by a new park proposal.

Climate change is causing everything in Canada's boreal regions to move and shift, even the land, and is adversely affecting boreal communities, species, infrastructure, rivers, and forests. More than 1,500 international scientists led by Nobel Prize–winning authors for the United Nations' Intergovernmental Panel on Climate Change have recommended that at least half of Canada's boreal forest be protected from any industrial activities. Yet permafrost, which normally begins to appear well below 60° then gradually expands northward, is now melting. Recent Mackenzie River Valley reports document the drastic results of this melting, and other studies have shown how it will impact northern and arctic communities.

Canada's boreal forests continue to provide services in the face of climate change. They scrub toxins from the water and air, and they help maintain river and lake ecosystems. They also store much of the world's terrestrial carbon, making boreal regions the second lung of the world.

Today Canada's boreal lands are a huge laboratory, where both stewardship and monitoring have become urgent, including to protect communities, species, and the economy of these regions. Scientists and concerned citizens are rushing to keep up with the movement of species, changes in range areas, and identification of species that will tell us the most about taking care of boreal regions in the future. Today woodland caribou are the bellwether for the future of Canada's boreal forests.

— GAILE WHELAN ENNS, *Director, Manitoba Wildlands*

Ferns and moss cover the Lake Superior shoreline in Pukaskwa National Park.

▶ PUKASKWA

ONTARIO
ESTABLISHED 1983
1,878 sq km/464,064 acres

The very act of getting to Pukaskwa National Park is an extraordinary experience. Whether you approach from the east or west, there are a hundred spots along the highway north of Lake Superior where billion-year-old cliffs plunge to the roadside, where banks of black spruce and jack pine ascend like Vesuvius from the ditches, where you crest a hill and feel a stab to the heart as the world's largest, most majestic, and sometimes most terrifying body of fresh water spreads out before you.

Pukaskwa is one of Ontario's last significant tracts of boreal forest untouched by human development or industry. The vast region of wilderness within its boundaries represents centuries of uninterrupted forest succession dating to the melting of the last glacier some 10,000 years ago. The park's Coastal Hiking Trail runs along the last undeveloped stretch of shore on the Great Lakes.

While Anishinaabe are known to have inhabited the area for thousands of years, one might well ask how such a sprawling area of wilderness remained largely unvisited by the mining and logging industries during the 19th and early 20th centuries, when almost all similar areas were being consumed by the advance of civilization. Harvesting of white pine and pulpwood occurred in the southern corner of the park during the early 1900s. However, the park at large was simply too rugged and remote for the ongoing cutting and removal of pulpwood or timber. A perceived absence of valuable metals or minerals in the rock discouraged mining. And when the transcontinental railway came through during the mid-1880s, it bypassed what is now Pukaskwa to the north. It bespeaks the ruggedness of the territory—the rock cliffs, marshes, and river chasms—that the stretches of rail in the vicinity of the park were not just the toughest to build and last to be completed by the Canadian Pacific Railway but in the end cost more than twice as much per hundred kilometres of track as did any 2,000-km (1,243 mi) stretch of rail in western or eastern Canada.

How to Get There

Drive east along Hwy. 17 from Thunder Bay, or west from Sault Ste. Marie, to Hwy. 627, which runs south 10 km (6 mi) east of the town of Marathon. The road will take you through the communities of Heron Bay and Pic River First Nation some 20 km (12 mi) into the public entrance at the park's north end.

Kayakers or canoeists coming from other parts of the lake can enter the park at Hattie Cove or wherever they can locate suitable moorage or beaches. White-water canoeists or kayakers generally enter on the park's east boundary, having come from White River Provincial Park, where most white-water river excursions into Pukaskwa begin.

When to Go

The most popular time to visit Pukaskwa National Park is June through September, when the days are long, daytime temperatures generally rise above 20°C (68°F), and most park programs are operational. In winter, the park offers snowshoeing, cross-country skiing, and camping to cold weather adventurers.

How to Visit

Many visitors to the park, especially those with children, will find all the stimulation they seek simply by pitching camp for a weekend or longer at the Hattie Cove Campground, near the park entrance, hiking the day trails, swimming in chilly Lake Superior, or paddling on the inlets of the cove. During high season, campers can experience local aboriginal culture through a traditional ceremony at the Anishinaabe Camp, where a First Nations interpreter will introduce visitors to native life and lore.

Those with a more ambitious agenda will undoubtedly want to venture along the 60-km (37 mi) Coastal Hiking Trail or paddle along the coast of Lake Superior or down the White or Pukaskwa Rivers through the park's remote interior.

COASTAL HIKING TRAIL
120 km/74.5 mi return; 1 to 2 days

Certainly, one of the most compelling of the many recreational opportunities available in Pukaskwa National Park is the hike down the **Coastal Hiking Trail.** This ancient pathway, one of Canada's most renowned and scenic hiking routes, stitches up a primeval line of granite headlands, pebble beaches, and old-growth forest. It also offers eleven primitive campgrounds with a total of 30 campsites (tent pad, privy, bear box, and fire pit) spread more or less evenly along the route. Parts of the trail make for tough hiking up and down the rock outcrops.

PUKASKWA

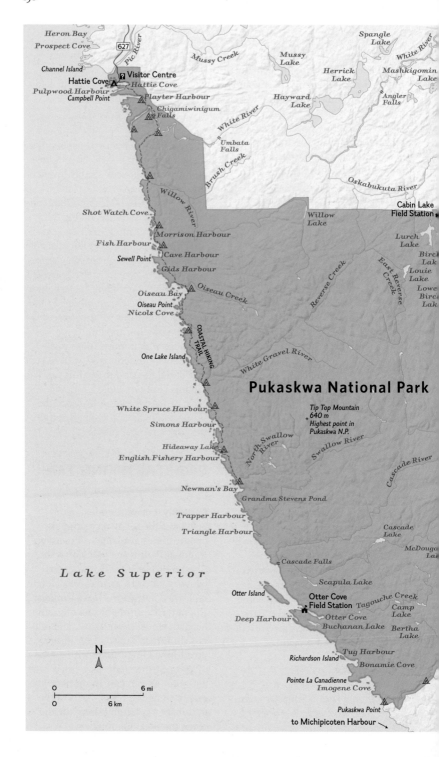

All backcountry users, including hikers, campers, and paddlers, must register with park staff upon arrival and departure. The park limits the number of hikers and canoeists permitted in the backcountry, so if you're planning either a coastal hike or paddle, or an interior river trip, call the park office well in advance to book.

HATTIE COVE

The interconnected hiking trails close to **Hattie Cove** range up to 3 km (1.8 mi) in length and offer everything from show-stopping views of the lake from atop the local headlands and close-ups of the intricacies of the boreal forest, to sunrise or sunset beach strolls within splash distance of the pounding surf.

Sharp-eyed hikers are apt to come across any number of small biological wonders in the park, including plants left behind by the Ice Age and nurtured in the park's "arctic" microhabitats hundreds of kilometres south of their normal range. The encrusted saxifrage produces showy white clusters of flowers in late June along the **Southern Headlands Trail.** Inasmuch as Lake Superior produces an "arctic" effect, it also, in its vastness, holds summer heat and humidity, creating microhabitats alongshore, where blueberries have appeared as late as mid-October.

Pukaskwa National Park is home to a small number of woodland caribou—a species that is considered threatened in Canada. The caribou population has been shown to be declining since Pukaskwa began aerial surveys more than 30 years ago. Experts have predicted that without recovery planning for the species, the park's caribou population could disappear by 2020. Ecological, social, and economic considerations play a large role in potential restoration efforts of woodland caribou and are being examined by Parks Canada, its partners, regional residents, and First Nations.

Those who prefer water travel can paddle the inlets around Hattie Cove or, if the wind and water are high, the more peaceful fetches of **Halfway Lake,** within walking distance of the campground at Hattie Cove.

CANOEING & KAYAKING

Canoeing the **White River** is possible during the open-water season but, because of the river's stiff current, requires getting to a point where downstream travel is possible. If you begin in **White River Provincial Park** to the east of Pukaskwa, expect to take four days or more to reach Lake Superior, from where it is an hour's paddle north along the coast to the visitor centre at Hattie Cove. The **Pukaskwa River** is also navigable but

Boardwalk trail through the woods

generally only during spring runoff in May and early June.

Between early summer and mid-autumn, paddlers enjoy the **coastal route** from Hattie Cove, down the west side of the **Pukaskwa Peninsula** and east to **Michipicoten Harbour.** In good weather, the trip can be accomplished in less than a week, but canoeists can also expect to spend one day in three wind- or wavebound at their shoreline campsites.

Lake Superior itself is of course a vast part of Pukaskwa's distinction— its vast and icy self-sufficiency; its unpredictability; its tendency to dwarf human endeavour. It is the world's largest lake by surface area, has more shoreline than the west coast of the United States (4,400 km/2,734 mi), and holds about a tenth of the world's accessible fresh water.

When the sun is out, the light above the lake is as hard and bright as sun reflecting off ice. Meanwhile, the light beneath the waves is as mysterious a medium as one is likely to encounter among the Earth's bodies of fresh water. Some would call Lake Superior a mythology unto itself, incorporating thousand-year secrets, the ghosts of old ships and drowned seamen and the gales and cataclysms that put them where they are.

Given the lake's profound ecological and historical significance, every attempt is being made by concerned agencies and individuals to protect and preserve it, as well as the surrounding shoreline and forest. In this, Pukaskwa National Park is leading the way, with its wildlife research and cultural and historical education programs. Once exposed to the park's extraordinary beauty and significance, visitors tend to include themselves among the growing number not just of Pukaskwa supporters but of wilderness preservationists at large.

PUKASKWA NATIONAL PARK
(Parc national Pukaskwa)

INFORMATION & ACTIVITIES

VISITOR & INFORMATION CENTRE
Visitor Centre located at the end of Hwy. 627. Open late May to early October.

SEASONS & ACCESSIBILITY
Park open year-round. Comfort stations open May to October. Campgrounds open year-round. Anishinaabe Camp open July to September.

HEADQUARTERS
P.O. Box 212, Heron Bay, ON P0T 1R0. Phone (807) 229-0801. www.parkscana da.gc.ca/pukaskwa.

FRIENDS OF PUKASKWA
P.O. Box 1840, Marathon, ON P0T 2E0. Phone (807) 229-0801 ext. 228. info@ friendsofpukaskwa.ca; http://friendsof pukaskwa.ca.

ENTRANCE FEES
$6 per adult per day ($3 in winter), $29 per adult per season.

PETS
Pets must be leashed.

ACCESSIBLE SERVICES
Two wheelchair accessible campsites on **Hattie Cove.** All facilities in the kiosk and visitor centre are accessible.

THINGS TO DO
Tour **Anishinaabe Camp** with First Nations interpreter. Hiking on the **Coastal Hiking Trail** (no bicycles permitted). In winter, skiing and snowshoeing. Calm paddling in the inlets of Hattie Cove, **Halfway Lake;** white-water paddling in the **White** and **Pukaskwa Rivers.** Sailing and boating on Lake Superior, not in Hattie Cove. Motorboats only permitted in areas accessible from Lake Superior. To register in and out, call (807) 229-0801 ext. 242.

SPECIAL ADVISORIES
- The park is prone to rapid weather changes. Take precautions against hypothermia, dehydration, and overexertion.
- Wear personal flotation device at all times when canoeing or kayaking.
- The Pukaskwa River is navigable only during spring runoff (May–early June).
- Lead sinkers and weighted lures for fishing are prohibited.
- If travelling by motorboat, note there are no refuelling opportunities in Pukaskwa. Motorboats prohibited in Hattie Cove.
- Keep food contained and out of reach of wildlife, especially bears. Do not leave food containers unattended.

OVERNIGHT BACKPACKING
Backcountry camping at primitive campsites available along the **Coastal Hiking Trail.** Random camping permitted at nondeveloped sites along the coastal canoe route. $10 per person overnight; $69 per year. Contact the park well in advance to reserve trip. Backcountry hikers and campers must register in and out of the park. Call (807) 229-0801 ext. 242.

CAMPGROUNDS
Hattie Cove has 67 campsites, 29 electrical ($29), 13 nonelectrical in the south loop; 25 nonelectrical sites including one walk-in site in the south loop ($26). Picnic table and fire pit at all sites; most have a sandy tent pad. Comfort stations with showers and flush toilets centrally located in each campground loop. Road to campground closed mid-November to mid-May; opened as snow conditions permit.

HOTELS, MOTELS, & INNS
(unless otherwise noted, rates are for a 2-person double, high season, in Canadian dollars)

Outside the park:
Heron Bay (Pic River), ON P0T 1R0:
Pic River Guest Suite 31 Rabbit Rd. One mini-apartment, 2 rooms, with kitchenette and private entrance. $110.
Marathon, ON P0T 2E0:
Lakeview Manor 24 Drake St. (807) 229-2248. www.bbcanada.com/3917.html. $90–$105.
Travelodge Marathon Hwy. 17 & Peninsula Rd. (807) 229-1213. www .travelodgemarathon.com. $87–$109.

▶ **NATIONAL MARINE CONSERVATION AREA**

LAKE SUPERIOR
ONTARIO

To understand the evolution of the Lake Superior National Marine Conservation Area, it helps to know that when the Welland Canal that links Lake Erie and Lake Ontario was built in the mid-1800s, bypassing Niagara Falls and allowing large boats to move from the St. Lawrence River into the upper Great Lakes, it inadvertently also allowed lamprey eels to bypass the falls for the first time.

A foggy morning in Lake Superior National Marine Conservation Area

By the mid-20th century, the voracious eels had severely reduced the lake's once teeming population of trout. Meanwhile, many of the 800 rivers and streams that flow into Lake Superior had become polluted and a daily rain of particulate poisons was settling on the lake from the air.

Although its ecology has drastically altered from what it was before the construction of the canal, Lake Superior is the cleanest of the Great Lakes.

The Ojibwe name for Lake Superior is Gichigami, meaning "big water." The size, power, and unpredictability have led many to think of Lake Superior as an "inland sea."

During the late 1990s, concerned shore dwellers and conservationists began promoting the idea of some form of protection for the lake and its islands. In 2007, after years of consultation between the federal government, regional First Nations, and stakeholders, a 10,000 sq km (2.5 million acres) section of the lake and its bed, stretching from

Thunder Cape in the west to past the town of Terrace Bay in the east and south to the U.S. border, was established as a national marine conservation area.

While the designation protects an enormous range of mammals, birds, and some 70 species of fish, it also preserves historic remnants such as shipwrecks, lighthouses, and ancient pictographs. In addition, it promotes the preservation and awareness of First Nations culture, past and present.

Unlike Canada's national parks, which permit no industrial activity within their borders, the mandate for Lake Superior support sustainable activities vital to the economy of the area such as shipping and commercial and sport fishing. At the same time, it prohibits waste dumping, mining, and oil and gas exploration, as well as any other industrial activity that might harm the area's ecology.

ON WATER & ON LAND: The best way to appreciate the waters and islands of Lake Superior is by boat, say on a fishing or kayaking venture out of one of the public boat launches on beaches in communities along the North Shore. There are areas in which the lake is so clear that boaters can see bottom and sometimes the wrecks of some 17 old vessels more than 20 m (66 ft) down. At Silver Islet, the shaft of the 19th-century silver mine, once the richest on Earth, is clearly visible in the lake bed.

The marine conservation area offers unparalleled waters for trout, whitefish, lake herring, and walleye. The waters surrounding the many islands near Rossport and Terrace Bay offer unique routes for kayakers.

Outfitters in the northern coastal towns offer tours and supplies. Camping sites, while rare to preserve the ecosystems, are available on the islands.

As an extension of its ecological and cultural aims, the marine conservation area supports the participation of local residents in stewardship and conservation initiatives and encourages their collaboration in directing the future of this vast and invaluable marine and boreal resource.

The headquarters for **Lake Superior National Marine Conservation Area** is located in Nipigon, Ontario. Call (807) 887-5467 for more information.

LAKE SUPERIOR

Kayaking through a rock arch in Lake Superior

PRAIRIE
PROVINCES

Page 144: top, Meadow Goatsbeard, a common Grasslands flower; middle, 70 Mile Butte, Grasslands National Park; bottom, Horseback riding in Prince Albert's Long Meadow. Page 145: Polar bear and cub, Wapusk National Park

PRAIRIE PROVINCES

The prairie parks zigzag across a huge landscape that stretches from Manitoba to Saskatchewan and the Northwest Territories. Wapusk protects a fragile subarctic environment on the shores of Hudson Bay where polar bears den. At Riding Mountain extensive wilderness trails lead hikers, bikers, and horseback riders through forests, over hills, and past lakes to a big draw: elk and captive bison. Visitors to Prince Albert seek out free-ranging bison, as well as

Above: A green curtain of the aurora borealis dances across a night sky in Wapusk National Park, where the upper atmosphere pyrotechnics are a common sight in winter due to the park's high northern latitude.

timber wolves, elk, and Grey Owl's cabin. Water sports abound in this park that is one-third water. Grasslands National Park is a semi-arid grassland punctuated by river valleys and badlands. Day hikes and horseback rides yield spectacular views and sites featuring Paleo-Indian medicine wheels. Wood Buffalo is characterized by forest, salt plains, and karst. It is known for buffalo, endangered whooping cranes, and a gigantic beaver dam.

Polar bears sparring

▶ WAPUSK

MANITOBA
ESTABLISHED 1996
11,475 sq km/2,836,000 acres

Manitoba's Wapusk National Park is one of the few places in the world where, in late February, visitors can watch tiny, three-month-old bear cubs explore, under the watchful eyes of their mothers, their snowy new world for the first time. But no roads or trails lead into this massive park made up of rough subarctic forest, tundra, muskeg, and part of North America's largest expanse of peat bog, which shelters one of the largest known maternity denning areas for polar bears. Wildlife-watching, especially for polar bears, is why people visit.

One of Canada's most accessible northern national parks, Wapusk—Cree for "white bear"—encompasses a good portion of the Hudson James Lowlands, a subarctic ecological transition region between Manitoba's boreal forests to the south and the Arctic tundra of Nunavut to the north. Hudson Bay itself is so vast (822,324 sq km/ 317,500 sq mi) that it creates its own chilly microclimate.

Wapusk National Park is home to polar bears and other wildlife, including many rare birds, moose, wolves, red and arctic fox, wolverines, lemmings, and the 3,000-strong Cape Churchill caribou herd, which winters here. While the climate can be inhospitable in winter for the region's aboriginal people, they continue traditional hunting practices within the park, primarily for the caribou. Winter's blank landscape of virtually nothing but snow would have an ill-equipped, unguided traveller lost and frozen within a day.

In summer, Wapusk National Park's peat bogs and marshy wetlands are nearly impossible for visitors to safely navigate. In the tundra, sedge meadows, peat bogs, and ponds cover the landscape, and in the subarctic forest, where the ground is firmer, tiny, stunted trees grow—hundreds of years old, less than 2 m (6.5 ft) in height, with branches only on their south-facing sides, thanks to constant harsh winds. The Hudson Bay shoreline habitat is peppered with salt marshes and flats, rocky beaches, and, because the bay has strong tides, an intertidal zone that stretches some 10 km (6 mi).

Come late October and early November, roughly a thousand polar bears, which have spent their summer shambling around the region's subarctic forest and tundra awaiting the freeze-up of Hudson Bay, move through the park's Cape Churchill area to the new ice. They spend the winter out on the frozen bay, gorging on seals to store up fat reserves for the following year's lean summer.

Visitors can access Wapusk through licensed local operators who provide guided trips into the park (see p. 153). Tours are also available into Cape Churchill Wildlife Management Area, a provincially designated buffer zone surrounding the park that affords additional protection for the polar bear denning area and the delicate ecological system here.

This ecological system attracts and supports some increasingly rare bird species. The habitat along the park's coastline lures more than 250 species of birds—including hundreds of thousands of waterfowl and shorebirds that come to nest or stage and feed en route elsewhere during annual migrations on this major North American flyway. Bird-watchers exploring accessible open tundra and shoreline northwest of the park can spot rare Caspian terns, great grey owls, sandhill cranes, stilt sandpipers, Hudsonian godwits, Ross's and ivory gulls, snow geese, Canada geese, arctic loons, gyrfalcons, and peregrine falcons.

Inexplicably, even grizzly bears have been spotted in the park: seven between 2003 and 2008.

How to Get There

From Winnipeg, Manitoba, fly north to Churchill using either Calm Air or Kivalliq Air. Flights take from 2 to 2.5 hours; some people opt to drive from Winnipeg to Thompson, Manitoba, on Hwy. 6 North—a distance of 700 km (435 mi)—then take a one-hour, less costly plane hop on Calm Air (Kivalliq does not service Thompson) to Churchill. Air schedules vary depending on the time of year and passenger demand, and in winter Arctic blizzards can disrupt flight schedules, delaying arrivals and departures, sometimes for days.

VIA Rail runs passenger service on the Hudson Bay Line from Winnipeg to Churchill twice weekly (Tues. & Sun. out, Thurs. & Sat. back). The train should take two nights to get there, but can be delayed if the track has been frost heaved and the train slows to about 15 km (9 mi) an hour, with frequent stops to check the track.

The train offers sleeper cars or economy class. The train also passes through Thompson, so visitors can

WAPUSK

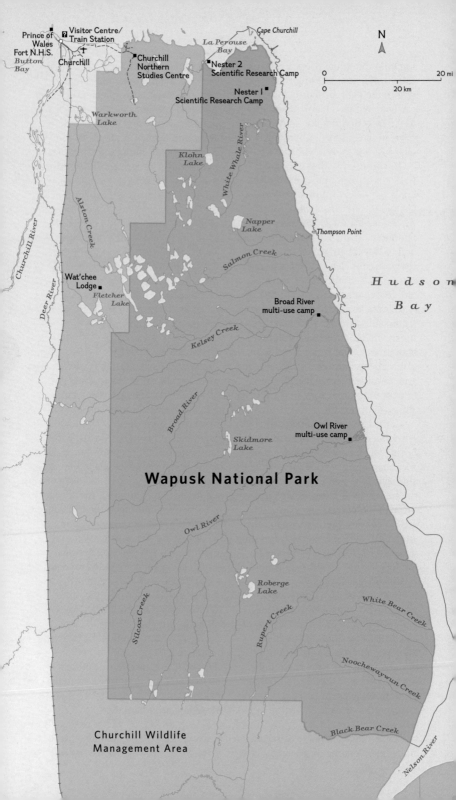

A caribou roams through Wapusk's tundra landscape.

WAPUSK

choose to drive to Thompson and take the train from there, or take the train to Thompson and fly the rest of the way on Calm Air, an option that requires taking a taxi from the train station to the airport or vice versa.

When to Go

The yearly polar bear congregation at the coast happens in late October and early November, while young cubs are visible at denning areas from mid-February to mid-March.

Wapusk National Park is accessible in summer via helicopter for guided tundra hiking and wildlife spotting. Birders and wildlife-watchers can also explore the tundra around the town of Churchill, 40 km (25 mi) northwest of the park. In July, visitors can don dry suits and frolic with hundreds of beluga whales and their calves in the Churchill River estuary. It is recommended that any hiking near Churchill be guided by trained escorts carrying firearms in case of encounters with polar bears. Keeping a vigilant eye out for wandering bears is critical; they sometimes come right into town.

How to Visit

Unescorted travellers are not permitted in Wapusk National Park. Escorting guides, operators, and local hotels usually book up well ahead, so early planning is a must. During "bear season," complete touring packages are the most common way to visit, with all travel details taken care of, from the Winnipeg arrival point on.

Wat'chee Lodge—Wat-chee is Cree for "a hill covered with trees in the middle of the tundra"—one of the few spots in the world where young polar cubs can be viewed, has limited capacity and is open for only four weeks from mid-February to mid-March. The lodge is reached by night rail from Churchill. Travellers detrain at a stopping point called Chesnaye, where lodge employees meet them with specially equipped all-terrain trucks and take them to the lodge.

BEAR VIEWING, BIG AND SMALL

a full day or weeklong excursion

The polar bear is the big draw for visitors to this subarctic part of Manitoba Province. Whether on a day excursion or on a weeklong visit or more, the traditional polar bear adventure involves boarding a giant tundra vehicle with massive snow tires roughly 3 m (10 ft) in height. The tires are tall enough to keep a

Heritage Railway Station, Churchill, Manitoba

curious, big bear from rearing up on hind legs for inspection of who's within the vehicle, but not too tall to prevent getting exciting views of the magnificent creatures.

Before heading out to the frozen tundra, visitors should make the effort to visit the **Parks Canada Visitor Centre** in Churchill's Heritage Railway Station. Its staff provide information and interpretive programs. The "Our Land, Our Stories" exhibit offers an introduction to both the park, covering its ecology and the great white bears it protects, and the cultural history of the region.

Healthy adult male polar bears can weigh up to a tonne; adult females weigh about half as much as the males. Polar bears eat almost

their entire year's worth of food in the winter, when they feed on ringed seals caught by waiting at the seals' breathing holes in the Hudson Bay ice. They must put on enough poundage to help them survive through food-sparse Arctic summers, when they subsist on occasional small mammals or wild berries.

Polar bear cubs, born in winter and often as twins, spend the first couple of months of their lives in dens scratched out of the ground above the permafrost by mother bears. The park protects an estimated 500 such dens, perhaps more. The dens are used repeatedly over the years, sometimes by different mothers.

The **Tundra Buggy Lodge** is run by Frontiers North Adventures (see opposite), the only operator besides Wat'chee Lodge allowed into the national park itself during migration season for bear viewing. The mobile lodge sets up in Wapusk National Park at Cape Churchill for one week in late November. Outfitted with a couple of bunk-bed-style sleeper cars, a lounge, and dining and utility cars—all with open decks in between the cars for better close-up polar bear viewing—the lodge can handle 38 guests at a time.

Similar experiences are offered in the neighbouring **Churchill Wildlife Management Area** in October and November.

For a truly unique opportunity, visitors should look to the **Wat'chee Lodge,** located in the Churchill Wildlife Management Area south of the townsite. Once a navy communications base, the lodge offers its guests day excursions to watch mothers and cubs as the youngsters experience their first tastes of the world outside their birth dens. Watchers must maintain a distance of at least 100 m (330 ft) to avoid distressing the mothers.

WAPUSK NATIONAL PARK
(Parc national Wapusk)

INFORMATION & ACTIVITIES

VISITOR CENTRE
Parks Canada Visitor Centre Churchill, MB R0B 0E0. Phone (204) 675-8863.

SEASONS & ACCESSIBILITY
The park is only accessible via commercial tour operators in Churchill. Contact park office for a list of licensed operators. Peak season for polar bear viewing is October and November.

HEADQUARTERS
P.O. Box 127, Churchill, MB R0B 0E0. Phone (204) 675-8863. www.parks canada.gc.ca/wapusk.

ENTRANCE FEES
Contact tour operators for fees.

PETS
Contact tour operators for regulations.

ACCESSIBLE SERVICES
No facilities in the park; contact tour operators for accommodations. Parks Canada Visitor Centre fully accessible.

THINGS TO DO
Parks Canada Visitor Centre, Churchill Heritage Railway Station. Interpretive exhibit "Our Land, Our Stories."
Tour the park with licensed operators:
Hudson Bay Helicopters, (204) 675-2576, www.hudsonbayheli.com. Sightseeing via helicopter.
Tundra Buggy Adventure by Frontiers North Adventures, (204) 949-2050, www.tundrabuggy.com. Polar bear viewing.
Wat'chee Lodge/M & M Ventures, (204) 675-2114, www.watchee.com. Polar bear-viewing opportunities in January and February.

SPECIAL ADVISORIES
• Weather is unpredictable and storms are frequent. Dress for extreme cold and wet conditions.
• Temperatures can drop below minus 40°C (minus 40°F), and to minus 62°C (minus 80°F) with wind chill. Skin freezes in less than 30 seconds of exposure. Wear appropriate clothing and good-quality glasses to avoid frostbite, hypothermia, and snowblindness.
• Open water is very cold. Sea, lake, and river ice may be unstable and unsafe to walk on at any time of year.
• Travel inland restricted to the winter.
• In summer, wear bug-proof jackets and hats and carry insect repellent to avoid biting insects.
• Avoid foxes, as they may carry rabies.
• Watch for polar bear and black bear encounters. Polar bears are a risk especially during ice-free periods from July through November.

HOTELS, MOTELS, & INNS
(unless otherwise noted, rates are for a 2-person double, high season, Canadian dollars)

Outside the park:
Churchill, MB R0B 0E0
Aurora Inn Box 1030. (204) 675-2071. www.aurora-inn.mb.ca. $235.
Bear Country Inn 126 Kelsey Blvd., Box 788. (204) 675-8299. $210.
Iceberg Inn 183 Kelsey Blvd., Box 640. (204) 675-2228. www.iceberginn.ca. Call for bear season rates.
Lazy Bear Lodge 313 Kelsey Blvd., Box 880. (204) 663-9377. www.lazybear lodge.com. $385 per night October–November; $193 July–August.

Adventure packages at Lazy Bear Lodge:
Beluga Whale Dream Tour, 2-night package, July–August boat tour to view beluga whales and Prince of Wales fort. $385 all-inclusive.
Ultimate Arctic Summer Adventure, 4-night package, July–August, tour to view polar bears and beluga whales, and cultural and heritage tour. $1,788 per person; prices do not include airfare.
Ultimate Polar Bear Tour, 3-night bear-viewing tour, October–November. $2,635 per person, including accommodation, meals, and 2 full days on the tundra and the cultural and heritage tour.

Additional accommodation/tour options:
Destination Churchill http://everything churchill.com.

Early morning mist blankets the rolling hills and meadows of Riding Mountain, softening and blurring the landscape.

▶ RIDING MOUNTAIN

MANITOBA
ESTABLISHED 1930
3,000 sq km/741,300 acres

Encompassing part of a postglacial age ribbon of high ground that stretches from South Dakota into northern Saskatchewan, Manitoba's Riding Mountain National Park "peaks out" at just under 800 m (2,625 ft) above a sea of surrounding prairie landscape. Within the park, a rich, diverse biosystem with everything from beavers to bison is based on a unique blend of different wilderness areas that offers a plethora of nature-oriented exploration options.

Geologically speaking, some 20,000 years ago a high beach ridge began forming along the western edge of Lake Agassiz, a postglacial inland sea that covered much of north-central North America. In the United States, the ridge is called the Pembina Escarpment or Gorge. The portion of the ridge in Canada is called the Manitoba Escarpment.

Whatever this abrupt rise in the prairie landscape is named, the stretch in Manitoba is a natural island of forests, lakes, and meadows that has been sheltered as a national park since 1930 (though it didn't officially open to the public until 1933) and became the core of the UNESCO-designated Riding Mountain Biosphere Reserve in

1986, one of just 15 such reserves in Canada.

Rich with aspen parkland and grasslands, marshes and small lakes, and spanning deciduous and boreal forests, Riding Mountain is a top wildlife-viewing locale. The park is favoured by hikers, backpackers, horseback riders, and mountain bikers in summer for its extensive series of wilderness trails—more than 300 km (186.5 mi) worth on more than three dozen trails—and cross-country skiers and snowshoers in winter, when dozens of trails are groomed for skiers, while snowshoers can explore at will.

Riding Mountain is also one of the few Canadian national parks that was founded during a time when recreation and public enjoyment of nature were the primary raison d'être for national parks—which is why there's an actual townsite here, Wasagaming, on the shores of Clear Lake, complete with souvenir and clothing shops, restaurants, movie theatre, marina, and a choice of lodges, inns, motels, and cabins for rent. A few of the town's buildings, including the visitor centre, date as far back as the late 1930s; they stand out because of their thick, rough-hewn log structures.

A national parks policy change eventually occurred. Now all Canadian parks now serve dual, sometimes potentially conflicting, roles: Protect key Canadian natural treasures from being loved to death, but still allow people to appreciate them as close-up as possible.

How to Get There

The park sits about 4.5 hours northwest by car from Winnipeg—via Trans-Canada 1 (for 98 km/61 mi) then Hwy. 16 (for 182 km/113 mi) to the park's south gate and, a short distance inside the gate, Wasagaming (known as Clear Lake by locals). The park's more scenic and geographically impressive entrance, the East Gate National Historic Site (see p. 161), is on Hwy. 19, which climbs the slope of the escarpment (take Trans-Canada 1 west to Hwy. 16, aka the Yellowhead Route, just past the city of Portage la Prairie, then head northwest on Hwy. 16 to Neepawa, then north on Hwy. 5, turning west on Hwy. 19).

Park passes can be bought at the north and south park gates.

When to Go

June, July, and August are peak season for vacationers who head to Clear Lake's sandy beaches and deep, cool water, settling into cottages or campsites at one of the park's half-dozen campgrounds (mid-May–mid-Oct.), or booking into the few hotels and B&Bs that edge the park's boundaries. Advance reservations are strongly recommended for campers at the fully serviced Wasagaming Campground; the outlying campgrounds are first come, first served.

Most of the public park facilities are closed in winter, except for occasional warming huts on cross-country ski trails, but Parks Canada staff do run a limited winter interpretive program, offering among other things animal tracking and snowshoeing.

How to Visit

A one-day drive handles both scenic roads in the eastern portion of the national park: Hwy. 10, which runs north and south through the park, and Hwy. 19 to the east. Off Hwy. 10, rounding the north curve of the lake,

Riding Mountain's lakes provide a variety of recreation.

another road leads to and through the national park's signature Lake Audy bison enclosure, where a large elevated, covered exhibit offers information and good views of the bison if the 30-member herd happens to be in this part of the meadow. When travelling through the enclosure, visitors should stay in their vehicles, keep their windows up, and not feed the animals. These beasts are still wild, still unpredictable.

But the park's real attractions are its vast swatches of nature, punctuated by dozens of trails negotiable only on foot, bicycle, or horseback. Dozens of trailheads, designed for long-distance or day hikes, are easily reachable by vehicle; the visitor centre can provide detailed maps. Most visitors should take at least a long weekend to explore the park's natural offerings, and backpackers can hike into remote campsites to spend a couple of nights under the stars.

The best hiking trails lead into the western high meadows and "prairie pothole" areas; the most isolated backcountry campsites are found here. Eastern park trailheads start on Hwy. 19, and western trailheads can be reached via Lake Audy or by driving west outside the

park, following Hwy. 45 to gravel roads 264 or 577, both of which run north to enter more remote areas of the park and reach the narrow, little-travelled trails that make this piece of the park a casual backpacker's heaven.

Most day trails are off-limits to mountain bikers, but the partly gravelled park warden patrol roads that cut through wilder areas of the park offer plenty of attraction for cycling enthusiasts. The Central, Baldy Lake, and Strathclair Trails are easy rides; the Packhorse, Jet, and Baldy Hill Trails are much more hilly and far tougher to handle.

WASAGAMING (CLEAR LAKE)

Wasagaming is "Clear Lake cottage country" and is the busiest part of Riding Mountain, bustling in summer with day-trippers, vacationers, and cottagers. Plenty of short hiking and cycling trails start and end at the edges of the townsite and its adjacent, fully serviced campground. One of the most popular, the **Ominnik Marsh boardwalk,** is just a five-minute stroll from the visitor centre, and runs just under 2 km (1.25 mi). The visitor centre loans out Marsh Kits with gear to keep kids interested and busy, even binoculars to spot marsh birds and wildlife.

Worth a stop for a little park natural history and orientation, the **visitor centre** is one of the few original log buildings in town, built in the 1930s. Another, the 1937 **Park Theatre,** is North America's largest log cabin theatre; it runs current films, changing them up every few days. The theatre sits on Wasagaming Drive, the town's main street. Most souvenir shops and restaurants are found along this street. (The Whitehouse Bakery is famous for its irresistible giant, gooey cinnamon buns.)

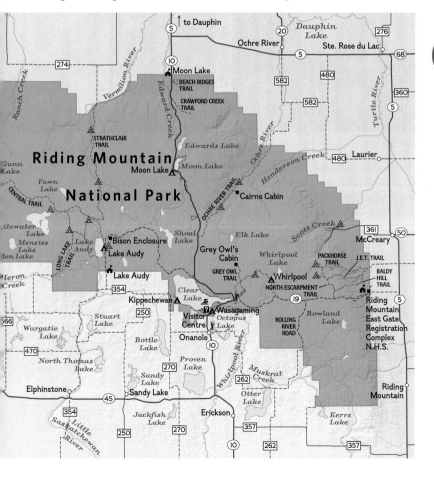

Sunlight strikes aspen trees in a boreal forest in the fall.

Bulrushes along Whirlpool Lake and reflections

Juvenile great horned owls *(Bubo virginianus)*

The 18-hole Clear Lake golf course—considered one of Canada's most beautiful golf courses—is located at the lake's east end and is open throughout the full summer season, as are the tennis courts. Other area golf courses include the new 18-hole Poplar Ridge Golf Course, on Hwy. 354 off Hwy. 10, near the village of Onanole just outside the park's south gate; the 9-hole Lakewood Hills Golf Course in Onanole; and a 9-hole course at the Elkhorn Resort.

Powerboats and pedal boats, canoes and kayaks, and fishing boats (fishing licences can be bought at the visitor centre; catch-and-release is practised here) can be rented at the town's main pier. Dinner and lake cruises are available on the *Martese* cruise ship. Bike rentals are easy to find in town, and horseback riding is available through the **Elkhorn Resort.**

WILDLIFE-WATCHING
predawn & dusk

Riding Mountain National Park is blessed with a bounty of wildlife, much of which can be seen by even casual visitors, much more so by wildlife enthusiasts. Wildlife-watchers favour the park in late April/early May and late September/ early October—the former because the wildlife's just waking up from being dug in for the winter and newborns tended through the snowy season are taking early steps into the wild outside world; the latter because it's both the fatten-up-for-winter season as well as the mating season for elk (Manitoba's largest population of elk lives in the park), moose, and other wildlife. In general, the animals are more active in the predawn and dusk hours, and thus are more easily spotted then.

Some wildlife-watchers stay in Wasagaming, at the Elkhorn Resort on the edge of the park near the South Gate entrance, or at Riding Mountain Guest Ranch, where sunset bear-watching is a "specialty of the house."

For optimum wildlife-viewing opportunities, join a guided hike led by local wildlife experts who know the park and daily wildlife movement patterns intimately. On these forays, wildlife-watchers are out on the back roads and trails before sunrise, when morning fog and mists cloak the quiet wetlands, and the only sounds are the flapping of wings or, in autumn, the scraping of elk antlers against trees and the eerie bugle of an elk in search of a mate.

These are the times when a moose could perhaps be spotted trotting along a gravel road or browsing the branches of low-hanging trees and bushes in a marshy meadow. A lone wolf or coyote may stand quietly at roadside, hoping not to be noticed, and beavers are easily visible dragging logs through patches of wetland to shore up lodges and dams in shallow ponds that are dotted with dozing waterfowl.

Lucky observers may catch glimpses of pine marten, fishers, mink, raccoons, coyotes, porcupines, and lynx. White-tailed deer herds, however, are easily spotted throughout the park, while fresh scat on narrow trails reveals the presence of black bears.

Pre-dusk bird-watchers in Riding Mountain will almost certainly spot bald eagles by **Moon Lake, Whirlpool Lake,** and **Lake Audy;** falcons and hawks overhead; plenty of songbirds in the trees; and grouse in the forest undergrowth pretty much anywhere in the park. Riding Mountain National Park boasts more than 260 species, so bird-watchers may easily find loons, ospreys, white pelicans, pileated woodpeckers, and great blue herons as well.

WHITEWATER LAKE
a half day

Before it became a national park, this area was a forest reserve, supplying firewood to surrounding farms and communities. During World War II, domestic fuel shortages meant it became a firewood source again—only this time, the wood was cut by German prisoners of war who lived in a **park encampment** at Whitewater Lake from 1943 to 1945.

Because it was so remote, the P.O.W. camp was neither fenced nor walled. Today, the crumbling ruins of building foundations remain and the site has become a campsite that can be reached by hiking, cycling, or horseback riding via the **Central Trail** to Whitewater Lake. Park interpreters also lead horse-drawn wagons to the site.

GREY OWL HIKE
17 km/10.5 mi return;
a full day

One of the park's most popular day trails is the 17-km (10.5 mi) round-trip **Grey Owl Trail**. Its trailhead is off Hwy. 19, 7 km (4 mi) from Wasagaming. The trail takes hikers to the remote cabin of Grey Owl,

RIDING MOUNTAIN

RIDING MOUNTAIN NATIONAL PARK
(Parc national du Mont-Riding)

INFORMATION & ACTIVITIES

VISITOR CENTRE
Wasagaming, MB R0J 2H0. Phone (204) 848-7228. Visitor information and interpretive programs, theatre, Discovery Room, and Nature Shop. Purchase park passes and fishing licences here, as well as book backcountry camping permits.

SEASONS & ACCESSIBILITY
Open year-round. Wasagaming Campground closed in winter. Visitor centre closed mid-October to mid-May.

HEADQUARTERS
Wasagaming, MB R0J 2H0. Phone (204) 848-7275. www.parkscanada.gc.ca/riding.

FRIENDS OF RIDING MOUNTAIN
Columbine Ave. in Wasagaming. Box 226, Onanole, MB R0J 1N0. Phone (204) 848-4037. friends.rmnp@pc.gc.ca; www.friendsofridingmountain.ca.

ENTRANCE FEES
$8 per person, $20 per group per day. $40 per person, $100 per group per year.

PETS
Pets must be leashed; they should not be left unattended.

ACCESSIBLE SERVICES
Most facilities are wheelchair accessible, including the washrooms at the visitor centre, Park Theatre, Wasagaming Campground, and Beach Bath House. Accessible wharf and tennis courts.

THINGS TO DO
Hiking, cycling, horseback riding, horse-drawn wagon rides, and fishing. Boating, sailing, swimming, and scuba diving. Interpretive programs ($4 per person) and guided hikes. Visits to the Pinewood Museum. Also, golfing at the Clear Lake Golf Course, (204) 848-4653; and tennis at the Clear Lake Tennis Courts, (204) 848-2649.

In winter, cross-country skiing on the surface of Clear Lake and along the park boundary, snowshoeing, skating, and ice fishing.

SPECIAL ADVISORIES
• Boil water before drinking at outlying campgrounds and backcountry campsites.

who was supposedly a native naturalist, sported braids and buckskins, and became the park's first official naturalist in the company of his pet beavers, Jelly Roll and Rawhide.

Grey Owl fooled everybody with his aboriginal act. He was really an Englishman named Archibald Belaney, who'd come to eastern Canada and "gone native," then moved west and passionately embraced ecological preservation. He quickly became a Canadian legend, preaching preservation of nature and wilderness. Then the national parks system offered him the job of park naturalist at Riding Mountain National Park, which he took. He served as the park's naturalist for six months in 1931, living in a two-room (one for his beavers, one for him) cabin park employees built for him. He then moved on to Prince Albert National Park (see pp. 162–167) in the neighbouring province of Saskatchewan. By then, Jelly Roll and Rawhide were the parents of four kittens; Grey Owl also had rounded up a few other beavers and begun raising them, too. Today, gnaw marks from Jelly Roll and Rawhide are still visible in places on the interior logs of the cabin beside **Beaver Lodge Lake.** The cabin is now a designated federal heritage building.

Mountain bikers are allowed to use the Grey Owl Trail as well, though it's a bit rough in spots.

- Boat motors must be either 4-stroke or direct injected 2-stroke engines. Park staff may inspect for compliance throughout the summer. Call (204) 848-7275.
- Swimming areas unsupervised. Coat skin with mineral or cooking oil to avoid swimmer's itch, a parasite in most park waters.

OVERNIGHT BACKPACKING

Permit required for backcountry camping. Call (204) 848-7275.

CAMPGROUNDS

Wasagaming Campground, water, sewer and electricity $38; electricity and water $35; electricity only $32; unserviced with washroom (toilets and showers) $27. Reservations recommended (877-737-3783 or www.pccamping.ca). **Moon Lake, Lake Audy, Whirlpool,** and **Deep Lake** outlying campgrounds, $16. All campsites contain a fire box, picnic table, and access to washrooms or pit privies. For group camping, yurt, **Cairn's Cabin,** and backcountry camping, reservations can be made by calling (204) 848-7275.

HOTELS, MOTELS, & INNS
(unless otherwise noted, rates are for a 2-person double, high season, Canadian dollars)

Inside the park:
Wasagaming, MB R0J 2H0:
Cottages at Clear Lake 109 Ta-wa-pit Dr. (204) 848-8489. www.cottagesatclearlake.ca. 2-bedroom cabin $800 per week.
Idylwylde Cabins 136 Wasagaming Dr., Box 130. (204) 848-2383. www.idylwylde.ca. $95–$285.
McTavish's Wasagaming Lodge 128 Wasagaming Dr., Box 99. (888) 933-6233. www.mctavishmotel.com. $122–$126.

Outside the park:
Crooked Mountain Cabins Southeast of Riding Mountain National Park. (204) 636-7873. www.crookedmountaincabins.ca. minimum 2-night stay in spring and fall, weekly rentals only in July and August ($910/week).
Elkhorn Resort & Conference Centre/Solstice Spa Box 40, Onanole, MB R0J 1N0. (204) 848-2808. www.elkhornresort.mb.ca. $120–$215.
Riding Mountain Guest Ranch Box 11, Lake Audy, MB R0J 0Z0. (204) 848-2265. www.ridingmountain.ca. $840 per person for 4-day package; $1,680 per person for 7-day package.

RIDING MOUNTAIN

EXCURSION

RIDING MOUNTAIN PARK EAST GATE REGISTRATION COMPLEX NATIONAL HISTORIC SITE
WASAGAMING, MB

Built in 1933 and 1934 as part of the Canadian federal government's Depression Relief Program, the park's East Gate Registration Complex National Historic Site is the only original national park gate still standing. Built from local logs and a prime example of 1930s rustic design style, the gate, its registration building, and two staff cabins make for a truly traditional picture-postcard photograph.

Kayaking on Waskesiu River

▶ PRINCE ALBERT

SASKATCHEWAN
ESTABLISHED 1927
3,875 sq km/957,500 acres

Typical of its era, Prince Albert National Park was created to serve as a recreational playground—its stewardship value would only be recognized much later. The park spans a slender transition zone between the northern boreal forest and the southern aspen parkland. Its rolling hills of spruce, pine, aspen, and birch shelter pockets of fescue and sedge meadows. Year by year, forestry concerns and encroaching civilization have threatened this ecosystem elsewhere, making Prince Albert today a precious preserve.

Prince Albert is also notable for the bison herd that roams along its southwestern border, the only free-range herd of wild plains bison in Canada that still occupies its ancestral territory. The herd is descended from a handful of animals once fenced along the south boundary of the park. It now boasts more than 200 head. Numbering many millions before near extirpation at the hands of European settlers, Canada's largest land mammal—a bull can weigh nearly a tonne—is still very much a threatened species. The animals do sometimes stray off parklands, much to the consternation of some neighbouring landowners.

When Prince Albert National Park was established, its land was occupied by the Cree, who had settled in the area in the mid-19th century; most of them were then obliged to move east to Montreal Lake. Soon afterward, the park became home to the renowned conservationist writer Grey Owl. Though he purported to be a member of the First Nations, he was in fact an Englishman named Archibald Belaney. The revelation of his true identity after his death was an international scandal. Nonetheless, Grey Owl's conservationist message—"Remember, you belong to Nature, not it to you"—has stood the test of time. His cabin on Ajawaan Lake is one of the country's best known hiking destinations.

How to Get There

Most visitors arrive by automobile via provincial Hwy. 2 and Hwy. 264, the quickest route to the Main Gate and the village of Waskesiu. Hwy. 263, a winding and scenic pavement that passes through the South Gate, is an alternate route. For access to the largely undeveloped West Side, visitors can use Hwy. 55. Saskatoon has the closest international airport and passenger rail service. The provincial bus line, STC, serves Waskesiu with daily departures from Saskatoon and Prince Albert. Service runs from early May to early September.

When to Go

The park is at its best between Victoria Day and Labour Day. The extra-long days around the end of June are especially glorious. The aspen and tamarack reach their height of tangerine colour around mid- to late September, when you will have the park mostly to yourself. However, many businesses will be closed, so call ahead. Freeze-up and winter arrives quickly and there is usually enough snow for skiing from early December through late March. Recreational options are most limited in April, when the lake ice is unsafe and the roads and trails are muddy.

How to Visit

Set inside the park, the resort town of **Waskesiu** (Cree for "red deer") offers accommodations, restaurants, shops, and services; hotel accommodations are available year-round. Typical visitors make the town their base for car-supported day trips on the **East Side** of the park, especially along Hwy. 263. Excellent sandy swimming beaches are found on **Waskesiu, Namekus,** and **Sandy Lakes.** There is an extensive trail network for day-use and backcountry hiking, cycling, and skiing on groomed trails. Backcountry paddling routes are limited, but there are many good day-trip options.

Visitors primarily interested in the park's **plains bison herd,** or in horseback- and wagon-riding trips into the park, should consider staying at one of the guest ranches operating on the park's **West Side;** park staff can make suggestions about accommodations and outfitters. In all cases, overnight backcountry stays require a permit from the Park Headquarters in Waskesiu.

EAST SIDE: KINGSMERE LAKE ROAD & GREY OWL'S CABIN
a full day

Kingsmere Lake Road heads north from the townsite of Waskesiu, following the shore of Waskesiu Lake, until it dead-ends at the Kingsmere Lake trailhead. Along

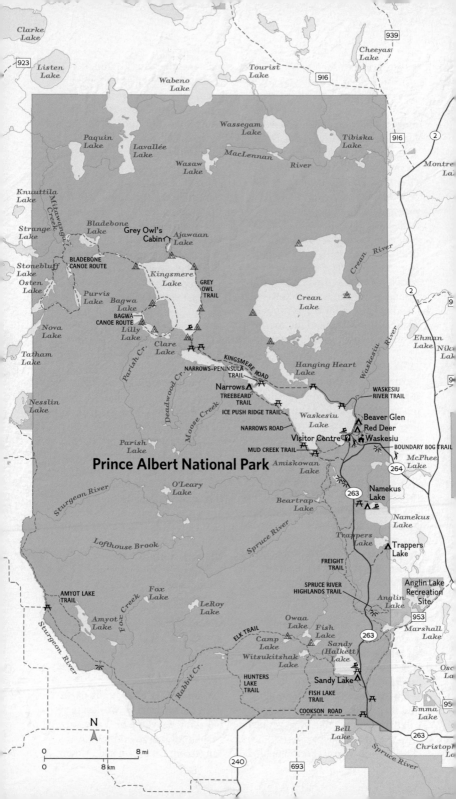

the way are many day-trip possibilities and backcountry entry points. Observant visitors might spot deer, wolves, black bears, grouse, elk, and bald eagles if they drive slowly and pay attention. A wheelchair accessible trail is located at the **Waskesiu River crossing.**

The **Waskesiu Lake Marina** has powerboats, canoes, and kayaks for rent. The big lake can be treacherous for any craft. Paddling close to shore is safer and more interesting. There are more rentals a little farther west along the Kingsmere Road at **Hanging Heart Lake.**

Hanging Heart Lake gets its name from a grim tale about Dene warriors who left the hearts of some vanquished Cree foes hanging in trees as a warning for others to stay outside their territory. This narrower, more protected waterway is inviting to paddle. Deer and bears often appear on its grassy foreshores. Get an early start, and you can paddle 8 km (5 mi) to glimpse **Crean Lake** before turning back. Or better yet, set up camp at one of the backcountry sites on the big lake. Pontoon boat trips with an interpreter are available along the route, too.

Farther west, the lovely **Narrows Peninsula Trail** gives views of Waskesiu Lake. The first **Narrows** was the location of a Cree village that was displaced when the park was created. The inhabitants moved east to Montreal Lake.

Kingsmere Road terminates at the **Kingsmere River,** where two trails lead north. One trail, a half-hour stroll following the winding ribbon of water, brings you to the south shore of **Kingsmere Lake.** In good weather, this beach is a lovely spot to picnic and swim; the lake has a sandy lake bottom that remains shallow a long way out.

Hawthorn tree berries (*Crataegus* sp.)

The second trail follows the eastern shore of Kingsmere Lake to **Grey Owl's cabin** on **Ajawaan Lake,** 20 km (12.5 mi) north. The Grey Owl hike has become a kind of pilgrimage. It started in the summer of 1936 when several hundred people made the journey to meet the famous author and his enigmatic Mohawk bride, who were famous across the British Empire. To this day the pilgrims keep coming, from all over the world. Grey Owl's personal life was sordid and unhappy at times, but his conservationist message was worthwhile. There is no better way to understand the beauty he wrote about than to hike to the cabin where he worked.

WEST SIDE: BISON HERD
a full day from Waskesiu

In contrast to the paved road and cottage-country developments on the park's East Side, Prince Albert's West Side retains a wild, frontier feel. Yet this hitherto virtually unvisited region is the focus of increasing attention—mostly because of

Canoeing on Bear Trap Lake

the plains bison herd that inhabits the **Sturgeon River Valley.** The burly animals can often be seen grazing in the sedge meadows in the area around **Amyot Lake.**

A double-track dirt road leaving from the parking area near the West Gate provides access to the Amyot Lake area; it is easy to walk or cycle,

The park becomes a snowy wonderland in winter.

though cycling will let you cover more ground and increase your chances of a sighting. Horseback riding or wagon trips are offered by outfitters along the West Side, who have the advantage of local knowledge in finding bison. The not-for-profit Sturgeon River Plains Bison Stewards *(www .bisonstewards.ca)* often has the most current information about the herd.

Always be cautious around bison. Despite their size and power, they are skittish grazing animals. Shy of people, they will generally move away if approached within, say, 100 m (330 ft). Keep your distance and the animals will stay put; push too close and you may find yourself in danger. Bulls in summer mating season can be aggressive, as can mothers protecting young. Bison are formidable when riled. Rely on a pair of binoculars for dramatic close-ups.

No road crosses the park, so getting to the West Side from Waskesiu means a long drive around the park's perimeter, mostly on gravel roads. Consider a West Side guest ranch stay to maximize your bison "hunting" time.

PRINCE ALBERT NATIONAL PARK
(Parc national de Prince Albert)

INFORMATION & ACTIVITIES

VISITOR CENTRE
969 Lakeview Dr., Waskesiu Lake, SK S0J 2Y0. Phone (306) 663-4522. panp.info@pc.gc.ca.

SEASONS & ACCESSIBILITY
Park open year-round. Main campgrounds operate mid-May through September; camping in Waskesiu and backcountry available year-round.

HEADQUARTERS
Box 100, Waskesiu Lake, SK S0J 2Y0. Phone (306) 663-4522. www.parks canada.gc.ca/princealbert.

FRIENDS OF PRINCE ALBERT
Waskesiu Heritage Museum, Box 11, Waskesiu Lake, SK S0J 2Y0. Phone (306) 663-5213. friends.panp@pc.gc.ca; www .waskesiu.org. Open June through September.

ENTRANCE FEES
$8 per person per day; $30 to $40 per person per year.

PETS
Pets must be leashed at all times. Ask staff about dog-friendly beaches. Boarding fees for cats, dogs, and horses $34 plus additional charge per day.

ACCESSIBLE SERVICES
The visitor centre, Beaver Glen and Red Deer Campgrounds, and some paths in Waskesiu are wheelchair accessible.

THINGS TO DO
Hiking trails of various lengths. Eight beaches on **Waskesiu, Namekus, Sandy** (Halkett), and **Kingsmere Lakes.**

Canoeing in **Spruce** and Waskesiu Rivers and **Amiskowan,** Shady, **Heart,** Kingsmere, or Waskesiu Lakes and the **Bagwa Canoe Route.** Rentals available at Waskesiu Lake Marina (306-663-1999). Powerboating on Waskesiu, **Crean,** Kingsmere, Sandy, and Heart Lakes. Fishing permitted with licence (obtain at visitor centre or marina facilities; check with park on limits).

Exhibits and videos at the nature centre in Waskesiu. Cycling on designated backcountry trails. Golf at the Waskesiu Golf Course (18 holes; 306-663-5300). In winter, cross-country skiing and snowshoeing.

SPECIAL ADVISORIES
• No open fires allowed on campgrounds.
• No boats or canoes allowed in buoyed beach areas. Beaches are unsupervised.
• Conditions highly variable on park lakes. Canoeists and kayakers advised to follow the eastern shore of Kingsmere Lake.
• Use bear caches for food, garbage, and toiletries.
• Boil lake water before drinking.

OVERNIGHT BACKPACKING
Overnight backcountry visitors must register at the visitor centre prior to the trip. Backcountry fees apply in some locations.

CAMPGROUNDS
In Waskesiu: **Red Deer Campground,** $30–$35 per night for campsites with water, sewer, and electricity; max. 1 RV and 1 tent (reservations: 877-737-3783, www.pccamping.ca). **Beaver Glen Campground,** $24–$30 per night with electricity; $20–$25 unserviced campsite with toilets and showers; max. 2 tents or 1 RV and 1 tent. Maximum stay 21 nights; maximum capacity 6 people per site.

In outlying areas: **Sandy Lake, Namekus Lake, Trappers Lake,** and overflow primitive campsites, $15 per night. **Narrows Campground,** unserviced campsite with toilets only; $22 per night, $127 per week, or $475 per month.

HOTELS, MOTELS, & INNS
(unless otherwise noted, rates are for a 2-person double, high season, Canadian dollars)

Waskesiu, SK S0J 2Y0
Elk Ridge Resort (800) 510-1824. www.elkridgeresort.com. $269–$389.
Hawood Inn (306) 663-5911. www.hawood.com. $129–$209.
Lakeview Suites (306) 663-5311. www.lakeviewhotel.com. $99–$279.

Additional visitor information:
Waskesiu Community Council
www.waskesiu.org

Blackfoot Worldview & Land

All societies, in one way or another, lay claim to a territory. Within the territory, a culture arises from a mutual relationship with the land. A culture consists of theoretical concepts, customs, and values. The theoretical concepts we can call paradigms. Paradigms are the tacit infrastructures members of a society utilize for their beliefs, behaviour, and relationships. To understand and appreciate a culture, one has to have a good understanding of that society's worldview.

Plains bison graze in Stoney Plain Meadow.

Thousands of generations of Blackfoot have dwelled in what is known as Blackfoot territory. Blackfoot territory roughly covers an area from the North Saskatchewan River to the Yellowstone River in Montana; from the Continental Divide of the Rocky Mountains to the confluence of the North and South Saskatchewan Rivers and the Cypress Hills in Saskatchewan. Within that territory the mutual relationship of humans, animals, plant life, the land, and the cosmos has resulted in a paradigm albeit not exclusive to Blackfoot.

The Blackfoot paradigm consists of constant flux, energy waves, everything being animate, interrelationships; reality requiring renewal, land, and language as a repository for Blackfoot knowledge. The notion of constant flux means for the Blackfoot that everything is in constant motion: Everything is undergoing a continuous process of change, transformation, deformation, reformation, and restoration. As Gary Witherspoon observes in *Language and Art in the Navajo Universe* (1977), the essence of life and being is movement. The constant flux consists of energy waves (physicists talk about the same thing but in terms of subatomic particles). For the Blackfoot, these energy waves can be referred to as the "spirit."

For the Blackfoot, everything is animate. All is animate because everything consists of energy waves. All existence has spirit including humans, plants, animals, the land, and the cosmos. The constant flux results in a complex relational network. Consequently, for the Blackfoot everything is interrelated. One will hear in many North American prayers the phrase, "all my relations." In other words, because all have "spirit," all are my relations including the land.

The Blackfoot paradigm incorporates the notion of renewal. There is a tacit belief that in the flux there is a combination of energy waves that makes up for the individual and collective existence of everything. In other words, when the particular combination of energy waves that constitutes a human, animal, rock, and so on dissolves or dissipates, death occurs. One can look at it as a disappearance into the flux. Or, one can look at it as being consumed by the flux. Recognizing that the energy wave combinations that make for our existence can dissipate, Blackfoot attempt to renew or sustain the existing reality through renewal ceremonies.

For the Blackfoot, land is very important. Blackfoot are so closely related to the land that they refer to it as "mother." Just as a mother is the source of human life, so is the land. The land is the source of life. Blackfoot are very respectful to "the mother," the land. In other words, the land is to be treated in the same manner that we treat our biological mothers. The land is important because it is where many observable manifestations of the flux occur. Manifestations such as cosmic events, patterns, cycles—and happenings such as migrations of animals, life cycles of plants, seasonal rounds—and so on are observable and occur on the land.

Language is important because it acts as a repository for the knowing in Blackfoot culture. Blackfoot language mirrors the constant flux because it is about motion, processes, and action, as opposed to English, which is noun oriented, and to a large extent, stagnant. Blackfoot language mirrors the flux because it allows for alliances and relationships between spirits, energies, and powers in ways very different from Indo-European languages such as English.

Short-eared owl (*Asio flammeus*)

When one comes to appreciate the paradigm of Blackfoot people and applies that paradigm to relationships with the land, one will find that sustainability, conservation, leaving the land as pristine as possible, leaving the land to bring about an ecological balance, and having humans fit themselves into that ecological balance are renewal goals of Blackfoot society. It seems that, in many ways, national parks have the same goals. One can say, if the Blackfoot paradigm were applied to all of our lands in Canada, all of Canada would become a "national park."

— LEROY LITTLE BEAR, *University of Lethbridge*

Enjoy the adventure of backcountry camping.

▶ GRASSLANDS

SASKATCHEWAN
ESTABLISHED 1981
565 sq km/139,600 acres

The prairie was once an ocean of grass where a million bison roamed and where summer wildfire was a rejuvenating force. Then settlement converted nearly the whole into the grid of agricultural townships that define the West today. Grasslands National Park, however, protects one of the largest remnants of pristine prairies along the U.S. border. Here, under the blue dome of prairie sky, great vistas run to the distant horizon—and small miracles are found underfoot.

One of Canada's newest parks, Grasslands is still growing as area ranchers reach retirement and sell their land holdings to the preserve. No land will be expropriated in creating the park which will eventually cover 900 sq km (347.5 sq mi) in two blocks. The West Block is dominated by the Frenchman River Valley; the East Block is known for the Rock Creek Badlands Wood Mountain Uplands. Both sections contain areas untouched by ice during the most recent glaciation, and fossils in the poorly consolidated bedrock of the hillsides record the last days of *Tyrannosaurus, Triceratops,* and other dinosaurs that roamed here.

In the valley bottoms you can walk through prairie dog towns that are as large as human towns, and perhaps spot rarities such as the black-footed ferret, an endangered species. Prickly pear cactus grows profusely on the sun-facing banks, mule deer and antelope browse in the cooler, lightly wooded hollows facing north. Short-horned lizards, western rattlesnakes, garters, racers, and bull snakes can all be found, too.

The ancient hills are graced by teepee rings, medicine wheels, and the stone tools of the First Nations people. Weathered, abandoned ranch houses tell of much more recent relationship with the land.

How to Get There

A vehicle is a practical necessity for trips into either block of Grasslands National Park. Regina and Saskatoon have the nearest international airports and other major transportation links.

Access to the West Block is via the village of Val Marie at Hwys. 4 and 18, where a stop at the visitor centre is recommended. The closest town to the East Block is Glentworth and Wood Mountain on Hwy. 18. In summer, staff at the Rodeo Ranch Museum in Wood Mountain Regional Park and the Rock Creek Campground can provide condition reports on the gravel roads leading into the park off Hwy. 18. From Wood Mountain, head south on Hwy. 18 for 22.4 km (14 mi), then turn west for 6.4 km (4 mi), then south for 6.4 km (4 mi), and then west for 2.4 km (1.5 mi) until you reach the park entrance.

When to Go

The park is open year-round. The heat of summer can be challenging. Afternoon thundershowers caused by daytime heating can be severe and can make roads impassable. Early morning and late evening, when temperatures have moderated, are good times to visit. Though the visitor centre is closed October to mid-May, the off-season has advantages. Winter temperatures can be very mild by prairie standards. Snowfall is generally quite low, so that hiking is a year-round possibility. The great vistas of Grasslands can be stunning in hoarfrost conditions. Warmer days arrive in early March, and flowers are abundant in May and June.

How to Visit

Grasslands is hypnotically beautiful, and accessible by car in dry weather. However, there are limited services, and roads become impassably muddy if it rains. The upland is wild and unmarked; it rewards hikers with transcendent natural beauty and the freedom to roam anywhere. But distances are deceiving and good navigation skills are required. Water is currently unavailable in the park, so you must bring your own— 2 l (0.5 gal) per person per day at a minimum. Summer conditions are hot and desertlike, and there is little natural shade. A one-day, self-guided Ecotour Road threads through the West Block, with interpretive signs at various stops.

To fully experience the subtle beauty of the park, get out on the trails. Day hiking into the hills using one of eight routes developed by Friends of Grasslands is perhaps the easiest and best way to experience the park. The volunteer group has produced a superb interpretive field guide, complete with maps and GPS waypoints, which can be bought at the park visitor centre or ordered online. Horseback riding is welcome; the park maintains a list of outfitters offering guided rides. Off-road cycling is not recommended due to cactus spines; however, the park is building its first sustainable trails and features multiuse trails to accommodate mountain bikes.

GRASSLANDS

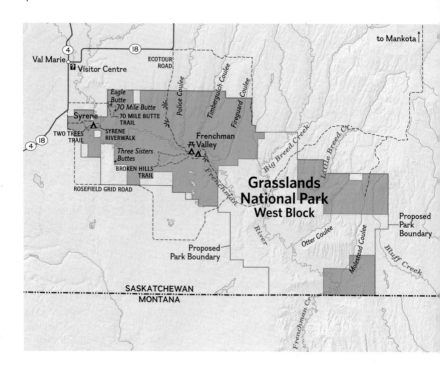

WEST BLOCK: 70 MILE BUTTE HIKE

a half day

A lovely introduction to the Frenchman River Valley, the 70 Mile Butte hike rewards visitors with stunning views from one of the highest points in the West Block. From the visitor centre in Val Marie, travel south on Hwy. 4, then turn east on the 70 Mile Butte Access Road that leads to the trailhead kiosk.

The trail climbs into one of the great landmark uplands of the Frenchman Valley and provides awe-inspiring views from atop the **70 Mile Butte**, rising 932 m (3,058 ft) above sea level. The 5-km (3 mi) loop route is moderately difficult and will take a leisurely morning to complete. Start at dawn to avoid the heat of the day and to see an array of wildlife at their most active.

The butte was a guiding landmark for the First Nations peoples for thousands of years; however, its name comes from the time when the Northwest Mounted Police patrolled the region via horseback. The butte was midpoint of the patrol—112.7 km (70 mi)—between Wood Mountain Post and Eastend Post and provided a reliable landmark.

Constable John George Donkin recorded in his journal of 1886: "These expeditions are fully armed of course and remain out on the prairie for a week. A transport wagon is attached to each, carrying tent, bedding, rations of tea, biscuit, bacon and oats, a spade, camp-kettles and frying pan, and wood."

The whole perimeter of 70 Mile Butte and the adjacent plateaus has archaeological remnants of native encampments. Make a side trip if your energy and map skills allow, and leave what you find untouched.

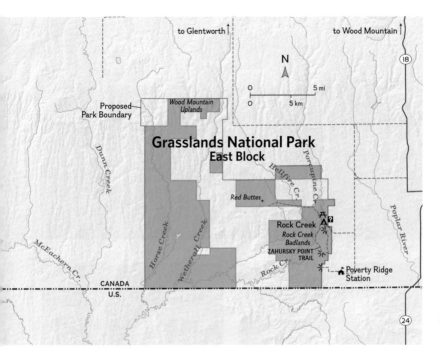

to Glentworth↑

to Wood Mountain↑

N

0   5 mi
0   5 km

Proposed Park Boundary

Wood Mountain Uplands

Grasslands National Park
East Block

Dunn Creek

Porcupine Cr.

Hellfire Cr.

Red Buttes

Horse Creek

Wetheral Creek

McEachern Cr.

Rock Creek

Rock Creek Badlands

ZAHURSKY POINT TRAIL

Rock Cr.

Poverty Ridge Station

Poplar River

CANADA
U.S.

18

24

EAST BLOCK: RIM HIKE

a half to full day

The **Rim Hike** offers a wonderful overview of the beauty of the East Block. The loop trail can be hiked in an hour or two, or extended to fill a day if side trips are made. To reach its trailhead, follow the directions to access Grasslands from Wood Mountain and park at the Rock Creek Campground and Picnic Area.

In 1911, James McGowan began to homestead in this area. After three generations of ranching, the McGowan family sold their lands to the national park in the 1980s. It is a familiar pattern, for making a living in this area has been a struggle. From 1850 to 1880, bison met their fate, and without the buffalo, Plains Indians and Métis could no longer live off the land. In the following years, cattle replaced buffalo, creating a new economy on the prairies and bringing in huge ranching companies. However, harsh winters, a massive die-off of cattle due to disease, and the Homesteaders Act of 1908 pushed the ranchers out.

The government enticed settlers from Europe and eastern Canada to "tame the west" and "break the land." Homesteaders faced many

Crocus (*Anemone patens*)

A hike through Eagle Butte provides breathtaking views and incredible scenery.

Sharp-tailed grouse (*Tympanuchus phasianellus*)

Black-tailed prairie dog (*Cynomys ludovicianus*)

hardships, including drought, frost, insect infestations, and disease. They soon learned that the land was more suited for grazing. Many picked up and left after only a few years, but their signature remains.

The land's fundamental low productivity has, more than anything, kept the grasslands intact. The grasses and forbs that thrive here are specialists, and many of them are visible on the Rim Hike. Needle-and-thread or blue grama grass, lichens, and moss phlox are characteristic ground cover plants. Sage is a staple for both antelope and grouse. Crocuses, avens, pin cushion cactus, and pale blue harebell

bloom throughout the summer. And an array of wildlife may be spotted, among them mule deer, badgers, jackrabbits, and coyotes.

One of the joys of hiking in Grasslands is the freedom to choose your own route. Exercise your option to descend to **Rock Creek** via a coulee from the rim. Its modest flow supports leopard frogs, crayfish, and many other aquatic species in this rich environment.

The dramatic **Rock Creek Badlands** are visible to the southwest. Just beyond the farthest reach of the last glaciations, these bluffs yielded in 1874 the first recorded dinosaur remains found in western Canada.

GRASSLANDS NATIONAL PARK
(Parc national des Prairies)

INFORMATION & ACTIVITIES

VISITOR CENTRE
Junction of Hwy. 4 & Centre St., Val Marie, SK. Near the West Block of Grasslands National Park.

SEASONS & ACCESSIBILITY
Park open year-round. Visitor centre open daily mid-May to early September; open Monday through Friday early April to mid-May and early September to late October. Limited hours rest of year; call in advance to ensure the office is staffed.

HEADQUARTERS
P.O. Box 150, Val Marie, SK S0N 2T0. Phone (306) 298-2257 or (877) 345-2257. www.parkscanada.gc.ca/grasslands.

FRIENDS OF GRASSLANDS
Prairie Wind and Silver Sage, P.O. Box 83, Val Marie, SK S0N 2T0. Phone (306) 298-4910. info@pwss.ca; www.pwss.ca.

ENTRANCE FEES
No entry fee.

PETS
Pets must be kept on a leash and at a safe distance from wildlife.

THINGS TO DO
Hiking: Two-day trips from **Ecotour Road** to **Broken Hills** in West Block; from **Rock Creek Campground** to **Zahursky's Point** in the East Block. Three-day trips from Ecotour Road to **Timbergulch Coulee** in the West Block or from Rock Creek to the **Red Buttes** in the East Block.

Weekly stargazing and astronomy programs from May to late September.

Guided hikes ($5 per person) and interpretive programs ($4 per person; $3 per person for school groups): "Cowboy Coffee" wagon ride interpretive program on ranching history; dinosaur safari program and fossil festival on paleontological resources of the park; interpretive programs on archaeological sites and their artifacts; guided tours with the park's bird, snake, and bison specialists.

SPECIAL ADVISORIES
• Portable stoves and campfires banned in the dry seasons. Be prepared to camp without a fire in designated areas when fire ban in effect in the East and West Blocks.
• Vehicles must remain on roads.

OVERNIGHT BACKPACKING
No designated backcountry campsites; backpackers must camp at least 1.6 km (1 mi) away from the road. Payment and registration at the visitor centre; self-registration available in the East Block. Backcountry camping $10 per night, $69 per year.

CAMPGROUNDS
Frenchman Valley Campground in the West Block has picnic tables, an outhouse, and road access. **Rock Creek Campground** in the East Block has picnic tables, an outhouse, camp shelters, and road access. Primitive camping with pit privies $16 per night. Group camping per night, per person (no showers) $5. Register at the visitor centre in Val Marie or the Rodeo and Ranch Museum in Wood Mountain. Full service campgrounds available in **Val Marie** and **Wood Mountain Regional Park.**

HOTELS, MOTELS, & INNS
(unless otherwise noted, rates are for a 2-person double, high season, Canadian dollars)

Outside the park:
Val Marie, SK S0N 2T0:
The Convent Box 209. (306) 298-4515. conventinn@sasktel.com; http://convent1.sasktelwebsite.net. $75. Summer only.
The Crossing Resort Box 31. (306) 298-2295. the.crossing.ken@sasktel.net; www.crossingresort.com. $65–$80.
Rosefield Church Guesthouse Box 14. (306) 298-2030. info@rosefield.ca; www.rosefield.ca. $105.

Mankota, SK S0H 2W0:
The Grasslands Inn Railway Ave. (306) 478-2909. $72.

Some 10,000 wood bison roam freely across Wood Buffalo, which was established to protect the species' habitat.

▶ WOOD BUFFALO

ALBERTA & NORTHWEST TERRITORIES
ESTABLISHED 1922
44,807 sq km/11,070,000 acres

Wood Buffalo is Canada's largest national park: Covering more territory than Switzerland, it sprawls across northeastern Alberta and juts into the southern part of the Northwest Territories. Designated a UNESCO World Heritage site, it is home to one of the last remaining free-roaming wood bison herds in the world, the nesting habitat for endangered whooping cranes, and the world's largest beaver dam.

The park's varied landscape includes boreal forest, salt plains, and gypsum karst landforms. The southern portion of the park features the Peace-Athabasca Delta, one of the largest inland freshwater deltas in the world. All four North American flyways converge over the delta each spring and fall. The last remaining flock of migratory whooping cranes nest in a remote corner of the boreal forest every summer.

In 1982, the International Union for the Conservation of Nature recognized Wood Buffalo for protecting the Peace-Athabasca Delta and the whooping crane nesting area. The two areas were designated as Ramsar sites under the Ramsar Convention, which focuses on identifying and protecting critical habitat for migratory birds. The Slave, Peace, and Athabasca Rivers flow through the park. Opportunities for backcountry hiking and camping include a trip down the Peace River followed by a 12-km (7.5 mi) hike into Sweetgrass Station, which features a restored warehouse and former bison corrals.

The boreal plains near the Northwest Territories town of Fort Smith are the most accessible and popular area of the park. Day hikes take visitors through boreal forests of spruce, jackpine, aspen, and poplar to see salt flats, underground streams, sinkholes, and saline streams. Wood Buffalo is home to such elusive species as black bear, wolf, moose, fox, beaver, and sandhill crane. But seeing these shy creatures is completely left to chance.

How to Get There

The park has two main gateway communities: Fort Smith and Fort Chipewyan. To reach Fort Smith, home to the park's headquarters, take the Mackenzie Hwy. from northern Alberta. Connect to Hwy. 5, an all-weather road of partly hard-packed gravel that starts near Hay River, Northwest Territories. Watch for black bears and bison that sometimes lumber across the highway.

The park office in Fort Chipewyan is only accessible by air or water, except for a few months every winter when an ice road links it to Fort Smith and Fort McMurray. Northwestern Air Lease offers commercial flights from Edmonton, Alberta. Flight-seeing tours into the park can also be arranged.

When to Go

The best time to visit the park is between the Victoria Day weekend and Labour Day, when the Pine Lake Campground is open. Summer temperatures range from 20°C to 30°C (68°F–86°F). Community events include the Pine Lake Picnic in mid-July and the Paddlefest Flotilla in early August. Contact the visitor centre for regularly scheduled programs and activities.

The park is open in winter. January and February are the best months for viewing the aurora borealis, due to the long nights. Temperatures hover between minus 25°C and minus 30°C (minus 13°F–minus 22°F). The winter road from Fort McMurray, up to Fort Chipewyan and through the park to Fort Smith, is an experience in itself. Driving the winter road requires proper preparation. Contact the park for road conditions and details.

How to Visit

A car provides the best means to see the park. A few pull-offs just past Hay River as well as the **Salt Plains Lookout** give visitors a chance to start experiencing the park before reaching the visitor centre in Fort Smith. Be sure to spend some time exploring **Fort Smith.** It was on the fur-trade route during the 18th and 19th centuries, and the administrative centre of the Northwest Territories until 1967. The town is a mix of mostly Chipewyan, Métis, and nonaboriginal people. Spend another day in the **Salt River Day Use Area** hiking, then head to **Pine Lake** to camp.

HAY RIVER TO FORT SMITH

270 km/168 mi; about 4 hours

Myriad sights lie along Hwy. 5 between Hay River and the northern boundary of Wood Buffalo National Park. Visitors should first stop to see the **Angus Sinkhole and Fire Tower.** Walk around the park's largest sinkhole, 100 m (330 ft) wide and 60 m (197 ft) deep. It formed when the top

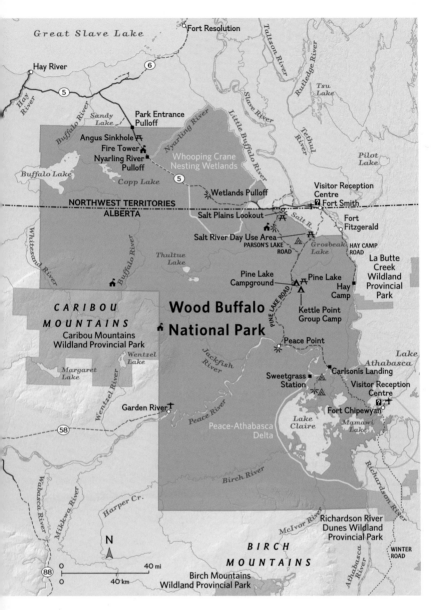

of an underground cave collapsed. Facilities here include interpretive panels, picnic tables, and washrooms. Continue along Hwy. 5 to the **Nyarling River Pull-Off.** The river flows for 26 km (16 mi), but you'd never know: Most of it flows underground. Interpretive panels explain why.

Closer to Fort Smith, the **Wetlands Pull-Off and Interpretive Trail** leads to a spot overlooking the boreal landscape, where endangered whooping cranes rear their young. Interpretive signs provide information on the Peace-Athabasca Delta and the whooping crane nesting area.

Back in the car, keep an eye out for a sign marking the side road to the **Salt Plains Lookout and Day Use Area.** This viewpoint offers a sweeping perspective of the 370 sq km (143 sq mi) salt plains. The lookout's high-powered telescopes can help visitors spot wildlife down below. Take the 500-m (0.25 mi) trail down the steep escarpment to the salt plains. There are no marked trails on this fragile, salt-encrusted landscape. Keen-eyed visitors might find delicate salt mounds and animal tracks indicating the passing of bears and bison.

Another lookout, the **Parson's Fire Tower,** lies a few kilometres down the 57-km-long (35.5 mi) dirt **Parson's Lake Road,** which leads from the day-use area deep into the boreal forest and connects with Pine Lake Road. This one-lane trail is not recommended for RVs and is impassable when wet. Keep an eye out for bison; you're on their land. The fire tower offers a panoramic view of the surrounding landscape. On a clear day, the salt plains might be visible in the distance. Return to Hwy. 5 and continue to Fort Smith.

Upon arriving in town, head to the park's visitor centre, which has an exhibit and a 20-minute DVD presentation about the park and its history. Parks staff can answer questions, provide maps, notify you of any bear sightings or fire bans in effect, and advise on backcountry trips and camping. They also offer regularly scheduled guided hikes and activities.

The centre also provides information about the various attractions in town, such as the **Northern Life Museum and Cultural Centre, Slave River rapids, Thebacha Trail,** and **Fort Smith Mission Historic Park.** You can stock up on snacks at Kaeser's or the Northern store for your second day in Wood Buffalo National Park.

PINE LAKE ROAD
120 km/74.5 mi; a full day

Just south of Fort Smith, the all-weather gravel Pine Lake Road runs southward from Hwy. 5 to the Peace River. Most people concentrate their visits to the Salt River and Pine Lake Day Use Areas.

The **Salt River Day Use Area** sits just inside the park's border. In early May this area is a mass of wriggling bodies: Hundreds of red-sided garter snakes emerge from their winter snooze underground to mate before slithering off to their summer feeding grounds. This is the species' most northerly hibernaculum. Parks interpreters are on hand to answer questions during this mating period. The snakes return each September to hibernate. The day-use area is also the starting point for several hikes.

The **Karstland Interpretive Trail** is an easy 750-m (0.5 mi) loop that wanders past active sinkholes and good examples of karst topography. Access the 7.5-km (4.5 mi) **North Loop Trail** from the day-use area or start at the trailhead 2.4 km (1.5 mi) beyond it, on the west side of Pine Lake Road. The hike offers a gentle climb to the top of an escarpment with a scenic view of **Salt Pan Lake.** There are also sinkholes, the Keg River geological formation, and outcrops.

The 9-km (5.5 mi) **South Loop Trail** starts at the Salt River on the east side of Pine Lake Road. The hike wanders over bridges and along a saline creek to the trail's highlight—the salt flats at **Grosbeak Lake.** This unique landscape features strangely shaped rocks and glacial erratics that have been formed by salt and frost. Look for animal tracks in the iron-rich mud, such as lumbering bear paws crossing the delicate prints of a sandhill crane. For a 20-minute

WOOD BUFFALO

A remote corner of Wood Buffalo serves as the nesting ground for the endangered whooping crane.

shortcut to Grosbeak Lake, start at the far end of the trail located 2.4 km (1.5 mi) past the Salt River Day Use Area on the east side of Pine Lake Road. Canoeing from bridge to bridge is also possible on the Salt River during spring runoff.

Continue along Pine Lake Road to the **Pine Lake Day Use Area,** accessed via Pine Lake Access Road. A sandy beach borders this startlingly aquamarine lake, which was created by the merging of several adjacent sinkholes, fed from underground springs. Blue-green algae at the bottom of the lake reflect back the sun's rays, giving the lake its brilliant colour. This is a good place to swim and picnic or paddle around in a canoe or kayak.

The easy 3-km (2 mi) **Lakeside Trail** connects the day-use area with the secluded Kettle Point Group Camp (a small campground on the eastern shore of the lake), which can also be accessed via the gravel Kettle Point Access Road off Pine Lake Road. About midpoint along the Lakeside Trail, the 6-km (3.5 mi)

Lane Lake Trail veers off and passes a chain of sinkhole lakes, ending at Lane Lake. The trail can also be picked up where it crosses Kettle Point Access Road.

Beyond Pine Lake, the road continues to the **Peace Point Reserve** on the Peace River.

The salt plains cover some 370 sq km (143 sq mi).

WOOD BUFFALO NATIONAL PARK
(Parc national Wood Buffalo)

INFORMATION & ACTIVITIES

VISITOR CENTRES
Fort Smith Visitor Reception Centre 149 McDougal Rd., Fort Smith, NT X0E 0P0. Phone (867) 872-7960.
Fort Chipewyan Visitor Reception Centre MacKenzie Ave., Fort Chipewyan, AB T0P 1B0. Phone (780) 697-3662.

SEASONS & ACCESSIBILITY
Park open year-round. Fort Smith Visitor Reception Centre open daily mid-May to Labour Day; weekdays rest of the year. Fort Chipewyan Visitor Reception Centre open weekdays year-round and most weekends in the summer.

HEADQUARTERS
Box 750, Fort Smith, NT X0E 0P0. Phone (867) 872-7960. www.parkscanada.gc.ca/woodbuffalo.

ENTRANCE FEES
No entry fee.

ACCESSIBLE SERVICES
Day-use area and two campsites wheelchair accessible at Pine Lake Campground. Kettle Point Group Camp is wheelchair accessible. Most interpretive exhibits are wheelchair accessible.

THINGS TO DO
Canoeing on **Pine Lake** for easy day paddling or on the **Peace, Athabasca,** and **Slave Rivers** for backcountry paddling. Paddling on the **Buffalo, Little Buffalo,** and **Salt Rivers** in spring. Canoe rentals available in Fort Smith. Fishing in some of the larger rivers (fishing permit $10 per day, $35 per year).

Hiking on seven frontcountry trails (easy–moderate) or two backcountry trails (moderate–challenging). Interpretive exhibits at **Angus Fire Tower** and Day Use Area, **Nyarling River** pull-off, **Wetlands** pull-off, **Salt Plains** Viewpoint and Day Use Area, **Salt River Day Use Area,** and the visitor centres. Taiga Tour Company is a licensed outfitter offering guided tours; call (867) 872-2060.

SPECIAL ADVISORIES
• Fish stocks are poor and difficult to reach, even in the larger rivers. Visitors should obey the daily catch-and-possession limit for grayling, whitefish, northern pike, goldeye, and walleye.
• Hikers should contact the Visitor Reception Centre at Fort Smith or Fort Chipewyan for trail updates and safety information on bear sightings or restrictions. Registration and check-out are mandatory for backcountry camping.
• Wear clothing layers that protect from bug bites. Mosquitoes are prevalent in June, July, and August.

OVERNIGHT BACKPACKING
Registration required for backcountry camping. Backcountry camping permitted off main trails. Backcountry camping at serviced sites including **Sweetgrass Station** and **Rainbow Lakes;** $10 per person per night, $69 per person per season. Paddle or hike to Sweetgrass Station starts at Peace Point; paddling downstream takes 10 to 12 hours.

CAMPGROUNDS
Pine Lake Campground and **Kettle Point Group Camp** open Victoria Day weekend to Labour Day. **Pine Lake** has fire pits, tent pads, picnic tables, water (boiling required), firewood, outhouses, and a playground; $16 per night. **Kettle Point** has a log shelter, tenting area, beach, fire circle and firewood, picnic tables, outhouses, and playground; $5 per person, $40 per group. Call (867) 872-7960.

HOTELS, MOTELS, & INNS
(unless otherwise noted, rates are for a 2-person double, high season, in Canadian dollars)

Outside the park:
Fort Smith, NT X0E 0P0:
Pelican Rapids Inn 152 McDougal Rd. (867) 872-2789. $140.
R House Bed and Breakfast 28 Cumming Ave., Box 395. (867) 872-5354. www.rhousefortsmith.com. $110–$120.

Additional visitor information:
Fort McMurray, Alberta
www.travelinalberta.com/FortMcMurray.cfm.

ROCKIES

Page 182: top, White-water rafting in Yoho National Park; middle, a mother grizzly bear and her two cubs, Banff National Park; bottom, Iceland poppies *(Papaver nudicaute)*, Banff. Page 183: Castle Mountain and boreal forest

ROCKIES

From Waterton in Alberta to Mount Revelstoke in British Columbia, these parks offer a photo-ready landscape of peaks, glaciers, rivers, lakes, and waterfalls. Waterton Lakes boasts scenic drives, horseback riding, boat cruises, and hiking through habitat for moose, elk, and deer. Banff is renowned for its waterfalls, historic hot springs, emerald green Lake Louise, and more than a thousand glaciers. In Jasper, visitors take the tramway to the top of Whistler's

reflected in lake, Banff. Above: The sun descends behind cedar trees and mountains near Athabasca Pass.

Mountain for a view of six mountain ranges, hikers follow trails grooved by wildlife and early First Nations peoples, and cavers explore a huge cave system. Hikers and skiers at Elk Island find plains and woodland bison, elk, and moose, or soak in the springs at Kootenay. Yoho attracts fossil hunters to the renowned Burgess Shale fossil beds, and hiking is popular at Glacier. The subalpine meadows of Mount Revelstoke brim with wildflowers.

Prince of Wales on the cliffs overlooking Waterton Lake

▶ WATERTON LAKES

ALBERTA
ESTABLISHED 1895
505 sq km/124,788 acres

The deepest lake in the Canadian Rockies (135.3 m/444 ft) and the first oil well in western Canada (1902) are both found in Waterton, a small park named in honour of English naturalist Charles Waterton. Set in a region renowned for its winds, Waterton has special significance as the Canadian portion of Waterton-Glacier International Peace Park.

Waterton sits in the extreme southwestern corner of Alberta, sharing boundaries with British Columbia and Montana in the United States. It's "where the mountains meet the prairies," as locals like to say. Indeed, lush native grassland rolls right up to the colourful peaks, which have been carved from sedimentary rock well over a billion years old.

With its outstanding scenery, sunny weather, easygoing wildlife,

and picturesque wind-raked trees, Waterton is a photographer's paradise. The park's isolation, far from any urban centre and off the beaten track, keeps the crowds small.

All three of the Waterton Lakes lie along the entry road. Other paved routes provide quick access to park highlights. One of the hiking trails is world famous, while mountain bikers will find several trails open to them, too.

How to Get There

The closest international airport is located at Calgary, 254 km (158 mi) away. From Calgary, take Hwy. 2 to Fort Macleod (164 km/102 mi), then turn west along Hwy. 3 for 97 km (60 mi) to Pincher Creek, where Hwy. 6 runs southward for 50 very scenic kilometres (31 mi) to the park gate. Hwy. 5 continues another 8.6 km (5.3 mi) to the "townsite" of Waterton Park, as Parks Canada describes the in-park community, summer population about 2,500. From east or west, take Hwy. 3 to Pincher Creek.

From the United States, you can enter the park directly. Take Mont. 17 north to the Chief Mountain border crossing and continue into Alberta on Hwy. 6. Be sure to inquire in advance of your visit for the Canadian post's hours of operation and seasonal closures.

When to Go

Waterton is open year-round, but windy weather discourages visitors in winter. Few services are available in the park between October and May, when some roads are subject to closure and the townsite population drops to less than 40.

Spring arrives in early May. The park is busiest in July and August, when daytime temperatures reach well into the 20s°C (over 70°F) and may hit the mid-30s°C (90s°F).

Low-elevation wildflowers are at their best in June, while the high country above tree line is most colourful in mid-July. Waterton's many aspen groves paint the valley floors and lower slopes brilliantly yellow in September.

How to Visit

You'll want a full day to tour the park's three byways, so get an early start.

Morning light on the mountain front is a spectacle best appreciated from the **Waterton Valley** viewpoint along the **Chief Mountain Highway** (Hwy. 6) in the eastern part of the park.

Return to the townsite for brunch and enjoy a breezy stroll along the shore of **Upper Waterton Lake.** The M.V. *International* and other passenger vessels cruise the lake. Since the waves may get bigger as the day goes by, morning is a good time to take the two-hour-plus cruise-boat ride down the lake and back.

Then head up scenic **Red Rock Parkway** to **Red Rock Canyon.** The canyon is aptly named, very photogenic, and great fun for the kids.

End your day by taking the **Akamina Parkway** to **Cameron Lake** to see stately peaks resplendent in the afternoon sun. The lake offers a smashing view to craggy peaks at the far end, just across the international boundary, plus rare botanical delights along the shoreline.

ENTERING THE PARK

60 km/37 mi; 1 hour

Travelling along Hwy. 6, Waterton comes into view at the **Pine Ridge Viewpoint,** 36 km (22 mi) south of Pincher Creek, well before you reach the park. Pull off and get out the camera, because this is one of the world's great vistas, 75 million years in the making.

Imagine the mountains creeping toward you at about 1 cm (0.4 in) per year, and gaining elevation as they go. Multiply by 40 million years, add 60 million years of landscape sculpture through erosion—the last three million years by glaciers—and this is what you get.

As you pass the park-boundary sign, watch for a turnoff on your

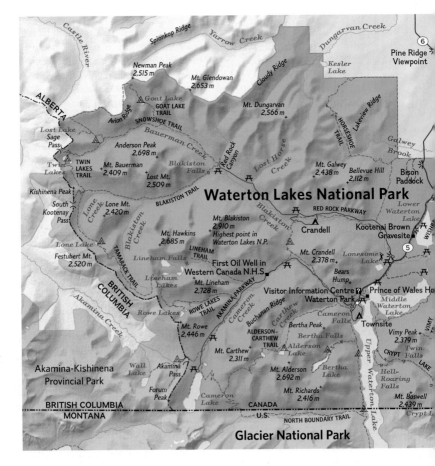

Castle River
Spionkop Ridge
Yarrow Creek
Dungarvan Creek
Pine Ridge Viewpoint
6
Newman Peak 2,515 m
Mt. Glendowan 2,653 m
Cloudy Ridge
Kesler Lake
ALBERTA
Goat Lake
GOAT LAKE TRAIL
Avion Ridge
SNOWSHOE TRAIL
Bauerman Creek
Mt. Dungarvan 2,566 m
HORSESHOE TRAIL
Lakeview Ridge
Galwey Brook
Lost Lake
Sage Pass
Anderson Peak 2,698 m
Red Rock Canyon
Lost Horse Creek
Bellevue Hill 2,112 m
Twin Lakes
TWIN LAKES TRAIL
Mt. Bauerman 2,409 m
Blakiston Falls
Mt. Galwey 2,438 m
Bison Paddock
Lost Mt. 2,509 m
Waterton Lakes National Park
Lower Waterton Lake
Kishinena Peak
South Kootenay Pass
Lone Mt. 2,420 m
BLAKISTON TRAIL
RED ROCK PARKWAY
Crandell
Kootenai Brown Gravesite
5
Lone Creek
Blakiston Creek
Mt. Blakiston 2,910 m Highest point in Waterton Lakes N.P.
Lone Lake
TAMARACK TRAIL
Mt. Hawkins 2,685 m
LINEHAM TRAIL
First Oil Well in Western Canada N.H.S.
Mt. Crandell 2,378 m
Lonesome Lake
Festubert Mt. 2,520 m
Lineham Falls
Lineham Lakes
Mt. Lineham 2,728 m
Bears Hump
BRITISH COLUMBIA
Rowe Lakes
ROWE LAKES TRAIL
AKAMINA PARKWAY
Cameron Creek
Buchanan Ridge
Carthew Creek
Visitor Information Centre
Waterton Park
Prince of Wales Hotel
Middle Waterton Lake
Akamina Creek
Mt. Rowe 2,446 m
ALDERSON–CARTHEW TRAIL
Alderson Lake
Bertha Peak
Bertha Falls
Cameron Falls
Townsite
Vimy Peak 2,379 m
Akamina-Kishinena Provincial Park
Wall Lake
Akamina Pass
Mt. Carthew 2,311 m
Mt. Alderson 2,692 m
Bertha Lake
Upper Waterton Lake
CRYPT LAKE
Twin Falls
Forum Peak
Cameron Lake
Mt. Richards 2,416 m
Hell-Roaring Falls
Mt. Boswell 2,439 m
BRITISH COLUMBIA
MONTANA
CANADA
U.S.
NORTH BOUNDARY TRAIL
Crypt L.
Glacier National Park

right. This narrow gravel track loops through the **Bison Paddock,** a grassy fenced-off area where bison graze. You can get photos of the animals in a natural setting, with lofty peaks in the background, but stay in your vehicle. Bison are dangerous.

The paddock is rolling kame-and-kettle topography, where part of the Waterton Valley's Ice Age glacier melted away under a cover of gravel some 15,000 to 20,000 years ago. The hills (kames) mark spots where the glacier was thin; the hollows (kettles, some with ponds in them) indicate thick spots. The low ridges are eskers, sinuous deposits of gravel left by streams flowing under the ice.

Farther on, **Lower Waterton Lake** occupies a depression in the landscape, an enormous kettle. You may see white pelicans on the water. They look much like their brown seashore relatives, but they scoop up fish from the surface rather than diving in after them from the air.

When you reach the townsite, stop at the park's **visitor information centre.** The **Peace Park Native Plant Garden** here reflects the region's exceptional botanical diversity. Also, it's only a short distance (0.4 km/ 0.25 mi) across the highway and up the access road to the charming **Prince of Wales Hotel,** a national historic site. Go around to the

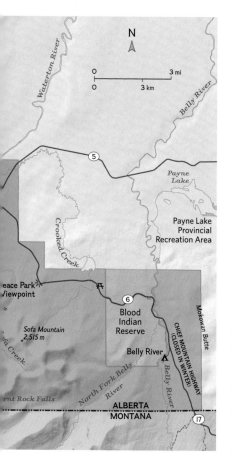

They make great photo subjects, but keep in mind that they are still wild animals. Don't feed or touch them. The deer are known to attack people, especially when the females have young, so give them plenty of room.

RED ROCK PARKWAY TO RED ROCK CANYON

14 km/8.7 mi; 1 to 3 hours

From the townsite, travel north on Hwy. 5 for 2.9 km (1.8 mi) to the turnoff. The road follows the valley of **Blakiston Creek**, truly a place "where the mountains meet the prairies." The grassy meadows and light tree cover beside the road, open from the first weekend in May to late October, allow open views of the mountains on either side. Much of the rock is ancient argillite, like shale but harder, in countless layers. Bears wander in the berry patches on the hillsides along the parkway.

The big, cliffy peak seen well up the valley is **Mount Blakiston**, 2,910 m (9,548 ft), the highest point in the park. A dark line low on the cliffs is the **Purcell Sill:** a zone of molten basalt that squeezed between the layers long before the Rockies began to rise.

WATERTON LAKES

south side of the building, where the view of **Upper Waterton Lake** is most impressive. So is the wind, which the seven-floor hotel has been battling ever since it opened in 1927. Though tied down with steel cables, the building still shudders in the gales.

Once in town, follow the signs to **Cameron Falls,** where Cameron Creek splashes over limestone of the Waterton formation. Dating to 1.5 billion years, this is the oldest sedimentary rock in Alberta.

You may see bighorn sheep right in the townsite. Mule deer, too. Habituated to humans, the sheep are very relaxed around people.

Cameron Falls runs red with argillite sediment.

The road ends at **Red Rock Canyon,** a shallow gorge stream-cut into red argillite and white sandstone of the distinctive Grinnell formation. The brick red colour in the rock is from hematite, which is oxidized (rusted) iron. This place is well suited to family recreation. A short, paved trail loops around the gorge, and interpretive signs add to the appeal. Another easy walk of 2 km (1.2 mi) from the parking lot takes you to the viewing platforms at **Blakiston Falls** and back.

AKAMINA PARKWAY TO CAMERON LAKE
16 km/9.6 mi; 1 to 2 hours return

Cameron Lake, elevation 1,660 m (5,440 ft), can be a chilly place in the morning. By afternoon the temperature is comfortable, while at lower elevations the day is becoming overly warm, so the lake makes a fine destination in hot weather.

The road starts where Hwy. 5 enters the townsite. From the initial switchbacks you get views of **Upper Waterton Lake.** Across the water lies **Mount Vimy** (2,379 m/7,950 ft), named during World War I for a battle won at great human cost to Canadian forces.

At 7.8 km (4.8 mi) you come to **First Oil Well in Western Canada National Historic Site** (see p. 192). Natural oil seeps here attracted drillers, who struck petroleum in 1902. The boom town of **Oil City** sprang up nearby, but it soon died when the flow tapered to practically nothing. Still, this was the first producing oil well in western Canada, and the hydrocarbons were found in extremely old rock, a rare situation.

At road's end, **Cameron Lake** stretches 2.5 km (1.6 mi) to the southwest, where the craggy visage of **Mount Custer** (2,708 m/8,883 ft) lies just across the international boundary in Montana.

The road opened in 1927, and much lakeside development followed. However, Parks Canada has removed it all, restoring the natural ambience. Commerce is limited to a canoe-rental concession. If you walk the shoreline trail in July or August, watch for showy red monkey-flowers and other species seldom seen north of Waterton. Botanical guidebooks and other useful publications are available at the Waterton Natural History Association shop in town.

HIKING & MOUNTAIN BIKING

If you're looking for a good workout, the hiking trail to the **Bear's Hump** climbs 240 m (790 ft) in only 1.2 km (0.8 mi). Despite its steepness, this is the most popular trail in the park. The view from the top stretches from the town, toy-like below, to the far end of **Upper Waterton Lake.** Start at the visitor information centre on the north edge of town. Allow one to two hours return, and bring water.

For adventurous hikers, Waterton Lakes National Park offers the world-renowned **Crypt Lake Trail.** Give yourself a full day, and bring pepper spray; the area is famous for grizzly sightings. Begin by taking the water shuttle across Upper Waterton Lake. From the dock to Crypt Lake you gain 675 m (2,215 ft) over 8.7 km (5.4 mi), including a cleverly engineered route through the cliffs below the lake. You'll climb an iron ladder, stoop through a short cave passage (enlarged for

Elk wander the plains of Waterton Lakes National Park.

easier negotiation), and run your hand along a fixed cable while crossing an exposed ledge. The lake sits in a glacial bowl at tree line—no glacier these days—and the south end is in the United States. Be sure you get back to the dock for pickup at the appointed time, or you'll be hiking an additional 14 km (9 mi) out to Hwy. 6 and then hitchhiking back to town.

The most popular trail to tree line and above is the well-graded path to **Carthew Summit,** elevation 2,311 m (7,582 ft). Be prepared for rough weather. Starting at Cameron Lake, the trail climbs steadily for 650 m (2,135 ft) in 8 km (5 mi) to the airy pass, with a view down the other side to the two sky-blue **Carthew Lakes,** each a classic glacial tarn sitting in a bedrock basin scooped out by the ice that once flowed down this valley. Return the way you came, or head down to the lakes and into the forest, passing by **Alderson Lake** to finish at **Cameron Falls** in the townsite, 12 km (7.5 mi) away, for a total hike of 18 km (11 mi). Since this is a one-way walk, it's handy to have two

cars. Alternatively, shuttle service to Cameron Lake is available. Inquire at Tamarack Outdoor Outfitters (214 Mountainview Rd., 403-859-2378, www .hikewaterton.com) in the townsite.

For a shorter hike with its own reward, do the first 4.2 km (2.6 mi) of the trail and stop at **Summit Lake,** surrounded by subalpine meadows full of showy white beargrass, the park's signature wildflower. The species blooms from early June to mid-July.

Of the park's several approved mountain-biking routes, perhaps the most pleasant is the **Snowshoe Trail** in the western part of the park. Start at the end of the **Red Rock Parkway.** A wide dirt track, closed to motor vehicles, continues up **Bauerman Creek** for 8.2 km (5 mi) at an easy to moderate grade. This is a fine ride for beginning trail cyclists, keeping in mind that it does entail some creek crossings. Another outing sure to become popular with cyclists is the new **Kootenai Brown Trail,** 6.5 km (4 mi) of paved pathway paralleling Hwy. 5 between the park gate and the townsite.

WATERTON LAKES NATIONAL PARK
(Parc national des Lacs-Waterton)

INFORMATION & ACTIVITIES

VISITOR CENTRE
Visitor Information Centre Phone (403) 859-5133. In the entrance parkway 6 km (4 mi) from the park entrance. Open mid-May to mid-October.

SEASONS & ACCESSIBILITY
The park is open year-round, but most park facilities are closed from late fall to early spring. Peak season is July and August; book accommodation well in advance. Reception services available year-round. No services on weekends from mid-October to mid-May.

HEADQUARTERS
Box 200, Waterton Park, AB T0K 2M0. Phone (403) 859-2224. www.parks canada.gc.ca/waterton.

FRIENDS OF WATERTON LAKES
Waterton Natural History Association Box 145, Waterton Park, AB T0K 2M0. Phone (403) 859-2624. wnha@tough country.net; www.wnha.ca. Heritage Centre, 117 Waterton Ave.

ENTRANCE FEES
$8 per person per day; $39 per person per year. $68 per person with Parks Canada Discovery Pass.

PETS
Pets must be kept on a leash at all times or in a kennel with a secure top.

ACCESSIBLE SERVICES
There are wheelchair accessible sites (serviced and unserviced) and washrooms at Townsite Campground.

THINGS TO DO
Boating, canoeing, and kayaking. Canoes, rowboats, and paddle boats available for rent at **Cameron Lake.** Powerboating on **Upper** and **Middle Waterton Lakes** and waterskiing on Middle Waterton Lake; dry suits or full wet suits recommended due to lake temperatures.

Hiking trails: 12 short hikes (20 min.-2 hrs.), 10 half-day hikes, 8 full-day hikes, and 1 multiday trail.

Visit the **Heritage Centre,** 111 Waterton Avenue, operated by the Waterton Natural History Association. Heritage Interpretation Programs offered by Parks Canada.

Self-guided tours available at **First Oil Well** in Canada (see below) and **Prince of Wales Hotel** National Historic Sites inside the park. Educational program at **Bar U**

EXCURSIONS

FIRST OIL WELL IN WESTERN CANADA NATIONAL HISTORIC SITE
WATERTON LAKES NP, AB

A small iconic derrick shelters the head of the first producing oil well in western Canada. Petroleum was struck at 312 m (1,024 ft) in 1902. Initial production of 300 barrels per day soon dwindled to nearly nothing, however, and other wells fared little better. Instead, one of them went out of control and created the first oil spill in western Canada. From the townsite, head north. Turn onto the Akamina Parkway to Cameron Lake, and follow it for 7.8 km (4.8 mi). (403) 859-2224.

Ranch, two hours north of the park (late May–mid-Oct.).

SPECIAL ADVISORIES

- Mule deer are defensive, especially in spring when they have fawns. Dog owners should keep their pets away.
- Keep food or other cooking waste in your vehicle to avoid attracting wildlife.
- Weather is highly variable, and winds average 32 kph (20 mph).
- When boating on Waterton Lakes, watch out for floating logs. Wash boats, motors, trailers, and other equipment before bringing them to the park to avoid the transfer of invasive species to the park's aquatic systems.
- Hunting, snowmobiling, paragliding, parachuting, hang gliding, or use of personal watercraft are forbidden.

OVERNIGHT BACKPACKING

Nine backcountry campsites. Wilderness Use Permit required for backcountry camping. For reservations, call warden office, (403) 859-5140, from April to mid-May and visitor information centre for the remainder of the year.

CAMPGROUNDS

Townsite Campground, 238 campsites, appropriate for RVs. With hot showers, flush toilets, food storage, and kitchen shelters $38 per night; with electricity only $32 per night; unserviced with toilets and showers

$27. Crandell Mountain Campground, 129 unserviced sites with piped water, flush toilets, kitchen shelters, some fire rings and firewood, food storage, recycling bins, and a dump station $22. Includes a campsite with five teepees ($11 reservation fee; $55 per night per teepee). Belly River Campground, group camping by reservation for groups of minimum 25 people ($5 per person). Call (403) 859-2224. Primitive campground. Pass Creek Winter Campground, (403) 859-5133. Privately operated campgrounds at Waterton Springs, (403) 859-2247, and Crooked Creek, (403) 653-1100.

HOTELS, MOTELS, & INNS
(unless otherwise noted, rates are for a 2-person double, high season, in Canadian dollars)

Waterton, AB T0K 2M0:
Crandell Mountain Lodge Box 114, 102 Mountainview Rd. (403) 859-2288 or (866) 859-2288. reservations@crandell mountainlodge.com; www.crandell mountainlodge.com. $140–$220.
Prince of Wales Hotel P.O. Box 33, Park entrance road. (403) 236-3500 (in Canada) or (406) 892-2525 (in U.S.). www .princeofwaleswaterton.com. $234–$299.
Waterton Lakes Resort P.O. Box 4, 101 Clematis Ave. (403) 859-2150. reserva tions@watertonlakeslodge.com; www .watertonlakeslodge.com. $185–$245.

WATERTON LAKES

BAR U RANCH
NATIONAL HISTORIC SITE
LONGVIEW, AB

Bar U Ranch, one of the more successful ranches in Canadian history (1882–1950), brings the Old West to life through its historic buildings, informative exhibits, and reenactments of daily life. Visitors learn everything from driving horses to throwing a lasso. You can also savour cowboy coffee over a campfire while listening to stories, poetry, and music. (403) 395-2212. Located 200 km (125 mi) north of Waterton, Hwy. 22.

Moraine Lake in Banff National Park

▶ BANFF

ALBERTA
ESTABLISHED 1885
6,641 sq km/1,641,027 acres

Simplicity marks the origin of Banff—Canada's first national park. In 1883, on the slopes of the Canadian Rocky Mountains, three railway workers discovered a natural hot spring, and from there the park was born. Nowadays, Banff is one of the world's premiere destinations, spanning a region of unparalleled majestic mountain scenery. Every year, millions of visitors make the pilgrimage to Banff to take in its stunning views and arsenal of activities.

Banff—the birthplace of the world's first national park service—is part of UNESCO's Canadian Rocky Mountain World Heritage site. Located in the heart of the Canadian Rockies, the park boasts a cornucopia of postcard-perfect mountains. These ancient monoliths range from 45 to 120 million years old, with the highest in the park, Mount Forbes, coming in at 3,612 m (11,850 ft).

The park encompasses Banff, the highest town in Canada at an elevation of 1,384 m (4,540 ft); the hamlet of Lake Louise (1,540 m/5,052 ft), the highest permanent settlement in Canada; several national historic sites (see pp. 202–203); Castleguard Caves, the largest cave system in Canada; more than a thousand glaciers; glacier-fed lakes such as Lake Louise as well as Moraine, Bow, and

Peyto Lakes; hundreds of hotels, restaurants, and retail shops, plus a 27-hole championship golf course.

In 2010, the park marked its 125th anniversary, commemorating some of the finest unspoiled ecosystems in the world. An integral part of the celebrations was the creation of the **Banff Legacy Trail,** a nonmotorized, paved trail for the likes of walking, cycling, and in-line skating. The 26-km (16 mi) trail connects users from the nearby town of Canmore through the park. Incorporating scenic views, it runs primarily along Trans-Canada 1 and the wildlife fence from the park's East Gate to the Bow Valley Parkway.

How to Get There

Banff National Park is located 129 km (80 mi) west of Calgary. Calgary's international airport is serviced by major national and international carriers with multiple flights arriving daily. From the airport, rent a car and take Trans-Canada 1 west from Calgary straight into the park, through Banff and Lake Louise. A direct bus service from the airport or downtown Calgary is also available to Banff and Lake Louise, as are shuttle services through tour operators.

When to Go

Open year-round, Banff offers amazing wildlife viewing and sightseeing, plus plentiful shopping and dining options, any time of the year. Summer is popular for hiking, paddling, mountain biking and cycling, photography, and climbing. The best time for viewing seasonal colour is fall, when the larch trees—the only coniferous trees to lose their needles in winter—turn yellow.

In winter, the mountain landscape makes for incredible downhill and cross-country skiing. In fact, three major downhill ski resorts operate within the park. Lake Louise Ski Area, Sunshine Village, and Mount Norquay combine to offer a large skiable terrain, not to mention the backcountry trails available throughout the park. The ski season, which runs from November to May, is one of the longest in North America. Visitors can also enjoy wildlife tours, ice walks, snowshoeing, and dogsled and horse sleigh rides.

Weather in the Canadian Rockies can change quickly. A single day can have a mix of sunshine, snow, wind, and rain, so dress in layers. Summers are warm with low humidity. Temperatures average a high of 21°C (70°F) and daylight lasts until 11 p.m. Autumn brings cool nights and crisp air. Winters can be frigid. In January, the average daytime high is minus 7°C (19°F), but by April it is 9°C (49°F).

How to Visit

Visiting the park by car or tour bus is most common. In the town of Banff you can also catch the ROAM bus, a publicly accessible and environmentally friendly hybrid outfitted with wildlife information. Pick up a map or bus schedule at the Banff or Lake Louise visitor information centres. GPS guides are also available.

To get the most out of the park, plan to spend a day in the town of Banff and the rest of your vacation outdoors, immersing yourself in the mountains, especially if you're an experienced skier or hiker.

TOWN OF BANFF
a full day

Start with a stroll down **Banff Avenue,** the main road into town and home

BANFF

to a bevy of retail shops and restaurants. Let the divine fragrances of the homegrown Rocky Mountain Soap Company seduce you, and select an all-natural bath product to take home.

But don't just stick to the main drag. Venture off the beaten path to the **Whyte Museum** *(www.whyte.org)* on Bear Street (1 block west) to learn about the area's cultural history, or succumb to the delicious tastes of Rocky Mountain cuisine at the Bison Restaurant & Lounge. Dine at the full-service restaurant or grab a delectable sandwich to go. If you have time, enjoy a cultural performance at **The Banff Centre** *(www.banff centre.ca)* on Tunnel Mountain Drive (up the hill on Buffalo St.).

If you prefer to stay outdoors, try a horseback ride. Saddle up with Warner Guiding & Outfitting *(www .horseback.com)* on Banff Avenue for a Rockies trail ride. You can explore the backcountry trails to a beautiful alpine lake or take a more daring weeklong trip into the backcountry and camp along the way.

At the end of Banff Avenue, after crossing the bridge, follow Mountain Avenue to take a dip at the **Banff Upper Hot Springs.** Canada's First Nations were the first to enjoy these waters, believed to be a place to cure illness and maintain health. Open year-round, this historic bathhouse gives you the chance to literally soak up the alpine scenery while relaxing in the natural springs after a long day of riding, hiking, or skiing.

Farther up Mountain Avenue, enjoy the best views of the park on the **Sulphur Mountain Gondola,** located five minutes from the town. You can hike up, but most visitors prefer the short gondola ride to the top of the mountain (an elevation of 2,282 m/

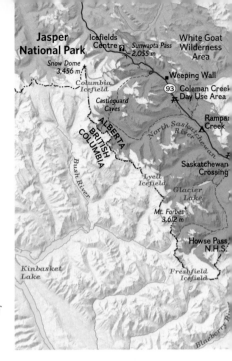

7,486 ft), where you'll come upon a panoramic view of six mountain ranges. Keep your eyes peeled for birds and wildlife such as the Rocky Mountain bighorn sheep. At the top, grab a bite at one of the restaurants. The two most popular trails here are the **Banff Skywalk Trail** (1 km/0.6 mi), a self-guided interpretive walkway to **Sanson Peak.**

BOW VALLEY PARKWAY TO LAKE LOUISE
56 km/35 mi; a half to full day

Head west from Banff on the **Bow Valley Parkway** (Hwy. 1A), the slower, more scenic alternative to Trans-Canada 1. From March to June, however, steer clear of this route between 6 p.m. and 9 a.m. to avoid disturbing the wildlife. Along the way, there are plenty of interpretive pull-outs, viewpoints, and picnic spots to choose from.

Drive about 18 km (11 mi) then detour at **Johnston Canyon,** where

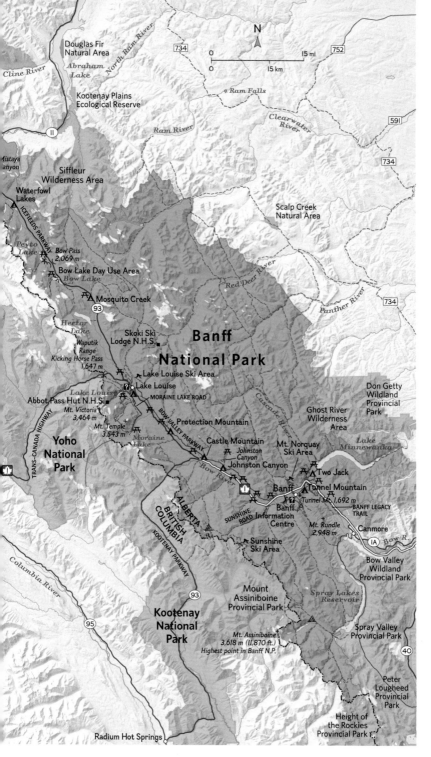

N

734   752

0   15 mi
0   15 km

Cline River

Douglas Fir
Natural Area

Abraham
Lake

North Ram River

Ram Falls

Clearwater River

591

Kootenay Plains
Ecological Reserve

Ram River

734

Mistaya
Canyon

Siffleur
Wilderness Area

Scalp Creek
Natural Area

Waterfowl
Lakes

ICEFIELDS PARKWAY

Peyto
Lake

Bow Pass
2,069 m

Bow Lake Day Use Area

Bow Lake

Red Deer River

Mosquito Creek

93

Hector
Lake

Waputik
Range

Kicking Horse Pass
1,647 m

Skoki Ski
Lodge N.H.S.

Banff
National Park

Panther River

734

Lake Louise Ski Area

Lake Louise

MORAINE LAKE ROAD

Don Getty
Wildland
Provincial
Park

Abbot Pass Hut N.H.S.

Mt. Victoria
3,464 m

Yoho
National
Park

TRANS-CANADA HIGHWAY

Mt. Temple
3,543 m

Moraine
Lake

BOW VALLEY PARKWAY

Protection Mountain

Castle Mountain

Johnston
Canyon

Johnston Canyon

Bow River

Cascade River

Mt. Norquay
Ski Area

Ghost River
Wilderness
Area

Lake
Minnewanka

Two Jack

Tunnel Mountain

Banff

Banff
Information
Centre

Tunnel Mt. 1,692 m

BANFF LEGACY
TRAIL

ALBERTA
BRITISH
COLUMBIA

Sunshine
Road

Mt. Rundle
2,948 m

Canmore

1A   Bow R.

KOOTENAY PARKWAY

Sunshine
Ski Area

Bow Valley
Wildland
Provincial
Park

Columbia River

95

93

Kootenay
National
Park

Mount
Assiniboine
Provincial Park

Spray Lakes
Reservoir

Mt. Assiniboine
3,618 m (11,870 ft.)
Highest point in Banff N.P.

Spray Valley
Provincial Park

40

Peter
Lougheed
Provincial
Park

Radium Hot Springs

Height of
the Rockies
Provincial Park

Fairmont Chateau Lake Louise

you can see the steep cliffs carved by rushing white water. From one of the viewpoints, you can actually feel the spray from the waterfalls. It's a 20-minute hike to the **Lower Falls** and 40 minutes to the **Upper Falls Trail.**

LAKE LOUISE & MORAINE LAKE

Approximately 5 km (3 mi) past the hamlet of **Lake Louise,** you'll find the glacial lake itself. Walk or ride a horse along the lake, marvelling at its emerald colours, or try one of the many hiking trails such as the classic Plain of Six Glaciers (4–5 hrs. round-trip). The popular **Lake Agnes Trail** (2.5–3 hrs. return) takes you past **Mirror Lake** to a backcountry teahouse at the top. Continue beyond (1.6 km/1 mi) to **Little Beehive** for a stunning view of the lake from above. For the more seriously adventurous, scramble up **Fairview Mountain** from **Saddleback Pass.** You can also rent a canoe and paddle your way across the lake, or hike the lovely trails surrounding the lake.

The **Fairmont Chateau Lake Louise,** a historic luxury resort hotel built in the early 20th century by the Canadian Pacific Railway, stands steps from the lake and is worth exploring. You may wish to stop in for its charming high tea service or for a high-end spa treatment.

Another place worth a visit is **Moraine Lake,** a beautiful glacially

fed lake situated in the Valley of Ten Peaks, which is part of the Continental Divide, the geographic point where waters flow either west to the Pacific Ocean or east to the Atlantic Ocean. The 13-km (8 mi) road from Lake Louise ends with a breathtaking view of Moraine Lake.

There are a few trails to explore around Moraine Lake. The easiest is the short **Rockpile Trail.** The view of the lake from the top of the rock pile is one of the most familiar sights in Canada; you may recognize the scene from older Canadian $20 bills. The 3.2-km (2 mi) **Consolation Lakes Trail,** with an elevation change of 90 m (295 ft), starts along the same trailhead.

The landscape between Lake Louise and Moraine Lake is not only highly attractive, it is also excellent grizzly bear habitat. To protect bears and people, visitors must hike in tight groups of four or more on some trails at some times of the year. Find more information at trailhead information kiosks or at the information centres.

ICEFIELDS PARKWAY
230 km/142 mi; a full day

From Lake Louise, proceed west along Trans-Canada 1. After 2 km (1.5 mi), exit and follow the signs for Hwy. 93 N, the **Icefields Parkway**—one of the world's most spectacular drives. Stretching between Banff and Jasper, this stunning stretch of road winds through mountain passes, around glassy turquoise lakes, centuries-old ice fields, hanging glaciers, waterfalls, and alpine meadows.

The parkway is open year-round, but in winter especially, check ahead for road conditions in case heavy snowfalls have caused closures. You

Top: Rocky Mountain bighorn sheep. Bottom left: Canoes resting on the dock at Moraine Lake. Bottom right: Skiing the Rocky Mountains.

also need to have snow tires and gas up beforehand as there are no services along the parkway from November to March. The summer months are a peak time for road cyclists. As a motorist, keep an eye out for them, or grab a bike and join them on the scenic ride.

The actual drive itself only takes about three hours, but its real charm can only be found if you stop along the way. So plan for at least five hours to experience the breathtaking mountain panoramas and discover some of the parkway's hundreds, if not thousands, of hidden and not-so-hidden treasures. You can spend hours at a single spot or visit several over the course of a day.

Be on the lookout for bighorn sheep, elk, moose, or even black bears. Chances of seeing wildlife on the parkway are very good in spring or fall, so take things slow, have your

BANFF NATIONAL PARK *(Parc national Banff)*

INFORMATION & ACTIVITIES

VISITOR & INFORMATION CENTRES

Banff Information Centre 224 Banff Ave., Banff, AB T1L 1K2. Phone (403) 762-1550. **Lake Louise Visitor Centre,** Samson Mall, AB T0L 1E0. Phone (403) 522-3833.

SEASONS & ACCESSIBILITY

Park open year-round.

HEADQUARTERS

Box 900, Banff, AB T1L 1K2. Phone (403) 762-1550. www.parkscanada.gc.ca/banff.

FRIENDS OF BANFF

Friends of Banff National Park, 214 Banff Ave., Banff, AB T1L 1C3. Phone (403) 760-5331. info@friendsofbanff.com; www .friendsof\banff.com.

ENTRANCE FEES

$10 per person, $20 per group per day; $68 per person, $136 per group per year with Parks Canada Discovery Pass.

PETS

Pets must be on a leash at all times and are not permitted to overnight in or outside the shelters.

ACCESSIBLE SERVICES

Public buildings are wheelchair accessible. Tunnel Village I, Tunnel Village II, Tunnel Village Trailer Court, Two Jack Lakeside, and Johnston Canyon campgrounds have wheelchair accessible washrooms, extended picnic tables, and raised fire pits. Sundance Canyon Trail and access to viewpoints at the promenade at Lake Louise are paved and wheelchair accessible.

THINGS TO DO

Hiking season runs from July to September; some lower trails may be hiked year-round.

On the water, canoes, kayaks, guided rafting tours, motorboat tours, and other nonmotorized boats allowed. Take a lake cruise or rent a motorboat at **Lake Minnewanka.** Canoes are available for rent in Banff, Lake Louise, and Moraine Lake. Raft tours are available on Bow River. Fishing (permit $10 per person per day, $34 per year) and swimming. **Upper Hot Springs** bathhouse and outdoor spring-fed pool open year-round.

Cross-country skiing, downhill skiing, and ski touring; ice skating; snowshoeing; and waterfall ice climbing.

Horseback riding, with maximum 3 nights at any grazing area; permit required (403-762-1470).

SPECIAL ADVISORIES

- Visit Lake Louise and Moraine Lake before 11 a.m. or after 5 p.m. to avoid congestion in peak season (July–Aug.).
- Be prepared for sudden changes in temperature, especially at higher elevations.
- When boating, be aware the water temperature is seldom over 10°C (50°F).

---

camera at the ready, and be safe. Pull over carefully off the highway, and never approach or disturb wildlife. If you plan to backtrack to Banff instead of proceeding to Jasper, try to leave enough travel time to drive back in daylight.

Designed for sightseeing, the parkway parallels the Continental Divide through the main ranges of the Canadian Rockies. The drive takes you through the Rockies' highest passes, the uppermost being **Bow Summit** at a lofty elevation of 2,069 m (6,787 ft) at km 40. Nearby you'll also find one of the world's best mountain panoramas at **Peyto Lake viewpoint.** On a typical sunny day, snowcapped peaks pierce the bright blue sky from every direction.

At km 19, stop to stretch your legs at the viewpoint for **Hector Lake,** formed in a glacial basin. From there you'll enjoy stellar views of **Mount Balfour** and the **Waputik Range** to the southwest. **Crowfoot Glacier** (km 33) once resembled a crow's foot with three large toes. The lower toe has

Small boats should stay close to shore, as capsizing could lead to hypothermia.
- Boaters should be ready for sudden strong winds and waves on the larger lakes, particularly in the afternoon.
- Water should be filtered and treated or boiled before drinking.

OVERNIGHT BACKPACKING

Fifty backcountry campgrounds, 2 trail shelters, 3 alpine huts, and 4 backcountry lodges. **Bryant Creek** and **Egypt Lake** public trail shelters available year-round, $7 per person. Mandatory Wilderness Pass for backcountry use $10 per person. Reservations for campsites and shelters can be made up to 3 months in advance. Safety registration recommended at the Banff Information Centre. Call (403) 762-1556. Paddlers must camp at designated roadside or backcountry campgrounds.

CAMPGROUNDS

Thirteen drive-to campgrounds. Call (877) 737-3783 or visit www.pccamping.ca. **Tunnel Mountain,** water, sewer, and electrical $38; unserviced with washroom building $27; electrical only $3. **Two Jack Main,** unserviced with toilets $22, and **Two Jack Lakeside,** unserviced with toilets and showers $2. **Lake Louise,** electrical $32 and overflow $11. **Johnston Canyon,** unserviced with toilets $22. **Castle Mountain** and **Protection Mountain,** unserviced with toilets $22. **Mosquito Creek,** primitive $16. **Waterfowl,** unserviced with toilets $22. **Rampart Creek,** primitive $16. Winter camping at Tunnel Mountain and Lake Louise only.

HOTELS, MOTELS, & INNS
(unless otherwise noted, rates are for a 2-person double, high season, in Canadian dollars)

Banff, AB:
Blue Mountain Lodge B&B 137 Muskrat. (403) 762-5134. www.bluemtnlodge.com. $119–$179.
The Fairmont Banff Springs 405 Spray Ave. (403) 762-2211 or (866) 540-4406. banffsprings@fairmont.com; www.fairmont.com/banffsprings. $350–$600.
Mount Royal Hotel 138 Banff Ave. (403) 762-3331 or (877) 442-2623. info@mountroyalhotel.com; www.mountroyalhotel.com. $109–$209.
Rimrock Resort Hotel 300 Mountain Ave. (403) 762-3356. www.rimrockresort.com. $275–$455.

Lake Louise, AB T0L 1E0:
Fairmont Chateau Lake Louise 111 Lake Louise Dr. (403) 522-3511 or (866) 540-4413. www.fairmont.com/lakelouise. From $349 per night.

Additional visitor information:
Banff Lake Louise Tourism Suite 375 Cascade Plaza, Banff, AB T1L 1B3. (403) 762-0270. info@bannflakelouise; www.banfflakelouise.com.

BANFF

melted away, leaving only two toes visible today. Nearby **Helen Lake** is the place for a gratifying day hike with meadows bursting with alpine flowers, noisy marmots, and a chance to scramble on rocky faces.

At km 71, **Mistaya Canyon** requires only a ten-minute trek along the trail. You'll find amazing canyon views, but watch your step and keep your distance from the edge as you gaze upon the rushing waters and eroding rock walls.

Back along the parkway, keep veering northwest until you come upon the **Coleman Creek day-use area** at km 99. It offers a pleasant picnic rest stop, where you might spy mountain goats perched on the cliffs above. Farther along, at km 106, you'll see the **Weeping Wall,** a very popular place with ice climbers, where meltwater from Cirrus Mountain pours over the steep rock face as a series of graceful waterfalls.

At km 126 sits a major highlight of the Icefields Parkway—the **Athabasca Glacier,** which is part of the huge Columbia Icefield (see pp. 210–211).

EXCURSIONS

ABBOT PASS REFUGE CABIN NATIONAL HISTORIC SITE
BANFF NP, AB

Built in 1922 by Swiss guides, the alpine shelter is one of 24 shelters managed by the Alpine Club of Canada. For generations, climbers have travelled to the stone cabin as a base for ascents up Mount Lefroy and Mount Victoria or as a destination in itself. The steep ascent to the hut should only be attempted by skilled mountaineers. Winter visits are not advised.

BANFF PARK MUSEUM NATIONAL HISTORIC SITE
BANFF, AB

The museum displays a historic collection of more than 5,000 specimens of Rocky Mountain mammals, birds, insects, plants, and geological wonders. Opened in 1895, it was moved to its current log building in 1903. Norman Bethune Sanson, the museum's curator from 1896 to 1932, developed the collections and was known as "nature's gentleman." Though the building was refurbished in 1985, the original exhibits still reflect museum interpretation practices from 1914. Located at 91 Banff Ave. (403) 762-1558.

CAVE AND BASIN NATIONAL HISTORIC SITE
BANFF, AB

Commemorating the birthplace of Canada's national parks system, this site received a face-lift as part of the 125th anniversary of the park in 2010. Naturally occurring, warm mineral springs along with the pungent smell of sulphur greet visitors inside the cave and outside in the emerald-coloured basin area. Walking trails and wetlands surround the site. Interactive activities, guided tours, and a café will open in the summer of 2012. (403) 762-1566.

HOWSE PASS NATIONAL HISTORIC SITE
BANFF NP, AB

This traditional aboriginal transportation route over the Continental Divide links the North Saskatchewan and Columbia River systems. David Thompson traversed it in 1807, and Canadian fur traders used it until 1810 to explore and establish posts west of the Rockies. Joseph Howse, the Hudson's Bay Company employee after whom the pass is named, first crossed it in 1809. It is located on the British Columbia–Alberta border, hiking 26 km (16 mi) west from the Icefields Parkway (Hwy. 93 N).

SKOKI SKI LODGE NATIONAL HISTORIC SITE
BANFF NP, AB

A throwback to the early days of ski tourism, the lodge exemplifies Banff's rustic design tradition. Opened for business in 1931, Skoki was built as a destination for backcountry skiers by a group of local ski enthusiasts, using timbers cut in the vicinity. Accessible only by ski- or hike-in, it was the first such facility to operate on a commercial basis in Canada and is still open year-round as a rest stop and social meet-up for backcountry skiers and hikers. (888) 997-5654.

SULPHUR MOUNTAIN COSMIC RAY STATION NATIONAL HISTORIC SITE
BANFF NP, AB

Located at the top of Sulphur Mountain, the cosmic ray station was completed by the National Research Council in 1956 for the 1957–1958 International Geophysical Year. Because of its high elevation (2,283 m/7,490 ft), Sulphur Mountain station was the most important Canadian site. Operational until 1978, the building was removed in 1981, leaving only the lab's foundation. It's accessible via hiking trail or the Sulphur Mountain Gondola. From the upper terminal, take the easy self-guided Banff Skywalk Trail along the summit ridge to the station.

BANFF

Painting the Parks

Canada's national parks and the Canadian Pacific Railway (CPR) that linked the country from east to west were early instruments in establishing a sense of national identity in the 19th century. But it was art that ultimately brushed the finishing touches on Canada's unique character.

Marmaduke Matthews, *Bow River (with Bourgeau Range in background)*, 1887, oil on canvas, Collection of Whyte Museum of the Canadian Rockies

In 1885, the CPR laid a ribbon of steel across Canada through the Canadian Rockies. The same year, a reserve was set aside around the hot springs at Banff, forming the basis of Banff National Park. Other mountain parks at Yoho and Glacier soon followed Canada's first national park, although it would be decades before Canada's parks were expanded into a truly national system.

William Cornelius Van Horne, the CPR's general manager, saw art as an inspirational means to promote mountain tourism and western settlement. By providing travel, lodging, and other benefits to artists, he encouraged them to paint and photograph the mountain landscapes.

Some of the first artists to travel to the Rockies in the late 1880s were John Fraser, Frederic M. Bell-Smith, Marmaduke Matthews, and Thomas Mower Martin, artists influenced by European landscape traditions and the Sublime Movement in American art. They primarily used watercolour to paint picturesque, romantic views that reflected the scale and grandeur of Canadian landscapes and popularized the West.

Banff and the other mountain parks continued to draw artists and photographers throughout the 20th century. Photographer Byron Harmon arrived in 1903, followed by artists Belmore Browne, Carl Rungius, Mary Schäffer, and Charlie Beil. Peter Whyte, born in Banff in 1905, was the first native of Banff to become an artist. He met fellow student Catharine Robb at the Boston Museum of Fine Arts School in the late 1920s, and after their marriage, they established a studio in their home and became the centre of a tightly knit, supportive artist community in Banff. Ultimately, they founded Banff's Whyte Museum of the Canadian Rockies in 1958.

With the inception of the Banff School of Fine Arts in 1935, Banff National Park became a magnet for artists from across Canada. Many great Canadian landscape artists taught and studied at the Banff School of Fine Arts, now the Banff Centre, from the 1930s until today. From Walter J. Phillips and A. C. Leighton to Robert Sinclair and Takao Tanabe—all of the artists who taught or studied here were inspired by the mountain parks. They, in turn, inspired the work of their students, contemporaries, and followers.

The Group of Seven, Franklin Carmichael, Lawren S. Harris, A. Y. Jackson, Frank H. Johnson, Arthur Lismer, J. E. H. MacDonald, and Frederick Horsman Varley, were artists committed to exploring the unique character of the Canadian landscape, and they developed a distinctive painting style that broke with English tradition.

Two of the Group of Seven, Jackson and Harris, taught at the Banff School of Fine Arts, and two other members, Arthur Lismer and J. E. H. MacDonald, painted in the mountain parks. Lismer visited only once, in 1928, while MacDonald, sponsored by the CPR, spent seven summers in the national parks from 1924 to 1930. He became a close friend of Peter and Catharine Whyte's.

Contemporary artists continue to paint the parks today. Their paintings are modern interpretations that capture the mystery and beauty of the mountain parks and national parks across Canada. Robert Sinclair, for example, has painted in national parks from Newfoundland to the West Coast. His works, painted from memory, capture the symbolic significance of the landscape.

The national parks, and particularly the mountain parks, have sparked and will continue to spark the imaginations of landscape artists who capture on paper, canvas, or in other mediums the incredible beauty of these natural places and contribute to our evolving national identity. For those who may have a chance

Peter Whyte, *Lake O'Hara, 1929,* oil on canvas, Collection of Whyte Museum of the Canadian Rockies

to visit only once in a lifetime, their works provide another way to experience the gift of Canada's national parks.

— MICHALE LANG, *Executive Director, Whyte Museum of the Canadian Rockies*

Spirit Island on scenic Maligne Lake in Jasper National Park

▶ JASPER

ALBERTA
ESTABLISHED 1907
11,228 sq km/2,774,500 acres

The largest national park in the Canadian Rockies, Jasper is wild in every sense of the word. Its landscape covers an expansive region of rugged backcountry trails and mountainous terrain juxtaposed against fragile protected ecosystems as well as the world-renowned Columbia Icefield. It's also chock-full of wildlife, home to some of North America's healthiest populations of grizzly bears, moose, and elk along with thousands of species of plants and insects.

The park comprises rough-and-tumble mountains, valleys, glaciers, forests, alpine meadows, and rivers along the eastern slopes of the Rockies in western Alberta. More than 980 km (615 mi) of hiking trails offer day and overnight trips. A number of spectacular mountain drives also beckon.

Established in 1907, Jasper protects what's left of the wildlife that was once commonplace in the West. While other areas have seen a dramatic decline in wildlife, strong populations of plants and animals persevere here. The park's elevation range, geology, geography, and climate serve as a safe habitat for a variety of species.

Due in part to the incredible diversity of wildlife found here, Jasper is part of the UNESCO Canadian Rocky

Mountain Parks World Heritage site, one of 15 World Heritage sites in Canada. It is home to nearly 70 species of mammals whose health and survival depend on the park. That's why it's crucial that visitors make as few disturbances as possible.

How to Get There

The town of Jasper is situated at the intersection of Hwy. 16 (Yellowhead Hwy.) and Hwy. 93 N (Icefields Pkwy.). It is straight west 362 km (225 mi) on Hwy. 16 from Edmonton and west from Calgary along Trans-Canada 1, then north on Hwy. 93 from Lake Louise, 412 km (256 mi) in total. Major national and international carriers service both Edmonton and Calgary's international airports, with multiple flights arriving daily. Renting a car at the airport is the easiest way to make the trip, but rail travel to the park is also available through VIA Rail *(www.viarail.ca)* and the Rocky Mountaineer *(www.rockymountaineer .com)*. Shuttle services are available through tour operators.

When to Go

The park is open year-round, but the weather and scenery are generally spectacular in late summer and early fall. Forest-fire season in North America also winds down in the fall, so the air is clearer—especially important for photo enthusiasts.

Wildlife viewing can happen any time of year, but your best bets are early in the morning or late in the evening during the slow seasons (fall and spring), particularly for bears, elk, and sheep. The best time to watch the annual elk rut, when males bugle and compete with each other for females, is August to September along the Athabasca River. Camping is very popular in summer. Most campgrounds are open until Labour Day weekend; some stay open later in the fall. There are winter campgrounds as well. Skiing and snowboarding at Marmot Basin typically runs from November to April.

How to Visit

Within the park, travel by car is most convenient. Drive with care and be prepared to avoid a collision with wildlife at all times. Be especially cautious at dusk and dawn, when many animals are most active and visibility is poor.

You can hike and bike along several trails in the park. Many of the backcountry trails were established first by wildlife, then by early travellers including First Nations people, fur traders, explorers, and adventurers. There are nearly 1,000 km (621 mi) of trails and 82 backcountry campsites in the park. Licensed commercial services include three backcountry lodges, several horse outfitters, and numerous hiking/ interpretive guides. The Alpine Club of Canada *(www.alpineclubofcanada .ca)* manages four alpine huts.

Plan to spend at least a half day in the town of Jasper and several days exploring the park.

MUNICIPALITY OF JASPER
a half to full day

Start your visit by talking to the knowledgeable staff at the information centre. Acquaint yourself with the town using the accessible **Jasper Discovery Trail,** an 8-km (5 mi) loop that borders Jasper and offers unique town vistas. Easy to navigate, the trail incorporates interpretive signs that inform trail users about special

JASPER

features of the area, including both cultural and natural heritage tidbits.

For a bird's-eye view of the town of Jasper and the surrounding area, head for the 2,277 m (7,472 ft) **Jasper Tramway** (April–Oct.; *www.jaspertramway.com*). You'll soar up Whistlers Mountain, the large rounded mountain just outside the town, into the alpine tundra for dramatic views of six mountain ranges, glacier-fed lakes, and the Athabasca River. Perfect for the whole family, it's the longest and highest guided aerial tramway in Canada. A tour guide accompanies you in your enclosed cabin on the seven-minute ascent.

As you reach the **Upper Station,** the mountains loom overhead, enticing you to hit the boardwalks adorned with interpretive exhibits. Watch for wildlife in this alpine life zone, the park's most fragile area. You can venture off the boardwalks to hiking trails leading to the breathtaking summit of the mountain, but be careful not to disturb the flora and fauna. Bring extra clothes in case of sudden weather changes.

Next, take a detour out of town to **Mount Edith Cavell** for impressive views of the mountain and of Angel and Cavell Glaciers. Travel south, following Hwy. 93A for 5 km (3.2 mi). After crossing the Astoria River, turn right onto Cavell Road, open from June to mid-October. Although it is paved, the road comprises several narrow switchbacks rendering it unsuitable for motor homes or buses. In winter, the road is closed until mid-February, even to skiing, for caribou conservation purposes. Continue 14 km (8.7 mi) up the road to the lush **Astoria Valley Viewpoint.**

Cavell Road ends at the Mount Edith Cavell parking lot. Here you will find a few climbing routes as well as two short interpretive trails.

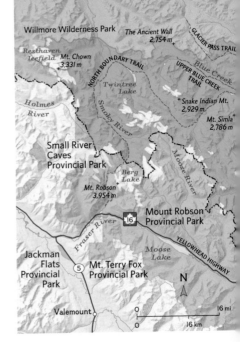

On the **Path of the Glacier Loop** (1–2 hrs. return), glacial debris from the Little Ice Age litters the trail, which takes you toward the north face of the mountain, across a rocky landscape cloaked with sparkling glacial ice. The trail ends at **Cavell pond,** which sometimes plays host to fallen icebergs and provides a good view of both glaciers. The moderately steep **Cavell Meadows Loop** (3–6 hrs.) guides you to alpine meadows flecked with flowers and striking views of powder blue **Angel Glacier.** Be alert as you will likely see wildlife on your trip—birds, squirrels, deer, goats, marmots, pika, and maybe a caribou. Take as many pictures as you like, but do not feed or disturb the animals.

MALIGNE VALLEY ROAD

45 km/29 mi; a half to full day

A side trip to Maligne (pronounced MAH-leen) Lake is a must-do when visiting Jasper. Go east on Hwy. 16,

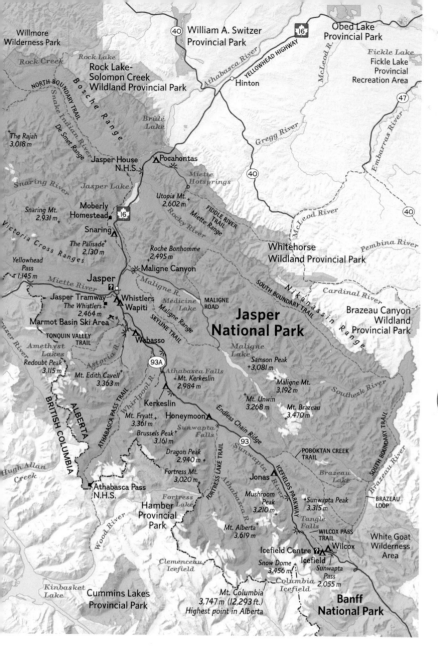

and turn right across the Moberly Bridge, 2.5 km (1.6 mi) east of the town of Jasper, and follow the signs. This stretch of road is home to a number of natural wonders including a deep canyon (which can be explored from the bottom in winter), a lake

that disappears down sinkholes, and Jasper's most picturesque lake.

Have your camera at the ready while you drive this winding road as animals of all kinds have been known to meander here. As always in the park, be on the lookout for bears, elk, deer, moose, sheep, and goats. Stay a safe distance away and remain in your vehicle if you do come upon wildlife.

At km 6, watch for the **Hanging Valley Viewpoint** on your left; the sign can be easy to miss. Take this exit for an exceptional panorama of the vast glacier-carved **Athabasca Valley,** the town of Jasper in the valley bottom, and across the valley, **Pyramid Mountain.**

At km 7, turn left into the **Maligne Canyon day-use area.** Created by Maligne River erosion between the Maligne and Athabasca Valleys, the canyon is up to 50 m (160 ft) deep at various places. Take a self-guided tour along the canyon's interpretive trail to learn about the geological history of the area. Cross the four bridges running across the gorge, each with its own special view. A short hiking loop takes you to the upper reaches of the canyon, while a longer trail follows the gorge. Stay on the trail and resist the temptation to climb past the railings for that perfect picture. Canyon walks, including winter ice walks, are available through various tour operators.

Continue on Maligne Road to km 20 to see **Medicine Lake,** which is not your average mountain lake. In summer, glacier meltwaters flood the lake, sometimes overflowing it. But in fall and winter, the lake disappears. With no visible channel draining the lake, it's unclear where the water goes—a veritable disappearing lake phenomenon.

In fact, the lake drains from the bottom like a bathtub. After Maligne River fills the lake, the water drains out through sinkholes in the bottom. It then streams through an underground cave network formed in the limestone rock, surfacing again downstream in the area of Maligne Canyon. It is one of the largest known underground river systems in North America and may be the world's largest inaccessible cave system. Thousands of gallons of water drain every second. During the summer runoff, enough water flows into the lake to surpass the drainage. By September, the runoff drops off, and the lake rapidly drains.

At the end of Maligne Road (km 45), you'll come to **Maligne Lake,** considered to be one of the most scenic spots in Canada. The largest natural lake in the Canadian Rockies at 22.5 km (14 mi) long, Maligne Lake is a popular site for interpretive boat cruises. From May to October, try the 90-minute boat tour to the famed **Spirit Island** in the middle of the lake for 360-degree views of the lake and mountains (the island is accessible only by boat).

Surrounded by snowcapped mountains, Maligne Lake stretches to the meltwater channels of **Coronet Glacier.** Amid the forest of spruce and lodgepole pine, you may once again catch a glimpse of wildlife including harlequin ducks along the Maligne River. Endless hiking and cross-country skiing trails make the lake a popular year-round getaway. Horseback riding, snowshoeing, and guided fishing are also available.

COLUMBIA ICEFIELD AREA & ATHABASCA GLACIER

a full day

Located off the Icefields Parkway (Hwy. 93), the **Columbia Icefield** is the largest reservoir of snow and ice in the Rockies and feeds three of the continent's major river systems. Straddling the borders of Alberta and British Columbia, the ice field

Exploring the narrows of Maligne Canyon

Bald eagle perched atop a fir tree in the shadow of Sirdar Mountain

Jasper Tramway

comprises 260 sq km (64,250 acres) of crystal-blue glacial ice and snow. And, almost three-quarters of the park's highest peaks are located nearby, fashioning a mantle of alpine majesty. A remnant of the last ice age, this frozen giant continues to gradually sculpt the scenery.

A 4.8-km (3 mi) tongue of the ice field, the **Athabasca Glacier** is the most accessible and visited glacier in North America, flowing within 1.6 km (1 mi) of the highway. Its ice is in continuous motion, creeping forward bit by bit every day. Spilling down the valley like a frozen river, the glacier has actually been receding for the last 125 years as the climate has warmed. It has lost half its original volume and has retreated more than 1.6 km (1 mi).

To experience the glacier up close, try a guided ice walk, where you can set foot upon the glacier itself. There are also specially designed Ice Explorer vehicles that can take you for a glacial expedition. See firsthand what glacier ice looks, feels, and even tastes like as you tread cautiously through ice-carved landscapes. Do not attempt to walk on the glacier on your own; glaciers can be hazardous.

Finish off with a visit to the **Columbia Icefield Centre and Glacier Gallery** (late April–mid-Oct.), located across from the Athabasca Glacier, to learn more about this frozen alpine world. Displays in the gallery explain how glaciers are formed as well as the ecology and history of the area.

JASPER NATIONAL PARK *(Parc national Jasper)*

INFORMATION & ACTIVITIES

VISITOR & INFORMATION CENTRES

Jasper Information Centre 500 Connaught Dr., Jasper, AB T0E 1E0. Phone (780) 852-6176. **Icefields Information Centre** Icefields Pkwy. Phone (780) 852-6288. 103 km (64 mi) south of the town of Jasper. Open April to October.

SEASONS & ACCESSIBILITY

Open year-round. Some seasonal restrictions for facilities and trails.

HEADQUARTERS

Box 10, Jasper, AB T0E 1E0. Phone (780) 852-6176. www.parkscanada.gc.ca/jasper.

FRIENDS OF JASPER

Friends of Jasper National Park P.O. Box 992, 415 Connaught Dr., Jasper, AB T0E 1E0. Phone (780) 852-4767. friends@incentre.net; www.friendsofjasper.com.

ENTRANCE FEES

$10 per person, $20 per group per day; $68 per person, $140 per group per year with Canada Parks Discovery Pass.

PETS

Pets not allowed in canvas tents. Dogs must be leashed at all times; not allowed on some trails.

ACCESSIBLE SERVICES

For information on accessible facilities, call the Jasper Information Centre (wheelchair accessible). Glacier Gallery in the Icefield Information Centre and Miette Hot Springs are accessible.

THINGS TO DO

Hiking, horseback riding, skiing, backpacking, and mountain biking. Rafting, canoeing, and swimming. Bathing in aquacourt with water from the Miette Hot Springs. Fishing permits $10 per day, $35 per year.

SPECIAL ADVISORIES

- If you encounter bears, slow down and make noise to alert them to your presence. Bear bells will not be enough.
- Never leave coolers, pet bowls, dishes and pots, food items, cooking stoves, garbage bags, or toiletries unattended.

CAMPGROUNDS

100 backcountry campsites; call (780) 852-6177 for information and reservations. **Pocahontas,** unserviced with toilets only $22 per night. **Whistlers,** with water, sewer, and electrical services $38; electrical services only $32; unserviced with toilets and showers $28; walk-in campground with toilets and showers $22. **Wapiti,** with electrical services $32; unserviced with toilets and showers $28. **Wabasso,** unserviced with toilets $21. **Snaring River, Mount Kerkeslin, Honeymoon Lake, Jonas Creek, Columbia Icefield,** and **Wilcox Creek** primitive campgrounds $16. Snaring overflow space $11. **Marmot** group camping $6 per person. **Whirlpool/Ranger Creek** group camping $5 per person. Serviced (hook-up) sites fill up quickly; arrive early. Cottage tents with space for 4 adults and 2 children, electric wall lights, and baseboard heaters. Reserve *(www.pccamping.ca)* in advance of peak season (June–Sept.). Fire, campsite day-use, and dump station permits $9 per day each.

HOTELS, MOTELS, & INNS

(unless otherwise noted, rates are for a 2-person double, high season, in Canadian dollars)

Jasper, AB T0E 1E0:
Jasper Park Lodge Old Lodge Rd. (780) 852-3301 or (866) 540-4454. jasperparklodge@fairmont.com; www.fairmont.com/jasper. $500–$800.
Maligne Lodge 900 Connaught Dr. (780) 852-3143 or (800) 661-9323. info@malignelodge.com; http://malignelodge.com. $120–$300.
Pine Bungalows 2 Cottonwood Creek Rd. (780) 852-3491. pinebung@telusplanet.net; www.pinebungalows.com. $125–$220.
Pocahontas Cabins Hwy. 16 E. (780) 866-3732 or (800) 843-3372. www.mpljasper.com/hotels/pocahontas_cabins. $130–$245.

Additional visitor information:
Jasper Tourism & Commerce, www.jasper.travel, or **Hostelling International Canada,** (778) 328-2220, www.hihostels.ca.

EXCURSIONS

JASPER HOUSE NATIONAL HISTORIC SITE
JASPER, AB

Built in 1813, the house served as a meeting and provisions place for fur traders and explorers journeying through the Athabasca and Yellowhead Passes throughout much of the 19th century. Originally named Rocky Mountain House, it was renamed after its first postmaster, Jasper Hawes. The Hudson's Bay Company moved the fur-trading post upriver in 1829, but by 1850 the post had declined. It closed permanently 50 years later. Today, access to the field where the house stood is via Hwy. 16, 40 km (25 mi) from Jasper.

JASPER PARK INFORMATION CENTRE NATIONAL HISTORIC SITE
JASPER, AB

A shining example of rustic architecture in Canada's national parks, the facility introduced a tradition of local building materials, namely cobblestone and timber. Completed in 1914, the centre originally housed park administrative offices, a museum, and living quarters for the park superintendent. The first major building in the townsite, it helped define the character of Jasper's early development. It continues to be a park contact point. 500 Connaught Dr. (780) 852-6162.

JASPER

Sunlight breaks through the fog in Elk Island National Park.

▶ ELK ISLAND

ALBERTA
ESTABLISHED 1913
194 sq km/47,938 acres

Elk had been hunted nearly to extinction in Alberta by the turn of the last century. Established originally as a fenced sanctuary for these animals, Elk Island was soon sheltering bison, too. Today the park is a favourite wildland recreation area for residents of nearby Edmonton, who enjoy wildlife viewing, birding, boating, hiking, and cross-country skiing in an interesting hilly landscape.

Elk Island National Park—Canada's only national park that is fully fenced off from surrounding lands—is an excellent example of Alberta's aspen parkland, meaning an open woodland of leafy trees and conifers that is transitional between the dense boreal evergreen forest of northern Canada and the grasslands of the Great Plains. These days the park is also thought of as a wilderness surrounded by agricultural land.

The park's landscape is a mosaic of hills and hollows, ponds and marshes, meadows and woods. This is knob-and-kettle topography, which is created when irregular masses of glacial ice melt away under a cover of gravel and till. The knobs are the hills; the kettles are the hollows. The topographic relief is about 60 m (200 ft), enough to sustain an ecosystem in which small differences in elevation produce large differences in plant communities. Biodiversity is high and the species list is long, especially the bird checklist. Both species of bison (plains bison and woodland bison) are represented.

The north and south portions of the park are separated by Hwy. 16 (Yellowhead Hwy.), which provides the main access to the park. All bison seen south of the highway are wood bison; to the north are the plains bison. There are no major north-south differences in the park's elk population.

The Elk Island Parkway takes visitors northward to the park's activity hub, the Astotin Lake Area. At 3.8 km (2.4 mi) long, Astotin Lake is the largest of the 250 water bodies in the park. One of the islands in the lake is named Elk Island, which may account for the park's name.

Birding and viewing the park's bison and elk are popular activities year-round. Visitors can walk and ski 11 maintained trails, most of them loops. One lengthy trail is paved and suitable for wheelchairs or strollers, but it has steeper sections that may be challenging for some wheelchair users. A boardwalk provides a short interpretive tour of a marsh near the visitor centre. Canoeing, kayaking, rowing, and sailing are popular; motorboats are not permitted. Boats can be launched from Sandy Beach. There is no fishing in the park. Cross-country skiing and snowshoeing are great ways to explore the peaceful serenity of winter trails.

Elk Island is a Dark Sky Preserve (see pp. 58–59) so artificial lighting in the park is minimal. Stargazing and aurora viewing are excellent, especially in winter.

How to Get There

Elk Island National Park is only 45 minutes from downtown Edmonton, Alberta. From Edmonton (closest airport), follow Hwy. 16 (Yellowhead Hwy.) east for 27 km (17 mi) and turn left onto the Elk Island Parkway. The parkway continues northward from the Astotin Lake Area to the northern park boundary, where it becomes Hwy. 831 to the town of Lamont.

When to Go

The warm months are June through August. In July, temperatures in the park typically reach into the 20s°C (70s–80s°F). Wildflowers begin to bloom in May and are at their best from late June to mid-July. The park's aspen groves turn a brilliant yellow in mid-September. By the end of October, the trees have lost their leaves and snow has started to accumulate. Be prepared for very cold days in January, when Arctic high-pressure cells can bring cold snaps of minus 40°C (minus 40°F).

How to Visit

Bison and elk roam freely through the park and may be seen nearly anywhere. The **Elk Island Parkway** (see p. 217), the park's main access road, is much better than Hwy. 16 (Yellowhead Hwy.) for observing wildlife. Take this low-speed paved road northward to the **Astotin Lake Area.** Once there, get out of your vehicle and explore.

Families will find much to enjoy at **Sandy Beach,** which has been developed with public recreation in mind. You can view several exhibits (including a full-size reproduction of a Ukrainian pioneer home), enjoy an interpretive program, and go boating or picnicking. Also available are a playground, soccer field, and horseshoe pits, and a nearby campground operates from May to October. Golfers can play a public

ELK ISLAND

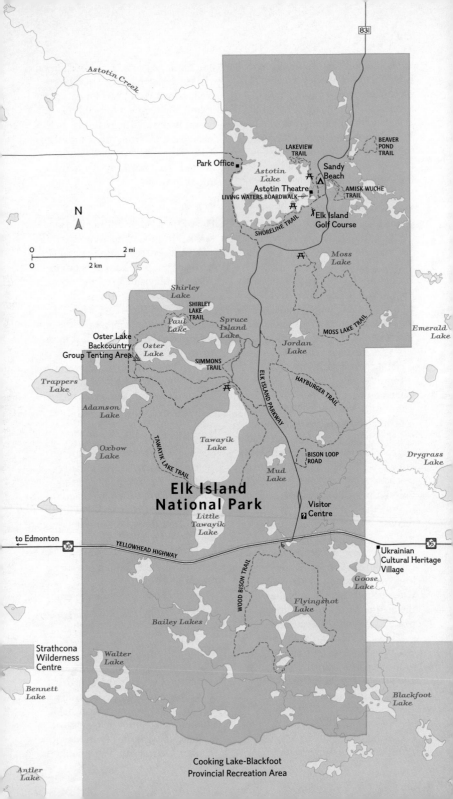

nine-hole course, and the golf club serves meals and snacks to the general public.

Despite all the facilities at the Astotin Lake Area, most of Elk Island National Park remains wild. Many visitors spend the day walking the trails that wind through the park's complex landscape, identifying bird species and taking photographs of wildlife in natural settings.

The park's bison are wild animals, and visitors need to exercise caution; a distance of at least 100 m (330 ft) should be kept at all times. The same applies to the park's elk, moose, and deer. Males become more aggressive during the mating season (summer for the bison, late summer and autumn for the others), and the females are especially dangerous when their young may be threatened. Keep your pets leashed at all times. Black bears are very rarely seen in the park.

Mountain biking is permitted, but confrontations with wildlife have led the park to recommend bicycling on roadways only.

WILDLIFE-WATCHING ALONG ELK ISLAND PARKWAY

20 km/12.4 mi; at least 1 hour

You will find many pull-offs and viewpoints with interpretive signs along this very popular park-access and wildlife-viewing route. Observe the speed limits, and be especially cautious at dawn, at dusk, and at night. The parkway is not fenced, and dark-coloured bison may be standing in the road.

Your best chance of seeing and photographing the park's plains bison is to turn off the parkway at the **Bison Loop Road,** 2.6 km (1.6 mi) from the start, where the animals

tend to congregate. The loop is 1.8 km (1.1 mi) long. Stay in your car during the midsummer mating period, when the male bison can be heard "roaring."

Elk, white-tailed deer, and mule deer prefer the open, grassy areas with woods nearby. During the autumn elk rut, the males "bugle," producing loud whistling sounds that carry to the females, and provide a challenge to other males. Give them plenty of room. Moose live in the park, too, mostly in the wooded wetlands. Other species to watch for include coyotes and beavers.

BIRDING

Elk Island has been described as a birder's paradise. The varied wet/dry ecosystems in the park provide habitat for some 250 species of birds, among them the distinctive American white pelican, the double-crested cormorant, and the trumpeter swan. Sandhill cranes frequent the park. Pileated woodpeckers—the largest woodpecker species in Canada—are often seen in aspen and poplar groves.

The short **Living Waters Boardwalk loop** at **Astotin Lake** is an easy-to-reach observation area for wetland birds and waterfowl, including red-necked grebes, cormorants, yellow-headed blackbirds, tundra swans, ducks, and shorebirds.

Any of the hiking trails at the lake will provide rewarding birding, especially the **Lakeview Trail,** 3.5 km (2.2 mi), one to two hours. The trailhead is located at the north end of the Astotin Lake Area. Birders looking for a longer walk will enjoy the **Shirley Lake Trail,** 10.5 km (6.5 mi), three to four hours, which is well known for views of the park's nesting waterfowl.

ELK ISLAND

HIKING

Trails in the Astotin Lake Area are very popular for short walks. The **Shoreline Trail** around the lake, 6 km (3.7 mi) return, two to three hours, is paved and wheelchair accessible. The easy and varied **Amisk Wuche Trail,** 2.5 km (1.6 mi), roughly one hour, is very popular with families.

Longer trails take visitors to some of the wilder parts of the park. (Do check with the park wardens or staff about restrictions and cautions concerning animals in rut in late summer and early fall.)

A favourite trail is the **Hayburger Trail,** 10 km (6 mi), three to four hours, with its "soap holes," which are patches of mineral salts formed by evaporation of groundwater. The **Moss Lake Trail,** 13 km (8 mi), 3.5 to 4.5 hours, explores the area southeast of Astotin Lake, while the **Wood Bison Trail,** 16 km (10 mi), four to five hours, is the only route into the portion of the park lying south of Hwy. 16 (Yellowhead Hwy.). This is the wildest area in the park, and you may, indeed, see wood bison here.

Cross-country skiing is popular at Elk Island.

SKIING & SNOWSHOEING

The winter activity season runs from November through March. The **Shirley Lake Trail** and the **Moss Lake Trail** are track-set each year, while other trails may be kept open by skiers on their own. Inquire at the visitor centre for conditions.

Snowshoers enjoy making their own paths, particularly on Astotin Lake and in rougher places that do not appeal to skiers. Snowshoers are asked not to travel on track-set trails because it ruins the track.

A bull moose sheds velvet from its antlers in Elk Island National Park.

ELK ISLAND NATIONAL PARK *(Parc national Elk Island)*

INFORMATION & ACTIVITIES

VISITOR CENTRE
Rural Route #1, Site 4, Fort Saskatchewan, AB T8L 2N7. Phone (780) 922-2950. einp.info@pc.gc.ca; www.parkscanada.gc.ca/elkisland.

SEASONS & ACCESSIBILITY
Park open year-round.

FRIENDS OF ELK ISLAND
Friends of Elk Island Society Box 70, 9920 63 Ave., Edmonton, AB T6E 0G9. (780) 895-7399. info@elkisland.ca; www.elkisland.ca.

ENTRANCE FEES
$8 per day for adults, $7 per day for seniors, $20 per day for families. Special rates apply for school and commercial groups (contact the park). Day Passes can be purchased at the South, North, and West Gates, Sandy Beach Campground, visitor centre, and administration office, or at the automated pass machines at the park gates.

PETS
Dogs must be leashed at all times.

ACCESSIBLE SERVICES
Washrooms and some sites at Sandy Beach Campground are accessible.

THINGS TO DO
Sailing, canoeing, and kayaking on **Astotin Lake** (no boat rental). Boat launch at the Astotin Lake Area parking lot.

Eleven trails for hiking.

Cross-country skiing and snowshoeing on and off trails.

Picnicking at **Tawayik Lake Picnic Area,** Astotin Lake, and **Moss Lake** trailhead.

Educational programs available mid-April to mid-October (advanced booking required). In summer, public programs offered free of charge with valid park pass. Explora, a new handheld GPS-activated device, is also available for rent in the park. Call (780) 992-2965 for more information.

A nine-hole golf course and pro shop are located in the Astotin Lake Area. Golf course (780-998-3161, *www.elkisland golf.com*) open May to October.

SPECIAL ADVISORIES
- Swimming is not recommended in Astotin Lake.
- Do not feed or chase squirrels and other small animals.
- Park Warden emergency phone (780) 992-6389.
- Fires and camping not permitted on islands in Astotin Lake.

OVERNIGHT BACKPACKING
Must obtain free permits from the visitor centre. Overnight backcountry camping is available at **Oster Lake** by reservation.

CAMPGROUNDS
Sandy Beach Campground, open May to September. 71 semiserviced sites (68 campsites and 3 teepees), unserviced overflow area. Flush toilets, showers. For reservations, call (877) 737-3783 or go to www.pccamping.ca. Maximum stay is 21 days. **Sandy Beach Group Camping Area** at Astotin Lake (minimum 10 campers). Not available on long week-ends and must be reserved in advance (780-992-0017). Winter camping area available in the RV loop and is free of charge (park entrance fee still applies). Additionally, winter camping is offered when the Sandy Beach Campground closes, typically after Thanksgiving weekend (October) until early May (weather dependent).

HOTELS, MOTELS, & INNS
(unless otherwise noted, rates are for a 2-person double, high season, in Canadian dollars)

<u>Outside the park:</u>
Lakeview Inn & Suites 10115 88 Ave., Fort Saskatchewan, AB T8L 4K1. (780) 998-7888. www.lakeviewhotels.com. $119–$139.
Prairie Sunset Bed & Breakfast 54140 Range Rd. 224, Fort Saskatchewan, AB T8L 3Y5. (780) 997-0551. reamc@telusplanet.net; www.prairiesunset.com. $90.

Vermilion Range and Floe Lake, Kootenay National Park

▶ KOOTENAY

BRITISH COLUMBIA
ESTABLISHED 1920
1,380 sq km/341,005 acres

"Kootenay" is an old spelling of the Ktunaxa (pronounced "k-тоо-nah-ha") First Nations. Comprising the corridor of Hwy. 93 in the Canadian Rockies west of Banff, this park features a fully developed hot spring and other popular geological attractions. New growth after major forest fires has been allowed to occur naturally, providing outstanding examples of ecological succession.

Since Kootenay is a narrow park with a highway down the middle, you can view much of its spectacular mountain scenery from the road. The park protects much of the headwaters of the Kootenay River and all of its tributary, the Vermilion, which Hwy. 93 follows closely for 56 km (35 mi) from the Continental Divide to the confluence. Travellers along the highway enjoy firsthand views of a textbook glacial river, complete

with milky blue water, gravel outwash flats, and big daily changes in flow. Farther on, the road passes through narrow, winding Sinclair Canyon, a stream-cut feature that contrasts with the glaciated landscape.

At 3,424 m (11,234 ft) high, Deltaform Mountain is the highest peak in Kootenay. The lowest point lies at only 901 m (2,956 ft) in the Columbia Valley at the park's west gate. This presents impressive topographic relief of 2.5 km (1.5 mi), in which all the elevational life zones of the Canadian Rockies are represented, from the grassy, juniper-clad lower slopes of the trench—the driest place in the region—through open montane woods to dense subalpine forests, windswept alpine tundra, high-elevation glaciers, and icy summits atop enormous cliffs.

How to Get There

From Calgary (closest airport), take Trans-Canada 1 west for 143 km (89 mi) to the junction with Hwy. 93 between Banff and Lake Louise (not the junction farther west, just past Lake Louise). Follow Hwy. 93 west for 10 km (6 mi) to the park.

From the south, take Hwy. 93/95 to the village of Radium Hot Springs, where Hwy. 93 branches east into the park. From the west, turn off Trans-Canada 1 at Golden and take Hwy. 95 south 102 km (64 mi) to Radium Hot Springs, then turn east onto Hwy. 93.

When to Go

Some spring wildflowers appear early in April at the park's west gate, but for better roadside displays wait until July, the warmest month. Daytime temperatures are typically comfortable through most of the park in July and August; nights are usually cool. The west gate area in the Rocky Mountain Trench can be hot.

Hwy. 93 is kept open all winter, plowed and sanded because it is a main highway. Still, the road can be icy after a snowstorm. Marble Canyon is particularly beautiful in the snow, and the hot springs pool is open year-round. The highway can be very busy on Friday evenings and Sunday afternoons, when Calgary weekenders drive to and from their vacation properties in the Rocky Mountain Trench.

How to Visit

A popular approach is to see the park from east to west along Hwy. 93, a distance of 104 km (65 m) from the junction with Trans-Canada 1 to Radium Hot Springs village. Once you've turned off the highway, allow 1.5 hours of driving time through the park and another hour or two for stops at **Marble Canyon** and the **Paint Pots,** plus additional time if you're planning to picnic and take a dip in the hot springs. There are 11 picnicking sites along the road. Restaurant meals, sandwiches, and coffee are available in summer at Kootenay Park Lodge *(www.kootenayparklodge .com)*, km 41.

KOOTENAY PARK HIGHWAY
104 km/65 mi; 1.5 hours

Originally named the Banff-Windermere Road, Hwy. 93 was the first auto route to reach entirely across the Canadian Rockies. It opened in 1920 as a rough gravel track after British Columbia ceded land for the park. The federal government, in exchange, provided money for road construction.

No fuel is available along this road. If you are headed westbound, the last chance for fuel in summer is at Castle Mountain Chalets (turn right at the junction with Trans-Canada 1; *http://castlemountain.com*). In winter, fill up at Banff or Lake Louise. Fuel is always available at Radium Hot Springs village, the end of the tour.

Turn west onto the parkway from Trans-Canada 1 between Banff and Lake Louise. As you crest **Vermilion Pass,** elevation 1,640 m (5,382 ft), you cross from Atlantic to Pacific drainage and from Alberta into British Columbia. In 1968, a forest fire in

this area restarted ecological succession, allowing lodgepole pines
and shrubs to replace the previous
climax forest of spruce and subalpine fir.

Soon the road enters a much
larger and more recently burned area,
in which 158 sq km (39,042 acres),
nearly 11 percent of the park, were
consumed by fire in 2003. Here the
succession is even younger, with
small pines growing rapidly through
a carpet of fireweed. All these fires
were started by lightning. Rather
than replanting the forest or trying to
influence its species makeup by using
chemicals, Parks Canada has allowed
regrowth to occur naturally. The
result is one of the better and more
accessible examples of ecological succession in the Rockies.

Past Marble Canyon, long, bright
green avalanche paths scar the steep
mountain slopes. Snowslides every
winter keep the trees cleared out of
these paths, but alders and other
shrubs survive by bending to let
the snow move by. Ahead looms
the **Rockwall,** a continuous line of
Cambrian limestone cliffs about
600 m (1,969 ft) high. Watch for
blue-white glaciers at the heads of
side drainages.

At **Mount Wardle,** where white
mountain goats often pick their
way along the rocky slopes to
natural mineral licks on the right
(north) side of the highway, the
river punches through the Rockwall.
The road climbs over a knoll and
descends to the wide, gentle valley of
the **Kootenay River,** a major tributary
of the Columbia.

Hwy. 93 follows the Kootenay
southwestward for 28 km (17 mi)
through forests of lodgepole pine
between the craggy **Brisco Range**
on the right (west) and the slabby
Mitchell Range on the left. The road

Ox-eye daisies flourish in Kootenay.

climbs up to the **Kootenay Valley
Viewpoint,** an excellent vantage point
with interpretive signs.

The route then turns west
and crosses wooded **Sinclair Pass**
(1,486 m/4,875 ft). Soon you enter
Sinclair Canyon, the steep, winding
stream course of Sinclair Creek.
Cliffs of brilliantly red Ordovician
rock indicate that you are approaching Radium Hot Springs. The
road passes right by the pool, then
squeezes through the canyon's nar-
rowest point to emerge into the
Rocky Mountain Trench, a 1,500-km-
long (932 mi) valley that marks the
western edge of the Rockies. Past
the park gate you're in the village of
Radium Hot Springs, which offers
food, fuel, and accommodation.

MARBLE CANYON

45 minutes

Marble Canyon is located along
Hwy. 93, 17 km (11 mi) west of the
junction with Trans-Canada 1, and
87 km (54 mi) east of Radium
Hot Springs village. Glacially blue
Tokumm Creek rushes through a
gorge 35 m (115 ft) deep and very
narrow, with a waterfall and natural
bridge at its upper end. The Cambrian
dolostone is similar to limestone but
with magnesium as well as calcium.
A short **interpretive trail** provides

KOOTENAY

KOOTENAY NATIONAL PARK (Parc national Kootenay)

INFORMATION & ACTIVITIES

VISITOR & INFORMATION CENTRE

Kootenay National Park Visitor Centre
7556 Main St. E, Radium Hot Springs, BC
V0A 1M0. Phone (250) 347-9505. Open
May to October.

SEASONS & ACCESSIBILITY

Open year-round. Book accommodations
months in advance if planning a trip in July
or August. Services offered at Radium Hot
Springs Chamber of Commerce (250-347-
9331) late October to early May.

HEADQUARTERS

**Radium Hot Springs Administrative
Office** Phone (250) 347-9615.
www.parkscanada.gc.ca/kootenay.

FRIENDS OF KOOTENAY

Friends of Kootenay National Park
Box 512, Radium Hot Springs, BC
V0A 1M0. Phone (250) 342-6525.
friendsofkootenay@gmail.com;
http://friendsofkootenay.ca.

ENTRANCE FEES

$10 per adult per day, $68 per adult
per year.

PETS

Keep pets on a leash.

ACCESSIBLE SERVICES

Wheelchair accessibility at Visitor Centre;
Kootenay Park Lodge Visitor Centre at
Vermilion Crossing; Radium Hot Springs
Pools; Redstreak, McLeod Meadows, and
Marble Canyon Campgrounds; Redstreak
Theatre; Olive Lake Area picnic site and
interpretive panels; Paint Pots area inter-
pretive trail to mining exhibits; Continental
Divide and Fireweed Trail interpretive
exhibits; and Sinclair Canyon, Kootenay
Valley, and Columbia Valley Viewpoints.

THINGS TO DO

Boating (nonmotorized), canoeing, rafting,
climbing and mountaineering (for conditions, call 250-347-9361), cycling and
mountain biking, fishing (permit $10 per
day, $35 per year), hiking, wildlife view-
ing, photography, camping. Swimming in
the Radium Hot Springs, call (250) 347-
9485 or (800) 767-1611.

---

guardrail-protected views into the
gorge. You may see American dip-
pers here, small brownish grey birds
that hop into the torrents to eat small
water insects.

PAINT POTS

1 to 2 hours return

An easy and very popular interpretive trail (1 km/0.5 mi) leads to three
small **ponds** (the "pots") fed from
deep below by acidic water containing
iron, zinc, manganese, and lead. Iron
oxide in the springwater has perme-
ated the silty soil here, and these red-
ochre deposits have attracted paint-
pigment collectors since prehistoric
times. From the early 1900s into the
1920s, the locality was mined. Water

flows from the Paint Pots into the
Vermilion River, staining the rocks
along one bank red for some distance downstream. The trailhead
lies along Hwy. 93, about 20 km
(12 mi) west of the junction with
Trans-Canada 1.

RADIUM HOT SPRINGS

Radium Hot Springs lies along
Hwy. 93, 3 km (2 mi) east of Radium
Hot Springs village. The water in
the large soaking pool averages 39°C
(102°F), comfortably warm in any
weather. Open year-round, the Parks
Canada facility here also includes a
cool pool for swimming, and lockers, plus Pleiades Massage and Spa
(*www.pleiadesmassage.com*).

SPECIAL ADVISORIES

- To avoid attracting bears and other predators, never leave coolers, pets or pet bowls, dishes, cooking stoves, garbage bags, wash basins, or toiletries unattended.
- Watch for black ice when driving on bridges or near water in winter.
- Be alert for rockfalls in steep terrain in the Rocky Mountains. Do not walk on or beneath overhanging ice or snow.
- Avoid stopping in avalanche zones.
- Do not approach elk, especially females during the May–June calving season and males during the September–October rut.
- Bring clothes and gear for a variety of trail conditions.

OVERNIGHT BACKPACKING

Primitive camping $10 per night. Five campgrounds along the rock wall: **Floe Lake, Numa Creek, Tumbling Creek, Helmet Falls,** and **Helmet Ochre Junction.** Tent pads and bear poles at each site.

CAMPGROUNDS

Four campgrounds, 431 campsites available in peak season (July–Aug.). Campsite day use, fire permit, and dump station $9 per day each. **Redstreak** open May to September. Water, sewer, and electricity $38, electricity only $32, unserviced with washroom (toilets and showers) $27. **McLeod Meadows** open June to September. Unserviced with washroom (toilets only) $22. **Marble Canyon** open June to September. Unserviced with washroom (toilets only) $22. **Crook's Meadow** group campsite open May to October, $6 per person. **Dolly Varden** day-use area open October to May.

HOTELS, MOTELS, & INNS
(unless otherwise noted, rates are for a 2-person double, high season, in Canadian dollars)

Outside the park:
The Prestige Radium Hot Springs 7493 Main St. W, Radium Hot Springs, BC V0A 1M0. (250) 347-2300. www.prestige hotelsandresorts.com. $130–$350.
Windermere Creek B&B Cabins 1658 Windermere Loop Rd., Windermere, BC V0B 2L2. (250) 342-0356 or (800) 946-3942. www.windermerecreek.com. $139–$159.

Additional visitor information:
Radium Hot Springs Chamber of Commerce (250) 347-9331. www.radium hotsprings.com.

EXCURSION

KOOTENAE HOUSE NATIONAL HISTORIC SITE
INVERMERE, BC

A stone monument and interpretive signs mark the location of the first fur-trade post in the Rocky Mountain Trench, built in 1807 by David Thompson of the North West Company and used for only five years. The site is located a short distance north of Invermere on Wilmer Rd., 0.7 km (0.4 mi) north of the intersection between Wilmer Rd. and Toby Creek Rd.

A view of Emerald Lake from the entrance to Emerald Lake Lodge

▶YOHO

BRITISH COLUMBIA
ESTABLISHED 1886
1,289 sq km/318,519 acres

A Cree exclamation of awe, "Yoho" applies perfectly to this park's big peaks, expansive glaciers, and impressive waterfalls. Add Yoho's famous fossils and it's easy to see why this park in the Canadian Rockies is part of a UNESCO World Heritage site. Although many of its highlights are accessible by road, Yoho is also a hiker's dream and a railway buff's delight.

Yoho National Park protects the upper watershed of the Kicking Horse River, a steep, unruly tributary of 53 km (33 mi). Much of the water comes from the Yoho River, ice cold and milky with rock flour from its source at the Wapta Icefield. Many other glaciers feed the Yoho and the Kicking Horse, which thunders over Wapta Falls before rushing through a steep-walled canyon to the Columbia River.

Trans-Canada 1 and the Canadian Pacific Railway follow the Kicking Horse through the heart of the park. Precipitous peaks sporting epaulettes of glacial ice rise more than 1.6 km (1 mi) above the transportation corridor. The highest point in the park is South Goodsir Tower, with a summit elevation of 3,562 m (11,686 ft). A side road leads to world-class Takakkaw Falls. Swollen with glacial meltwater on summer afternoons, the falls plunges 380 m (1,250 ft) to the floor of the Yoho Valley. Other roads lead to appropriately named Emerald Lake.

Among this spectacular terrain lies the Burgess Shale, a layer of half-billion-year-old rock that holds paleontology's most valuable fossils. Specimens are on display at the park information centre.

How to Get There

From Calgary (closest airport), follow Trans-Canada 1 west for 200 km (125 mi) to the small community of Field, near the centre of the park.

From the south, take Hwy. 95 to Golden, then turn east onto Trans-Canada 1 and follow it 60 km (36 mi) to Field.

When to Go

Yoho is accessible and enjoyable year-round. The western valley floors green up in May, and by mid-June the side roads are open. By mid-July the higher trail passes are snow free, and later in the month the alpine wildflowers reach their peak. In late September, subalpine larch rewards visitors with a showy band of gold at tree line. Winter in Yoho, which lasts from November to March, offers Nordic skiing, snowshoeing, ski touring, and world-renowned waterfall ice climbing.

How to Visit

Give yourself a full day to take in the roadside views and enjoy some easy walking. Emerald Lake makes a fine morning destination, with a stop at Natural Bridge en route. Have a stroll at the lake, then head back to Trans-Canada 1, catch some lunch in Field, and keep going east to the Yoho Valley Road for a drive to jaw-dropping Takakkaw Falls, at its best in the late afternoon.

DRIVING ACROSS THE PARK

46 km/28 mi; 1 to 2 hours or
70 km/44 mi to Golden; 2 hours

If you want to drive across Yoho, begin your journey on Trans-Canada 1, at **Kicking Horse Pass,** elevation 1,632 m (5,353 ft). Located 10 km (6 mi) west of Lake Louise at the eastern park boundary, the pass marks the Continental Divide as well as the boundary between Alberta and British Columbia. All water in the park flows to the Pacific.

Ahead of you, the castle-like peak on the left is 3,073-m-high (10,083 ft) **Cathedral Mountain.** Past small **Wapta Lake,** you descend the **Big Hill,** originally a railbed that had by far the steepest grade (4.5 percent) on the Canadian Pacific Railway (CPR). Pull off at the **Spiral Tunnels Viewpoint** to learn how the CPR lowered the grade to 2.2 percent by cutting two semicircular tunnels into the mountain.

Near the base of the hill you will cross the **Kicking Horse River.** Look low on the cliffs to the right to see small entrances to the **Kicking Horse Mine.** The limestone and dolomite rock contains a lead-and-zinc ore deposit that was mined from 1888 to 1952. Having acquired a major tributary from the **Wapta Icefield**—50 sq km (20 sq mi) of glacial ice straddling the divide—the river rushes across gravel flats in many shallow, shifting channels, more evidence of its Ice Age character.

At the turnoff for Field, stop at the **visitor centre** operated jointly by Parks Canada and Travel Alberta (*www.travelalberta.com*). On display are fossils of trilobites and much stranger creatures from the Burgess Shale, science's window on the

YOHO

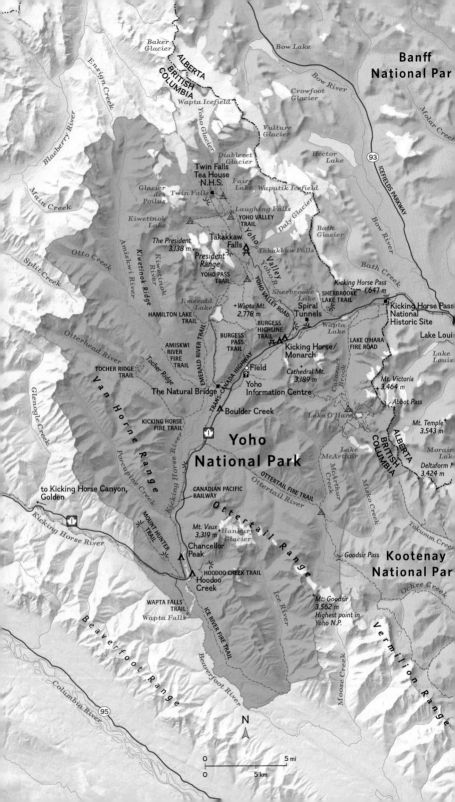

Baker Glacier

Bow Lake

Banff National Par

ALBERTA
BRITISH COLUMBIA

Ensign Creek

Wapta Icefield

Crowfoot Glacier

Bow River

Yoho Glacier

Vulture Glacier

Hector Lake

93

ICEFIELDS PARKWAY

Blaeberry River

Diableret Glacier

Twin Falls Tea House N.H.S.

Fairy Lake

Waputik Icefield

Daly Glacier

Bath Glacier

Bow River

Main Creek

Glacier des Poilus

Twin Falls

Kiwetinok Lake

Laughing Falls

YOHO VALLEY TRAIL

The President 3,138 m

Takakkaw Falls

Takakkaw Falls

Bath Creek

Split Creek

Otto Creek

Kiwetinok Ridge

President Range

YOHO PASS TRAIL

Emerald Lake

Sherbrooke Lake

SHERBROOKE LAKE TRAIL

Kicking Horse Pass 1,647 m

Kicking Horse Pass National Historic Site

HAMILTON LAKE TRAIL

+ Wapta Mt. 2,778 m

Spiral Tunnels

Wapta Lake

Lake Loui

BURGESS HIGHLINE TRAIL

Otterhead River

AMISKWI RIVER FIRE TRAIL

EMERALD RIVER TRAIL

BURGESS PASS TRAIL

LAKE O'HARA FIRE ROAD

Lake Louise

TOCHER RIDGE TRAIL

Tocher Ridge

Kicking Horse/ Monarch

Cataract Brook

Mt. Victoria + 3,464 m

Glenogle Creek

The Natural Bridge

TRANS-CANADA HIGHWAY

Field

Yoho Information Centre

Cathedral Mt. 3,189 m

Abbot Pass

ALBERTA
BRITISH COLUMBIA

KICKING HORSE FIRE TRAIL

Boulder Creek

Lake O'Hara

Mt. Temple 3,543 m

Porcupine Creek

1

Yoho National Park

Lake McArthur

McArthur Creek

Morain Lak

Deltaform 3,424 m

to Kicking Horse Canyon, Golden

1

CANADIAN PACIFIC RAILWAY

OTTERTAIL FIRE TRAIL

Ottertail River

Misko Creek

Kicking Horse River

Kicking Horse River

Mt. Vaux 3,319 m

Hanbury Glacier

Tokumm Cre

MOUNT HUNTER TRAIL

Chancellor Peak

Goodsir Pass

Kootenay National Par

HOODOO CREEK TRAIL

Hoodoo Creek

Ice River

Mt. Goodsir 3,562 m Highest point in Yoho N.P.

WAPTA FALLS TRAIL

ICE RIVER FIRE TRAIL

Wapta Falls

Ochre Creek

Beaverfoot Range

Beaverfoot River

Moose Creek

Vermilion Range

Columbia River

95

N

0   5 mi

0   5 km

Cambrian world. Fuel and snacks are available at Yoho Trading Post opposite the visitor centre.

West of Field, you cross the Kicking Horse River again as it pours noisily into a gorge cut in Cambrian slate. The next time you see the river, however, it will be flowing more placidly westward through a wide U-shaped glacial valley between the big limestone peaks of the **Ottertail Range,** on the left, and the gentler, shaly peaks of the **Van Horne Range** on the right. The water colour has changed to powder blue from dilution by clear tributaries.

Near the western park boundary, the highway turns west and climbs away from the river again. Fifteen km (9 mi) ahead lies **Kicking Horse Canyon,** viewed spectacularly as you drive over the **Park Bridge,** 405 m (1,330 ft) long and 90 m (295 ft) high. At this point, you might as well continue another 13 km (8 mi) to the town of **Golden** in the **Rocky Mountain Trench—**a great valley between the western edge of the Canadian Rockies and the eastern edge of the older Purcell Mountains. Straight-walled and more than 1,500 km (930 mi) long, this is one of the world's great topographic features, queried by the Apollo astronauts as they orbited the moon.

NATURAL BRIDGE & EMERALD LAKE

9.1 km/5.7 mi one way; a half day

About 1.6 km (1 mi) southwest of Field, turn west off Trans-Canada 1 and follow the branch west then north toward Emerald Lake. The opening stretch has some long road cuts in limy Cambrian slate about 510 million years old. If you drive slowly, you may be able to spot the small, wavy-looking folds in the rock. Heat and extreme pressure hardened and deformed these originally flat-lying layers of seabed mud during the building of the Rockies 55 to 100 million years ago.

At **Natural Bridge,** km 2.4, the Kicking Horse River splashes through a bedrock slot roofed in one spot by the slate. A footbridge across the water provides excellent views.

At road's end, **Emerald Lake** itself is dammed by a rockslide heap, now overgrown with tall conifers and home to Emerald Lake Lodge. One look at the water reveals its namesake deep-green glacial colour, photogenic at any time of day.

Directly across the lake lies the glacier-mantled President Range, where the highest summit, **The President,** stands a lofty 3,138 m (10,296 ft). To the right, across the forested gap of **Yoho Pass,** is the high ridge between **Wapta Mountain** and **Mount Field,** site of the Burgess Shale fossils discovery in 1909 (see p. 231). Farthest right is **Mount Burgess** itself, whose craggy image once graced the Canadian $10 bill.

The trail around the lake offers 5.2 km (3.2 mi) of easy walking. Give yourself two hours to enjoy the fragrant spruce and fir forest at this elevation (1,300 m/4,300 ft). You may see three-toed woodpeckers, grouse, red squirrels, a marten, or perhaps even a black bear.

YOHO VALLEY & TAKAKKAW FALLS

13.5 km (8.4 mi) one way; 2 hours

Leave your trailer behind for this drive because it entails two tight switchbacks near the start. Otherwise the road is easy. En route, note the avalanche tracks on the mountainsides. Sliding snow rumbles down

YOHO

Top: Crossing Little Yoho River. Bottom left: Kicking Horse River at Natural Bridge. Bottom right: A rarely seen mountain lion.

these ski-run-like swaths nearly every winter, keeping them clear of trees.

From the parking lots, walk toward the bridge for ever improving views of the falls. "Takakkaw" is another Cree exclamation, this one along the lines of "Magnificent!"

Once across the fast-flowing, green-grey Yoho River, you'll find that the path gets rougher and steeper as you approach the roaring spectacle. The water free-falls for about 254 m (833 ft) out of its 380 m (1,250 ft) total drop over a

cliff of Cambrian limestone. Out of sight above is the water's source: the **Daly Glacier,** part of the **Waputik Icefield,** 15 sq km (5.8 sq mi).

Near the base of the falls you feel fine spray in the air. In late afternoon, with the sun behind you, a standing rainbow makes the scene magical. Closer yet, the waterfall's wind blast turns most people around. That's a good thing because anyone venturing nearer risks being hit by one of the boulders that come crashing down in the torrent.

LAKE O'HARA

11 km/7 mi (accessible only by bus—reservations required—or on foot); a full day

Justifiably popular for its well-built hiking trails and great scenery, uncrowded Lake O'Hara is subject to daily visitor quotas and not accessible to private cars or tour buses. Public transport to the lake runs from mid-June until late September. Call (250) 343-6433 for information.

The bus drops you by the shore, elevation 2,020 m (6,565 ft) and not far below tree line, so be prepared for cool temperatures and cold rain. Upon arrival, you may wish to stroll over to Le Relais Day Shelter, operated by the Lake O'Hara Trails Club, to get the latest information on trail conditions. Le Relais also offers snacks, trail maps, and guidebooks.

The 2.7-km (1.7 mi) **Lakeshore Trail** loop is mostly level, with one climb and descent. **Linda Lake** (3.5 km/2.2 mi one way) is a forest walk with gentle grades, perfect for kids. **Lake Oesa** (3.2 km/2 mi one way) climbs steeply into the rough and spectacular terrain below the continental divide. **Opabin Plateau** (5.9 km/3.7 mi loop) is a moderate hike with steep sections through tree-line meadows.

BURGESS SHALE

9 to 22 km/6 to 14 mi return; a half to full day

Workers building the Canadian Pacific Railway in the early 1880s discovered what they called "stone bugs" (trilobite fossils) in the Field area that attracted the attention of paleontologist Charles Walcott, Secretary of the Smithsonian Institution. In 1909, Walcott found bizarre soft-bodied forms in what he named the Burgess Shale. The quarry he opened and returned to repeatedly, collecting many Cambrian species previously unknown to science, became a World Heritage site in 1980. In 1988, all of Yoho was included in the much larger Canadian Rocky Mountain Parks World Heritage site.

The Burgess Shale is famous enough to tempt fossil thieves, so Parks Canada has made the two more accessible localities off-limits except to groups led by authorized guides. Getting to either place entails a steep hike to higher elevations, where the views are as wonderful as the ancient animal remains in the rock. Contact Parks Canada at (800) 759-2429 or the Burgess Shale Foundation at (800) 343-3006.

HIKING TRAILS & THE RAILWAY

If you enjoy a two-hour walk, do not miss **Wapta Falls,** west of Field. If you are a fit day hiker, visit emerald **Lake O'Hara** and explore the spectacular high-country trails that radiate from the lake. Or spend the day on the aptly named **Iceline Trail,** which takes you through rugged, recently glaciated terrain high on the west wall of the Yoho Valley. Backpackers can include this trail on an overnight circuit, tenting at a secluded backcountry campground in the **Little Yoho Valley.** Mix strenuous exercise and fascinating science on a hike to one of two Burgess Shale locations (see above).

If you love railways, stop at the **Lower Spiral Tunnels Viewpoint,** partway up the long Trans-Canada 1 grade east of Field. Watch the freights enter the tunnels then emerge going the opposite direction on the mountainside.

YOHO

YOHO NATIONAL PARK (Parc national Yoho)

INFORMATION & ACTIVITIES

VISITOR CENTRE
Yoho National Park Visitor Centre
Trans-Canada 1, Field, BC V0A 1G0.
Phone (250) 343-6783. Open year-round.

SEASONS & ACCESSIBILITY
Park open year-round. Reservations
required for Lake O'Hara day use and
camping. Make reservations by telephone
up to three months in advance, (250)
343-6433.

HEADQUARTERS
P.O. Box 99, Field, BC V0A 1G0. Phone
(250) 343-6783. www.parkscanada
.gc.ca/yoho.

FRIENDS OF YOHO
P.O. Box 100, Field, BC V0A 1G0. Phone
(205) 343-6393. info@friendsofyoho.ca;
www.friendsofyoho.ca.

ENTRANCE FEES
$10 per adult per day; $68 per adult
per year.

PETS
Leashed pets permitted but not at
Lake O'Hara.

ACCESSIBLE SERVICES
Multiple disabled-access facilities.
Contact visitor centre for information.

THINGS TO DO
Guided tours of **Burgess Shale fossil
beds** and exhibit at the visitor centre.
Whitewater canoeing and kayaking on the
Kicking Horse River.
Contact the visitor centre for climbing
and mountaineering route descriptions,
and the Association of Mountain Guides
for guided tours (403-678-2885, www
.acmg.ca). Also mountain biking on designated trails, fishing (permits $10 per day,
$34 per year), and hiking. Guided hikes to
Mount Stephen Fossil Beds $50 to $55
per adult, to **Walcott Quarry** $63 to $70.

SPECIAL ADVISORIES
• Never leave coolers, pets or pet bowls,
  dishes, cooking stoves, garbage bags,
  wash basins, or toiletries unattended.
• Watch for black ice when driving.
• Be alert for rockfalls. Do not walk on
  or beneath overhanging ice or snow.
• Avoid stopping in avalanche zones.
• Do not approach elk.
• Prepare for a variety of trail conditions.

OVERNIGHT BACKPACKING
Primitive camping $16. Four camp-
grounds in Yoho Valley: **Laughing Falls,
Twin Falls, Little Yoho,** and **Yoho Lake,**
and **McArthur Creek Campground** in
Ottertail Valley (links to the Rockwall in
Kootenay). Tent pads and bear poles at
all sites.

CAMPGROUNDS
Call visitor centre for campground
availability. Campsite day-use permit
and fire permits $9 per day. **Takakkaw
Falls** (35 sites), **Monarch** (44 sites),
and **Chancellor Peak** (54 sites) walk-in
primitive campgrounds, $18. **Hoodoo
Creek,** 30 sites, unserviced campground
with washroom (toilets only), $22.
Kicking Horse, 88 sites, unserviced
campground with washroom (toilets
and showers), $27.

HOTELS, MOTELS, & INNS
(unless otherwise noted, rates are for a
2-person double, high season, in Canadian
dollars)

Field, BC V0A 1G0:
Cathedral Mountain Lodge Yoho Valley
Rd. (250) 343-6442. info@cathedral
mountain.com; www.cathedralmountain
.com. $224–$386.
Emerald Lake Lodge P.O. Box 10. (403)
410-7417. www.crmr.com. From $109.
Kicking Horse Lodge P.O. Box 174.
(250) 343-6303. oink@trufflepigs
.com; www.trufflepigs.com/the-lodge.
$120–$190.

Lake Louise, AB T0L 1E0:
Lake O'Hara Lodge Lake O'Hara, P.O.
Box 55. (250) 343-6418 or (403) 678-
4110. www.lakeohara.com. $580–$845.

Additional accommodations:
Field, BC www.field.ca.

EXCURSIONS

TWIN FALLS TEA HOUSE NATIONAL HISTORIC SITE
YOHO NATIONAL PARK, BC

Built by the Canadian Pacific Railway to serve its hiking and horseback-riding hotel guests, the log-cabin "teahouses" of the Canadian Rockies are still welcome sights along the trail. The 1908 teahouse at Twin Falls, 8.5 km (5.3 mi) up the Yoho Valley from the trailhead at Takakkaw Falls, is a worthy choice to commemorate them all. (403) 228-7079.

KICKING HORSE PASS NATIONAL HISTORIC SITE
BANFF & YOHO NP, BC

In 1882, the Canadian Pacific Railway chose this pass instead of a much easier route across the Rockies farther north. The length of the line was reduced by 122 km (76 mi), but construction and day-to-day operation proved to be very costly. The site commemoration is found at the Spiral Tunnels Viewpoint along Trans-Canada 1 between Lake Louise and Field.

YOHO

Migrations

A female wolf—captured and radio-collared near Banff, Alberta, in 1992—got everyone thinking about large-scale migration and the role of national parks. Fitted with a satellite transmitter, Pluie, as the wolf came to be known (French for the rain that poured down that June morning), recovered and set off on an epic journey that challenged every boundary drawn on a map.

Wolves are found throughout most of Canada and play an integral part in keeping the ecosystem in balance.

As an ecological imperative, migration is well understood. Animals move in order to find mates, avoid predators, escape diseases, find seasonal foods, recolonize areas swept by fire and flood, and search out safe places to rear their young. Indeed, migration patterns are the reasons behind the establishment of many Canadian national parks over the last 125 years. Point Pelee National Park in southern Ontario, for example, protects a major stopover point for 380 species of migratory birds, and Ivvavik National Park, set aside in 1984 in the northern Yukon, protects the calving grounds of the 120,000-member Porcupine caribou herd. But these are just pieces in a much larger conservation puzzle that, like the individual words in a beautiful poem, hold little value when removed from the larger whole.

What was so impressive about Pluie's journey was its scale: Driven by urges as old as the world itself, she moved from Alberta to Montana to northern Idaho to south-central British Columbia and back again, crisscrossing hundreds of roads, ranches, forests, meadows, rivers, and mountain ranges in the process. Her movements encompassed more than 120,000 sq km (46,332 sq mi), the equivalent of 20 Banff National Parks. It took two years for her to complete her zig-zag journey, and the message it left scrawled across biologists' maps has reverberated through the conservation community ever since: Think Big; Be Bold; Act Now.

Such slogans can't be found directly within Canada's National Parks Act but they exist between the lines, which is why Parks Canada signed a memorandum of agreement with the U.S. Park Service in 1999. Dubbed Y2Y for short, the Yellowstone to Yukon Conservation Initiative puts forth a bold new vision for conservation in North America: Establish and manage national parks and other protected areas not as stand-alone entities but as components in a much larger system of core reserves linked by wildlife corridors.

The focus of Y2Y is the Rockies and the wide-ranging species— like elk, caribou, grizzly bears, wolves, and wolverines—that still roam its many folds. But there are other, equally important reserve network proposals cropping up all over the continent, including Adirondacks to Algonquin (A2A) in the east and Baja to Bering Strait (B2B) along the Pacific Coast.

The role of Canadian national parks within these reserve networks is to preserve the connections critical to the continuation of migratory life. This involves looking both inside and outside park boundaries. The most visible example is the construction of wildlife overpasses and underpasses across Trans-Canada 1 in Banff National Park, but one can also point to the recent sixfold expansion of Nahanni National Park (2009) and the addition of a 3,500 sq km (1,313 sq mi) Marine Conservation Area to Gwaii Haanas National Park Reserve (2010).

Much remains to be done. As temperatures rise due to climate change, not only will animals need to move across borders, but plants will too. Entire forests will need to migrate, seed by seed, to find the cooler environments they require to survive.

The need for continuity and connectivity in our landscapes is more important than ever. As visitors to national parks, we need to take the lessons and inspirations offered by the animals we're lucky enough to see and apply them in our everyday lives. How much wood, oil, gas, and other raw materials we consume and where they come from has a direct impact on the wildlife corridors between national parks.

We need to think big. We need to be bold. And yes, we need to act now.

— KARSTEN HEUER, *seasonal park ranger and author of* Walking the Big Wild

MIGRATIONS

Illecillewaet Valley and the Selkirk Mountains

▶ GLACIER

BRITISH COLUMBIA
ESTABLISHED 1886
1,349 sq km/333,345 acres

Experience the Columbia Mountains—what used to be called the Interior Ranges—of British Columbia in Canada's Glacier National Park. Glacier protects the heart of the Selkirk Mountains, the highest range in the Columbias. Trans-Canada 1 crests the Selkirks at historic Rogers Pass, while the Canadian Pacific Railway punches through far below in the longest standard-gauge train tunnel in the Americas.

Glacier National Park is best known for its deep valleys, thick coniferous forests, and spectacular mountain scenery, all seen by millions annually as they travel Trans-Canada 1 through Rogers Pass. Pyramidal Mount Sir Donald, elevation 3,284 m (10,774 ft), stands nearly 2 vertical km (1.4 mi) above the pass. From the highway you can also see the Illecillewaet Névé (ill-uh-SILL-uh-wet neh-VEIGH), a famous ice field and the best known glacier in the park. The park protects the headwaters of the Illecillewaet, Beaver, and Incompappleux Rivers. The highest point is Mount Dawson at 3,377 m (11,079 ft).

How to Get There

The park is located between Golden and Revelstoke along Trans-Canada 1.

The closest major international airport is at Calgary, 330 km (205 mi) east of Rogers Pass. The highway can be busy in summer, and only half the distance is four-lane divided highway, so budget four to five hours of travel time from Calgary.

When to Go

Trans-Canada 1 is open year-round through the park. From December into May, however, expect short-duration road closures—typically two hours or less—through Rogers Pass for avalanche control. While the valleys at lower elevations may green up in May, and June brings a fine wildflower display, the park receives so much snow that trails at and above tree line can be blocked by snow into July. Alpine wildflowers are at their best in mid-August.

Temperatures at Rogers Pass are often cool in summer (mid-20s°C/mid-70s°F); however, extended hot spells of 30°C (86°F) occur every year. If you're camping or planning to spend the day outside, be prepared for rain and mosquitoes.

How to Visit

It's possible to cover the distance between Golden and Revelstoke in less than two hours, but you'll miss plenty. There are several must-see places along the 45 km (28 mi) of highway through the park, including the Rogers Pass Discovery Centre, the Hemlock Grove Boardwalk Trail, and the summit of Rogers Pass. Your time in the park will be extended by an hour or two, but your travel experience will be much richer.

This park has much to offer hikers, mountaineers, and skiers. Easy loop trails with interpretive signs show off Glacier's big trees and impart railway lore. Steeper, longer trails lead to the high country, where the landscape is Ice Age and so is the weather. Most of the park's trails can be hiked in a day,

and many provide access to classic Selkirk Mountains climbing routes. Several trails have backcountry campsites, but the only multiday backpacking trek in the park is the Beaver River–Copperstain route.

Experienced cavers can explore the Nakimu Caves system with the approval of the superintendent, and a number of guided caving tours are offered during the summer months.

In winter, skiers willing to head up the slopes under their own steam—there are no lifts in the park—can enjoy the park's outstanding wilderness ski routes.

ROGERS PASS
a half day

Centrally located along Trans-Canada 1, the summit area of the pass has the park's only visitor centre. There is also a convenience store here, as well as a hotel with restaurant and cafeteria.

The pass is named for American Albert Bowman Rogers, a retired Army major, civil engineer, and surveyor who was responsible for establishing the route of the Canadian Pacific Railway (CPR) across the country's western mountains. Following a suggestion from an earlier surveyor, Rogers discovered the avalanche-prone pass in 1881.

The railway was built through in 1885. After the deaths of 200 railway workers and countless snowslide delays, however, the CPR gave up on the Rogers Pass in 1911 and blasted the 8-km (5 mi) Connaught Tunnel under it. In 1988, the company completed the Mount Macdonald Tunnel. At 14.7 km (9.1 mi) long, it is the longest standard-gauge tunnel in the Western Hemisphere.

Trans-Canada 1 was completed through the pass in 1962. Several concrete snowsheds (strong-roofed structures that allow snow to slide harmlessly over the road), plus the most thorough avalanche forecasting and control program in the world, have succeeded where the railway could not. Still, the road closes 30 times each winter, on average, for crews to shoot the snow down with artillery before it avalanches on its own.

Try to reach the **Rogers Pass Discovery Centre** well before it closes for the day. Designed to resemble a historic railway snowshed, it offers a multimedia experience, including landscape models, interactive exhibits, and lively theatre programs.

Travelling across the pass in winter, when the highway has been plowed through very deep snow, gives an appreciation of what it takes to keep this nationally important transportation corridor open. Parks Canada's excellent 25-minute film *The Snow War* tells the full story of people versus avalanches in the park. You can view it at the visitor centre.

SHORT SELF-GUIDED TRAILS

Step into the wilderness on one of seven interpretive trails along the highway. The **Hemlock Grove Boardwalk Trail** is located in the western part of the park. A wheelchair-accessible loop of 400 m (0.25 mi), this pleasant stroll takes you through a typical Glacier forest of old-growth western hemlock.

The **Loop Brook interpretive trail**, located 6.4 km (4 mi) west of Rogers Pass, is at Loop Brook Campground. The path threads its way among stone trestle supports built by the CPR to elevate the rails along portions of two adjoining semicircles.

Inquire at the visitor centre about other interpretive trails.

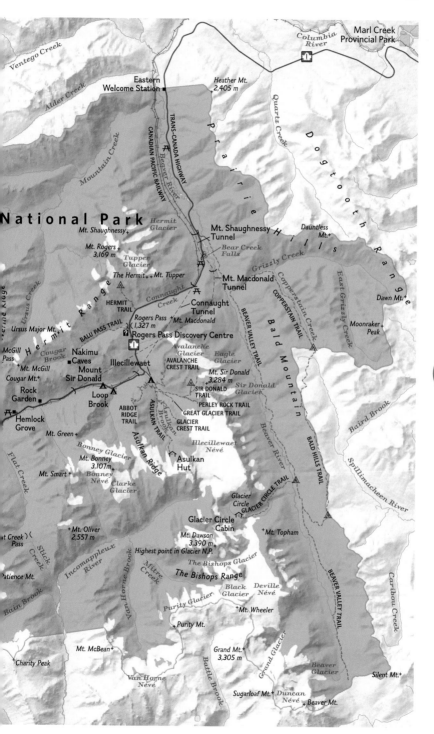

LONGER HIKES

Illecillewaet Campground, located 3.5 km (2.2 mi) west of Rogers Pass, is the jumping-off point for several steep but popular day-hiking trails to exceptional viewpoints. Trail maps and current information are posted at the trailheads. Purchase guidebooks and maps at the visitor centre.

All of Glacier is bear country, so hikers should take proper precautions—make noise, hike with others, keep your dog on a leash, and never approach a bear. The **Balu Valley** is prime grizzly habitat, and hikers are required to walk in groups of four or more. You may find that other trails have been restricted or closed to prevent disturbance of grizzly bears.

BEAVER RIVER BACKPACKING
42 km (26 mi); 3 days

The trailhead for the **Beaver River Trail** is located 10 km (6 mi) east of Rogers Pass along Trans-Canada 1. Expect the wet and muddy trail conditions typical of the backcountry in the Columbia Mountains.

The thickly forested trail functions as a valley-floor trunk route for side trips up to the high country. Considerably tougher, these trips include the **Copperstain Trail** and the **Caribou Pass.** As of 2011, the Beaver River cable car crossing is not operational. Trail access in the upper Beaver Valley (beyond 20 Mile Cabin and including the Glacier Circle Trail) is under review. Check at the visitor centre for up-to-date information about these routes.

CAVING

A cluster of limestone caves is found 5 km (3 mi) northwest of Rogers Pass, near Balu Pass. First described in 1902 and known collectively as the **Nakimu Caves,** the passages total more than 5 km (3 mi). Despite being cold, wet, and dangerous, some of the caves were developed for public tours early in the history of Rogers Pass, when the CPR was maintaining its Glacier House hotel not far away.

After the CPR abandoned Glacier House in 1927, the caves were rarely visited. Nowadays Parks Canada strictly controls access. The caves can only be reached by a circuitous 9-km (5.6 mi) route that avoids the grizzly bear habitat in the Cougar Valley. Persons wishing to enter the caves should inquire at (250) 837-7500 or revglacier.reception@pc.gc.ca.

BACKCOUNTRY SKIING

In an average winter, 9.3 m (31 ft) of snow falls at Rogers Pass, 15 m (49 ft) at higher elevations. With 2 m (6.5 ft) of snow lying on the ground at the pass in February and March, and 3 m (10 ft) or more higher up, it is no wonder that backcountry skiers are attracted to the park. They need to be highly skilled and well equipped, because the weather is often stormy and avalanche danger is a constant concern.

A winter permit system allows backcountry users to enter restricted areas affected by the highway avalanche control program when artillery gunfire is not anticipated. This avalanche control work is conducted to keep the transportation corridor open and does not make the slopes safe for recreation. Anyone travelling into the backcountry in winter must be able to assess avalanche terrain and conditions. Before taking off in winter, check the park website for the most up-to-date information on conditions and permit requirements.

GLACIER NATIONAL PARK *(Parc national des Glaciers)*

INFORMATION & ACTIVITIES

VISITOR CENTRE
Rogers Pass Discovery Centre Phone (250) 837-7500. Opening hours vary by season.

SEASONS & ACCESSIBILITY
Park open year-round. Contact visitor centre for facility openings if planning to visit in spring or fall.

HEADQUARTERS
P.O. Box 350, Revelstoke, BC V0E 2S0. Phone (250) 837-7500. www.parks canada.gc.ca/glacier.

FRIENDS OF GLACIER
Friends of Mount Revelstoke & Glacier National Parks 301-B Third St. W, Revelstoke, BC V0E 2S0. Phone (250) 837-2010. fmrg@telus.net; www.friends revglacier.com.

ENTRANCE FEES
$8 per adult per day; $20 per group per day. Annual passes available.

PETS
Leash all pets. No pets in Balu Pass.

ACCESSIBLE SERVICES
Illecillewaet Campground, Abandoned Rails Trail, and the summit of Rogers Pass Picnic Area accessible June to October. Hemlock Grove Boardwalk is barrier-free with interpretive panels, accessible picnic area, and toilets. All-terrain wheelchair for loan at the Illecillewaet Campground welcome station. Tactile topographical map, low-level viewing scope available year-round at Discovery Centre. Barrier-free facility at Heather Hill welcome station.

THINGS TO DO
Day hikes from Illecillewaet Campground. Backpacking trails. Ski touring in **Rogers Pass,** mountain climbing, and tours of **Nakimu Caves.** For more activities, visit the Discovery Centre. Check website for weather conditions.

SPECIAL ADVISORIES
• Challenging or complex avalanche terrain. A valid winter permit is required to enter restricted areas in the park. For avalanche bulletins call (250) 837-6867.
• Skiers should wear avalanche transceivers and be prepared for self-rescue.
• Compass and navigation skills necessary to hike **Copperstain/Bald Mountain Trail**.
• Rain forest park: be aware of extremes in temperature and precipitation.

OVERNIGHT BACKPACKING
Wilderness pass required (available at Discovery Centre and Illecillewaet Campground). Backcountry campsites: **Copperstain Pass, Caribou Pass, 20-mile, Sir Donald,** and **Hermit.** Open fires not permitted. For information about winter camping and random camping, visit the Discovery Centre. Four backcountry huts: **Sapphire Col Hut, Glacier Circle Cabin, Asulkan Hut,** and **Wheeler Hut.** Contact Alpine Club of Canada (403-678-3200) for reservations.

CAMPGROUNDS
Illecillewaet (60 sites), **Loop Brook** (20 sites), and **Mount Sir Donald** (15 sites) **Campgrounds.**

HOTELS, MOTELS, & INNS
(unless otherwise noted, rates are for a 2-person double, high season, in Canadian dollars)

Inside the park:
Glacier Park Lodge Bag 6000, The Summit at Rogers Pass, Revelstoke, BC V0E 2S0. (250) 837-2126. innkeeper@ glacierparklodge.ca; www.glacierpark lodge.ca. $119–$149.

Outside the park:
Canyon Hot Springs P.O. Box 2400, 7050 Trans-Canada 1, Revelstoke, BC V0E 2S0. (250) 837-2420. www.canyonhotsprings .com. $115–$175.
Heather Mountain Lodge Box 401, Golden, BC V0A 1H0. (250) 344-7490 or (866) 344-7490. www.heathermountain lodge.com. $129.
Purcell Mountain Lodge P.O. Box 1829, Golden, BC V0A 1H0. (250) 344-2639. www.purcellmountainlodge.com. Accessible by helicopter only. $1,820 for 3 nights (includes helicopter travel and meals).

GLACIER

Meadow wildflowers in Mount Revelstoke National Park

▶MOUNT REVELSTOKE

BRITISH COLUMBIA
ESTABLISHED 1914
260 sq km/64,247 acres

The park is best known for its scenic parkway linking the town of Revelstoke with the summit of Mount Revelstoke, which is a surprisingly gentle parkland of tree-line woods and flowery meadows. Short self-guided trails loop through the area, while longer ones reach northeastward toward the park's wilderness peaks and glaciers.

From base to top, Mount Revelstoke rises through 1,500 m (5,200 ft) of topographic relief. Park staff describe the elevational life zones in the park as, lowest to highest, "rain forest, snow forest, and no forest." You can see all three in one short visit.

The panorama from the summit of Mount Revelstoke, summit elevation 1,938 m (6,360 ft), takes in dozens of peaks in the Selkirk and Monashee Ranges of the Columbia Mountains. On a clear day, the view

alone is worth the 26-km (16 mi) drive up the switchbacking Meadows in the Sky Parkway.

At the summit, the park's other great attraction spreads out before you: carpets of wildflowers. Nowhere else in the mountains of western Canada can you step out of your car into subalpine meadows as richly floral as these. Through the course of the summer, which can be condensed to the single month of August in a year with lingering snow, the display changes colour week by week. White anemones, yellow glacier lilies and buttercups, red paintbrush species, and blue lupines put on quite a show.

How to Get There

Trans-Canada 1 runs along the southern edge of the park. The only other road in the park, the Meadows in the Sky Parkway, is accessible from the town of Revelstoke. From Calgary, the closest international airport, follow the Trans-Canada 1 west for 380 km (236 mi) to the turnoff for the Meadows in the Sky Parkway at Revelstoke.

When to Go

The park's low-elevation trails are typically snow free in mid-May, and most facilities are open by Victoria Day. In a typical year, the Meadows in the Sky Parkway is open all the way to the top of Mount Revelstoke by mid-July, but the road cannot be fully opened until the deep summit-area snowpack has melted, which can be as late as the first week in August. Lower elevation sections of the parkway open earlier than the summit portion. The road always closes at Halloween.

From December to May, cross-country skiers can enjoy the first 8 km (5 mi) of the parkway as a track-set trail. Skiers continuing 11 km (6.8 mi) farther can overnight at the Caribou Cabin. Register for the cabin by calling (250) 837-7500 or at revglacier.reception@pc.gc.ca.

How to Visit

If you wish to see the park's high-country wildflowers at their best, visit in the first or second week of August. Weekend traffic on the Meadows in the Sky Parkway can be heavy, so go in mid-week if you can.

The park's wild and extremely rugged northeastern wilderness attracts experienced backcountry travellers. Mountaineers are drawn to the glaciers and granite summits found there. At the other elevational extreme, self-guided loop trails along the Illecillewaet River show off old-growth rain forest and a valley-floor wetland.

MEADOWS IN THE SKY PARKWAY

26 km/16 mi one way; 1 hour

Completed in 1927, the Meadows in the Sky Parkway is the premier attraction in Mount Revelstoke National Park. In addition to taking visitors to the summit of **Mount Revelstoke,** this road also provides access to the historic fire lookout tower there. The parkway opens at 7 a.m. and closes at 10 p.m. in June and July, with shorter hours during the rest of the summer and fall.

The parkway is hard surfaced (chip sealed), with grades any standard vehicle can handle, but it is narrow and there are 16 switchbacks. Trailers and buses are not permitted, and Class A motorhomes are not recommended because the summit parking lots are very small. You can drop your trailer off before reaching the first switchback. Leave it in the parking lot for the **Nels Nelsen Historic Area,** worth visiting for its own sake. Nelsen was a world-champion ski jumper, and the early days of the sport in British Columbia are commemorated here at what was for many years Canada's premier ski-jumping hill.

If you are planning to drive the road early in the summer, check with Parks Canada to see whether it is open. Deep snow can keep the upper

MOUNT REVELSTOKE

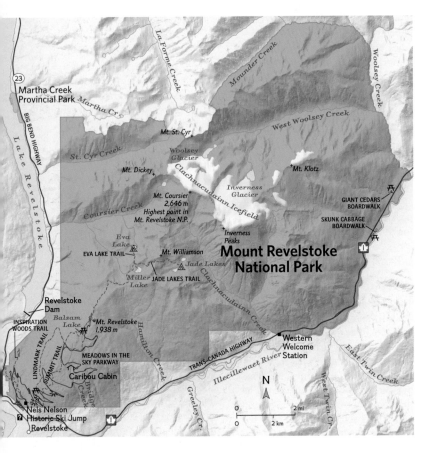

section closed well into July. There is no fuel available on the parkway, so be sure you have enough to make the climb and return to Revelstoke. Nor is food available, but there are picnic tables at three spectacular viewpoints along the way.

To start the drive, take the Trans-Canada 1 bypass around Revelstoke. The turnoff for the parkway is 1.2 km (0.75 mi) east of the intersection of Victoria Road and the highway. The first half of the route is a steady climb through heavy forest, including western redcedar and hemlock, two species characteristic of the wet Columbia Mountains ecosystem. Higher up the views expand, with scenic pull-offs. At km 19, you pass the **Caribou Cabin,** an overnight stop for ski tourers ascending the parkway in winter.

The summit is a particularly photogenic place at sunset, but you'll want to be back through the gate at the lower end before closing time or risk being locked in and having to call the park to let you out.

HIKING

From mid-July to mid-September, a free shuttle service runs the last kilometre (0.6 mi) from the parking lot at the end of the parkway at Balsam Lake to the summit area (10 a.m.–4 p.m.). Or you can walk the pleasant **Summit Trail** to get there.

Bring a sweater with you. It's cool up there, nearly 2 km (more than 1 mi) above sea level. You'll also want mosquito repellent, water, and a jacket to keep the rain and wind off. Guidebooks, maps, and other essentials are on sale at the Balsam Lake Bookstore by the Friends of Mount Revelstoke and Glacier National Parks.

Give yourself an hour or two for exploring the easy interpretive trails that loop through the summit area, especially the popular **First Footsteps Trail,** a 1-km (0.5 mi) loop from **Heather Lake.** The trail features sculptural pieces that evoke the long First Nations history in the Columbia Mountains, and it passes by the **Icebox,** a deep cleft in the rock that holds snow all summer. The **Koo Koo Sint interpretive loop** develops the story of early fur-trade explorer David Thompson. Another trail takes you to the **Historic Firetower,** which has been restored to its original look.

Day hikers can make it to **Eva Lake** and back in a few hours, while backpackers eager to spend the night outdoors can camp at Eva Lake or at the more distant Jade Lakes.

Persons using wheelchairs should contact the park in advance to get permission to take their vehicle up to the shuttle drop-off at Heather Lake. The trail from there to the **Parapets Viewpoints** is fully accessible by wheelchair.

BOARDWALK TRAILS IN THE ILLECILLEWAET VALLEY

En route to or from the park, consider stops at the Giant Cedars Boardwalk Trail and Skunk Cabbage Boardwalk Trail. These short, low-elevation interpretive paths present a striking ecological contrast to the subalpine plant community atop Mount Revelstoke. Both offer picnic areas and flush toilet washrooms.

Near the eastern park boundary, 30 km (19 mi) from Revelstoke, watch for the turnoff to the **Giant Cedars Boardwalk Trail.** As you follow this short loop through peaceful

Visitors at Heather Lake

MOUNT REVELSTOKE

old-growth forest, it's hard to believe that a major highway lies close by. Interpretive signs provide information about British Columbia's interior wet belt. The trees here were seedlings when Christopher Columbus reached the shores of North America.

Located 2 km (1.2 mi) closer to Revelstoke, the **Skunk Cabbage Boardwalk Trail** takes you into a classic Columbian forest marsh, where yellow skunk cabbage, with its enormous leaves, predominates. If you arrive in May, the skunk cabbage may look quite different. Large yellow flower sheaths protect the musty-scented blooms, which come before the leaves. Birds banded here have been tracked to their winter homes in tropical South America.

Top left: Woodland caribou. Top right: Alpine lily. Bottom: The serene summit of Mount Revelstoke in winter.

MOUNT REVELSTOKE NATIONAL PARK
(Parc national du Mont-Revelstoke)

INFORMATION & ACTIVITIES

VISITOR & INFORMATION CENTRE
Parkway Welcome Station On the parkway. Open from mid-May to late October.

SEASONS & ACCESSIBILITY
Park open year-round. Many facilities not accessible in winter. Lower Meadows in the Sky Parkway, Giant Cedars, and Skunk Cabbage open mid-May to late October. Upper parkway open mid-June to early October. Park open for cross-country skiing December to April.

HEADQUARTERS
P.O. Box 350, Revelstoke, BC V0E 2S0. Phone (250) 837-7500. www.parkscanada .gc.ca/revelstoke.

FRIENDS OF MOUNT REVELSTOKE
Friends of Mount Revelstoke & Glacier National Parks 301-B Third St. W, Revelstoke, BC V0E 2S0. Phone (250) 837-2010. fmrg@telus.net; www.friends revglacier.com.

ENTRANCE FEES
$8 per person, $20 per group per day; $29 to $39 per person, $74 to $98 per group per year.

PETS
Pets must be on a leash at all times.

ACCESSIBLE SERVICES
West Welcome Station, Monashee picnic area, Balsam Lake day-use area, and Heather Lake day-use area are wheelchair accessible.

THINGS TO DO
Hiking on self-guided trails (**Giant Cedars, Skunk Cabbage, Meadows-in-the-Sky**); cycling on Trans-Canada 1, **Meadows in the Sky Parkway,** and trails at the foot of Mount Revelstoke.

The Moonlight Ski and Moonlight Drive are special events in January and September respectively. Celebrate the Summit in August is a mountaintop children's festival that includes an evening of stargazing and meteor-watching.

SPECIAL ADVISORIES
• Open fires not permitted except in Monashee Lookout fireplace.
• Rain forest park: be aware of extremes in temperature and precipitation.

OVERNIGHT BACKPACKING
Eva Lake and **Jade Lakes** backcountry campsites, with tent pads, outhouses, and food storage poles. Wilderness pass required (available at Parkway Welcome Station and park headquarters).

CAMPGROUNDS
There are no frontcountry (vehicle accessible) campgrounds. **Blanket Creek Provincial Park,** 63 campsites (30 reservable), open May to September. Call (800) 689-9025. **Martha Creek Provincial Park,** 25 vehicle accessible campsites and 3 tent pads, open May to September. First come, first served. **Caribou Cabin,** open in winter only, is ski accessible. Call park office to reserve. **Canyon Hot Springs** serviced (power and water) and nonserviced sites.

HOTELS, MOTELS, & INNS
(unless otherwise noted, rates are for a 2-person double, high season, in Canadian dollars)

Revelstoke, BC V0E 2S0:
Courthouse Inn B&B 312 Kootenay St., Box 3180. (250) 837-3369 or (877) 837-3369. info@courthouseinnrevelstoke .com; www.courthouseinnrevelstoke.com. $140–$179.
The Hillcrest Hotel Box 1979. (250) 837-3322. www.hillcresthotel.com. $159–$239.
Inn on the River (B&B) 523 Third St. W, P.O. Box 1284. (250) 837-3262. www .innontheriverbc.com. $150–$250.
The Nelsen Lodge 2950 Camozzi Rd. (250) 814-5000. www.sandmansignature .com. $345–$800.

For additional accommodations:
See Glacier National Park (p. 241).

PACIFIC RIM

Page 248: top, Hiking on the West Coast Trail in Pacific Rim; middle, A herring boat at twilight in the Gulf Islands; bottom, Hiking above Kathleen Lake in Kluane. Page 249: Winter in Kluane National Park.

PACIFIC RIM

The four national park reserves in the Pacific Rim region stretch from Yukon's Kluane with its giant ice fields, south to Gulf Island, where small islands between Vancouver Island and the mainland bask in the sun. Kluane National Park and Reserve offers spectacular views of mountains and glaciers. Gwaii Haanas National Park Reserve and Haida Heritage Site, ranging across forested islands almost 500 miles north of Vancouver, allows visitors

Above: Relaxing at East Point, Saturna Island, in Gulf Islands National Park Reserve, a couple enjoys the sunrise over Boundary Passage, which separates the island from the San Juan Islands in the United States.

to see the villages and archaeological sites of the Haida people as well as unique subspecies of wildlife and vegetation. A sliver of land and islands west of Vancouver Island, Pacific Rim National Park Reserve boasts a pristine beach, waterways for kayakers, and a challenging rain forest hike. Gulf Islands encompasses meadows, hills, and headlands with rare vegetation; its waters are home to seals, sea lions, and killer whales.

A watery playground, the Gulf Islands offer a wealth of ecological and cultural attractions.

▶ GULF ISLANDS

BRITISH COLUMBIA
ESTABLISHED 2003
62 sq km/15,321 acres (36 sq km/8,896 acres on land and water; 26 sq km/ 6,425 acres of adjacent marine area)

Nurtured by a unique Mediterranean climate, Gulf Islands National Park Reserve supports a stunning diversity of rare bird-, plant, and marine life spread across 15 islands and innumerable islets and reefs in the northern reaches of the inland Salish Sea.

There's no gate or interpretive centre at this national park reserve: Much of the nearly 36-sq-km park is spread over 699 sq km (270 sq mi) of sheltered ocean separating mainland Vancouver from the city of Victoria on Vancouver Island, and some of it is under water. Much of the park is located on the bigger southern Gulf Islands, including Saturna, North and South Pender, and Mayne.

The abundant marine life, climate, and physical beauty of this archipelago—protected in the rain shadow of two mountain chains—have attracted people for more than 5,000 years. First were the Coast Salish, thriving on the bountiful shellfish, plants, and game; Spanish explorers followed, adding their names on waterways and islands. The British joined the Hawaiians and other Europeans as pioneer farmers, clearing great swaths of the forest to plant apple orchards and graze sheep.

The latest wave of settlers—mostly artists, seasonal cottagers, and retirees—have created enormous new development pressures across the southern Gulf Islands in the later part of the 20th century and into the 21st, threatening the endangered ecosystems found only in this microclimate, including the multitude of rare life-forms associated with the meadows and rocky outcrops occupied by the Garry oak, British Columbia's only native oak. The demand for waterfront property has also threatened the last critical habitats for fish, seals, sea lions, and killer whales.

In 2003, Canada's federal government gathered together a patchwork of existing ecological reserves, provincial parks, and newly acquired lands under the banner of a national park reserve. The park reserve remains a work in progress, with new acquisitions ongoing.

How to Get There

There is regular car/passenger ferry service (BC Ferries) to the larger southern Gulf Islands throughout the year from Swartz Bay (near Victoria) and the Tsawwassen ferry terminal accessible from Vancouver. The rest of the parklands and marine protected waters open to the public are only reachable via private means—passenger ferry, water taxi, boat, or even kayak.

When to Go

The dry, warm season between June and early October is the best time for most activities in the park. Services and some park access are limited in the winter.

How to Visit

In the absence of visitor centres, the Parks Canada website provides maps and information about hiking routes, boating, and other activities.

If you have only one day, take a car ferry to Saturna Island, the biggest and least developed of the southern Gulf Islands with national park land on them. Home to about one-third of the park's total land area, it offers short trails, day-use areas, and some of the most commanding views in the region. Accommodations are limited; book ahead if you want to stay overnight, especially in summer. There are no reservable campsites on Saturna Island.

For a very popular but no less spectacular view of the park, spend a second day exploring Sidney Spit on Sidney Island, wandering the beautiful sandy beaches, forests, and meadows.

Note: There are no garbage cans throughout the park: Pack out what you pack in. Bring your own drinking water, too, as it is in short supply during summer across the Gulf Islands.

GULF ISLANDS

Bald eagle (*Haliaeetus leucocephalus*)

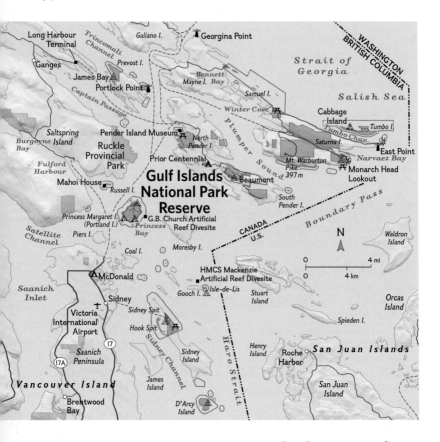

SATURNA ISLAND

a full day

Largely undeveloped and home to just 350 people, **Saturna Island** provides visitors with a glimpse of what the Gulf Islands were like a hundred years ago.

To stand atop **Mount Warburton Pike**—at 397 m (1,303 ft) the second highest peak in the park—take East Point Road from the ferry terminal for about 2 km (1.25 mi), turning right onto Harris Road for about five minutes; a left turn onto Staples Road, a steep winding gravel route, will take you to the top, named for a British explorer and author who bought several large parcels on the island in the 1880s to farm sheep.

On a clear day you can see from Victoria's Oak Bay to the Olympic Mountains and the San Juan Islands in the east. Directly across Plumper Sound is **South Pender Island.** From this vantage point falcons, eagles, and feral goats are common sights—the latter have roamed wild on Saturna Island for more than a century, descendants of livestock kept by early settlers.

Now backtrack to the junction of East Point Road and Narvaez Bay Road, turn right, and follow Narvaez Bay Road to its end, where there is parking for a short trail down to stunning Narvaez Bay, named for Spanish explorer José María Narváez, who captained the naval schooner *Santa Saturnina* (thus the island's name) through these waters in 1791.

One of the most beautiful little bays in the park, **Narvaez Bay** penetrates for almost 2 km (1.25 mi) into the island's southeast shore. Walk down the former driveway past the bike rack for about 1 km (0.5 mi), through to the field at the bottom—turn left and walk down to the campsites and the bay. Narvaez Bay is remote and secluded, except for the odd sailboat that anchors in its protected clear green waters. Be cautious on the cliff edges and rocky promontories, particularly if it is wet.

The easiest way to get to the **Monarch Head lookout** at the head of the bay is to walk about 40 m (130 ft) up Narvaez Bay Road from the parking lot and take the trail on the left (two large rocks mark the trail). Follow the trail until it comes out into a small clearing, then follow the signs up another little logging road; the route is steep, but it only takes about ten minutes to hike up

to the lookout. From atop the bluff, watch for killer whales and porpoises in **Boundary Pass,** amid the busy shipping lane and boat traffic using the nearby international border.

Exploration of the western Saturna parklands begins with a hike to **Boat Passage** in **Winter Cove,** a picturesque, sheltered spot that is a popular day-use area, especially with private boaters. From Narvaez Bay Road, turn right on East Point Road, then left on Winter Cove Road, then take the first right, which will take you into the national park at Winter Cove. Here a gravel-groomed trail (about 1.6 km/1 mi round-trip) loops through Douglas-fir and red alder forests to the water. If possible, time your visit close to low tide: That's when the currents pushing between the point and Samuel Island create fast-flowing rapids.

To get back to the parking lot, follow the loop trail that parallels the shoreline around two saltwater lagoons and follow the boardwalks back to the trailhead.

GULF ISLANDS

As dusk falls, kayaks lie at rest on the southwest side of Princess Margaret Island. Sea kayaking is one of the best ways to explore the Gulf Islands, offering an intimate experience with nature.

East Point, on the far eastern tip of the island, is home to an automated light station and restored fog alarm/heritage centre. It also offers close proximity to an offshore marine oasis that regularly attracts killer whales, sea lions, and seals.

Follow East Point Road for 10 km (6.2 mi) (it eventually becomes Tumbo Island Road), much of it with ocean views, to the road's terminus. Walk through an open grassy field to the restored **1938 Saturna fog alarm building**—the island's most photographed building. A local historical group hosts a heritage centre here, detailing local island history and the nautical feats of the Spanish explorers who "discovered" the island.

A five-minute walk takes you to the tip of East Point, where on a clear day, spectral Mount Baker rises in the northeast—an active volcano almost 3,353 m (11,000 ft) high in Washington's nearby North Cascades—looming above all else. Arrive at low tide, when the flow of water rushing through **Tumbo Channel** is at its greatest—and behold the water accelerating to up to 14 knots—so fast that it is audible.

The unusual concentration of marine life here is the result of the upwelling and collision of nutrient-rich currents: Just offshore, the waters of Boundary Pass, the Strait of Georgia, and Washington's Puget Sound collide. The aptly named **Boiling Reef,** situated in the midst of this aquatic chaos, is a resting place for seabirds and a haul-out for seals (year-round) and sea lions (fall to spring). Resident and transient killer whales, which patrol these waters between spring and fall, often appear along the cliff immediately below the light station, seemingly so close one could jump on their backs as they swim by.

Across the water from the point is **Tumbo Island,** now a park property. Bring binoculars, and look upon one of the best examples of pristine Garry oak grassland meadow, an ecosystem endemic to this region; this is what a Garry oak ecosystem would have looked like 150 years ago.

SIDNEY & HOOK SPITS
1 to 2 days

At the northern end of Sidney Island, in Haro Strait, you will find Sidney Spit along with the hook spit, the main attractions of this 4 sq km (990 acres) chunk of park reserve.

Through time Sidney Island has been used by humans for First Nations clam harvesting, as a brick factory, then later a provincial and now federal park. Most of the island is still in private hands.

A private 12-m (40 ft) passenger ferry travels the 3.7 km (2 nautical mi) between the town of Sidney on Vancouver Island and Sidney Island from May to September (call for times; Alpine–Sidney–Spit Ferry 250-474-5145). There is pay parking at the Sidney Pier Hotel or Port Sidney Marina, from which you can walk in two minutes to Beacon Pier dock; remember to pack snacks and water.

The ferry lands at a day-use area situated at the base of **Sidney Spit**—a thin, white arm of sand that reaches more than 2 km (1.2 mi) into Haro Strait; you can walk its entire length, right to the light beacon at the point.

Hook Spit—a second spit that is equally long—is located to the west, curling into a hook creating a lagoon. This inner lagoon is closed to boating in order to protect the sensitive eelgrass beds, which provide important bird and fish habitat. Hiking is permitted on the outside of Hook Spit, provided visitors stay out of the vegetated area and walk along the beach. The inner lagoon side of the spit is a special preservation area; there is no access.

Because the lagoon is situated on the Pacific flyway, migratory birds use it as a stopover for their spring and fall migrations; in all, at least 150 species of resident and migratory birds can be seen here—including bald eagle, great blue heron, purple martin, and multiple species of grebe and cormorant.

To explore the spit, take the 2-km (1.2 mi) loop trail (about 40 minutes to complete) that can be picked up directly from the day-use area at the ferry dock and follow it through Douglas-fir and arbutus forests heavily thinned by the island's very large population of fallow non-native deer. These small, reddish-coloured deer (the males often display impressive palmated antlers) were likely brought to the island in the early 1900s, where they have thrived ever since without predators. Each winter since 2005, the park closes for several months to facilitate a First

Nations hunt for the invasive deer on Sidney Island.

Follow the trail along the eastern edge of the island; a staircase leads down to a beautiful eastward view facing the United States at **East Beach.** Continue on the trail; at the campground the route loops back across toward the lagoon, where you will approach a large clearing. It is a gathering point for large herds of deer. (Remember: It is a federal offence to disturb the deer.) The trail passes an old ranger station and returns to the ferry dock.

Pink seablushes and purple camas carpet a meadow.

GULF ISLANDS

Steller sea lions

GULF ISLANDS NATIONAL PARK RESERVE
(Réserve de parc national des Îles-Gulf)

INFORMATION & ACTIVITIES

HEADQUARTERS
Sidney Operations Centre 2220 Harbour Rd., Sidney, BC V8L 2P6. Phone (250) 654-4000 or (866) 944-1744. www.parkscanada.gc.ca/gulf.

SEASONS & ACCESSIBILITY
Sidney Operations Centre open weekdays, year-round.

ENTRANCE FEES
No entry fee.

THINGS TO DO
Kayaking, powerboating, and whale-watching. Road cycling, hiking, beach walking.

You can picnic in **Winter Cove** or **East Point** on Saturna Island, **Sidney Spit** on Sidney Island, or **Roesland** on North Pender Island.

Interpretive programs offered on Saturna, Mayne, Sidney, Russell, and Pender Islands from June to early September. Naturalist presentations are given on some ferry rides.

SPECIAL ADVISORIES
- Bring water supplies and containers for packing out garbage.
- No bike lanes or paved shoulders for cyclists on Saturna, Mayne, and Pender Islands. Cycling on park trails not allowed.
- Visitors should remain on designated hiking trails.
- Consult the Canadian Hydrographic Service website *(www.charts.gc.ca)* for tide timetables before visiting tide pools.

CAMPGROUNDS
Backcountry campgrounds with tent pads or tent platforms and pit or composting toilets are available on **Cabbage Island;** at **Narvaez Bay** on Saturna Island; **D'Arcy Island; Isle-de-Lis; Portland Island; James Bay** (Prevost Island), accessible by water only; and **Beaumont** (South Pender). Camping at **Sidney Spit** is accessible by seasonal foot passenger ferry from **Sidney** (Vancouver Island). For schedule and fee information call (250) 654-4000. **Beaumont, Cabbage Island, Narvaez Bay** campgrounds and **Sidney Spit** open mid-May to late September. **D'Arcy Island, Isle-de-Lis,** and **James Bay** campgrounds open June to late September. For group camping reservations, contact the park office at (866) 944-1744.

Mooring buoys at **Sidney Spit, Beaumont,** and **Cabbage Island** are $10 per night, 14-day maximum stay. Vehicle accessible camping is available at **McDonald Campground** (mid-May–early Oct.) on Vancouver Island and at **Prior Centennial Campground** (May–early Oct.) on Pender Island; reservations can be made by contacting the Parks Canada Reservation System at (877) 737-3783 or www.pccamping.ca.

Camping fees are $14 per party or $5 per person in backcountry campsites. Call park office for special rates and group campsite reservations. Visit park website for updated fees.

HOTELS, MOTELS, & INNS
(unless otherwise noted, rates are for a 2-person double, high season, in Canadian dollars)

Outside the park:
Saturna Island, BC V0N 2Y0:
Saturna Lodge 130 Payne Rd. (250) 539-2254. innkeeper@saturna.ca; www.saturna.ca. $120–$170.

Sidney, BC:
Beacon Inn at Sidney 9724 Third St., Sidney by the Sea, V8L 3A2. (250) 655-3288 or (877) 420-5499. info@beaconinns.com; www.thebeaconinn.com. $150–$260.
Cedarwood Inn & Suites 9522 Lochside Dr., V8L 1N8. (250) 656-5551 or (877) 656-5551. info@thecedarwood.ca; http://thecedarwood.ca. $125–$425.
Sidney Waterfront Inn & Spa 9775 First St., V8L 3E1. (250) 656-1131 or (888) 656-1131. stay@sidneywaterfrontinn.com; www.sidneywaterfrontinn.com. $135–$314.

EXCURSIONS

GULF OF GEORGIA CANNERY NATIONAL HISTORIC SITE
RICHMOND, BC

In Steveston, Canada's busiest fishing community, the 1894 Georgia Cannery has been transformed into an interactive museum dedicated to Pacific salmon and the history of the west coast fishing industry. Experience how European, Chinese, Japanese, and native fishermen and workers caught and processed mountains of Fraser River salmon through interpretive tours, thousands of artifacts, images, and a restored (and still noisy) canning line. Open daily. (604) 664-9009.

FISGARD LIGHTHOUSE NATIONAL HISTORIC SITE
COLWOOD, BC

Perched at the tip of a causeway jutting into the sea, Fisgard Lighthouse has been a homeward beacon to mariners plying the turbulent waters of the Juan de Fuca Strait since 1860. Explore the museum housed in the former keeper's residence next door—one of the oldest homes in the city of Victoria—where visitors can enjoy colourful interactive exhibits. Abundant wildlife and stunning views of Washington's Olympic Mountains complete the experience. (250) 478-5849.

FORT RODD HILL NATIONAL HISTORIC SITE
COLWOOD, BC

This intact 1890s British artillery fort was designed to protect the Royal Navy base at Esquimalt Harbour and the city of Victoria from naval attack. Visitors can explore underground magazine complexes, walk the original ramparts of three gun batteries, and examine original artillery pieces. Interpretive displays and summer historical reenactments (including the "Firepower" weapons demo) show how technology and perceived enemies shifted right up to 1956, the year the fort closed. (250) 478-5849.

Inviting white sand beaches stretch for miles at Pacific Rim National Park.

▶ PACIFIC RIM

BRITISH COLUMBIA
ESTABLISHED 1970
512 sq km/126,500 acres

Few people forget the first time they walk out onto seemingly infinite Long Beach, a 16-km (10 mi) strip of undeveloped coastline set against a backdrop of lush emerald rain forest and distant mountains. One of Canada's most visited tourist attractions, the beach attracts surfers, beachcombers, and marine life enthusiasts.

Skirting the western fringe of Vancouver Island, Long Beach is the most northern of three park units, a 141-sq-km (34,800 acres) chunk of beach-fronted coastal temperate rain forest, and since 2000, a core protected area of the Clayoquot Sound UNESCO World Biosphere Reserve. Unknown to the world before 1959, when a road was punched across the width of Vancouver Island, the beach became an end-of-world refuge for draft dodgers, hippies, and surfers until 1970, when the beach settlements were evicted for the new national park. Much of the laid-back vibe of that earlier era remains. The shoreline stretches roughly between the town of Tofino in the north and Ucluelet in the south.

Directly to the east of Ucluelet are the Broken Group Islands—an archipelago of more than a hundred tiny, rugged islands at the centre of Barkley Sound, a popular kayak destination. Only about 16 sq km (3,950 acres) of land is found across the 107 sq km (26,440 acres) of ocean park area; this maze of waterways and channels is accessible by watercraft only.

The southernmost area is the 264 sq km (10,130 acres) West Coast Trail unit, named for the 75-km (47 mi) hiking path through pristine rain forest between Port Renfrew and Bamfield. The trail was established in 1907 as an emergency rescue path for shipwrecked mariners after 120 people died when the *Valencia* ran aground on a reef near Pachena Point during a gale.

The unifying elements of these three different units are water, rain forest, and the native Nuu-chah-nulth culture. Present in the Pacific Rim area for thousands of years, these master mariners and whale hunters utilized the natural resources for trade and sustainability and often battled the waves of Spanish then British (and later Americans) who descended on the coast in the late 18th century to exploit furs, timber, and whale oil. Today 7 of 15 Nuu-chah-nulth tribes maintain at least 22 small reserves within the park boundaries and 9 at the border of the park; they are active partners in park administration and interpretive programs.

How to Get There

Long Beach is the only one of the park's three units that can be explored by car—and you will need one. From Victoria: travel northwest on Hwy. 19, take the Hwy. 4 exit about 34 km (21 mi) past Nanaimo. *(Hwy. 4 is beautiful but dangerous: It has steep grades, little room for passing, and traffic congestion in the summer.)* Budget three hours for the drive from Nanaimo. From Vancouver, take a ferry from West Vancouver's Horseshoe Bay ferry terminal to Nanaimo and proceed to Hwy. 4.

A right turn at the Tofino–Ucluelet junction leads to the Long Beach area. The highway runs through the park for 22.5 km (14 mi), with the town of Tofino at its end.

When to Go

For most activities at Long Beach, visit between June and Labour Day. (Book ahead for accommodation during this time.) For storm-watching and advanced surfing, the winter is best—fearsome winter gales can rip this coastline, conjuring waves 8 m (26 ft) high, and dropping up to 48 cm (19 in) of rain in a single day. The West Coast Trail is open between May and late September.

How to Visit

Most visitors stay for longer than a day, basing themselves in Tofino or Ucluelet. If a day is all you have, focus on **Long Beach**—roughly between the Tofino-Ucluelet junction and Wickaninnish Beach—where rain forest hikes, beach and tide-pool exploration, and a surf lesson will easily fill a day.

Spend a second day whale-watching and exploring the northern reaches of the park: Walk the sand dunes and tidal pools in **Schooner Cove** and look for wildlife in the sheltered, kayak-friendly **Grice Bay.** End the day with a dinner and walkabout in **Tofino** or **Ucluelet** (just beyond the northern park boundary), the best bases of operations for any park visit.

The weeklong **West Coast Trail** requires both advanced backcountry experience and substantial advance planning. The best way to see the **Broken Group Islands** is by boat. The Port Alberni–based M.V. *Frances Barkley,* a 120-foot passenger ferry, offers day trips through the islands June through mid-September *(www .ladyrosemarine.com/index.html).*

PACIFIC RIM

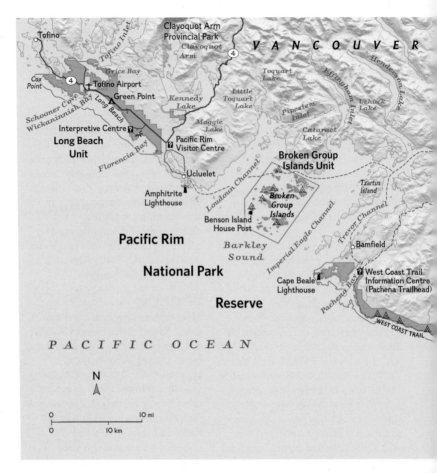

PACIFIC RIM HIGHWAY

Tofino–Ucluelet Jct. to North Long Beach; about 15 km/9 mi; at least a full day

Start at the **Pacific Rim Visitor Centre** at the Tofino–Ucluelet junction for maps, suggestions for tours and activities, and tide tables, then drive 5 km (3 mi) to the turnoff to the Kʷisitis Visitor Centre, which stands about 3.5 km (2 mi) away, at the end of the road.

Wickaninnish Bay and **Beach** are named after the great Clayoquot chief of the late 18th century, who traded local sea otter pelts, then in great

demand in Asia, with the Americans and British. The **Kʷisitis Visitor Centre** offers exhibits, films, and interpretive information about Nuu-chah-nulth culture and history, rain forest ecology, and the diversity of marine life found on the coast.

To explore the sand dunes at **Wickaninnish Beach,** set out northwest along the beach in front of the visitor centre and walk for some 10 to 15 minutes toward **Combers Beach.** The dunes here are the highest in the area, towering to 27 m (88 ft), running a length of about 3 km (2 mi). In summer, even if the winds that rip the beach are quite cool, the dunes

The warmest the water ever gets is about 14°C (57°F)—so the best way to get in the water (and best vantage point of the entire beach) is on a surfboard. There are at least four private surf schools between Tofino and Ucluelet that provide friendly novice instruction, including a wet suit and board rental. Instructors will take students to waters that are relatively shallow, with smaller swells (3-m/10-ft swells are common in summer). Many beginners succeed in standing up on their first day.

Step back from the shore at the **Shoreline Bog Trail;** the trailhead is about 300 m (1,000 ft) south of the Florencia Bay turnoff. This 800-m (2,625 ft) boardwalk trail loops through one of the wettest areas of the park—coastal bog, which accounts for about 5 percent of the forested Long Beach area. Rain forest species like western redcedar and hemlock grow grudgingly in this acidic soil; shore pine does better, some hundreds of years old, their grey limbs topped with vivid green tufts. (Self-guided walking pamphlets are usually at the trailhead.)

Drive back to Hwy. 4 and turn left; drive about 4 km (2.5 mi) to the **Rainforest Trail** (about 6.4 km/ 4 mi northwest from the Pacific Rim Visitor Centre). This interpretive loop trail consists of two 1-km (0.6 mi) loops on either side of Hwy. 4, leading beneath a canopy of breathtaking 800-year-old redcedars, 300-year-old hemlock, and amabilis fir.

GRICE BAY TO TOFINO
about 12 km/7.5 mi; at least a full day

Pacific Rim National Park falls along a migratory route for Pacific grey and humpback whales, and its coastal waters are also frequented

are always several degrees warmer. (Dress in layers; be prepared for rain, even in summer.)

To explore the intertidal zone, walk ten minutes southeast from the centre: Walk out on the rocks as far as the tide allows. Time your exploration for low tides: The difference between low and high tide can be as much as 4 m (14 ft). Tide-pool denizens include big purple and yellow ochre sea stars, sea palm algae, and giant green sea anemones, as well as raucous seagulls, harlequin ducks, and black oystercatchers. (While exploring, watch your footing and incoming waves, as well as the tide.)

Salal (*Gaultheria shallon*)

offshore; they make for interesting tide-pooling at low tide.

Walk to the far north end of this 2-km-long (1.25 mi) beach, where a system of sand dunes stretches about 470 m (1,500 ft) behind the beach.

The tidal mudflats at **Grice Bay** offer a glimpse of a more protected marine environment—and a spectacular stopover for the enormous number of migratory waterfowl travelling the Pacific flyway, one of four major migratory routes for North American birds. From the Schooner Cove parking lot, follow the highway north to the turnoff for the Grice Bay public boat launch.

There are no hikes or trails along this sensitive shoreline. The best way to bird-watch is from a canoe or kayak, or with a spotting scope from the boat launch. The absence of large waves and rocky reefs makes this a sheltered spot for a relaxing paddle—but not during low tide, when the shallow bay transforms into a mudflat.

Winter provides the best opportunities to see the greatest numbers and diversity of birds: Huge numbers of Canada geese, trumpeter swans, and ducks by the thousands descend on the flats, including mallards, buffleheads, and goldeneyes. (April and May are also a good time to see ducks and a variety of sandpipers in the thousands.) Great blue herons favour the tidal shallows as a summer hunting ground; bald eagles are regulars; and the bottom-feeding Pacific grey whales come into the bay to feed on ghost shrimp, although their presence is not consistent year to year.

End your day in **Tofino:** The quality (and laid-back friendliness) of the indie coffee shops, bakeries, art galleries, and resort restaurants is widely renowned. A walk through the downtown core takes half an hour.

by killer whales. Pacific grey whales and humpbacks are a common sight from March to late October; transient killer whales can be seen alone or in pods year-round. Harbour sea lions, seals, and porpoises are year-long residents as well.

Boarding a private whale-watching boat for what is usually a three-hour tour is the best way to see any combination of the marine mammals. The park visitor centres can provide information on the tours and a listing of companies that offer them.

Back on dry land, **Schooner Cove** is the most northerly beach in the national park, easily accessed at low tide by a 1-km (0.6 mi) hike from the Schooner Cove parking lot (4.8 km/3 mi north of Green Point Campground on Hwy. 4). The hike down to the beach winds through a mixed cedar/hemlock forest, passing a small salmon stream along the way.

Emerging at the beach at low tide, turn right and walk north up and around the jutting point of land. About 1 km (0.6 mi) up the beach, a series of small rocky islets lie just

PACIFIC RIM NATIONAL PARK RESERVE
(Réserve de parc national Pacific Rim)

INFORMATION & ACTIVITIES

HEADQUARTERS
2040 Pacific Rim Hwy., P.O. Box 280, Ucluelet, BC V0R 3A0. Phone (250) 726-3500. www.parkscanada.gc.ca/pacificrim.

SEASONS & ACCESSIBILITY
Pacific Rim Visitor Centre, Kʷisitis Visitor Centre, Pachena Bay Information Centre, and Green Point Theatre Programs open seasonally. West Coast Trail closed October to May. See park website for up-to-date seasons and hours of operation.

ENTRANCE FEES
Fees vary. See park website for current information.

PETS
No pets permitted at walk-in sites.

THINGS TO DO
Birding and fishing (licence required). Nightly presentations from late June to early September at indoor theatre in **Green Point Campground. Long Beach Unit:** Walking along 10 km (6 mi) of trails and kayaking in **Grice Bay.** Consult Fisheries & Oceans Canada for tide time-tables *(www .lau.chs-shc.gc.ca).* **Broken Group Islands:** Boating and kayaking. **West Coast Trail:** Hiking and the School Discovery Program ($55 per student).

SPECIAL ADVISORIES FOR BROKEN GROUP ISLANDS
• Boaters need to be wary of strong winds, particularly westerlies during the after-noon, due to daytime heating.
• Boaters should know how to navigate through fog and should carry a marine VHF radio and Canadian Hydrographic Service Chart #3670 for navigation.
• If you want to eat shellfish you catch, you need a valid Tidal Fishing Licence and should check the daily PSP warnings.

OVERNIGHT BACKPACKING
West Coast Trail: 5 to 7 days. May to September. Reservations recommended for trips planned between mid-June and mid-September. Check park website for more information on reservations and lim-itations. Register for a permit and orienta-tion at Pachena Bay Information Centre or Port Renfrew (south end).

CAMPGROUNDS
94 drive-in sites, 20 walk-in sites, and 1 group walk-in site at **Green Point Campground** located on Hwy. 4. Flush toilets, picnic tables, garbage cans, and firewood for sale. Open mid-March to mid-October. For drive-in sites, call (905) 566-4321 or (877) 737-3783 or visit www.pccamping.ca for reservations. For group walk-in site, fax request to (250) 726-3520. Maximum stay 7 nights. Backcountry camping on **West Coast Trail** ($128 overnight use fee) and **Broken Group Islands** ($10 per person per night May–late Sept.). Camping permit $24 (unserviced with washroom building) or $18.

HOTELS, MOTELS, & INNS
(unless otherwise noted, rates are for a 2-person double, high season, in Canadian dollars)

Outside the park:
Bamfield, BC V0R 1B0:
Marie's Bed & Breakfast 468 Pachena Rd. (250) 728-3091. mariesbedand breakfast2@gmail.com; www3.telus.net/ marie/. $90.

Port Renfrew, BC V0S 1K0:
Bayview Accommodations 16975 Parkinson Rd.(250) 217-2977. info@ bayviewaccommodations.com; www .bayviewaccommodations.com. $135.

Tofino, BC V0R 2Z0:
Cable Cove Inn 201 Main St., Tofino. (250) 725-4236. info@cablecove.com; www.cablecoveinn.com. $225–$340.

Ucluelet, BC V0R 3A0:
Pacific Rim Motel 1755 Peninsula Rd. (250) 726-7728. info@pacific rimmotel.com; www.pacificrimmotel .com. $85–$200.

Festivals in Canada's National Parks

Festivals have been around for centuries and, in early days, were most often associated with religious celebrations. They are now more likely to celebrate some unique aspect or common set of values of a particular community.

A Stoney Indian brave performs a ceremonial dance at a festival in Banff.

This is true of festivals that occur in and around Canada's precious protected areas as well, where people come not only to appreciate nature but also to celebrate their common traditions and culture.

Loggers Days & Edge of the World Music Festival

On the Queen Charlotte Islands, or Haida Gwaii, the locals say, "When you've reached the edge of your world, ours begins." Perched off the west coast of British Columbia, Canada's most remote archipelago is rich with unique natural endowments and is steeped in culture.

Gwaii Haanas National Park Reserve is unique in Canada for being the first national park to be cooperatively managed by a joint board of First Nations and the Canadian government. First settled around 13,000 years ago, the early inhabitants of the islands developed a culture that was informed by the abundance of the land and sea. They became known as the Haida, a linguistically distinct group with two main clans, the Eagles and the Ravens. When Europeans arrived in the area, they too stamped their cultural presence. The depth of the cultural heritage of Gwaii Haanas illuminates two of its festivals. Loggers Days, held in July, speaks to the strong roots of the islands' logging industry, and in the languid days of August, local musicians with names like Honey Brown and Crabapple Creek Electric Jug Band headline the aptly named Edge of the World Music Festival.

Banff Mountain Festival

Straddling the Canadian Rockies, Banff National Park is probably Canada's most famous national park, as well as a UNESCO World Heritage site. Rugged mountains, glaciers, and ice fields; flower-filled alpine meadows; impossibly turquoise alpine lakes; steaming mineral hot springs; mysterious canyons; and silt-laden rivers dominate the landscape. Home to elk, bighorn sheep, bears, wolves, and cougars, the park is also home to adventurers. Climbers, kayakers, trekkers, and skiers flock to the pristine wilderness in all four seasons.

There is one month—a month almost *between* seasons—when the flow of mountain enthusiasts reaches stampede proportions. November is Banff Mountain Festival month, when more than 10,000 people come to celebrate mountain culture, mountain traditions, and the spirit of adventure. This annual festival pays tribute to the common values of mountain people from around the world: love of nature, concern for the environment, and a healthy appetite for vertically induced adrenalin. Often referred to as a "tribal gathering," the festival features film, literature, photography and mountain art, mountain-inspired crafts, music, and vertical dance that blend creative mentality with a spirit of adventure. The result is an amazingly vibrant sense of energy. For nine action-packed days, Banff theatres and lobbies are crammed with those who come to be inspired, and to connect with like-minded people. The town of Banff swarms with festival-goers clad in fleece and down, and the surrounding canyons and peaks enjoy a resurgence in activity, from ice climbing to hiking to skiing.

Festival of Birds

Southern Ontario's Point Pelee National Park marks its unique position in the world of birds with its annual spring Festival of Birds, when birders from around the globe flock to the park to experience the melodious avian migration in Canada's southernmost mainland.

Bird-watcher, Point Pelee National Park

Over the course of three-plus weeks, bird-watchers can partake in guided hikes and birding workshops, all while adding numerous species to their life lists.

— BERNADETTE MCDONALD, *author of* Tomaz Humar

Even with some figures weathering in the moist climate of the Haida Gwaii, the long-standing mortuary poles at SGang Gwaay still impress with their artistry.

▶ GWAII HAANAS & HAIDA HERITAGE SITE

BRITISH COLUMBIA
ESTABLISHED 1988
1,500 sq km/371,000 acres

Unique in the Parks Canada system, this entity consists of the park reserve, the heritage site, and the marine conservation area (see p. 275) encompassing everything from the seafloor to the mountaintops. Gwaii Haanas, "islands of beauty" in the Haida language, is world renowned for its cultural heritage and natural splendour. It boasts an unparalleled biological richness, more than 600 archaeological sites, and a cultural history that dates back more than 12,000 years.

At its southernmost end lies the ancient village of SGang Gwaay, a UNESCO World Heritage site home to around two dozen cedar totem poles that represent family and clan crests like eagle, raven, and bear; carved more than 100 years ago, many of them honour past chiefs.

Gwaii Haanas is located in the southern end of the archipelago of Haida Gwaii (formerly known as the Queen Charlotte Islands), 120 km (74.5 mi) west of Prince Rupert and 770 km (478.5 mi) north of Vancouver. Efforts to protect what is now Gwaii Haanas began in the 1970s, when logging of the region began. In 1985, the Haida blocked logging roads on Lyell Island to protest the destruction of the area. Their efforts paid off in 1988 with the creation of the park reserve. In a unique arrangement, the Council of the Haida Nation and the government of Canada cooperatively manage the site.

Before European contact in the late 1700s, the Haida have been estimated to have numbered between 10,000 and 30,000 people, scattered throughout 20 permanent villages in Haida Gwaii. Smallpox—a European import—devastated the Haida, killing almost 95 percent of the population, and by 1900 only 600 Haida remained, congregated in the villages of Skidegate and Masset. Today, the Haida number 2,500 and the people are still tied to their land and waters, using the Gwaii Haanas area to harvest food and run a cultural youth camp. Although there are no permanent residents in the old village sites, hereditary chieftainships of the villages are still passed down through the generations and all areas remain of great significance to the lives of the Haida. Today, Haida Gwaii Watchmen (cultural guardians) can be found in five key village sites during the summer months.

What makes this park reserve remarkable is not only its cultural significance but also its biological richness: Many species are different from those in mainland British Columbia. Some common species are not found here at all and some that are have evolved into their own subspecies (Haida Gwaii has its own subspecies of black bear—the largest found anywhere).

How to Get There

Gwaii Haanas is very remote—there are no services, facilities, or designated hiking trails. Gwaii Haanas is accessible only by BC Ferries from Prince Rupert or by a two-hour flight from Vancouver, with airports in Sandspit (southern end) or Masset (northern end). Most licensed operators leave from the village of Queen Charlotte or Sandspit. A wide range of accommodations are available in the towns. The visitor centres at the Sandspit Airport and in the village of Queen Charlotte can provide information about tour operators. Tour operators offer a variety of experiences and transportation options, from flight-seeing to day trips by motorboat to multiday kayak and sailing expeditions.

Only a limited number of visitors are allowed to visit Gwaii Haanas each day. All visitors must first attend an orientation session, a legal requirement. Orientations for independent travellers are provided at the Haida Heritage Centre at Ḵaay Llnagaay in Skidegate. Orientations for visitors travelling with a licensed tour operator are given by their guide on the trip.

Independent visitors travelling by kayak or motorboat most often launch from Moresby Camp, reached by the logging road on Moresby Island north of the Gwaii Haanas boundary. Check in at the visitor centres for up-to-date road conditions and procedures for travelling on active logging roads.

When to Go

The best time to visit Gwaii Haanas is between May and the end of September. June days enjoy about 18 hours of daylight and the summer months have calmer waters. Fall and

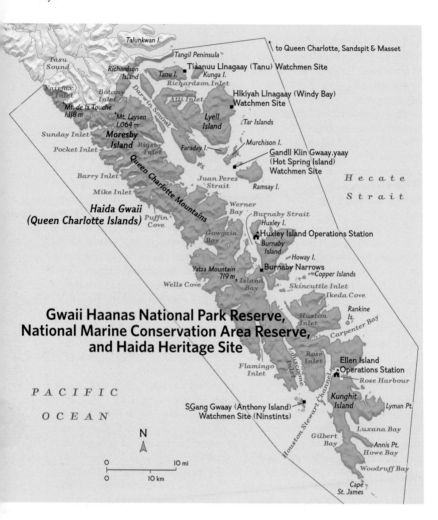

winter both feature unpredictable weather and storms that may prevent boats or planes from travelling. May and June are the best months for seeing large concentrations of whales and dolphins, although you may spot one or two anytime. The best place to see large pods of whales is near Tanu and the best place to see bunches of dolphins is near Hot Spring Island.

How to Visit

Because of its remoteness and the fact that travel by air and water is often weather dependent, it is necessary to be flexible when planning a trip to Gwaii Haanas. Many sites can be visited within a day on a floatplane or boat, but some require more time. Many kayakers have floated and paddled weeks away, immersed in a place so far removed from their home. Independent travellers not only need time but also skills in navigation and water safety—even in good weather, help is hours away at best.

A highlight for many visitors is their interactions with the Haida

Gwaii Watchmen. The Watchmen (elders, adults, and youth) live at the old village sites during the summer months. The mandate of this program is to protect culturally sensitive sites and educate visitors about the cultural and natural heritage of Gwaii Haanas. The Watchmen can also provide information about safety and marine forecasts. Because only 12 people are allowed onshore at any one time, it is necessary to radio ahead on VHF radios to request permission to come ashore. There is no camping permitted at the village sites (except **Windy Bay**) and visits should be limited to daytime hours. Composting toilets are available at all Watchmen sites.

Skedans and **Tanu**, although not formally within the national park reserve boundaries, are within the Haida Heritage Site.

SKEDANS
a half day

Skedans—also known as K̲'uuna Llnagaay, or "village at the edge" and "grizzly bear town"—is the most northern and most accessible of the old Haida village sites. It is one of the few remaining villages with standing poles (in various stages of decay) and remnants of longhouses. The village is located on the eastern tip of Louise Island and can be visited easily as a day trip by boat or floatplane.

The Watchmen cabin can be found behind the village facing the opposite side of the peninsula. Skedans is also home to the largest red alder tree in British Columbia; it has a circumference of 7.1 m (23 ft) and can be found at the western end of the village trail.

TANU
a half day

Tanu (T'aanuu Llnagaay or "eelgrass town") is named for the eelgrass that grows in the shallow water around the village. It has also been called Klue's Village after the original village chief, a name that can be found on some of Emily Carr's work after she came here to paint in 1907. The village follows the shoreline of two beaches separated by a rocky shoal. Many of the logs littering the ground were actually the posts and beams of old longhouses. There are no standing poles here but if you look closely, you may find carvings barely visible as they have been polished smooth over time and half buried in furry moss. The Watchmen cabin is at the northeast end of the village. Tanu can be visited on its own or as part of a day trip in combination with Skedans and/or Hot Spring Island.

HOT SPRING ISLAND
a half day

Hot Spring Island (G̲andll K'in or "hot water island") is well known for the healing and spiritual properties of its natural thermal pools. It has been a sacred place for the Haida for thousands of years. At one time, a village stood on the east side of the island, but it isn't visible today. The best place to come ashore is on the northeast side of the island, where a trail takes you through lush forest to the Watchmen cabin. The nearby bathhouse has showers fed by the natural hot springs. The island has three main thermal pools. The largest pool nestles amid crabapple trees and salal bushes near the bathhouse. A trail leads over the meadow to the cliffside pool, a small pool that overlooks **Juan Perez**

Strait and boasts spectacular views of the mountain peaks of Moresby Island. The third pool is found farther down the trail and is an intimate beachside pool, merely steps from the ocean. Two other cabins are found adjacent to the Watchmen cabin—these are privately owned by Haida families.

WINDY BAY
a full day

Popular with kayakers and other independent travellers, **Windy Bay** (Hlk'yah G̲aawG̲a) is located on the exposed eastern coast of **Lyell Island,** at the site of what was once a major village called Hlk'yah Llnagaay or "falcon town." The village is not visible today. This island is also where the Haida stood their ground, blocking logging roads in their fight to protect what is now Gwaii Haanas. The longhouse-style cabin named **Looking Around and Blinking House**

A bat star edges across sea lettuce.

honours this victory and provides camping-style accommodation for one night for kayakers. A trail winds through an old-growth forest of huge Sitka spruce and western redcedar; some of the trees are more than a thousand years old and reach 70 m (230 ft) in height. Look carefully at the trees: Some have been culturally modified while others bear ancient test holes, made to see if the tree would make a good canoe or standing pole.

SG̲ANG GWAAY
1 to 2 days

SG̲ang Gwaay is the southernmost Haida village site on the small island of SG̲ang Gwaay, which is also known as Anthony Island. The name SG̲ang Gwaay refers to the wailing sound made when the wind pushes through the rocks at a certain tide level. The village was also named NangSdins Llnagaay (Ninstints) after one of the village chiefs. SG̲ang Gwaay has the park reserve's most impressive array of longhouse remains and standing poles; it was declared a UNESCO World Heritage site in 1981. Although 11 of the best preserved poles were removed in 1957 to southern museums, about two dozen poles stand in various stages of decay, as well as posts and pits from several longhouses.

Because of a protected bird colony and a ban on air traffic, visitors who fly to SG̲ang Gwaay actually land in nearby Rose Harbour and then take a Zodiac boat the rest of the way. The boats drop anchor at the north end of the island, where visitors disembark. A boardwalk trail winds through a lush forest, leading visitors to the village. After passing

Soaking in a natural hot spring

the Watchmen cabin, visitors are suddenly confronted with a row of monumental mortuary poles, dating from the mid- and late 1800s. Many people sense that spirits still remain, making this village site a spiritual experience for some. At low tide, canoe runs are visible on the beach— these are areas that have been deliberately cleared of rocks (making it easier to bring canoes to safety).

The Looking Around and Blinking House at Windy Bay

Because of its distance and extra issues of accessibility, SGang Gwaay is often visited as part of a multiday trip and accommodations are available at Rose Harbour. However, flight operators are able to offer the trip as a one-day excursion.

up to 74 per square metre! Not only is the marine life abundant, it is also easy to see: At low tide, most of the 293 species are visible in the roughly half-metre-deep (1–2 ft) water.

BURNABY NARROWS
a half day

Burnaby Narrows is a 50-m-wide (164 ft) shallow channel of water between Moresby and Burnaby Islands. It has one of the highest levels of living biomass of any intertidal zone in the world. The bat star, for instance, which can be found in almost every brilliant colour, is found in quantities

IKEDA COVE
a half day

Ikeda Cove, on the southeast coast of Moresby Island, is named for the Japanese fisherman who discovered copper here and later operated a mine between 1906 and 1920. The remnants of a small, former mining town can still be seen set against the lush rain forest.

GWAII HAANAS NATIONAL PARK RESERVE, NATIONAL MARINE CONSERVATION AREA RESERVE, AND HAIDA HERITAGE SITE *(Réserve de parc national, réserve d'aire marine nationale de conservation, et site du patrimoine haïda Gwaii Haanas)*

INFORMATION & ACTIVITIES

VISITOR CENTRES
Queen Charlotte Visitor Centre 322 Wharf St., Queen Charlotte. Phone (250) 559-8316. www.qcinfo.ca.
Haida Heritage Centre at Kaay Llnagaay, 60 Second Beach Rd., Skidegate, Queen Charlotte, BC V0T 1S0. Phone (250) 559-7885. www.haidaheritagecentre.com.

HEADQUARTERS
60 Second Beach Rd., Skidegate (Haida Heritage Centre). P.O. Box 37, Queen Charlotte, BC V0T 1S0. Phone (250) 559-8818. www.parkscanada.gc.ca/gwaii haanas.

ENTRANCE FEES
$20 per adult, $50 per group per day; $120 adult, $295 group per season.

PETS
Pets not allowed at Haida Gwaii Watchmen village sites. Dogs must be on a leash when on shore.

THINGS TO DO
Kayaking, boating, and saltwater fishing (licence required). Electrical hookups for boats available in Queen Charlotte, Sandspit, and Masset.
Interpretive tours of ancient Haida villages with Haida Gwaii Watchmen at **K'uuna Llnagaay** on Louise Island, **T'aanuu Llnagaay** on Tanu Island, **SGang Gwaay Llnagaay** on SGang Gwaay island, **Windy Bay** on Lyell Island, and **Gandll K'in Gwaayaay** on Hot Spring Island.
For information contact the Haida Gwaii Watchmen Program, P.O. Box 1413, Skidegate, Haida Gwaii, BC V0T 1S1. Phone (250) 559-8225.

SPECIAL ADVISORIES
- Hikers should have good compass and orienteering skills.
- Hike in groups and make loud noises to avoid contact with bears.
- No maintained hiking trails.
- Emergency assistance at operations stations on Ellen and Huxley Islands, Haida Gwaii Watchmen sites, and Rose Harbour residences. Prince Rupert Coast Guard (800) 567-5111.
- Ferry reservations needed from Prince Rupert to Skidegate. BC Ferries (888) 223-3779. www.bcferries.com.

CAMPGROUNDS
No designated campsites. Beaches above high tide line recommended. Consult tide timetables before selecting campsite. Practise no-trace camping.

HOTELS, MOTELS, & INNS
(unless otherwise noted, rates are for a 2-person double, high season, in Canadian dollars)

Outside the park:
Masset, BC V0T 1M0:
Copper Beech House 1590 Delkatla. (250) 626-5441 or (855) 626-5441. info@copperbeechhouse.com; www.copperbeechhouse.com. $90–$120.

Queen Charlotte City, BC V0T 1S0:
Dorothy and Mike's Guest House 3127 Second Ave. (250) 559-8439. doromike@qcislands.net; www.qcislands.net/doromike. $80–$245.
Premier Creek Lodging 3101 Third Ave. (250) 559-8415 or (888) 322-3388. premier@qcislands.net; www.qcislands.net/premier. $35–$95.

Sandspit, BC V0T 1T0:
Northern Shores Lodge 455 Alliford Bay Rd. (250) 637-2233. $100–$140.

LICENSED TOUR OPERATORS
Anvil Cove Charters (250) 559-8207. anvilcove@qcislands.net; www.queen charlottekayaking.com.
Queen Charlotte Adventures (250) 559-8990 or (800) 668-4288. mail@queencharlotteadventures.com; www.queencharlotteadventures.com.

▶ **NATIONAL MARINE CONSERVATION AREA RESERVE**

GWAII HAANAS
BRITISH COLUMBIA

Setting a global precedent, Gwaii Haanas National Park Reserve, National Marine Conservation Area Reserve, and Haida Heritage Site is the first protected area to extend from the seafloor to the mountaintops. It is a victory recognizing that for the Haida, the land, sea, and people are interconnected and inseparable.

A colourful sunflower star lurks in the shallows of an inlet.

Gwaii Haanas extends approximately 10 km (6.2 mi) offshore and encompasses 3,400 sq km (1,313 sq mi) of the Hecate Strait and Queen Charlotte Shelf. It is the first national marine conservation area reserve established under Canada's National Marine Areas Conservation Act. The designation aims to protect the ecological and cultural resources of the area so that ecologically sustainable use can continue. The area supports the Haida's traditional harvest of marine resources as well as commercial fisheries that include herring roe, halibut, salmon, rockfish, geoduck clam, and red sea urchin.

These nutrient-rich waters support some of the most abundant, diverse, and colourful intertidal communities found in any temperate waters. From ocean abyss to continental slope to shallow shelf to rugged islands, this marine area is one of biological richness and is home to more than 3,500 marine species, including species at risk, and 20 species of whales, dolphins, and porpoises. Above the waters, the area provides nesting for more than 370,000 pairs of seabirds.

As a protected region, safeguarded from large-scale fishing and petroleum interests, Gwaii Haanas offers visitors an unparalleled opportunity to appreciate and enjoy the beauty and abundance of the oceans.

GWAII HAANAS

▶ NATIONAL MARINE CONSERVATION AREA

DIVING: This rich and colourful underwater world teems with kelp forests, sea stars, anemones, sea urchins, and a vast array of fish species and offers spectacular diving opportunities. The best diving is in spring when the area boasts crystal clear waters; in the summer, warm waters create algae blooms that can compromise visibility. Because of the remoteness and logistical difficulty in transporting tanks and refilling them, it is easiest to join a guided dive trip. Diving in Gwaii Haanas is not for beginners—divers should be experienced cold-water dry suit divers and should bring their own suits. (Note: The closest hyperbaric chamber is in Vancouver, which could take several hours to reach even by air.) One local dive operator is **Moresby Explorers** (800-806-7633, *http://divegwaiihaanas.com*).

SNORKELLING: While diving might be reserved for only the experienced, snorkelling offers a way for everyone to enjoy the underwater beauty of Gwaii Haanas. The thermal springs at **Hot Spring Island** make the underwater plant life extra colourful and **Burnaby Narrows** offers unparalleled snorkelling in an incredibly rich area of biodiversity.

KAYAKING: There are several ways to enjoy kayaking in Gwaii Haanas. Kayakers who are experienced and self-reliant and have the gift of time may choose to spend days or weeks exploring the park. Those less experienced but still ambitious may choose a guided kayaking trip. Even novice kayakers may still have the chance to paddle in paradise, as many of the sailing tour operators carry kayaks with them on their voyages.

BOATING & SAILING: There are 11 buoys spread throughout the marine park—they range from large can buoys that can accommodate several vessels to smaller buoys suitable for only one boat. In some places, boats may need to anchor without buoys. The general anchoring policy for the park is that a vessel is permitted to stay in any one place for up to three nights, but after that it must move locations, weather permitting.

SALTWATER FISHING: The Haida people have since time immemorial used these waters to harvest food and continue this practice today. A licence is required for all saltwater fishing in Gwaii Haanas and these can be obtained online from Fisheries & Oceans Canada (*www.pac.dfo-mpo.gc.ca/fm-gp/rec/licence-permis/index-eng.htm*) or at local retail outlets. Freshwater fishing within the park is prohibited. In addition, there are some areas within Gwaii Haanas Marine Area that are closed to all fishing or have fishing restrictions.

MARINE MAMMAL-WATCHING: Marine mammals inspire awe, spark our imaginations, and fill our hearts. It can be hard to control excitement but please use caution in areas of marine mammal activity, show courtesy by slowing your speed, and keep a distance of at least 100 m (330 ft). It is never safe to swim with or feed the marine life.

At the southern tip of Gwaii Haanas near **Cape St. James** is a

Dusk over the islands

large sea lion rookery with a large breeding colony of Steller sea lions. There are also several other haul-outs in Gwaii Haanas, one located near **Cumshewa Head.** Sea lions are particularly vulnerable during the breeding and pupping season (May–July). Female sea lions (cows) give birth high on the rocks to protect their young from being swept away by waves and drowning. Use caution and leave at the first sign of agitation. Any disturbance that causes the mother to change spots risks her pup falling into a crack in the rocks or into the ocean and drowning.

More than 20 species of whales, dolphins, and porpoises can be seen in the Gwaii Haanas Marine Conservation Area, including orcas (killer whales), humpbacks, minkes, and grey whales. Humpback whales, known for their acrobatics, arrive each April to feed on herring. They have spent the winter in either Mexico or Hawaii and pass through on their migration. Grey whales also pass through each spring on their way to their summer feeding grounds in the Bering Sea. Large aggregations of a hundred or more whales can often be found just north of Tanu feeding in the plankton-rich outflow waters.

There are some guidelines to keep in mind when encountering these majestic sea creatures: Travel parallel to whales and dolphins and never travel through them with the intent of having them ride your bow. When approaching, do so from the side instead of from the front or behind.

In the spring, thousands of dolphins, killer whales, salmon, and halibut can be found in the nutrient-rich waters near Hot Spring Island.

Gwaii Haanas National Marine Conservation Reserve: Gwaii Haanas National Park Reserve and Haida Heritage Site, Queen Charlotte, BC V0T 1S0. Phone (250) 559-8818. gwaiihaanasmarine@pc.gc.ca.

Approximately 70 km (43.5 mi) long and some 5 km (3 mi) wide at its terminus, Lowell Glacier ends at Lowell Lake, through which the Alsek River flows.

▶ KLUANE

YUKON
ESTABLISHED 1972
21,980 sq km/5,431,000 acres

They say the Yukon's soul resides in Kluane, and the giant peaks, glaciers, and abundant wildlife in Kluane National Park and Reserve make it clear why. Vast ice fields form the park core—crowned by Mount Logan, Canada's highest peak at 5,959 m (19,550 ft) high— and glaciers spill into broad valleys populated by grizzly bears, Dall sheep, and mountain goats.

Kluane's landscape is in flux. The geologically active St. Elias Mountains stretch from Alaska to northern British Columbia, breached just once by the Tatshenshini-Alsek River flowing to the Pacific Ocean. Dynamic forces like surging glaciers, silt-laden rivers, and forest fires constantly reshape the land. The rain shadow of the St. Elias Mountains creates a dry continental climate in much of the park, while some areas are heavily influenced by moist Pacific air masses. The result is highly changeable, sometimes turbulent weather: Picture icy winds howling out of the ice fields or wildflowers peeking out from under a summer snowfall.

Kluane National Park and Reserve's grandeur is about size as much as it is about beauty. It's one of Canada's largest parks, covering an area four times the size of Prince

Edward Island. Combined with three adjacent parks—Tatshenshini-Alsek Provincial Park in British Columbia and Wrangell–St. Elias National Park and Preserve and Glacier Bay National Park and Preserve in Alaska—it forms the largest international protected region in the world, a UNESCO World Heritage site. Mount Logan is believed to be the most massive mountain in the world. It towers over a dozen 4,600-m (15,000 ft) peaks, all enveloped by the planet's largest nonpolar ice fields.

North America's most genetically diverse population of grizzly bears make their home in Kluane, as do snowshoe hares, lynx, wolves, and moose. This wild remote region is also part of the homelands of the Southern Tutchone People, who travel, hunt, and live in the area. Along with Parks Canada, two First Nations—and possibly a third in the future—share in the management of the national park.

How to Get There

From Whitehorse, drive 160 km (100 mi) west on the Alaska Highway to Haines Junction, where the visitor centre and park headquarters are located. Paved highways follow the park boundary: From Haines Junction the park can be explored northwest along the Alaska Highway or south along the Haines Road. In both directions, the road skirts along the base of the Kluane Front Ranges. Flight-seeing and air charters into the park operate out of Haines Junction airport and the Silver City airstrip at Kluane Lake.

When to Go

Summer is an energetic time of long sunny days, while fall is colourful but chilly. Winter is cold, bright, and snowy, and spring is notable for late season skiing and early wildflowers. Kluane receives up to 40,000 visitors per year—with most coming in the summer—so you can find uncrowded wilderness experiences anytime of the year. Backcountry hiking and rafting trips occur from June to September. Climbing season in the ice fields is late April to late June.

How to Visit

Most people explore Kluane's frontcountry from the road, where wildlife is often visible and well-maintained trails lead into nature. Haines Junction is a good base for a lengthy stay in the area. The town has a full range of tourist services, including the Kluane National Park and Reserve Visitor Centre, which will be housed within the First Nations cultural centre Dä Ku by summer 2012. The park visitor centre is the place to learn about the park and register for backcountry trips.

The best way to experience Kluane is through hiking, canoeing, river rafting, cultural experiences, nature walks, and other outdoor pursuits. The Kathleen Lake Campground and day-use area 27 km (16.5 mi) south of Haines Junction is one hub of activity: Its setting is spectacular and it's the easiest place to access the park. A second hub is the Tachäl Dhäl Visitor Centre, about 70 km (43 mi) north of Haines Junction on the Alaska Highway, surrounded by hiking trails, great wildlife viewing, and eye-popping scenery.

Discovering some of Kluane's gems involves some effort and adventure, requiring overnighting in the Kluane backcountry. Wilderness tour operators guide multiday hiking trips on several major routes, and rafting companies lead expedition-style trips down the Alsek River.

KLUANE

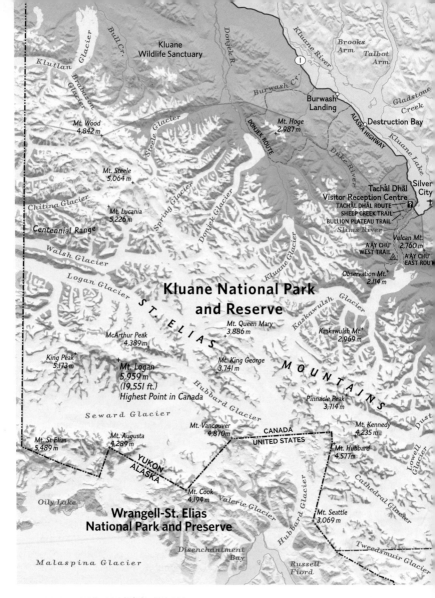

HAINES ROAD

64 km/40 mi to Klukshu; at least 2 days with day hikes

In addition to great scenery, abundant wildlife, and adventure thrills, many of these trips include views of Kluane's prized glaciers. Flight-seeing tours offer an alternative means of seeing the rivers of ice.

If you plan to go walking or hiking, be bear aware. The park visitor centres have good information about travelling in bear country.

Kluane is big, and summer's extended daylight makes it easy to put in long days. Before setting out on **Haines Road** from Haines Junction, gas up and stock up on food, so you can be ready to explore in any direction.

Crocus (*Anemone patens*)

KLUANE

packers can camp in the basic campsite near the midpoint.

Located 27 km (16.5 mi) south of Haines Junction, **Kathleen Lake** is a focal point for activities in Kluane. Parks Canada maintains a campground, day shelter with picnic tables, outhouses, boardwalk, boat launch, and trails. Many people start hikes here or launch canoes from the curving pebble beach. Wheelchair accessible **Kokanee Trail** is an easy 0.5-km (0.3 mi) stroll a short distance along the shore. The trail to **King's Throne** also starts at the lake. The 5-km (3 mi) steep ascent to an enchanting alpine cirque is hard, but the wildflowers and views are worth the effort.

Haines Road has plenty of other diversions. **Rock Glacier Trail** (0.6 km/0.4 mi) leads to a fine example of a rock glacier, with interpretive panels and segments of boardwalk along the way. An alternative to the Kathleen Lake Campground is the Yukon Campground at **Dezadeash Lake,** outside the park. Depending on the month, you might see spawning salmon and traditional fish traps at **Klukshu,** a Southern Tutchone village at the park's edge.

Driving south out of town on the Haines Road, the **Kluane Ranges** parallel the road and fill your view on the right. Just 7 km (4 mi) south of Haines Junction is one of the park's most pleasant and accessible hikes. The **Auriol Trail** is a moderate 15-km (9 mi) loop trail that winds up through spruce and aspen forest into subalpine meadows. It's a popular day hike with great views, and back-

Top: Hiking on Sheep Mountain Trail. Middle left: Winter in Kluane. Middle right: Remnants of the gold rush town of Silver City at Kluane Lake. Bottom: Dall sheep, in full winter coat.

ALASKA HIGHWAY
61 km/38 mi to Kluane Lake; at least a full day

North of Haines Junction, the **Alaska Highway** provides the means to explore the Tachäl Region of Kluane National Park and Reserve. The park is harder to access along here, but some key attractions and the stunning scenery make the drive memorable. Spruce bark beetles have infested these forests, leaving large stands of dead trees while the forest regenerates damaged areas back to their full beauty. The 2-km (1.25 mi) interpretive **Spruce Beetle Trail,** 17 km (10.5 mi) north of Haines Junction and outside the national park, reveals the devastation—and subsequent rejuvenation—of the boreal forest.

Beyond **Bear Creek Summit,** the highest point on the Alaska Highway between Whitehorse and Fairbanks, the mountain vistas just get more breathtaking. **Kluane Lake** and the **Tachäl Dhäl Visitor Centre,** where more park features are clustered, lie about 75 km (46.5 mi) from Haines Junction, roughly an hour's drive from the town. Dall sheep are often visible on the mountain flanks rising above the centre, which sits in the middle of the **Ä'ay Chù' Delta.** Chilly, dusty outflow winds often blast down this valley from the Kaskawulsh Glacier. Knowledgeable park staff are on hand to share information about sheep or to answer questions about Kluane's natural and cultural history. You can also plan park explorations here or register for trips into the backcountry.

Hiking options range from an easy 1-km (0.5 mi) walk to **Soldiers Summit,** to moderate day hikes to **Sheep Creek** or **Bullion Plateau,** to a challenging multiday trek up the **Ä'ay Chù' River.**

BACKCOUNTRY ADVENTURES
4 to 10 days

Seen from the road, Kluane National Park and Reserve is like an iceberg: Only its tip is visible. Beyond that imposing front range of mountains lie giant peaks, broad valleys, glacial rivers, and the vast St. Elias Icefields. To get a sense of this grand landscape, take a flight-seeing tour or go on a multiday wilderness trip. People come from around the world to participate in extended backcountry trips—backpacking and river rafting are the two main activities—into the park.

A multiday rafting trip on the Alsek River is a life-changing journey down one of the world's wildest river systems. The **Alsek River** is designated a Canadian Heritage River, and a float down it through this raw, primordial landscape featuring calving glaciers and grizzly bears will reveal why. This icy river delivers a thrilling ride and the backdrop is spectacular, even when the weather is grim.

Adventurous visitors can plan independent hikes into Kluane National Park and Reserve or hire a commercial guide. The 85-km (53 mi) **Cottonwood Trail** is a popular four- to six-day loop that starts at either Kathleen Lake or the south end of Dezadeash Lake. The Cottonwood is the longest true trail in the park and, even though it is well maintained, it challenges hikers with a tough traverse across two alpine passes. Another long-distance trek, the 64-km (40 mi) **Ä'ay Chù'** hike can take three to five

KLUANE

KLUANE NATIONAL PARK & RESERVE
(Parc national et réserve de parc national Kluane)

INFORMATION & ACTIVITIES

VISITOR CENTRES
Kluane National Park and Reserve Visitor Centre at Haines Junction open daily mid-May to late September and by appointment rest of year. Phone (867) 634-7207.

Tachäl Dhäl Visitor Centre open daily mid-May to early September. Phone (867) 841-4500.

SEASONS & ACCESSIBILITY
Road access to parking areas from Haines Junction, which is 160 km (100 mi) west of Whitehorse, Yukon, via the Alaska Highway, or 250 km (155 mi) north of Haines, Alaska, via the Haines Road. Topographic map available at visitor centre. Road access at **Kathleen Lake** and **Tachäl Dhäl.** Most park access is by foot, raft, or mountain bike. Four campsites at Kathleen Lake open for winter camping.

HEADQUARTERS
P.O. Box 5495, Haines Junction, YT Y0B 1L0. Phone (867) 634-7250. www.parks canada.gc.ca/kluane.

ENTRANCE FEES
No entrance fee for daily use. $30 per landing.

ACCESSIBLE SERVICES
Wheelchair-accessible boardwalk on Kokanee Trail (0.5 km/0.3 mi one way) along the shore of Kathleen Lake.

THINGS TO DO
In summer: Mountain biking on **Mush Lake Road, Alsek Trail,** and **Ä'ay Chù' East Road.** Rafting or kayaking down the **Alsek River** (pre-booking of Alsek trips is mandatory). Mountaineering in the **Icefield Ranges** (application and waivers required; call 867-634-7279). Flight-seeing tours over ice fields, motorized boating on Kathleen and Mush Lakes, fishing (permit required; $10 per day and $35 per year). Hiking on trails (easy–moderate) and routes (advanced). Guided walks $5 (1–2 hrs.) or $20 (4–6 hrs.) per person.

In winter: Skiing on **St. Elias Lake, Shorty Creek, Cottonwood, Auriol,** and **Dezadeash River Trail.** In February and March, cross-country skiing, snowshoeing, dogsledding, snowmobiling.

CAMPGROUND
Kathleen Lake Campground: 39 sites open mid-May to mid-September, first come, first served; 4 sites open in fall and winter. Outhouses, bear-proof storage lockers, and firewood for sale. $9 per day for camping services; $16 per night for campsite or $5 per person per night for group sites. Backcountry permits $10 per night and $70 per year.

HOTELS, MOTELS, & INNS
For information, contact the Village of Haines Junction, Box 5339, Haines Junction, YT Y0B 1L0. (867) 634-7100. vhj@yknet.ca; www.hainesjunction yukon.com.

LICENSED TOUR OPERATORS
Yukon Department of Tourism and Culture (800) 661-0494. vacation@gov .yk.ca; www.travelyukon.com.
Wilderness Tourism Association of the Yukon (867) 668-3369. http://yukon wild.com.

days. The hike begins on a trail, but eventually it steps off the trail and requires route finding; the hike has difficult creek crossings as well. Only hikers with good orienteering and backcountry skills should attempt this route, or any other overnight hikes in the national park.

The reward is a view overlooking **Kaskwulsh Glacier.**

Registration is mandatory on overnight hiking trips, and you may need bear-resistant food canisters. Kluane has a significant population of grizzly bears; bear awareness and good practices are key to safe travels in bear country.

EXCURSIONS

CHILKOOT TRAIL NATIONAL HISTORIC SITE
BENNETT, BC

The Chilkoot Trail is a 53-km (33 mi) scenic hiking trip from Dyea, Alaska, through the Coast Mountains to the Yukon River headwaters in Canada. Canada's largest national historic site, the Chilkoot Trail commemorates the historic gateway to the Yukon once tread by Tlingit First Nations traders and Klondike gold rush prospectors. Hikers should be well equipped, self-sufficient, and in good physical condition for the rugged three- to five-day wilderness trek. Daily departures are limited, and hikers must have a permit. Call Parks Canada well in advance to reserve your hike. (800) 661-0486 or (867) 667-3910.

S.S. KLONDIKE NATIONAL HISTORIC SITE
WHITEHORSE, YT

The S.S. *Klondike* was the largest stern-wheeler to ply the Yukon River in the decades following the Klondike gold rush of 1898. This carefully restored ship is now a national historic site on the riverbank in Whitehorse surrounded by lawn, boardwalks, and views of the Yukon River. Parks Canada operates this popular attraction daily from mid-May to mid-September, with guided tours every half hour 9:30 a.m. to 5 p.m. (867) 667-3910.

KLUANE

FAR NORTH

Page 286: top, Arctic blueberries at Ford Lake, Ukkusiksalik; middle, Beaufort Sea, near Firth River, Ivvavik; bottom, narwhals resting in a hole in the sea ice, near Sirmilik. Page 287: A helicopter below a mountaineer in the Cirque of

FAR NORTH

Although remote and isolated, Canada's northernmost parks are not inaccessible. But only skilled and experienced adventurers—or those with a guide or outfitter—should go. Pristine land, abundant wildlife, and the warm welcome of indigenous peoples await visitors. At Vuntut or neighbouring Ivvavik celebrate the annual migration of 100,000 caribou with the local Gwich'in people. At Nahanni, canoers and kayakers negotiate the South Nahanni River,

the Unclimbables, Nahanni. Above: A hiker pauses to take in the view near Black Fox Creek Valley, Vuntut.

while at distant Tuktut Nogait paddlers reach the Arctic Ocean. Aulavik
attracts visitors for its archaeological
sites and wildlife that includes
muskox and arctic fox. Ski tour on glaciers at Quttinirpaaq, only 725 km (450
mi) from the North Pole. The waters
of Sirimilik provide food for seals
and polar bears. A boat is the best
way to see Ukkusiksalik as it wraps
around Wagner Bay. At Auyuittuq
top-notch mountaineers tackle the
Thor Peak and Mount Asgard.

A migrating Porcupine caribou herd

▶ VUNTUT

YUKON
ESTABLISHED 1995
4,345 sq km/1,073,673 acres

Vuntut National Park may be one of the most remote and least visited national parks in Canada, but it's far from unpopulated. Vuntut is the domain of the Porcupine caribou herd and half a million migratory birds, and is also the cultural homeland of the Vuntut Gwich'in people. In the Gwich'in language, Vuntut means "among the lakes," a fitting moniker for this Arctic landscape, which is dotted by fertile wetlands, winding rivers, and rolling mountains.

Vuntut National Park was established through a land claims agreement in 1995, and is thus a relatively recent addition to Canada's national parks system. It realized the vision the Vuntut Gwich'in people of North Yukon have of preserving the land and their way of life, and they work together with Parks Canada to manage the park.

The Gwich'in people live in about 15 communities across northeast Alaska, the North Yukon, and the Northwest Territories, and are united by their language and a culture founded on a dependence on the Porcupine caribou herd. A number of nations and bands comprise the Gwich'in people throughout their vast territory; the Vuntut

Gwich'in First Nation in Old Crow is one of these.

Vuntut lies north of the village of Old Crow, a fly-in community of 300 located at the confluence of the Crow and Porcupine Rivers. Wetlands are protected in the Old Crow Flats part of the park, but Vuntut also plays a significant role in a much larger protected area. Vuntut's neighbouring national parks include Ivvavik to the north (see pp. 296–301) and the Arctic National Wildlife Refuge across the international boundary to the west.

Caribou is an important species in this northern ecosystem, and Old Crow is located on the migration path of the Porcupine caribou herd. The annual migration of this herd is the largest of any land animal on Earth, and a portion of the herd ranges in Vuntut National Park at various times of the year. Caribou are important to the local communities not only as a source of food but for their role in Gwich'in culture. Historically, Gwich'in hunters built caribou fences to capture the animals, and the remains of several of these fences are important heritage sites in Vuntut National Park.

Hundreds of thousands of nesting or migrating waterfowl visit the Old Crow Flats complex of shallow lakes each year, and moose and muskrat thrive in the wetlands. The park is also home to grizzly bears, wolves, wolverines, raptors, and many small mammals. Interestingly, parts of Vuntut remained unglaciated in the last Ice Age, and those parts of the landscape served as a refuge for plants and animals trying to survive in the barren environs.

How to Get There

Access to the park is challenging. The closest road, the Dempster Highway, is about 175 km (109 mi) away, so one good option is to fly to Old Crow and stage a trip into the park from there. Air North flies from Whitehorse to Old Crow, Dawson City, and Inuvik several times a week. Vuntut National Park is 50 km (31 mi) north of Old Crow by air, or 190 km (118 mi) via river. Boats may be available for hire in Old Crow. An aircraft landing permit is required to land in Vuntut National Park; if you are planning a journey there, you need to contact Parks Canada in advance.

When to Go

Summer is short north of the Arctic Circle, and June, July, and August are the most pleasant months for a visit to Vuntut National Park. Unfortunately, insects also peak in the summer, so a bug jacket is essential gear for a summer trip. Many families from Old Crow go out to seasonal camps in the spring and fall to partake in traditional activities like

VUNTUT

Anglican church in the village of Old Crow

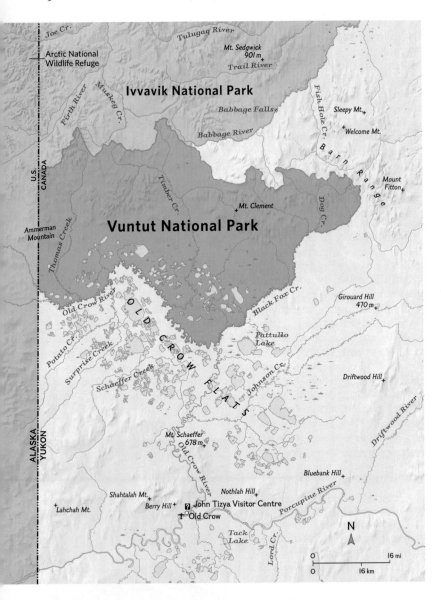

hunting, trapping, fishing, and berry picking, so even though a visit to the community is special at any time of the year, you'll see more and enjoy a richer cultural experience if you visit between March and September. Your best chance to see caribou near Old Crow is in spring (April–May) or fall (Sept.–Oct.).

How to Visit

Vuntut National Park is a destination for experienced, self-sufficient adventurers. Fewer than 25 people visit the park each year (not including locals); it's complete wilderness that is difficult and expensive to access. There are no facilities or services to assist visitors—in short, you're left mostly to your own devices if you plan a visit to the park. Those who make the effort, though, will encounter a wilderness adventure unlike any other, in a place pristine and unspoiled.

Visitors to Vuntut will get to enjoy exceptional wildlife viewing—with 500,000 birds and 100,000 caribou passing through, you can't fail to spot some interesting species. Hardy souls may wish to hike and backpack through the park's distinctive unglaciated mountains, or you can also canoe the Old Crow River or plan a winter ski trip through the park. Please note that extended backcountry journeys in the park require careful advance planning and logistics.

If you can, make time to visit Old Crow and stop by the new visitor centre, which stands in the middle of the traditional village. A few of the residents of Old Crow also offer tours, accommodation, and excursions to view wildlife or partake in cultural activities.

OLD CROW

Old Crow is the Yukon's most northerly and isolated community. While the climate may be harsh, people are friendly and hospitable, and the village is known as one of the most authentic destinations in the North. It's also a "dry" community, meaning that alcohol is prohibited. If you visit in the summer you'll experience round-the-clock daylight, while for a few months in winter it's cold and dark, day and night. But whenever

Lichen in Vuntut National Park

VUNTUT

Wetlands of Old Crow Flats—breeding habitat for several aquatic mammals

Camping near Black Fox Creek

A former Hudson's Bay Company fort on the Porcupine River

you visit Old Crow, you're guaranteed a memorable cultural adventure.

There are only a couple of places to stay in Old Crow, so book ahead. If you are tenting, someone from the village will show you where you can camp. A crowd from the village always greets the daily incoming flight, and even if you haven't arranged to be met planeside, someone will be sure to help you sort out your arrangements. The airport is at the edge of town, and the village is fairly cohesive. Most people simply walk and ride snow machines or ATVs; if you find a vehicle, you will have to ask for a ride. Stroll around the rustic village to see the log homes, smokehouses, and caribou antlers that serve as a reminder that Porcupine caribou are in the blood of this tiny North Yukon community.

If you're on a quest to learn more about the caribou that migrate through Old Crow, the impressive **John Tizya Visitor Centre**—part museum and part welcome centre—offers visitor information, park interpretation, and extensive natural and cultural history exhibits on the Porcupine caribou. Don't miss artifacts like the photographs of Gwich'in elders and youth out on the land. Fur-lined audio sets play recordings as part of an interpretive display. Like most large public buildings in Old Crow, the minimalist-modern visitor centre is elevated on posts to protect both the building and the permafrost. Excavating a conventional foundation would cause the permafrost to melt and the building to sink. Parks Canada has an office in the visitor centre.

VUNTUT NATIONAL PARK
(Parc national Vuntut)

INFORMATION & ACTIVITIES

VISITOR CENTRE
Old Crow Visitor Centre Phone (867) 966-3626. www.oldcrow.ca.

SEASONS & ACCESSIBILITY
Park open year-round. No road access. Air North offers scheduled service to Old Crow from Whitehorse and Dawson City in the Yukon and Inuvik in the Northwest Territories. Call (867) 668-2228.

HEADQUARTERS
Yukon Field Unit–Parks Canada Room 205, 300 Main St., Whitehorse, YT Y1A 2B5. www.parkscanada.gc.ca/vuntut.

ENTRANCE FEES
Access fee $25 per day, $147 per year.

PETS
Permitted; must be on a leash at all times.

ACCESSIBLE SERVICES
None.

THINGS TO DO
No facilities or developed trails. Caribou Days is a three-day festival to view Porcupine caribou herd as they begin their migration. For more information about the area, visit www.oldcrow.ca.

SPECIAL ADVISORIES
- Be aware of procedures for bear encounters, food storage, camping, and hygiene.
- Firearms not permitted.
- Dense concentrations of blackflies and mosquitoes, summer (late June–July).
- Weather and temperatures vary. Snow can fall at any time of the year, and temperatures can swing by as much as 16°C (60°F) in a few hours.
- Search and rescue operations limited.
- Removal of natural or cultural objects is prohibited.

OVERNIGHT BACKPACKING
Registration and deregistration at the Parks Canada office in Old Crow required.

CAMPGROUNDS
None.

HOTELS, MOTELS, & INNS
(unless otherwise noted, rates are for a 2-person double, high season, in Canadian dollars)

Outside the park:
Old Crow, YT Y0B 1N0:
Porcupine Bed & Breakfast P.O. Box 55. (867) 966-3913. blue fish_kennels@ hotmail.com. $120.

Cn'oo Deenjik Accommodations P.O.Box 25. (867) 966-3008. choodee@northwestel .net; http://choodee.oldcrow.ca. $160.

VUNTUT

Hiking near Black Fox Creek

Aerial view of the Firth River

IVVAVIK

YUKON
ESTABLISHED 1984
9,750 sq km/2,409,277 acres

High in the northwest corner of Yukon, stunted spruce trees pitch from the permafrost at wild angles. Arctic willow grows like a carpet low on the ground, where it's safe from the wind and close to sunlight-warmed soil. The Firth, Canada's oldest flowing river, cuts a turquoise trail through the rolling, unglaciated hills of the British Mountains.

A visit to Ivvavik National Park gives one a special sort of bragging right—this site sees an average of only 200 visitors yearly. Its Arctic location means it can be tough to access, but the pristine beauty of the place makes it well worth the challenge. Ivvavik (meaning "nursery" or "birthplace" in Inuvialuktun) was the first Canadian national park created as the result of an aboriginal land claim settlement. One of the many provisions of the 1984 Inuvialuit Final Agreement (a constitutionally protected legal agreement that protects and preserves Inuvialuit culture in the North) established Ivvavik on the Yukon North Slope, which some of the Porcupine caribou herd use as calving grounds, while other parts of the herd continue each year to coastal calving grounds in Alaska.

Despite the rugged, isolated nature of the land here, human presence stretches back thousands of years. Radiocarbon-dated bison bones, found along the frigid Firth River, bear butchering marks that speak to hunting activity more than 10,000 years ago.

The remnants of tools—both primitive and advanced—are found in Ivvavik today. The park is more than a collection of ancient artifacts; it is a living cultural landscape on which Inuvialuit continue traditional practices including subsistence harvesting, all of which are provided for in the land claim.

Throughout the park, you'll find evidence of stone and sod remains of Dorset, Thule, Eskimo, and Inuit habitation, tools used by Paleo-Arctic communities, and old fishing sites along the shores of the Firth.

Evidence of European occupation also exists in the form of fur-trading posts on Herschel Island, artifacts from the mini gold rush at Sheep Creek in the 1970s, and traces of the Cold War—the remnants of one of America's Distant Early Warning Line stations at Komakuk Beach and Stokes Point.

How to Get There

Drive north from Dawson City, Yukon (670 km/420 miles), on the Dempster Highway or fly into Inuvik airport. From here, you must charter a plane into the park.

When to Go

Considering that winter conditions can occur from mid-September to mid-May, summer is the best time to visit. Temperatures hover around 14°C (57°F) and the summer sun lasts 24 hours.

How to Visit

There are no licensed outfitters running single-day trips into the park, but visitors can organize self-guided excursions. Fly into Ivvavik for an afternoon and hike from a mountain-top airstrip down to **Babbage Falls** or land at **Sheep Creek** and hike the hills. If you have a couple of weeks, book a **Firth River** rafting trip with one of the licensed outfitters that offers trips on the Firth.

BABBAGE FALLS TRIP
5-km/3-mi hike; 6 hours

Aklak Air is the only charter airline that can land on the ridgetop runway at **Babbage Falls,** so it's best to build your trip around their availability. As soon as you have confirmed dates, notify Parks Canada of your plans. When you arrive in Inuvik, you'll have to register at their downtown Mackenzie Road office and attend a mandatory orientation session.

Be sure to give yourself a two-day buffer when arranging transportation in and out of Inuvik. Weather in the Arctic can delay departures,

King eider (*Somateria spectabilis*)

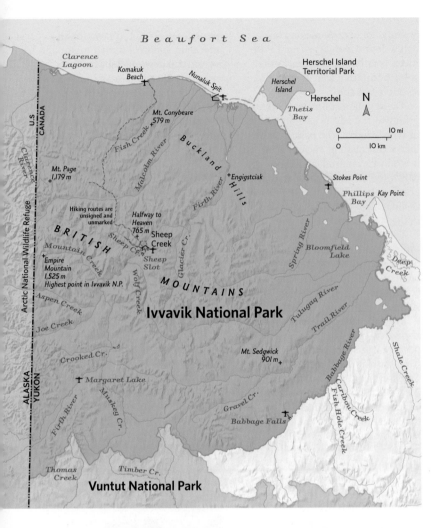

Beaufort Sea

Clarence Lagoon

Komakuk Beach

Nunaluk Spit

Herschel Island Territorial Park

Herschel Island

Herschel

Thetis Bay

N

Mt. Conybeare ×579 m

Buckland Hills

Engigstciak

Stokes Point

Phillips Bay   Kay Point

0   10 mi
0   10 km

U.S CANADA

Clarence River

Mt. Page 1,179 m

Fish Creek

Malcolm River

Firth River

Spring River

Bloomfield Lake

Deep Creek

Arctic National Wildlife Refuge

Hiking routes are unsigned and unmarked

BRITISH

Sheep Creek

Halfway to Heaven 765 m

Sheep Creek

Glacier Cr.

Empire Mountain 1,525 m Highest point in Ivvavik N.P.

Mountain Creek

Sheep Slot

Wolf Creek

MOUNTAINS

Tuluaq River

Trail River

Babbage River

Shale Creek

Aspen Creek

Ivvavik National Park

Joe Creek

Crooked Cr.

Mt. Sedgwick 901 m

Margaret Lake

Muskeg Cr.

Gravel Cr.

Babbage Falls

Carbou Creek

Fish Hole Creek

ALASKA YUKON

Firth River

Thomas Creek

Timber Cr.

Vuntut National Park

particularly at **Babbage Falls** where the site's proximity to the Beaufort Sea can make for foggy, cool, and windy conditions. Flying into the park, you'll pass over the **Mackenzie Delta,** one of the world's great river deltas, made up of a spectacular complex of lakes and streams that flow north into the Arctic Ocean. Watch for the transition from pancake-flat delta to the rounded, emerald peaks of the **British Mountains.** This range makes up two-thirds of the park's total area and is typical of Ivvavik's nonglaciated landscape. Thirty thousand years ago, a wide land bridge (called Beringia) stretched west to Alaska and Siberia. The unique landscape visitors experience in Ivvavik is one of the oldest in the world, as it was unaffected by Ice Age glaciation.

The coast of the Beaufort, frozen eight months of the year, is fringed with ice. Babbage Falls is one of a number of places to spot *aufeis,* thick sheets of ice that form when underground springs freeze in the

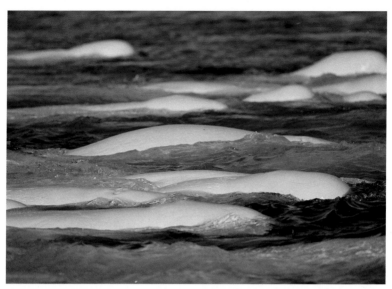

Beluga whales in Ivvavik National Park

winter, often over existing river ice, and over such an expanse (several square kilometres) that these sheets frequently do not melt before the winter weather begins freezing them again.

From the airstrip, the hike to Babbage Falls descends 420 m (1,380 ft) over about 5 km (3 mi) and generally takes two to three hours to walk. The terrain here is dry tundra until you reach the base of the falls where small peat hummocks crop up. Beside the slopes immediately alongside the Babbage River, you can find the worn trail made by generations of grizzly bears passing through the area. Fortunately the short, sparse vegetation makes for easy trailblazing.

SHEEP CREEK TRIP

17 km/11 mi; 1 to 2 days

Until 1986, a placer gold mine operated on **Sheep Creek**. Today, where this winding waterway drains into the **Firth River,** you'll find Ivvavik's only Parks Canada station—a collection of small buildings including the park's single outhouse. The station is used by Parks Canada for school camps, research and monitoring, and an artist's residency, but visitors are welcome to camp outdoors here. Keep an eye open for wildlife. Ivvavik is the northernmost extension for Dall sheep, and Sheep Creek is more than just a catchy name.

While there are no marked paths here, it is a hiker's paradise. Visitors can choose from an assortment of ridges and hikes, until they've expended their energy. Routes with names like **Halfway to Heaven, Inspiration Point, Dragons Ridge,** and **Dragons Tor** give you a sense of the possibilities. If you're feeling less adventurous, take a stroll along the nearby Firth River and check out some of the Class V rapids at **Sheep Slot**—they contribute to the Firth River's reputation as a life list river for paddling fanatics. Keep an eye out for Dolly Varden char and Arctic grayling in the crystal clear pool.

IVVAVIK

Top: A snowy owl. Middle: Arctic willow. Bottom: A walrus.

FIRTH RIVER RAFTING TRIP

130 km/81 mi; 13 days

Ninety-five percent of Ivvavik's visitors come to raft the **Firth River**—a stunning Class IV waterway with temperatures as low as minus 7°C (19°F). Because of this, private groups must be able to deal with emergencies and self-rescue in a remote Arctic setting. Those who are not so well equipped should look into booking a guided trip with a licensed outfitter.

The rafting season is late June to early August. Charters drop off at **Margaret Lake,** at the southwest corner of Ivvavik, close to the Alaska border, where rafters put in to begin the journey to **Nunaluk Spit** on the Arctic Ocean, a distance of 130 km (80 mi).

From here, north is the only direction you can go. The wide river valley at Margaret Lake narrows near **Joe Creek,** speeding up to Class II and III rapids as it moves toward the boulder gardens of **Sheep Slot.** Before **Engigstciak,** narrow canyons (10 m/ 33 ft across in some places) lead the way to Class IV rapids.

For those who still have energy (or adrenalin) at the end of the day, there are a number of hikes along the way. An 11-km (7 mi) loop at Margaret Lake summits a series of three peaks, offering views of the **Firth River Valley** and the **aufeis field** to the south and north. The hike at **Crooked Creek** is an easy 6-km (4 mi) trek to a scenic ridge overlooking the Firth River. Watch for hummocks and tussocks as you hike—it's easy to twist an ankle on their shaggy heads.

During the final leg of the trip, the river enters the coastal plain and mingles with sandbars to form a long delta. **Nunaluk Lagoon** is the take-out location for the trip. In the late summer months, it's one of many coastal lagoons that host moulting sea ducks like the white-winged scoter and common eider. A 100-m-wide (328 ft) band of warm water near the shore here also acts as a major migration corridor for the least and arctic cisco of the Mackenzie River. Newborn caribou and cows, seals, and, rarely, polar bears can be seen from the spit.

IVVAVIK NATIONAL PARK
(Parc national Ivvavik)

INFORMATION & ACTIVITIES

HEADQUARTERS
Western Arctic Field Unit P.O. Box 1840, Inuvik, NT X0E 0T0. Phone (867) 777-8800. www.parkscanada.gc.ca/ivvavik.

SEASONS & ACCESSIBILITY
Charter aircraft services from Inuvik, 200 km (124 mi) east of the park, to **Margaret Lake, Sheep Creek, Stokes Point, Nunaluk Spit,** and **Komakuk Beach.** Landing sites are not maintained. Landing permits issued when registering for trip. Recommended winter travel between March and April.

ENTRANCE FEES
Camping and backcountry excursions $25 per person per day, $147 per person per year. Fishing permits $10 per day, $34 per year.

PETS
Pets permitted; must be under physical control at all times.

ACCESSIBLE SERVICES
None.

THINGS TO DO
Rafting on the **Firth River** (Class IV wilderness). Limited rescue assistance. Hiking along the mountain ranges to coastal lowlands. Twenty-four-hour daylight in summer months.

Wildlife viewing of Porcupine caribou migration between June and early July from central Yukon to calving grounds in the park and neighbouring Alaska. Fishing in early June to August for Dolly Varden char. Fishing catch-and-possession limit is one Dolly Varden char with an aggregate of three game fish total. Permit required.

Hiking: No marked hiking trails; journey should be accompanied by topographic maps. Air access points at Sheep Creek, Margaret Lake, Komakuk Beach, and Stokes Point.

Aircraft charter companies such as Aklak Air, (867) 777-3555, www.aklakair.ca, must have valid national parks business licence to land in the park. Winter access via aircraft equipped with skis or by snow machine as far as park boundary. More information available at the Parks Canada office in Inuvik (see opposite).

SPECIAL ADVISORIES
• No facilities, services, established trails, or campgrounds in the park. Visitors must be entirely self-sufficient.
• Flash flooding potential hazard.
• Ivvavik is home to grizzly bears and, on the coast, the occasional polar bear. All necessary precautions should be followed. Contact Parks Canada for more information on travelling in bear country.

CAMPGROUNDS
Camping permitted throughout the park except at archaeological sites. Recommended sites included in Firth River map and guide available at Parks Canada office. Wind-resistant tents recommended. Campfires forbidden. Camp stoves and bottled fuel must be used.

HOTELS, MOTELS, & INNS
(unless otherwise noted, rates are for a 2-person double, high season, in Canadian dollars)

<u>Outside the park:</u>
<u>Inuvik, NT X0E 0T0:</u>
Nova Inn Box 3169, 300 Mackenzie Rd. (866) 374-6682. inuvik@novahotels.ca; www.novainninuvik.ca. $109–$175.

Polar Bed & Breakfast 75 Mackenzie Rd., P.O. Box 2258. (867) 777-2554. kaufman@permafrost.com; www.polarbedandbreakfast.com. $125.

IVVAVIK

Travelling on Sea Ice with Paniloo Sangoya

Sirmilik means "land of glaciers" in Inuktitut, which refers to its northern location and the many glaciers that extend from the summit of the mountains down the recently shaped valley to the ocean. Inuit inhabiting the area have lived here since A.D. 1000 and have traditionally travelled vast distances to harvest terrestrial and marine life. Today, they still travel extensively, and in the absence of roads, sea ice remains the best means of reaching some of these same areas.

A dogsled with Inuit guide

We asked Paniloo Sangoya, Inuit Elder from Mittimatalik (Pond Inlet), to share his knowledge of Arctic travel and, in particular, sea ice travel. At this high latitude, winter presides and the temperatures get cold in early September.

In November, the sea ice is almost always formed. For that reason, we say Tusaqtuuq in Inuktitut to refer to the time of year when people could visit again. After a summer separated from each other and without communication, the sea ice allowed people to travel again and meet.

Paniloo says sea ice travel presents unique challenges as the seasons progress. Depending on the amount of snowfall, recent and current temperatures, wind direction and strength, moon cycles, salinity of the water, and solar radiation, the density and thickness of the ice can be drastically different. Dark ice indicates water-saturated, thin, unsafe ice, but Paniloo says that even white ice can be treacherous.

Even though the ice is white, it can also be thin ice if the patch used to be qinuaq. What I called qinuaq *is the white ice, well-formed ice but still thin. It always has to be tested with a harpoon. I fell through ice that looked like that, all nice and white and it turns out that the wind had broken it up, it was white while being very thin, not dark . . . looking exactly like the rest of the ice. Because I had failed to notice the edges, I ended up falling in . . . only the harpoon can expose the thin ice. The harpoon is your best companion.*

Even in the high Arctic, in areas of strong current, the water never freezes in winter. These areas are called *polynia* and Paniloo says that you can find polynia in front of Igluluarjuit, Tunnuujaqtalik, and Iqalugaarjuit, and in these places you simply need to know that the ice is never safe. Open water in winter is also found at the floe edge where the ice extends and recedes with the season—the newly formed ice is thin, layered, and can break away. Although a valuable hunting area for narwhals, seals, and polar bears, the conditions at the floe edge can be extremely hazardous.

In springtime, the ice changes, large cracks open up and turn into leads, the snow starts to melt, and water accumulates. Depending on the strength and structure of the ice, the water drains differently.

At the beginning of July when we lived at Qaurngnak, we went to Pond Inlet to get some provisions for the summer. The sleds were heavily loaded when coming back, the melt pools were deep, and we had to go slow. Nowadays, you don't encounter deep melt pools—the pools are very shallow.

The ice is not very solid anymore and the water doesn't accumulate in deep pools. The time of breakup is also earlier.

Back then, on August 1st—the Commissioner's holiday—although the ice had shifted, we travelled on the sea ice trying very hard to go west, trying to make it through. We couldn't do this now, the ice breaks up sooner and it is all open water at the beginning of August . . . Today, the ice is snowlike: When you check the ice with a harpoon, it bores down quite a bit.

Paniloo and other elders are concerned that changes in climate are greatly affecting the characteristics of the sea ice.

If the conditions continue to change and the sea ice stops forming or becomes more hazardous, we would have no means to travel in winter.

The travel routes are everywhere; they traverse every fjord, the coastline, and span thousands of kilometres. Sea ice travel is important to the Inuit, and knowledge of the environment is critical in informing their travel, and yours, if you are to fully appreciate the richness, diversity, and beauty of these Arctic national parks.

— MICHELINE MANSEAU, *Ecosystem Scientist, Parks Canada & Associate Professor, Natural Resources Institute, University of Manitoba*
— GARY MOULAND, *Manager Resource Conservation, Nunavut Field Unit, Parks Canada*
— *Interview conducted by* SAMSON ERKLOO *and translated by* MORGAN ARNAKALLAK

A view of Death Lake and the surrounding forests and cliffs

▶ NAHANNI

NORTHWEST TERRITORIES
ESTABLISHED 1972
over 30,000 sq km/413,000 acres

In the summer of 1928, American adventurer Fenley Hunter paddled up the South Nahanni River hoping to find a huge waterfall that seemed largely the stuff of Dene legend at the time. Hunter thought he would never make it. Halfway upstream he wrote: "The Nahanni is unknown and will remain so until another age brings a change in the conformation of these mountains. It is an impossible stream, and a stiff rapid is met on average every mile, and they seem countless."

The subsequent decades have proved Hunter wrong. Multiday canoeing, kayaking, and rafting trips on the South Nahanni, and to a lesser extent on the Flat and Little Nahanni Rivers, are now the main attractions in Nahanni National Park Reserve. The park is more than 30,000 sq km of wilderness that rolls out of the ice fields, mountains, alpine tundra, and boreal forest along the Continental Divide separating the Yukon and Northwest Territories.

For experienced paddlers, the South Nahanni is what Everest is to mountaineers—remote, breathtaking, and mystical. The river may not be the most difficult in the world, but neither is it for the faint of heart. It plunges through a series of four spectacular canyons, churning up rapids, boils, and whirlpools with sinister names such as Hell's Gate, or misleading ones like Tricky Current and Lafferty's Riffle, which can be equally challenging. Here, grizzly bears, black bears, moose, mountain caribou, trumpeter swans, and upland sandpipers are among the 42 species of mammals and 180 species of birds found in the park.

Nahanni is rich with legends of lost gold, murder, and headless men, along with airier lore of tropical gardens and Dene spirits that dwell in the vents of the river valley's tufa mounds and hot springs. Undisturbed by roads or seismic lines, Nahanni was, along with Yellowstone, one of the first parks to be listed as a World Heritage site.

While river trips are recommended only for skilled paddlers or those travelling with licensed outfitters, visitors of all ages can fly into Virginia Falls, which is twice the height of Niagara.

How to Get There

You can get to Nahanni by flying to Fort Simpson via Yellowknife, and then to the river by floatplane from Fort Simpson. Alternatively, you can make the 18-hour, 1,470-km (913 mi) drive from Edmonton to Fort Simpson in two days along the Mackenzie Highway. For those driving north from Edmonton looking for a hotel, High Level in Alberta is the best stopover. Twin Falls Park, 72 km (45 mi) north of the Alberta/Northwest Territories border, offers good camping.

Note: One can drive to Fort Simpson via the Alaska and Liard Highways.

When to Go

The South Nahanni is in a serious spring flood up until early June and sometimes later. The risk of severe weather toward the end of August makes it unwise to go any later, so the best time is between June and August.

How to Visit

Take a day trip from Fort Simpson, Fort Liard, and Muncho Lake in northern British Columbia; trips involve a 90-minute to two-hour flight to **Virginia Falls** and the surrounding area. Air charter service information can be found at www.pc.gc.ca/pn-np/nt/nahanni/visit/visit3.aspx#air.

A Parks Canada interpreter is usually on hand at Virginia Falls to give visitors a briefing about the area and what they can see. You can then take a very easy 30-minute hike to the **Virginia Falls viewpoint,** which offers a breathtaking view of **Sluicebox Rapids** and the waterfall. The more demanding portage trail around the falls takes about an hour. Pack a rain jacket or an extra sweater if you choose to do this. While it might be sweltering at the top of the falls, the temperature drops by at least 10 or 15 degrees down below in the mist.

You can also plan canoe, kayak, and raft trips—they'll take from eight days to three weeks. Parks Canada highly recommends that people go with a registered, licensed outfitter (see p. 308). Starting points are the **Moose Ponds** (21 days), **Island Lakes** (14–18 days), **Rabbitkettle Lake** (10–14 days), and **Virginia Falls** (7–10 days). The ending points are **Blackstone Territorial Park** for campers and **Lindberg Landing** (250-233-2344) for those who want a cozy cabin. (Deregistration takes place at the Nahanni National Park Reserve Office in Nahanni Butte.)Both are located on the **Liard River** near the confluence of the South Nahanni.

If you wish to paddle on your own, Nahanni River Adventures

NAHANNI

(a licensed outfitter) has a guide *(www .nahanni.com/rentals/selfguided.html)* which you should bring along with your 1:250,000 topographical maps.

Advanced reservations and permits are required. Visitors must register and check out at the beginning and end of their trip.

CHALLENGING WHITE-WATER ROUTES

Apart from the Moose Ponds route, which has about 50 km (31 mi) of very challenging, continuous white water, experienced paddlers have little to be concerned about until they get to Virginia Falls. Immediately downstream of the falls, however, is some challenging white water: **Canyon Rapids** followed by **Figure Eight Rapid** (Hell's Gate), **Wrigley Whirlpool, George's Riffle,** and then **Lafferty's Riffle.** Spray covers are recommended.

Difficulty of these rapids depends entirely on river water levels.

HIKES & HIGHLIGHTS ALONG THE NAHANNI

The **Cirque of the Unclimbables** was so named by Arnold Wexler and a small group of American rock climbers in 1958. When they encountered this cluster of jagged peaks and sheer rock walls, they were haunted by what they saw before them. It looked like the craggy spires of Yosemite, which Ansel Adams had made famous during his mountain photography expeditions in the 1920s.

When Wexler and his colleagues got over the shocking head-on view of the 2,740-m-high (9,000 ft) fins of wind and ice-polished granite standing tall and angular and facing one another in a half circle, the adjoining

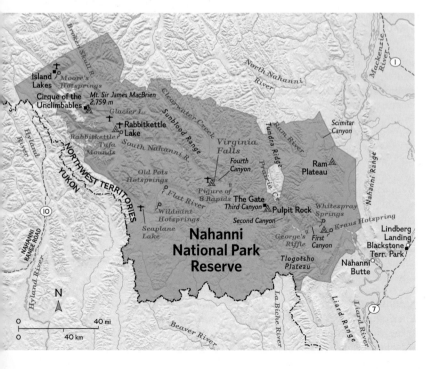

mountains suddenly looked small and terribly ordinary. Turning toward his partners, Wexler declared most of the peaks "unclimbable."

Most trips into the Unclimbables begin at **Glacier Lake,** a designated landing spot in the park. It is also possible (but not easy) to get to the Unclimbables from **Brintnell Creek** along the South Nahanni, an easy day's paddle from Island Lakes. The trail from here is at best indistinct.

From Brintnell Creek, hike upstream for 1 km (0.6 mi) until you get to a snye (a side channel) coming off the South Nahanni. Watch out for a heavily blazed pine tree. The trail eventually makes an abrupt left turn. Follow the trail over rolling hills until it nears Brintnell Creek, then follow the north bank of the creek west to Glacier Lake. Count on losing the trail a number of times along the way. Allow a day to get to Glacier Lake, and another half day to get to the **Fairy Meadows,** which is located at the foot of the Unclimbables.

Continue along to **Rabbitkettle Lake** (Gahn Hthah Mie) and its famous tufa hot springs, the largest in Canada. Some of these terraced mounds of calcium carbonate precipitate are 27 m (89 ft) high and 70 m (230 ft) in diameter. Yambadezha, "protector of the people," is said to inhabit one of the vents. It is this spirit, so the Dene legend goes, that went down to Nahanni Butte and drove away two giant beavers that would drown boaters with a slap of their enormous tails.

From the campground at Rabbitkettle, one can hike to the **Secret Lakes**—a series of small, deep lakes nestled in the sides of the mountain valley. There are two 10-km (6 mi) routes in the area; ask the staff based at Rabbitkettle for advice. Note that Rabbitkettle is a

Kayaking on the South Nahanni River

hot spot for grizzly bears and black bears, so tread cautiously.

Downriver the **Sunblood Mountains** trailhead (8 km/5 mi one way) is located across the river from the Virginia Falls Campground. To get there safely, paddle upstream a few hundred metres and cross the river to the sign that marks the beginning of the trail. Follow this trail to an open scree ridge and continue to the peak of Sunblood. Start early, bring water, and enjoy the spectacular views of the river and waterfalls below.

Marengo Falls (4 km/2.5 mi one way): There are two ways to get to this small waterfall that drops 30 m (98 ft) over a series of limestone ledges. Parks Canada interpreters will be happy to point you to the two routes from **Virginia Falls.** All you'll need is a GPS or map and compass.

THE THIRD CANYON

In **Third Canyon,** the river takes a sharp turn before cutting a narrow, steep-sided slit through rock streaked red with iron, known as **The Gate.** Passing through this peaceful stretch of water in 1927, author/adventurer Raymond Patterson wrote, "The whole thing was like a great gateway through which I glided silently, midget like.

NAHANNI

NAHANNI NATIONAL PARK RESERVE
(Réserve de parc national Nahanni)

INFORMATION & ACTIVITIES

VISITOR CENTRE
Nahanni National Park Reserve office Fort Simpson. Phone (867) 695-3151. Open daily June to October; weekdays rest of year. **Nahanni Butte** (867) 602-2024. Duty officer on call 24 hours a day, June–Sept. (867) 695-3732.

SEASONS & ACCESSIBILITY
Park open year-round, peak season May to August. No roads lead to the park; accessible by chartered floatplane from licensed company. Park permits required for landing at Virginia Falls and Rabbitkettle Lake. Floatplanes accessible from Fort Simpson, Fort Liard, and Yellowknife, NT; Fort Nelson and Muncho Lake, BC; and Watson Lake, YT. Licensed charter companies: Simpson Air, Ltd. (867) 695-2505; South Nahanni Airways (867) 695-2007; Wolverine Air (867) 695-2263; Air Tindi (867) 669-8200; Alpine Aviation (Yukon) Ltd. (867) 668-7725; Kluane Airways/Inconnu Lodge (250) 860-4187; Liard Tours/Northern Rockies Lodge (250) 776-3482.

HEADQUARTERS
10002 100 St., P.O. Box 348, Fort Simpson, NT X0E 0N0. Phone (867) 695-3151. www.parkscanada.gc.ca/nahanni.

ENTRANCE FEES
Backcountry excursion and camping permits are $25 per person per day, $147 per person per year. Reservation requests, member list form, and emergency contact and equipment list forms must be provided to park office.

PETS
Pets permitted but not recommended; must be on a leash at all times.

ACCESSIBLE SERVICES
None.

THINGS TO DO
Most visitors start their trips from **Virginia Falls** (typically 7–10 days) or **Rabbitkettle Lake** (10–14 days). Other starting locations include **Island Lakes** (14–18 days; flat, with Class II rapids), the **Little Nahanni River** (6–7 days to paddle to Rabbitkettle Lake and join South Nahanni; Class II–IV rapids), or **The Moose Ponds** (outside park boundary; 21 days; Class II–IV white water). Alternate routes include **Seaplane Lake/Flat River** (4–5 days; Class II–V rapids) and **Glacier Lake.** Permits required. River guide pamphlets available for $5. Reservations must be confirmed with park office.

Canoeing in the **South Nahanni River** between June and September.

Hiking in the **Cirque of the Unclimbables; Glacier Lake** (accessed from South Nahanni River north of park boundary); **Secret Lakes** (6–10 km/4–6 mi, one way); **Sunblood Mountain** (8 km/5 mi,

I have seen many beautiful places in my lifetime, but never anything of this kind."

Just past **Big Bend,** where the **Funeral Range** ends and the **Headless Range** begins, is where the headless bodies of the McLeod brothers, Willie and Frank, were found after they went missing in 1903 searching for an Indian tale of gold piled high in the region. A note carved in a sled runner that read, "We have found a prospect," resulted in a mini gold rush and murderous incidents that are why the Nahanni has been called the "Valley of the Vanishing Men."

Prairie Creek (4 km/2.5 mi one way) is a large alluvial fan that can't be missed. Stay left of Prairie Creek's channels when you begin the hike; when Prairie Creek exits the mountains, climb over a saddle to the west of the gap, to get to a floodplain flanked by the vertical canyon walls.

The dry gravel fan of **Dry Canyon Creek** (10 km/6 mi one way) is at the one way); **Marengo Falls** (4 km/2.5 mi, one way); **Scow Creek/Headless Range** (8 km/5 mi, one way); **Prairie Creek** (4 km/2.5 mi, one way); **Sheaf Creek–Tlogotsho Plateau** (10 km/6 mi, one way); **Dry Canyon Creek** (10 km/6 mi, one way); **Ram Creek** (15 km/9 mi, one way); **Lafferty Creek** (10 km/6 mi, one way).

Fishing permitted in all park waters at any time of year with five fish limit for daily catch-and-possession. Fishing permits are $34 per year.

Licensed river outfitters include: Black Feather—The Wilderness Adventure Company (705) 746-1372 or (888) 737-6818; Nahanni River Adventures (867) 668-3056; Nahanni Wilderness Adventures (403) 678-3374.

SPECIAL ADVISORIES

• Open fires for cooking or heat not permitted. Fire-box and fire-pan rentals available at Deh Cho Hardware, Fort Simpson. Phone (867) 695-2320.
• Campsites forbidden near staff cabins.
• Solid experience in white-water paddling or rafting, self-rescue skills, and knowledge of travelling and camping in remote wilderness environments recommended.
• Consult park map for boundaries.

CAMPGROUNDS

Virginia Falls Campground by reservation. Maximum group size 12 people, 2-night stay, $25 per person per day or $147 per person per year. Collection box at kiosk at Virginia Falls. Travel time to campsite is 2 to 3 days paddling time if starting from Rabbitkettle Lake; 6 to 7 days if starting from Island Lakes; 10 days if starting from the Mooseponds. Travel time depends on weather conditions and off-river hiking time. Canoe racks, food caches, and composting toilets available. Use caution when approaching portage landing. **Rabbitkettle Lake** campgrounds are off the shores of the lake 300 m (984 ft) north of staff cabin, and on an island in the South Nahanni River across from portage landing. Both campgrounds have food caches and outhouses. No camping permitted at portage landing. **The Gate (Pulpit Rock)** is a designated campsite. Composting toilet available. **Kraus Hotsprings** former homestead of Mary and Gus Kraus. Hot springs along river's edge. Check-in station, food cache, and outhouse available. Use of soap prohibited.

HOTELS, MOTELS, & INNS
(unless otherwise noted, rates are for a 2-person double, high season, in Canadian dollars)

Outside the park:
Fort Simpson, NT X0E 0N0:
Deh Cho Suites 10509 Antoine Drive, Box 60. (867) 695-2309 or (877) 695-2309. $175–$195.
Maroda Motel 9802 100th St. (867) 695-2602. $115–$170.
Nahanni Inn Box 258. (867) 695-2201. $115–$170.

Nahanni Butte, NT X0E 0N0:
Nahanni Butte Inn and General Store Box 149. (867) 602-2002.

far eastern end of **Deadmen Valley.** Hike along gravel beds of the steep-walled canyon. Several draws and ridges to the east will take you to the **Nahanni Plateau.** Note that the canyon can flood in a thunderstorm.

OTHER RIVERS

Lafferty Creek (10 km/6 mi one way) joins the South Nahanni near the bottom of First Canyon at km 260. Some boulder walking and scrambling will be necessary to get through.

Kraus Hotsprings, located a kilometre downstream of Lafferty Creek at the end of a long rapid (Lafferty's Riffle), is the site of an old homestead. Here, weary paddlers can soak their bones in one of the warm springs percolating from the gravel.

The **Flat River** and **Little Nahanni River** both flow from the Yukon Divide and provide alternative and somewhat more challenging ways of exploring Nahanni National Park.

NAHANNI

Brock River Canyon, Tuktut Nogait

▶TUKTUT NOGAIT

NORTHWEST TERRITORIES
ESTABLISHED 1996
16,340 sq km/4,037,702 acres

In an expanse of tundra, scattered with rolling hills, barren plateaus, and remote lakes, three wild rivers carve their way across a vast landscape to the Arctic Ocean. Spring melt rushes through sheer vertical canyons over chiselled beds of limestone, shale, and sandstone; roars through rapids; and crashes over waterfalls. This exceptional canyon scenery is reminiscent of that found in the more populated American Southwest, but here, standing on the wide open tundra above the Arctic Circle, you are likely to enjoy it in nearly total seclusion.

Although the Hornaday River runs for 360 km (224 mi), it was the last Canadian river of its size to be discovered. In its upper reaches, it is shallow, wide, and meandering, but downstream it transforms into 45 km (28 mi) of wild, white water. Red canyon walls soar 120 m (394 ft) above it. At one dramatic spot, the river is funnelled through a canyon 3 m (10 ft) wide before it plunges over the magnificent La Roncière Falls.

The tundra itself has varied features and climates. Long, harsh winters give way to summers that bring the landscape to life. Cliffs formed by the canyon walls provide nesting sites for one of the greatest concentrations of peregrines and gyrfalcons in Canada. Ancient, well-worn migration trails wind along the canyon rims and across plateaus, marking the route of thousands of caribou from the Bluenose West herd as they travel to their traditional calving grounds in the Melville Hills. And tracks of wolves, grizzlies, and wolverines along the sandy edges of the upper Hornaday testify to the presence of these hard-to-glimpse species.

Evidence of early cultures, such as the Thule and Copper Inuit (A.D. 1200–1500), can still be seen. Remnants of campsites on top of hills, food caches, graves, and kayak rests—some more identifiable than others—all suggest that this vast landscape has been in use by indigenous people for hundreds of years.

Today the Inuvialuit people from the nearby community of Paulatuk still rely on the lands encompassed by the park to provide a healthy start for young caribou born in early summer. In fact, it is from their language, Inuvialuktun, that the park is named—*Tuktut Nogait* means "young caribou" and refers to moment after a caribou's birth, when it first stands, shakily, on the tundra.

How to Get There

Tuktut Nogait is a remote park located 40 km (25 mi) east of the community of Paulatuk and 460 km (286 mi) northeast of the town of Inuvik. To access the park for backpacking or paddling trips visitors typically fly from either Inuvik or Norman Wells in the Northwest Territories. Only water-based landings are permissible. As charter flights are very expensive, investigate sharing or splitting the costs with another group—contact the Parks Canada officer in Inuvik or Paulatuk for a list of planned trips.

Alternatively, if you're backpacking (and thus don't need to transport a canoe or kayak), take a scheduled flight (available three days a week) with Aklak Air from Inuvik to Paulatuk. From Paulatuk you can access the park on foot, or save some time and get a little closer to your destination with the aid of a locally hired boat shuttle service that can get you to the lands north of the park. Either option will take you across privately owned Inuvialuit lands, and you are asked to contact the Inuvialuit Land Administration prior to your trip. Be aware that all modes of travel may be delayed due to unexpected weather and environmental complications such as fog, high river water, pack ice, strong winds, or snow.

When to Go

Go after the ice has melted on the lakes and before the snow begins to fall. In the Arctic, that's mid-June to mid-August. During the summer months, expect anything from blue skies and warm breezes to fog and freak snowstorms. In late June, the tundra explodes into a carpet of wildflowers, and caribou are out in numbers. In early July, the river water levels are ideal, and the diversity of birds rich. In August, the land is ablaze with fall colours, and you'll finally be able to pack away your bug spray.

How to Visit

Extended backpacking or paddling trips of 10 to 12 days are the preferred methods to take in this remote Arctic wilderness. All trips require extensive logistical preparation several months in advance, and it is mandatory to register and receive an orientation session at the start of your trip. Detailed backpacking and paddling guides for the Hornaday River are available, and additional but limited

TUKTUT NOGAIT

information on other areas is available upon request.

Given the park's remote location and the potential for weather-related complications in air travel, be aware that in the event of an emergency, assistance could be days away. Therefore, it is highly recommended that visitors have backcountry survival skills and extensive knowledge of wilderness first aid.

HORNADAY RIVER CANYONS
About 7 to 10 days

La Roncière Falls, Hornaday River

Paddling the 45-km (28 mi) stretch of white water through the **Hornaday River Canyons** is not an option for the amateur adventurer. However, trekking along the rim is a thrilling experience, and you'll spend days soaking in the dramatic scenes of frothing water and jagged rock. Hiking on either side is mostly level terrain with a mix of tundra and tussocks. Both hikes allow you to view the impressive 20-m-high (66 ft) **La Roncière Falls** (in the third canyon).

To backpack the west rim, fly into Cache Lake and hike back out to Paulatuk. From Cache Lake, 2 km (1 mi) from the first of three Hornaday Canyon sections, hike for several days until you reach the delta, approximately 10 km (6 mi) from the coast, and continue overland to **Paulatuk.** Allow ten days for this 107-km (66 mi) hike. Given that this route does not require crossing the Hornaday River, it's the one most frequently taken by visitors.

To backpack the east rim, fly in to a small lake 4 km (2.5 mi) southeast of Roncière Falls. This seven-day hike follows the east rim of the canyons and river edge to the delta. From here, you must either have arranged for a boat pickup at a predetermined time

and location, or make a river crossing on foot. The latter should only be attempted by experienced backpackers at low-water levels.

HORNADAY (UPPER SECTION) & LITTLE HORNADAY RIVERS
About 10 days

Upstream of the canyons is a vast river valley scored by meandering waterways and large sweeping sandbars. Experience this section of the river by backpacking or paddling.

To backpack, fly to **Erly Lake** near the south border of the park. Hike across the open tundra for a couple of kilometres (1 mile) to reach the river. For 105 km (65 mi), you will follow the west bank to **Cache Lake,** the aircraft pickup spot just before the canyons begin. Mats of pink moss campion and white mountain avens guide the way.

In early July, 145 km (90 mi) of the **upper Hornaday** is navigable by canoe. Off the river, there are side valleys that offer hiking excursions among small hills and lakes. It takes a minimum of ten days to complete

White water in a slot canyon

this route from **Canoe Lake** (south end of the park) to Cache Lake (upstream of the canyons). You'll need flights in and out, as well as a short portage to and from the lakes.

Upstream from its confluence with the Little Hornaday (its one major tributary, see opposite), the **Hornaday River** is shallow, and alternates between short, calm, slow sections and long, fast, rocky riffles and chutes, though none of the white water is designated as anything over Class II. Good campsites are plentiful in this area. Downstream of the confluence, the current slows and the channel widens. Some stretches, which are up to 800 m (2,625 ft) wide, resemble a lake more than a river. Lined by vast sandbars and dunes, the river wanders through an old bedrock river valley modified by

glacial erosion. Suitable campsites are more difficult to find in this section.

You can access the Hornaday River via the **Little Hornaday River,** which forms the outflow from **Hornaday Lake.** Fly to the eastern park boundary where Hornaday Lake borders Nunavut. Hornaday Lake is the park's largest lake and is located in the **Melville Hills** 512 m (1,680 ft) above sea level. The Little Hornaday River drops 150 m (492 ft) between the lake and the Hornaday River 89 km (55 mi) downstream. Spirited and fast flowing, the Little Hornaday is ideal for experienced Class III white-water paddlers. The river is narrow and shallow with riffles, rock gardens, and rapids. A trip from Hornaday Lake to the Hornaday River and then to Cache Lake is 185 km (115 mi). Allow a minimum of ten days.

TUKTUT NOGAIT NATIONAL PARK
(Parc national Tuktut Nogait)

INFORMATION & ACTIVITIES

HEADQUARTERS
Box 91, Paulatuk, NT X0E 1N0. Phone (867) 580-3233. www.parkscanada.gc.ca/tuktutnogait. **Western Arctic Field Unit,** Box 1840, Inuvik, NT X0E 0T0. Phone (867) 777- 8800. Inuvik.info@pc.gc.ca.

SEASONS & ACCESSIBILITY
Park open year-round; peak visitor season in July. Overland hiking from **Paulatuk** (40 km/25 mi) or charter boat. Boat shuttle services via Paulatuk Community Corporation (867) 580-3601 or Paulatuk Hunters and Trappers Committee (867) 580-3004. Flights from Inuvik, available via Aklak Air, Tuesday, Wednesday, and Friday, (867) 777-3777. Charter aircraft from **Norman Wells** via North-Wright Air Ltd. (867) 587-2288. Twenty-four-hour daylight June and July. Winter access by aircraft equipped with skis, snow machine up to park boundary, or skiing from Paulatuk. Optimal skiing and snowshoeing late March until May.

ENTRANCE FEES
$25 per person per day, $147 per person per year. Fishing permits $10 per person per day, $34 per person per year.

PETS
Pets permitted; must be on a leash or under physical control at all times.

ACCESSIBLE SERVICES
None.

THINGS TO DO
Hiking, fishing for arctic char and lake trout, paddling for novice and expert paddlers with strong wilderness first aid and backcountry travel skills. No established hiking trails. Access to **Hornaday River** for paddling via the **Little Hornaday River** (Class III rapids) starting at **Hornaday Lake** (185 km/115 mi) or starting directly on main river (145 km/90 mi). Total paddling time is 8 to 12 days. Copies of "Hornaday River Guide" available at park office in Inuvik. More than 350 archaeological sites dating back to A.D. 1200.

SPECIAL ADVISORIES
- No campfires permitted. Camp stove and bottled fuel for cooking can be purchased in Inuvik or Paulatuk.
- Fishing permits allow limit of one game fish. Daily catch-and-possession limit is one of either arctic char, lake trout, or grayling in addition to one broad whitefish. Permits required for anyone above age 16.
- Commercial and sport hunting not permitted.

CAMPGROUNDS
No designated campsites. Camping permitted everywhere; avoid areas around archaeological sites. Appropriate camping sites along the Hornaday River recommended.

HOTELS, MOTELS, & INNS
(unless otherwise noted, rates are for a 2-person double, high season, in Canadian dollars)

Paulatuk Visitors Centre Hotel P.O. Box 52, Paulatuk, NT X0E 1N0. (867) 580-3051. paulatuk_hotel@airwave.com. $349.

TUKTUT NOGAIT

ROSCOE & BROCK RIVERS

The beautiful waterfalls and deep, narrow canyons of **the Roscoe,** in the northeast, and **the Brock,** in the mid-north, are also worth exploring though few visitors do, given the increased logistical challenges of accessing these areas. Less information is available for these routes. Hiking here is more challenging than on the Hornaday because of creek crossings and uneven ground. On both rivers, expect Class II and III white water upstream of unnavigable canyon sections. Note that weather conditions can delay travel for several days.

Muskoxen sightings are frequent along the lower Thomsen.

▶AULAVIK

NORTHWEST TERRITORIES
ESTABLISHED 1992
12,200 sq km/3,014,686 acres

While the rest of the world marches forward to the drums of progress, Aulavik National Park's spectacular wildlife-rich lowland tundra seems content to remain a timeless Arctic treasure. In this remote park, one can hear the howl of wolves, the *kee-yee-yip* of arctic foxes, the grunt of the muskoxen, and the relentless rush of wind. The tundra of Aulavik is home to 150 species of flowering plants that explode in a kaleidoscope of colour, making it easy to feel as though you have landed in a world totally removed from the one we live in.

In addition to the park's rich biodiversity, the western Arctic lowlands of Aulavik are breathtakingly beautiful, and the park protects over 280 archaeological sites, some of which date back 3,500 years. A visitor with sharp eyes will spot metal knives, tools crafted from bone and antler, and stone points scattered amid the remains of ancient meat caches and tent rings. The more recent historical drama of the European quest for the Northwest Passage is evoked by the shore cache of the obsessed Capt. Robert M'Clure, whose British naval ship H.M.S. *Investigator* was frozen fast in Mercy Bay in 1851. The desperate crew was finally rescued in 1853, and the icebound vessel became a source of rare wood and metal for the Copper Inuit.

The level of commitment and cost required to access Aulavik prevent much human traffic: The park sees an average of 15 visitors per year—over 80,000 Arctic hectares (197,680 acres) per visitor. Translated as "the place where people travel" in Inuvialuktun, the language of the Inuvialuit, Aulavik is a must for any serious Arctic wilderness lover, despite the challenges of getting there.

How to Get There

Aulavik is one of Canada's most remote parks, and visitors must plan their visit well ahead. Charter a Twin Otter from Inuvik for the four-hour, 750-km (466 mi) flight northeast to the park. There is one stop en route to refuel in the only permanent settlement on Banks Island, Ikahuak (Sachs Harbour), population approximately 100. The expense of the plane charter may motivate you to book with the park's only licensed commercial operator, Whitney & Smith Legendary Expeditions (403-678-3052). Most

A black-bellied plover

visitors fly to Inuvik via Edmonton, or drive the famous Dempster Highway via Whitehorse—an adventure in itself.

When to Go

Aulavik is best enjoyed at the fleeting height of the high Arctic summer. Paddlers will want to arrive after the river breaks up, usually in mid- to late June, and before the snowmelt ends in mid-July. After this, water levels drop dramatically, leaving the upper Thomsen River a shallow, rocky riffle, and the silty lower reaches become a frustrating maze of shifting sand and mud bars. Visit from late June to mid-July to hit the best paddling, peak flowers, and good bird- and wildlife-watching.

How to Visit

A visit to Aulavik requires detailed advance planning. This is a very isolated high Arctic wilderness and visitors need to be self-sufficient and prepared to meet a large range of obstacles and complications, some more foreseeable than others.

All visits begin with a park orientation from Parks Canada staff in Inuvik. This one-hour presentation will acquaint you with the remote and sensitive nature of the unusual landscape on northern Banks Island. In a place where average July temperatures rarely exceed 10°C (50°F), you'll need to be prepared for cold weather conditions, and be aware of the risks of hypothermia. Although temperatures on south-facing, sheltered slopes can reach 25°C (77°F), midsummer snow is still likely. Inland encounters with polar bears are less likely, but grizzly bear encounters are possible. With the changing conditions of glacial ice and the unpredictable bear behaviour observed in recent years, bear spray

AULAVIK

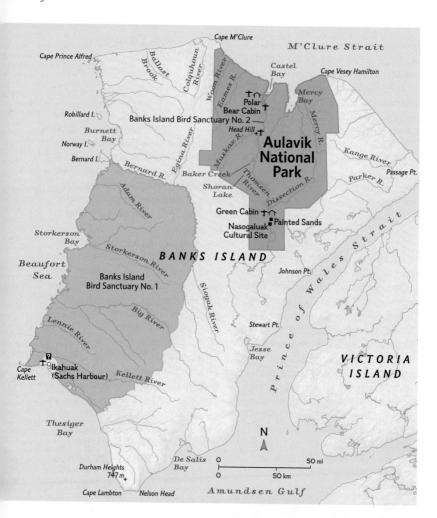

and approved protocols for travelling in bear country are necessary parts of safe travel in Aulavik. A new policy on firearms in northern national parks where polar bears are present has been introduced. Speak to Parks Canada officials in Inuvik for details. Visitors must also pick up the requisite Parks Canada landing permit for air access to the park.

While most visitors to Aulavik canoe or kayak the **Thomsen River,** billed as the world's most northerly navigable waterway, some prefer to ramble across the rolling tundra, an option that affords glimpses of Arctic wildlife from nearly every mountable ridge. Given the expense and travel time of an expedition to Aulavik, most parties wish to spend ten days to two weeks exploring the park. This is sufficient time to canoe or kayak the entire length of the Thomsen River within the park, and have plenty of time for hiking excursions along the way. This is also the minimum time needed to thoroughly explore part of the park on foot from a base camp, or to hike between two of the established airstrips. You need to factor in a couple of days for weather-related delays when you plan your trip.

FLOAT TRIP—THOMSEN RIVER

About 7 to 10 days

Although the park offers rewarding (if somewhat sodden) hiking, Aulavik is best experienced from a kayak or canoe. The entire 150 km (93 mi) from the south boundary to **Castel Bay** is an easy Class I float, with few hazards, save for some visible rocks and secondary channels. The valley is notorious for frigid headwinds howling inland off the ice-covered **M'Clure Strait,** sending whitecaps rolling upstream, so expect some lining and bumping. Many expedition groups prefer collapsible canoes and kayaks to cut down on the size and weight of their cargo, bearing in mind the Twin Otter payload restrictions.

There are four established tundra airstrips and one gravel strip inside the park. Paddlers often put in at **Thom Up** (Upper Thomsen) strip near the park's southern boundary. For shorter trips, or if low water levels preclude paddling the upper river, a good strip exists at **Green Cabin,** at the confluence of the Thomsen and **Painted Sands Creek.** The forest green plywood building is the only permanent structure near the Thomsen River, and is a popular put-in or pickup location for visiting groups. The ideal, two-week float takes parties from Thom Up or Green Cabin to established landing strips at the **Muskox River** or Castel Bay, where the Thomsen empties its snowmelt into the ice-choked M'Clure Strait. Do not attempt to establish a new landing strip, as pilots are wary of soft tundra, and are unlikely to agree to land on it except in the case of an emergency. Parks Canada also discourages this, as landings can scar the tundra with tire marks for decades.

Upstream of Green Cabin, crystal clear water hurries over a shallow, bouldery bed. A vibrant community of poppies, louseworts, and purple saxifrage dance in the wind on a gently rolling tundra. Plover, sandpipers, snowy owls, jaegers, and sandhill cranes all nest here, and several active wolf dens have been established near the

A hiker looks over the lower falls of Mercy River.

An arctic tern nesting

Arctic oxytrope

riverbanks. Overlooking the river, Xanthoria-encrusted stone cairns mark archaeological sites, which attest to centuries of human activity in the region.

The **lower Thomsen** boasts rugged topography, with rocky outcrops and steep banks, many of which are home to nesting pairs of peregrine falcons or rough-legged hawks. Although the lower river becomes muddier, the hiking becomes more interesting, and muskox encounters are virtually guaranteed. Aulavik boasts the highest density of these Ice Age mammals on the planet.

ARCHAEOLOGICAL TREASURE

Though often overshadowed by the prolific Arctic wildlife and birdlife, Aulavik's archaeological sites are a major attraction for many visitors. **Nasogaluak,** 8 km (5 mi) upstream and across the river from Green Cabin, is an incredible assemblage of more than 30 meat caches, wind breaks, and tent rings spread over a large area. Farther downstream near **Baker Creek** sprawls an impressive ruin, with meat caches, tent rings, and muskox skulls strewn along a prominent ridge from the water's edge to the top of the ridge. The most impressive site, however, is **Head Hill,** where the remains of hundreds of muskoxen dot a prominent rise just up the Muskox River from its confluence with the Thomsen.

In addition to the lure of these fascinating historical artifacts, the microclimate here produces some of the most diverse and dense Arctic flower growth imaginable, and the

AULAVIK NATIONAL PARK OF CANADA
(Parc national Aulavik)

INFORMATION & ACTIVITIES

VISITOR CENTRE
Box 29, Sachs Harbour, NT X0E 0Z0.
Phone (867) 690-3904.

SEASONS & ACCESSIBILITY
June until mid-August, accessible by
airplane. Twenty-four-hour daylight
between June and mid-August. Darkness
throughout winter makes it difficult to
land a plane.

HEADQUARTERS
Western Arctic Field Unit P.O. Box
1840, Inuvik, NT X0E 0T0. Phone
(867) 777-8800. www.parks canada
.gc.ca/aulavik.

ENTRANCE FEES
$25 per person per day, $147 per person
per year. Fishing permits $10 per person
per day, $34 per person per year. Landing
permits are mandatory for charter flights.

PETS
None permitted.

ACCESSIBLE SERVICES
None.

THINGS TO DO
Paddle down the **Thomsen River.** Hiking
terrain throughout the park. Contact park
outfitter Whitney & Smith Legendary
Expeditions P.O. Box 8576, Canmore, AB
T1W 2V3. (800) 713-6660.

Visit pre-Dorset archaeological sites
near **Shoran Lake.**

View Peary caribou, muskoxen, arctic
foxes, arctic wolves, ermines, arctic hares,
and both brown and collared lemmings.
Marine mammals along the north coast
include polar bears, ringed seals, bearded
seals, beluga whales, and bowhead whales.

SPECIAL ADVISORIES
• Note daily fish catch-and-possession
limit of one arctic char, one lake trout,
and one grayling.

CAMPGROUNDS
There are no designated campgrounds.
Camping permitted everywhere in
the park except in or around archaeological sites.

HOTELS, MOTELS, & INNS
*(unless otherwise noted, rates are for a
2-person double, high season, in Canadian
dollars)*

Polar Grizz Lodge Box 15, Sachs Harbour,
NT X0E 0Z0. (867) 690-3614. $250 per
person per night, continental breakfast
and full kitchen access included.

AULAVIK

south-facing slopes below Head
Hill support nesting peregrines and
rough-legged hawks, and are also
home to several fox dens.

Hikes from the main river valley
can include trips to **Shoran Lake** and
3,500-year-old pre-Dorset archaeological sites, and to **Mercy Bay** to
view all that's left of M'Clure's
ambitious quest for the Northwest
Passage and to check out **Gyrfalcon
Bluff.** You can easily spend several
days exploring the region around
the confluence of the Muskox and
Thomsen Rivers, looking for the
scattered archaeological sites, searching for rare Arctic plants like the
giant mastodon flower, and watching for wildlife.

Complicated logistics and heavy
expense deter some prospective
visitors from independently planning their trip, and many opt to visit
Aulavik with the park's only registered commercial outfitter, Whitney
& Smith Legendary Expeditions.
Several other outfitters currently list
Aulavik as a destination—be sure to
ask to see their commercial licence
before you sign up.

View of ice floes in Discovery Harbour from Fort Conger

▶ QUTTINIRPAAQ

NUNAVUT
ESTABLISHED 1988
39,500 sq km/9,760,663 acres

Quttinirpaaq National Park is a sprawling expanse of a high Arctic park, the most remote in Canada, and situated at the northern end of Ellesmere Island, the last piece of land before Canada gives way to the Arctic Ocean. Visitors to Quttinirpaaq will encounter wildlife that has almost certainly never laid eye on humans, including arctic wolves, Peary caribou, muskoxen, and arctic hares. One can also trek through a glacier-eroded landscape in the brilliance of a 24-hour sunlit day.

Quttinirpaaq (pronounced Kooo-tin-i-paaack) means "place at the top of the world" in Inuktitut. Originally created as Ellesmere Island National Park Reserve in 1988, this expanse of land became Quttinirpaaq National Park in 2001 after the Nunavut Land Claim was settled. This park is the second largest national park in Canada, and is also the most northerly. It is only 720 km (447 mi) from the North Pole

and is the last stop on land for adventurers headed to the Pole.

Visitors to the North Pole begin their journey at Ward Hunt Island, which is also a part of this vast park. Before they step off these islands and out of the park, these adventurers must be utterly self-sufficient and skilled in wilderness travel and survival, because designated trails do not exist. Rescue capabilities are limited and may take several days. Pickup must be arranged in advance with the air company that visitors use to start their North Pole journey.

Visitors who come to Quttinirpaaq to hike, ski, mountain climb, or mount expeditions across the ice caps or glaciers in the park must have and be able to read topographical maps, as hiking in this backcountry does not involve groomed trails but, instead, suggested routes. Quttinirpaaq is a land of contrasts. It's home to the highest peak in eastern North America—Barbeau Peak. It has an ice cap a kilometre (0.6 mi) thick, but also shelters a very productive thermal Arctic oasis at Lake Hazen, which at 70 km long and 10 km wide (43 mi by 6 mi) is one of the largest and deepest lakes in the circumpolar world. Quttinirpaaq also contains some geological features that suggest that perhaps this part of the world was not always situated so far north.

Inside the park, visitors can hike different loops, or can ski and hike between Lake Hazen and Tanquary Fiord. Accompanied by Parks Canada staff, visitors can explore the historic base camp at Fort Conger, site of American Robert Peary's North Pole expeditions. From Fort Conger on a clear day, you can see Greenland 20 km (12 mi) away.

In summer, temperatures can reach 23°C (73°F) at Lake Hazen, warmer than Nunavut's capital of Iqaluit 2,000 km (1,240 mi) to the south. However, weather is always unpredictable and any visit demands advance planning and preparation.

How to Get There
Get to Iqaluit daily by air from Ottawa and Montreal, or three times a week from Yellowknife via Edmonton by First Air, Canadian North, or Air Canada. In summer there are five flights a week from Iqaluit to Resolute Bay by First Air. You can also fly from Yellowknife to Resolute Bay via First Air once a week.

Quttinirpaaq is 800 km (497 mi) northeast from the community of Resolute Bay, which is the last leg of the journey you can make via scheduled flights. Beyond Resolute, unless you fly your own plane, Kenn Borek's chartered aircraft are the only option available. These ten-seat charter Twin Otters are the workhorses of the high Arctic. Charter costs vary from year to year, depending on the cost of fuel. In 2010, a return flight to Tanquary Fiord for ten passengers and their gear cost $30,000.00 to charter. Contact park staff to help organize shared flights with other visitors in advance of your trip.

When to Go
Park staff spend the spring and summer in Quttinirpaaq, usually from

QUTTINIRPAAQ

An arctic hare

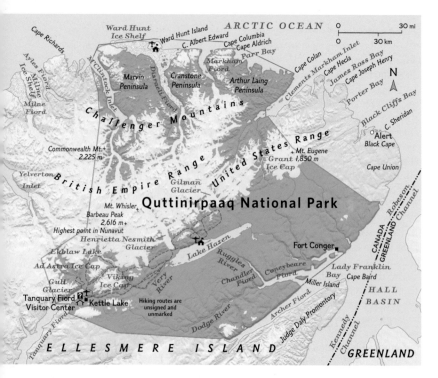

ARCTIC OCEAN

Quttinirpaaq National Park

ELLESMERE ISLAND

GREENLAND

mid-May until about mid-August. It is not recommended that visitors venture into the park when staff is not there, as this is an extremely isolated and remote location. May is still snowy and cold, although 24 hours of bright sun light any adventure. With thousands of square kilometres of glaciers and skiable terrain, the opportunities for ski touring for the experienced visitor in Quttinirpaaq are almost endless.

Mid-June until mid-August is the best time for hiking in the park. Hikers can explore the park from drop-off points at Tanquary Fiord or Lake Hazen, but should be mindful that in such a remote high Arctic location, any sort of weather is possible, even in summer. From September to March even charter flights to the park are not possible, as pilots won't fly into the park during these bleak, dark months.

How to Visit

Because of the high cost of charters and because most flights are shared, it is very rare for anyone to schedule day trips into the park from Resolute Bay. However, if price is no object, day trips can be arranged. Most visitors choose to travel in guided groups, plan one- or two-week excursions, and take advantage of shared flights in and out of the park. Costs for charter flights increase beyond Tanquary Fiord, the first staff camp from Resolute, where planes refuel.

Visitors alone or in guided groups must arrange mandatory registration and orientation in advance of their arrival in the park. This will ensure that Quttinirpaaq park staff are available at Tanquary as visitors arrive and will be there for their debrief at the end of their journey. Visitors must be self-sufficient, and bring their own gear, tents, clothing, stoves, fuel, and food. It's a good idea to pack even more supplies than you think you'll need, in case weather-related delays extend the length of your trip.

Between 1992 and 2010 expedition cruise ships visited the park almost every year for either day or multiday visits to Tanquary Fiord, and occasionally to Fort Conger. However, due to changes in marine shipping laws, icebreaker class ships using heavy oil can no longer ply high Arctic or Antarctic waters, and as of this writing, it is unknown whether expedition cruises to Quttinirpaaq will resume. The result is that increasingly, the park is accessible only to the hardiest of adventurers.

TANQUARY FORD

At Tanquary Fiord, visitors can see a small **museum** with exhibits on the Cold War–era Defense Research Board's influence in the area, prior to the park's establishment. Military interest in the North was high during the height of the Cold War, and the displays illustrate Canada's response to the tensions. The park was also the site of committed academic research: In 1957–1958, which was an International Polar Year, McGill University students wintered here in semipermanent structures and research tents while they conducted extensive scientific research.

Travel in Quttinirpaaq will introduce you to the remains of an ancient culture predating the modern Inuit: The Paleo-Eskimo (Independence I and Independence II cultures) lived in what is now the national park 4,500 years ago. Evidence of their inhabitation can be found in various locations of the park. Park staff can educate you further on the resilient and adaptive people who called this land home.

ARCTIC LIFE CYCLES

Because the park is in the extreme high Arctic, the landscape is unlike anything most visitors will ever have seen. Vegetation is sparse across most of the landscape, though it is lush in a few locations, such as **Lake Hazen.** The life cycle of organisms

QUTTINIRPAAQ

Camping in one of the park valleys in Quttinirpaaq National Park

QUTTINIRPAAQ NATIONAL PARK
(Parc national Quttinirpaaq)

INFORMATION & ACTIVITIES

VISITOR CENTRE
Contact Pangnirtung park office for mandatory registration and orientation. Phone (867) 473-2500.

SEASONS & ACCESSIBILITY
Park open year-round, summer season lasts late May to late August. Notify Tanquary Fiord Warden Station of arrival. Park accessible by charter aircraft from **Resolute Bay** or **Grise Fiord** (depending upon the season and fuel prices, flights typically cost $30,000 to $50,000). Kenn Borek Air provides Twin Otter aircraft. Call (867) 252-3845.

HEADQUARTERS
P.O. Box 278, Iqaluit, NU X0A 0H0. Phone (867) 975-4673. www.parkscanada.gc.ca/quttinirpaaq.

ENTRANCE FEES
$12 per person per day for commercial groups. $25 per person per day or $147 per person per year for backcountry excursions and camping.

PETS
None permitted.

ACCESSIBLE SERVICES
None.

THINGS TO DO
Hike in **Lake Hazen** and **Tanquary Fiord** in the summer. Take an expedition to the North Pole starting on **Ward Hunt Island** along the northern coast. Guided historic tour of **Fort Conger** by special permission. Ski-touring or ski-mountaineering on the ice cap and glaciers in the spring. If accessing the North Pole from parklands, inform park staff at Iqaluit headquarters.

SPECIAL ADVISORIES
- Contact Pangnirtung office for pre-trip information. Contact park staff in advance to book registration and orientation (mandatory) and to learn about sharing flights. During orientation, you must provide park staff with a detailed itinerary, including side trips.
- Weather may delay flights to the North.
- Allow for flexibility in scheduling.
- Practise proper food management when camping to avoid problems with wildlife.
- Be able to recognize and prevent the onset of hypothermia.

seems to operate in slow motion here: An array of wildflowers and other plants take years to produce seeds, though in the meantime they support a range of herbivores that roam the area. Insects like the woolly bear caterpillar also may take up to 14 years to mature from egg to butterfly.

Migrating birds from Africa, Europe, and the southern tip of South America come to the area to nest and raise their young. Muskoxen, the endangered Peary caribou, arctic wolves, and arctic hares remain in Quttinirpaaq year-round and raise their young during the brief, bright summer months. The ice cap that covers much of the park results in the creation of many glaciers; the peaks seen barely poking through this ice are called *nunataks,* which is a Greenlandic word for a ridge or a peak surrounded by ice. **Barbeau Peak** is the highest of these. Guided or very experienced independent visitors can ski and climb Barbeau Peak, which is near Lake Hazen.

At the north end of the park, near **Ward Hunt Island,** the last fragments of 300,000-year-old ice shelves remain. Until recently, the **Ward Hunt Ice Shelf** acted as a dam at the mouth of the **Disraeli Fiord,** containing a giant epishelf lake. A crack began to develop in the ice shelf, and in 2002 the lake drained into the Arctic Ocean.

- When crossing glaciers, travel with ropes. Individuals should be experienced in crevasse rescue.
- When hiking, avoid rock walls and cliffs with bare, freshly broken rock. Be particularly careful when it is raining and during the spring and fall.
- Visitors should be experienced in recognizing avalanche hazards, have good route-finding skills, and be skilled in self-rescue techniques.
- Water should be fine filtered and treated or boiled before drinking.
- Be cautious on riverbanks when crossing rivers and streams. Cross major waterways early in the day (2 a.m.–7 a.m. if possible, and if water levels are high, wait for them to drop).
- Emergency radios provided in the park buildings at Tanquary Fiord and Lake Hazen. In case of emergency call dispatch line (780) 852-3100.

CAMPGROUNDS

No designated campgrounds. Select campsites in durable locations where signs of your occupation will be minimized, such as areas with little or no vegetation. Avoid camping in steep terrain or near potential wildlife habitat, such as sedge meadows. Do not dig trenches around tents or build rock windbreaks.

HOTELS, MOTELS, & INNS

(unless otherwise noted, rates are for a 2-person double, high season, in Canadian dollars)

Outside the park:
Grise Fiord, NU X0A 0J0:
Grise Fiord Lodge Box 11. (867) 980-9913. $210 per person.

Resolute Bay, NU X0A 0V0:
The Qausuittuq Inn Box 270. (867) 252-3900. www.resolutebay.com. $225 per person.

LICENSED TOUR OPERATORS

Tour companies licensed to operate in Quttinirpaaq National Park: **Black Feather—The Wilderness Adventure Company** 250 McNaughts Rd., Parry Sound, ON P2A 2W9. (888) 849-7668. info@wilderness adventure.com; www.blackfeather.com. **Northwinds Arctic Adventure** Iqaluit, NU. (867) 979-0551. north@northwinds-arc tic.com; www.northwinds-arctic.com. **Quark Expeditions** 93 Pilgrim Park, Waterbury VT 05676. (203) 803-2888. enquiry@quarkexpeditions.com; www .quarkexpeditions.com. **Whitney & Smith Legendary Expeditions** P.O. Box 8576, Canmore, AB T1W 2V3. (800) 713-6660. info@legendaryex.com; www.legendaryex.com. Contact Nunavut Tourism at http://nunavut tourism.com for more options.

QUTTINIRPAAQ

A polar bear and cub

Moonrise over snow-blanketed mountains

▶SIRMILIK

NUNAVUT
ESTABLISHED 2001
22,200 sq km/5,485,739 acres

Sirmilik National Park is home not only to breathtaking views of the sea, mountains, and broad valley vistas, but also to an amazing variety of marine and avian wildlife. One of Canada's most accessible high Arctic parks, Sirmilik is truly a jewel in Canada's celebrated national parks network. Bylot Island offers stunning sights: deep, navy blue waters setting off the glistening white glaciers and icebergs that rise out of them, tinged with turquoise. Visitors may also catch sight of some of the hundreds of narwhals and seals that inhabit the park.

For thousands of years, right up to the present, the rich diversity of Arctic wildlife in the park supported the nomadic Inuit people. For centuries, they centred their existence around the demands of the land and its weather: Their survival depended on it. When the wind blew and the temperature plummeted, they stopped and found shelter, and continued only when the weather eased. Their culture and history is still well documented today for visitors to Sirmilik National Park.

Sirmilik, pronounced Siir-mi-lick, means "place of glaciers" in Inuktitut. The park covers much of the north tip of Baffin Island,

and is bordered by the communities of Arctic Bay and Pond Inlet. Established as a national park as the result of the Nunavut Land Claim Agreement in February 2001, Sirmilik is still a fairly unknown expanse of land. The park encompasses the Bylot Island Bird Sanctuary, jointly managed by Parks Canada and the Canadian Wildlife Service, where greater snow goose research has been conducted for more than three decades. Bylot Island is the nesting site for more than 40 species of migratory birds.

How to Get There

From Iqaluit, travel to Pond Inlet (one of the two gateway communities into Sirmilik National Park) is possible in six or seven days with either First Air or Canadian Northern airlines. First Air also offers flights that will take you to the other, smaller gateway community of Arctic Bay. Air travel between Arctic Bay and Pond Inlet is possible only via Iqaluit, although spring travel by snow machine and summer travel by boat can also get you from one to the other.

From Pond Inlet or Arctic Bay, hire a snow machine for transport, or engage an outfitter or guide to lead you into Sirmilik National Park, preferably in spring when the ice is still safe to traverse. You can also ski across the ice of Eclipse Sound—approximately 25 km (16 mi) from Pond Inlet—in spring to get to the park. Floe edge tours from the sea ice are also available in the spring.

If travelling with the comfort of modern conveniences appeals to you, you can visit the park in summer as a passenger on one of the many expedition cruise ships that spend up to two days sailing the sounds and inlets around Sirmilik. Depending on the itinerary of the cruises, passengers

may be able to go ashore for some exploration within the park. In summer, you can also hire a kayak guide to lead you on a trip into the waters of the park.

When to Go

Sirmilik is in the high Arctic wilderness, so the best time to go is in spring or summer, which in this region means May through September when the sun is shining for the better part of 24 hours. July is ice breakup month and the park is not accessible, as the ice will no longer support ski or snow machine travel. Boats and ships can't travel the waters around this time either, because of the hazards posed by the breaking ice. August to mid-September is the best season for boating and hiking in the park. From late September to late March, Sirmilik's weather turns harsh and stormy. The dark season, during which the sun is hardly in evidence at all, lasts for two solid months around the time of the winter solstice.

How to Visit

Sirmilik offers a variety of activities for hardy travellers eager to learn about the park's geology and wildlife. If you're willing to put forth some effort, you can get a close-up look at glaciers, icebergs, and the marine life residing off the floe edge. The park's population of Arctic seabirds make it a wonderful destination for the avid bird-watcher. If you're feeling adventurous, you can dive under the sea ice for intimate encounters with the marine life living in the waters, including narwhal and beluga whales and walruses. Summer is the best time to meet Inuit residents and learn about their culture, ancient and modern. Watch craftsmen at work, and take in Inuit art and performances in either Pond Inlet or Arctic Bay.

SIRMILIK

To ensure your safety on kayak, boat, ski, or hiking expeditions, rely on the skills of outfitters and guides to arrange your visit into the park. As in all national parks in Nunavut, Sirmilik expeditions are backcountry adventures and are generally not suitable excursions for small children or elderly travellers. As this is still a relatively new park, it doesn't yet have established routes for you to follow through the park. However, by the same token, Sirmilik offers you the opportunity to blaze your own trails, depending on what you wish to see and how skilled a hiker you are. Make sure you bring a good camera with you: The beauty and awesome vastness of Sirmilik National Park afford visitors a wealth of photo opportunities.

HIKING & PADDLING

One of the most frequently hiked areas of the park is the **Mala River Valley** on the **Borden Peninsula**. Some camping and hiking around **Pond Inlet** is possible, though these excursions won't necessarily take you into the park. Exploring the area around Pond Inlet will give you the opportunity to examine the remnants of sod huts built in past centuries by the North Baffin Inuit, which are a testament to their resilient culture.

Outfitters will take you into Sirmilik to explore the cultural sites protected within the park's boundaries. A single row of ten sod houses built at the foot of the mountains along the north coast of Borden Peninsula is one of the most important and evocative cultural

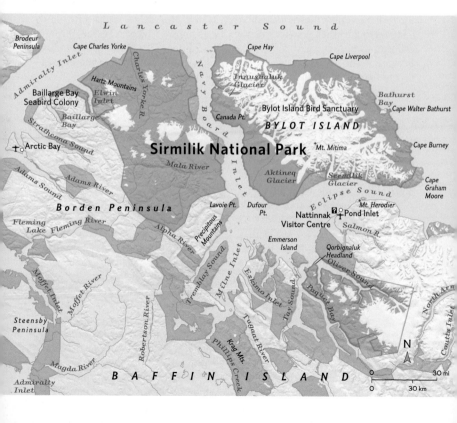

Black-legged kittiwake gull rookery on a cliff

sites along this coast. These durable Thule-era houses are constructed of stone, whalebone, and sod.

BYLOT ISLAND & BORDEN PENINSULA

Guided kayak trips of various lengths and to various parts of the park can be arranged. Floe edge excursions near **Bylot Island** will give you close-up encounters with marine mammals and can be booked in the spring. You can also arrange to partake in diving expeditions, guided by outfitters, and based out of **Arctic Bay.** Only the most experienced skiers and climbers should attempt spring glacier crossings on Bylot Island.

Many of Bylot Island's 16 alpine glaciers are visible from the waters of **Eclipse Sound** and from **Navy Board Inlet. Oliver Sound**'s deep waters, glaciers, and sheer cliffs shelter a rich variety of sea life from the inclement weather of North Baffin Island. The sprawling Borden Peninsula is also within park boundaries. Partially covered with glaciers, its tortuous geo-

logical formations are composed of red sandstone that's layered, striped, and folded with shades of ochre and magenta. These cliffs are home to thousands of nesting seabirds. Colonies of murres, kittiwakes, and fulmars come here to prey on fish from Lancaster Sound to feed their nestlings. The **Baillarge Bay bird sanctuary,** a small crescent of cliffs that is habitat for seabirds, is also protected as part of the park.

Sirmilik National Park's high concentration of seabirds and other Arctic life like narwhals, seals, and polar bears is a result of the rich, highly productive waters of **Lancaster Sound,** just north of Bylot Island and the Borden Peninsula. The waters of the sound are capable of supporting a hugely diverse array of life, and Parks Canada is studying the feasibility of creating a national marine protected area in Lancaster Sound to extend the park's protection to this rare Arctic marine ecosystem.

There's a healthy polar bear population in this park, especially along the Lancaster Sound area, so if you're planning to traverse parts of the

SIRMILIK NATIONAL PARK
(Parc national Sirmilik)

INFORMATION & ACTIVITIES

VISITOR CENTRE
Nattinnak Visitor Centre Phone (867) 899-8225. **Sirmilik Park Office** phone (867) 899-8092

SEASONS & ACCESSIBILITY
Park office open year-round. The park is inaccessible during ice breakup in mid-June to late July and when the ice freezes in mid-October to early November. Travel to the park is not advisable November to February. Access is by boat from late July to September or by snow machine from late September to early July from **Pond Inlet** or **Arctic Bay.** Contact Nattinnak Visitor Centre to make arrangements with outfitters. Endless daylight May–August; no daylight in December and January. Late March–early June is the best time of year for winter activities.

HEADQUARTERS
P.O. Box 300, Pond Inlet, NU X0A 0S0. Phone (867) 899-8092. www.parks canada.gc.ca/sirmilik.

ENTRANCE FEES
The daily backcountry excursion fee per person is $25, or $147 for a season's pass. For large commercial groups the fee is $12 per person for short stays on shore (such as a cruise ship visit).

PETS
Pets are not recommended as they can attract polar bears. If a pet is taken into the park it must be leashed at all times.

ACCESSIBLE SERVICES
None.

THINGS TO DO
Skiing, mountaineering, and winter camping. Windslab is the common form of snow; deep powder rare. In late July to early September, sea kayaking and boating in **Oliver Sound** south of Pond Inlet; **Lancaster Sound** between Devon Island and Sirmilik; **Eclipse Sound** waterway to Bylot Island, **Navy Board Inlet,** and **Borden Peninsula.**

SPECIAL ADVISORIES
- Before visiting, contact the park to book an appointment for mandatory registration and pre-trip orientation, during which you will need to provide park staff with a detailed itinerary of your planned trip and arrange a post-trip deregistration.
- Weather may delay flights to the North.
- Allow for flexibility in scheduling.
- Talk to park staff to identify areas with thinner ice. Sea ice close to river mouths is generally thin. Do not approach areas with deep snow and water on top, as this indicates open water beneath. Avoid travelling through bays and inlets with

Iceberg on Pond Inlet dwarfs human visitor.

landscape on foot, it is very advisable to travel with a qualified guide who knows the region and can provide you the necessary gear for a safe trek.

INUIT COMMUNITIES

Hotel accommodations are available in the local communities, or you can also arrange a home stay with an Inuit family. If you'd rather brave the elements, Arctic camping is possible at **Salmon River** just outside Pond Inlet. If you do plan to camp narrow channels, as they often have strong currents in spring.

- Boaters should be prepared for strong winds, floating ice, and strong tides.
- No campfires allowed. Campers are advised to bring white gas and portable stoves.
- Visitors must be prepared for whiteouts, avalanches, and extreme weather. Travel in groups of at least four is advised. Individuals must have training in glacier travel and crevasse rescue.
- Avoid polar bears, which are most active along the coast of the Borden Peninsula and along the north, west, and east coasts of Bylot Island. Avoid females and cubs in March and April and from July to October.

CAMPGROUNDS

No designated campgrounds. Select campsites in durable locations where signs of your occupation will be minimized. Avoid camping in steep terrain or near potential wildlife habitat, such as sedge meadows. Do not dig trenches around tents or build rock windbreaks. Camping near floe edge can be dangerous.

HOTELS, MOTELS, & INNS

(unless otherwise noted, rates are for a 2-person double, high season, in Canadian dollars)

Pond Inlet, NU X0A 0S0:
The Sauniq Hotel Box 370. www.pondinlet hotel.com. (867) 899-6500. $225 per person.

Arctic Bay, NU X0A 0A0:
Tangmaarvik Inn P.O. Box 130. (867) 439-8005. $215 per person.

LICENSED TOUR OPERATORS

Tour companies licensed to operate in Sirmilik National Park:

Adventure Canada 14 Front St. South, Mississauga, ON L5H 2C4. (800) 363-7566. info@adventurecanada.com; www .adventurecanada.com.

Arctic Kingdom Marine Expeditions Inc. 3335 Yonge St., Suite 402, Toronto, ON M4N 2M1. (888) 737-6818. adventures@arctic kingdom.com; www.arctickingdom.com.

Black Feather Wilderness Adventure Company 250 McNaughts Rd., Parry Sound, ON P2A 2W9. (888) 849-7668. info@wilderness adventure.com; www.blackfeather.com.

Cruise North Expeditions Inc. 111 Peter St., Suite 200, Toronto, ON M5V 2H1. (416) 789-3752. info@cruisenorthexpeditions .com; www.cruisenorthexpeditions.com.

Polar Sea Adventures (tour and equipment rentals) P.O. Box 549, Pond Inlet, NU X0A 0S0. (867) 899-8870. info@polarsea.ca; www.polarseaadventures.

Quark Expeditions 93 Pilgrim Park, Waterbury, VT 05676. (203) 803-2888. enquiry@quarkexpeditions.com; www .quarkexpeditions.com.

Whitney & Smith Legendary Expeditions P.O. Box 8576, Canmore, AB T1W 2V3. (800) 713-6660. info@legendaryex.com; www.legendaryex.com.

SIRMILIK

in Sirmilik, be sure to confirm with an outfitter what equipment and supplies you should bring with you. If you're eager to immerse yourself in local culture, some outfitters can arrange a visit with the Inuit at their outpost camps. This may give you a chance for a taste of local cuisine too: Recently harvested local food is sometimes offered as part of this experience. Near the communities of Arctic Bay and Pond Inlet, there are opportunities to fish for arctic char or to pick berries in the late summer.

Community visitor centres provide a rich offering of local art, including hand carvings, dolls (Pond Inlet is known for dolls that reflect the culture and customs), fabric painting, hats, jewellery, and items crafted from narwhal tusks. These unique pieces are also available for purchase at the local co-op store. This is a wonderful opportunity to come away from your trip with a locally made item that evokes the culture and traditions of the people of Sirmilik.

Reversing Falls, at the mouth of Ford Lake, with 8-m (26 ft) tides surging in and out.

▶UKKUSIKSALIK

NUNAVUT
ESTABLISHED 2003
20,000 sq km/4,942,108 acres

Ukkusiksalik National Park surrounds the inland sea of Wager Bay and is Nunavut's only unglaciated national park. The park has extraordinarily rich concentrations of marine wildlife, and the Inuit came to harvest it hundreds of years ago and remain on the land today. In the wake of centuries of human activity, Ukkusiksalik has become the site of more than 500 documented archaeological sites that date back more than a thousand years.

Ukkusiksalik National Park was signed into existence on August 23, 2003, by an agreement between the government of Canada and the Kivaaliq Inuit Association. Since then, final park boundaries have been established and the park is expected to be gazetted in the Canadian Parliament as a fully established national park in 2011.

Ukkusiksalik (pronounced Oo-koo-sick-sa-lick) is the Inuktitut word meaning "place where there is stone to carve pots and oil lamps." Given the size of Wager Bay, and the fact that the park completely encompasses this large body of water, the best way to see it is by boat.

There's a great deal to see and do in Ukkusiksalik. Venturing into

Wager Bay places you in the territory of the explorers who once sought the Northwest Passage—the first "Qablunaat" (white man) sailed into Wager Bay in 1742 hoping it was the long-sought-after passage. Wager Bay has been called an inland sea, and visiting it by boat will help visitors understand how the early explorers might have mistaken it for a passage to the Pacific.

This history of exploration, the archaeological record of the Inuit on the land, and the more recent presence of the Hudson's Bay Company's trading post in Ukkusiksalik make this park an exciting destination for the history buff. The historic Hudson's Bay Company buildings date from the 1920s and are where Iqungajuk, the only Inuk Hudson's Bay post manager, lived and worked. The site is located on Ford Lake and can be accessed through the reversing tidal falls.

There are numerous archaeological sites scattered around the shoreline of Wager Bay. Inuksuit—stone cairns used by the Inuit people—are plentiful across the landscape. An Inuksuit could be used to mark a trail, or served as a cache to store meat from the harvest and protect it from carnivorous wildlife like wolverines or foxes. Some trails of caribou herds are marked with these Inuit cairns, which could also serve as hunters' blinds for when the caribou passed by.

Ukkusiksalik is located on a continental flyway, and visitors will encounter a great number of migratory birds nesting in or passing through its sprawling landscape. These include species like predator hawks and peregrine falcons. The peregrine falcon, while rare in other parts of the continent, is quite plentiful in the park.

The park is also well populated with polar bears. Any travel to Ukkusiksalik is best done in the company of guides and outfitters who are trained and equipped to deal with the hazards of polar bear country. But the beauty of this park, with its rolling ochre and grey hills, its waterfalls and rare tidal reversing falls, will make travel to Ukkusiksalik well worth your while.

How to Get There

Fly from Winnipeg, or Yellowknife via Edmonton, to Rankin Inlet to get to the central Arctic (called the Kivalliq Region), where Rankin is the hub community. Charter flights can access the park from Baker Lake or Rankin Inlet. Check with Ukkusiksalik park staff about the status of airstrip conditions prior to chartering an aircraft, because the runways are remote and often unmaintained. Access to Ukkusiksalik National Park can also be achieved by contracting a licensed outfitter and chartering a boat from Repulse Bay (the closest community to the park) or from Rankin Inlet and other communities in the Kivalliq Region.

Spring snow-machine access is also possible in April and May using licensed outfitters. Make sure you factor the time needed to cover the distances to Ukkusiksalik by land or by water into your travel time, and always allow an additional couple of days in case weather intervenes.

When to Go

July and August are the best months to see the park. While it may be possible to fly into the park by charter earlier or later in the spring and summer season, July is when the area is awash in wildflowers. You can see the fall colours beginning to

UKKUSIKSALIK

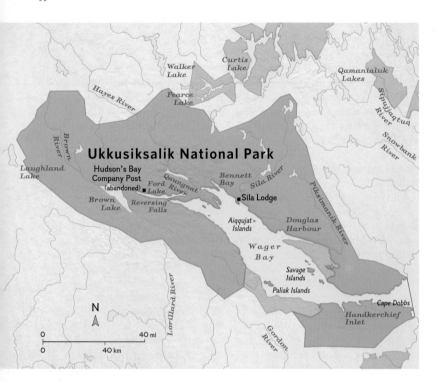

Ukkusiksalik National Park

Hudson's Bay Company Post (abandoned)

Sila Lodge

form on the tundra, along with ripening berries, in August. Travelling to the park in April by airplane or snow machine is also possible, since the sun will be high in the sky and you'll have 16 hours a day of bright sunlight glinting off the snow.

How to Visit

If **Sila Lodge** (Wagner Bay) is operating, the staff there can arrange guided hikes and guided boat trips. If the lodge is not operating, however, visitors will need to seek tour operators and guides to facilitate onshore excursions from a base camp, and use a chartered boat to explore the park. For more information on Sila Lodge, contact the park office. A few intrepid visitors have explored small parts of the park via kayak, but the presence of polar bears in the water and along the shores of Wager Bay make this a highly inadvisable approach.

Park staff are located year-round at the administration and operations centre and office in **Repulse Bay** and are available to discuss your trip throughout the planning stages.

Once the park is gazetted (in 2011), registration, orientation, and a post-trip debrief will be mandatory. Before the park is gazetted, it is recommended that you receive an orientation before entering the park so that staff can monitor your trip and assist if you have any problems. Government of Nunavut Territorial regulations remain in force until ownership of the lands that make up Ukkusiksalik is officially transferred to Parks Canada.

WILDLIFE

A trip to Ukkusiksalik centres upon life on the inland sea—**Wager Bay.**

Top: A visitor at Thule site near Brown River. Middle left: Astarte fritillary. Middle right: Arctic ground squirrel. Bottom: Aurora borealis near Wager Bay.

UKKUSIKSALIK NATIONAL PARK
(Parc national Ukkusiksalik)

INFORMATION & ACTIVITIES

HEADQUARTERS
P.O. Box 220, Repulse Bay, NU X0C 0H0. Phone (867) 462-4500. ukkusiksalik .info@ pc.gc.ca; www.parkscanada.gc.ca/ ukkusiksalik.
Field Unit Office Box 278, Iqaluit, NU, X0A 0H0. Phone (867) 975-4673.

SEASONS & ACCESSIBILITY
Park open year-round; park office open weekdays. Park accessible by boat in July and August from **Rankin Inlet, Repulse Bay, Chesterfield Inlet, Baker Lake,** or **Coral Harbour,** or a charter flight from Baker Lake or Rankin Inlet. Travel restricted or impossible during ice breakup in May and June. Travel to the park not recommended in fall and winter. Flights and charters to Repulse Bay, Chesterfield Inlet, Baker Lake, and Coral Harbour available from Winnipeg via Rankin Inlet, or from Ottawa via Iqaluit, or Edmonton via Yellowknife. Kenn Borek Air provides Twin Otter aircraft. Call (867) 252-3845. Charters into the park must be by Single Otter if the runway is suitable. Contact the park office for information about current air companies flying charters in the area.

ENTRANCE FEES
None until the park is gazetted.

PETS
All pets must be on a leash.

ACESSIBLE SERVICES
None.

THINGS TO DO
Once the park is gazetted, contact Repulse Bay office for mandatory registration, pre-trip orientation, and post-trip deregistration. At the orientation, visitors must provide park staff with a detailed itinerary of the trip, including side trips. The park is mostly navigable by water. Boating and paddling in **Wager Bay,** hiking with experienced guides and outfitters and wildlife viewing (polar bears, seals, beluga whales, narwhals). Archaeological sites can be seen throughout the park, including an ancient gymnasium-like structure, food caches, and tent circles. To find outfitters contact Nunavut Tourism office in Kivalliq (866-686-2888) or Parks Canada office in Repulse Bay.

TOUR COMPANIES
There are currently no tour companies licensed to operate in Ukkusiksalik; however, once the park is gazetted, business licences and guide permits will apply. There are currently tour companies operating in the area that visitors can approach to access the park:
Adventure Canada Lochburn Landing
14 Front St. South, Mississauga, ON L5H

Boating from place to place around the shore offers visitors the quickest and best way to access the myriad smaller bays along the coast of Wager Bay. One of these excursions can expose visitors to several of the park's most exciting features, such as the archaeological sites, fabulous views, and hilltop and river valley hikes. Moreover, from the boat you'll get a good look at some of the marine life and wildlife that inhabit the park, too.

Ukkusiksalik National Park is first and foremost about Arctic wild-life. Visitors to the park may see caribou wandering by, alone or in groups. In the waters, whales and fish abound; the sky is filled with a huge range of bird species. Sik-sik (ground squirrel) will sit on their haunches and chatter at you. You may see a fox or a wolf, but you're almost guaranteed to catch sight of a polar bear and probably more than once, sometimes at a distance, but perhaps much closer.

You may see polar bears with their cubs, harvesting seals,

2C4. (800) 363-7566. info@adventure canada.com; www.adventurecanada.com. **Arctic Odysseys** 3409 E. Madison, Seattle, WA 98112. (206) 325-1977. www .arcticodysseys.com. **Canadian Arctic Holidays** 151 Basswood, Aylmer, QC J0X 1N0. (877) 272-7426. canadianarctic@serioussports.com. **Grand Nord/Grand Large (GNGL)** 15, rue Richelieu, 75005, Paris, France. +33 40 46 05 14.

SPECIAL ADVISORIES
- Exercise polar bear safety procedures.
- Twenty-four-hour daylight in summer.
- Tides and currents may affect boating. Boating only possible between July and September. Consult the Canadian Ice Service on the Environment Canada website for sea ice conditions.
- If travelling in the spring, talk to park staff to identify areas with thinner ice. Do not approach areas with deep snow with water on top, as this indicates open water beneath. Avoid travelling through bays and inlets with narrow channels, as they often have strong currents in spring.
- Be able to recognize and prevent the onset of hypothermia.
- Water should be fine filtered and treated or boiled before drinking.
- Be cautious crossing rivers and streams and do not cross during episodes of high water—wait for water levels to drop.
- Visitors should be experienced in recognizing avalanche hazards, route-finding skills, and self-rescue techniques.

- Visitors must be self-sufficient and able to handle medical or wildlife-related emergencies.
- In case of emergency call Jasper National Park Emergency Dispatch (780) 852-3100.

CAMPGROUNDS
No designated campgrounds. Visitors must stay in hard-sided accommodations or camp with bear fencing or overnight in closed boats. Campsites and food containers should be bear-proof. Camping near floe edge can be dangerous.

HOTELS, MOTELS, & INNS
(unless otherwise noted, rates are for a 2-person double, high season, in Canadian dollars)

Baker Lake, NU X0C 0A0:
The Iglu Hotel (867) 793-2801. www .bakerlakehotel.com. $215 per person.

Rankin Inlet, NU X0C 0G0:
The Turaarvik Hotel (867) 645-4955. www.rankininlethotel.com. $205–$245. **Nanuq Lodge** P.O. Box 630. (867) 645-2650. www.nanuqlodge.com. $200.

UKKUSIKSALIK

scrounging along the coastline looking for fish or a whale carcass, or feeding on seaweed. Because the polar bear population is so high, it is important for visitors to travel with licensed tour operators once the park is gazetted and guides who are familiar with polar bear behaviour and know how to keep bears at a safe distance from humans. Contact park staff for the latest information on the companies providing services to the park.

Barren-ground caribou at Ford Lake

A climber on Mount Thor

▶ AUYUITTUQ

NUNAVUT
ESTABLISHED 1976
19,089 sq km/4,716,995 acres

Auyuittuq (pronounced Ow-you-wee-took) is the most geologically dynamic of the national parks in Nunavut. It is a relatively young landscape, with new mountains thrusting sharp granite peaks skyward. Sculpted by glaciers, this park is 85 percent rock and ice. It encompasses the Penny Ice Cap, which is bisected by Akshayak Pass, the main travel route through the park. Countless glaciers have flowed off the ice cap and into the pass.

Auyuittuq has the highest peaks in the Canadian Shield, and the internationally famed Thor Peak and Mount Asgard are dream destinations for rock climbers all over the world. Marine life, like the narwhal and ringed seal, thrive in the coastal fjords of Auyuittuq. You'll find evidence of the changing geology of the park and of the erosive effects of ice, wind, and water everywhere as you explore the park's challenging terrain.

Auyuittuq means "land that never melts" in Inuktitut, the language of the region's Inuit citizens. Auyuittuq was the first national park established in what is now Nunavut. It was signed into existence as a national park reserve in 1976 and became Auyuittuq National Park with the signing of the Nunavut Land Claim Agreement and the creation of Nunavut in 1999.

Other parks in Nunavut have more Arctic wildlife, but Auyuittuq is the most visited because the Akshayak Pass offers a natural route through the heart of the park and provides access to the park's interior peaks, glacier-fed rivers, and lakes. The park's late June and July explosion of wildflowers, the potential for encounters with foxes, weasels, or hares, and the diversity of marine life make a visit to Auyuittuq an incredibly rewarding backcountry experience.

Auyuittuq's world-famous sheer cliff faces and tumbling scree slopes, glaciers and mountain peaks, and crystal clear air will make your visit unforgettable. Adventurers can test themselves in a rugged, wild landscape that is still only a day's travel from Nunavut's capital, Iqaluit. This proximity to Iqaluit makes Auyuittuq the most accessible and affordable of Nunavut's national parks.

Its terrain is great for multiday backpacking trips and mountain climbing in summer. Glacier expeditions and ski trips in spring are more easily organized in Auyuittuq than in any of the other national parks in Nunavut. A day trip to the Arctic Circle marker is possible from Pangnirtung. It's even possible to enjoy a boat ride to the park, take a short hike, and still manage to spend the night in a local hotel. With planning, you can also enjoy an Inuit homestay in the local community. Additionally, each year a select few cruise companies access the park as part of their itinerary.

How to Get There

Fly to Iqaluit daily from Ottawa and Montreal with Air Canada, First Air, or Canadian North. Flights to Iqaluit from Edmonton via Yellowknife by First Air and Canadian North are scheduled three times a week. Iqaluit serves as a hub for all air travel in the eastern Arctic.

Daily scheduled flights leave from Iqaluit on First Air or Canadian North to either Pangnirtung or Qikiqtarjuaq; these communities are the gateways to the park. If you plan a ten-day through-hike or a five-day ski trip, as about 25 percent of visitors to this park do, start your trip in Qikiqtarjuaq and make your way toward Pangnirtung; then fly out from there. If you plan a climbing expedition of specific mountains or of the Penny Ice Cap, plan a hiking or ski loop trip of the pass to the Arctic Circle, Windy Lake, Glacier Lake, Thor, or Summit Lake, and start and end your trip in Pangnirtung.

To access the park via Qikiqtarjuaq you will need either a boat or snow-machine outfitter to bring you to the start of Akshayak Pass at the inner tip of the North Pang Fjord, a trip of about 85 km (53 mi). From Pangnirtung, your boat or snowmachine outfitter will take you to the start of the Akshayak Pass that begins at Overlord, some 32 km (20 mi) from the community. To access this point, the tide must be high in the Pangnirtung Fjord. It is also possible to hire a local outfitter during the spring season to take you by snow machine or dog team through the entire pass, or as far as the Arctic Circle marker.

When to Go

Auyuittuq's spring season for ski and glacier expeditions and ice cap travel is from mid-March to late April. For much of May and most of June, the park is not accessible because the

AUYUITTUQ

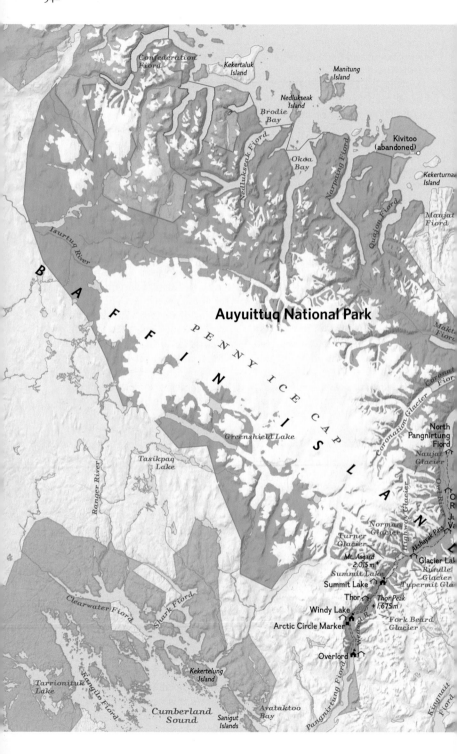

Auyuittuq National Park

PENNY ICE CAP

BAFFIN ISLAND

Confederation Fiord
Kekertaluk Island
Manitung Island
Nedlukseak Island
Brodie Bay
Okoa Bay
Kivitoo (abandoned)
Kekerturnae Island
Naujat Fiord
Narpaing Fiord
Quajon Fiord
Isurtuq River
Nedlukseak Fiord
Makta Fiord
Coronation Glacier
Coronat Fior
North Pangnirtung Fiord
Greenshield Lake
Naujat Glacier
Tasikpaq Lake
Ranger River
Highway Glacier
ORJUVE
Akshayak Pass
Norman Glacier
Turner Glacier
Mt. Asgard 2,015 m
Summit Lake
Glacier Lak
Rundle Glacier
Typermit Gla
Summit Lake
Thor
Thor Peak 1,675 m
Clearwater Fiord
Shark Fiord
Windy Lake
Weasel R.
Arctic Circle Marker
Fork Beard Glacier
Overlord
Kekertelung Island
Tarrionituk Lake
Kangilp Fiord
Cumberland Sound
Sanigut Islands
 Avataktoo Bay
Pangnirtung Fiord
Kingnait Fiord

ice is soft and dangerous to traverse by snow machine yet still too dense for boat travel. Day trips, backpacking, hiking, and expedition climbing start the last week of June from Pangnirtung. Hiking through the entire pass starts in late July from the Qikiqtarjuaq side, and activities continue until early September. Expedition cruise visits occur in either August or September. After that, conditions in the park deteriorate: Waning hours of daylight, high winds, and extreme cold blowing off the Penny Ice Cap make the park an uncomfortable and dangerous place to be.

How to Visit

Auyuittuq, like all the national parks in Nunavut, is a wilderness backcountry experience. All visitors must register, pay the park visitor fee, and take the mandatory orientation at the park office/visitor centre in either Pangnirtung or Qikiqtarjuaq before entering the park. Book your appointment in advance with park staff. Auyuittuq National Park also has a free Visitor Information Package which is available by email (Nunavut .info@pc.gc.ca). It also can be mailed to you in advance of your trip. Park staff are happy to answer your questions by phone (867-473-2500) or email as you plan your itinerary. After your trip, you will be required to meet with park staff again to deregister and provide a post-trip debrief.

Very few visitors bring young children into the park, unless it is for a day trip within a kilometre or two of Overlord. Skiers, hikers, backpackers, and expedition climbers are expected to be experienced. Otherwise, visitors should consider hiring a qualified and licensed outfitter or guide. Park staff recommend visitors travel in groups of at least six people.

A harp seal

HIKING

Within Auyuittuq you will find routes rather than trails. The park is a spectacular destination because of its active, changing landscape, but be aware that the weather is variable too: Prepare for fierce winds, storms, and periods of low visibility due to fog and snow. Also be prepared to deal with rushing cataracts of glacier meltwater following a few warm days or a rainstorm. Include enough extra time in your itinerary that you won't be rushed if weather conditions slow you down.

Within the park, visitors need to be self-sufficient, and bring with them tents, enough food for their trip, stoves, first aid kits, and all the gear necessary (including spares) for their planned activities. Consider hiring a licensed outfitter and guide to help ensure a safer journey and to provide the gear you need. There are no lodges or stores in the park, though emergency shelters and outhouses are stationed about 15 to 29 km (9–18 mi) apart.

Most visitors experience Auyuittuq National Park by going into the park via **Akshayak Pass** but for seasoned hikers, there are other ways to see the park. From the pass, it's possible to take side trips up the valleys that radiate off the pass. You can also gain access to the park using other fjords with the help of local boat outfitters, depending on the season. It also is possible to spend most of your trip on the **Penny Ice Cap,** which covers an area the size of Prince Edward Island. This is recommended only for veteran explorers, as it's difficult to access and requires a high level of glacier travel skills.

If your trip takes you through the community of **Pangnirtung,** which has a population of approximately 1,300 people, be sure to include enough time in your itinerary to take in the **Uqqurmiut Centre of the Arts** and spend some time looking around the tapestry and printmaking studios. You can also take a side trip to hike **Mount Duval** or visit the site of the former whaling station at the **Kekerten National Historic Site.**

AUYUITTUQ NATIONAL PARK
(Parc national Auyuittuq)

INFORMATION & ACTIVITIES

VISITOR CENTRES
Angmarlik Interpretive Centre Pangnirtung, NU X0A 0R0. Phone (867) 473-8737.
Auyuittuq Visitor Centre, exhibit and office in Pangnirtung, NU X0A 0R0. (867) 473-2500. nunavutinfo@pc.gc.ca.

SEASONS & ACCESSIBILITY
Visitors can access the park either using licensed outfitters or independently. If you are using a snow machine, motorboat, or dog team, you must hire a licensed outfitter. Visitors can ski, hike, and mountain climb independently. Travel is discouraged between October and February. Contact park for ice conditions.

HEADQUARTERS
Pangnirtung Office Phone (867) 473-2500; **Qikiqtarjuaq Office** Phone (867) 927-8834. www.parkscanada.gc.ca/auyuittuq.

ENTRANCE FEES
Park backcountry user fees are $25 per day per person or $147 for a season pass. For large commercial groups such as cruise ship groups, the fee is $3 per person in an educational group, $12 per person for short group for backcountry excursions.

PETS
Pets not recommended, but if brought to the park, must be leashed at all times.

ACCESSIBLE SERVICES
None.

THINGS TO DO
Snow-based activities take place in the park from early March to late April when fjords are frozen, or by boat after ice breakup from Pangnirtung Fjord (late June–Sept.) or Broughton Island (late July–Sept.). Skiing and hiking in **Akshayuk Pass** (97 km/60 mi) between North Pangnirtung Fjord and Overlord. No designated ski or hiking trails.

Boat tours from Qikiqtarjuaq. Dogsledding and snow-machine rides with outfitters, ski-touring on the ice fields, and mountain climbing.

Licensed outfitters: Alivaktuk Outfitting (867) 473-8721; Iceberg Outfitting (867) 927-8457; Jaco Qaqasiq Outfitting (867) 473-8055; Nunavut Experience Outfitting Service (867) 927-8518; Qumuatuq Tours & Outfitting (867) 473-4065; Whitney & Smith Legendary Expeditions (800) 713-6660.

SPECIAL ADVISORIES
- Contact Pangnirtung or Qikiqtarjuaq offices to register, participate in orientation, provide skiing or hiking itineraries, and deregister.
- Travel not advisable between October and February.
- Emergency shelters with two-way radios found at Overlord, Windy Lake, Thor, Summit Lake, Glacier Lake, June Valley, Owl River, and North Pangnirtung.
- No cooking or sleeping in emergency shelters. Use only in an emergency.
- Carry satellite phones.
- To prevent encounters with wildlife, avoid camping near wildlife habitats or leaving food around campsites.

CAMPGROUNDS
In **Akshayuk Pass,** warden cabins and emergency shelters with radio and outhouse on trail one-day hike apart. Visitors can camp wherever they like, but near emergency shelters recommended. In Pangnirtung there is the **Pisuktinu Tungavik Territorial Campground** (minimal services) or homestays; contact Angmarlik Interpretive Centre.

HOTELS, MOTELS, & INNS
(unless otherwise noted, rates are for a 2-person double, high season, in Canadian dollars)

Outside the park:
Pangnirtung, NU X0A 0R0:
Auyuittuq Lodge (867) 473-8955. www.pangnirtunghotel.com. $225 per person.
Kilabuk Lodge (867) 473-8229. $190 per person.

Qikiqtarjuaq, NU X0A 0B0:
Leelie Homestay and Lodge (867) 927-8002. www.leelieenterprises.ca. $120–$175 per person.
The Tulugak Hotel (867) 927-8874. www.qikiqtarjuaq.com. $225.

▶ NATIONAL HISTORIC SITES OF CANADA

57-63 St. Louis Street N.H.S. Part of an historic significant streetscape. Québec, QC

Abbot Pass Refuge Cabin N.H.S. Early stone alpine cabin used by climbers, 1922. Banff NP, AB

Alexander Graham Bell N.H.S. Commemorates famous inventor. Baddeck, NS

Ardgowan N.H.S. Residence of Father of Confederation William Henry Pope, circa 1850. Charlottetown, PE

Athabasca Pass N.H.S. Major fur trade transportation route. Jasper NP, AB

Banff Park Museum N.H.S. Early natural history museum in Rustic style, 1902-03. Banff NP, AB

Bar U Ranch N.H.S. Historic ranch in AB foothills, 1883. Longview, AB

Batoche N.H.S. Métis village; site of 1885 Battle of Batoche; Northwest Rebellion. Batoche, SK

Battle Hill N.H.S. Site of Battle of the Longwoods, 1814; War of 1812. Wardsville, ON

Battle of Cook's Mills N.H.S. Site of British victory; War of 1812. Cook's Mills, ON

Battle of the Châteauguay N.H.S. Site of 1813 battle in defence of Lower Canada; War of 1812. Allans Corners, QC

Battle of the Restigouche N.H.S. Site of last naval battle in Seven Years' War. Pointe-à-la-Croix, QC

Battle of the Windmill N.H.S. American invasion mission foiled, 1838. Prescott, ON

Battle of Tourond's Coulee/ Fish Creek N.H.S. Site of battle between Métis and Canadian forces, Northwest Rebellion 1885. Fish Creek, SK

Battlefield of Fort George N.H.S. War of 1812,

capture of Fort George by Americans, 1813. Niagara-on-the-Lake, ON

Beaubassin N.H.S. Major Acadian settlement; pivotal place in the 17th- and 18th-century North American geopolitical struggle between the British and French empires. Fort Lawrence, NS

Beaubears Island Shipbuilding N.H.S. Archaeological site associated with nineteenth-century shipbuilding in NB. Beaubears Island, NB

Bellevue House N.H.S. Important Italianate villa 1840's; home of Sir John A. Macdonald, Prime Minister (1867-73, 1878-91). Kingston, ON

Bethune Memorial House N.H.S. Birthplace of Dr. Norman Bethune, a national hero to the Chinese and possibly Canada's most prominent international humanitarian. Gravenhurst, ON

Bloody Creek N.H.S. Site of two French-English combats, 1711 and 1757. Bridgetown, NS

Bois Blanc Island Lighthouse and Blockhouse N.H.S. Wooden blockhouse part of the defences of Fort Malden, 1839; point of attack by Canadian rebels and their American sympathizers; January 1838. Bois Blanc Island, ON

Boishébert N.H.S. Acadian refugee settlement, 1756-59. Beaubears Island, NB

Butler's Barracks N.H.S. Complex represents 150 years of military history. Niagara-on-the-Lake, ON

Canso Islands N.H.S. Site of fishing centre, 16th- to 19th-century. Canso, NS

Cape Spear Lighthouse N.H.S. Oldest surviving lighthouse in Newfoundland, 1836. Cape Spear, NL

Carillon Barracks N.H.S. Early 19th-century stone military building. Carillon, QC

Carillon Canal N.H.S. Operational canal; site of two earlier canals, 1826-33. Carillon, QC

Carleton Martello Tower N.H.S. Fortification built to defend Saint John during War of 1812. Saint John, NB

Carrying Place of the Bay of Quinte N.H.S. Site of 1787 treaty between British and Mississauga. Carrying Place, ON

Cartier-Brébeuf N.H.S. Wintering place of Jacques Cartier, 1535-36. Québec, QC

Castle Hill N.H.S. 17th- and 18th-century French and British fortifications. Placentia, NL

Cave and Basin N.H.S. Hot springs, birthplace of national parks. Banff NP, AB

Chambly Canal N.H.S. Operational canal; nine locks, swing bridges. Chambly, QC

Charles Fort N.H.S. Charles Fort (formerly known as Scots Fort) was built in 1629 by the son of Sir William Alexander. Annapolis Royal, NS

Chilkoot Trail N.H.S. Transportation route to Klondike gold fields. Chilkoot, BC

Coteau-du-Lac N.H.S. 18th-century transportation and defence structures. Coteau-du-Lac, QC

Cypress Hills Massacre N.H.S. 1873 attack on Assiniboines by wolf hunters, North West Mounted Police restored order. Fort Walsh, SK

Dalvay-by-the-Sea N.H.S. Queen Anne Revival summer home, 1896-99. Prince Edward Island NP, PE

D'Anville's Encampment N.H.S. Encampment of failed French expedition to recover Acadia, 1746. Halifax, NS

Dawson Historical Complex N.H.S. Important collection of buildings from

the Klondike gold rush. Dawson, YT

Dredge No. 4 N.H.S. Symbolizes importance of dredging operations (1899-1966) with the evolution of gold mining in the Klondike. Bonanza Creek, YT

First Oil Well in Western Canada N.H.S. First commercially productive oil well in the West. Waterton Lakes NP, AB

Fisgard Lighthouse N.H.S. First permanent lighthouse on Canada's West Coast, 1859-60. Colwood, BC

Forges du Saint-Maurice N.H.S. Remains's first industrial village. Trois-Rivières, QC

Former Territorial Court House N.H.S. Substantial frame judicial building, 1900-01. Dawson, YT

Fort Anne N.H.S. 1695-1708 fortifications. Annapolis Royal, NS

Fort Battleford N.H.S. North West Mounted Police headquarters, 1876. Battleford, SK

Fort Beauséjour – Fort Cumberland N.H.S. Remnants of 1750-51 French fort; captured by British and New England troops in 1755. Aulac, NB

Fort Chambly N.H.S. Restored and stabilized 1709 stone fort. Chambly, QC

Fort Edward N.H.S. Played a role in the struggle for predominance in North America, 1750-1812; oldest blockhouse in Canada, 1750. Windsor, NS

Fort Espérance N.H.S. Remains of two North West Company fur-trade posts. Rocanville, SK

Fort Gaspareaux N.H.S. Military ruins and cemetery of 1751 French fort. Port Elgin, NB

Fort George N.H.S. Reconstructed British fort from War of 1812. Niagara-on-the-Lake, ON

Fort Henry N. H. S. British fort completed 1836 to defend Rideau Canal. Kingston, ON

Fort Langley N. H. S. Early 19th-century Hudson's Bay Company post. Langley, BC

Fort Lawrence N. H. S. English fort, 1750-55. Fort Lawrence, NS

Fort Lennox N. H. S. Outstanding example of early 19th-century fortifications. Saint-Paul-de-l'Île-aux-Noix, QC

Fort Livingstone N. H. S. Original headquarters of North West Mounted Police. Pelly, SK

Fort Malden N. H. S. 19th-century border fortification; Fort Amherstburg; War of 1812. Amherstburg, ON

Fort McNab N. H. S. Fort built in 1889 to defend Halifax Harbour. Halifax, NS

Fort Mississauga N. H. S. 19th-century brick tower within star-shaped earthworks; War of 1812. Niagara-on-the-Lake, ON

Fort Pelly N. H. S. Remains of Hudson's Bay Company fur trade post. Pelly, SK

Fort Rodd Hill N. H. S. Late 19th-century fort to defend Victoria-Esquimalt fortifications. Colwood, BC

Fort Sainte Marie de Grace N. H. S. First permanent French settlement in Acadia, 1632. LaHave, NS

Fort St. James N. H. S. Fur trade post founded by Simon Fraser, 1806; Hudson's Bay Company. Fort St. James, BC

Fort St. Joseph N. H. S. British military outpost on western frontier, 1796-1812; War of 1812. St. Joseph Island, ON

Fort Ste. Thérèse N. H. S. Site of French fort for defence against Iroquois, 1665. Chambly, QC

Fort Témiscamingue N. H. S. Remains of French fur trading post. Ville-Marie, QC

Fort Walsh N. H. S. Early North West Mounted Police post. Merryflat, SK

Fort Wellington N. H. S. Military remains of 1813-38 fortifications; War of 1812. Prescott, ON

Fortifications of Québec N. H. S. 4.6-km (2.9 mi) network of walls, gates, and squares. Québec, QC

Fortress of Louisbourg N. H. S. Reconstruction of 18th-century French fortress. Louisbourg, NS

Forts Rouge, Garry and Gibraltar N. H. S. Fort Rouge, - La Vérendrye, 1728; Fort Gibraltar, - North West Company, 1810; Fort Garry – Hudson's Bay Company, 1822. Winnipeg, MB

Frenchman Butte N. H. S. Site of 1885 battle, Cree and Canadian troops; Northwest Rebellion. Frenchman Butte, SK

Frog Lake N. H. S. Site of Cree uprising, Northwest Rebellion 1885. Frog Lake, AB

Georges Island N. H. S. Harbour fortification; contains Fort Charlotte. Halifax, NS

Gitwangak Battle Hill N. H. S. 18th-century Gitwangak hilltop fortification surrounding five longhouses, Tawdzep. Gitwangak, BC

Glengarry Cairn N. H. S. Conical stone monument, with stairway, to the Glengarry and Argyle Regiment, erected in 1840. Cairn Island, ON

Grand-Pré N. H. S. Commemorates Acadian settlement and expulsion. Grand Pré, NS

Grassy Island Fort N. H. S. Centre of English fishery in 18th-century. Canso, NS

Grosse Île and the Irish Memorial N. H. S. Quarantine station for immigrants from 1832-1937. Grosse-Île, QC

Gulf of Georgia Cannery N. H. S. Outstanding West Coast fish processing complex, 1894. Richmond, BC

Halifax Citadel N. H. S. Restored British masonry fort, 1828-56. Halifax, NS

Hawthorne Cottage N. H. S. Picturesque cottage, home

of Captain Bob Bartlett from 1875-1946. Brigus, NL

HMCS Haida N. H. S. Last of World War II tribal class destroyers. Hamilton, ON

Hopedale Mission N. H. S. Symbol of interaction between Labrador Inuit and Moravian Missionaries; representative of Moravian Mission architecture in Labrador. Hopedale, NL

Howse Pass N. H. S. First crossed by David Thompson in 1807. Banff NP, AB

Inverarden House N. H. S. Important 1816 Regency cottage with fur-trade associations. Cornwall, ON

Jasper House N. H. S. Archaeological remains of 1829 fur trade post, Hudson's Bay Company. Jasper NP, AB

Jasper Park Information Centre N. H. S. Picturesque fieldstone park building of Rustic design, 1913-14. Jasper NP, AB

Kejimkujik N. H. S. Important Mi'kmaq cultural landscape. Kejimkujik NP, NS

Kicking Horse Pass N. H. S. Traversed by Palliser expedition, 1857-60; adopted by Canadian Pacific Railway as their new route through the Rockies, 1881. Yoho NP, BC

Kingston Fortifications N. H. S. Protection for the Royal Naval Dockyard and the entrance to the Rideau Canal; War of 1812. Kingston, ON

Kootenae House N. H. S. Site of North West Company post, 1807-12. Invermere, BC

L.M. Montgomery's Cavendish N. H. S. Intimately associated with Lucy Maud Montgomery's formative years and early productive career. Cavendish, PE

La Coupe Dry Dock N. H. S. Site may represent 18th-century Acadian construction. Aulac, NB

Lachine Canal N. H. S. Operational canal; five locks, railway/road bridges. Montréal, QC

L'Anse aux Meadows N. H. S. Only authenticated Viking settlement in North America. St. Anthony, NL

Laurier House N. H. S. Second Empire home, built in 1878, of two prime ministers, Sir Wilfrid Laurier and William Lyon Mackenzie King. Ottawa, ON

Lévis Forts N. H. S. Part of Québec fortification system. Lévis, QC

Linear Mounds N. H. S. Aboriginal burial mounds from 1000-1200 AD. Melita, MB

Louis S. St. Laurent N. H. S. Childhood home of Louis S. St. Laurent, Prime Minister, 1948-57. Compton, QC

Louis-Joseph Papineau N. H. S. Stone house built in 1785, associated with Louis-Joseph Papineau. Montréal, QC

Lower Fort Garry N. H. S. Major centre in 19th-century fur trade, Hudson's Bay Company. Selkirk, MB

Maillou House N. H. S. Fine example of 18th-century QC town architecture, 1736. Québec, QC

Manoir Papineau N. H. S. 19th-century manor, home of Patriot leader, Louis-Joseph Papineau. Montebello, QC

Marconi N. H. S. Site of first wireless station in Canada. Table Head, NS

Melanson Settlement N. H. S. Pre-expulsion Acadian farm community, 1664-1755. Lower Granville, NS

Merrickville Blockhouse N. H. S. Part of lock system of Rideau Canal, 1832-33. Merrickville, ON

Mississauga Point Lighthouse N. H. S. Site of first lighthouse on great lakes, 1804. Niagara-on-the-Lake, ON

Mnjikaning Fish Weirs N. H. S. Largest and best preserved wooden fish weirs known in eastern North America, in use from about 3300 B.C. Atherley, ON

Montmorency Park N. H. S. Site of bishop's

palace; Parliament 1851-55. Québec, QC

Monument-Lefebvre N.H.S. Multi-function building, symbol of Acadian cultural revival. Memramcook, NB

Motherwell Homestead N.H.S. Farm of William Richard Motherwell built in 1882, noted politician and scientific farmer. Abernethy, SK

Murney Tower N.H.S. Mid 19th-century British imperial masonry fortification. Kingston, ON

Nan Sdins N.H.S. Remains of Haïda longhouses and totem poles. Gwaii Haanas National Park Reserve, BC

Navy Island N.H.S. Archaeological remains related to ship building. Niagara Falls, ON

Peterborough Lift Lock N.H.S. World's highest hydraulic lift lock, 1896-1904. Peterborough, ON

Point Clark Lighthouse N.H.S. Imperial tower and lightkeeper's house, 1859. Amberly, Point Clark, ON

Pointe-au-Père Lighthouse N.H.S. Early reinforced concrete lighttower at strategic location. Pointe-au-Père, QC

Port au Choix N.H.S. Pre-contact burial and habitation sites. Port au Choix, NL

Port-la-Joye–Fort Amherst N.H.S. Remains of British and French forts. Rocky Point, PE

Port-Royal N.H.S. Reconstruction of 1605 French settlement. Port Royal, NS

Prince of Wales Fort N.H.S. 18th-century stone fur trade fort; Hudson Bay Company. Churchill, MB

Prince of Wales Tower N.H.S. Late 18th-century stone defence tower, 1796-99. Halifax, NS

Province House N.H.S. Neoclassical birthplace of Confederation. Charlottetown, PE

Québec Garrison Club N.H.S. Only private military club in Canada

perpetuating the British colonial tradition of assembling military officers in a social environment, 1879. Québec, QC

Queenston Heights N.H.S. Site of 1812 Battle of Queenston Heights; includes Brock Monument; War of 1812. Queenston, ON

Red Bay N.H.S. 16th-century Basque whaling industry complex. Red Bay, NL

Rideau Canal N.H.S. Operational canal; 202 km route, forty-six locks. Ottawa/Kingston, ON

Ridgeway Battlefield N.H.S. Site of battle against Fenian raiders, 1866. Ridgeway, ON

Riding Mountain Park East Gate Registration Complex N.H.S. Three rustic buildings built under depression relief programs. Riding Mountain NP, MB

Riel House N.H.S. Family home of Métis leader Louis Riel. Winnipeg, MB

Rocky Mountain House N.H.S. Rival Hudson's Bay Company and North West Company posts. Rocky Mountain House, AB

Rogers Pass N.H.S. Canadian Pacific Railway route through Selkirk Mountains. Glacier NP, BC

Royal Battery N.H.S. Role in the 1745 and 1758 sieges of Louisbourg. Louisbourg, NS

Ryan Premises N.H.S. East Coast fishing industry complex. Bonavista, NL

S.S. Keno N.H.S. Wooden steamboat built 1922, 140 feet x 30 feet, three decks. Dawson, YT

S.S. Klondike N.H.S. Largest and last YT commercial steamboat. Whitehorse, YT

Sahoyúé-Şehdacho N.H.S. Expression of cultural values through the interrelationship between landscape, oral histories, graves and cultural resources. NT

Sainte-Anne-de-Bellevue Canal N.H.S. Operational

canal; site of earlier 1843 canal. Sainte-Anne-de-Bellevue, QC

Saint-Louis Forts and Châteaux N.H.S. Integral part of Québec's defence system; the seat of colonial executive authority for over 200 years. Québec, QC

Saint-Louis Mission N.H.S. Site of Huron village destroyed by Iroquois in 1649. Victoria Harbour, ON

Saint-Ours Canal N.H.S. Operational canal; 1933 (and remains of 1849) lock. Saint-Ours, QC

Sault Ste. Marie Canal N.H.S. First electrically-powered lock, 1888-94. Sault Ste. Marie, ON

Shoal Tower N.H.S. Mid 19th-century British imperial masonry fortifications. Kingston, ON

Signal Hill N.H.S. Commemorates defence of St. John's; includes the Cabot Tower. St. John's, NL

Sir George-Étienne Cartier N.H.S. Double house of prominent 19th-century politician, 1830s. Montréal, QC

Sir John Johnson House N.H.S. House of famous Loyalist, 1780s. Williamstown, ON

Sir Wilfrid Laurier N.H.S. House interprets life of Sir Wilfrid Laurier, Prime Minister (1896-1911). Laurentides, QC

Skoki Ski Lodge N.H.S. Ski lodge in rustic vernacular, 1930-31. Banff NP, AB

Southwold Earthworks N.H.S. Rare and well-preserved example of an Aboriginal fortified village completely surrounded by earthworks; Attiwandaronk Indian village, circa 1500 AD. Iona, ON

St. Andrews Blockhouse N.H.S. Restored wooden blockhouse from War of 1812. Saint Andrews, NB

St. Andrew's Rectory N.H.S. Example of mid 19th-century Red River architecture, 1852-1854. St. Andrews, MB

St. Peters N.H.S. French trading post and fort, 1650-1758. St. Peter's, NS

St. Peters Canal N.H.S. Operational canal; structures dating from 19th century. St. Peter's, NS

Stanley Park N.H.S. Outstanding large urban park, 1890s. Vancouver, BC

Sulphur Mountain Cosmic Ray Station N.H.S. Remains of high altitude geophysical laboratory. Banff NP, AB

The Forks N.H.S. Historic meeting place, junction of the Red and Assiniboine rivers. Winnipeg, MB

The Fur Trade at Lachine N.H.S. Stone warehouse used as depot, 1803; North West Company and Hudson's Bay Company. Lachine, QC

Trent–Severn Waterway N.H.S. Operational canal; 386 km route, forty-five locks. Trenton/Port Severn, ON

Twin Falls Tea House N.H.S. Early rustic tea house in Yoho National Park, 1923-24. Yoho NP, BC

Wolfe's Landing N.H.S. Successful landing led to capture of Louisbourg, 1758. Kennington Cove, NS

Woodside N.H.S. Boyhood home of William Lyon Mackenzie King, Prime Minister (1921-26, 1926-30, 1936-48). Kitchener, ON

Yellowhead Pass N.H.S. Transportation route through Rocky Mountains. Jasper NP, AB

York Factory N.H.S. Hudson's Bay Company's principal fur trade depot from 1684-1870's. York Factory, MB

York Redoubt N.H.S. Major seaward defences of Halifax Harbour from the American Revolutionary War until World War II. Halifax, NS

National Historic Sites information from the Parks Canada website: www .pc.gc.ca/progs/lhn-nhs/ index_e.asp

ACKNOWLEDGEMENTS

We are indebted to the many individuals that have helped prepare this guide, especially to John Thomson, France Faucher, Dawn Allen, Gerry Boulet, Guy LeBlanc, and all the staff of Parks Canada and the individual parks.

ILLUSTRATIONS CREDITS

The following images were provided by and are © Parks Canada:

4: W. Lynch; 6-7: E. Le Bel; 8: Dale Wilson; 12 (LOW): Dale Wilson; 14-15: Dale Wilson; 17: Rod Cox; 18: W. Lynch; 20: Nick Langor; 25: Dale Wilson; 26: Dale Wilson; 27: André Cornellier; 28: Heiko Wittenborn; 31: Heiko Wittenborn; 32 (LEFT): Heiko Wittenborn; 32 (RIGHT): Heiko Wittenborn; 34: Dale Wilson; 39: Dale Wilson; 40: Dale Wilson; 41: Ron Garnett; 42: Dale Wilson; 47 (UP): Chris Reardon; 47 (MIDDLE): Dale Wilson; 47 (LOW): A. Fennel; 52: John Sylvester; 54: Wayne Barret; 56 (UP): Wayne Barrett & Anne MacKay; 56 (LOW): John Sylvester; 57 (UP): Wayne Barrett & Anne MacKay; 57 (MIDDLE): John Sylvester; 57 (LOW): John Sylvester; 60: Wayne Barrett & Anne MacKay; 61: Chris Reardon; 63: Wayne Barrett & Anne MacKay; 65: Chris Reardon; 66: Brian Townsend; 70 (LOW): Chris Reardon; 73: Brian Townsend; 74 (UP): Mark Mills; 74 (MIDDLE): Jacques Pleau; 74 (LOW): Willy Waterton; 75: Brian Morin; 80: Éric Le Bel; 81: Éric Le Bel; 85: Éric Le Bel; 88 (LOW RIGHT): Jean-François Bergeron; 91: Marc Loiselle; 92: Marc Loiselle; 93 (UP): Louis Falardeau; 93 (LOW): Nelson Boisvert; 94: Jacques Pleau; 97: André Guindon; 98 (UP): Jacques Pleau; 98 (LOW): Jacques Pleau; 98 (LOW RIGHT): Jacques Pleau; 99: Jacques Pleau; 101: Jacques Pleau; 104: Brian Morin; 107: André Guindon; 108 (UP): Ted Grant; 108 (LOW): André Guindon; 110 (UP): André Guindon; 110 (MIDDLE): John R Butterill; 110 (LOW): Simon Lunn; 111 (MIDDLE): John Butterill; 111 (LOW): John Butterill; 112: Willy Waterton; 115: Parks Canada; 118 (UP): Fred Cattroll; 119: John Butterill; 120: Don Wilkes; 126: D. Wilkes; 128: S. Kenney; 131: A. Guindon; 133: Parks Canada; 144 (UP): Wayne Lynch; 144 (LOW): Kevin Hogarth; 154: Éric Le Bel; 156: Sandy Black; 158 (LOW RIGHT): Wayne Lynch; 161: Parks Canada; 162: Parks Canada/Prince Albert National Park; 166 (UP): Brad Muir; 166 (LOW): Kevin Hogarth; 168: Glen & Rebecca Grambo; 169: Wayne Lynch; 170: Robert Postma; 173: Wayne Lynch; 174 (UP): Greg Huszar; 176: Wayne Lynch; 180 (LOW): Jean-François Bergeron; 192: Parks Canada; 193: Jacques Pleau; 202 (MIDDLE): Amak Athwal; 202 (LOW): John Evely; 203 (UP): Rafa Irusta; 203 (MIDDLE): Parks Canada; 203 (LOW): Patricia Kell; 213 (UP): Rogier Gruys; 213 (LOW): Ted Grant; 214: Parks Canada; 218 (UP): D. Tuplin; 220: Chris Siddall; 225: Parks Canada; 230 (UP): Chris Siddall; 230 (LOW LEFT): Chris Siddall; 230 (LOW RIGHT): Wayne Lynch; 233: Parks Canada; 234: Jacques Pleau; 236: John Woods; 242: R.D. Muir; 245: Jacolyn Daniluck; 246: (UP LEFT): Wayne Lynch; 246 (LOW): John Woods; 248 (UP): Josh McCulloch; 248 (LOW): John Butterill; 249: Fritz Mueller Photography; 250-251: Josh McCulloch; 252: Josh McCulloch; 255: Chris Cheadle; 257 (UP): Emily Gonzales; 257 (LOW): Christian J. Stewart; 259 (UP): Ken Mayer Studios; 259 (MIDDLE): Chris Cheadle; 259 (LOW): John Butterill; 260: Josh McCulloch; 267: Wayne Lynch; 273 (LOW): Chris Cheadle; 275: Mark Hiebert; 277: Chris Cheadle; 278: Wayne Lynch; 282 (UP): Jean-François Bergeron; 282 (MIDDLE LEFT): Fritz Mueller; 284 (UP): Wayne Lynch; 285 (LOW): Fritz Mueller; 286 (UP): Lee Narraway; 288-289: Wayne Lynch; 291: Wayne Lynch; 293 (UP): Wayne Lynch; 293 (LOW): Wayne Lynch; 294 (UP): Wayne Lynch; 294 (LOW): Wayne Lynch; 295: Wayne Lynch; 297: Wayne Lynch; 299: Wayne Lynch; 300 (UP): Wayne Lynch; 300 (MIDDLE): Wayne Lynch; 300 (LOW): Parks Canada; 302: Wayne Lynch; 307: D. Harvey; 310: Ian K. MacNeil; 313: Ian K. MacNeil; 314:

Rob Buchanan; 316: Wayne Lynch; 317: Wayne Lynch; 319: Wayne Lynch; 320: Wayne Lynch; 322: Wayne Lynch; 323: Wayne Lynch; 325: David Andrews; 327: Wayne Lynch; 332: Lee Narraway; 334: Lee Narraway; 337 (UP): Lee Narraway; 337 (MIDDLE LEFT): Lee Narraway; 337 (MIDDLE RIGHT): Lee Narraway; 337 (LOW): Lee Narraway; 339: Lee Narraway; 344: Parks Canada.

Additional images were provided by the following:

Cover: Jason Kasumovic/Shutterstock; 2-3: Carr Clifton/Minden Pictures/NG Stock; 12 (UP): Raymond Gehman/NG Stock; 12 (MIDDLE): Chris Alcock/Shutterstock; 13: Raymond Gehman/NG Stock; 16: Michael S. Lewis/NG Stock; 22: Duncan de Young/Shutterstock; 48: V. J. Matthew/Shutterstock; 53: Taylor S. Kennedy/NG Stock; 58: Steve Irvine/National Geographic My Shot; 70 (UP): Melissa King/Shutterstock; 76-77: Richard Olsenius/NG Stock; 78: Pierdelune/Shutterstock; 82: Michael Melford/NG Stock; 84: Jean-Francois Rivard/Shutterstock; 87: Jean-Francois Rivard/Shutterstock; 88 (UP): Daniel Zuckerkandel/Shutterstock; 88 (LOW LEFT): Jean-Paul Lejeune/iStock; 102: © Whyte Museum of the Canadian Rockies/V263/NA-3436/Byron Harmon; 103: Library of Congress/LC-USZ62-94387; 111 (UP): Eric Ferguson/iStock; 116: Marc Filion/Shutterstock; 118 (LOW): Wayne Adam; 122: Kateryna Dyellalova/Shutterstock; 124 (UP): Carr Clifton/Minden Pictures/NG Stock; 124 (LOW): Scott Currie; 134: Michael S. Lewis/NG Stock; 136: Carr Clifton/Minden Pictures/NG Stock; 140: Rob Huntley/Shutterstock; 142: © GaryandJoanieMcGuffin.com; 143: © GaryandJoanieMcGuffin.com; 144 (MIDDLE): Raymond Gehman/NG Stock; 145: Linda Drake/National Geographic My Shot; 146-7: Norbert Rosing/NG Stock; 148: David Schultz/National Geographic My Shot; 151: Norbert Rosing/NG Stock; 152: Keith Levit/Shutterstock; 158 (UP): Raymond Gehman/NG Stock; 158 (LOW LEFT): Raymond Gehman/NG Stock; 165: Raymond Gehman/NG Stock; 174 (LOW LEFT): Raymond Gehman/NG Stock; 174 (LOW RIGHT): Raymond Gehman/NG Stock; 180 (UP): Klaus Nigge/NG Stock; 182 (UP): Michael Melford/NG Stock; 182 (MIDDLE): Raymond Gehman/NG Stock; 182 (LOW): James Blair/NG Stock; 183: Tim Fitzharris/Minden Pictures/NG Stock; 184-185: Maria Stenzel/NG Stock; 186: Lowell Georgia/NG Stock; 189: Rochelle Coffey/National Geographic My Shot; 191: Michael Melford/NG Stock; 194: Caleb Foster/Shutterstock; 198: Adrian Baras/Shutterstock; 199 (UP): IPK Photography/Shutterstock; 199 (LOW LEFT): Artifan/Shutterstock; 199 (LOW RIGHT): morganry/iStock; 202 (UP): Raymond Gehman/NG Stock; 204: Marmaduke Matthews, *Bow River (with Bourgeau Range in background)*, 1887, oil on canvas, Collection of Whyte Museum of the Rockies; 205: Peter Whyte, *Lake O'Hara*, 1929, oil on canvas, Collection of Whyte Museum of the Canadian Rockies; 206: Raymond Gehman/NG Stock; 211 (LEFT): Alaska Stock Images/NG Stock; 211 (UP RIGHT): Raymond Gehman/NG Stock; 211 (LOW RIGHT): Jason Kasumovic/Shutterstock; 218 (LOW): Raymond Gehman/NG Stock; 223: Raymond Gehman/NG Stock; 226: Michael Melford/NG Stock; 246 (UP RIGHT): 2009fotofriends/Shutterstock; 248 (MIDDLE): Paul Nicklen/NG Stock; 253: naturediver/Shutterstock; 264: Rich Reid/NG Stock; 266: Raymond Gehman/NG Stock; 268: Pete Ryan/NG Stock; 272: Raymond Gehman/NG Stock; 273 (UP): Taylor S. Kennedy/NG Stock; 281: George F. Mobley/NG Stock; 282 (MIDDLE RIGHT): Murray Lundberg/Shutterstock. 282 (LOW): Michael S. Quinton/NG Stock; 286 (MIDDLE): Michael Melford/NG Stock 286 (LOW): Paul Nicklen/NG Stock 287: Gordon Wiltsie/NG Stock 290: Peter Essick/NG Image Collection; 296: James Blair/NG Stock; 304: Raymond Gehman/NG Stock; 328: Paul Nicklen/NG Stock; 331: Gordon Wiltsie/NG Stock; 340: Michael Nichols/NG Stock.

INDEX

MAP LEGEND

AREAS

■ Featured national park

■ Other national park

■ Other parkland

■ Canadian aboriginal land

LINES

═◫═ Freeway

—⑪— Main highway

—⟨831⟩— Other road

------- Unpaved road

············ Winter road

------- Trail or suggested hiking route

⊢——⊣ Railroad

POINT SYMBOLS

○ Town

■ Point of interest

🛈 Visitor or information centre

▲ Campground

⚠ Backcountry campground

⯬ Picnic area or shelter

⸌ Overlook, viewpoint

⌂ Ranger station, warden cabin, operation station

⌂ Emergency cabin

🛆 Lighthouse

✝ Airport, landing strip

🏌 Golf course

🏊 Swimming, beach

⛷ Downhill skiing

+ Peak

⌣ Pass

) (Tunnel

— Dam

‖ Waterfall

ℓ Spring

NOTE: Parks Canada excludes all representations, warranties, obligations and disclaims all liabilities in relation to the use of the maps included in this book.

NATIONAL GEOGRAPHIC
GUIDE TO THE

National Parks
of Canada

Allan Casey, Dawn Chaffe, Teresa Earle, Garry
Enns, Ben Gadd, Helena Katz, Amy Kenny, Ilya
Klavana, Samia Madwar, Sandra Phinney, Jacques
Pleau, Christopher Pollon, Dave Quinn, Colleen
Seto, Pauline Scott, Ed Struzik, Masaji Takei,
Michelle Theberge, Judy Waytiuk, Charles Wilkins,
Janna Wilson, *Writers*

Published by The National Geographic Society

John M. Fahey, Jr., *Chairman of the Board and*
   Chief Executive Officer
Timothy T. Kelly, *President*
Declan Moore, *Executive Vice President; President,*
   Publishing
Melina Gerosa Bellows, *Executive Vice President,*
   Chief Creative Officer, Books, Kids, and Family

Prepared by the Book Division

Barbara Brownell Grogan,
   Vice President and Editor in Chief
Jonathan Halling, *Design Director, Books and*
   Children's Publishing
Marianne Kozorus, *Director of Design*
Barbara Noe, *Senior Editor*
Carl Mehler, *Director of Maps*
R. Gary Colbert, *Production Director*
Jennifer A. Thornton, *Managing Editor*
Meredith C. Wilcox, *Administrative Director,*
   Illustrations

Staff for This Book

Caroline Hickey, Bridget English, *Project Managers*
Kay Kobor Hankins, *Art Director*
Susan Blair, *Illustrations Editor*
Olivia Garnett, Mary Stephanos, Jane Sunderland,
   Text editors
Michael McNey and XNR Productions, *Map*
   Research and Production
Lynsey Jacob, *Researcher*
Judith Klein, *Production Editor*
Robert Waymouth, *Illustrations Specialist*
Rick Boychuk, Rachael Jackson, Erin Monroney,
   Lise Sajewski, John Sweet, Julie Woodruff,
   Contributors

Manufacturing and Quality Management

Christopher A. Liedel, *Chief Financial Officer*
Phillip L. Schlosser, *Senior Vice President*
Chris Brown, *Technical Director*
Nicole Elliott, *Manager*
Rachel Faulise, *Manager*
Robert L. Barr, *Manager*

The National Geographic Society is one of the
world's largest nonprofit scientific and educational
organizations. Founded in 1888 to "increase
and diffuse geographic knowledge," the Society
works to inspire people to care about the planet.
National Geographic reflects the world through its
magazines, television programs, films, music and
radio, books, DVDs, maps, exhibitions, live events,
school publishing programs, interactive media
and merchandise. *National Geographic* magazine,
the Society's official journal, published in English
and 32 local—language editions, is read by more
than 35 million people each month. The National
Geographic Channel reaches 320 million households in 34 languages in 166 countries. National
Geographic Digital Media receives more than 13
million visitors a month. National Geographic has
funded more than 9,200 scientific research, conservation and exploration projects and supports an
education program promoting geography literacy.
For more information, visit nationalgeographic.com.

For more information, please call 1-800-NGS LINE
(647-5463) or write to the following address:

National Geographic Society
1145 17th Street N.W.
Washington, D.C. 20036-4688 U.S.A.

For information about special discounts for bulk
purchases, please contact National Geographic
Books Special Sales: ngspecsales@ngs.org

For rights or permissions inquiries, please contact
National Geographic Books Subsidiary Rights:
ngbookrights@ngs.org

ISBN: 978-1-4262-0805-8

All photographs and marks have been reproduced
with the permission of the Parks Canada Agency.

All maps have been produced by the National
Geographic Society based on data provided by the
Parks Canada Agency or made available through
GeoConnections and GeoGratis (Natural Resources
Canada). The incorporation of data sourced from
the Parks Canada Agency or made available through
GeoConnections and GeoGratis (Natural Resources
Canada) within this book shall not be construed
as constituting an endorsement by them of this
book. Data provided by the United States Geological
Survey was also used in compiling certain maps.

Parks Canada excludes all representations, warranties, obligations and disclaims all liabilities in relation to the use of the maps included in this book.

Printed in Canada

11/FC/1

Made in the USA
Coppell, TX
04 May 2021

54991100R00178

BLACK SHIP

Also by Carola Dunn

THE DAISY DALRYMPLE MYSTERIES

BLACK SHIP

A Daisy Dalrymple

Mystery

CAROLA DUNN

MINOTAUR BOOKS

NEW YORK

BLACK SHIP. Copyright © 2008 by Carola Dunn. All rights reserved. Printed in the United States of America. For information, address St. Martin's Press, 175 Fifth Avenue, New York, N.Y. 10010.

www.minotaurbooks.com

The Library of Congress has catalogued the hardcover edition as follows:

Dunn, Carola.
   Black ship : a Daisy Dalrymple mystery / Carola Dunn. — 1st ed.
     p. cm.
   ISBN 978-0-312-36307-9
   1. Dalrymple, Daisy (Fictitious character)—Fiction. 2. Women journalists—Fiction. 3. Police spouses—Fiction. 4. Americans—England—Fiction. 5. Liquor industry—Great Britain—Fiction. 6. Smuggling—England—Fiction. 7. Criminals—England—Fiction. 8. Nineteen twenties—Fiction. 9. London (England)—Fiction. I. Title.
PR6054.U537B53 2008
823'.914—dc22

2008020345

ISBN 978-0-312-59865-5 (trade paperback)

To my "full-service" agent,
Alice Volpe of Northwest Literary Agency, Inc.,
and to Alan (and Slick), with thanks

ACKNOWLEDGMENTS

My thanks to Scott T. Price, historian, of the U.S. Coast Guard, for the book *Rum War at Sea*, by Commander Malcolm F. Willoughby, which, with *The Black Ships* by Everett S. Allen, provided a great deal of invaluable information about rum-runners and their opponents. Thanks also to Drs. Larry Karp and D. P. Lyle for medical information; Lynne Connolly for help with Manchester speech and Kate Dunn for New England speech; Norma and Dick Huss for nautical tips; and my brother Tony for rugger and cricket details.

BLACK SHIP

ONE

A last teeth-rattling sneeze escaped Daisy as she stepped out to the front porch. The tall, spare solicitor, locking the door behind them, gave her a worried look. That is, she thought she detected anxiety, though the layer of dust on his pince-nez obscured his expression.

Having dusted off his hat, Mr. Irwin carefully settled it on his thinning hair, then took out a large white linen handkerchief to polish the pince-nez. "Oh dear, I expect I ought to have had cleaners in before I showed you the house."

Being too well brought up to voice her hearty agreement, Daisy said politely, "It wouldn't have been so bad if I hadn't taken the dust sheet off that rocking chair and wafted it about a bit." Glad she'd worn grey gloves, she brushed down her lovat green costume.

"I'm afraid the late Mr. Walsall's staff let things slide. The butler and housekeeper were as aged as he himself, having been with him for a great many years. The unfortunate condition of the interior may deter you from taking up your abode in the house; perfectly understandable."

"You said the electrical system is quite new."

"It was installed in 1910, I believe. I should not describe fifteen years as precisely new. There have been great improvements in such things in the past fifteen years."

"New enough. The building itself seems sound. No damp patches in the attics, no creaking floorboards, no smell of drains."

"Structurally," he said with obvious reluctance, "I believe the house is comparatively sound."

"I'm glad to hear it."

"Though there's no knowing what defects a surveyor might find. Dry rot, perhaps? If you decide to sell the property, I shall, of course, be happy to handle the conveyancing for you."

"But, if I understand you correctly, the way my husband's great-uncle left things, we don't inherit his money unless we live in the house. It goes to the Home for Aged Donkeys."

"Superannuated and Superfluous Carriage Horses."

"I suppose there must be a great many about, what with motor-cars and all."

"I dare say," Irwin grunted. He didn't seem any happier at the prospect of the horses getting the money than at the prospect of the Fletchers moving into his late client's house. "It is only one of several worthy causes to be benefited according to the instructions in Mr. Walsall's last will and testament, should you decline to reside in the house."

"Does that include the proceeds of the sale of the house?"

He cheered up. "No. The proceeds would be yours—your husband's—free and clear. Apart from any taxes due, naturally. So you'll be able to purchase a more suitable residence elsewhere."

More suitable? Daisy gazed across the cobbled street at the communal garden in the middle of the ring of houses. In central London, it would have been a square, but one couldn't very well call it a square, because it was round.

In the slanting sun of the late September afternoon, it was bright with neat beds of chrysanthemums and the red and gold leaves of bushes and the ring of trees that enclosed the whole.

2

Directly opposite her, a paved path sloped down across the lawn, levelling off to circle the marble-rimmed pool in the centre, with park benches on either side. The pool had a fountain, a marble maiden in vaguely Greek draperies holding an urn on her shoulder from which water spilled.

Three small children toddled about under the watchful eyes of a pair of uniformed nannies. In next to no time, Miranda and Oliver would be old enough to play with them.

"Mrs. Fletcher?" the lawyer ventured tentatively.

"Sorry, Mr. Irwin, I was thinking. Is that an alley I see between those houses down there, on the other side of the communal garden?"

"Not exactly an alley. It might better be described as a foot passage, leading down to Well Walk."

"How convenient! And where is the Heath?"

"The Heath?"

"Hampstead Heath. It can't be too far away?"

"Oh, the Heath. Just around the corner—literally. If you would care to descend the steps and walk to the corner . . ."

Running up the side of the house and garden was a cobbled alley leading to a block of carriage houses now used as garages for motors. Beyond these, the way narrowed to another foot passage ending with a gate onto a lane, and on the other side of the lane was the Heath. It couldn't be more perfect for Belinda and her friends, and for the twins when they were old enough. They'd have many of the advantages of both town and country life.

Not to mention being able to give the dog a good run without the dreary trudge through the streets to Primrose Hill. Daisy would walk Nana much more often when it was so easy, and perhaps at last she'd take off a few of those extra pounds.

"Ahem!"

Once again, Daisy apologised for her abstraction. As she pondered, she had strolled back to the foot of the steps up to the front door of number 6, Constable Circle. Now she stepped backwards to the edge of the pavement and looked up at the

façade. It was an attractive place, a detached house built in the last decade of the nineteenth century of red brick, the first floor hung with matching tile in alternating bands of plain and patterned. The front porch was set back between protruding wings, and the paired gables in the tile roof had a dormer between. Four stories from semibasement to attics, it was considerably larger than their semidetached in St. John's Wood.

Now that the twins were mobile, Nurse Gilpin really had to have a nursery maid whether they moved or not. Their present house would be terribly crowded when Belinda came home from school for the holidays. Besides, poor Bel deserved more than the tiny box of a room she had nobly put up with over the summer. For Alec, the journey to Westminster would actually be easier from Hampstead when he went in by tube, not having to change at Baker Street, and by car it was very little farther. Nor would Daisy and Belinda be far from their St. John's Wood friends.

The rates were bound to be higher, plus their share of the upkeep of the garden, and Mrs. Dobson would need the help of a house-parlour maid as well as a full-time daily woman. But if they kept the house, they'd keep old Mr. Walsall's fortune, as well.

Logic told her to jump at the prospect. Then why did it make her so uneasy?

Perhaps her reluctance was just sentimental, an atavistic—was that the word she wanted?—attachment to family land, bred in the blood by her aristocratic ancestors. But, Daisy's brother having been killed in the War, the Dalrymple estate now belonged to a distant cousin. The suburban semi bought two or three decades ago by Alec's father was scarcely in the same category as Fairacres.

More likely, Daisy decided with cynical honesty, she just didn't want to face the disruption of the move. Yet if they sold, the sensible thing to do with the money would be to buy a bigger house elsewhere, which would involve hunting for one, as well as the horrors of moving.

"We'll keep it!"

"But Mr. Fletcher hasn't even seen it yet."

"He said it's for me to decide." Though Daisy might wish Alec had not left the decision to her—it was *his* great-uncle's legacy, after all—she wasn't going to acknowledge that to the solicitor.

"But . . . but—"

"I'm the one who'll be spending most of my time here, with the babies and working."

"Working!"

"Yes, Mr. Irwin, working. I'm a journalist."

"Oh. How . . . how enterprising," he said weakly. Then he rallied. "Mr. Fletcher will have to sign all the documents, of course."

"Naturally. Mr. Walsall was his relative. I'm afraid he's out of town at present, though, and I don't know when he'll be back."

"I suppose in his . . . er . . . his occupation, he is often away."

Daisy was inured to the way even the most law-abiding people looked askance at a Scotland Yard detective, not to mention his wife. The average suburban solicitor rarely, if ever, came into contact with a criminal investigation.

Mr. Irwin must have carried out his own investigation into Alec's life before approaching him about his great-uncle's will, if only to make sure he was really the heir. Old Mr. Walsall seemed to have cut off all connection with his sister's family long ago. Alec had only the vaguest memory of his mother once mentioning a rich uncle.

Naturally, Daisy was dying to know the reason for the breach.

She wouldn't dream of asking her mother-in-law, though. The elder Mrs. Fletcher would not only undoubtedly refuse to tell her, she'd make snubbing remarks about people prying into other people's business and curiosity killing cats. Which was most unfair, as what was Alec's business was surely his wife's business, and if one didn't ask questions, how was one ever to find out anything?

Daisy resolved on the spot that nothing should be allowed to suppress her own children's sense of curiosity. Besides, Alec's mother had obviously failed with him, or he wouldn't have become a detective.

"Yes, his work often takes him away. But I know he'll love the house." She looked up at it again, already with a proprietorial pride.

It was altogether a substantial house, the sort of house even her own mother could not possibly object to. The Dowager Lady Dalrymple might even consider it worthy of her spending the odd night in the spare bedroom.

Now there was a prospect that failed to please. "Oh dear!" said Daisy.

"Are you having second thoughts, Mrs. Fletcher?" the solicitor enquired hopefully. "You have time to consider, and to consult Mr. Fletcher. Mr. Walsall set a time limit for the decision, to ensure the funds reaching his chosen charities without excessive delay should you decline to live here, but he was not unreasonable. You have two months from the date Mr. Fletcher received my communication with regard to the will. I'm sure he ought to visit the house. He may take it in dislike."

"I'll ask him, but I'm sure he's much too busy. I expect Tommy—Mr. Pearson, that is, our solicitor—will want to go over the figures with you to make sure we won't be biting off more than we can chew. But assuming, as you say, that we'll have enough funds to cover increased expenses, we'll move in as soon as possible."

Mr. Irwin sighed heavily. He seemed less than thrilled by her decision. In fact, thinking back over the past hour, she suspected he had done his best to present the house in the worst-possible light, without going so far as to claim an infestation of deathwatch beetle. She could only suppose that he had hoped to profit from the conveyancing fees if they sold it.

"In that case," he said gloomily, "perhaps you would not be averse to meeting your future next-door neighbours?"

"The neighbours?" Daisy asked in astonishment. Though she had never been in precisely this situation before, she couldn't believe the duties of a solicitor included introducing neighbours to one another.

"My daughter, Mrs. Aidan Jessup, resides at number five. She and her mother-in-law expressed a wish to make your acquaintance should this situation arise, if you would be so kind as to step in for afternoon tea."

Had he told his daughter that Daisy's father had been Viscount Dalrymple? He must have found out while investigating Alec. She gave him a frosty look with eyebrows raised, one of the Dowager Lady Dalrymple's armoury of pretension-depressing weapons. Much as Daisy abhorred the possibility of becoming in any way similar to her mother, she was fed up with people whose only interest in her was the accident of her aristocratic birth.

It was even worse than their shying away on learning her husband was a detective. That, at least, had been her own choice.

The solicitor responded to her chilliness with stiff rectitude. "I've told Audrey and Mrs. Jessup only that you and Mr. Fletcher may move in next door. Any other information I may have gathered is, of course, confidential."

"Of course," Daisy said apologetically. This was the third or fourth time she'd had to apologise to him. However perfect the house, did she really want to live next door to a relative of someone who kept putting her in the wrong? "I'll be happy to make their acquaintance."

What else could she say?

The house next door was similar in style to number 6 but lacked the pleasing symmetry. A neat young parlour maid answered Mr. Irwin's ring.

"Good afternoon, Enid. Tell your mistress I've brought Mrs. Fletcher to meet her."

"Oh, yes, sir, madam told me you might." The maid admitted them to the hall, trotted off, and returned a moment later

7

to usher them to the back of the house and into a vast, glittering room.

After a startled moment, Daisy realised that the room was actually quite small. A multitude of mirrors created an illusion of illimitable space, reflecting one another and themselves and the windows in endless reduplication. Practically everything that wasn't mirror was gilt, she observed, dazzled. Even the rococo plasterwork of the ceiling (not mirrored, thank heaven) was picked out in gilt. In the centre hung a ballroom-size chandelier. Countless crystal drops sparkled in the glow of its electric bulbs.

From the midst of this outré magnificence came forth a petite silver-haired lady with bright, shrewd blue eyes. Her milky skin was beautifully made up, with a discreet touch of rouge, and she wore a well-cut navy silk tea frock. In contrast to the flamboyance around her, her only jewellery was a triple strand of superb pearls and a large diamond on her ring finger.

"Mrs. Fletcher, I'm Mrs. Jessup." Her voice was unexpectedly resonant for such a small frame, and had an intriguing hint, the merest flavour, of an accent. "How do you do? It's very kind of you to accept our unconventional invitation."

"Not at all. It's kind of you to invite me." Daisy smiled at the younger woman who came up behind her hostess.

Mrs. Jessup introduced her daughter-in-law. Mrs. Aidan Jessup's peaches and cream complexion would never need powder or rouge, nor develop freckles, Daisy thought enviously. She was as thin as her solicitor father; the still-current straight up and down style with hip-level waistline suited her boyish figure. However, she had considerably more hair than Mr. Irwin—a smooth flaxen bob—and less twitchiness.

"We ought to have waited for you to move in and then left our cards," she said placidly, returning Daisy's smile. "We hoped you might be encouraged to know you have friendly neighbours. Father seemed to doubt that you'd want to come to live here."

Mr. Irwin shot her an irritated glance. "Not at all," he muttered. "But the house has been standing empty, and there's no knowing what condition—"

"That's just it, Father," Audrey Jessup broke in, her tranquillity undiminished; "we don't care for living next door to an empty house."

"As for the condition," said Mrs. Jessup robustly, "it's only a couple of months since Mr. Walsall went to his reward, and Maurice—my husband, Mrs. Fletcher—visited him twice a week right up to the end for a game of chess. These past few years, he was the only person the poor old fellow would see. He was nervous of burglars, so Maurice always checked upstairs and down before he left to make sure all was secure. He'd surely have noticed if anything was seriously amiss."

So much for Mr. Irwin's excuse for trying to put Daisy off the house.

She was intrigued by these first hints of Alec's great-uncle's personality. All she'd known of him before was that he had cut off all communication with his sister, but mightn't that have been the sister's fault as much as his? Judging by her offspring, Alec's mother, she could well have been an extremely difficult person to get along with.

"You will stay for tea, won't you, Mrs. Fletcher? And Jonathan? Audrey, ring the bell, please."

"You must excuse me, ladies," said Mr. Irwin. "I have another appointment. The taxicab should be at the door any minute. Mrs. Fletcher, you'll let me know when your husband returns to town?"

"Of course. In the meantime, please arrange for a surveyor to inspect the house."

"When Mr. Fletcher—"

"I see no need to wait." Daisy was growing impatient with his incomprehensible delaying tactics. "You said yourself that it would have to be surveyed anyway if we decide to sell. I should like to have a report to show Alec when he gets home."

"I'll see what I can do," he promised glumly. "These things

9

take time. Audrey, you'd better telephone for a taxicab when Mrs. Fletcher is ready to leave."

"Thank you for the thought, Mr. Irwin, but I don't need one. I left my car in Well Walk."

"Your car!" Shaking his head at the shocking state of the modern world, the solicitor departed.

"I'm afraid Father is frightfully old-fashioned," said Audrey Jessup as they all sat down on chairs upholstered in gold brocade. "What kind of car is it?"

"An Austin Chummy. Alec didn't need it today, and I was in a bit of a rush. I don't usually drive in town, but it's nice for a ride in the country, just big enough to squeeze in my twelve-year-old stepdaughter, two babies and their nurse, and a picnic."

"Good heavens!" the elder Mrs. Jessup exclaimed, laughing.

"You have little ones?" her daughter-in-law asked. "You absolutely must come to live here. How old are they?"

"Seven months."

"And the other?"

"Both seven months. They're twins, boy and girl."

"Double trouble," said the elder Mrs. Jessup with a smile. Daisy had heard the comment often enough to be mildly irritated without feeling any need to retort.

"Double joy, Mama Moira! Marilyn, my five-year-old, will be thrilled to death. She adores babies. Percy's getting too old to appreciate being smothered in kisses."

The parlour maid brought in the tea trolley. As Mrs. Jessup poured, Daisy and Audrey Jessup compared notes on their children.

"They change so fast," said the elder Mrs. Jessup with a sigh. "Aidan, my eldest, was such a staid, sensible child. Then he went away to school. Next thing we knew, we were being congratulated on his becoming a positive demon on the Rugby football field!"

Daisy believed her. Her friend Lucy had married a quiet,

mild-mannered man who turned into a ravening beast on the rugger field.

"But Aidan's very staid and sensible now," Audrey observed with a touch of wistfulness.

"I should hope so, with a growing family of his own. My youngest, on the other hand, was a rough-and-tumble boy, always looking for trouble." A shadow of anxiety crossed Mrs. Jessup's face, and Daisy wondered if her youngest was still looking for trouble. "Yet he took up cricket, which has always seemed to me a rather sedate affair."

"Compared to rugger, positively placid!" Daisy agreed.

"And my daughter, Deirdre, wasn't at all like Audrey's little Marilyn. She never cared much about dolls or babies. All she ever wanted was a horse, and though we couldn't manage that, she took riding lessons for years. Somewhat to my surprise, she's turned into a devoted mother."

"How many grandchildren have you?"

"Five. Just wait until you're a grandmother, Mrs. Fletcher. The pleasures of motherhood are nothing to it."

Daisy wished her mother and Alec's could bring themselves to enjoy Belinda, Miranda, and Oliver instead of always finding fault. She also envied the easy relationship between the two Mrs. Jessups, so different from her own with her exacting mother-in-law.

She finished her second cup of tea and was about to say regretfully that it was time she was going, when the maid came in.

"There's someone to see the master, madam. A foreigner. On business, he says. I told him Mr. Jessup don't do business at home, but he said the master wouldn't take kindly to him turning up at the shop, and it's not my place, 'm, to tell him the master's gone abroad. So!"

Mrs. Jessup looked dismayed, even alarmed. "Didn't he give his name, Enid?"

"No'm. I ast for his card, but he didn't have one. He's a foreigner." In the maid's eyes, this fact clearly explained any and all peculiarities of conduct.

"I suppose I'd better speak to him. Please excuse me, Mrs. Fletcher." She stood up.

Daisy also rose. Her curiosity aroused, she had to force herself to obey the dictates of manners. "I really must be off," she said. "Thank you so much for tea. I'm looking forward to our being neighbours."

Mrs. Jessup went out. Daisy stayed chatting to Audrey for a few minutes before going into the hall, where the maid waited to usher her out.

A door towards the front of the hall was slightly ajar. Stopping at the looking glass hanging over the hall table to straighten her hat and powder her nose, Daisy heard a man's voice. He spoke too low to make out his words, but something about the intonation sounded to her distinctly American, rather than any more exotic incarnation of English. On the other hand, Mrs. Jessup's voice, when she spoke, was unmistakably Irish. That brogue was what she had caught a hint of earlier, Daisy realised.

"As it happens," Mrs. Jessup said coldly, "my husband is travelling on the Continent. He moves about a great deal from country to country—France, Spain, Italy, Portugal, even Germany. I have no way to get in touch."

The visitor's voice rose. "Aw, don't give me that, lady! You must know when you're expecting him home at least."

"I don't. His plans often change, so he sends a telegram when he's on his way home."

"OK, if you say so." He sounded disgruntled, almost threatening. "But you better tell him I came looking for him, and tell him I'll be back."

The door swung open. A short, wiry man in a blue suit strode out into the hall. In passing, his dark eyes gave Daisy a sidelong glance. Something about it made her shiver. She glimpsed black slicked-back hair before he clapped a grey-blue fedora on his head, pulling it well down over his swarthy face. A black-avised devil—the phrase surfaced from somewhere in the depths of Daisy's memory.

He reached the front door before the maid could open it for him. Letting himself out, he failed to shut it behind him. He ran down the steps and walked quickly away around Constable Circle.

"Well, I never!" the maid exclaimed. "Manners!"

"Born in a barn," Daisy agreed with a friendly smile. "I take it he's not a frequent visitor?"

"Never set eyes on him before, madam, and I'm sure I hope I never do again. We get plenty of foreign visitors, the family being in the importing business, but most of 'em are polite as you please, in their foreign sort of way. Begging your pardon, 'm, but is it right what I heard, that you're taking the house next door? If you was to be wanting a parlour maid, my sister's looking for a new situation. . . ."

Daisy promised to let her know as soon as their plans were certain. Down the steps she went and started across the street, intending to cross the garden by the path.

"Excuse me, madam!" A man came towards her, hurrying up the path. Well dressed in an unobtrusive dark grey suit and carrying a tightly rolled umbrella, he looked very respectable, a banker perhaps, in no way an alarming figure.

Daisy paused. The man came closer, raising his hat politely. He was quite young, early thirties at a guess, though his dark hair was already greying a little at the temples.

"I beg your pardon for accosting you, ma'am. I saw you come out of my house. I'm Aidan Jessup."

The staid, sensible older son? Lucy's Gerald would have let himself be boiled in oil before he'd have accosted in the street a lady to whom he had not been introduced, even having observed her departure from his house. Unless the house was going up in flames . . . But a quick backward glance showed Daisy such was not the case. However, she was not the sort to cut off a possible source of information just because of a certain disregard of etiquette.

"Afternoon tea," she explained, and added encouragingly, "Can I help you?"

13

"You noticed the fellow who came out just before you? Who dashed off at such a pace?" He stared frowning after the American, now out of sight. "I don't suppose you know who he was?"

"I'm afraid not. I didn't meet him. I imagine Mrs. Jessup—your mother—can tell you."

"Mother spoke to him?"

"I believe so. I did hear his voice, and he sounded as if he came from America."

His already-pale face blanched. "Oh Hades!" he groaned. "I knew it was a terrible idea. Thank you, madam, and once more, my apologies." He raised his hat again and made for the Jessup house at a hasty pace.

Interesting! Daisy thought, making her way back to the car.

There seemed to be enough secrets and mysteries at number 5 to furnish a half-ruined Gothic mansion. They ought to have an old crone for a housekeeper, instead of a smart young parlour maid.

She had liked both the Jessup ladies, though. If they were aware of her aristocratic background, they had showed no signs of toadying. In fact, their unaffected manners were very much at odds with the flamboyance of their interior decorating. Could it be Mr. Jessup's taste that ruled?

If anything, the mysteries associated with the Jessups made Daisy keener to get to know them better. Who was the intrusive, aggressive American whose arrival so alarmed Aidan Jessup? What was the "terrible idea" that had apparently led to his arrival? Was the younger brother in trouble with the law?

Could that explain Mr. Irwin's reluctance to have a CID detective move in next door to his daughter?

FIRST SEA INTERLUDE

There was three men came out of the west,
Their fortunes for to try,

14

And those three made a solemn vow,
John Barleycorn should die.
They ploughed, they sowed, they harrowed him in,
Throwed clods upon his head,
And these three men made a solemn vow,
John Barleycorn was dead.

—OLD ENGLISH BALLAD

" 'It was a dark and stormy night . . . ' "

Clinging to the rail, sleet streaming down his neck, Patrick muttered the words to himself. He'd have had to shout to be heard above the howl of the wind in the rigging, and in any case, he doubted his present companions would appreciate the literary allusion.

At the best of times, the seamen had little regard for the supercargo.

Bulwer-Lytton's London couldn't possibly have been as dark and stormy as the North Atlantic in a September gale, at night, on board a ship with all lights extinguished. The best that could be said for the situation was that the U.S. Coast Guard was not likely to find the *Iphigenia*. If they had any sense, they wouldn't even be afloat tonight.

On the other hand, nor would *Iffie*'s customers find her.

Captain Watkins had insisted that the supercargo must be on deck, ready to keep tally of the merchandise handed over when the inshore boats arrived. Teeth chattering, Patrick suspected—to the point of near certainty—that Watkins had been having him on. Surely on a night like this the captain couldn't even guarantee that the black ship was in the vicinity of Rum Row. If she was, one could only hope that a dozen—or a score or more—unlighted ships were not circling blindly in the area, waiting for the storm to ease.

At least they were not likely to be blown ashore, Patrick was glad to realise. Last year, in May 1924 to be precise, the old three-mile limit had changed to twelve, so Rum Row was now some fifteen miles from the coast.

15

A song ran through his head:

> *Oh, 'twas in the broad Atlantic,*
> *Mid the equinoctial gales,*
> *That a young fellow fell overboard . . .*

His frozen hands gripped the rail tighter. Not that he was afraid. He had, after all, chosen to come, in search of adventure. But he was so cold, he hardly felt the touch on his arm until the bo'sun's voice bellowed in his ear, "You'd best come below, lad. The runners won't be out tonight."

Turning, he was grateful for the man's steadying hand on his elbow. Thank heaven he wasn't seasick. That would have been the ultimate humiliation.

A faint light glimmering through the downpour showed the position of the open deckhouse door. Finding his feet on the heaving deck, he made for it, the bo'sun a step behind.

Once sheltered from the storm's savagery, Patrick felt the steady, reassuring thump of the engines. His breath caught in his throat as he stepped into the cabin. After the bracing air outside, the fug seemed thick enough to scoop with a ladle. On the outward voyage, everyone but the captain slept, ate, smoked, and drank in the narrow space, to allow room for more bottles and barrels of their precious cargo—of which one cask had been broached since he went on deck. The watch below greeted him with a steaming tankard.

"Not to worry, mate," said one bewhiskered mariner, grinning. "'T ain't the ten-year-old Haig and Haig."

He reached for the toddy eagerly. "Th-thank you." His teeth were still not quite under control. He took a swig and started to warm up inside. "I'll put it d-down as lost overboard."

"That's the spirit." The bo'sun's witticism raised a laugh.

One of the men threw Patrick a towel. "Better get out o' them wet duds."

The ordeal outside seemed to have been some sort of test. Apparently, he had passed. The son of the cargo's owner could

never really be one of the crew, though someone made room on the steam pipes for him to hang his dripping clothes among theirs.

But he remembered the story of the Norwegian black ship *Sagatind:* The crew had broken into the cargo, drunk their fill, quarrelled and fought, and, when the Coast Guard seized the ship, were found blotto and bloody belowdecks.

TWO

"*What I* want to know," said Daisy, "is why Alec's great-uncle's solicitor is nervous about having a policeman move into that house."

Alec and Tommy Pearson had just joined her and Madge in the sitting room. It was a pleasant, comfortable room, half the size of Mr. Walsall's drawing room and without a scrap of the Jessups' flamboyance.

Tommy liked his glass of port after dinner, but Alec had promised Daisy they wouldn't discuss Mr. Walsall's will in her absence. They hadn't kept the ladies waiting more than a quarter of an hour.

Daisy's demand brought a frown to the face of the stocky, bespectacled solicitor. "That, I can't tell you," he said, accepting a cup of coffee. He helped himself to a lump of sugar. Tongs poised to take a second, he glanced at his wife and regretfully forbore.

Madge's blond curls nodded approval, but as he sat down beside her, she said tartly, "He *won't* tell you, more likely. Tommy's refused to say a word to me about why you invited us to dinner tonight."

"For the pleasure of your company, of course, darling," said Daisy.

"Well, of course! But I know he has business to discuss with Alec, too. Do you want me to go and powder my nose while you talk? Or I could go up and admire the babies. They're always so angelic when they're asleep."

"As far as I'm concerned, you're welcome to stay, Madge," Daisy assured her. "Only it's really Alec's business. . . ."

"There's no reason you shouldn't stay," said Alec, "but it's not particularly interesting business, unless Pearson's going to drag some hitherto unsuspected family skeleton out of the cupboard?"

"Good Lord, no!" Tommy was shocked. "Nothing like that."

Daisy was always somewhat taken aback by evidence of Tommy's earnest outlook on life. She had heard tales of his derring-do during the War, in the course of which he had been badly shot up. In fact, he had met Madge—then Lady Margaret Allinston—in the military hospital where she had been a VAD nurse and Daisy had worked in the office. Since returning to the long-established law firm of Pearson, Pearson, Watts & Pearson, Tommy had reverted to the conventions with a vengeance.

Although he *had* been extremely helpful in that extremely unconventional business in Worcestershire, Daisy reminded herself.

Doubtless his retreat into stolidity was his way of coping with the horrors he had lived through. People had different ways of dealing with the memories, some more efficacious, some less so. Tommy and Madge and their little boy were a happy family, and he was doing well in his profession. A certain degree of gravity was required of solicitors, as well as of policemen.

Alec wasn't being a policeman this evening, though, just a hopeful heir.

Tommy took some papers out of an attaché case. "Let me say right away," he stated, "that William Walsall was a very wealthy man. He left considerable sums to various charities—"

"Buying his place in heaven," said the irrepressible Madge.

Her husband gave her an affectionately exasperated look. "There's no reason to suppose so. He made generous provision for his butler and housekeeper, a married couple, though given their advanced ages, the annuities could not have been expensive. Be that as it may, I can assure you, Fletcher, your income from investments will be quite sufficient to cover the increased cost of a larger household, without—"

"That's what Mr. Irwin told me," said Daisy, "but with the utmost reluctance, which I don't understand at all."

"Perhaps he's been misappropriating funds," Madge suggested.

"My dear, you mustn't say such things, even in jest," Tommy remonstrated. "Phelps, Irwin, and Apsley is a highly regarded firm. Besides, the sale of the property would be equally likely to bring to light any discrepancy in the accounts."

"We might not have delved deep, as we'd be happy to get the funds from the sale," Daisy pointed out. "It would have been the horses he cheated, and they'd not likely complain."

Madge had to be told about the Home for Superannuated and Superfluous Carriage Horses. "No," she agreed, laughing, "they'd never look a gift horse in the mouth."

"Probably not," said Alec. "Whereas if he'd left us skint, or without sufficient funds to keep up the house—"

"Either way, I shall have everything checked by an accountant, though I'm sure Madge is quite mistaken. Still, it is odd that Irwin appeared not to want you to move in."

"Entirely Daisy's rampant imagination, I expect," said Alec.

"It was not! Don't be beastly, darling."

He grinned at her. "You were saying, Pearson, 'without' . . . ?"

"Without? Oh yes, without considering the leases."

"Leases? Mr. Irwin didn't mention leases, only investments. I told you he was holding out on us, Alec."

"Land is an investment," Tommy said patiently. "Assuming you keep the house, you appear to own the freehold of the whole of Constable Circle."

"Constable Circle!" Madge burst out laughing. "You'll have to change it to Chief Inspector Circle."

"I must admit the name was something of a shock," said Alec with a smile. "It's called after the painter, of course."

"John Constable lived in Hampstead," Daisy confirmed. "In Well Walk, actually, just around the corner. There's a Gainsborough Gardens nearby, too."

"As I was about to say," Tommy continued, "the ground rents don't amount to much in modern terms, as the ninety-nine-year leases were signed in the mid-1890s, when prices were much lower than since the War. Under certain circumstances, you can raise them, of course."

"What circs?" Daisy enquired.

"It's a complicated subject, as leases are all different. I'll have to have time to study them before I can explain properly. But if you were ever in need of capital, you could sell the freehold. It must be worth a pretty penny. Not that I'd recommend such a course unless you found yourselves in desperate straits. Land is an excellent investment."

"How clever of your great-uncle to buy it up," Madge congratulated Alec.

"He didn't actually buy it," said Tommy.

"Aha, the skeleton in the cupboard!" Madge crowed. "He was a gambler and won it in a game of cards."

"Stuff and nonsense. No one could have been more respectable. Jonathan Irwin's father was Walsall's solicitor back then, and knew him quite well. Irwin told me his history—in confidence, of course."

"Tell all," Daisy commanded. "Do you know what caused the breach with Alec's grandmother?"

Tommy looked at Alec, who shrugged. "Surely you can tell me, and Daisy will find out one way or another. I gather the next-door neighbour—"

"The one with the Versailles sitting room?" Madge interrupted. She exchanged a glance with Daisy, who had described the Jessups' sitting room to her as a miniature Galerie des Glaces.

Not that Daisy had ever seen the original, but she'd read descriptions. "That's the one," she said. "Mrs. Jessup told me her husband used to visit the old man regularly."

"So it's quite likely Mr. Jessup and perhaps his wife know all there is to know about my forebears, in which case Daisy'll have it out of them in no time. You may reveal the worst, Pearson."

"It's not so bad. More old-fashioned, really, though I have plenty of clients who still have the old attitudes. Mr. Walsall acquired the land that became Constable Circle in payment of a debt. He owned the majority of shares in a bank, which he sold when he retired, to one of the bigger banks. Barclay's, if I remember correctly."

"Never mind that," Daisy said impatiently. "What about Alec's grandmother?"

"It's all tied together. His sister—your grandmother, Alec—married his chief clerk, against his bitter opposition."

"I suppose he gave my grandfather the sack," Alec guessed. Tommy nodded.

"That's disgraceful!" Daisy burst out. "Even my mother didn't behave as badly as that when I married Alec. Darling, we ought to reject his house and his blasted money!"

Aghast, Tommy was speechless. Madge intervened. "Daisy, don't you think Mr. Walsall was trying to make amends when he left everything to Alec?"

"Ha! When he was already dead and it didn't cost him anything!"

"Calm down, love. My grandparents did all right, and my mother ended up as a bank manager's wife. You could call that a revenge of sorts."

"Besides," said Madge, "it would be cutting off the twins' and Belinda's noses to spite their great-great-uncle's face, and he won't even know about it."

Daisy laughed ruefully. "True. As a gesture, it wouldn't give the same satisfaction as throwing a bag of gold in his face. But what—" She stopped and listened. "That's the doorbell. Who on earth, at this time of night . . . ? Darling, you promised—"

"I told them we'd be out. Anyway, the Yard would telephone, not send someone to my doorstep. Mrs. Dobson's getting it."

The heavy footsteps of the cook-housekeeper were heard in the hall. Called from the washing up, she was probably wiping her hands on her damp apron as she went and tucking wisps of hair behind her ears. Soon, perhaps, they'd have a neatly uniformed house-parlour maid. . . . Still, Mrs. Dobson was more than capable of getting rid of unwanted visitors.

They heard the rattle of the chain, the murmur of voices, a door closing with a decided thud, then Mrs. Dobson's footsteps again, coming to the sitting room.

The door opened. "It's an American with a carpetbag, madam. He says you know him, you and the master. 'Mr. and Mrs. Fletcher,' he said. It's pouring cats and dogs, it is," added Mrs. Dobson, "and he's ever so wet. Sopping wet."

Another mysterious American visitor? "Didn't he give his name?" Daisy demanded.

"No, madam. I ast him, and he looked behind him, sort of shifty like, and said he better not tell. So I shut the door on him."

"Very wise," said Tommy.

"Shall I tell him to go away, madam?"

"Heavens no!" Daisy started to get up. "I'll go and see who it is."

Alec put out his hand to stop her. "Stay here. I'll go. You made friends with some pretty strange people over there."

"So did you," she retorted as he went out, followed by Tommy.

Alec had told her some rather odd stories about the director of the new Federal Bureau of Investigation, J. Edgar Hoover, with whom he'd briefly worked. Judging by the peculiar behaviour of the man on the doorstep, he could well be one of Hoover's agents. He had claimed to know both of them, though, and events had prevented her joining Alec in Washington, D.C.

So much had happened in her life since the American trip that it seemed like aeons ago. But come to think of it, she had met one FBI man, and he, of all people, might conceivably turn up on their doorstep without notice, sopping wet, and refuse to give his name.

"Wait, Alec! I shan't be a minute," she excused herself to Madge.

"I'm coming, too. You don't think I'd miss the excitement, do you?"

They went after the men.

Alec had his hand on the chain, about to unhook it and open the door, when he hesitated.

"What is it?" Pearson asked.

"Probably nothing. You may have read reports from America about the rise of large criminal gangs, fuelled by the vast sums to be made by evading Prohibition. It's been in the *Times*, I think."

"Small-time hoodlums—mostly Italian, Irish, and Jewish, aren't they?—joining together into well-organised groups, leading to a rising level of violence. There were some pretty virulent letters about the idiocy of the Volstead Act. It's unenforceable over here, though, nothing to do with Scotland Yard."

"Bootlegging, no, but the violent crimes are extraditable offences. Not long ago, the FBI asked us to collar an Irish fugitive, an American with family in Dublin, and I got landed with the job."

"Because of your American expertise? So you think someone's out for blood because you arrested—"

24

"Actually, we didn't arrest him. He got away to the Irish Free State. But—"

"Oh come on, darling," said Daisy, reaching past him to open the door. "I bet I know who it is." She peered through the three-inch gap allowed by the chain. The electric light was on in the porch. She saw a huddled, dripping figure of misery, who raised his head hopefully, revealing spattered horn-rimmed glasses, and lifted his trilby. "I knew it, it's Mr. Lambert. Just a minute, Mr. Lambert!" She closed the door and unfastened the chain.

"Lambert? Who . . . ? Oh, your watch-sheep." Alec had not held a high opinion of Lambert even before the youthful agent had abandoned them somewhere in the middle of the United States. "I suppose we'd better take him in." Sighing, he opened the door.

"Darling," Madge said to Daisy, "I'm simply dying to hear all about it!"

Half an hour later, Lambert was ensconced in a chair by the fire, the damp change of clothes from his bag steaming gently, as was the glass of whisky toddy in his hand. Judging by the rate at which the latter was disappearing, he was no great devotee of Prohibition.

Daisy decided to offer coffee rather than a refill.

While the American was changing, she had told Madge a bit about their mutual adventures in the States. Subsequently, Tommy had tried, without success, to persuade his wife it was time they went home. She gazed in fascination at the American.

Alec stood leaning against the mantelpiece, tamping tobacco in his pipe, frowning down at Lambert. "All right," he said, "now let's hear just what exactly you're doing here."

"Here?" Lambert bleated. Since their last meeting, two years ago, his face had not lost its youthful ingenuousness.

"Here in London. Here in my house. Here—"

"Oh, *here*! My pocket was picked—on the boat train. Luckily,

Mrs. Fletcher's letter was in a different pocket, so I still had your address."

"Her letter?" Alec threw an accusatory glare at Daisy.

"Don't you remember, sir? After . . . after what happened, I wrote you in care of the Bureau to apologise, and I enclosed an apology addressed to Mrs. Fletcher. She kindly wrote back."

"So you came here because you have no money for a hotel?"

Lambert blushed. "It's worse than that, I'm afraid, sir. The thief took my passport as well as my money, and my credentials, too."

"You're still with the FBI?"

The blush deepened, even his ears reddening as he sheepishly put down his now-empty glass and pushed it away. "No, sir. I'm with the Treasury Department, Bureau of Internal Revenue, Prohibition Division."

"Then what the deuce are you doing in England?" Tommy gave the empty glass a pointed look. "Alcohol is not illegal here."

"I know that, sir." Turning to Alec, the hapless Prohibition agent asked, "Sir, who is this guy . . . er, gentleman?"

"Mr. Pearson is a solicitor—that is, a lawyer. You may place absolute trust in his discretion. Mrs. Pearson's also, I believe."

"Oh yes, I shan't breathe a word." Madge was entranced.

Lambert stood up, bowed to Madge, shook Tommy's hand, and said solemnly, "Pleased to meet you, ma'am, sir. If Mr. Fletcher vouches for you, I guess that's good enough for me. The thing is, I know we can't enforce the Volstead Act here, not even for American citizens, but what we can do is find out who's shipping the stuff to our bootleggers. Your British government says there's no law stops us doing that."

"Outrageous!" sputtered Tommy. "Spying on our citizens? I shall speak to my MP."

"Member of Parliament," Daisy explained to the American.

"Kind of like a congressman? Well, I guess that's your right, sir."

"But how do you do it, Mr. Lambert?" asked Madge. "Surely you can't keep watch on every wine merchant in the country?"

"Gee whiz, no, ma'am. We're kind of shorthanded at best. I guess it's OK to tell you. See, the Coast Guard's gotten itself some new ships, fast ones, and they're keeping the black ships on the move—"

"Black ships?" Daisy queried.

"That's what they call the rumrunners, ma'am. There're the freighters from Europe and Canada—they're wholesalers—and the inshore boats that pick up the liquor out at sea, on Rum Row. But the Coast Guard's disrupting business now, forcing the ships to keep moving so they can't meet up. The rumrunners have started using radio to arrange new meeting places, but we're listening in, so they have to transmit in code. Some of these bootleggers, the big guys, are sending contact men over here to arrange codes. Also to figure out how to pay without the risk of the cash being confiscated if they get caught."

"And your job is to follow the contact men?" Alec suggested.

"That's right, sir. They're real tough guys, though," he added despondently, "and your Customs took away my gun."

"I should hope so!" Tommy exclaimed. "This isn't the Wild West, you know. Even the police are rarely armed."

Lambert came very close to pouting. "OK I guess, if that's the way you do things."

"How do you propose to find these tough guys?" Alec asked.

"The embassy's supposed to help, but the public desk was closed when I got there and I didn't have my credentials, so they told me to come back in the morning."

"Did you report your loss to the police?"

"Yes, sir, I walked on over to Scotland Yard and asked for you, but I didn't have—"

"Your credentials, yes, I realise that."

"And I guess you're too important to disturb for a pick-pocket. A bobby took a report and said they'd get in touch if

my passport was found, but I couldn't tell them where I'd be at because I didn't have—"

"Money for a hotel," Daisy put in.

"You got it, ma'am. So seeing I had your address, I asked the way to your home. He gave me directions and a dime—a shilling?—for the bus ride, and here I am. I'm mighty sorry to intrude like this, Mrs. Fletcher, but I didn't know what else to do."

He was so disconsolate, Daisy hadn't the heart to say anything but that he was more than welcome and she'd have Mrs. Dobson make up a bed. "I expect you haven't eaten," she said kindly. "If you wouldn't mind coming to the kitchen, I'm sure Mrs. Dobson will find you something."

Lambert followed her docilely, and she left him in the cook-housekeeper's competent hands.

Returning to the sitting room, she sank into a chair. "Well! Still singularly lacking in eptness."

"*Eptness*, darling?" said Madge.

"Should it be *eptitude*, do you think, like *aptitude*?"

"He's not merely inept," Alec snorted, "he's incompetent. I can't imagine how he got another government job after leaving the FBI, except that I've heard that Prohibition agents are exempted from the usual civil service requirements."

"It sounds," Tommy remarked, "as if someone didn't want them to be too efficient! Come along, Madge, we really must be going." The Pearsons left.

"Two unexpected American visitors within just a few days," Daisy mused.

Surprised, Alec asked, "Have we had a visitor you haven't mentioned?"

"No, darling, the Jessups, remember? Our neighbours-to-be. I told you."

"None of our business."

"Don't you think it's an odd coincidence?"

"Coincidences happen. Perhaps Lambert called on them, too."

"No, it wasn't him. I caught a glimpse of the man's face. You don't doubt Lambert's story, do you?"

"Great Scott no. If I were a pickpocket, he's just the sort of feckless-looking mark I'd head straight for. Besides, I don't believe he has the wits to invent it."

"True. He'll have to have Bel's room tonight."

Alec sighed. "I suppose you expect me to take him with me tomorrow and sort him out."

"After all, he did *try* to protect me in New York," said Daisy.

SECOND SEA INTERLUDE

Then they let him lie for a very long time
Till the rain from heaven did fall,
Then little Sir John sprung up his head,
And soon amazed them all.
They let him stand till midsummer
Till he looked both pale and wan,
And little Sir John he growed a long beard
And so became a man.

The dark of the moon, and not a lamp showed on either vessel, yet Patrick could see the motor launch bobbing alongside *Iphigenia* as clearly as if they were sailing the Solent on a sunny Sunday afternoon. By the starlight reflected off the inky, satin-smooth swells, he watched the last sack lowered to the deck of the inshore boat and hastily stowed by the men below. She was considerably lower in the water than when she had arrived at Rum Row.

"Your turn, lad, if you're up for it."

"I'm ready, Captain." Patrick slung his kit over his shoulder.

"Just sign my copy of the manifest here—the true manifest, not the one we show the Yanks if they stop us." White teeth glinted in a grin. "So there's no trouble when we get back to Blighty."

Shading the torch beam with his hand, he pointed to the spot on the top sheet of his sheaf of papers. Patrick scribbled his name.

"Thanks, Captain. You may be sure I'll tell my father he can rely on you in any future business of this kind."

"You've not done too badly yourself. Watch your back when you get among those cutthroat bootleggers. They owe you plenty, and who knows how keen they are to pay. Right, over you go."

The bo'sun himself took charge of the sling to which Patrick now entrusted himself. Dangling from the side of the black ship, he looked down at the strip of inky water between the freighter and the launch and prayed he wouldn't get a dunking. He was concerned less about an icy soaking than the humiliation involved.

With a thud, he dropped safely to the deck. A waiting seaman disentangled him from the sling and tugged twice on the rope. As Patrick waved good-bye at the darkness above, the idling engines of both vessels took on a more urgent note and they began to move apart.

He hadn't paid much attention to the captain's warning. His father had been doing business with the same people—at least, the top man—since before Prohibition. A Boston Irishman whose father owned a bar, he had a ready market for good stuff, the best wines and Champagnes and, in particular, Haig & Haig and Gordon's gin, both for some reason especially popular with the smart set.

In view of all the tales of piracy on Rum Row, they had arranged a code between them, so that no cash need change hands at sea. In a belt pouch sewn by Patrick's mother were the playing cards, torn in half, used as identification by the inshore boats as they arrived at the *Iphigenia* to pick up their loads. Now matched with the halves Patrick had brought with him, they would prove to the agent ashore that business had been properly transacted as planned. No cash to be seized by pirates, Coast Guard, or Treasury men—the agent would trans-

fer payment to a New York bank to be transmitted to the firm's London account.

But first, Patrick must reach the Irishman's agent. *Iffie*'s bo'sun had warned him that the Coast Guard, rather than merely firing warning shots at suspected boats, had actually killed several seamen.

He had chosen adventure, yet he watched *Iffie*'s shadowy shape disappear into the night with a shiver of apprehension. Behind her spread her wake, pointing at her as plainly as a white arrow painted on tarmac.

THREE

The day after Lambert's arrival, having gone into town with Alec in the morning, he turned up in St. John's Wood again in the middle of the afternoon. When Mrs. Dobson showed him into the small office Daisy shared with Alec, he stood before her desk, more sheepish than ever.

"Mr. Fletcher told me to come back," he mumbled miserably.

"Still no money for a hotel?" Daisy enquired with resignation, lowering her hands from the typewriter.

"No, ma'am. The guy at the embassy took the chief inspector's word that I'm Absalom Lambert, but—"

"You are?" Trying to hide her incredulity, she wondered what sort of person could saddle a child with such a name. It was tempting Fate to kill him by way of a nasty accident. Of course, he wore his hair cut too short to get entangled in a tree, but still . . . "I don't believe I ever heard your Christian name before."

Lambert blushed. "I guess you never asked me to show my credentials back home, but I did show Mr. Fletcher in New York. So today he told them I used to be a federal agent, but he

couldn't vouch that I still am, though with a different department. They wired Washington."

"With any luck, then, they'll hear back tomorrow."

"Gee whiz, don't I wish! The trouble is, the embassy wants a photograph, so it'll take at least a week, maybe more."

"Good gracious! I'd have thought they'd be more cooperative, more helpful to a citizen in distress."

"I expect they are, normally. See, they don't like the Prohibition Division. No one—well, hardly anyone—does. They don't understand over here how bad things are getting in the big cities, what with the bootleggers, like I was telling you. They'll have to help, though, soon as they get my credentials."

"In a week or so. Did Alec invite you to stay here in the meantime?" Daisy enquired dangerously, ready to be furious.

"Oh no, Mrs. Fletcher! He said it's entirely up to you."

Pipped at the post. With Lambert standing in front of her, unhappily studying the toes of his shoes, how could she not offer to put him up?

"I suppose I'd better drive you to the station to retrieve your bags from left luggage," she said with a sigh. "Or was your luggage ticket pinched, too?"

Lambert perked up. "No, I stuck it in my hat band. It got soaked, but Mrs. Dobson kindly dried it out for me, and I think it's OK. Here," he said, handing it to her, "don't you?"

The man at left luggage gave Lambert an extremely dubious look. He examined both sides of the wrinkled scrap of cardboard carefully, while Daisy held her breath. But a glance at Daisy, who was wearing her most respectable coat, reassured him and he handed over Lambert's belongings.

Lambert fitted himself into the household with remarkable ease. He had a good appetite, which endeared him to Mrs. Dobson. The helpless quality, which sometimes made Daisy

want to scream, appealed to Nurse Gilpin. He was always welcome in the nursery, where he soon made himself popular with the twins. Daisy would feel quite jealous when she went upstairs and found Miranda sitting on his lap, studying a picture book, or Oliver shrieking with laughter as he climbed over the American's recumbent form.

Not that there was much room to recline, what with all the babies' stuff as well as Mrs. Gilpin's bed and chest of drawers. The Hampstead nursery was going to be a great improvement.

Daisy's pangs of jealousy abated when Miranda held out her chubby arms to her mama to be picked up for a kiss and Oliver raced across the floor with his spiderlike crawl to pull himself up by her leg to a wobbly standing position. Daisy's stockings might suffer, but she reaffirmed her determination to be a modern mother, not the sort who left her children's upbringing to a nurse, however capable. Besides, the older the babies grew, the more fun they were.

Lambert was popular with the dog, too. He was always ready to take Nana for a walk, whatever the weather. What was more, on returning, he washed her down if she was muddy and dried her off when she was wet.

In fact, such were his domestic virtues that Daisy thought it a great pity he was so determined to make a go of it in the cloak-and-dagger world. He ought to go home to a safe if dull job in his father's business—insurance, she recalled him mentioning—marry a nice girl, and have a family.

Whatever his failings as an agent of the law, however, he was an excellent guest. It was just as well. Ten days passed and still the American embassy had not received any response to their wire.

"Perhaps they never will," Alec said morosely at bedtime, wrenching off his tie. "Is one evening alone, just the two of us, too much to ask?"

"I could give him money for the cinema," Daisy proposed, "though it seems a bit inhospitable when he's so helpful during

the day. Darling, you don't think he actually did make up the whole story, do you?"

"Not really. Why would he choose to foist himself indefinitely on *us*?"

"I expect it's just that his department has lost his photo. On purpose, I shouldn't be surprised. Or they haven't got one. Oh dear, I hope they don't have to get in touch with his family to ask for one. Goodness knows how long that might take."

"More likely they're happy to have lost him and hope he'll disappear for good."

Daisy giggled as she helped him undo his collar stud. Though they didn't usually change for dinner, he'd had a meeting that afternoon with the Assistant Commissioner (Crime), who didn't approve of soft collars.

"Now that we *are* alone," she said, "don't let's waste time talking about Lambert."

So they didn't.

The very next day, Tommy Pearson telephoned to say the Fletchers could move into the Hampstead house as soon as they wanted. Daisy was startled. With memories of Jarndyce and Jarndyce, she had anticipated a *Bleak House*-like sluggishness in the windings of the law. Certainly she hadn't expected to be able to leave St. John's Wood before the new year.

"Did you just say what I think you said?"

"What do you think I said?" Tommy asked patiently.

"I can start putting the Hampstead house in order?"

"That's not precisely what I said, but that's what it amounts to. There are a few *i*'s to be dotted and *t*'s to be crossed, and Alec'll have to sign more papers. However, I've managed to convince Irwin that given Walsall's explicit instructions, the sooner you take possession, the less likely the will is to be contested."

"He really doesn't want us there, does he."

"So it would appear," said Tommy with lawyerly caution. "At least, he's unenthusiastic. I dare say he was had up for

pinching a bobby's helmet in his salad days and has developed an inhibition about the police."

"A complex, I think, not an inhibition. Is one allowed to become a lawyer after pinching a bobby's helmet?"

"Yes, as a matter of fact."

"Oh Tommy, you, too? What is the fascination of bobbies' helmets for young men?"

"Daisy, I do have other clients—"

"Sorry, but you raised the subject. To return to Mr. Irwin, complex or no, he could have refused the Jessup ladies' request to introduce me to them, or vice versa, but he didn't. They were friendly and welcoming. I should think they'll be good neighbours, and the house is perfect, except for a lot of cleaning and a lick of paint. I wonder whether we'll be able to move in before Bel comes home for half term."

"Is that odd Yankee still hanging about? Have him give you a hand with packing up and so on. He must be good for something. Tell Alec to give me a ring, will you?"

"Right-oh."

"Speaking of which, you'll want to get the house wired for telephone service. The old man electrified, but he didn't believe in the infernal apparatus."

"Oh bother! Thanks, Tommy. Love to Madge and Robin." Daisy rang off.

Lambert came down the stairs and found her sitting in the hall, feeling rather stunned.

"Gee whiz, Mrs. Fletcher, are you OK? I hope you haven't had bad news?"

"No, good news. At least, it's what I was hoping for. The trouble is, I just don't know where to start!"

Alec was called away to the outer reaches of the kingdom, whether by good (from his point of view) luck or good management. Lambert, still without papers or money, offered to accompany Daisy to the new house to go over it thoroughly

and see what needed to be done before the Fletchers could move in.

After touring the house in increasing consternation, they stood in a sitting room at the rear, peering out into the dusk—made duskier by the grimy French windows—over the paved terrace and the weed-grown terraced garden to the leafless trees at the top. Though Mr. Irwin had had the furniture uncovered and dusted, Daisy was dismayed anew by how dismally dingy the old man had let his home become.

"It's a nice room," Lambert said doubtfully.

"It could be. Before, I was concentrating on the size and number of the rooms," she explained. "But after a proper cleaning, the whole place is going to have to be painted and wallpapered from top to bottom. Bother! Choosing colours and patterns could take ages, and then Alec might not like my choices. I wish he hadn't gone away just now. I'd hoped to have it ready for Belinda's half-term holiday."

His ears turned red. "It looks like Miss Belinda will need her old room. Don't worry about me, Mrs. Fletcher. I'll find somewhere to stay."

"I wasn't exactly worrying." Daisy couldn't keep a note of asperity from her voice, and his flush deepened. "All the same, I would have liked to move before she comes home."

"How about you just paint everything white? That way, it'd look nice and fresh, and it wouldn't be too hard to paint or paper over if you wanted to change."

"Light and bright." Perhaps even a judicious use of looking glasses here and there at strategic points, avoiding the excesses of the house next door! "Yes, that might work. I'll think about it. Thank heaven Mr. Walsall preferred good-quality, comfortable furniture rather than the latest fashion. Much of it is perfectly all right."

"And so little used, it's hardly worn."

"The cleaners are going to be here for the next couple of days and I can't— Isn't that the doorbell? Someone at the front door? Who on earth . . . ?"

"Must be a Fuller Brush man."

"A what?"

"Don't you have them here? A door-to-door salesman. Shall I get rid of him?"

"Yes, please."

As he went out, Daisy turned away from the window. The room was larger than their only sitting room in St. John's Wood, and there was the drawing room at the front, as well. The furniture really wasn't bad, though she might use the St. John's Wood stuff in here. White paint and new curtains—yes, she could see the possibilities. Once the electricity was turned on, and the boiler stoked and lighted to run the radiators—

"It's a maid from next door, Mrs. Fletcher," Lambert announced buoyantly. "We're invited for cocktails."

"Oh dear! I can't possibly go. I'm covered in dust and cobwebs."

The maid had followed him in. "It don't show, ma'am," she said.

"That's because I wore brown tweed, on purpose."

"I'll fetch you a clothes brush."

"Thank you. But no amount of brushing will transform a coat and skirt into a cocktail dress."

"Not to worry, 'm. It'll just be family. Mrs. Jessup said to tell you it's just so's the master can meet the new neighbours, seeing he came home yesterday from foreign parts. Mr. Aidan's back from the shop, too."

As usual with Daisy, curiosity overcame any reluctance to appear incorrectly dressed. With the gentlemen present, perhaps she'd get the answers to some of her questions about the Jessups.

A few minutes later, the maid preceded them into a large drawing room at the front of the Jessups' house. It was furnished—to Daisy's disappointment—in a thoroughly conventional manner.

"Mr. and Mrs. Fletcher, madam," the maid announced.

"Who, me?" bleated Lambert, at his most inane.

"Oh, this gentleman isn't my husband," Daisy said at the same time. "This is Mr. Lambert. He's visiting from America."

Mrs. Jessup, rising to greet them, sank back into her chair as if her legs had suddenly lost their strength. Already on their feet, the two men froze. After a moment, they exchanged a silent glance of consternation.

Audrey Jessup stepped into the breach. "How do you do, Mr. Lambert? Mrs. Fletcher, Father says you've definitely decided to move in. I'm thrilled!"

By the time she had made all necessary introductions, the others had recovered their sangfroid. Her husband made no mention of his previous meeting with Daisy in the garden, so she followed his lead, despite wondering about the reason for his reticence.

His father, Maurice Jessup, a portly man, was wearing a well-cut suit designed to disguise that fact. His jowls hung over the knot of his tie, and his forehead was receding towards the crown of his head. His present worried frown looked out of place on a face that seemed essentially genial. He offered drinks: "Anything you fancy," he said, gesturing at a cabinet standing open to display bottles of every conceivable shape, size, and colour. "Aidan, you do the honours, will you?"

While his son poured and mixed, he turned to Lambert and asked warily, "Are you over here on business?"

"Not really, sir. Well, kind of."

This response—to Daisy's ears, typical of Lambert's vagueness—appeared to hold some sinister significance to the Jessups. She was tempted to tell them he was on government business, just to see what their reactions would be. She resisted temptation, remembering how chary he'd been of revealing his "business" to the Pearsons. It was quite conceivable that he was being obfuscatory on purpose.

"Which part of America are you from?" asked Audrey, the only one not disturbed by Lambert's presence.

"Arizona, ma'am."

"Is that in the South?"

"Southwest. It's mostly desert and mountains, no real big cities. The population of the whole state's not much above three hundred thousand. My father owns the biggest insurance company in the state. Both our senators are customers. That's how he got me a job in . . . er, hmm, on the East Coast."

Daisy came to the rescue. "We met in New York a couple of years ago. I was over there on a writing assignment."

"Oh yes, Father mentioned that you're a writer. How marvellous!" Audrey exclaimed. "What do you write? Do you use a pen name?"

"Magazine articles, under my maiden name, Daisy Dalrymple."

"In *Town and Country*?" asked Mrs. Jessup. "I've read several. You always have such fascinating snippets of the history of the places you write about."

Everyone seized on this new topic and worried it to death. Then they moved on to the house next door and Daisy's plans for it.

Mr. Jessup was given to colourful notions, such as enclosing the front porch and turning it into a conservatory for hothouse orchids. Recalling his Continental travels, Daisy decided the miniature Galerie des Glaces must be blamed on him rather than on his wife. She, in contrast, made several helpful suggestions about the kitchens and servants' rooms. Aidan took after his mother in practicality, offering the name of a housepainter whose work and charges they had found satisfactory. His wife seconded everyone's proposals with enthusiasm, but her chief interest was in the nursery, which she was longing to see.

"As soon as it's been cleaned and painted," Daisy promised. "I'm sure you'll be able to give me some ideas."

When Daisy started making "time we were getting home" noises, Mr. Jessup said, "If by any chance you're thinking of having a housewarming party, I'll be glad to let you have any wines and spirits you want at wholesale."

Daisy must have looked as blank as she felt, because Aidan

added, "We're in the business, you know, Mrs. Fletcher. Jessup and Sons of New Bond Street, since 1837."

"Oh, I didn't realise." That would explain Mr. Jessup's travels, visiting wine growers, no doubt. About to comment, she recalled just in time that she had been eavesdropping when she overheard Mrs. Jessup's mention of his whereabouts. "That's awfully kind of you."

"Just a gesture to welcome new neighbours," said Aidan, perhaps with an eye to depressing future expectations.

"I'm afraid," Daisy went on regretfully, "my husband's job precludes our accepting favours."

"Civil service?" he asked.

"Yes, sort of."

"No one need know," said his father.

"Thank you, but it's just not on." The inevitable moment had come when Mr. Irwin's discretion went for nothing and all must be revealed. "Alec's a policeman, you see. Scotland Yard. He's a detective."

"Too thrilling!" Audrey exclaimed.

The rest of the Jessups appeared more dismayed than thrilled.

"Of course he can't accept a gift, then," said Mr. Jessup with a jovial laugh that didn't quite come off. "Are you a policeman, too, Mr. Lambert?"

"Who, me?" Lambert said blankly.

"Lambert's usual idiotic response to any question about himself," Daisy told Alec later that evening when he rang up, "but it averted further interrogation and they dropped the subject."

"They were alarmed, though, to hear I'm a copper?"

Daisy considered. "*Perturbed* is the word. They didn't seem as worried as Mr. Irwin was."

"Perhaps Irwin, as a lawyer, is more aware of the legal ramifications of whatever they're doing. You say the Jessups run an off-licence?"

"I should think they call themselves 'Purveyors of Fine Wines and Spirits to the Aristocracy.' Premises in New Bond Street, and the elder Jessup trots around the Continent, presumably visiting vineyards."

"Most likely they're evading duty somewhere. Not my headache, thank heaven. I don't feel obliged to tip off Customs and Excise, especially as the whole thing may exist only in your imagination."

"It's not!" said Daisy indignantly. "You don't think it could have something to do with their unwanted Yankee visitor?"

"Great Scott, Daisy, it's not against the law to have visitors from America, even unwanted ones, or we'd be in trouble ourselves! It's probably just the shiftiness the law-abiding public so often display when coming face-to-face with the police. Are you having second thoughts about moving in next door?"

"Oh no, darling. I like them. Mrs. Jessup's read my articles—"

"A sure way to a writer's heart."

"And she didn't tell the others about my writing as 'the Hon.,' which was jolly decent of her. It would have been frightfully embarrassing! Of course, maybe she didn't notice or had forgotten."

"I wish you could persuade your editors to leave it off."

"Believe me, so do I. At least in England. I don't care if—"

"Your time is up, caller," the exchange operator announced. "Do you want another three minutes?"

"Let me see if I have change. Daisy, I'll be home tomorrow late, but I have to leave again early the next—"

Click click bzzzz. They were cut off. With a sigh, Daisy hung up the receiver.

"Gee whiz!" Lambert stood on the stairs, staring at Daisy. "Are you telling me some guy from the States called on the Jessups?"

"No."

"They didn't have an American—?"

"I wasn't telling you anything."

Lambert looked confused. "You mean there *was*—?"

"I mean it's not really any of your business. Or mine, come to that."

"Aw, gee, come on, Mrs. Fletcher! I'm here to do a job for the government—"

"Not my government. As it happens, I can't tell you anything for certain anyway. I overheard what sounded to me like an American accent, but I could well have been mistaken."

"And old Jessup's a wine merchant. What a stroke of luck! It gives me somewhere to start looking. As soon as my papers arrive," he added sheepishly.

"Let's hope it's soon," said Daisy in heartfelt tones.

THIRD SEA INTERLUDE

They hired men with the scythes so sharp
To cut him off at the knee.
They rolled him and tied him by the waist,
And served him most barbarously.
They hired men with the sharp pitchforks,
Who pricked him to the heart,
And the loader he served him worse than that,
For he bound him to the cart.

"Welcome aboard *Barleycorn*," grunted the seaman who had helped Patrick to descend from *Iffie*. A couple of others were busy stowing sacks and crates. "Skipper's in the wheelhouse."

Taking this as an invitation—or perhaps an order—Patrick made his way cautiously forward by starlight, making for the blacker black rectangle in the bow. The wheelhouse was much lower than he would have expected. He couldn't imagine how a man might stand upright inside.

Beneath his feet, the deck surged as the *Barleycorn* put on

speed, her engines running smooth and quiet. Having found his sea legs weeks ago aboard *Iphigenia*, Patrick adjusted easily to the motion.

"And these three men made a solemn vow, John Barleycorn was dead . . . ," he sang silently to himself.

"Then little Sir John sprung up his head, and soon amazed them all."

Whoever had christened the bootleggers' boat had a sense of humour, though somewhat lacking in common sense. Her name would surely arouse suspicion in anyone who knew the old ballad.

He was quite close to the wheelhouse before he could make out the windows, faintly illuminated by the binnacle lamp within. But glancing back, he saw the wide white curve of the wake. If Coast Guard vessels were about, they could hardly miss that signal. Then, the very absence of required lights would be cause enough to stop her.

The wheelhouse roof was just above his waist level. Stooping, he peered through the side window and saw the silhouette of a mariner in a peaked cap. He knocked.

The man at the wheel gestured to him to enter. He had to crouch to enter and climb down a short ladder to reach the deck inside.

"Sir, I'm Patrick—"

"No names," growled the skipper.

"Right-oh. I mean, aye, sir. But I'm supposed to be meeting a man. . . ."

"The Irishman."

"Is he aboard?"

"Nope. Waiting ashore."

"Oh." While not exactly gushing, the skipper didn't seem actually hostile. Patrick ventured a question. "May I ask why the wheelhouse is lower than the main deck?"

"So there's somewhere to duck down when the bullets start flying."

"Gosh, I'd hoped the stories I've heard were exaggerated. The Coast Guard actually shoot to kill?"

"Ayup. Leastways, I don't say they mean to kill, but when you turn a machine gun on a manned ship, accidents happen."

"I suppose so."

"Even with bulletproof glass and armour plating."

"Which she has?"

"Purpose-built."

Patrick was silent for a moment, contemplating the degree of adventure he was encountering. "Are you ... er ... are we expecting to meet any Coast Guard ships?"

"Regular patrol cutter hereabouts is paid off. Shore station likewise. But there's no knowing where they'll pop up. We can outrun 'em, given half a chance, even their new cutters."

"I thought your engines sounded sweet. Where do you intend to land the stuff?"

"No names. We'll get you where you're bound. You don't need to know how."

"Sorry!"

Patrick expected to be dismissed ignominiously to join the crew. However, the nameless captain ignored him henceforth. After waiting for a few minutes, he found a stool and sat down, leaning back against the rear window. He even managed to sink into an uneasy doze without falling off the stool.

He dreamt he was standing in the middle of Piccadilly Circus, with motor-car horns blaring all around him. The noise woke him.

A brilliant white light flooded the small cabin. The moon? No, much too bright, and it moved with a disconcerting unsteadiness. "What ... ?" he asked, confused.

"Get down! Last thing we need is them to find a limey aboard. Go nap on those sacks." The captain pointed at a pile in the corner. "Pull one over you. If you're questioned, you're my sister's deaf-mute boy."

"Aye, sir." As Patrick ducked below window level and scuttled over to the sacks, a Klaxon horn bellowed again, followed by a loud-hailer.

"Ahoy, *Barleycorn*! U.S. Coast Guard. Stand by to be boarded."

The beam of the searchlight remained on the wheelhouse. "Damn their eyes!" the captain swore. "It's illegal to throw a searchlight on the bridge of a ship! Pity I'm in no position to report them, though if it comes to trial. . . ." He let roll a slew of oaths but throttled back the engine. He hauled himself up the short ladder to the main deck.

Huddled among the sacks, which smelled of a curious mixture of fish, spirits, and tar, Patrick heard only fragments of the ensuing conversation.

". . . Double-crossing whoreson skunk . . ."

"Hey, take it easy. Me and the boys just figured . . ."

". . . Had a deal . . ."

". . . Spare a coupla crates . . ."

Concluding that he was not going to be arrested in the immediate future, Patrick stopped cowering and made himself as comfortable as possible on his odiferous bed. He was half-asleep again by the time the captain returned with another man.

"Greedy bastard's made us run late," the captain growled. He resumed his post at the wheel and the purr of the engines swelled. "It'll be daylight before we're in signalling distance."

"What we need's one of those radio transmitters," said the other in the dogmatic tone of one who was repeating oft-unheeded advice.

"That's what the limey's here for." Without turning his head, the captain asked, "You awake, son?"

"Yes, sir." Patrick scrambled to his feet.

"You're here to set up radio codes, that right?"

"That's right, sir. We've heard your Coast Guard is intercepting uncoded messages from ship to shore, so my father hired a top-notch cryptographer—a chap who worked for the War Office during the War—to set up a code for us. It's not hard to use, and it can be changed at irregular, prearranged intervals, so they won't get a chance to work it out. I'm going to set it up with Mr. . . . uh . . ." He recalled the warning against naming names. "With our buyer's agent."

"What did I say, skipper? These days, you gotta have radio."

The captain gave an unenthusiastic grunt. When nothing more was forthcoming, the seaman went out and Patrick subsided on his pile of sacks again.

When next he roused, day was breaking. A light mist swirled over the sea. The captain still stood at the wheel, steady as a rock. Feeling chilly, Patrick yawned and stretched. He was dying for a cuppa, but he knew one didn't ask New Englanders for tea.

"Good morning, sir."

The captain, now revealed as a tall, lean man with a long, seamed face fringed with grizzled whiskers, hooked a laconic thumb over his shoulder. "Bread and cheese in the locker."

"Thanks. Will you have some?"

"Ayup."

With the half loaf and hunk of cheese in the locker, Patrick found a thermos flask of coffee and a couple of battered tin mugs. Having acquired a seaman's knife aboard the *Iphigenia* (for which he now felt a nostalgic affection), he cut a doorstep of bread and a slab of the cheese. The coffee smelled very strong. He poured a cup and carried the makeshift meal to the captain.

When Patrick tasted the coffee, he discovered the aroma disguised a healthy slug of whisky. It wasn't the breakfast he'd have chosen, but it warmed him through. Evidently, the captain of the *Barleycorn* believed in his work, unlike the Boston Irishman, who, according to Patrick's father, was a teetotaller.

An Irishman, a *Catholic* Irishman, who didn't drink was oddity enough. A teetotaller who broke the law to import booze for his fellow citizens boggled the mind, Patrick mused, gnawing on his bread and cheese. Love of money was the root of all evil, they said. Not, of course, that he considered dealing in high-quality alcoholic beverages to be an evil.

A young seaman burst into the wheelhouse. "Skipper, Jed spotted a destroyer astern!"

Startled, Patrick choked on a crumb.

The captain swore a brief but pungent oath. "He's sure?"

"Just a glimpse, but he's using the spyglass."

"Did they see us?"

"She ain't hailed us. Nor shot at us . . . yet."

"Which way's she heading?"

"Dunno, skipper. He couldn't tell."

"This fog's going to burn off soon as the sun rises. So much for the weather forecast! Tell the boys to hold on to their hats. We'll run for it."

By the time Patrick got over his choking fit, the heavy-laden *Barleycorn* was ploughing through the swells at her top speed. The mist turned to gold as the sun's first rays touched it, and soon its wraithlike wisps dissipated.

The young seaman returned, bursting with excitement. "She's turning, skipper. She's spotted us for sure. A mile and a half astern, Jed says. D'you want us to chuck the stuff overboard?"

"Send a hundred thousand bucks' worth of good liquor to Davy Jones's locker? Not danged likely," said the captain grimly. "We'll give her a run for her money."

FOUR

A smell of paint still hovered in the hallways when Belinda came home for her half-term holiday. That the Fletchers had managed to move from St. John's Wood by then was in no small part due to Lambert.

Though he still spent every weekday morning haunting the American embassy, an unhappy ghost who had lost his obol for Charon, he would then go to the Hampstead house to "ginger up" cleaners and workmen, as he put it. Daisy didn't tell Alec that when she dropped in to see how things were going, Lambert was generally standing at a window with borrowed binoculars, watching the doings of the next-door neighbours.

Daisy wasn't sure what he was looking for, but she was pretty sure he hadn't seen it. He couldn't have hidden his subsequent excitement from her.

Be that as it might, the refurbishment was completed in record time. The house was light and bright. Bel loved her new bedroom, three times the size of the one she had occupied since the twins' arrival.

The very morning after she came home, Lambert returned

from the embassy with his passport and papers, and took his leave.

His gratitude for the Fletchers' hospitality was so heartfelt that Daisy began to feel quite mean for having scoffed at him and resented his intrusion into their lives.

"You've been a great help," she said. "I hope you'll come back to say good-bye before you leave England."

He cast a furtive look behind him and whispered, "You may see me around, Mrs. Fletcher. If you do, please pretend you don't know me. Don't speak to me, and don't tell anyone. Except Mr. Fletcher, of course."

She bit her lip to hold back a laugh. He was so keen to be a hero out of Anthony Hope's romances, or John Buchan's, or the American equivalent, and he just wasn't cut out for the role. "I won't," she promised.

He stood on the threshold for a moment, scanning his surroundings before he ventured forth. As he went down the steps, Daisy saw him turn up his coat collar and pull down his hat.

She told Alec when he turned up in the middle of the afternoon and announced that he was taking three days off while Belinda was at home. To her surprise, her news made his dark brows lower in a frown.

"What's the matter, darling? Aren't you glad he's gone at last?"

"Naturally. I just hope he's not going to cause any trouble."

"What kind of trouble?"

"The Americans are pushing us to help them enforce their stupid law. It started last year with extending territorial waters from three to twelve miles. Well, the government approved that treaty for our own reasons, and a lot of grief it's caused already. They've seized a number of British-registered ships, some actually outside the new limit, when they've caught them off-loading alcohol, or even just with alcohol aboard. Now they're sending agents over here to investigate the shippers. The last thing we need is trigger-happy idiots like Lambert wandering about."

"Customs took away his gun, remember?"

"Thank heaven for small mercies! Let's forget about him, for the present at least. No doubt he'll turn up again sooner or later, like a bad penny. Where's Bel?"

"She went with Mrs. Gilpin and Bertha. . . . Don't look blank, darling. Bertha's our new nursery maid. They've taken the babies and Nana for a walk on the Heath. It's such a beautiful day, let's go to meet them."

"Right-oh. Just let me get changed."

A two-minute walk took them to the edge of the Heath, eight hundred acres of woodland and meadow practically on their doorstep. From their high position, on this clear October afternoon, they could see the glint of the sun's slanting rays on the Crystal Palace, far off beyond St. Paul's. At the foot of the hill, a large pond gleamed between leafless trees.

Quite a number of people were taking advantage of the weather: boys kicking balls, well-wrapped pensioners chatting on benches, dog walkers, pram pushers, and, combining the last two, a small group coming up the slope towards Daisy and Alec.

Nana was first to spot them. Off her lead, she came bounding up to them, tail gyrating wildly. Behind her, at a snail's pace, came Belinda, bent double with Oliver clutching her forefingers and staggering along on his own two feet. Next was Bertha, a plump, toothy girl with a soft West Country voice, carrying Miranda. Keeping an eye on her charges, Nurse Gilpin brought up the rear with the empty pushchair, a newfangled contraption she had fought tooth and nail until it was made plain to her that Daisy's brother-in-law, *Lord* John, had had it specially designed and built for the twins. Nurse Gilpin was a snob.

Belinda looked up to see where Nana had gone. Of course, Oliver promptly sat down. He opened his mouth to yell but stopped when Bel picked him up, the burden making her look

skinnier than ever. She had been a thin child as long as Daisy had known her, and since going back to boarding school after the summer hols, she seemed to have grown an inch without putting on an ounce. Daisy hoped she was getting enough to eat. She didn't seem to have any trouble carrying the baby, though, and gave him up reluctantly to Daisy when they met.

Alec relieved the nursemaid of Miranda and sat her on his shoulders, wincing as she buried her little hands in his dark, springy hair.

"Hold on tight, Daddy. She doesn't understand she mustn't let go."

"Da-da," Miranda observed with satisfaction.

With a smug smile at Daisy, Alec said, "Da-da before Ma-ma."

"It's just babbling at this age, isn't it, Mrs. Gilpin?"

"I'm sure I can't say, madam. In the old days, I'd've said so, but what with all these modern notions, who can tell?" The nurse had reluctantly given in to Daisy's "modern notions" about parents actually being allowed free access to their children, but she didn't pretend to approve. Now and then, she managed to get in a dig on the subject.

An elderly man came down the hill towards them. He walked stiffly, with the aid of a stick, and was dressed in tweed knickerbockers, like a country squire out to view his estate. He had a pair of binoculars dangling on a cord around his neck and a pair of fat spaniels waddling at his heels. Nana rushed to meet the dogs.

"You'd better put her on the lead, Bel," said Alec.

The man heard him. "It's all right, they know one another. Nana, isn't it? They met in the garden when your maid let her out one morning." Pale, washed-out eyes scrutinized them from under bushy eyebrows. "You'll be the new people at number six. My sister and I are at number ten. Bennett's the name, two *t*'s. Settling in all right, eh?"

"Yes, thank you," said Daisy. "I'm Mrs. Fletcher. My husband. Our daughter Belinda."

"And who was the young fellow I saw leaving this morning with bag and baggage, eh?"

"A guest," Alec said repressively.

"A guest, eh? We thought he might be a relative, the way he's been popping in and out the last couple of weeks, before you moved in. Or a decorator. You've spent a fortune having the place done up nicely, I expect?"

"Nothing terribly exciting," said Daisy. "We've kept it quite simple."

"Haven't you even bought new furniture? We haven't seen a furniture van pull up, only Pickford's moving van."

"We've kept it simple," Daisy repeated. Feeling Alec seething beside her—he was more accustomed to interrogating than to being interrogated—she went on: "I hope you'll excuse us, Mr. Bennett. We must get on home before the little ones catch a chill."

Mr. Bennett peered at the babies. "Twins, eh? Not identical, though!" he said disagreeably.

Oliver's face crumpled, preparatory to a yell, but as the old man stumped off, he decided to blow a raspberry instead, a skill he had recently mastered.

"Why did he ask so many questions, Daddy?" Belinda whispered.

Alec grunted.

Daisy said diplomatically, "It's natural to be interested when new people move in nearby."

"Which doesn't mean you have to answer any questions he may ask you, Bel," said her father.

"Certainly not," Daisy agreed. "But try not to be rude."

"Like you, Mummy. You didn't really tell him anything, but you were perfectly polite. I don't expect I can do it so well."

"Practice makes perfect," said Alec with a grin.

"I expect he's grumpy because he's feeling rheumaticky," Daisy said forgivingly.

As they reached the top of the hill, Alec started to swing Miranda down. She refused to let go of his hair.

"Bel, you're quite wrong. She understands about hanging on. What she doesn't understand is that Da-da doesn't care for a damp collar."

"Oh, Daddy!" Belinda giggled, and a muffled snort came from Bertha. "Bend down and I'll make her let go. There you are. Mirrie, darling, I'm not carrying you wet. You'll have to go back in the pushchair."

Daisy deposited Oliver, too, who was beginning to smell less than fragrant. It was Mrs. Gilpin's turn to look smug. "They should have gone on the pot half an hour ago," she announced, "but Miss Belinda *would* walk on." Stately as a dowager duchess, she sailed ahead with the pushchair, Bertha trotting at her side, receiving low-voiced instruction.

Belinda skipped along between Daisy and Alec, arms linked through theirs. "I'm glad I don't have to change nappies," she said.

"You'd better learn how, darling," said Daisy. "I have the best of both worlds, playing with the twins as much as I want but not having to do the dirty work. When I was little, Nanny ruled supreme, and we hardly ever saw my parents. Of course," she mused, "I'm not at all sure Mother ever had the least desire to challenge Nanny's rule. But by the time you have children, who knows how the world will be?"

Bel wrinkled her nose. "All right, Mummy, I'll ask Bertha to show me how. I'll even do it myself. Practice makes perfect! I do like helping to give them baths, though. It's such fun watching them splash."

When they reached the house, the parlour maid met them with a folded note. Daisy opened it.

"From next door. An invitation to drinks before dinner tomorrow, to meet the neighbours."

Alec groaned. "Must we?"

"I'm afraid so, darling." She checked that the parlour maid had returned downstairs. "Unless you want to hide behind closed curtains with all the lights off. But we'd never get away with it anyway. Remember, Elsie's sister is parlour maid next door."

"And a rotten idea that will probably prove to be! I bet that's how the Jessups know I'm home for a few days. We could try for theatre or concert tickets?"

"We could, but we'll have to take the plunge sooner or later. After all, we're not only neighbours, we're their landlords. We don't want to behave as if we're high-and-mighty, and turn them against us. Besides, the Jessups are nice people. Mr. Jessup did offer to provide drink at cost for a housewarming party."

"Trying to worm his way into my good graces. We don't have to have a party, do we?"

"I thought the best thing would be to wait till Christmas and hold an open house for everyone, your friends, my friends, relatives—"

"Mothers?" Alec asked with deep foreboding.

"We'll have to sometime, darling. This way, they'll be sort of diluted."

"You have a point." He sighed. "All right, drinks next door tomorrow. I suppose that nosy old man from the Heath will be there."

"Diluted," Daisy said hopefully.

"She was on the stage, you know," said Miss Bennett in an insinuating tone. A pudgy woman with pepper-and-salt hair, confined in a net, and a round, pale, doughy face, she had cornered Daisy.

"Our hostess?" Chorus girl? Music hall turn? Though dying to know, she wouldn't have asked for the world. To do so would only encourage the beastly woman's tattling, and she didn't need any encouragement. Obviously, the Bennetts were going to be the flies in the ointment. One ought to be able to interview one's prospective neighbours before moving.

"We all know about actresses. And Irish, into the bargain!" said Miss Bennett darkly.

"Such charming people, I've always found."

Miss Bennett looked at her as if she were mad. "Charming? Always blowing up policemen—"

"I don't suppose Mrs. Jessup's career left her any time for blowing up policemen. Mine certainly doesn't."

"Your career?" Her nose positively twitched. "You have a job?"

"I write. Oh, excuse me, Miss Bennett, I believe my husband wants to speak to me."

"Write? Write what?" Her nose twitched eagerly, but Daisy was already moving away with an insincere smile. "*Novels*, no doubt," came a mutter behind her, the inflexion leaving no doubt about the kind of novels Miss Bennett was imagining.

Aidan Jessup, bottle in hand, intercepted Daisy on her way across the room towards Alec. "Now what has that dreadful woman been saying to put you in such a pucker?" he asked with a wry look. "Let me fill up your glass. Dubonnet, wasn't it?"

"Yes, thanks. No doubt you'll soon be hearing that I write blue novels."

"But you write magazine articles, don't you? I'm afraid I don't read much besides the trade journals, but Mother enjoys your work. Good Lord, you didn't tell Miss Bennett—?"

"Not I. It's what she prefers to assume."

"Oh yes, Always Assume the Worst is their motto. I suppose they've told you Mother was a chorus girl."

Daisy willed herself not to blush. "Just that she was on the stage."

"As a matter of fact," he said a trifle belligerently, "she started as a soubrette in the provinces and was playing decent roles in London—Celia and Nerissa and that sort of thing—when she met Father. She might have gone on to Rosalind and Portia if she hadn't retired when they married."

"Not the Lady Macbeth type, I take it."

That made him laugh. "No, Mother's not made for tragedy. She doesn't even take the Bennetts' mischief making too seriously. If you ask me, it's a great pity my revered papa-in-law didn't put a spoke in the Bennetts' wheel when they decided to

buy here." He nodded towards Mr. Irwin, who stood staring gloomily into his glass, his expression suggesting that the stout, prosperous-looking citizen holding forth at his side might be asking for free legal advice.

"Could a reputable lawyer do that?"

"There must be a way, don't you think? As it is, unfortunately, one can't easily exclude them from a gathering of Constable Circle residents. It doesn't do to be at odds with one's neighbours."

"No, of course not. Their tales would only grow the wilder. Otherwise, everyone seems to be very pleasant."

"Not a bad lot. Is there anyone you haven't met yet?"

"I've talked to all the neighbours, I think. Your brother and sister aren't here? Your sister's married, I understand, but I didn't gather where she lives. I had the impression that your brother lives here, though."

Aidan looked disconcerted. "Deirdre lives in Birmingham," he said. "My brother often goes on buying trips with our father, to learn that side of the business. I've never been much of a one for travel. I prefer to stay home, and one of the family has to be here to mind things at this end. There's Audrey and the children to be considered, too. Have you travelled much on the Continent?"

"Just one flying visit, a few days last summer. If it hadn't been for the War, I'd undoubtedly have been shipped off to finishing school, like my sister Violet. I'm glad to have avoided that—I don't think it would have suited me at all—but I'd like to see some of the rest of the world. Besides America, that is."

"Ah, yes, I'd forgotten you were in America." He turned with obvious relief to Alec, who came up just then. "May I get you another drink, Mr. Fletcher?"

"Thank you, no. We ought to be making our adieus, ought we not, Daisy?"

People were beginning to drift away, and the Fletchers had to run the gauntlet of new acquaintances saying "So glad to have met you." A few last good nights were exchanged on the pavement before they attained their own front steps.

Daisy tucked her hand into Alec's arm as they went up.

"Did you talk to the Bennetts?" he asked, delving into his pocket for the door key. "He asked me if it's true I'm a peeler—a peeler! I thought the word went out of use decades ago. And then he had the nerve to say he hoped not, because many respectable people don't care to associate with the police."

"Don't worry, at least Miss Bennett seems to disapprove of blowing up policemen. She told me in the most horridly insinuating way that Moira Jessup is Irish and pointed out that the Irish have a habit of blowing up policemen. They're in luck, as I have no intention of associating with them any more than absolutely unavoidable."

Small wonder if Daisy forgot Aidan's odd reactions and patent attempt to change the subject of his brother's whereabouts. She did remember next morning but decided against telling Alec. He'd only say she was imagining things.

FOURTH SEA INTERLUDE

They wheeled him round and round the field
Till they came unto a barn,
And there they made a solemn mow
Of poor John Barleycorn.
They hired men with the crab-tree sticks
To cut him skin from bones,
And the miller he served him worse than that,
For he ground him between two stones.

The moment the Coast Guard destroyer was sighted, *Barleycorn*'s skipper had changed course. Now, though he knew they were on his tail, he held steady.

"Can we outrun them?" Patrick asked.

"Not with this load. But they're slow to turn. Just watch. Go out on deck if you want."

Two considerations weighed against Patrick's reluctance to leave whatever cover the wheelhouse offered: He didn't want to appear a coward, and surely the skipper wouldn't let him go out if they were in range of the destroyer's guns. Would he?

He climbed the short ladder to the low door. Two deckhands had opened several of the lockers lining the port and starboard rails and were spreading fish from a large crate over the illegal contents.

Glancing around, Patrick saw the lookout standing on the railed roof of the wheelhouse, gazing astern with his spyglass to his eye. Now and then he would swing round to scan the horizon. Near him, smoke poured from the smokestack as the *Barleycorn*'s engines put forth their utmost effort. Though the smoke quickly dissipated in the wind created by their speed, it must appear as a banner to the pursuing destroyer. Staring sternward into the glare of sea and sky, Patrick could just make out the distant banner of smoke from the Coast Guard ship's four funnels.

He was about to ask the lookout man for a turn with the spyglass when one of the others called to him. "Bear a hand here," he requested, holding out a bucket.

"What are you doing?"

"Can't hurt to tell 'em we're innocent fishermen," the other drawled. "Not that they'll believe it, 'less they're looking for an excuse to let us go."

Patrick took the bucket and scooped up a mess of fish. They were very dead, with dull eyes, and beginning to smell. Fresh fish might have better helped the deception, he thought, crossing to an open locker to slosh the contents of his bucket across the bulging sacks within. Perhaps the bootleggers hoped the smell would deter the Coast Guard from further investigation.

Perhaps they were right. Holding his nose, he returned for another bucketful. No wonder they didn't want to attempt this ruse unnecessarily. When time came to unload, not only would the fish have to be disposed of but the burlap swathing the bottles would have absorbed the stench. Patrick could only hope he would not be expected to help with that, too.

As he worked, he kept an eye on the destroyer. At first, the four smoke trails grew more indistinct. The distance between her and *Barleycorn* must be increasing, Patrick realised. Gradually, the four appeared to merge into one as she came around to chase the rumrunner. And then the intervening distance began to shrink.

Patrick started to wonder what American gaols were like. It was a happier alternative to wondering what it felt like to be shot.

The lookout on the roof shouted to his shipmates, "OK, go ahead!"

One of the men put down his bucket and moved aft, where he crouched to fiddle with three cylindrical canisters. Puzzled, Patrick stopped mucking about with fish and moved closer to watch. The man delved into the pockets of his pea jacket, came up empty-handed, and called to Patrick, "Matches?"

Patrick threw him a box, his aim sure despite the motion of the boat.

The seaman caught it. Cupping his hands, he struck a match and applied it to the top of one of the canisters. He paused to study the result. No effect was visible to Patrick, but the man nodded in satisfaction and proceeded to light the other two canisters.

The third failed to ignite on the first try. By the time he got it going, smoke billowed from the first and streamed out behind the *Barleycorn*.

"Tell the skipper to give it a couple of minutes," he directed Patrick.

Grinning, Patrick hurried forward. The destroyer was already invisible. Therefore, he presumed, *Barleycorn* was invisible to the destroyer.

Leaning down, he passed on the message. The skipper glanced back through the rear window at the thickening, spreading screen, then gestured to him to enter.

He obeyed. "They'll never catch us now," he said with enthusiasm.

"*They* won't."

"Oh." Patrick pondered. Of course, the destroyer would have a radio transmitter. At this moment, they were doubtless sending out wireless messages to all Coast Guard ships within reach, with details of *Barleycorn*'s course. "Oh," he said again, crestfallen. Given the hint, the conclusion was obvious, and he should have worked it out for himself right away.

The skipper glanced back again at the smoke screen, then changed course.

Since the skipper didn't dismiss him, Patrick stayed below, dropping onto the stool. This time, the result of his subsequent cogitations was still less cheering: The skipper expected shooting, and since the codes Patrick carried were important to the success of the lucrative business, he was to be protected.

He didn't exactly want to be on deck, dodging flying bullets, yet he felt like a coward, hiding out of sight while the others risked their lives on deck. If he had fought in the War, would he have been one of those who did his duty, even a hero, perhaps, or would he have funked it? He couldn't help wondering, though it was a futile question. He had been too young to bear arms for king and country.

Not that his present business was in any way comparable. He was doing nothing illegal by English law, but he was deliberately flouting American law. In American terms, he was a criminal.

Too late to worry about that. He had a job to do for his family, and he'd do it unless prevented by force majeure.

The approach of force majeure was announced just a few minutes later.

"Cutter on the starboard bow." The man relaying the sighting from Jed on the wheelhouse roof stayed by the open door.

Patrick stared through the windscreen, or whatever it was called on a boat. He couldn't see the cutter, but what had been a shadow on the horizon was now unmistakably land, green and grey and growing clearer by the moment.

"He's spotted us. Changing course to intercept, and there's another on the port bow."

61

The skipper's mouth took on a grimmer set, but he held steady on their course.

"Jed reckons they'll fall astern afore they're in range."

That sounded like good news to Patrick. However, this time he paused before voicing his relief. The cutters would be behind *Barleycorn*, but within firing range nonetheless. One on each side, they could rake the launch from stem to stern if she refused to stop—or they could hold their fire, follow her to her landing place, and make their arrests on shore.

Now there were low headlands on either side as *Barleycorn* entered a bay.

A Klaxon horn blared, followed by a loud-hailer: "U.S. Coast Guard. *Barleycorn*, stand by to be boarded."

The skipper's response was to shout to the man at the door, "Get Jed off the roof, and all of you lie flat!"

"But skipper—"

"Get your heads down!"

The man disappeared.

Another hail was followed by a warning shot screaming overhead. A fountain of water and mud arose where it landed in the shallows. The *Barleycorn* veered left, then right, then left again. Patrick assumed they were dodging further shots, until he realised the banks were closing in as they sped up a narrowing, winding inlet.

And ahead loomed a low drawbridge—a *very* low bridge.

"Skipper—"

"Duck!"

Patrick flung himself to the floor, arms covering his head. Above him, the roof splintered and disappeared, the smokestack crumpled, and windows shattered as they struck the bridge.

The skipper bobbed up and resumed steering, his gaze fixed on the river ahead. His cap had been knocked off and shards of glass glittered in his hair and whiskers. He spared a quick glance back at Patrick, prone amid the wreckage, and a manic grin bared his teeth.

"Too shallow for the cutters," he explained, "and they can't fire in case there's people around."

"Geez, skipper!" came a choking protest from the deck to the rear.

Half-hidden by smoke billowing from the truncated smokestack, three wobbly figures were picking themselves up from the backswept rubble of the roof. *Barleycorn* was now moving too slowly in the narrow channel to disperse the pungent fumes. Coughing, the men stumbled forward, one of them dabbing at a trickle of blood running down his cheek.

"Geez, skipper, there ain't much of that drawbridge left. The township's not gonna be too happy."

"We'll tell 'em a Coast Guard shell demolished it. They can try for compensation. Jed, get forward and watch for shoals. The rest of you, watch for the shore signal."

Patrick said hesitantly, "There's a chap over there who seems to be trying to attract our attention." He pointed at a couple of men on the wooded bank, one waving both arms, the other launching a dory.

Throttling back, the skipper kept just enough way on the launch to hold her in place against the current in the middle of the stream. The dory pulled alongside and the oarsman hung on to a fender. On his face, a naturally dour expression seemed to be warring with inward amusement.

"You're to unload in town," he said laconically.

"In town?" Turning his head, the skipper stared at him.

"Ayup."

"What's going on?" Patrick asked uneasily in a low voice. "Has something gone wrong?"

"Looks that way."

"Is it safe to go into the town? Won't the police be waiting for us?"

"We'll find out."

"You trust the man who told us—?"

"My brother."

Patrick didn't like to point out that history was full of brothers

betraying brothers, starting with Cain and Abel. After all, he trusted his own brother, the old stick-in-the-mud!

Meantime, the oarsman had briefly conferred with his passenger. He hoicked a thumb at Patrick and asked his brother, "That the fella you picked up out there?" The thumb hoicked seaward.

"Ayup."

The thumb indicated his companion. "This fella's come to pick him up."

In contrast to the overall-clad boatman, the other was wearing a yellowish brown suit, of a colour and cut that would have raised eyebrows in London—but Patrick had no way of knowing whether it was proper business dress in America. The passenger started to stand up, subsiding abruptly as the dory rocked but raising his brown fedora enough to show reddish hair and bright blue eyes in a pale face scattered with pale, blotchy freckles.

An Irishman, if ever Patrick had seen one.

"Now?" asked the skipper.

"Ayup."

Patrick retrieved his kit bag from under a heap of debris and clambered out of the remains of the wheelhouse. He turned to thank the skipper, receiving a silent nod in response. With a wave to the deckhands, he went over the side and landed nimbly enough in the dory to preserve his self-respect. His natural inclination was to introduce himself, but he recalled the ban on naming names and refrained, uttering merely, "How do you do?"

"Uh, howdy."

"What went wrong, sir?" Patrick asked the local man as he rowed them towards the riverbank. "Why is the *Barleycorn* going into the town?"

"Farmer called the feds."

"After taking our money for the use of his barn!" the Irishman exclaimed. He sounded more American than Irish, and very angry.

"Changed his mind," the skipper's brother said mildly. "It's a free country. Man's allowed to change his mind."

"Not after taking our money. He's going to regret it, I can tell you."

"Not too badly, if you want folks hereabouts to cooperate in future."

"He called the feds."

"And his boy called us. So what happens? The feds rope in the local cops and every last one of 'em heads out to the farm to set an ambush. So 'stead of a dozen men tramping to and fro through the mud from river to farm with their arms full, *Barleycorn* sails into town and unloads at the dock, straight onto the trucks. Sounds like a good deal to me."

He shipped his oars as the dory nosed into the bank. Patrick jumped ashore with a painter. He tied up securely to a stake he found there, then turned to take the oars and boat hook from the boatman.

"Thanks." The man joined him, handed him his kit bag, and took the oars.

"Thank *you*, for ferrying me from *Barleycorn*."

Patrick used the boat hook to bring the dory close and then gave the Irishman a hand up onto the bank. The air was so thick with animosity, he felt a nervous desire to chatter but managed to keep his mouth shut. The local man led the way into the woods, along a barely visible path. Birds fell silent as they passed.

In the rear, the city man, wearing utterly inappropriate shoes, picked his way with care through the damp leaf mould. Patrick paused to let him catch up.

"Where are we going?" he ventured to ask.

"To see a man. You don't need to know his name, but he works for the Eyetie who works for the big boss, your customer. That is, you are Patrick Jessup, I presume?"

"Yes. And you?"

The man considered a moment. "I guess you'll have to know sooner or later, seeing I'm going to England with you."

"You are?" Patrick exclaimed.

"Yeah, so they tell me. Someone's gotta make sure our competitors don't get at you. But don't let's talk about that here. It's none of the hick's business." He nodded towards the man trudging ahead. In a low voice he added, "You can call me Mickie Callaghan. Pleased to meetcha."

"Callaghan! That's my mother's maiden name."

"No kidding. Well, is that a coincidence or what?"

The local man was waiting for them beside an unpaved road. He had stowed the oars in a farm cart pulled off onto the verge. The cart horse was looking back at him with patient hope.

A little farther along, a large Packard was parked; half-concealed by bushes, it faced in the opposite direction from the cart. Callaghan pointed. "That's us." He looked Patrick up and down. "Mary Mother of God, you're a mess altogether. You brush yourself down before you get into my auto. I guess I better pay this guy off, or he'll be calling the feds on us."

Patrick handed the boat hook to the boatman and went on to the car. As he took off his jacket and shook the wood and glass debris out of it, he watched Callaghan hand over a wad of banknotes. Both he and the recipient looked grim.

Patrick was glad he was not the object of their anger. His energy was beginning to flag. He hoped he wouldn't be expected to crank the Packard. When Callaghan came over and curtly gestured to him to get in, he realised with relief that the car had a self-starter. Callaghan climbed in behind the wheel.

He stuck his hand inside his jacket, pulled out a pistol from a shoulder holster, and chucked it onto the backseat.

The Packard failed to start on the first attempt. Before Callaghan could press the button again, the local man came up from behind. Boat hook in hand, he loomed over Callaghan.

"I'm telling you," he said, and his voice carried no less conviction for being calm and quiet, "you and your buddies better

not be seen in these parts ever again if any harm comes to that family."

The motor caught and they spurted away in a cloud of dust. Like it or not, Patrick was committed to travelling with the aggressive, vengeful, and armed Irishman.

FIVE

Daisy wanted to reciprocate for the Jessups' drinks party, but with Alec's schedule so erratic, a similar evening do was impossible. Besides, the Fletchers simply could not compete in variety or quality with the wine merchant's vast selection. Worse, she'd have to choose between inviting the Bennetts, who would ruin the affair, or offending them by not asking them.

She decided afternoon tea for the Jessup ladies would be the proper response, especially if she included an invitation to the children for nursery tea. Her St. John's Wood friends, Melanie and Sakari, would round out the party.

Sakari couldn't come because of a prior engagement at India House, where her husband was something important. Daisy rang up Madge.

"The people with the Versailles room? Darling, I'd love to meet them."

"Here, not at their house."

"Of course. Just watch me wangle an invitation. Will Lucy be there?"

"Lucy? Gosh no. Afternoon tea in suburbia is definitely not Lucy's . . . well, cup of tea."

Madge laughed. "True. I'm not so choosy. I'll be there. Shall I be Lady Margaret, do you think? Are they that sort of people?"

"I don't think so," Daisy said doubtfully. "I suspect they'd be *less* likely to invite you. But I don't know them very well yet."

"Then Mrs. Pearson it is."

"Bring Robin, too, if you like. There's to be nursery tea, as well."

"Heavens, darling, you are becoming positively domesticated."

"It's all right, we don't have to watch feeding time at the zoo. There will be nurses aplenty to scrub their jammy faces. But the little Jessup girl adores the twins, and Mrs. Jessup—Mrs. Aidan Jessup—is very motherly, so I thought it would please her."

"You want to please Mrs. Aidan Jessup? What are you up to, Daisy?"

"Nothing!"

"Aidan? Isn't that Irish?"

"I believe so. The elder Mrs. Jessup was Moira Callaghan when she was on the stage."

"A chorus girl?" Madge sounded amused.

"Shakespearean," Daisy said severely.

"And Irish. Have you moved in next door to a nest of Republicans?"

"Not at all! Aidan is frightfully English, in spite of his name. So is his father, in spite of all his travels on the Continent. It's the younger son . . . Irish Republican—I hadn't even considered that possibility. I think he's in America, not Ireland."

"I'll come early and you can tell me all about it."

"Right-oh. Yes, I'd better ring off now or Alec's going to be asking nasty questions about the telephone bill. Cheerio, darling."

Hanging up, Daisy went down to the kitchen to discuss the tea party with Mrs. Dobson. The cook-housekeeper was delighted at the prospect of showing off her baking skills. Daisy

left her to make out a shopping list, and went up to the nursery to tell Oliver and Miranda about their coming treat—and to warn Nurse Gilpin.

Oh dear, she thought, realising she ought to have consulted Nurse first. Mrs. Gilpin would be offended, but then, she was offended with Daisy most of the time anyway.

The new nursery was light and bright, with plenty of room for two cribs, dressers, toy chests, a rocking horse, and all the other necessary accoutrements. The walls were hung with paintings by Belinda of bunnies, kittens, squirrels, and puppies, some more recognisable than others. A small room connected to it was Mrs. Gilpin's bedroom, so that she had some privacy but, with the door open, could hear the slightest sound from the babies at night. She had grudgingly approved the arrangement. It meant Alec could go into the nursery with good-night kisses even when he got home very late.

Nana, the subject of one of Belinda's paintings, lay sprawled on the floor. She had been allowed into the nursery occasionally on sufferance for several months. Then Daisy thought to mention to Mrs. Gilpin that, during her own childhood, a couple of dogs were always to be found in the nurseries at Fairacres. After that, Nana was made welcome. Oliver and Miranda crawled over her, cooing with delight, the way they had over Lambert.

Watching them, Daisy found it impossible to believe in a nest of Irish Republicans next door. Did they still go around blowing up English policemen, now that they had their own country? She hadn't heard of any such incidents recently, but she'd never been much of a newspaper reader.

When she was growing up, any young lady taking an interest in politics was assumed to be a suffragette—horror of horrors! Men still had a tendency to go into a female-excluding huddle when the subject arose. But the suffragettes had won, and there were already several women MPs. Daisy was twenty-eight years old. In two years, she'd be thirty (more horrors!) and able to vote in national elections, and she hadn't the

foggiest what it was all about. She decided she had better start reading Alec's morning paper.

In the meantime, with Miranda crawling towards her crying "Ma-ma"—indubitably "Ma-ma"!—Daisy couldn't put off much longer broaching the delicate subject of nursery tea.

Oliver raced after his sister, shouting "Ga-ga-gak."

Daisy sat down and the babies climbed onto her lap. Inhaling the sweet milk and talcum smell of them, she gave each a kiss and said over their heads, "I've invited the children next door to tea, Mrs. Gilpin."

"Indeed, madam!" said Nurse with a sniff. "I hardly think Master Oliver and Miss Miranda are old enough to entertain guests."

"Their nanny will come, too, of course."

"Indeed, madam."

"Besides, I expect Miss Marilyn will entertain the twins. You know how she dotes on them when they meet in the gardens. And there will be another two-year-old to play with Percy Jessup—Mrs. Pearson's Robin."

"Lady . . . Mrs. Pearson's little boy? How nice for our little ones to make his acquaintance."

What a change of tune! Daisy assumed Mrs. Dobson must have told her that Madge was Lady Margaret. If Nurse knew, then the nursery maid surely knew, and what Bertha knew the parlour maid knew, and what Elsie knew, her sister next door was bound to know. So no doubt the Jessups would also find out within a short time. It would be interesting to see whether they were more impressed by someone with the genuine title of "Lady" than by someone with a mere "Honourable" before her name.

Alec came home early for once. He had obtained tickets for that night's concert at Queen's Hall, a rare occasion, given his erratic schedule. Daisy didn't want to spoil the evening, so she postponed asking him whether the Irish Republicans were still in the habit of blowing up policemen. Perhaps she'd learn enough about the Jessups at the tea party not to have to ask him at all.

It was quite late when they got home. As it was drizzling, Alec stopped the Austin right in front of the house to let Daisy out, then went to put the car in the garage in the alley. As Daisy started up the steps, the Jessups' front door opened, silhouetting a man against the lighted hall. Then the door slammed shut and the figure hurried down the next-door steps. Daisy couldn't see his face, but something about the way he moved seemed familiar.

She was in the house and taking off her coat before she made the connection: Surely he was the American visitor who had so upset Mrs. Jessup. Judging by his hasty retreat, his reception hadn't been any better today.

When Alec came in, rain dripping from his hat, Daisy almost told him. But he had other plans for what was left of the evening.

"Time for bed," he said firmly, and with his arm snug about her waist, she wasn't going to argue.

The next afternoon, Madge arrived in good time for a chat, as she had promised. They went straight up to the nursery, however, and by the time Robin, Oliver, and Miranda had been introduced and induced to play more or less nicely with one another, it was too late for Daisy to tell Madge any details of the mysteries surrounding the Jessups. She did warn her, though, that her title was no secret.

When they went downstairs, Elsie was just opening the door to Melanie. Madge had met Mel a couple of times but didn't know her at all well. Besides, Melanie, the very proper wife of a bank manager, was rendered acutely uncomfortable by gossip that involved speaking ill of anyone. Though Daisy had no intention of maligning the Jessups, discussing the possible involvement of one or more members with the Irish Republicans was bound to distress Mel.

The Jessup ladies, children, and nanny arrived a few moments later. After greetings and introductions and the des-

patching of the nursery party upstairs, Daisy poured tea. Elsie passed it around, along with watercress sandwiches (Mrs. Dobson was a genius at cutting bread practically paper-thin) and a variety of homemade biscuits (including Daisy's favourite macaroons, which she allowed herself only on special occasions).

Once everyone was served, Daisy dismissed Elsie. Madge and Audrey Jessup, both cheerful, practical women with two-year-old boys, were already getting on like a house on fire. Mel and Mrs. Jessup, on the other hand, were making polite conversation, so Daisy joined in.

It wasn't difficult to introduce the subject of foreign travel. The Germonds had taken the whole family to Brittany in the summer. Daisy asked Melanie about the difficulties of travelling with children, and went on to mention quite naturally that Mr. Jessup took his younger son with him on his business trips to the Continent.

"How old was he the first time he went abroad with your husband?" she asked Mrs. Jessup.

"Fifteen or sixteen." Mrs. Jessup did not elaborate.

"And now he goes by himself," said Daisy.

"You must worry about him," said Mel.

Since Mrs. Jessup didn't respond, Daisy pointed out, "Surely if he's old enough to do business on his own, he's old enough not to worry about."

"Oh Daisy, I don't think one ever stops worrying about one's children. Wouldn't you agree, Mrs. Jessup?"

"Absolutely," she agreed with an amused smile. "Even into one's dotage, I dare say, when the 'children' themselves are growing elderly."

Daisy thought that behind the calm façade, the smile was forced, stagy even, but perhaps she was influenced by knowing Mrs. Jessup had been an actress. She ventured another probe. "He isn't in Germany, is he? As far as I can recall, most German wines come from the Rhine and Moselle, and that part of Germany has been pretty unsettled recently, even more so than the rest."

"There are some vineyards farther east, but yes, most are in the Rhineland. Maurice doesn't handle many German wines, though, because there's still a lot of prejudice against them. But I don't want to bore you with business talk, Mrs. Germond. Are you an aficionado of the theatre?"

"I should be happy to go more often than I do."

"Perhaps Mrs. Fletcher has told you that I was on the stage. It's an odd world." She proceeded to entertain them with stories of theatre life. Madge, who was a great playgoer, joined in, while Audrey Jessup prompted her mother-in-law, suggesting particularly interesting incidents. Once again, Daisy envied their easy relationship.

Mrs. Jessup was very amusing, but when everyone departed, a frustrated Daisy was no wiser about the whereabouts of her younger son.

Madge was last to leave. "I wish I could stay and talk," she said. "I must say, they seem like nice people. Not a single 'your ladyship' to be heard, thank heaven! Mrs. Aidan has invited me to go and see the Galerie des Glaces one of these days."

"Madge! How did you manage it?"

"I just mentioned that you'd mentioned it," Madge said airily, "and that it sounded interesting. She told me her father-in-law had it made as a compliment to her mother-in-law, because she was so beautiful, he wanted to see her everywhere he looked. Mr. Jessup must have been quite a romantic, though nowadays apparently he uses it mostly to entertain foreign businessmen and their wives."

"And there I've been tiptoeing around the subject for weeks!"

"I even found out that the ladies entertained you in there that first time because the children had been playing in the drawing room earlier and little Percy threw a wooden train through a windowpane."

"Well, that's one little mystery cleared up. I trust they don't let him play in the Galerie?"

"Catastrophe! But Mrs. Jessup sounds like a very affectionate, not to say indulgent, grandmother. I can't believe she's in-

volved in any dastardly plots. Here's my taxi, so we'll have to talk about that another time. Bye, darling."

They kissed cheeks, and Daisy waved as Madge stepped into the cab. As it pulled away, her eye was caught by a movement in the garden opposite. Many of the bushes were leafless now, but there was a clump of laurels and rhododendrons. The evergreen leaves were waving in an unnatural manner, even considering the slight breeze that was chasing clouds across the sky.

Daisy watched. Someone was lurking there.

She was as certain as certain could be without actually confronting him that it was Lambert. She had glimpsed him once or twice in the streets of Hampstead but had obeyed his instructions to pretend she hadn't. Could anyone else who made a practice of lurking possibly be so inefficient at it?

"Alec?"

"Mmm-hmm?" He looked up from the *Daily Chronicle*.

"Do the Irish still go around blowing up policemen?"

"I can't promise they've given up the practice, love, but at the moment they seem more intent on blowing up one another."

"Oh. I suppose that's a good thing, in its way. Sort of."

Alec grinned. "Sort of. They'd probably give it up if they didn't get endless support, guns and money, from their fellow countrymen who have emigrated to America. But it's not my problem at the moment, thank heaven."

"Leave me the paper, will you, darling? Do you realise I'm going to be old enough to vote soon? I ought to know what's going on in the world."

"You mean you're not going to vote as your husband directs you?"

"Alec!"

"Ah well. As long as you don't start writing political diatribes." He folded the newspaper and passed it over. "Here you go. Have fun."

Daisy wrinkled her nose at him. "I don't suppose it'll actually be fun, but I'm sure it must be my duty to king and country, so I'll give it a try."

He drained his coffee and left for work. Daisy spread the *Chronicle* on the table in front of her, but instead of reading the headlines, she found herself considering what he had said.

The bellicose Irish Republicans obtained arms and money from their compatriots in America. So the younger Jessup son—she realised she still didn't know his name—might be in America raising funds. Why were the Irish fighting among themselves? It was all very muddling. Perhaps something in the newspaper would help her sort it out.

The first headline that caught her eye informed her that the French were bombing Damascus. Fighting in Ireland was bad enough, she decided; she simply didn't want to know why the French were bombing Damascus. Thankfully, she remembered that she had to get started on an article about Hampstead Heath, and of course she had to go and see the babies first.

It was a couple of days later that Daisy came out of the High Street stationer's with a packet of carbon paper and a heavy sigh. She nearly bumped into Audrey Jessup.

"Oh, Mrs. Fletcher, good morning. Whatever is the matter?"

"Mrs. Jessup! I beg your pardon. I wasn't looking where I was going. It's nothing, just a minor irritation, but . . . irritating."

"I know just what you mean. I expect Mr. Knowles can't find what you need."

"A typewriter ribbon, for the commonest make of machine available, an old one that everyone has. I suppose I'll just have to go back to the stationer in St. John's Wood. He always has the right one."

"Knowles is the most disorganised person, and if he can't lay hands on something immediately, he gets flustered and de-

nies the possibility of ever being able to get it. But one just has to be patient and firm."

"Is that all? Then if you'll excuse me, I'll just go back in and be firm."

"He's probably standing there now with the ribbon in his hands, wondering what to do with it." Audrey smiled. "If you're not in a great hurry to get back to work, would you like to meet for coffee after you sort him out? There's a Kardomah just down the street, opposite the bank."

Daisy was only too glad to agree. It was the first opportunity she'd had to talk to Audrey alone. Perhaps, on her own, Mrs. Aidan Jessup would be more forthcoming about her husband's family.

Her mother-in-law always evaded talk about the younger son's whereabouts. Why, if he were simply visiting vineyards in Europe, or even relatives in Ireland? Daisy was practically convinced he was in America. Whether he was rumrunning or gunrunning, she couldn't be sure, but he must be up to something fishy, or his mother wouldn't be so worried. Further questions also remained to be answered. Who, for instance, was the angry American? Might he be another agent, unknown to Lambert? After all, no one could expect poor Lambert to actually accomplish anything.

These reflections were no hindrance to dealing firmly with Mr. Knowles. Daisy reemerged into Hampstead High Street with a typewriter ribbon nestling alongside the carbon paper in her basket.

As arranged, Audrey had gone into the Kardomah to bag a table before the morning rush hit. When Daisy entered, she was standing next to a table for four, talking to a pair of seated women. Daisy hoped she wouldn't want to join them.

Seeing her, Audrey waved. Daisy went over and was introduced as the mother of adorable twins. The two ladies invited her and Audrey to sit down, but Audrey said she had already taken possession of a table for two by the window. They stood for a couple of minutes, chatting about their various offspring.

Quite the most annoying thing about having children, Daisy decided, was being forced to listen politely while other people talked about theirs.

Mrs. Vane's and Mrs. Darby's coffees arrived, accompanied by toasted tea cakes. Daisy had resolved to be good, but the spicy, buttery aroma of one of her favourite treats undermined her resolve. She and Audrey repaired to their table, saved by a scarf flung over one chair and a basket on the other.

"My treat," said Audrey as they sat down. "You will have something to eat, won't you? Otherwise, I can't, and I'm simply starving." She lowered her voice. "I'm pretty sure we'll be having an addition to the family in the spring."

"Congratulations!" More baby talk, Daisy thought, but perhaps she'd be able to lead it round to Mrs. Jessup's missing offspring.

A waitress, neat in black, with a frilly white apron and cap, came to take their order—two coffees, a tea cake, and a Bath bun.

As she left, Daisy added, "No wonder you're blooming."

Audrey beamed. "I'm so happy. We're all happy. Not just about the baby. My father-in-law has heard from Patrick at last—my brother-in-law, you know. Mama Moira's been dreadfully anxious about him. Being an actress, she doesn't show it, but I always know. Now Patrick's on his way home, we can all be comfortable again."

Before Daisy could think of a polite way to enquire where Patrick was coming home from and what he'd been doing there, the waitress arrived with a tray. And then it was too late. Audrey revealed that she had read Daisy's latest article in *Town and Country*, because "Mama Moira said I ought, with you living next door. I'm not much of a reader," she confessed, laughing. "I just don't seem to have time. But I really enjoyed your article."

She had lots of questions, and Daisy never managed to steer the conversation back to Patrick Jessup. At least she now knew his name!

HOME SWEET HOME

Here's little Sir John in a nut-brown bowl,
And brandy in a glass;
And little Sir John in the nut-brown bowl
Proved the stronger man at last.
And the huntsman he can't hunt the fox,
Nor so loudly blow his horn,
And the tinker he can't mend kettles or pots
Without a little of Barleycorn.

As a child, Patrick had found the long lift ride at Hampstead tube station spooky, though he'd have died rather than admit it to his brother or his friends. Once he was old enough, he preferred to climb the three hundred steps to the surface from the deepest platforms in the whole Underground network. Though the staircase was pretty grim and gloomy, at least he wasn't shut up in a cage. He used to say it was to keep himself fit for cricket.

Arriving in London on a rainy afternoon with Mickie Callaghan in tow, he assumed they would take a taxi from the boat train to Constable Circle.

"Nix," said Callaghan. "Cabs can be traced. We take the subway, or whatever you ride in in this burg."

The implications did not make Patrick happy. He was already unhappy about taking the Irish American home to his family. They had crossed the Atlantic together, Callaghan hiding in their cabin most of the way in a most unsettling manner. Patrick still wasn't sure what the man was after, but it seemed impossible to get rid of him.

His father had set up this whole affair. Patrick had carried out his part successfully. His father would have to deal with Callaghan.

They reached Hampstead station just early enough not to

have to stand in line for the lift, but Callaghan took one look at the lift attendant and said, "We take the stairs."

"He takes thousands of people up and down every day. He won't remember you."

"We take the stairs."

Maliciously, Patrick failed to inform him that they were not much less than two hundred feet below ground level. Callaghan, silent in his rubber-soled shoes, set off at a fast pace that would have taken him quickly to the top of a four-story building. Patrick didn't attempt to keep up. He was not at all surprised when he caught up with Callaghan plodding upward, looking disgruntled. Knowing from experience that taking the climb too slowly was as exhausting as attempting to take it too fast, Patrick kept going, giving the disgruntled American a wave as he passed.

"See you at the top."

Callaghan scowled.

The last step behind him, Patrick was pleased to find that he was less out of shape than he had feared. He was breathing hard but by no means winded. Leaning against a poster advertising *The Lost World*, starring Bessie Love, he waited for Callaghan, who appeared at last, after a considerable interval. He came up the final flight breathing easily. Patrick was sure he had stopped to rest on the last landing. If he had learnt anything about Mickie Callaghan, it was that he'd go to considerable trouble to avoid being caught at a disadvantage.

As always, it was a relief to exit into the open air. The rain had stopped, but dark clouds hung overhead, bringing an early twilight. Patrick turned left and left again, into Flask Walk. Callaghan, silent and morose, kept pace with him along the narrow paved lane, past the Flask public house. It was just opening.

"Let's stop in for a pint," Patrick suggested, trying to postpone the moment when he'd have to introduce his companion to the family.

"Nix. I bet you're known in there. They'd remember me."

The two-story workmen's cottages opening directly onto

the pavement gave way to larger houses and big trees as they crossed into Well Walk. At the old Chalybeate Well monument, they left the street and took a passage uphill between two large redbrick houses. They came out on the south side of Constable Circle.

"We'll cut across the garden," said Patrick, turning his head to speak to Callaghan, who had fallen a step or two behind.

"Nice place. Which is your house?"

"To the left of the one at the top." He pointed. Someone was coming down the steps. "I think that's my brother." In the dusk, he couldn't be sure.

The man crossed the street and started down the path. It *was* Aidan. Good old Aidan! Patrick had never in his life been so glad to see the old sobersides. He waved. Aidan waved back and they both walked faster. Callaghan fell behind Patrick.

A man stepped out of the bushes and accosted Aidan. He spoke too softly for Patrick to hear at that distance, but his gestures were forceful. Aidan brushed him off and kept going. The man persisted, striding along at Aidan's side, gesticulating. He seemed to be angry.

They all converged on the fountain.

The stranger's rant cut off abruptly, as if he had suddenly noticed he and Aidan were not alone. He stared towards Patrick.

"You!" he exclaimed, his tone venomous. Thrusting his hand inside his coat, he took a couple of quick paces forward. His hand reappeared gripping a pistol.

SIX

"*Madam!*" *Elsie* burst into the dining room in a manner most unlike her usual parlour-maidenly propriety. "Oh madam!"

"What's the matter?" Daisy sloshed tea over the *Chronicle* as she jumped up in alarm. "Not the twins—?"

"Oh no, 'm, not the babies."

Flooded with relief, Daisy took a closer look at the maid. "You're white as a sheet, Elsie. Here, sit down. What's wrong?"

"It's the little dog, 'm. I let her out same as usual to go over to the garden—"

"Don't tell me she's been run over!"

"Oh no, madam. Nothing drives that fast round the Circle. But usually she's that good about coming right away when I call her, and this morning I called and called and she didn't come—"

"She's run away?" Daisy asked incredulously.

"Oh no, 'm. I went up the area steps to the pavement to look if I could see her, and there she was in the garden, over by them bushes, the evergreen ones? And she was barking and whining fit to bust, and she just wouldn't come away, so I went to fetch her. And I grabbed her collar and she kept on

whining and I was scolding her like anything when I saw it."
The maid fell silent, her eyes and mouth round with remembered shock.

Daisy mustered all her patience. "What did you see, Elsie?"

"A glove, madam. Someone dropped it, I thought, and I went to pick it up—a good leather glove, someone'd be looking for it—but it had a hand in it, and I thought, 'Oh it's one of them nasty drunkards. What cheek sleeping in our garden!' And I moved the branches, like, to give him a piece of my mind, but he wasn't drunk, madam. He's dead! As a doornail."

"Good gracious! Oh dear, I suppose he must have died of exposure. It was cold and wet last night."

"I must say, 'm, he didn't look like a common drunk." Elsie was regaining her sangfroid. "Good-quality clothes he has on. He looked sort of familiar, but I can't quite place . . . Has the master gone already?"

"I don't think so. He went up to say good-bye to the twins." Daisy had got up early to have breakfast with Alec, who had to leave for Scotland Yard earlier than usual to finish writing a report before a meeting with Superintendent Crane and the AC (Crime). "You're right, Elsie. He'll have to be told."

What, after all, was the point of being married to a policeman if one had to cope oneself with dead bodies carelessly strewn around? It was no use, however, expecting him to be pleased.

Daisy went upstairs. She met Alec on the landing, as he came down.

"I'm off, love. I shouldn't be too late tonight."

"Darling, I'm afraid you're going to be late this morning. There's a tramp lying under the bushes in the garden, and it looks as if he's dead."

"Daisy, if you *must* fall over bodies wherever you go, could you not at least wait until I've left for work?"

"It wasn't me! Elsie found him."

"Not me, 'm!" Elsie, who had come up the stairs behind Daisy, was equally anxious to disclaim responsibility. "It was the little dog, sir."

"Where is she?" Daisy asked. "Where's Nana?"

"Oh madam, I must've forgot her, what with the shock and all. She'll be out there guarding him still, I 'spect. And I don't think he's a tramp, sir, not by his clothes."

Alec groaned. "Couldn't we just pretend you found him when I was already gone?" When Elsie looked almost as shocked as she had in reporting the body, he went on quickly: "No, of course we couldn't. Daisy, you'd better ring up the local station, but I suppose I'll have to take a look."

"Elsie, go with Mr. Fletcher and fetch Nana in."

"Oh madam, not me. I'm not going anywhere near that body again, not for nobody, not if you was to tell me to pack my box this instant."

Daisy looked at Alec. Alec looked at Daisy.

He sighed. "Right-oh, you'll have to come and get the dog. I can't cope with her as well as a corpse. Telephone the locals first. Elsie, I suppose you're quite sure he really is dead?"

"I saw bodies in the War, sir, when they bombed the East End. He looked to me about as dead as a jellied eel." She paused to consider. "No, not a jellied eel, not really. Dead as—"

"Never mind," Alec said hastily, "I'll take your word for it." He looked at his wristwatch. "I'm not going to make it to that meeting. Daisy, after you've spoken to the locals, you're going to have to ring up the Yard and tell the Super what's going on."

"Darling, he's bound to blame me!"

"Can't be helped." His grin was infuriating. Daisy wondered whether on the whole it might be preferable to have a husband who was *not* a policeman if one had to cope with a body. "If he carries on at you, say you have to secure the dog. In the meantime, no doubt she'll show me where to look."

With that, he bounded down the stairs and disappeared through the front door.

Before she followed, Daisy fixed the parlour maid with a stern eye. "This is police business now, Elsie. You mustn't talk about it to anyone. Not a soul, not even your sister, or you'll be in serious trouble. Did you talk to anyone outside?"

"No one was about, 'm. Leastways, I didn't see anyone, but then after I saw it, I wasn't looking. There could've been someone I didn't notice."

"When you talk to the police, just tell them exactly what you saw, not what or who might have been there."

Her eyes went round again. "Ooh, madam, will I have to talk to the police?"

"Very likely not, but if so, it's nothing to be afraid of. You speak to Mr. Fletcher every day, don't you?"

"Yes'm, but he's the master. It's not the same."

Daisy wished she had never embarked upon the subject. "Well, I dare say they won't want to see you, with the master to explain what happened. I must go and telephone."

The desk sergeant at Hampstead police station sounded bored. She gave him her name.

"Mrs. Fletcher, what can I— Mrs. Fletcher?" The voice perked up. "Mrs. DCI Fletcher, by any chance?"

"Yes, actually."

"What can we do for you, ma'am?"

"I'm ringing for my husband. Could I speak to a detective, please?"

"Of course, Mrs. Fletcher. DS Mackinnon is on duty."

"Oh good, I know him." And she liked him. Alec approved of him, too. "At least I think I do. Was he in St. John's Wood?"

"Moved here a few months ago, ma'am. Half a jiffy. I'll get him right on the line."

There were advantages to being notorious, Daisy thought with a sigh.

A moment later: "Mrs. Fletcher?" The rolling Scottish *r*'s were unmistakable, as was—she hoped—the pleasure in his voice as he continued. "Good morning, ma'am. What can I do for you?"

"Good morning, Mr. Mackinnon. I'm afraid it's a body."

"You've found a body?" he asked cautiously.

Silently, Daisy blessed him for not saying *"another* body." "Not exactly. That is, my maid found it. Or rather, the dog."

"Your dog found a body. Where, exactly?"

"In the garden—it's a sort of park, actually, or circular square, if you see what I mean." Daisy discovered she was more upset than she had supposed. "I'm explaining it very badly."

"Not at all. Chust take your time, Mrs. Fletcher. It isna the private garden of your own house, then?"

"No, not exactly. It's communal, for all the residents of Constable Circle. In Hampstead. Did you know we moved to Hampstead? Constable Circle, number six."

"Got it. You've seen this body, ma'am?"

"No, but my husband has gone to take a look. He told me to telephone."

"DCI Fletcher is on the scene? Excellent," Mackinnon said soothingly. "Nae doot it'll be best if I wait for his confirmation, sin ye've only the maid's word for it. What do you think?"

"No . . . Yes . . . Yes, perhaps. Right-oh, I'll tell him. You'll be standing by?"

"Of course, Mrs. Fletcher. I'll be ready."

"Thank you." Reluctantly, Daisy depressed the hook and asked the operator for Whitehall 1212. She did not want to speak to Superintendent Crane. She wasn't responsible for the body in the bushes; she hadn't even been the one to find the body in the bushes; but she knew perfectly well that, because of certain unfortunate incidents in her past, Crane would find some way to persuade himself it was all her fault.

A glance at old Mr. Walsall's grandfather clock suggested a ray of hope. Surely it was much too early for so exalted a person as the Super to be in his office. She would have to leave a message.

"I would like to leave a message for Superintendent Crane, please," she told the Scotland Yard operator.

"Who is calling, please?" came the inevitable question.

"This is Mrs. Fletcher, with a message from DCI Fletcher."

"Oh, Mrs. Fletcher, I'm sure the superintendent will want to speak to you directly. One moment while I connect you."

Daisy managed to suppress a howl of "NO," though a click told her it was too late anyway.

"Superintendent Crane's office. May I help you?"

"This is Mrs. Fletcher." She went on quickly: "My husband asked me to let Mr. Crane know he's been unavoidably delayed and won't—"

"Just a minute, Mrs. Fletcher. You can tell him yourself."

"But I don't want—"

"Good morning, Mrs. Fletcher." Crane sounded irritable, though she hadn't told him yet about the body. "What's up? Has he forgotten we have an important meeting this morning?"

"No, Mr. Crane, he's well aware of it. But he simply can't get away in time." She absolutely could not think of an easy way to break the news. "I'm afraid our dog found a body. Alec has to wait for the local police to come."

There was dead silence on the line. Then Crane asked with a sort of incredulous resignation, "Did I hear you correctly, Mrs. Fletcher? You've found another murder victim?"

"No! *I* didn't find him, and I don't know if he was *murdered* or not. I haven't even *seen* him yet."

"Yet!" exploded from the much-tried superintendent. "I dare say he's a particular friend of yours?"

"I don't know who he is. Believe me, I sincerely hope I shan't have to look at him. However," Daisy said firmly, "I told Alec I'd go and get the dog out of his way, so I'm afraid I shall have to hang up." And she did. Shockingly bad manners, but he was already annoyed with her. She might as well be hanged for a sheep as a lamb.

"Oh madam!" Elsie hovered anxiously by the green baize door to the stairs down to the kitchen. "I'm sure I wish I'd never gone after the little dog."

"Nonsense. It was your job, and if you hadn't found the man, someone else would have." As she spoke, Daisy took her coat from the coat tree. She started to put it on before she realised

she was still wearing her dressing gown. "Bother! Oh well, it's perfectly decent, and Alec can't wait." She buttoned the coat to the neck and tied a scarf over her head.

For once, Nana's lead was hanging in its proper place on the coatrack. Daisy reached for it.

"Madam, your slippers!" Elsie pushed through the swing door and returned immediately with a pair of galoshes, ancient enough to have belonged to Mr. Walsall.

Daisy put them on over her slippers and at last went outside.

Descending the steps—with care, because the galoshes were not hers and were too big—she called to Nana. She could see the little dog's rear end sticking out of the bushes, tail wagging now that Alec had joined in the excitement.

Nana backed out and came to meet Daisy, whining. She submitted docilely to having the lead clipped to her collar, but she had no intention of tamely returning to the house. With a couple of sharp barks—*Come and see what I found*—she pulled towards the bushes. In the oversized galoshes, Daisy had no traction to resist. She slip-slopped across the grass after the dog, losing one galosh halfway there.

Squish. "Oh blast!"

"Daisy! For pity's sake, you're going to muck up any footprints."

"It's murder?"

"It doesn't look good," Alec admitted, backing out of the bushes.

"Not someone we know?" Daisy removed a twig from his hair. "Not one of the neighbours?"

"No one I've met."

"Alec, it couldn't be . . . The Jessups are expecting the younger son home."

"I don't think so. This poor chap looks about the same age as Aidan Jessup, or a year or two older, though it's hard to tell once they're dead. Are the locals on their way?"

"It's DS Mackinnon. Remember him? He said he'd wait till

he had confirmation from you that there really is a corpse, but he's ready to get moving."

"Good. Go and get him moving. And in the meantime, I need someone stationed at each end of the path until Mackinnon arrives, to keep people out of the garden. I've done all I can here. I'll take the top end. People are more likely to come that way at this time of day."

"Oh for a good, solid, authoritative butler! I suppose I'd better take the bottom." Glancing down the slope, Daisy saw the local beat constable about to start up the path.

"Stop!" she and Alec cried in unison.

PC Norris hesitated.

"He'll do. Daisy, give Mackinnon the word," Alec ordered. "I'll deal with this."

Just as well, Daisy thought, remembering she hadn't dressed before coming out. She looked down at her feet, abandoned the second galosh, and tugged Nana back across the lawn, careful to place her ruined slippers in the marks she had already made. She didn't want to be accused of messing up the evidence.

SEVEN

The beat bobby had recognised Alec and was staying put, as instructed. Alec picked his way towards him by the route he thought least likely to disturb any traces of the night's doings. It was pure guesswork at this stage, so he examined the ground ahead intently before he took each step.

The grass was lush, having been too wet for mowing for a couple of weeks. So far, October had brought lots of rain and little frost. When Alec looked back, his trail was clearly visible, but blurred, unlikely to convey any useful information except direction. No, not even that; just where he had walked.

And if he wasn't mistaken— He held out his hand, palm up. Yes, it was starting to rain again.

PC Norris looked up at the lowering grey overcast. "More to come, sir," he opined. "Came down heavy in the night, it did. What's happened, sir? Anything I can do to help?"

He was a burly middle-aged man. Talking to him when the Fletchers first moved to his district, Alec had found him intelligent but unambitious, with no desire for promotion. He enjoyed patrolling his beat, one of the pleasantest in the metropolitan area, and he knew all the residents by sight, most by name.

"Yes," Alec said grimly. "We have a suspicious death. Right now, I want you to stay exactly where you are and make sure no one enters the garden from this end. Later, I'll have you take a look at the deceased."

"Right you are, sir. Will I blow my whistle for help?"

"No. It would bring every servant in the Circle running, and half their masters and mistresses." Alec eyed the nearest house, number 10, where the nosy Bennetts lived. He was happy to see all the blinds still closed. "We don't want to alarm people more than we must. The chaps from your division HQ should be here shortly."

"Right, sir, but there'll be them that see me here and come to ask. What do I tell 'em?"

"Tell them you have no idea what's going on."

Norris grinned. "No more I don't," he said.

"True." Alec left him, treading on the edge of the paving on the side of the path closest to where the body lay. He had considered going around the outside of the garden to see if there were any signs of the body having been deposited from that direction, but that would have made it impossible to see or prevent people walking down the path. He kept a close watch on the edge of the lawn and was rewarded, just before he reached the fountain, with clear evidence of something heavy having been dragged across the wet grass.

He was about to stoop to examine the traces, when a loud voice hailed him. "I say, Fletcher! What's up?" His neighbour from number 7, George Whitcomb, was on his way to whatever he did for a living.

"Stop! Not another step!" Alec yelled, and hurried up the slope.

Though Whitcomb obeyed, he looked affronted and indignant. Alec had met him at the Jessups' party and had exchanged cordial greetings when their paths happened to cross thereafter. The man knew he was a police officer—but that was theory; this was practice. Apparently, Whitcomb either had not expected to encounter Alec in his official

capacity or didn't like being ordered about by the police—or both.

At that moment, Alec realised he could not take on this case. All his neighbours would have to be questioned, as possible witnesses, if not as suspects. He was not only a fellow resident of Constable Circle, he was their leaseholder.

He could hold the fort until DS Mackinnon arrived, and then he'd have to bow out.

Yet Daisy, who knew the neighbours considerably better than Alec did, was sure to be an important source of information. However peripherally she was involved, Superintendent Crane and the Assistant Commissioner would expect Alec to keep her from meddling. Unless, he thought hopefully, they had at long last realised that nothing and nobody was capable of keeping Daisy from meddling.

It was all in the lap of the gods, alias the AC and the Super. Right now, Alec's job was to keep Whitcomb from marching down the garden path.

Whitcomb was armoured for the day's battle in pinstriped trousers, a fur-collared overcoat, and a bowler hat, and his chosen weapon was a tightly furled black umbrella. He was respectability personified and respectability outraged.

"I say, what the deuce . . . ," he spluttered. "You're not thinking of closing off the garden to the rest of us, are you, Fletcher?"

"Great Scott no! I wouldn't dream of it. The thing is, there's been a spot of bother down there and I'm just lending a hand while the local chaps gather their forces."

"Forces? Ah, the police, eh? Splendid chaps. Anything I can do?"

Civil servant, not businessman, Alec guessed. "Not at present, thank you," he said. "I expect the detective in charge will be in touch. You won't mind walking round instead of across the garden, I hope."

"No, no, of course not. Don't suppose you can give me a hint? No," he said hastily as Alec shook his head, "of course not." And off he went.

Alec didn't foresee objections from the Jessups, who were amiable types. For the rest of the inhabitants of the Circle, going around by the street was actually a more direct route than crossing the garden.

His thoughts turned to Detective Sergeant Mackinnon. The young Scot was competent and cooperative, if a little too inclined to believe Daisy walked on water. Still, Alec had worked with him once or twice since the case in which she had been involved, and his own feet seemed firmly grounded. He had matured, but he was still on the young side to lead a murder investigation.

And pending the doctor's report, Alec was pretty certain this was going to be a murder investigation.

The local police surgeon, Ridgeway, was also a good man. With luck, he was available and on his way. Not that it really mattered to Alec, as this wasn't going to be his case, but if people were going to get themselves bumped off not a hundred yards from his front door, he wanted the murderer under arrest. The sooner the better.

In fact, for once, when it was out of the question, Alec really wanted to be in charge. He wanted to be on his knees in the leaf mould beneath the bushes, rain dripping down the back of his neck, looking for clues anyone else just might miss.

The rain was belting down, blurring still further the already-indistinct traces of activity on the lawn. Daisy came down the steps towards him, fully dressed at last under her red umbrella, bringing him his conventional black one.

"Darling, you'll be soaked. Mackinnon's on his way, and so's that nice Dr. Ridgeway. And Mr. Crane rang back. He was a bit grumpy, but he said he'll try to soothe the AC's savage breast. No, that's not what he actually said, but that's what it amounted to. I've been thinking—"

"Please don't, Daisy! Besides, there's no point in passing on your speculations to me. I can't take the case. You must see that."

"Because of the neighbours? I wondered if interrogating

them was going to be a problem. But you have to find a way to do it, or we won't have any servants left."

"*What?*"

"The only reason they aren't quitting en masse is that they trust you to bag the murderer quickly. Yes, they all know. I made Elsie promise not to tell a soul, but one can't expect something like this to remain a secret from the rest, not when they can see out of the windows that something's going on. She swore, cross her heart and hope to die, that she wouldn't talk to her sister about it."

Alec snorted. "Fat chance!"

"There is a chance. She likes working next door to her sister, and I told her she wouldn't be any longer if she breathed a word about police business."

"It sounds as if, one way or another, we're doomed to lose all our servants."

"It's no laughing matter, you wretch! Mrs. Dobson won't desert us, come what may, but Mrs. Gilpin says if you aren't put in charge, she's not staying to see her babies murdered in their beds. *Her* babies, forsooth!"

"Did I just hear you say 'forsooth'?" Alec queried.

"Yes, and it just goes to show how upset I am. If she really thought of them as her babies, she wouldn't threaten to desert them. But I can tell you, if you're not busy solving the murder, you're going to be busy changing nappies!"

"Calm down, love. Such things have happened before in your vicinity without your getting in such a state."

"It's never happened right on my front doorstep before," she wailed. "So close to the twins!"

Alec would have put an arm around her to comfort her, but the umbrellas got in the way. "You know it's up to the Super whether I get the case," he pointed out. "But if Crane should be so ill-advised as to give it to me, we might have to move. The neighbours wouldn't take kindly to being interrogated by a fellow resident of the Circle."

"Couldn't you direct the investigation without actually seeing

people yourself? You could stay at the Yard, or the local station, and tell your men what questions to ask. Mackinnon, Tom, Ernie Piper, and DC Ross, they're all good detectives, I've heard you say so."

With a sigh, Alec conceded. "If Crane doesn't absolutely forbid my having anything to do with it, I'll pass on your suggestion."

"For pity's sake, don't tell him it's mine."

"I shan't. But if it works and I get stuck behind a desk for the rest of my natural, I'll know whom to blame!"

To his relief, she smiled. "I expect you'll soon find out it was nothing to do with anyone in the Circle, so you'll be able to take a more active part. You did say you didn't recognise him, so it's not one of the neighbours."

"Are you sure we met all of them at that party?"

"No, not absolutely. Mrs. Jessup told me they had invited everyone, but I don't suppose she'd have mentioned it if some sent their regrets. I'm glad the victim is too old to be her younger son."

"Daisy, I can't swear to it. Death changes appearances. Don't go telling them it's not young Jessup, when one of them may have to identify the body."

"I shan't, don't worry. Here come your reinforcements."

She pointed down the hill and Alec turned, to see a cluster of men around PC Norris, some in uniform with waterproof capes, some in plainclothes macs. In turn, Norris pointed up the slope.

"I'd better go down to them," Alec said hastily, "before the whole troop troops up and destroys any clues there may be. Would you stay here just for a moment, till I can send a man around, just in case someone else tries to walk down this way?"

"Of course, darling," Daisy said to his retreating back.

Shivering, she hoped he meant "just for a moment." The rain was coming down harder than ever, with sideways gusts that splashed her legs, though the umbrella kept her upper half dry. Trousers! she thought longingly. Why couldn't one of

those fashion tyrants who dictated what women should wear design warm tweed trousers instead of slinky evening frocks that made most figures look terrible?

She couldn't even distract herself by watching what the men were up to, as she was supposed to look out for encroaching pedestrians.

She turned her back on the garden just in time to see a man come out of the Jessups' front door. Swathed in an overcoat, umbrella held low, he was unrecognisable, but presumably one of the Jessup men. Daisy wondered how to bar his way down the path without telling him more than she ought about what had happened.

The problem didn't arise. Somewhat to her surprise, he didn't approach her, but hurried away down the pavement on the other side of the street. Perhaps he was late for work—no, she rather thought that as proprietors they usually didn't go to the shop till half past nine or so, and it couldn't be that yet. Of course, the weather was not exactly suitable for chatting outdoors. One of the household had no doubt observed from a window that no one was being allowed to cross the garden.

Yet Daisy couldn't help recalling the man she had twice before seen hurrying down those same steps, the American visitor. It couldn't be him. Surely he would not have been invited to spend the night at the Jessups'? The very night when someone was murdered in the garden?

EIGHT

"*Mr. Fletcher!*" DS Mackinnon greeted Alec thankfully, raising his hat to reveal short-cropped red hair. "Good morning, sir. Ye've a body in the bushes, Mrs. Fletcher said. Those evergreens up there, it'd be?"

"That's right." Alec curbed his irritation at Daisy's immediate intrusion into the case. "You'd better have one of your uniform chaps go up to the top to take over from my wife and keep people out. I suggest you send him round by the street."

Mackinnon duly nodded to one of the men, who set off up the hill as directed, but his dismay was apparent. "*Suggest*, sir?"

"This is your case, Sergeant. At least for the present." Drawing the Scotsman off to one side, Alec explained the situation.

"I see, sir. But I've never handled a murder case before. Not on my own."

"Your superintendent will probably put one of his DIs in charge."

"Yes, sir. But in the meantime, you're here, sir, and you know what's happened and what needs to be done. Can ye no stay and make *suggestions*?" he pleaded. "Or at least warn me if I'm missing something, or going wrong."

"Damn it, man, I should have been at the Yard half an hour ago!" But it was impossible now to have that report finished for the meeting with the AC, and Crane wasn't expecting him. And he did want to know what had happened practically on his doorstep while he slept. And Mackinnon was regarding him hopefully, like a persistent Scottish terrier—a dripping-wet terrier. Clues were washing away. "All right, let's get on with it."

"Thank you, sir! Dr. Ridgeway should be here any moment."

"I see you've brought photographic equipment."

"Yes, sir." He turned back to the group. "This is DC Ardmore, sir. He's pretty good with it."

"Going to be tricky under them bushes in the rain," said Ardmore dispassionately.

"Do what you can," said Mackinnon. "But keep your big boots out of there till we've seen what else there may be to see."

Alec listened to his instructions to his men, giving a slight nod now and then when Mackinnon glanced at him for approval. The young Scot had the theory down pat. Whether he had that indefinable other sense, the ability to see beneath surface appearances, to spot the detail that didn't quite fit, and to weave apparently unrelated facts into a coherent story, remained to be seen. Part of it could be developed with experience, but part was sheer instinct.

He had shown definite promise on the previous occasions when he had worked with Alec. Running an investigation was another kettle of fish.

He knew PC Norris's name. That was a good sign, whether he was already acquainted or had checked to see who was the copper on the beat before coming out. Alec was not one of those detectives who considered the humble beat bobby a lesser breed. Without those flat-footed plodders to prevent countless crimes, the CID would be even more overworked than it already was.

The second uniformed man Mackinnon had brought with him was sent to complete Norris's round, so that Norris would

be on the spot when the body was available for viewing. There was always the chance the local man might have noticed the victim earlier, alive, and be able to give some hint of a reason for his presence.

Before starting up the path, Mackinnon turned to Alec and said, "I don't suppose you could have taken a proper look without leaving traces, sir. You'll point them out when we come to them?"

"Of course." He was pretty sure the circuitous routes he had taken had not obliterated anything of significance. The effects of the maid's movements were less certain.

The signs of something having been hauled across the grass were still visible, and Mackinnon spotted them at once.

"You can see the troughs where his heels dragged," he said. "They caught on some blades of grass and uprooted them. And these indentations could be the footprints of someone heavy, or pulling a heavy load, moving backwards, with *his* heels digging in. They're nowhere near clear enough for identification, though, and there's not much point looking for footprints on the paving in this weather."

"I'm afraid not," Alec agreed. "It rained heavily during the night and everything was mushy by the time I came out this morning."

"Better take some snaps anyway, Ardmore. Warren, give him a hand."

As DC Ardmore started to erect his tripod and DC Warren put up the enormous umbrella he had been carrying over his arm, Mackinnon set off across the grass on one side of the trail. Alec went with him. They studied the marks as they walked. Alec agreed with Mackinnon's analysis.

"And look over there. The rain's just about washed them out, but you can just about see several more sets of tracks converging on the spot—mine, my wife's, the maid's, and the dog's. These are much clearer, fortunately."

They reached the shrubbery. A leather glove was visible, and a few inches of the sodden sleeve of a dark blue sharkskin jacket.

"You won't see much more under there without a torch," said Alec.

Mackinnon took an electric torch from the pocket of his mackintosh and switched it on. The light gleamed on the wet leaves framing the scene. "Looks as if a couple of branches have been hacked off with a pocketknife. Probably broke them getting him in and removed them so as not to draw attention. What do you think, sir?"

"That was my conclusion. The branches are lying beside the body."

"But in the dark, he didn't realise the hand was showing."

"He?"

Grasping Alec's meaning at once, Mackinnon looked back along the trail and said, "I hae my doots a woman could have carried anything so heavy."

"Possibly that's why it was dragged. In these days of sportswomen, it doesn't do to jump to conclusions. Even pre-War, there were plenty of farm women and market women capable of moving quite a weight, though neither is very likely in Hampstead."

"But sporting ladies are quite likely, tennis players and such. I'll keep yon in mind, sir."

"I must apologise for any footprints I left beyond the edge of the grass, by the body. I stood—or rather, crouched—as far back as possible, but there's not much room, I couldn't see very well, and I had to make sure he was dead. I hope I haven't mucked anything up."

Without comment, Mackinnon directed the beam at Alec's wet, muddy shoes, then crouched and shone it into the bushes. "He looks pretty dead to me." He prodded the hand with the torch. "Rigor well established. Dr. Ridgeway should be here by now."

Alec looked back. No doctor, but Ardmore was diligently photographing the lawn while Warren held the umbrella over him and his camera.

Mackinnon inserted his upper body beneath the leaves,

which released their burden of raindrops in a cascade onto his back. "One or two prints I'd say are yours, sir. The rest seems to have been deliberately smoothed. A hardened villain, would you say, sir?"

"Or anyone who's ever read detective fiction."

"Och, aye, nae doot." He hesitated. "If I squeeze in to take a closer look at the deceased, sir, I'm bound to leave more footprints. I shan't see anything you haven't already found out, not to mention what the doctor will tell us. Could ye no tell me—"

"I could, but how much are you going to learn if I spoon-feed you? I understand your reluctance, believe me. However, you chose to become a detective, and if you want to rise—"

"I'll go." Mackinnon visibly braced himself and ducked into the shrubbery.

His body blocked Alec's view of what he was doing. Leaves rustled and a twig snapped underfoot.

"Mud on the heels," he observed. "Feels as if his clothes are pretty dry underneath him, for what that's worth."

A voice came from behind Alec. "Done what I could, sir." It was the photographer, tripod and attached camera in his hands, Warren at his heels with the umbrella held high and a flashpan under his arm. "The prints aren't going to be any too clear, though."

"The impressions aren't any too clear." Alec eyed the pair. "I hope you're going to be able to get your stuff in there."

"Not till the sergeant comes out, any road," said Warren. "Then we'll just have to see. It'll be pretty close quarters."

Mackinnon backed out. He had taken off one glove and was eyeing his fingertips with distaste. "I couldn't see anything amiss, sir," he said, "but it feels as if the hair on the top of his head is matted with blood from a wound. That's aboot all I can tell. Enough, with the removal of the body, to make it murder."

"To make it, at the very least, distinctly fishy," said Alec.

They stood back to let Ardmore and his assistant scuffle

their way into the bushes. Entering last, the huge black umbrella completely blocked their view of what was going on.

Minute examination of his finger having apparently revealed no bloodstains, Mackinnon put his glove back on. "I didn't search his pockets, sir," he said a trifle defensively. "It seemed best to leave everything undisturbed until it's been photographed, since there's no hurry over identifying the deceased."

"What makes you think that, Sergeant?"

Mackinnon flushed. "Well, sir, if it was urgent, you'd have—"

A muffled thump interrupted him, coincident with the brilliant flash of magnesium powder igniting, visible in spite of the umbrella.

The umbrella went up in flames. Alec and Mackinnon stepped back as, along with the usual cloud of white powder, black, glowing fragments floated down.

"I take it, Fletcher," said the police surgeon, arriving at this inopportune moment, "that you won't want a report in the autopsy on any superficial burns."

A fit of coughing overtook Alec as he breathed in the acrid fumes of burning silk. Before either he or Mackinnon had a chance to respond to Dr. Ridgeway's quip, Ardmore's voice issued from the bushes: "Said it was close, didn't I? Good job everything's wet, or the whole bloody lot'd've gone up in flames."

Still clutching the skeleton of the umbrella, Warren backed out, muttering, "Cor, strike me pink! If it wasn't wet, we wouldn't've needed the bloody brolly, would we."

He turned, revealing a powder-whitened face with black crescents above his eyes.

"Better take off your hat, laddie," said Ridgeway, "the brim's smouldering. I'll put some ointment on your eyebrows. Where they were, that is."

Warren raised his hand towards his face and almost put out an eye with a spoke of the denuded umbrella frame. Mackinnon removed it from his shaking hand.

"Sarge, I feel kind of funny."

"You look kind of funny," said DC Ardmore unhelpfully. He, too, was coated in white powder, but his eyebrows appeared to be intact.

"Shock," Ridgeway diagnosed. "Sit down and put your head between your knees."

Warren dropped to the wet grass and the doctor took his pulse. "Not too bad. Does your face feel hot?"

"Yes, Doc, like I got sunburn."

"Scorched. I'll want to take a look at it, but you'll have to wait till I've had a gander at our dead chum. Fletcher, can we get him out of this rain?"

"He could take my umbrella and sit on one of those benches." Seeing Ridgeway's frown, he sighed and went on: "But I expect he'd better go up to my house, number six." He pointed. "My housekeeper will take care of him." Which Daisy would regard as a heaven-sent invitation to meddle, he thought gloomily.

"Strewth, I think I'm going to be sick," Warren mumbled.

"Keep your head down till the feeling goes away," advised Ridgeway. "Anything you want to tell me about the corpse, Fletcher?"

"He's not mine, Doctor; he's the sergeant's."

"Oh? Mackinnon, isn't it?"

"Yes, sir."

"Well?"

"I . . . uh . . ." He looked to Alec, who gave a slight shrug. "I don't think so, sir. Go ahead. Would you like my torch?"

"Hmm, yes, thanks." Without further ado, Ridgeway dived into the shrubbery. For a few minutes, the only sound was the rustle of leaves; then his voice emerged. "He was bashed on the head, but I rather doubt that was the cause of death. Probably occurred very shortly before death, judging by the amount of blood. Are you getting this down, Mackinnon?"

Mackinnon whipped out his notebook. "Yes, sir."

"Rigor is fully established. He died at least twelve hours ago, not more than twenty-four, probably of deliberate compression of the carotid arteries, though I'll have to get him on the table to be certain. Not something he could do to himself. It looks as if you've got a murder on your hands, Sergeant."

NINE

Left to guard the northern approaches, Daisy frowned as she looked up at the Jessups' house. The more she thought about it, the odder it seemed that the man who had come out of their front door and hurried off down the street had not at least waved a greeting. Furthermore, though not all the world matched her own inquisitive nature, surely he must have wondered what was going on in the garden.

Unless he already knew, perhaps because Elsie had disobeyed orders and told her sister, Enid, what she had seen, which Daisy considered unlikely. But even if she had, and Enid had relayed the news to her employers, wouldn't they want to know more and from a more reliable source than a parlour maid?

That was assuming the man hurrying away had, in fact, been one of the Jessups. Daisy couldn't put out of her mind the unwelcome visitor who had pushed past her in the Jessups' front hall and torn off down the steps, nor that she was fairly certain she had seen him again later. He was an American. She suspected Patrick Jessup had been in America, and she knew he was expected home. There *must* be some connection.

Suppose the man she had just seen was the American. Had he met Patrick in America and come to look for him, and if so, as a friend or an enemy?

She recalled Aidan's remark when she told him about the American's first visit: "I knew it was a terrible idea." Perhaps "the idea" seemed terrible to him, the stay-at-home member of the family, only because it was unconventional. As she didn't know what it was, she couldn't tell.

At any rate, his words had reinforced her impression that the American was not a desirable acquaintance, as her mother would put it. Friend or enemy to Patrick, he would hardly be invited to spend the night at number 5, Constable Circle.

Not the American, then. But why had Mr. Jessup, or Aidan, not greeted her?

He was in a hurry.

Not even a wave? When hordes of police had just arrived in the garden opposite his house?

Number 5 was awfully quiet. Suppose—

The tramp of heavy boots diverted her attention. Round the bend came a constable, a comfortingly solid figure in his cape and helmet. "Mrs. Fletcher, ma'am, I've been sent to relieve you," he announced, saluting.

"Th-thank you."

He looked at her with concern. "You're half-froze, ma'am. Better get inside quick and get something hot inside you."

"Yes, thanks, I will." She couldn't tell him it wasn't just the cold that made her shiver; she'd scared herself silly with idiotic imaginings.

But once indoors, sitting at the kitchen table in dry stockings and shoes, with her hands wrapped around a mug of hot cocoa, she couldn't shake the thoughts. What if something had happened to the Jessups, and she did nothing? She managed to steer clear of picturing exactly what might have happened.

"You're still pale as ice, madam," said Mrs. Dobson. "Shock as well as cold, I shouldn't wonder. I'll fill a hot bottle you can put on your lap."

As if alerted by the last word, Nana, who had been lying good as gold under the table, sat up and placed a comforting, if still slightly damp, paw on Daisy's lap.

Daisy stroked her head and said absently, "Good girl." The dog had, after all, done her duty, and it was no good wishing she had left it to the Bennetts' horrid fat spaniels to discover the body.

Now Daisy had to decide what was *her* duty. Alec would say it was to go straight to the police with her fears. But she'd feel very silly if the Jessups, except for one bound for Bond Street, were just having a lie-in after a late celebration of the prodigal's return.

Was the prodigal home already? Could it have been he himself who had hurried past without so much as a wave? He didn't know her, after all.

Before she said anything to the police, was there a way to find out whether anything was amiss? Go and knock on the door, and they'd wonder what on earth she wanted so early in the morning. If they were up and about and she was invited in, she could hardly avoid mentioning the body in the garden, which would make Alec furious. She could telephone, but again, she'd need an excuse. Suppose she invited the ladies and children to afternoon tea. No, it would look as if she wanted to gossip about the murder.

The cook-housekeeper presented her with a hot-water bottle, neatly shrouded in a woolly cover. The faint rubbery smell was somehow comforting. "There you go, dearie, that'll help, I hope."

"Lovely. I'm sure it will. Mrs. Dobson, are you on cup-of-sugar borrowing terms with next door?"

"Certainly, madam. Their Mrs. Innes is a very good sort of woman."

"Then could you please think up something you need to borrow right now?"

"Well, I don't know, madam, I'll be popping round to the shops this morning anyway. . . . Well, now, I could say I want

to make some biscuits for elevenses before I do the shopping, though there's plenty in the tin, perfectly good."

"Perfect. And who knows, you may have a kitchenful of frozen bobbies to feed by then."

"And a finer body of men I couldn't wish for, though I says it as shouldn't."

Daisy was diverted. "Why shouldn't you, Mrs. Dobson?"

"Because of working for a police detective, madam. Looks like boasting, doesn't it? But I must say, madam, all these years of working for the master, and I never thought something like this'd happen so close to home."

"Nor did any of us," Daisy helplessly. "I know you won't desert us, Mrs. Dobson."

Mrs. Dobson put her hands on her hips and glared. "As though I would, madam! Me that's been with Mr. Fletcher through thick and thin. And if that Mrs. Gilpin says another word, I'll give her the rough side of my tongue, so I will."

"Oh dear, Nurse Gilpin is still threatening to leave?"

"Now don't you fret, madam. She won't leave the babies. You can say what you will of her, and nobody's perfect, but I will say this: She's proper fond of the babies. There now, I never meant to say nothing about that dreadful murder, and you upset already—"

"I started it, talking about frozen bobbies. I know you won't say anything to anyone else."

"That I won't. Now I'll just find Elsie and tell her to go next door and borrow a bit of brown sugar."

"Couldn't you go yourself, Mrs. Dobson?"

"Oh no, madam, it wouldn't be proper, not now we've got a parlour maid. They'd think it ever so queer next door."

"Really? We don't want that. I'll tell her, then. I'm feeling much better, thanks to your cocoa and hot-water bottle. How much brown sugar do you need?"

"None at all, seeing I've a canister full in the larder, but she can ask for a quarter of a pound. Right, madam, I'll just get on with weighing out the ingredients."

Elsie was dusting the drawing room. "I'll go and put my hat on this instant, madam," she said when Daisy asked her to beg, borrow, or steal a quarter of a pound of brown sugar from next door.

"You'll need an umbrella. Elsie, Mr. Fletcher will be quite annoyed that you didn't obey my order not to talk to anyone about what you found in the garden."

"I only told Mrs. Dobson, 'm. That's not the same, is it? Mrs. Dobson isn't just anyone."

Daisy could hardly deny this, having just involved Mrs. Dobson in a somewhat mendacious scheme. Nor did she feel up to getting into a discussion of what she had meant by "anyone." With a sigh, she said, "Well, if you breathe a word to your sister, you'll find it a lot more difficult to chat with her in future, because you won't be working here."

"Oh, I know, 'm. I wouldn't want that. I won't say a word next door, honest."

The moment Elsie left, Daisy had second thoughts. She must be crazy to trust the rattle-tongued girl to be discreet. But on the point of calling her back, she hesitated. She really was desperate to know whether the Jessup household were all right.

She returned to the kitchen to wait, as Elsie would no doubt take the sugar straight there. She watched Mrs. Dobson measure, melt, mix, and stir together butter, golden syrup, rolled oats, and brown sugar.

"Flapjacks," she said. "Quick and easy, 'cause I've got to be off to the shops if lunch isn't to be late." Heaven forbid a mere murder on the doorstep should make lunch late. "The twins like 'em, and they're good and filling if those frozen coppers turn up. I'm making a double batch in case, and I've used the last of the brown sugar, so it's not stretching the truth too much borrowing from Mrs. Innes."

"I'm sorry I made you stretch it at all."

"That's all right, madam. I know you wouldn't without good reason." She scooped the mixture into a couple of baking tins

and flattened it with the back of a spoon. Stooping, she listened to the oven. "Still heating up. Wonderful invention, these thermo whatchamacallits, aren't they? No more guesswork. I'm that glad the house had a gas stove. It'd be hard to go back to a coal range."

"We'd have bought you a gas stove if there hadn't been one already installed, Mrs. Dobson."

"I don't know how I'd get on without one, and that's the truth. There, the burners have stopped; that's hot enough now." Mrs. Dobson put the tins in the oven and started clearing up. "And the geyser for the hot water, too, always ready to hand. When I remember all the carrying of coal, with coal dust everywhere, and blacking the range to stop it rusting, and the hot oven too hot and the cool oven too cool . . ." She went on reminiscing about the bad old days.

Daisy half-listened, wondering why Elsie had not yet returned. Surely she should be back by now with the unneeded brown sugar. Suppose she, too, had been attacked. . . . No, much more likely everyone was perfectly all right and she was having a good chin-wag with the Jessups' cook. But what could she have to talk about if not the dead man in the garden?

"Where's that dratted girl got to?" said Mrs. Dobson. "If I'd really needed that sugar, it'd be too late by now. Ah, sounds like her now."

Elsie came in through the kitchen door from the paved area outside. "I didn't see my sister, madam," she announced, crossing the kitchen to deposit her dripping umbrella in the scullery. "Here's your sugar, Mrs. Dobson. I didn't say a word to Mrs. Innes about that out there in the garden, 'm, no matter what she asked me, but she'd a good deal to say on her own account, so I let her talk."

"Oh?" Daisy didn't exactly want to encourage servants' gossip, but how else was she to find out what was going on?

The monosyllable was encouragement enough. "Seems Mr. Patrick came home last night from foreign parts. He's been gone ever such a long time, not but what him and Mr. Jessup

don't go off a-travelling for weeks on end every year, but they usually go together. Mr. Patrick's old enough now to do business by himself, seemingly. But Mr. Aidan must've been waiting for him to get back to go off himself. He's already left to visit some customers up north somewheres."

"He left as soon as his brother came home?"

"Yes, 'm."

"Did they have a disagreement? A quarrel?" Horrible possibilities raced through Daisy's mind—but Aidan was the one who had disappeared, and Alec would have recognised his body.

"No, 'm. Leastways, my sister didn't hear nothing like that, she told Mrs. Innes. The only thing is, Mrs. Aidan's ever so upset. Crying her eyes out, poor thing, Mrs. Innes said. Course, Mr. Aidan's the one that usually stays home, but it's not like he's going abroad, is it? And her always cheerful as anything."

Daisy was so relieved to hear the Jessups were still in the land of the living, not, as in her direst imaginings, weltering in their own blood, that some time passed before she began to wonder what had so upset Audrey. She was in the nursery by then, so naturally her thoughts flew to the Jessup children. But Mrs. Innes would know if Marilyn or Percy was hurt or ill.

Could Audrey and Aidan have quarrelled unbeknownst to the servants, leading to his precipitate departure? More likely— if one did not know the couple. Daisy had seldom met a less quarrelsome, more peaceable, even-tempered pair.

Whatever the cause of her woes, Audrey might be glad of a shoulder to weep on other than her mother-in-law's. Daisy just had to come up with an excuse to call next door, one that would satisfy both the Jessups and Alec.

Which left her right where she had started, except that she knew the Jessups were alive, thank heaven.

It was time to stop worrying about them and concentrate on the twins. Seated cross-legged on the nursery floor, she built an umpteenth tower of wooden blocks, which Oliver knocked down with as much delight as he had the first one.

"Gak!" he shouted.

Meanwhile, Miranda, in Daisy's lap, turned the pages of a cloth picture book and chanted in a language of her own invention.

"Going to be a bookworm, that one," said Nurse Gilpin disapprovingly.

"I do hope so," said Daisy. "I was one myself."

Sparring with Mrs. Gilpin, she almost managed to forget what was going on outside. Then Elsie came in.

"Madam, it's that Mr. Crane on the telephone. He wants to speak to Mr. Fletcher. I told him he's not here, but he says if he's not here, why isn't he at Scotland Yard, and I'm sure it's not my place to say, so I thought maybe you'd better talk to him."

For one craven moment, Daisy was on the brink of saying, "Tell him I'm not here, either." Then sanity returned. Getting up from the floor, she straightened her stocking-seams—Lucy always claimed crooked seams sapped one's self-confidence. "I'm on my way," she sighed.

TEN

Stiff as a board, the body had not been easy to move without wrecking the shrubbery. By natural light, however grey, Dr. Ridgeway had confirmed the probable cause of death, so slight as to have escaped Alec's and Mackinnon's notice by torchlight. The obvious injury to the scalp, from a blunt instrument wielded without a great deal of force, had knocked him out and the wound had bled a good deal. Innocent-looking but deadly, there was a small bruise on either side at the base of the neck.

"Thumb marks," said Ridgeway, "though I don't imagine you'll be able to get prints from them. Once the fellow was unconscious, it would have been the easiest thing in the world to apply enough pressure to shut off the arteries. A couple of minutes is all it takes."

"How long after the head bashing d'you reckon, sir?" asked Mackinnon.

"Almost immediately. The scalp bleeds freely, so it wouldn't take long to produce this much blood. But, as I'm sure you're aware, Sergeant, dead men don't bleed, or he'd have lost considerably more before it clotted. Not likely to bleed to death, though."

"What about the rain?" Alec asked, before he recalled that this was not his case. "Is it possible a significant quantity of blood simply washed away?"

"Certainly, for a brief period. Clotting usually starts in three to ten minutes. If that happened, if he bled significantly more than appears here, then the time between the blow and the application of pressure to the arteries might have been longer than a minute or two. Since it seems impossible that he was hit under the bushes, as there's no room to raise a weapon, you'd have to find out where he was killed and exactly when it was raining there, in relation to the time of death. That, I shall endeavour to discover for you, but it's unlikely to be accurate within an hour or two, or more."

"Never is," Warren grumbled. He had recovered enough not to retire to the house.

The doctor grinned. "I'll be able to tell you more, if not enough to satisfy you, when I've had a go at him."

"Will you be able to tell us the shape of the weapon?" Mackinnon asked.

"Possibly. Roughly. I'll do what I can, but now I must get back to my surgery." Ridgeway departed.

Mackinnon told Ardmore to take a few more photos of the body. "And try not to set anything else on fire," he added.

"Don't need the flash in this light, if I can do some long exposures," Ardmore said. He set to work, anxious to atone for the flaming umbrella.

"We'd better start looking for the weapon, don't you reckon, sir?" Mackinnon asked Alec.

"Sounds like a good idea. Where will you start?"

"He—or she—might have thrown it in the bushes, but likely he wouldna carry the weapon while moving the body. The way those drag marks run, I'd no be surprised if it was in the fountain. Warren, take a look."

DC Warren looked gloomily down at his feet. "S'pose I can't get much wetter," he said.

"The water's not too scummy," said Alec. "Take a look first;

then if you need to wade, go up to my house and borrow a pair of rubber boots."

Warren thanked him, looking a trifle happier, and tramped off to circle the fountain.

Lips pursed, Mackinnon watched Ardmore photographing the corpse. "There's something a wee bit odd about his suit," he declared. "Would ye no agree, sir?"

"Not Savile Row, as far as one can tell when it's soaking wet."

"Not English."

"Scottish?" Alec suggested with a grin.

"Foreign, I'm thinking."

"Could be."

"Is it too much to hope that he'll have a passport on him?"

"We can hope. Looks as if Ardmore's finished, so you can go through his pockets."

"Would ye care to—?"

"This is not my case," Alec said firmly.

"Ardmore, ye can start searching the shrubbery for a weapon."

As Mackinnon stooped over the body, Alec saw a black van pull up at the bottom of the garden. PC Norris went over to speak to the driver. Two men got out, opened the back doors, and started pulling out a stretcher.

"The mortuary people are here," Alec told Mackinnon.

The sergeant had folded back the man's jacket and was staring down at his chest. "Will ye look at that, sir! He's wearing a shoulder holster."

"Great Scott! Empty?"

"Yes, sir. Ardmore! Keep your eyes peeled for a gun, as well as yon blunt instrument."

"A gun!" came an astonished voice from the bushes. "You're kidding."

"I am not."

"Right, Sarge. A gun it is."

Mackinnon straightened with an air of triumph.

"Here's his pocket-book. Lots of cash, so it wasna robbery. And look here, sir!" He opened a thin water-stained booklet and read, "'The United States of America—Passport.' He's a Yank! From New York, it says. And there's a photograph, which will come in handy. The rain hasna damaged it."

"Excellent."

"I canna read the name, though. The signature's a scribble, and where it's written out at the top, by a clerk, likely, the water's seeped in and the ink has run. It looks as if the Christian name might begin with an *M*. And the surname—this could be a *C*, or a *G*. Quite a long name, more than one syllable."

Alec took the passport and examined it. "Yes, *M*, and this blur suggests the dot of an *i*, wouldn't you say? I wouldn't like to swear to your *C* or *G*, but this looks as if it might be a double *l*. You'd think they'd use India ink. Has he a watch?"

"Not in his fob. Ah, a wristwatch. Gold. Looks like an expensive one. Let's see—no inscription on the back."

"It might be worth checking his hands for rings before they cart him off. American men are more apt to wear rings than the English. Or Scots."

"Stiff as he is, I'll have to cut his gloves off," Mackinnon said doubtfully.

"Let's not do that if we can help it. It'd be difficult without marking the skin, which could mislead the doctor. The leather seems to be thin and flexible. Perhaps you can feel whether he has any."

Mackinnon grimaced. Alec agreed with his implied comment: For some reason, feeling the dead man's fingers for rings seemed even more distasteful than anything they had so far put the poor chap through.

But the sergeant obeyed—or rather, followed Alec's suggestion—and reported, "Nothing, sae far as I can tell. He could be wearing a flat band o' some sort, like a wedding ring."

"We'll leave that for Dr. Ridgeway to find out."

The stretcher arrived and Mackinnon told the men they

could remove the body. "Let PC Norris down there take a look at his face."

He and Alec, sheltering under the latter's umbrella, took off their hats as a gesture of respect as the dead man was lifted onto the stretcher, covered with a sheet, and borne off.

Mackinnon offered the passport, pocket-book, and watch to Alec, who was tempted but managed to resist.

"You'd better come up to the house and telephone your super," he said as Mackinnon tucked the objects into his pocket.

"Thank you, sir. Och, here comes Mrs. Fletcher."

The pillar-box red umbrella came down the garden path towards them, in a hurry.

"Alec," she called, "Superintendent Crane just rang up. He wants you to ring back immediately."

"I'm on my way. Daisy, DS Mackinnon needs to use our telephone, too, as soon as I've finished, and can we find a pair of rubber boots for DC Warren?"

"I should think so."

Warren came over. "Can't see anything, sir, but the water's pretty murky. I could do with a rake or summat like that."

"I expect we have one," Daisy said vaguely. "Don't we, darling? Or does the gardener bring his own? We could borrow one from the neighbours."

"On no account are the neighbours to be involved! There's a rake in the shed." Alec was the member of the family who took most interest in the garden, though he rarely had time to work in it.

"Good." Daisy smiled at Warren. "Are you fishing in the fountain for clues?"

"For the weapon, ma'am."

"Was he shot?"

"Daisy!" Alec exclaimed in exasperation.

"Sorry," she said unrepentantly. "Why don't you all come to the kitchen for tea and biscuits before you do anything else. You must be frozen, and Mrs. Dobson has them ready."

Mackinnon and Warren gave Alec hopeful looks, and Ardmore emerged from the bushes to do likewise.

Alec gestured to Mackinnon.

"Thank you, Mrs. Fletcher," he said. "That will be verra welcome. Nobody can interfere with the scene of the crime with the bobbies on duty."

"You can bring them a hot drink when you come back here," Daisy proposed, reminding Alec of why he loved her, however infuriating she was at times.

They all trooped up the path to the house, Daisy leading the three local detectives down the area steps to the kitchen while Alec went straight up to the front hall to ring up the Yard.

The switchboard girl put him through. "What's going on, Fletcher?" barked Superintendent Crane.

"I'm on my way, sir. I should get that report to the AC by noon."

Crane's sigh of relief gusted along the wires. "So it's not a homicide on your front doorstep. Thank heaven for that."

"I'm afraid it is, sir. Well, not quite on my front doorstep, but, in fact, it's almost certainly murder."

"Damn it all, are you sure?"

"The divisional surgeon says so, and he's a good man. And I have to agree with him. But it's not my pigeon."

"Oh yes it is. I've had the S Division super on the line. Claims he's shorthanded, and if it's homicide, he wants you on the case."

"But we're shorthanded, too. It's chronic—"

"You know what the Commissioner said just the other day about cooperation with the divisions, Fletcher. It's your case."

"But sir, it's going to mean questioning all my close neighbours, for a start. I can't—"

"No, I see that. But someone else can do that part while you direct behind the scenes. You can come in and write up that report while you're waiting for them to report to you."

"I suppose so," Alec said reluctantly. He liked to have his finger directly on the pulse of an investigation.

But his neighbours were no lords and ladies, merely wealthy cits, in the idiom of the eighteenth century, which Alec had studied at university. Tom Tring could cope perfectly well with interrogating nobs as long as he wore his best suit, not one of his checked monstrosities.

Could Mackinnon? He didn't know him well enough to count on it. "I'll want DS Tring, sir, and DC Piper. They've worked well before with the S Division detective sergeant on the job."

"Done. And you'll have the report by noon?"

"I said that before you dumped this case in my lap, sir! I need to discuss it with Tring and Mackinnon so that they can get going. And the American embassy will have to be notified."

"What? What?" Crane demanded wildly. "The American embassy?"

"Yes, sir. The victim was a U.S. citizen."

"Are you sure?"

"Passport in his pocket. The photo and description match."

"If the divisional chappie had known that, he'd have handed it over to us anyway." The superintendent sounded slightly mollified.

"No doubt. Come to think of it, sir, I'd like your permission to get in touch with the New York police, and perhaps the FBI."

"FBI?"

"Federal Bureau of Investigation, sir. In Washington."

"Oh yes, those chappies you gave a helping hand to over there. Why? Do you suspect he was a wrong 'un?"

Alec chose his words with care. "Let's just say there are aspects of the case that point to the possibility. Or perhaps it would be more accurate to say that it wouldn't surprise me." It dawned on him that the holster might equally well mean the man was an agent, like Lambert. Like Lambert, he could have had his gun confiscated by Customs—but then he'd have had no reason to wear the holster. Alec didn't have time just now to

think it through, what with Crane panting on the other end of the line. "Would you like details?"

"No, no. Go ahead and cable whomever you need to." This time, his sigh expressed long-suffering rather than relief. "I'll try to explain to the AC why he won't be getting the report for a while. If you can *possibly* spare me a moment, you might pop in and tell me what you've learnt so far about your Hampstead murder. By the by, how is Mrs. Fletcher holding up? She sounded pretty chipper when I spoke to her just now, but it must have been a shock to her, finding *yet another* body."

One cannot tell one's superior in the police force that sarcasm does not become him. "She didn't actually find this one, sir," Alec reminded him. "She hasn't actually seen him."

"I dare say, Fletcher, but it is, to my recollection, the first to be found on—I beg your pardon—*practically* on her own doorstep." With that, he rang off, which was just as well, as the retort that sprang to Alec's lips was most improper.

Alec arranged for Ernie Piper to come out to Hampstead to help with the search, and for Tom Tring to meet him and Mackinnon at the Yard. He had to get copies of the passport photo made, and some good photographs of the entire passport to show at the U.S. embassy and to send to the NYPD and FBI. In the meantime, he could cable the passport number to them.

He went down to the kitchen, where Daisy and Mrs. Dobson were presiding over the consumption of tea and flapjacks. "You can go up and ring your station," he said grumpily to Mackinnon, "but I can tell you what your super's going to say: He's talked mine into handing over the case to me."

"Good!" said Mackinnon. "I mean, I'm sorry you're being troubled with it, but I'm glad to be working with you again, sir."

"DC Piper's coming to give your men a hand. You and I will go to the Yard."

"Yes, sir." Mackinnon went off to telephone.

"Ardmore, Warren," said Alec, "off you go to see if you can find that weapon before Piper arrives."

There was some scurrying about while boots and a rake were procured for the fountain-fishing expedition; then the two detective constables departed, carrying a couple of thermos flasks and flapjacks wrapped in wax paper for the uniformed men. Alec sat down at the kitchen table.

"Darling, you're not going to have to interrogate the Jessups, are you?" Daisy poured him a cup of tea. "And the Whitcombs and everyone?"

"I sincerely hope not. Initially at least, the others can do it, but if it turns out any of them are involved, then all bets are off." He helped himself to a flapjack, chewy and still slightly warm from the oven. A large bite effectively stopped his mouth, allowing Daisy to have her say.

"I hope it doesn't come to that. We shan't dare poke our noses outside the door, Mrs. Dobson."

"Not to worry, madam," said the cook-housekeeper, clearing cups and plates and sweeping away crumbs. "You know how it is. There's some as'll blame you no matter what, and others that'll know it's none of it your fault. That's how you tell your true friends."

"Very true. Come to think of it, Alec, you can give the Bennetts the 'third degree' with my goodwill. Do you have any reason to think one of the neighbours may be involved?"

"I can't talk about it here."

Mrs. Dobson drew herself up, her hands on her hips. "If it's because I'm here, sir, I take leave to tell you there's many and many a secret I've known that's never crossed my lips, and I'm sure I never gave you cause—"

"Of course not." Harassed on every side, Alec tried to sound soothing. "I just meant that at present it's a matter to be discussed only with my colleagues in the police."

"Hmm."

"I suppose you won't tell us who he is, either," said Daisy.

"I don't know his name. If I did, you're right, I wouldn't tell you."

Mackinnon came in. "All settled, sir," he said cheerfully. "I'm to take my orders from you, and I don't even have to give my super a report until we've made an arrest."

"Assuming we do. Let's get going. There's one good thing about crime on the doorstep, Daisy, I should be home on time for dinner, if not before."

ELEVEN

"*Will you* look at that, madam! Those policemen haven't left hardly enough flapjacks to be sent up to the nursery."

"I've already eaten more than my share, Mrs. Dobson," Daisy said guiltily.

"Then I'll just put what's left on the tray here for the kiddies and Mrs. Gilpin's morning coffee and be off about the shopping. It's to be hoped that butcher hasn't already sold his best cuts, the master being home for dinner tonight."

She put on her hat and coat, took up her basket and umbrella, and set off, leaving Daisy once again pondering a way to infiltrate the Jessups' house. She still wanted to talk to them, though at least she was no longer worried about their safety.

Another cup of tea failed to inspire her. Perhaps a bath would help. Having dressed in a tearing hurry, she had omitted even a lick and a promise earlier.

On her way up the kitchen stairs, she heard the front doorbell ring. As she pushed open the baize door at the top, Elsie opened the front door. Though she couldn't be seen, Daisy didn't step out into the passage. She held the door ajar and listened.

A man's voice asked for Detective Chief Inspector Fletcher.

"He's left for the Yard," said Elsie. No *sir*, Daisy noted. "You from the papers?"

"That's right. You're a sharp girl, you are."

"Seeing you got a notebook and a cam'ra, and any copper'd be ashamed to go about looking like a ragbag, it weren't too difficult."

"Sharp in mind and sharp in tongue." The reporter sounded disconcerted. "I bet you wouldn't mind making a couple of pounds telling me what's going on in the garden there?"

"Go on, you really think I'd risk losing a place like this for a couple of quid? No, not for ten, not for twenty, no thank you! They treat me proper, and it suits me. So you can just get along with you and—"

"Here, hold on! Don't be so hasty. What about your missus, eh? I bet she'd like to see her name in the paper, and maybe her face, too."

"Not likely! Madam's a real lady, not the sort that'd want to see her picture on every street corner. 'Sides, she's not at home." The parlour maid closed the front door with a brisk thud. "Not at home to the likes of you, anyway!" she added.

Daisy came out of hiding. Elsie turned and saw her.

"Oh, madam, I hope I done right. There was this nasty reporter—"

"I heard every word. You were wonderful, quite perfect. Anyone would think you'd been turning newshounds away from the door for years. I'm afraid you may have to do it again, once word gets around."

"Now I know what they're like, I'll get rid of the next one in half the time. You just watch me!"

Daisy went upstairs and took a bath, which thawed the bits of her still chilled in spite of hot tea and the warmth of the kitchen. She was almost dressed when Elsie tapped on the bedroom door and announced, "Mrs. Jessup's called, madam. I said I'd see if you're at home."

"Yes, I'm at home! Tell her I'll be down in just a minute. Offer

her a cup of coffee." *If Mahomet can't think of an adequate reason to go to the mountain,* she thought, *then let him wait until the mountain comes to him!*

She went down a few minutes later, to find Mrs. Maurice Jessup—she had for some reason expected Audrey—standing at the window of the drawing room, gazing out over the garden. It had stopped raining. As Daisy crossed the room, she could see that Ernie Piper had joined Ardmore and Warren. They stood by the fountain, Warren waving the rake like a magic wand, as if he hoped to bring the nymph in the centre to life.

"Good morning, Mrs. Jessup," said Daisy.

Swinging round, Mrs. Jessup said, "Oh, good morning! I didn't hear you come in. You gave me quite a start."

"Isn't it odd how something one is expecting sometimes startles one more than the unexpected?"

"Yes indeed. Especially when you're waiting by the telephone for a particular call, and when at last it rings, you jump out of your skin. At least I do."

"Exactly! Won't you sit down? Elsie's bringing coffee, I hope."

Moving with the studied grace of an actress, Mrs. Jessup sat down on the edge of a chair. After a moment's hesitation, she shifted back and relaxed. "Mrs. Fletcher, as you have no doubt guessed, we are dying of curiosity about the very unexpected goings-on down in the garden. I'm afraid our Enid has taken quite a pet because her sister refused to talk about it."

"I sympathise," Daisy said with a smile. "That's just how I feel when Alec won't tell me what's happening."

"He won't? How very irritating men can be. I suppose Audrey will just have to go away wondering."

"Go away? Where is she off to?"

"Oh, didn't she tell you? Of course, when the two of you are together, you never need any subject of conversation beyond the children. She's taking Marilyn and Percy to her sister's, in Lincolnshire. The visit has been planned for ages, but the exact date was uncertain. You see, Aidan has business

in the North, customers to see and so on. He's been postponing the trip until Patrick's return—my younger son, you know. So when we heard from Patrick that he was on his way home, Aidan made arrangements to take the night train last night."

"And Audrey's going to her sister's while Aidan's away?"

"That's right. Vivien married a country squire, and he and Aidan simply have nothing in common. Besides, Aidan loves his own children, but you know how men are with other people's offspring."

"Better to visit without him."

"Much better. The taxi will be here any minute to take them to Liverpool Street. Patrick's going to see them off, to help Audrey cope with children and Nanny and luggage and all at the station. She's dreading the journey."

"I'm sure it takes a good deal of coping, even if she wasn't expecting."

Mrs. Jessup seized on this remark. "That's another reason to go right away, while she's feeling well and not showing yet."

"I travelled quite a bit while I was pregnant, but I haven't tried it with the twins yet."

"It's a difficult journey anyway, changing trains twice. I just hope they don't miss any connections."

"How nice that your Patrick is home to give her a hand at this end at least. When did he—"

Her question was interrupted as Elsie came in with the coffee tray. While dispensing coffee and biscuits—the flapjacks were all gone, but as Mrs. Dobson had said, the biscuits from the tin were perfectly good—Daisy pondered the situation.

Alec would be unhappy to have potential witnesses scattering to all corners of the kingdom, but there wasn't anything Daisy could do about it. In any case, many of the residents of Constable Circle must have departed about their lawful occasions before the police got things organised out there.

On the other hand, most of them had probably gone no farther than the City, whereas Audrey was bound for the ru-

ral fastnesses of Lincolnshire. Daisy wondered whether she ought to suggest that Audrey wait until she had talked to the police.

Daisy was sure she had only to drop a word in Piper's ear and he'd stop the taxi leaving, but he might get into trouble for it. Also, it would make Audrey's journey even more difficult, if not impossible. Imagine having to start all over again tomorrow, getting the children ready for travelling—it didn't bear thinking of.

If Alec wanted to know why she hadn't attempted to foil their departure, she'd tell him it was his own fault for not giving her more information.

The unknown Patrick was going only to the station and back, so he would be available for questioning. Daisy wondered exactly what time he had arrived. Not that she knew the time of the murder.

"You must be happy to have your son safe at home again," she said.

"Yes, I was a little worried, I confess. He's not been gone so long on his own before, and it's hard to recognise that he's an adult now. He's still my little boy."

"When did he—"

"Listen!" Mrs. Jessup held up one hand. The chimes of the grandfather clock in the hall were heard. She rose. "I didn't realise it was so late. They'll be leaving as soon as the luggage is loaded into the taxicab, and I must be there to say good-bye. Thank you for the coffee, Mrs. Fletcher. It was very bad of me to interrupt your morning just for the sake of vulgar curiosity. I know you write in the mornings."

"Not today."

"No, I dare say not. Well, vulgar or not, my curiosity remains unslaked." She moved towards the window and glanced out. "I hope you'll pass on any account of the police activity out there that you glean from your husband. He surely must give you some sort of explanation!"

"I can't count on it." Daisy laughed. "He's quite capable of

leaving me entirely in ignorance if it suits him. I'll pop out with you to say good-bye to Audrey and the children."

"Oh no, don't do that. It looks to me as if it's going to pour with rain again any moment. I'll tell Audrey you sent your best wishes."

"Please do, and bon voyage."

Daisy accompanied Mrs. Jessup to the front door. A taxi was just pulling up next door. As the cabbie climbed out, Mrs. Jessup hurried down the steps to the pavement. Both of them started up the Jessups' steps together.

Daisy would have liked to watch, perhaps to manage a word or two with Audrey. Mrs. Jessup might call it vulgar curiosity, but Daisy had long ago accepted that, like Kipling's Elephant's Child, she was cursed with "satiable curtiosity." She had a hundred questions.

Had her friend really been crying, as the servants reported? If so, what about? Had she quarrelled with Aidan, or was she unhappy because they were to part for an unknown period, or was she merely overtired from preparing for her trip? Pregnancy could be exhausting, too, even right at the beginning. Daisy remembered morning sickness all too clearly.

Where had Patrick been, and exactly what time did he arrive home? Daisy wanted to meet him. What was he like? Adventurous, his mother had said, yet with the patience and coolness to be a good cricketer.

He sounded interesting, more interesting than Aidan. Surely Audrey wasn't in love with him, was she? It would explain his long absence, her distress coincident with his return, Aidan's sudden departure, followed by hers. . . . But Mrs. Jessup would never let Patrick accompany Audrey to Liverpool Street if such were the situation.

What was more, Daisy remembered Audrey saying that once Patrick came home, they could all be comfortable again. That didn't sound like an illicit passion. No, once again, she realised, she was wandering in the realm of pure speculation.

Any moment, the Jessups would come out and see her stand-

ing there staring. Besides, it was cold on the doorstep, though no sign of impending rain was apparent.

She went in, pausing on the threshold for one last backward glance. The sun gleamed palely through thinning clouds.

The twins should go out for an airing before it disappeared again. All nannies agreed on the health-giving effects of fresh air on children. Nana ought to go out, too. If Daisy managed to get Mrs. Gilpin to hurry, they could all take a walk before either the rain or Alec returned. In the latter case, she might get a chance to talk to Ernie Piper.

Her timing was perfect. As the group set out towards the path to the Heath, Ernie backed out of the bushes, took off his hat, and shook the drips from it. It was natural for Daisy to wave the others onwards while she stopped to speak to him.

"Good morning, Mr. Piper. Any luck?"

"Morning, Mrs. Fletcher." He paused to respond to Nana's rapturous greeting. They were old friends. "I haven't found anything, and I expect Ardmore or Warren would've shouted if they had."

"What exactly are you looking for? 'A weapon' is a bit vague."

"That's what we don't know, Mrs. Fletcher," said DC Warren, joining them. His face, eyebrowless and scorched red, was gloomy. He had indeed been struck pink, Daisy thought. It was lucky he hadn't had a moustache. He would have got flames up his nose, assuredly a horribly painful experience. "Could be a stick or a stone or some weird African knobkerrie like in the detective stories."

"You read too many of those." Ardmore had arrived. "Dr. Ridgeway should be able to tell us what shape we're looking for."

"Doesn't much matter what shape," Piper pointed out, "seeing none of us has found anything that could be it. Leastways, I don't see either of you carrying a life preserver or a crowbar or even a heavy walking stick."

"Whatever it is," said Warren, "it's not in the pond. No

need to call in divers. It's less'n a foot deep and there's nothing in it bigger'n a twig."

"The children drop toys in regularly," said Daisy, "but the nannies always fish them out. If it's a walking stick, I can't see how you'd ever find it. I mean, the murderer could just have walked off with it and stuck it in an umbrella stand somewhere, or thrown it in the river."

"Prob'ly has done just that," said Warren.

"It's not that bad," Piper insisted. "This here's a private garden, isn't it, Mrs. Fletcher?"

"Yes, sort of. Not belonging to one family, but to all the residents of Constable Circle."

"Not like a public park at any rate. You don't get Tom, Dick, and Harry using it. It's not by way of being a shortcut either, is it? I looked at a map before I came."

"No, not really. There are footpaths to the Heath up here and to Well Walk down there, but they don't really cut corners for anyone not living here."

"Right. So chances are, if the victim wasn't a resident, which he prob'ly wasn't, or the Chief'd've recognised him, then he was somehow connected to a resident. These houses here, they're big houses and you can bet they all have servants. It's not likely he could have called on anyone without being seen by someone else, so it shouldn't be too hard to find out which house he was connected with. And chances are, it was someone in that house that killed him, and chances are, he just went home afterwards and stuck the walking stick in the umbrella stand, like Mrs. Fletcher said," Piper concluded triumphantly.

"Always s'posing it was a walking stick he used," Warren said sourly.

"Whatever it was, he'd have trouble getting rid of it this morning," Ardmore put in. "He'd've looked funny carrying anything but a brolly."

"Whatever it was," said Daisy, "it probably doesn't have nice helpful fingerprints on it. Last night was so cold and wet, no one would have gone out without gloves."

"True." Warren sank still further into gloom.

"Might the weapon have been chucked down into an area?" Daisy proposed. "That would be a quick and easy way to get rid of it without going far."

Piper nodded. "It's a thought. Only thing is, it must have been heavyish, would have made a noise landing. Unless the servants were listening to the wireless or something . . . but still they'd've found it this morning."

"Might not think anything of it," said Ardmore. "Not enough to call it to our attention anyway. It needn't be very big. Dr. Ridgeway was pretty sure it wasn't getting clobbered that killed him."

"Really?" said Daisy. "What killed him?"

All three men looked at her. She realised at once that she had inadvertently stepped over an invisible boundary. She had reminded them, even Ernie Piper, that they ought not to be discussing the case with her, even though she was the chief inspector's wife. On his own, Ernie might have answered her question, but not with the other two as witnesses.

"Gosh," she said, "Nurse and the babies are out of sight! I'd better catch up with them. Come along, Nana. Good luck!"

Hurrying along the footpath, she pondered what she had learnt and found herself impressed by Piper's chain of logic. Unfortunately, it led to the inescapable conclusion that one of her neighbours was a murderer.

TWELVE

"*Mackinnon, you* give Mr. Tring the details, please." Alec started skimming through the papers on his desk, but as he initialled some and put them on a new pile, and set others in a third pile to be read more thoroughly, he was listening intently.

He wanted to know whether the young detective sergeant understood and remembered all the information they had gathered so far and what conclusions—if any—he had drawn. It was also possible that he had picked up something Alec himself had missed.

Tom Tring listened with appropriate gravity, making a note now and then. His amusement every time Daisy's name came up was apparent to Alec, but sufficiently discreet to evade Mackinnon's notice. His moustache, the magnificent hirsuteness compensating for the vast baldness of his head, twitched occasionally as Daisy and her red umbrella wove their way through the narrative.

Tom was very fond of Daisy, and vice versa. In fact, he was Oliver's godfather. But his fondness didn't make him consider her an infallible oracle, as Ernie Piper did.

Mackinnon's view seemed to be somewhere in between. He was a fervent admirer, but he failed to believe she was always right.

His exposition brought out one fact that Alec had failed to enquire after. "Constable Norris didn't recognise the deceased," Mackinnon said. "He was pretty certain he'd never seen him about. As he pointed out, though, he's been on the early-morning beat for several weeks, so unless the Yank was an early riser, he could well have missed him."

"We'll give the local station a copy of the photo," said Tom, "and make sure everyone takes a look at it. You want to circulate it elsewhere, Chief?"

"Not yet. Go on, Mackinnon."

"Well, sir," Mackinnon said tentatively, "Norris did say a different American has been seen aboot the area, a laddie that was known to be staying with you and Mrs. Fletcher, it seems."

"Lambert. He left us some time ago."

"But he's still aboot, sir, according to PC Norris."

"The devil he is! I wonder what bee he has in his bonnet now. Two shady Americans haunting Hampstead—it's not quite beyond the bounds of coincidence, but . . ." Alec sighed in exasperation. "I can't see Lambert as the murderer of his fellow countryman, but he may conceivably have useful information for once. Next time he's spotted, or if they can find out where he's lodging, he'll have to be brought in."

Tom made a note. "You have a picture of him, Chief?"

"No. The embassy does, and may even know where to find him, as he's supposed to be on official business, but for heaven's sake, let's not get them involved yet."

"Mrs. Fletcher'll be able to identify him for us," said Tom with an innocent expression.

Alec scowled at him. "For heaven's sake, let's not get Daisy involved, if we can possibly avoid it."

Tom made no attempt to hide his grin. "We'll do our best, Chief."

Mackinnon continued to brief Tom, laying out the known facts without attempting interpretation.

When he finished, Tom asked, "Mrs. Fletcher didn't actually view the body, then?"

"I believe not, Mr. Tring. Sir . . . ?"

"No." Alec abandoned the papers with relief. He hated desk work. "At most, she saw the outstretched hand, gloved."

"I'm glad to hear it, Chief. It's an odd business, for sure. This empty holster now. I'll be blowed if I can think of any reason he'd go out wearing it without a gun, bloody uncomfortable as they are. So what was he doing walking about London with a gun? And where is it now?"

"They're looking for it in the garden, for a start," said Mackinnon, "along with whatever was used to bash him over the head."

"Ah." Tom ruminated for a moment. "Now that's another odd thing. Just supposing the victim started this whole bit of bother by drawing his gun. Hitting him on the head could have been self-defence. But the business with the pressure on the arteries, that's plain cold-blooded murder."

"That's what it looks like," Alec agreed. "We'll have to wait for the autopsy to be certain of the cause of death."

"Why go so far as murder when the chap's out of it and you could just run away?"

"Because you were afraid he'd come after you?" said Mackinnon, hazarding a guess. "When he came round, I mean."

"Which makes it sound like it's the victim that's the real villain."

"Cold-blooded murder," Alec reminded them. "You can speculate to your hearts' content on your way to Hampstead. I've got this damn report to finish and an irate AC to placate. Tom, between the two of you, can you work out what questions you need to ask my neighbours in this preliminary round?" Alec was being tactful. He knew Tom was perfectly capable of doing the job, but he wasn't sure of Mackinnon. Now, Tom would instruct the young sergeant under the guise of a discussion.

134

"I reckon so, Chief. Let me just get the times straight. The doctor saw the body about eight o'clock this morning and said he'd been dead twelve to twenty-four hours?"

"That's right."

"So he was killed before eight in the evening. Sounds like the body must have been pretty much out in the open before it was moved, so not before dusk, probably. Say around five o'clock. Between five and eight."

"Close enough, for the present. They should have finished photographing that passport by now, and made a couple of quick prints for you to take with you."

"D'ye want us to drop the passport—the original—off at the American embassy, sir?"

"Ah," Tom said weightily.

Alec grinned at him. "Are we of one mind on this, Tom? As soon as they know an American is involved, or possibly two, they'll want to 'muscle in,' as they themselves would put it. We can't turn over evidence in a murder case at the drop of a hat. It will have to go through the proper channels—as many channels as we can dig."

"We'll give 'em the number and a copy of the photo in a couple of days?"

"Depending on how our enquiries proceed."

"Right, Chief. Any questions you want to ask Mr. Fletcher before we go, Mr. Mackinnon?"

"I canna think of any," Mackinnon said hesitantly.

"If there's anything we can't work out between us, there's always the telephone. Let's be off, then."

Alec had a sudden thought. "Hang on a sec, Tom. Do you happen to recall the name of that chap at the British Museum who was a cryptographer in the War? The one who helped us round up the Gloucester Customs raid gang last year? Poplar, Pollard, something like that."

"Peplow? I couldn't swear to it, Chief, but young Piper will know. Or if there's no hurry, you could always ask Records, but don't hold your breath. Why?"

"His job at the museum is actually deciphering palimpsests."

"And what may a palimpsest be when he's at home?"

"Another useful word to add to your dazzling vocabulary. It's a used parchment that's been scraped clean and written on again. Often the obliterated text is of more interest than the overwriting. This chap—Popkin? Yes, I believe it's Popkin—he's an expert at making out the original writing. Perhaps he can get the victim's name from the passport."

"Worth a try," Tom agreed.

"Will he need the original, sir?" Mackinnon asked. "I doot a photograph will do as well."

"Good point. I'll deal with it when I've dealt with the AC." He turned to his report at last as the two sergeants went out.

By the time Daisy and her entourage returned homeward from the Heath, the sun was shining. The change in the weather, as much as the change of scene and the passage of several hours, made the murder in the garden seem like a bad dream, or at least an event that had taken place aeons ago.

Reality intruded all too soon. From the end of the alley, Daisy saw DS Mackinnon and one of the detective constables coming down the steps of number 8. They turned down the hill, then ascended the steps of number 9.

Number 9, the Ormonds, she thought. Inherited money; four children, all away at school; Mr. Ormond dabbled in painting and had turned up at the Jessups' drinks party with longish hair and a flowing cravat; Mrs. Ormond, very smart, kept busy with the sort of committees that organised charity balls. Disappointed to learn that Daisy didn't play bridge, she had attempted without success to co-opt her onto one of these committees. The lure she held out was the chance to hobnob with the aristocracy.

Unlured, Daisy had been relieved that the Jessups had not revealed her own family background, though doubtless Mrs.

Ormond would find out sooner or later. In the meantime, the Ormonds were pleasant enough neighbours, but she didn't anticipate their becoming great friends.

The same applied to all the residents of Constable Circle apart from the abominable Bennetts at one end of the scale and the Jessups at the other.

Perhaps by now, Mackinnon had talked to the Jessups and they had given him satisfactory answers to all the questions Daisy hoped he had confronted them with. She wished she had had a chance to suggest exactly what questions ought to be posed.

Or perhaps she didn't. If there was something fishy about the Jessups' conduct, she didn't really want to be the one to draw it to the attention of the police. They would soon enough uncover it without her help. Wouldn't they?

Nor could she make up her mind whether she had rather talk to Alec, who would know at once if she prevaricated, or to one of the others, who might not notice.

She wondered whether Mackinnon had already called at number 6 in her absence. She was tempted to wait for him to come out of the Ormonds' house to ask if he had any questions for her. She nobly resisted temptation, the more easily because she was carrying Miranda, who was hanging on to her with a death grip.

A few minutes ago on the Heath, when she had tried to put her daughter in the pushchair to give Oliver a turn in her arms, Miranda had produced an eldritch screech that turned all heads for a hundred yards. The audience included Mr. Bennett and his spaniels. Daisy was certain he would subsequently spread the word that she was cruel to her children. She only hoped he wouldn't go so far as to report her to the NSPCC. Not likely, she thought. He and his wife preferred "insinuendo" to outright accusations that could be disproved.

Thus, despite Nurse Gilpin's protests about spoiling the child so that she would always expect to be carried in future, Daisy had Miranda on her hip when they reached the Circle.

Somewhere in the back of her mind she could hear her mother rebuking her, saying she looked like a gypsy, carrying a baby on her hip, but it was quite the most comfortable way to do it.

What with one thing and another, she simply hadn't much attention to spare for a police investigation just at that moment.

Even with three adults in attendance, steps up to the front door and down to the area door made getting two babies and a pushchair into the house a complicated matter. Daisy kept Miranda until they reached the front hall, by which time she was unhappy even in her mother's arms.

"She's hungry, poor lamb," said Nurse accusingly, taking her.

Daisy felt as guilty as if she had deliberately withheld food from her child, in spite of knowing that was exactly what Mrs. Gilpin intended.

"So's Oliver," said Bertha.

"Well then," snapped Mrs. Gilpin, "hurry and take him upstairs so you can come down for their lunch."

Lunch sounded like a good idea to Daisy, too, but the parlour maid was hovering at the rear of the hall, having obviously kept a lookout for their return.

"Oh madam!" she exclaimed as the nursery party headed up the stairs.

"What is it, Elsie?"

"Oh madam, a policeman came by while you were out!"

"As we expected," Daisy pointed out reassuringly.

"Yes'm." The girl sounded as doubtful as if the possibility had never crossed her mind.

"Come into the sitting room and tell me about it."

To the left of the stairs was a small sitting room that caught the afternoon sun. Daisy had furnished it with the chintzes and cheerful paintings of Paris scenes that Alec's first wife had chosen to brighten the house in St. John's Wood. Daisy and Alec used it far more than the formal drawing room at the front of the house.

Daisy sank into a chair, glad that they were the kind of chairs one could sink into. "Sit down, Elsie."

"Oh madam, I didn't ought!" She twisted the corner of her apron in agitated fingers. "It was the Scottish one, madam. Detective Sergeant Mackinnon, he calls himself. He wanted to know exackly what I saw and what I did, and I told him I already told the master, but he said I had to tell it all over again."

"So you did?"

"Oh yes'm. And the other one, Detective Constable Warren, the one with his eyebrows burnt off—you know?—he wrote it all down. Like as if he thought I might tell it all different next time!"

"Did you happen to think of anything you hadn't already mentioned to me or to Mr. Fletcher?"

"Oh no'm. I told you every single thing, just like it happened."

"Good. I'm sure Mr. Mackinnon didn't mistrust you, Elsie. He was just doing his job, following the rules."

"Well, that's as may be. It's not very nice for a girl to have every word she speaks wrote down."

"No, it's never nice being mixed up in a police case." Not nice, Daisy thought, but always interesting. "Did he ask for me?"

"No'm. I said did he want to see the mistress, because you'd gone for a walk, but he said he was sure you'd told the master all you knew. Like as if I hadn't!"

"I'm sure you did," Daisy assured her, and the girl departed soothed.

Daisy, however, was left quite indignant. She would have liked a chance to go over the whole affair with Mackinnon, or, better still, with Tom Tring. What she really wanted, she realised, was to be reassured that they knew all about the Jessups' comings and goings and were certain they had nothing to do with the stranger's death.

In fact, she was not a little peeved at being ignored. On the

other hand, as long as they didn't want her contribution, she didn't have to make up her mind what she really ought to reveal about the Jessups.

Her next aim, she decided, must be to meet Patrick Jessup. Though it was his elder brother who had fled, if the family was somehow caught up in the murder in the garden, could Patrick's return from America that very night have been pure coincidence, or had it set the affair in motion? Only by talking to him could she judge to her own satisfaction—if not that of the police—whether the fatal outcome was inadvertent or the result of malice aforethought.

What was the cause of death? Ernie Piper might have had the decency to tell her!

Mackinnon might be an easier mark. He didn't know her as well, and besides, she would be very careful not to alarm him with a direct question. He must be tired and hungry by now, tramping up and down the hill and all those steps. She would invite him to lunch.

THIRTEEN

As soon as she stepped out of the front door, Daisy saw Tom Tring approaching the Jessups' house. He and Mackinnon must have split the circle between them, she deduced.

What was more, Ernie Piper was at his side. She had forgotten that when she saw Mackinnon, he'd had a DC accompanying him.

She sighed. Tom wasn't in the least likely to reveal any information he didn't intend to, but even if he hadn't been a dear friend, she couldn't possibly invite Mackinnon to lunch without him, and Piper and the other chap. That made four detectives for lunch. She hoped Mrs. Dobson had plenty of eggs, cold meat, bread, and cheese on hand.

Then after eating, she thought, cheering up, she would take Tom up to the nursery to see Oliver. Surely he couldn't be so heartless as to refuse to pass on a tip or two to the mother of his godson.

Piper saw her, waved, and pointed her out to Tom. She gestured to them to come over.

"Tom, Mr. Piper, you must be hungry, and I'm about to sit

down to a lonely meal. Won't you and Sergeant Mackinnon join me? And DC Warren, of course."

"That's very kind of you, Mrs. Fletcher." The twinkle in his eyes told her he was well aware of her ulterior motive. "I was just hoping to catch Mr. Mackinnon and Mr. Warren and suggest we go for a quick bite, rather than disturbing people at their lunches."

"Perfect! There they are now, just leaving number nine."

Mrs. Dobson, warned to expect a guest before Daisy went out to find Mackinnon, had refused adamantly to have her kitchen cluttered again with constabulary. "Once in one morning is enough, madam. I'll never get a thing done today. It'll have to be the dining room."

Leading her horde into the house, Daisy was afraid it would be awkward when they found the table set for two. But Elsie—a veritable paragon of a parlour maid!—had looked out of the window and seen them all arriving, as she told Daisy later. Five place settings welcomed them, and Elsie carried in laden platters, as well as several bottles of beer. Mrs. Dobson had done her proud. Signs of haste might have been apparent to the housewifely eye, but that was something Daisy had never claimed to possess. As far as she could tell, fussing about whether everything was perfect never caused anything but grief.

Soon the sound of contented munching filled the room. Daisy was careful to ask no questions of more significance than "Another slice of bread, Mr. Mackinnon?"

Her forbearance was rewarded when Warren, the first pangs of hunger assuaged, grumbled, "I hope you had better luck than we did, Mr. Tring."

"Not much!" said Piper. "Mostly, there was no one home but the servants, and not a one of them heard or saw anything out of the ordinary, nor recognised the photo."

Photo? No one had shown Daisy a photo. She managed not to voice her outrage, but Tom caught her eye and raised ques-

tioning eyebrows. She shook her head very slightly. He answered with an equally infinitesimal nod, perceptible only by the shifting sheen on the reflective dome of his head.

"Same here with the photo," Warren confirmed. "Leastways, there was a housemaid swore she'd seen him peeping in her bedroom window one night, but seeing she sleeps in the attic—"

The others laughed.

"And it was her mistress," Warren continued, apparently forgetting Daisy's presence, "who didn't sleep a wink all night for the screams and groans. Sarge asked why she hadn't reported the disturbance to us, and she said her husband was in such a temper at breakfast because his egg was boiled too long that it put everything else right out of her mind."

Daisy knew exactly whom he was talking about. She ought not to listen to their discussing her neighbours, but it was irresistible. What was more, Tom, who could have put a stop to it anytime, let them continue. Perhaps he hoped their talk might spark a useful idea or two in Daisy's brain. After all, much as it pained Alec to admit it, she had occasionally been helpful in the past.

However, nothing occurred to her. She simply didn't know most of the neighbours well enough to have more than the most superficial impressions of them.

Elsie brought in coffee.

"Tom," said Daisy, "would you like to bring yours up to the nursery to say hello to your godson?"

"I would indeed, Mrs. Fletcher, thank you very much. Mr. Mackinnon, I shan't be long. I'd appreciate a word with you before you finish up down the road. How is the little fellow?" he continued, following Daisy from the room with the light tread that revealed his mountainous bulk as mostly muscle.

She closed the door. "*I'd* appreciate a word with *you*," she echoed. "'Word' first or babies first?"

His grin made his moustache wiggle. "Let's get the word over with, so that I can enjoy the twins in peace."

"Come into the office." She led the way through a door next to the foot of the stairs.

The room had two desks, as she shared it with Alec. His had little on it besides an inkwell and blotter, since he did most of his paperwork at the Yard. Hers, a massive rosewood creation inherited from Mr. Walsall, was dominated by her aged, secondhand, but trusty Underwood typewriter. Around it were piles of paper and reference books. No one could have called the result tidy, but Daisy could generally find what she needed when she needed it.

More books filled the shelves against the wall backing the stairs. When Belinda was home and young feet had thundered up and down those stairs, the books had muffled the noise. Under the window facing north onto the terraced garden stood the Georgian writing table, one of the few objects Daisy still possessed from her childhood home. She sat there to write personal letters, and sometimes just to think, when she was at the planning stage of future articles. Beside it, a glass-paned door led out onto the paved lowest terrace, where green-painted wrought-iron chairs awaited the return of summer.

Daisy perched on the corner of her desk and waved Tom to a chair by Alec's desk, one he had occupied before, talking police business with Alec.

"Well?" she said severely. "Why haven't I seen the photograph?"

"I understand you were out when Mr. Mackinnon came to speak to your household. And, strictly between ourselves, Mrs. Fletcher, the Chief was most adamant that you shouldn't be involved any more than absolutely necessary. It's possible the lad took his words rather too much to heart. Or he felt the Chief should cope with you himself! Or both."

"So you do concede I ought to have a go at identifying the victim? Not that I exactly want to study a picture of a corpse, mind you, but in the interests of—"

"Not to worry. It's not a picture of a corpse we're showing

around." Tom reached into the breast pocket of his green-and-maroon check jacket. He was wearing one of his more sober outfits today. "The deceased had a passport in his pocket, so we're using the photo from that."

"A passport? British?"

"Ah." Tom pondered as he handed over the photo. "I don't see why you shouldn't know. American."

"Oh!" Dismayed, Daisy took a moment to focus on the face. Then, instantly, she recognised it. "Oh no!"

"You've seen him before. You're quite sure?"

"Yes."

"Do you know who he is?"

She shook her head. "I just saw him in passing."

"Where?"

Slipping down from the desk, she went over to the garden door and stood there staring out at the dank flower beds, tidy now but bleak. She couldn't avoid telling Tom she had seen the American at the Jessups', but need she report that he was dashing away after an acrimonious meeting with Mrs. Jessup? Did she have to reveal Aidan's dismay on hearing of his visit? After all, the former was hearsay, not proper evidence, and the latter just her reading of Aidan's emotion.

She knew what Alec would say to that rationalisation!

Turning, she found Tom regarding her with a steady gaze, part quizzical, part stern. "Where did you see him, Mrs. Fletcher?"

With a sigh, she admitted, "At the Jessups' house, number five, next door. Several weeks ago." She made up her mind. "And I really think that's all I can tell you, at least until you've talked to them yourself."

He nodded. "Fair enough. They're next on my list, the last. You didn't react much to anything the others were saying over lunch. I take it there's nothing to tell about the rest of the residents?"

"Nothing I know of." Daisy hesitated. "No one mentioned the Bennetts, at number ten."

"Number ten was last on Sergeant Mackinnon's list, so he probably hasn't got there yet. Why?"

"I can't help thinking that anyone who had talked to them would have had plenty to say on the subject."

"As you do?"

"Just that you shouldn't believe a word they say. They're the worst kind of gossips, avid for any breath of scandal even if they have to make it up themselves. If they have no meat for outright rumourmongering, they're expert insinuators."

"I shall so advise Mr. Mackinnon," Tom said gravely. "Thank you, Mrs. Fletcher. Now we'd better go on up to the nursery before the others start wondering where we've got to."

At New Scotland Yard, with the Assistant Commissioner and Superintendent Crane pacified at least for the present, Alec returned to his office. An internal message form lay on his desk. Dr. Popkin had telephoned to say he'd be delighted to pop round and take a dekko at anything the chief inspector wished to set before him—the message Alec had left for him at the British Museum switchboard had been a model of discreet nonspecificity.

Regarding the piles of paper still awaiting his attention, Alec decided he could, if forced to do so, justify going to the museum, rather than inviting the expert to come to him.

Beside the message was a large manilla envelope with the photography department's stamp in the corner. Inside were a dozen enlargements of the dead man's passport photo, four of the entire passport, and the passport itself.

Alec studied the photo with interest. They had blown it up to the point that it was just barely beginning to blur. While agreeing with Shakespeare that "There is no art to find the mind's construction in the face," he judged the subject of the portrait to be a tough man. His eyes were hard beneath dark slicked-back hair, and his thin-lipped mouth was a straight line with no sign of softness or humour. Not that that made him a

criminal, of course. Besides, as well as the unreliability of features as a guide to character, passport photos were notoriously uncomplimentary.

And regardless of the victim's character, his murderer must be punished.

He made arrangements for copies of the passport to be sent to the FBI and the New York police, to follow up his cables. He couldn't expect a response for at least five days, probably longer. With any luck, he wouldn't have to wait that long to find out the man's name. If Dr. Popkin managed to read it, perhaps he'd have wrapped up the case by then. Slipping the passport into his pocket, he set off for Bloomsbury.

Hunger overtook him en route, and he popped into an Express Dairy milk bar in Oxford Street for a quick lunch.

When he reached the British Museum, he showed his warrant card and asked for Dr. Popkin, saying he was expected. A messenger led him at a great rate into the labyrinth of corridors hidden away behind the equally labyrinthine public halls, galleries, and libraries.

"Do you ever lose visitors in here?" Alec enquired.

"Hardly ever," the man replied in a lugubrious tone that suggested he wished the answer was "Frequently."

At last they stopped in front of a door labelled DR. N. POPKIN. The guide knocked.

"Come in!"

Opening the door, the guide announced, "It's the police, Dr. Popkin." Now his tone implied that he expected Dr. Popkin to be hauled off to prison on the instant.

"Police? Ah, Mr. Fletcher." The tall, lean man wore a white coat and white gloves. He had the permanently disappointed look of a basset hound.

"I'm afraid I'm interrupting you, Dr. Popkin," Alec said, entering and closing the door firmly on his guide. They shook hands.

"Not at all. After all," Popkin pointed out, gesturing at a sloping glass table with a bright light underneath and a couple

of ancient manuscripts on top, their curling corners held down by broken clay tablets incised with strange markings, "these have been lying around for a millenium or two. A few minutes longer won't hurt them. I beg your pardon if I seemed unwelcoming. The truth is, I was looking forward to escaping this mausoleum for a visit to Scotland Yard."

"I'm sorry to have deprived you of the outing, sir. I hoped to disturb your work as little as possible. Though if we're telling the truth, my desire to escape from my office was probably as strong as yours."

The basset hound grinned disarmingly. "Oh, by all means, let's have the truth. It's rare enough here, where practically everything I produce is a matter of inference and interpretation. What have you got for me?"

Alec handed him the passport. "Water has seeped between the pages, and the name is unreadable. I don't know if there's any chance you might be able to suggest what it might be."

"No bloodstains," Dr. Popkin noted, disappointed again. "No bullet hole."

"I'm afraid not."

"Ah well, we must work with what we have." He opened the booklet. "Odd, I'd have expected India ink in an official document of this nature."

"So would we. What do you think?"

"Oh, I expect I can give you something. This may take a few minutes. Do sit down."

"I'd like to watch, if I may."

"Certainly, though there won't be much to see. It's a matter of training the eye to read shadows. I dare say it's not unlike police work in some ways, eh?"

"Very like. Only our shadows tend to come in larger sizes. Man-size, for the most part."

Popkin laughed. He took the passport to his glass table, which had brilliant lights above as well as below, and picked up a magnifying glass. He studied the open page closely, first looking straight down, then squinting sideways. Then he set

down the magnifying glass, turned off the underneath lights, and stuck a jeweller's loupe in one eye. Picking up the passport, he examined it at an angle.

"Easy. They used an inferior pen nib as well as inferior ink. It has scratched the paper. If you wouldn't mind passing me that notebook on the desk there—"

"I'll write it in my own, sir, if you'll dictate the letters to me."

"*M I C H E L E*, capital *C*, *A S T E*, double *L*, *A N O*. Michele Castellano. Italian, wouldn't you say?"

"Yes, I would," Alec said thoughtfully. "Thank you, sir. I never dreamt you'd be able to give me so definite an answer, let alone so quickly."

"We aim to please."

"Needless to say, the matter is confidential."

"Of course," Popkin agreed cordially. "Dare I hope to learn what it's all about when you have bagged your villain?"

"I'd say of course, sir, if it weren't for the possibility of international ramifications. . . . Oh, what the hell, after what you did in the War, you know all there is to know about international ramifications! I'll be glad to send you a report."

Popkin beamed. "Thank you, Chief Inspector. I'll look forward to it."

Rather than ring for a messenger, he himself escorted his guest out to the great portico, so not until Alec was descending the steps to Great Russell Street was he able to consider what he had learnt.

Michele Castellano. Italian American. His mind went back to that evening a couple of months ago, in St. John's Wood, when the Pearsons had come to dinner and an unexpected American had turned up.

Pearson had spoken of reading about Irish, *Italian*, and Jewish bootleggers in America organising into increasingly violent gangs. Scotland Yard were naturally most concerned about the Irish aspect. In spite of the Irish Free State, the Irish were in general anti-British, yet fugitives from the American police were quite likely to have relatives living in Britain.

Despite a growing number of Italian restaurants in London, the community of Italian expatriates was minuscule in comparison.

The subject of American gangs had arisen because of Lambert's advent, and, lo and behold, Lambert had turned out to be a Prohibition agent. The young idiot had babbled about following gangsters to England, but Alec hadn't paid much attention. In his opinion, Lambert's superiors had probably sent him across the Atlantic to get him out of their hair.

What was it he had claimed to be his purpose in England? All Alec could recall was that he had tried to bring a gun into the country—which implied a willingness to use it.

Lacking the firearm, could he have resorted to other methods with one of the villains he purported to be chasing? Had the apparently ingenuous Lambert hit Michele Castellano over the head and then, with his thumbs, compressed both carotid arteries until the man lay dead? *Lambert*, who would lose his head if it weren't firmly attached to his body? He would never have found the right spots to compress.

Lambert, who was still to be seen out and about in Hampstead, even after leaving the Fletchers'.

Still, the only reason to connect Lambert with Castellano was that they were both Americans. Except that Castellano had been found murdered in Constable Circle, where Lambert had spent considerable time . . . What had Daisy said about Lambert and their next-door neighbours, and about the Jessups' mysterious American visitor?

Once again, it seemed he ought to have paid more attention to Daisy's guesswork, or intuition, or whatever it was that made her so often and so infuriatingly right. His sigh was so heartfelt that the woman sitting next to him on the number 24 bus he had unthinkingly boarded gave him a look of sympathy and said, "Never you mind, ducky. The night is darkest before the dawn."

He nodded an acknowledgement, but as the bus negotiated Trafalgar Square, with Nelson's Column in the middle, he

found himself dwelling on the admiral's death in battle. Then the Charing Cross statue of Charles I brought to mind the king's execution.

The bus trundled down Whitehall, with all the panoply of government on either side and the Houses of Parliament ahead. Alec reminded himself that Nelson's fleet had won a glorious victory at Trafalgar, and that Cromwell's grim rule had ended with the restoration of Charles's son to the throne in a constitutional monarchy with no claims of "divine right."

Alec swung down from the bus at the Cenotaph stop and hurried into the Yard. Things were really not going too badly. He had far more information than when Daisy had broken the news of the body in the garden to him, just a few hours ago. More important, he had a good idea of where to look for more answers. The most frustrating moment in any police investigation came when one didn't know where to turn next.

This time, he knew. First, he had to cable Michele Castellano's name to Washington and New York. And then he needed to talk to Daisy.

FOURTEEN

"Daisy?"

"Darling! You've rung just in time. Tom wants to interrogate me."

"So do I. Tell him to hold off with the thumbscrews until I arrive."

"Right-oh. Are you at the Yard still? I'll give him a cup of tea in the meantime. And all the others, too, I suppose. Mrs. Dobson's getting a trifle fed up."

"What are they all doing there? No, don't tell me! Doubtless I shall find out in due course. I'm on my way."

Daisy hung up. If he was coming home, surely he wouldn't then take Tom and Mackinnon back to the Yard, or even to the local station, to give their reports. With any luck at all, she would manage to listen in.

Instead of trying to guess from Tom's questions what the Jessups had told him, she would hear it from his own mouth. It wasn't that she intended to lie on their behalf, but nor would she disclose everything unless she was convinced that the police needed to know. In her experience, they were all too apt to read a sinister significance into the most innocent actions.

Tom and Ernie had arrived first. When Elsie announced them, Daisy had told her to show them into the dining room. No sooner had she joined them there than Mackinnon and Warren turned up, looking for Tom. Before Tom had made up his mind whether Daisy ought to leave while he and Mackinnon discussed the results of questioning the Jessups and the Bennetts, the telephone rang.

But Alec's call had been very brief. Returning to the dining room, Daisy hoped she hadn't missed anything.

As she pushed open the door, Ernie Piper was saying in an incredulous voice, "Shopping? The biggest gossip in the neighbourhood, with a murder on her doorstep, and she goes *shopping*? You're having us on."

Daisy slipped in and sat down as quietly as possible. Tom and Ernie were staring at Mackinnon, Ernie looking quite indignant.

"Simmer down, lad," said Tom calmly. "Mr. Bennett told you his sister went shopping, Mr. Mackinnon?"

"So did the servants."

"Ah. Well, that'd be what they were told."

"It's not as odd as it sounds," Mackinnon protested. "It seems she has a school friend living in the country who comes up to town once a month. The ladies go out to a show and supper, and then, rather than come home late—I gather Bennett objects to being disturbed after midnight—his sister stays at the friend's hotel. And next day, they go shopping together. Sometimes, if they manage to get tickets for something good, they'll stay over another night."

"Sounds to me like a load of codswallop," said Warren.

Though Daisy would have used a less vulgar term, that was exactly what it sounded like to her. Why on earth had the Bennetts—or Mr. Bennett—invented such a farrago? Surely not to give Miss Bennett time to escape the police? It just wasn't possible that she had murdered the man in the garden. She wasn't capable of killing anything but reputations.

"He claims he doesn't know what hotel she stayed at last

153

night," Mackinnon went on. "Nor whether she intends to come home today."

Tom glanced at Daisy. She should have known her return had not escaped his eagle eye. She shook her head. She'd never heard of Miss Bennett's monthly outing, or her school friend, come to that, and she hadn't had time to develop any theories.

"Tell it to the Chief," Tom said. "I take it no one in the house saw or heard anything last night?"

"The servants didn't. Mr. Bennett was . . . What would you say, Warren? Evasive, perhaps."

"Kept on and on about how they hadn't thought anything of it at the time and he wouldn't want to say anything that might get someone into trouble when he wasn't absolutely sure—"

"Ha!" escaped Daisy inadvertently.

They all looked at her. She was afraid they'd stop talking about the Bennetts, though they'd find it difficult to ask her to leave her own dining room.

However, Tom turned back to Mackinnon, produced an *ah* laden with meaning, and asked, "Anything else?"

"It's what he refused to say that seems to me significant, Mr. Tring," said Mackinnon. "He refused to tell us anything more until he talks to his sister to see if she remembers the same."

"Never heard that one before, Mr. Mackinnon! Now, Mrs. Fletcher knows the Bennetts. What do you think he meant by it, Mrs. Fletcher?"

"I wouldn't say I know them. In fact, I've gone out of my way to avoid them. But if you ask me, neither of them saw anything and they're waiting to see which way the wind blows before they invent a story."

"Waiting to find out what happened and who's suspected, you mean?"

"Exactly. I simply can't believe she'd go off to a show and a day's shopping if they had really seen anything. She's keeping out of the way to give him an excuse to postpone telling what they'll claim to have seen, so that when she returns, they can concoct a tale to fit the facts."

"I bet that's it," said Ernie Piper enthusiastically. "I bet you've hit the nail on the head, Mrs. Fletcher."

"Ah," said Tom, his eyes twinkling. "We'll see."

"Nae doot the chief inspector will try to persuade Mr. Bennett to tell his tale before he has a chance to learn the facts from servants and neighbours and pass them on to Miss Bennett."

"Not much hope of that, Sergeant," Warren put in with his accustomed gloom. "We've talked to every servant in the Circle, and you can bet they're all comparing notes by now. However careful we've been, they'll have a good idea of what it's all about."

"In any case," said Daisy, "I should think Alec's more likely to send you to do it, Tom. He doesn't like the Bennetts any better than I do, and I expect they know it. Not that he'd let his dislike get in the way of the truth, but if he disbelieves them, they might make a fuss and start spreading nasty rumours about prejudice."

"Sounds to me like they'll do that anyway," said Warren.

"Probably, but there's no point adding fuel to the flames. One thing's certain: Whatever they claim to have seen will be aimed at making trouble for someone. That's what they live for. Don't you think you should have a go at him, Tom?"

"It's for the Chief to decide. In the meantime, now that I've talked to the Jessup household, I've a few questions for you, Mrs. Fletcher, before we go back to the Yard to report to him."

"That was Alec I talked to on the phone just now, and he said he's on his way here." Daisy sighed. "*He* wants to ask me questions, too. So, since I'm so popular at the moment, why don't we just wait till he arrives? We can have a cup of tea while we wait."

She was pouring second cups all round when the front doorbell rang again. Elsie ushered in DC Ardmore. He looked somewhat nonplussed at finding himself in the middle of a tea party.

"Do sit down, Mr. Ardmore," Daisy invited.

"Another cup, madam?" asked the parlour maid resignedly.

"Yes, please, Elsie, and some more hot water."

"I telephoned in, Sarge," Ardmore told Mackinnon, "and they told me the chief inspector left a message to meet him here."

"That's right. Any luck?"

"Depends how you look at it. No one at the Hampstead station recognised the passport photo. Me and a couple of the uniformed lads covered Well Walk, Flask Walk, and the High Street and we found four people who thought they might have seen him. Only not a one of 'em would swear to it, and they didn't know anything about him anyway, just seen him about. We went to a couple of hotels and lodging houses, but no luck there. It'll take more time or more men to check everywhere in the area."

"And he could be staying anywhere," said Tom. "Doesn't have to be Hampstead. I expect we'll have to circulate the picture to all stations. Go on."

"The other American, your friend Lambert, Mrs. Fletcher—lots of people recognised the description, and the woman at the newsagent's told me where he lodges. So I went along there and had a chat with the landlady—it's a widow who lets out a couple of rooms. Hodge is the name."

"He wasn't there?" Mackinnon asked.

"No, nor he didn't come in last night," Ardmore said with heavy significance.

"She doesn't know where he went?"

"No, but she does say he's often away for a night or two," the detective constable conceded, "so she wasn't worried. She says she doesn't usually let to foreigners, but he speaks English quite well, and he's a nice young chap. Keeps his room tidy and very helpful about the place when he's home."

"That sounds like Lambert all right," said Daisy. "Did he tell Mrs. Hodge why he's here? In England?"

"It seems he said he's in the import business and looking for suppliers."

Daisy laughed. "It's true, in a way." She didn't know how much of Lambert's clandestine mission Alec had entrusted to the others, so she didn't explain that he was in the business of preventing imports and looking for the suppliers of bootleggers.

The coincidences really were too much to swallow: A Prohibition agent who was interested in a wine merchant who was visited by a mysterious American who turned up dead a hundred yards from his house. Although Daisy couldn't see Lambert as a cold-blooded killer, she couldn't forget the irresponsible way he had waved his gun around at their first meeting, when she and Alec were in the States. Yet if anyone was going to get bumped off, an agent of the law seemed the most likely victim.

Into the middle of a discussion of which she hadn't heard a word, Daisy dropped the question: "What if Lambert has been murdered, too?"

Everyone stared at her in silence.

Tom was first to recover. "Have you any reason to think he might be?"

"Alec didn't tell you why he came to England?"

"Not just to visit you and see the sights, I take it."

"No. Oh dear, if Alec didn't, I'd better not. I can tell you that Lambert seemed to think it was a dangerous business. He even tried to smuggle a gun into the country. Well, not exactly smuggle, because he apparently didn't know he wasn't supposed to have one, and he was quite upset when Customs took it away. Admittedly, he's given to exaggeration for the sake of excitement, but still, it does seem to me possible that he could be another victim."

As she spoke the last few words, the dining room door opened and Alec came in, with DC Ross on his heels.

"Who could be another victim?" Alec asked sharply.

"Lambert. He's disappeared, darling!"

"Not exactly disappeared," Ardmore protested. "We found his lodgings, sir, and it's true he didn't come home last night, but his landlady said he often goes away for a few days."

Alec sat down at the table and motioned to Ross to do likewise. "Lodgings?" he said. "A private house, not a flat or a hotel?"

"A furnished room, sir, let by the week. He's paid up to the end of next week."

"What's the landlady like?"

"Uh, fiftyish, grey hair—"

With an impatient gesture, Alec said, "Her character, Constable! Is she likely to allow you to search Lambert's room without a fuss? And preferably without telling all her neighbours."

"Yes to the search, sir. She was quite friendly and helpful. About the neighbours, I dunno. She didn't seem like the gossipy sort, but you never can tell with women. Oh, she did say she was glad I wasn't in uniform, because she wouldn't want people to know she'd had the police in the house."

"Right-oh. Do your best to impress upon her that it's best to keep quiet, and also that we have no reason to suspect Lambert of any wrongdoing. We're just concerned for his safety."

"Oh, darling, do you really think—?"

"You're the one who started this hare, Daisy. We have to chase it."

Ardmore stood up. "So you want me to search his room, sir? What'm I looking for? A gun?"

"Great Scott no! At least, I sincerely hope not, but if you find one, you'll confiscate it, of course. No, see if he's taken his toothbrush with him. If he has, we can stop worrying."

"And if he hasn't?" Daisy asked.

"Then we'll start worrying. Ardmore, give Piper the name and address, if you haven't already, then off you— No, come to think of it, a few more minutes won't make much difference. You'd better stay and hear a bit more."

Ardmore sat down again.

"Chief," said Tom, "can you tell us a bit more about Mr. Lambert? Why we may be worried about him? Mrs. Fletcher decided she shouldn't, as you hadn't."

"How uncommonly discreet!"

"Don't be beastly, darling. He did make a point of telling us in confidence. If he's missing, though . . ."

"You probably remember a good deal more of what he said than I do. Why don't you explain."

Daisy gave him a suspicious look. He was actually inviting her to get involved? It was true she knew Lambert much better than he did.

"Right-oh. Shall I start with New York?"

"Great Scott no! All that need be said about New York is that when you met him there, he was an agent of the Federal Bureau of Investigation."

"And a very enthusiastic one, but hopelessly incompetent. When he turned up here—or rather, in St. John's Wood—we weren't a bit surprised to find out he'd lost all his papers and his money. He said he'd transferred from the FBI to the— What was it, darling? Something to do with money."

"Treasury."

"That's it. Though why they should put the Treasury in charge of enforcing their law against drinking is more than I can understand. Still, they did, and Lambert was working for them."

"Over here? Not trying to stop *us* drinking, I hope, Mrs. Fletcher?" asked Mackinnon, only half joking. "The English might stand for it, but the Scots, never."

Four English detective constables glared at him in outrage. Whether they were outraged by the idea that the Americans might try to keep them from their pints, or by the suggestion that they wouldn't fight as hard for those pints as the Scots would for their drams, or both, Daisy didn't wait to discover.

Hastily, she reassured them, "No, they couldn't do that."

"They better not try," muttered Warren.

"Lambert was sent to try to stop the export of alcohol from England—Britain—to America."

"Single-handed?" Tom asked dryly.

"Well, that's the thing. Surely they must have sent more

159

than one agent. Suppose the dead man was another? What if a bootlegger unmasked both him and Lambert and murdered both of them?"

"What would a bootlegger be doing over here, Mrs. Fletcher?" asked Piper.

"It was something about codes, wasn't it, Alec? I don't remember exactly what Lambert said. Something about the Prohibition people intercepting the rumrunners' radio messages, so the gangs are sending men here to arrange codes with their suppliers."

"Gangs!" Ardmore exclaimed. "Don't say they're exporting their gangs now!"

"Not wholesale, and just visiting, I gathered."

"And the enthusiastic but incompetent Lambert is supposed to stop them?" Tom enquired in a tone of deep interest. "By shooting them?"

"Heavens no! He's supposed to identify them and follow them to see which English wholesalers they get in touch with. Oh, and try to find out what ships they use to deliver the stuff. You can imagine he was quite thrilled when we moved in next door to a wine merchant."

"The Jessups," said Tom.

"The Jessups," Daisy confirmed. "He used to watch them through binoculars, believe it or not. Then, after he moved out, I'd see him lurking in the undergrowth, presumably still spying on them."

"You never told me that, Daisy!"

"You were so relieved when he left. Besides, I couldn't swear it was him. I never came face-to-face with him. But he's such a rotten lurker, I'd catch glimpses now and then. It reminded me of the old days in New York."

"We'll have to find out if he's been seen 'lurking' around the homes or business premises of any other large-scale licensed victuallers. Piper, that's a job for you. Get a list of all the major wine merchants in London for a start, and call on them."

"Right now, Chief?"

"Yes, let's get cracking on this. Lambert's been lurking in the bushes, Castellano's body was found—"

"Castellano?" said three or four voices simultaneously.

"Michele Castellano," said Alec, trying to be nonchalant but looking smug. "The chap at the British Museum read the name in the passport without the slightest difficulty." He spelt it out and all the detectives wrote it down in their notebooks. "You'd better take his photo, Ernie, and make enquiries about him, too. He may have nothing to do with the booze trade, but we might as well kill two birds with one stone."

"Right, Chief."

"Ring up now and then to see if there have been any developments you need to know about."

"Uh . . . where?"

Leaning back in his chair, Alec ran his fingers through his hair. Dark, thick and springy, it showed no signs of depredation. "Uh, Daisy," he said reluctantly, "would it be very disruptive if we used this room as our headquarters, just until we finish our enquiries in the immediate area?"

Daisy quickly changed a burgeoning grin into a frown. "I haven't planned any dinner parties for the next few days," she said—she seldom did, never knowing when Alec would be home. "We could eat in the office or the kitchen, I suppose. It'll mean extra work for the servants, though. They're sure to kick up a dust."

"I suppose it wouldn't work—"

"But I expect I can talk them round," Daisy interrupted before he could dismiss the idea out of hand, the last thing she wanted. "In fact, with half a dozen policemen in the house, perhaps Nurse Gilpin will stop declaring that the murderer will have to climb over her dead body to get at the babies. If she carries on much longer, she'll end up giving them a complex. All right, darling, I should think we can manage."

And just let them try to keep her out of her own dining room!

FIFTEEN

Ernie Piper and Ardmore departed, the latter with instructions to search Lambert's room for anything that might connect him with Castellano, as well as for his toothbrush and other overnight necessities.

Alec turned back to Daisy. "Any more revelations about Lambert?" he asked.

"Not that I can think of."

"Can you, by any chance, remember how he found out that the Jessups are in the wine trade?"

"It was when they invited us, him and me, for cocktails. I'm sure I told you. He was helping me go over the house and decide what to do. It was an awful mess when Alec inherited it," she informed Tom and the others in an aside. "Mrs. Jessup sent her maid to ask us over for a drink, under the impression that Lambert was my husband."

"The Jessups knew Castellano, too, Chief," said Tom, his voice carefully neutral. "Mrs. Fletcher recognised him."

"What? Great Scott, Daisy—"

"I *told* you they had an American visitor, an unwelcome visitor. You just said so did we, and that it's not against the law."

"And forgot about it," Alec admitted ruefully.

"No one showed me Castellano's passport, not until Tom showed me a copy of the photo after lunch. How was I supposed to know it was the same man?"

"You're sure of that?"

"Not absolutely. I didn't get a really good look at his face. I wouldn't swear to it in court, but if I wasn't pretty certain, I wouldn't have mentioned it." Or rather, she wouldn't have let Tom wring it out of her.

"How do you know he was unwelcome? Did they tell you so?"

"No, I overheard him trying to bully Mrs. Jessup. I wasn't eavesdropping. I happened to be leaving and couldn't help passing the door of the room where they were."

Alec gave her a sceptical look but didn't comment. "What was he bullying her about?"

"I didn't hear much. I gathered he wanted to see Mr. Jessup, who was travelling on the Continent. He seemed not to believe that Mrs. Jessup didn't know exactly where he was or when he was due to come home. He gave up while I was still in the entrance hall, and I caught a glimpse as he left, but he'd already put on his hat and turned up his collar. He didn't look at me, so, as I said, I didn't get a good look at his face."

"Tom?"

"You want the lot, Chief, or just the Jessups? Not that there's much else."

"Apparently we're going to be concentrating on the Jessups, so let's get the rest over with first. Mackinnon, did you get anything of interest?"

"Not a bite till I got to the Bennetts, sir. And then nothing actually useful, just a hint that they might have seen something."

"You couldn't get it out of them? They're usually only too ready to spread stories."

Mackinnon explained about Miss Bennett's absence and Mr. Bennett's evasions.

"I'd better have a word with him myself," Alec said with a sigh.

"Darling, you're not going to believe anything they say, are you? They'll concoct a story just to make trouble. They're utterly poisonous!"

"I know, Daisy, and I promise I'll take their claims with a pinch of salt, but the fact is, they have the best view of the garden of anyone but us and the Jessups, and they're notorious for keeping an eye on what's going on. It's just conceivable they actually did see something."

"Then why wouldn't he tell? Why did she go off with her mythical school friend?"

"Is the school friend mythical?"

"I don't know," Daisy conceded. "I've never heard of her before, but I don't exactly go out of my way to chat with Miss Bennett."

"Mackinnon?"

"I talked to the servants first, sir, before I talked to him. They told me she had gone to meet an old friend. When he told the same story, it never dawned on me that the friend might not exist."

"No, why should it?"

"Well, sir, Mrs. Fletcher had warned us about the Bennetts not being entirely reliable."

"She did, did she?" He glared at Daisy.

"Be reasonable, darling. I couldn't let him walk into their lair assuming they were nice, normal people."

"All the same, I should have—"

"Never mind, Mackinnon. It was natural to believe them, and it may even be true. But someone in the Circle may know if she exists. Ross, I'll leave that to you. Ask the Bennett servants first whether they have heard of her before, or seen her. If not, go round the Circle, asking the ladies of the house whether Miss Bennett's ever mentioned her. We may not get an answer, but it'll give them all something to think about."

And distract attention from the Jessups, Daisy hoped. The situation was beginning to look pretty black for them.

"I've got it, sir," said Ross. "Right away?"

"Yes. It's probably just a distraction, so let's clear it out of the way. You can skip the Jessups, at number five. Report back here."

Ross went out. Alec gazed thoughtfully at the remaining DC, Warren, whose cheeks were still fiery red from the flaming umbrella. He had had a hard day. His shoulders were slumped, and if it weren't for the scorching, his eyebrowless face would probably be pale and wan, Daisy thought. He straightened under Alec's gaze.

"How are you feeling, Warren?"

"A bit sore, sir, but I can carry on all right."

"Good man. Go to the kitchen and ask Mrs. Dobson to give you some more ointment for that burn; then I want you to ring up the Yard and tell them to transfer calls to this number. Stay by the phone—there's a chair beside it—ready to answer if anyone rings. We don't want the parlour maid going on strike."

Alec, Tom, and Mackinnon remained—and Daisy, who wondered if she was about to be ejected.

Alec subjected her to the same thoughtful gaze he had turned on Warren. She, too, felt the urge to straighten her shoulders. She resisted it.

"You know the Jessups quite well, don't you?" he said.

She nodded. "As well as one can after being next-door neighbours for a few weeks."

"You'd better stay. But you are not to pass on to them a single word of anything that's said here."

"Of course not, darling."

"Tom, Mackinnon, as I'm sure you realise, I'm caught between the devil and the deep blue sea. The Jessups are my neighbours, and I've no desire to have to move out. The connection with the victim is not proof that any of the family had any hand in his death, even if he was here because of that connection. I'm not saying we will in any way compromise the

investigation. I'm saying tread gently, and above all, don't talk about the case to anyone outside this room."

"Right, Chief."

"Yes, sir."

"All right, Tom. Your turn."

"Nothing of interest at numbers one to four. No one recognised Castellano's photograph; no one had seen or heard anything. Three of the men had gone to work, and one housekeeper was out at the shops, so we'll have to go back, but I doubt we'll have any luck there."

"All the ladies were at home?"

"Every one of 'em, Chief, and dying to know what's happened. Miss Bennett leaving like that, it's not natural."

"Alec, you don't suppose Miss Bennett could have killed Castellano?" Daisy asked.

"Highly unlikely. It must have taken considerable strength to move the body."

"But if he helped her—"

"Then why didn't he scarper too?" asked Tom.

"He's verra arthritic and not a big man," Mackinnon commented.

"We'll keep them in mind, of course, Daisy, but don't get your hopes up."

Daisy was afraid he guessed that not only would she be happy to dispense with the Bennetts as neighbours but she was also doing her best to provide an alternative to the Jessups as chief suspects. Whenever she "interfered" (as he put it) in one of his cases, he accused her of trying to protect someone she was fond of, even to the extent of ignoring evidence against them. It wasn't true. She never ignored real evidence, and he himself was always telling her hearsay and speculation were not evidence. It wasn't her fault if sometimes it was not clear which was which.

Tom was continuing his report. "Before I reached number five, Mrs. Fletcher had a look at the photograph and recognised the victim, so I already knew he had visited the Jessups.

Their parlour maid, Miss Enid Bristow, identified him at once. She didn't know his name—she said he had terrible manners and never gave it to her—but she'd admitted him to the house twice, before she was ordered not to. A smart girl, that."

"Our maid's sister," said Daisy.

"Ah. I thought I detected a resemblance."

"So you should. You're a detective."

Impatiently, Alec asked, "Did she know Castellano's business?"

"Not much more than what Mrs. Fletcher happened to hear. He wanted to see Mr. Jessup and got pretty shirty when Mrs. Jessup wouldn't tell him where her husband was."

"I wonder why he didn't go to the shop and talk to Aidan?" Daisy muttered. Then she wished she hadn't.

Suppose Castellano had known Aidan—or, more likely, had known something about Aidan that he was going to report to Mr. Jessup. What was it Alec had mentioned as a possible reason for the Jessups and Mr. Irwin to be nervous of a policeman moving in next door? Evasion of duty on wine and spirits, that was it. Aidan was in charge of the financial side of the business. Suppose he had been paying the tax money to himself instead of the government? Aidan was Mr. Irwin's daughter's husband, so if the solicitor knew, he'd have every reason to be worried sick.

What a gift to a blackmailer! He could threaten Aidan with telling his father and threaten Mr. Jessup with telling Customs and Excise, which would probably ruin the business.

But how on earth could Castellano possibly have found out?

Not merely groundless speculation, but a wild flight of fancy, Alec would say if she told him. Much better not to.

"What did you say, Daisy?" he enquired, his tone of voice suggesting it was not the first time of asking.

"Oh, nothing."

He raised his eyes to heaven in exasperation but did not press her. "Go on," he said to Tom.

"The housekeeper only knew what Enid Bristow had told her, but at least she confirmed the girl wasn't making it up on the spot for my benefit. There's no lady's maid. The nanny's away, and the daily help 'don't know nothin' about nothin',' and doesn't want to. The others don't take her into their confidence."

"What time does she leave?"

"Four o'clock. She has children coming home from school and her husband wanting his tea at six. She walks down through the garden, but she would have been too early to see anything yesterday evening. That's assuming nothing happened before dusk. Mrs. Innes—that's the cook-housekeeper—and Enid Bristow were busy from five to eight clearing up tea things and preparing dinner. I'm pretty sure neither could have got away without the other knowing about it."

"And what about the family?"

"Ah, now that's another story, Chief. Comings and goings like a merry-go-round." Tom put on the wire-rimmed glasses he had recently taken to wearing for reading and took out his notebook. "Let me get this straight. I'll start with what the servants told me."

Alec nodded.

"First—being neighbours you'll know this, I expect—the younger son, Patrick Jessup, has been abroad for some time, on his own. He's always gone with his father before on these buying trips to the vineyards on the Continent."

Daisy knew all that, and she was fairly certain she had told Alec. She couldn't tell from his expression, though, whether he had actually been listening at the time, and remembered.

Tom moved on to the events of the previous night. "Patrick Jessup came home last night. They're not sure exactly what time, just that it was after dark. He came in through the kitchen—said he wanted to surprise his parents, and besides he was starving and could do with a bite before dinner. He gave 'em each a kiss, and they agree he had beer on his breath. He said he'd stopped in at the Flask public house for old times' sake."

"We might be able to get a check on the time from the pub, but he was certainly out and about between five and eight."

"Only thing is, Chief, he'd left the country before the first time the American turned up. Miss Bristow—Miss Enid Bristow's sure of that."

Alec frowned. "That does rather— No, it doesn't. They could have met abroad. Possibly their meeting set the whole peculiar business in motion." He scribbled a note to himself. "We'll consider it later. Go on."

"Patrick Jessup goes on up the back stairs. Next thing they know in the kitchen, before the maid's had time to lay a place at table for him, is Mrs. Jessup coming down to say not to bother. With Patrick home, Aidan was going to catch the night express to the North."

"Great Scott! Were they on such bad terms?"

"On the contrary, according to what I was told. Not to say there wasn't an occasional spat. Like, f'rinstance, Aidan didn't approve of this trip of Patrick's. Mostly, they got on about as well as brothers can. No, it seems Aidan had been on the fidget for a couple of weeks on account of some urgent business needed doing up north, but his mother—their mother—didn't want him to go while his brother was abroad."

"They'd known about this for a couple of weeks, or they were told last night he'd been fretting to get away?"

"They knew, though it was a bit of a surprise that he up and left so quick. A cab pulled up and he was off and away before the others sat down to dinner. He was going to get a bite to eat at the station, so as to be sure of not missing the train."

"He was in a tearing hurry, wasn't he! Did you get any further explanation? What his urgent business was?"

"Yes, Chief." Tom started to thumb through his notebook.

"Never mind; when you get to it. Go on with what the servants had to say."

"Let's see, now. Enid Bristow doesn't serve at dinner. She takes the dishes in and they help themselves, so she only heard bits and pieces when she fetched plates and took in the next

course. Mr. Patrick seemed happy to be home, and Mrs. Jessup was happy he was home safe, and Mr. Jessup was pleased with some business he'd done. They all seemed cheerful, 'cepting Mrs. Aidan, who was in the dumps because of her husband leaving. Leastways, that's what Miss Bristow assumed was wrong with her."

"She didn't actually hear it said?"

"Not in so many words. But after dinner, when she took coffee to the drawing room, Mrs. Aidan asked her to help Nanny pack, because she was going to take the children to visit her sister while he was away. And this morning, off they went, with Patrick along to lend a hand."

"Don't tell me Patrick Jessup's left town, too?" Alec demanded in dismay.

SIXTEEN

"*Hold on,* Chief!" said Tom. "Patrick didn't go off with Mrs. Aidan. He just went to the station to see her and the children onto the train. Mrs. Fletcher telephoned the shop, or showroom, or whatever they call it. . . ." He looked at Daisy.

"I was afraid you might think I ought to have stopped Audrey leaving," she admitted, "though I really don't see how I could have. But it seemed to me at least I could find out for you whether Patrick had hopped it, too. I rang up Jessup and Sons and asked for Aidan—"

"For Aidan!"

"Because I knew he wasn't there."

"For pity's sake, Daisy!"

"Patience is a virtue," she reminded him severely. "It worked just as I intended. The receptionist said he wasn't available but either Mr. Jessup or Mr. Patrick could help me. I told her I really needed to speak to Mr. Aidan and asked when was he expected back. She said he was travelling on business and the date of his return was uncertain. So there you are. One flown, one in the bag."

"I hope you didn't leave your name," Alec said acidly.

"Of course not, darling. And I put on Mother's *grande dame* voice."

"Thank heaven for small mercies!"

"Heaven had nothing to do with it. It was entirely my own notion."

"And I suppose the notion didn't dawn on you to warn me that Mr. and Mrs. Aidan were flitting?"

"Be reasonable! Last night, not only did I not know Aidan was going; I didn't even know there was a body in the bushes. This morning, Mrs. Jessup told me only a few minutes before Audrey left that she was departing, and that Aidan had already gone. But I still didn't know the victim was an American, let alone that he was the Jessups' mysterious visitor. I had no idea they were any more involved than any of the neighbours. If you'd shown me the passport right away, I could have chained myself to the bumper bar of Audrey's taxi, like a suffragette. Not that I think for a moment that she had anything to do with whatsisname's death."

"Castellano," Mackinnon put in, checking his notebook. Both he and Tom seemed to be enjoying the skirmish between Daisy and Alec. "Michele Castellano."

"Italian-American," Daisy exclaimed. "I knew it!"

"Knew what? What else haven't you mentioned? And what the deuce do you mean, Mrs. Jessup told you about Aidan leaving? I wish for once you'd start at the beginning instead of dropping bits and pieces here and there."

"It all goes back to Lambert's arrival. And all I have are bits and pieces, like a jigsaw puzzle, half of them *pure speculation* you wouldn't have wanted to hear. But the picture is beginning to come together."

"Let's have it."

"Only it's more like a jigsaw than a consecutive story, so starting at the beginning isn't going to—"

"Great Scott, Daisy, start where you want, but let's have the whole of it! Or as many damn bits and pieces as you have."

"On the other hand, perhaps Lambert *is* the best place to

start," Daisy said reflectively. Alec looked about to explode, so she hurried on. "No, actually, it was Tommy, not Lambert. Tommy Pearson. Do you remember, he said something about gangs of criminals in America being Irish, Italian, and Jewish? We were worried about the Irish because of their habit of blowing up policemen, but even though Mrs. Jessup is Irish, it looks as if it's one of the Italians who's ended up dead on our doorstep."

"There are plenty of law-abiding Italians in America. Castellano may even be another Prohibition agent, sent to check up on Lambert."

"I *said* a lot of my picture is speculation. The next bit is Lambert, of course, who came to England to find out who are the wicked Englishmen whose shipments of alcoholic beverages are corrupting the morals of America."

"Excuse me a moment, Mrs. Fletcher," said Tom. "I assume Lambert's on the up-and-up, Chief? You checked his credentials? He couldn't be a non-Irish, non-Italian, non-Jewish crook?"

"No," Alec said regretfully. "It would have given me great pleasure to extradite him to America."

"He lost his papers," Daisy reminded Tom, "and it took forever to get them replaced, but he did. Which makes me wonder: You didn't find similar papers in Castellano's pockets, presumably. If he was an agent, he would have had them, and if his passport wasn't stolen, it seems unlikely his credentials would have been."

"Good point, Daisy. It doesn't prove he was a gang member, however."

"Don't forget the shoulder holster, sir," said Mackinnon.

"A shoulder holster!" said Daisy. "What else haven't you told me?"

"You're supposed to be telling us," Alec reminded her. "You're right, though, Mackinnon. With or without a gun in it, it's significant. We'll take it as a working hypothesis that Castellano was up to no good. Go on, please, Daisy."

"Right-oh. Next was finding out we were moving in next to a wine merchant. Lambert was instantly on the qui vive. Asinine, because there must be hundreds of wine merchants in the country who have nothing to do with bootlegging, but these were convenient for him to keep a watch over. And—let me see—after that, I discovered the younger Jessup son was abroad, not with his father as always before, but on his own. I can't remember what made me suspect he'd gone to America. No reason at all, really, just being mixed up with Lambert and his obsession."

"Do you know now for a fact that Patrick was in the USA?"

"No, actually. That's one thing that made me wonder: the way no one ever mentioned where he'd gone for such a long time. That and Mr. Irwin's jitters at the prospect of a policeman moving in next door to the Jessups. Mr. Irwin is Audrey's father, and a solicitor," she explained to Tom and Mackinnon, "so it seemed probable something a bit fishy was going on."

"Tom, did you by any chance ask Mrs. Jessup where Patrick had come home from?"

" 'Fraid not, Chief."

"What I canna understand," said Mackinnon, "is what Castellano was here in England for, assuming he was a gangster, if Mr. Patrick had gone over there on that verra same business of codes and such. It doesna make sense to me."

"No, it's odd," Daisy agreed.

"We'll be able to tell from Patrick's passport if he was in the States," Alec pointed out. "Daisy, let's get back to your jigsaw puzzle."

"Where were we?"

Mackinnon consulted his notebook. "Mr. Irwin," he said.

"Oh yes, his having the wind up was a small piece. So was Mrs. Jessup's anxiety. In general, she seems such a calm, practical person, but she worried about Patrick, and why should she if he was just across the Channel, where he'd been often before with his father? Then we have a murder in our quiet, secluded garden, followed by the news that Patrick came home

and Aidan went off the very evening it took place. And then"—she glowered at the three men—"*much* later, I'm shown a photograph of the victim and recognize him as . . . Well, you know that bit. There's definitely a picture emerging, but it has too many holes left to make out what it is."

"The one part that's clear as a bell," said Tom, "is that square in the middle of your picture are the Jessups."

"However," said Alec, "we've no proof that Daisy's picture bears much relationship to reality. It's made up of a few facts and a lot of inference and sheer guesswork. Tom, did Mrs. Jessup tell you anything you didn't already get from the servants?"

"She explained Aidan's rush to leave. Seems he usually visits some of their customers up north at this time of year. The customers expect him. In particular, one gentleman, a Mr. Dalton, rang up to say his shooting party had depleted his cellar. He wanted to place a big order but wouldn't do it without the personal guidance of Aidan, on the spot. He telephoned several times and they were afraid he'd take his business elsewhere if Aidan didn't get there pretty quick."

"At least we know exactly where he went today, then."

"Mrs. Jessup didn't know the address. We'll have to get the details from the shop."

Alec looked at Daisy. "I don't suppose . . . ?"

"Of course I didn't ask, darling. I didn't want them to know who was calling, remember? Or that I had any connection with the police. In fact, I didn't even know Mrs. Jessup hadn't given Tom the information."

Tom gave his rare rumbling laugh. "You see, Chief, it doesn't pay to keep Mrs. Fletcher in the dark!"

"Mackinnon, go and ring the shop. This is official. You're a police detective and you want to know the whereabouts of Mr. Aidan Jessup today and his planned itinerary. Make sure you speak to Mr. Jessup himself, though. There's no need for his staff to know what's up. While you're about it, tell him I want—no, make that 'would like'—to speak to him and to Mr.

Patrick at home." Alec checked his wristwatch. "Half past six this evening. Got it?"

"Yes, sir. A command disguised as a polite request."

"Exactly."

Mackinnon went out.

"Tom, anything else from Mrs. Jessup?"

"I asked what time the gentlemen generally came home from work. She said it varies. The shop closes at eight. The Jessups generally leave at five-thirty or six, but quite a few of their better customers like a private appointment later on. Whichever of the Jessups stays on to deal with them sometimes goes in late or comes home early the next day, depending on how busy they are. Yesterday, though, both Mr. Jessup and Aidan came home earlier than usual because they were expecting young Patrick. Mr. Jessup went in early this morning to make up."

So much for that hurrying figure that had so alarmed Daisy! She wasn't going to tell them about that.

"They knew what time Patrick was coming home?" Alec asked.

"Not exactly. He sent a cable from the steamer as it approached the Liverpool docks—"

"Liverpool!" Daisy exclaimed. "So he *was* in America."

"Or Ireland, Mrs. Fletcher. You said Mrs. Jessup was Irish. Patrick could have been visiting relatives, or maybe calling on breweries and distilleries."

"Or talking to Irish Republicans about bombs," she said darkly.

"Not impossible," said Alec, "and I'll keep it in mind, but I'm inclined to believe your original notion was right, Daisy." He grinned at her look of triumph. "I think Patrick was in America, on business concerned with outwitting their forces of law and order. Tom, if he was still on board when he cabled, the Jessups didn't know what train he'd catch?"

"No. The men came home about four o'clock, she said, which agrees with what the servants told me. Just in case Pat-

rick disembarked and got through Customs quickly, to be there to welcome him."

"Or—I wonder—to meet Castellano? I'm assuming Castellano refused to go to the shop because he knew Prohibition agents were over here on the watch. Suppose Jessup had at last agreed to talk to him at home, to find out what he wanted? And when they found out, they didn't like it."

"But they wouldn't *kill* him," Daisy protested, "not deliberately."

"Pending the autopsy report, I'm afraid we're virtually certain he was killed deliberately. I'm not yet prepared to swear he was killed by one of the Jessups, but with the information we have, I have no choice but to work on that basis. I realise it's no earthly use trying to tell you what to do, but I hope you'll steer clear of the family, all of them, until we have this sorted out. And while we're on the subject, how did you happen to be chatting to Mrs. Jessup this morning?"

Tom, who in the middle of this peroration had gazed up at the ceiling as if trying to pretend his considerable bulk was elsewhere, returned his attention to the proceedings.

"She came round," said Daisy, feeling somewhat subdued but on the whole heartened that Alec seemed at last to have grasped that he couldn't order her about. "She told me Audrey was just leaving to visit her sister, and before she went, she wanted to know what was going on in the garden."

"What did you tell her?"

"That I couldn't enlighten her because you never tell me anything."

A muffled snort emerged from the depths of Tom's moustache.

Alec visibly relaxed. "Good. What did you make of her manner?"

Daisy thought back. "As far as I remember, she seemed perfectly relaxed. Or at least as relaxed as one can be with hordes of policemen quartering the neighbourhood. But don't forget, darling, she was an actress."

"Ah, was she now?" said Tom. "Then it's no good reading anything into her reactions."

"How did she seem to you, Tom?"

"Just the right amount of concern if there's hordes of policemen quartering the neighbourhood and you don't know what's going on and one of them comes to ask you nosy questions about your family's movements. And you can't give satisfactory answers, and you have to admit you recognise the victim. I wish I'd seen her on the stage. She must have been pretty good."

"Or else she doesn't know what's going on," Daisy suggested.

"That's always a possibility," Alec agreed, "but I think I have enough to apply for search warrants for the house and shop. He looked around as Mackinnon came in. "Did you find out where Aidan is?" he asked.

"No such luck, sir. Apparently this chap Dalton lives in some godforsaken part of the country. Aidan's the only member of the firm who's ever been there. He has the address and telephone number in his address book—"

"Which he took with him."

"Which he took with him. What's more, he took the only list of the customers he has to call on, all of whose names and addresses are only to be found in his address book. All they know is that they're scattered all over the North, including Scotland. He takes the train up and then hires a car and driver. Mr. Jessup said he could probably come up with a few names if he put his mind to it, but he can't recall any with unusual names we might be able to run to earth."

"They must have an order book with the names and addresses of people they ship stuff to."

"Yes, but a lot of them just write with their orders; they dinna insist on a visit from a knowledgeable representative."

"There should be letters in their files, Chief," said Tom. "It may take a bit of digging, but we should be able to sort it out. Course, that won't tell us where he'll be on any particular day."

"Search warrants," said Alec crisply. "Tom, I'm leaving you to find a friendly magistrate. Mackinnon, you come with me to take notes. It's about time I had a word with Mrs. Jessup for myself."

Not five minutes after Alec went over to the Jessups, the doorbell rang. Daisy was still sitting in the dining room, writing down everything she had heard, which she hadn't dared to do with Alec present. She ignored the bell, thanking heaven that Elsie had proved quite capable of dealing with nosy reporters. However, the parlour maid showed in DC Ross, who had returned from his errand.

"You've been quick," said Daisy. "If I remember your instructions correctly, that means the Bennetts' servants confirmed the existence of Miss Bennett's old school chum. What a pity."

"Is it?" Ross asked. "To tell the truth, Mrs. Fletcher, I don't feel I've really got the hang of this case, coming in on it late, so to speak. I don't s'pose you'd be kind enough to explain what's going on?"

"I'd be glad to. It would help get it straight in my own head." About to add that she didn't actually know everything, as Alec refused to tell her, she realised just in time that nothing could so effectively cut off future confidences from Ross. She told him all she had already told the others, as well as what she had learnt from them, adding to her notes as she spoke.

He had his notebook out, too, but unlike Ernie Piper, he didn't have an endless supply of well-sharpened pencils. She had to wait while he shaved one into the fireplace. He did know shorthand, though, like Ernie, and unlike Daisy's version of Pitman's, his was probably legible to anyone who had studied the subject.

"Thanks," he said when she finished her exposition. "That was very clear. I see what you mean about the Bennetts. I wish I could report no one had ever heard of Miss Lagerquist."

"Lagerquist—is that the friend's name? They could never have invented that, alas. Pity her name's not Smith. Of course,

even if she's real, she's just an excuse, giving the Bennetts time to make up a credible story. But if Miss Lagerquist were a figment of their imaginations, then the police could dismiss the Bennetts' story as another figment. Now they'll have to take it seriously, whatever they come up with."

"With a pinch of salt, Mrs. Fletcher, seeing they didn't see fit to come to us right away."

"Oh, the Chief will take anything they say with a pinch of salt. He knows them. It's because he knows them that he'll have to act on what they'll say they saw."

Ross looked somewhat confused. Daisy was about to elucidate when the doorbell rang again. Poor Elsie was going to be run off her feet, Daisy thought, but it was DC Warren who ushered in DC Ardmore.

"Hope it's all right, madam," Warren said, "if I answer the door. Miss Bristow passed a remark when Ross here arrived and I offered to do it for her."

"Thank you," Daisy said warmly. "With all of you coming and going, I was beginning to worry about Elsie. What about the telephone? No one has rung up yet?"

"Not yet. D'you mind if I leave this door open a bit? Then I'll be able to hear it ring from here, and the front doorbell, too. I'd like to know what's been found out."

"Of course, leave it ajar. Mr. Ross found out that Miss Bennett's school friend is real."

"And Miss Bennett spends a day with her in town every month, and sometimes doesn't come home for the night."

"What about you, Mr. Ardmore?" Daisy enquired.

"Bad news, I'm sorry to say, Mrs. Fletcher, him being a friend of yours. Mr. Lambert didn't take his toothbrush with him, nor his hairbrushes or anything else he'd need for a night away. Any way you look at it, it don't look good."

"Oh dear, I wonder what can have happened to him! He's so helpless and hopeless and hapless, I can't help feeling a bit responsible for him. Surely Castellano's murderer can't have got him, too."

The three men exchanged glances.

"We've no reason to think so," Ross said soothingly.

Warren inevitably looked on the gloomy side. " 'Cepting he was int'rested in the Jessups, same as Castellano."

Ross frowned at him. "Mr. Lambert was . . . is a sort of policeman, and it looks like Castellano might've been a crook."

His slip of the tongue didn't make Daisy feel any better. Clearly he, too, had a feeling Lambert was dead. Equally obviously, he assumed the Jessups were responsible. Daisy refused to believe any of them was a cold-blooded killer.

She had to remind herself that she had never met Patrick Jessup. He had been described to her as "adventurous," often a euphemism for *reckless*, or even for *aggressive*. Was it possible that he had come home from America to find his family being persecuted by Castellano, and decided to do something drastic about it?

Yet Aidan, not Patrick, had done a moonlight flit. Staid, sober, sensible Aidan, father of two small children—and adept of the rugger field. Rugby football was above all a game invariably associated with physical aggression.

Daisy felt she was going round in circles again. Then suddenly a new idea struck her. Whichever brother was a murderer, if either was, she would expect the family to rally round to protect him. Could Aidan have left to draw suspicion away from Patrick?

There were too many unanswered questions. She wished she knew how Castellano had been killed, not in too much gruesome detail, of course. And she wished she knew what he had been doing in England.

"It's all very well saying Castellano may have been one of a bootlegging gang," she interrupted the subdued discussion of the others, "and that they've started sending people to England to coordinate codes with their suppliers. It doesn't explain why the Jessups didn't want anything to do with him, does it?"

"It would if they're not selling booze to America," Ross

pointed out, "and he's been trying to persuade them to join the trade, and they don't want to."

"Oh. Yes." Daisy had been assuming Jessup & Sons were rumrunners, if the word could be applied to British wholesalers. It fitted so well with her theory that Patrick had been in America. Or had she first guessed that they were shipping to America and from that deduced Patrick's whereabouts? She couldn't remember. And then there was Mr. Irwin's nervousness, suggesting some sort of illegal carrying-on. Perhaps evasion of duty owed was behind that after all. How dull!

Whichever, it didn't make sense for Patrick to be sent over to arrange the deal while the bootleggers sent an envoy in the opposite direction on the same business.

She badly wanted to meet Patrick. Normally, she would expect to have him introduced to her shortly after his return from abroad, but circumstances were anything but normal. After this, innocent or guilty, the Jessups might never again want to have anything to do with the Fletchers.

"Tea," she said, and rang the bell.

SEVENTEEN

Opening the Jessups' front door to Alec and Mackinnon, Elsie's sister Enid bristled. He hoped her obvious disapproval would not be transferred to his own parlour maid.

"The mistress is resting, sir," she announced forcefully. "She's already talked to them other policemen and she's wore-out."

"I know. I'm afraid I have a few more questions to ask her."

"It's not right to keep on at her like this!"

"It can't be helped. We have a job to do. Mrs. Jessup may be able to help us catch a murderer. You wouldn't want to leave him running around, would you?"

"No-o. Long as you don't think the poor lady did it." Enid changed her tack. "I hope as my sister's giving satisfaction, sir?"

"Absolutely." He assumed he'd have heard from Daisy if she wasn't.

"She didn't tell me nothing about this dead body she found," the maid said resentfully, "her and the little dog. Not till after the police came here and I knew anyway, she didn't."

"I'm glad to hear it." From a police point of view, Elsie was definitely giving satisfaction if she'd managed to hold her

tongue in such circumstances. "She had strict instructions not to talk about it and would have been in serious trouble if she had. Did Mrs. Jessup instruct you not to let us in?"

"Oh no, sir, it just doesn't seem right."

"Then be a good girl and tell her we're here to see her."

"Beg pardon, I'm sure." The girl allowed them across the threshold and went off up the stairs.

His gaze following her, Alec saw at the top of the first flight a most attractive painting of a vineyard, a grape-harvest scene, in the French Impressionist style. Hanging there, it was at the perfect distance for proper appreciation, and he allowed himself to be distracted for a moment.

He tore himself away. He needed to put his thoughts in order and he didn't know how quickly Mrs. Jessup would put in an appearance.

"D'ye know Mrs. Jessup well, Chief?" Mackinnon asked.

"I've met her three or four times, but always in passing or in a social setting."

Where, he thought, it was impossible to gauge anything but her social proficiency, and that she had aplenty: charming, good-looking (well preserved, one might say, but he disliked the phrase, with its suggestion of mummification), well dressed and groomed, and an excellent hostess.

"Best face forward, as you might say," Mackinnon suggested.

"She's always seemed very pleasant. Bear in mind the fact that she was a serious actress." The ability to project unreal emotions was a skill like riding a bicycle—once learnt, never wholly forgotten. "Mrs. Fletcher likes her," Alec continued, "and she knows her much better than I do. However, she's been acquainted with her for only a few weeks, and I gather she spent more time with the daughter-in-law, Audrey, than with Mrs. Jessup herself."

True, Daisy always expected to like people. At the same time, she was a fairly shrewd judge of character. She would disregard minor flaws and quirks, but face her with people like the Bennetts . . .

After that first meeting on the Heath, Daisy had looked for an excuse for Mr. Bennett's rudeness. After the party, she had written him and his sister off as irredeemable. Though he didn't suspect them of murder, Alec had a nasty feeling they were going to cause problems.

Mrs. Jessup, on the other hand, was likable. The trouble was, the most likable and otherwise-admirable people frequently had—or imagined they had—reasons for trying to bamboozle the police. On present evidence, Mrs. Jessup's reasons might be sound.

Enid came down. "If you'll come this way, sir, madam will be with you in a minute." She turned towards the back of the house.

Alec had been shown the Versailles room on the occasion of the Jessups' party for the neighbours. He remembered well its startling, bewildering effect. He wondered whether Mrs. Jessup had chosen to see Tom therein. Tom hadn't mentioned it, but with Daisy constantly interrupting his report, that was hardly surprising. Bedazzlement might explain why he had extracted less information from the interview than Alec expected of his right-hand man. The endless mirrored reflections were confusing and distracting. How could one concentrate on a person's expression when she was repeated ad infinitum in all directions? Alec did not intend to be lured into a similar situation.

Instead of following the girl, he opened the door to the drawing room and said firmly, "We'll see Mrs. Jessup in here."

She turned back. "Oh, but—"

"I don't mind if you haven't dusted yet."

"Of course I've dusted!" she said, bridling. "Hours ago."

"Then we needn't worry." He went on into the room, Mackinnon at his heels.

Another painting caught his eye, a bar scene in the style of Renoir. In the crush of people at the party, he hadn't noticed the pictures on the walls. This one was quite small, so he went closer to have a good look. He didn't know much about art, and

most of what he did know was about the artists of the period he had studied, Gainsborough (of the Gardens) and Constable (of the Circle) among them. He had no idea what Impressionists sold for in these days of Cubism, Surrealism, Expressionism, or whatever the latest fad might be, but he recalled a terrific fuss when a couple had been stolen. Presumably they were valuable.

"The real thing, d'ye reckon, Chief?"

"It's not a print. It could be a good copy, or 'after the school of Renoir,' but I'm inclined to think it genuine. The wine business must be much more lucrative than I had imagined."

Or Jessup & Sons had made a huge profit on a cargo or two to America.

"Could be Mr. Jessup's father or grandfather picked it up for a song before the Impressionists became popular, on one of their business trips."

"You know a lot about art?"

"Nay, not me. I'm one of those people the connoisseurs despise: I know what I like."

Alec laughed. "That's about my level. I like this, and the subject might well appeal to a wine merchant!"

When Mrs. Jessup joined them, she showed no sign of being ruffled by his change of venue. She didn't even mention it, as would have been natural, which made him suspect that she was, in fact, disturbed. If so, she hid it well.

"More questions, Mr. Fletcher? Do sit down, both of you," she said, taking a chair by the fireplace. She held out her hands to the flames as if chilled, though a pair of radiators made the room quite warm.

"This is Detective Sergeant Mackinnon, Mrs. Jessup. He's here just to take notes, so that there can no misunderstanding later about what was said." Also to dispel any suggestion that this was a friendly chat between neighbours.

She nodded to the sergeant and turned back to Alec. "This is a dreadful business!"

"Murder is always dreadful."

"It's . . . You're quite sure it was murder? Yes, of course; the other sergeant said you're certain it was not an accident."

"So it would appear."

"And not random. Not a robbery, that is, or a madman."

"We can never rule out a madman, Mrs. Jessup, but in this case, it seems highly unlikely."

"So we needn't be afraid to leave the house, for fear of meeting a like fate?" she asked, wide-eyed.

Alec was taken by surprise. If he were not already fairly sure that one or more members of her family were involved, the question would tend to disarm suspicion. In the actual circumstances, it made him wonder whether whatever had happened had somehow been kept from her.

Or was it a calculated, subtle plan to throw him off balance, and if so, was the subtlety hers, her husband's, or that of one of her sons? The best way to find out, he decided, was not to ask questions but to get her talking.

"You're more likely to be run down in the street by a careless motorist than attacked by a madman," he assured her. "I gather you had a busy evening yesterday. Tell me about it."

Her face lit up. Alec could see her as Nerissa, reunited with Gratiano, as Hero, exonerated and reunited with Claudio, but it was no young lover she had awaited; it was her son. "Patrick came home!" she said joyfully. No hint of unease marred her delight. "My younger son—no doubt you've heard he was travelling?"

She paused. Alec looked at her attentively but did not speak. For the first time, a shadow of anxiety crossed her face. Silence must be peculiarly difficult for actors to bear, he thought. In the theatre, it usually meant someone had fluffed his lines.

At any rate, only a few seconds passed before Mrs. Jessup resumed. "I was rather worried about him. Silly, really. He's not a boy anymore. But I must admit I was quite annoyed, when at last he came home, to find he'd stopped in at a public house on the way from Euston. As though we didn't have here any drink

he could possibly want! Young men can be very thoughtless, can't they?"

She stopped again, and again Alec provided no answer.

"And then, to top it all, instead of all the family under one roof for a change, Aidan decided he couldn't postpone his business up north any longer. He dashed off to catch the night express from St. Pancras."

St. Pancras was a terminus for trains to the North, but also for boat trains to Tilbury. If Aidan had run for the Continent, he'd have been well on his way across the Channel by the time Castellano's body was found. The family had plenty of acquaintances on the other side to give him shelter.

Or was Mrs. Jessup's mention of St. Pancras a bit of "corroborative detail intended to lend verisimilitude to an otherwise bald and unconvincing narrative," à la *Mikado*? The whole exposition was beginning to sound like a well-rehearsed speech, and who better to memorise and deliver it than the ex-actress! The Jessups couldn't rely on Audrey to be word-perfect, so Audrey went to her sister's—assuming that was really where she had fled—as Mrs. Jessup was now relating.

She hadn't told him anything she had not already told Tom. In this case, perhaps direct questioning was the better way to go.

"What is the sister's name and address?" he asked, glancing at Mackinnon to make sure he was ready to take down the information in black and white.

"Her name is Vivien . . . Oh dear, I simply can't remember her surname." She gave a faint smile. "I suppose I'll have to pronounce those hateful words, 'I'm not as young as I was.' I refuse to believe one's memory fails. It just gets so cluttered, one can't find the needed fact. Enid shall fetch my address book."

She rang the bell and sent the parlour maid to find the address book in the bureau in her bedroom.

While they waited, Alec asked, "Does your daughter-in-law often visit her sister?"

"Every autumn, when Aidan has to travel on business. Au-

drey and Vivien are quite close, as their mother died young, but Aidan has nothing in common with Vivien's husband, so it works out very well."

The regularity and timing of the visits would be easy to check with the servants, so that was probably true. "Why did Aidan leave so abruptly, when his brother had just returned after a lengthy absence? Did they quarrel?"

For the first time, she looked disconcerted. She hadn't expected the question. Tom had asked the servants and been satisfied with their answer.

"Patrick and Aidan quarrel with each other?" She frowned. She not only hadn't expected the question, she didn't like it one little bit. "No, they've been good friends since childhood. Just the occasional squabble. You know how siblings are."

"I was an only child," Alec said woodenly, further disconcerting her.

"Oh, I'm sorry. And your two aren't old enough . . ." She remembered Mackinnon's presence and veered away from a cosy chat about the twins. "My sons do have the odd disagreement, inevitably. I find it hard to believe they had a . . . fight in the short time they were both here. But I wasn't with them every second, of course."

Apparently, she had decided on the spur of the moment that it might be advantageous to leave open the possibility that Aidan and Patrick had quarrelled, even come to blows. The obvious inference was that Aidan had sustained some presumably minor injury in his encounter with Castellano and had fled because the marks could not be hidden. But in that case, his mother must surely have noticed when she said good-bye, even if she had not witnessed her sons' putative battle. Alec wondered how long it would take her to realise that her red herring would not fly, to coin a phrase.

He had to assume Aidan was still in England and track him down before the bruises faded. A hired car and driver might be traceable, with the driver possibly ringing up to report daily. All they had to do was find the car-hire firm.

"Sergeant Tring tells me Aidan has the only list of customers he's gone to call on, but no doubt he mentioned where he intended to start out, which city he took a railway ticket to."

A mantle of vagueness settled over her. Like Tom, Alec wished he had seen her on the stage.

"Oh . . . No, I don't believe he told me. As he was not going to stay, there wouldn't have been any point, would there?"

"I dare say not, but I'm sure his father or brother must know. I'll ask when I see them here this evening."

There was nothing stagy about her passionate plea. "No, not here! If the Bennetts see you haunting the house, they'll make up some horrible story, and half the neighbours will believe it!"

"You have a point," Alec acknowledged wryly. "I'll make arrangements to see them at their place of business, after hours."

"Mr. Fletcher, why are you hounding us? Why are you hunting down Aidan? He hasn't done anything wrong. None of us has."

"Then you have nothing to worry about. Except the Bennetts. But a man has been murdered, and that man is known to have associated with your family, however briefly or unwillingly on your part. Would you have the police ignore it? I can ask to be relieved of the job, but whoever might take my place will follow the same trail."

"No. No, I'd rather have you, I suppose."

"What was Michele Castellano's business with your husband?"

"I don't know. I only know that Maurice didn't want anything to do with him." She turned with relief to Enid, who came in carrying a small green leather-bound book.

"Sorry I've been so long, madam. It wasn't where you said, in the cubbyhole. I found it in the top drawer."

"That's all right, Enid. Thank you." She took the address book and started to riffle through it as the maid went out. "The one thing I'm certain of is that Vivien lives in Lincoln-

shire, in or near some small village. Funny, I can't find a single Lincs address. *X Y Z*. Nothing." She turned back to the beginning.

"Allow me." Alec rose to take the book, and continued to stand, examining each page swiftly but with care. Most of Mrs. Jessup's friends and acquaintances lived in London and the Home Counties, with a few, very likely relatives, in Ireland. Almost all of the latter were in the Six Counties, he noted, rather than the Free State. Not that Northern Ireland lacked disaffected citizens.

He found no addresses in Lincolnshire, no one named Vivien or listed with the initial *V*, and no sign of a page torn out. Closing the book, he handed it back. "That's a pity."

"I suppose I've always been able to ask Audrey for the address if I needed it, though, to tell the truth, I can't remember ever having written to Vivien, nor can I imagine why I ever should. Sending kind regards via Audrey has always been perfectly adequate."

Alec felt he was wasting his time with her. "One last question, for the present," he said. "Where—"

"Not another word!" Mr. Irwin burst into the room. "My dear Moira, I hope you haven't been answering questions. You cannot be required to do so. Mr. Fletcher, I am shocked to find you questioning Mrs. Jessup without her solicitor present. It's against all the rules."

"On the contrary, sir. As I have absolutely no intention of arresting Mrs. Jessup, it's her duty as a citizen to aid the police in a murder enquiry."

"In any case, Jonathan, I'm afraid I've been most unhelpful to Mr. Fletcher. I don't seem to know anything he wants to know."

Irwin regarded Alec with suspicion. "What have you been asking, Chief Inspector? I'm sure it's most irregular."

"I was about to ask one last question. May I proceed?"

"I suppose so," he said grudgingly. "Now that I'm here."

"Mrs. Jessup, where has your younger son been these past weeks, and on what business?"

The solicitor turned apoplectic red and his mouth opened and closed several times, but no words emerged.

"Patrick's been in America," said Mrs. Jessup with the utmost calm. "Something to do with exporting 'the demon rum' to the deprived citizens of that country. I'm assured that no English laws have been broken in the process. Jonathan, you look as if you'd better sit down at once. Let me get you a whisky."

"My dear Moira! Law is Law! And these are policemen!"

She guided the horrified man to a chair and went to the drinks cabinet.

"I'm sure you'll feel better for a whisky, sir," Alec said soothingly. "In the meantime, I'd be grateful for your daughter Vivien's surname and address."

It was Mrs. Jessup's turn to look appalled. She froze with the decanter in her hand. Her reaction suggested Audrey really had gone to her sister's, not abroad. Alec breathed a silent sigh of relief.

Irwin looked merely astonished. "What can Vivien possibly have to do with a murder in London? She married a farmer called Bessemer. West Dyke Farm, Butterwick, near Boston." Noticing Mackinnon writing down the name and address, he clarified: "That's the Lincolnshire Boston, not the American one. Vivien has no connection with America whatsoever. Nor does her husband."

"I'm glad to hear it, sir. Do you happen to remember the telephone number?"

"They're not on the telephone."

"Thank you." Alec glanced at Mrs. Jessup. She had regained her self-possession and was pouring whisky with a steady hand, though Irwin no longer appeared to be in need of fortification. Perhaps she intended to drink it herself. "May I ask what brought you here?"

"An impertinent telephone call from one of the neighbours,"

Irwin said angrily. "He advised me that the entire family was about to be arrested for murder. Naturally, I hurried to my daughter's assistance."

Alec and Mrs. Jessup exchanged a look. Simultaneously they said, "Mr. Bennett."

EIGHTEEN

Returning home, Alec arrived with Mackinnon just in time to follow the parlour maid into the dining room.

"Tea, please, Elsie," said Daisy.

"How many for, madam?" the parlour maid enquired pointedly.

Daisy looked at Alec.

"Six," he said. "Tom may not be back for a while, and Piper certainly won't."

"I'll come and help you carry the tray, miss," offered Warren. "If that's all right, sir?"

Elsie looked mollified. Daisy gave Warren a grateful smile. His assistance might serve to avert mutiny in the kitchen.

Alec waved his permission and the two went out.

"Ross?"

"Miss Bennett's friend exists, sir. I talked to all the servants. None of 'em's been there more than a few months, and none of 'em's planning to stay more'n a few months, but as long as they've been there, she's spent a day or two each month with a Miss Lagerquist. They saw the lady a couple of months ago, in the summer, when she came in a hired car to pick up Miss Bennett for a

jaunt in the country. There was some argument as to was it July or August, but they all agreed it happened."

"I don't suppose you asked whether this is the usual time of the month?"

"I did, and it is, and she told 'em yesterday she wouldn't be in for lunch or dinner today."

"Good work," said Alec, "even if it's not the answer I'd hoped for. Ardmore?"

"No trouble with Mr. Lambert's landlady, sir. She went up to his room with me and pointed out all the stuff he usually takes with him when he goes away for a night or two. She cleans a couple of times a week, so she's had a good nose around and knows exactly how many pairs of socks he owns, and how many pairs of under— Begging your pardon, Mrs. Fletcher! And what's at the laundry, too."

"All right, we don't need a list of every item of clothing he possesses! The conclusion is that he didn't plan his departure."

"That's right, sir. He's never gone off without warning like this before, seemingly. Proper worried about him is Mrs. Hodge."

"Daisy, you know him best. What do you think would make him dash off without his traps?"

"The slightest hope of getting mixed up in some sort of havey-cavey business where he could use what he fondly imagines to be his undercover skills. I'm worried about him, too, Alec. If the Jessups' connection with bootlegging isn't utter piffle, then Lambert was on the scent."

"It's not utter piffle," said Alec. "Mrs. Jessup admitted it."

"She didn't!"

"It's not illegal here, as she pointed out."

"Then Patrick was in America?"

"He was. She must have realised we had only to ask to see his passport to find that out. Of more immediate use to us, Mr. Irwin gave me Audrey's sister's address. Mackinnon, I'm going to send you to take a statement from her—from Mrs. Aidan, that is. The children's nurse, as well. What we need most is

Aidan's whereabouts. But who knows, it's always possible one of them will provide some revelation about what happened last night."

"Aye, sir."

"Ring up the Boston police and request a car and driver to take you to the farm. You'd better get going. Goodness only knows how you get to Boston."

"Mrs. Jessup said it's two changes. There's a *Bradshaw's* in the drawer of the little table beside the phone," Daisy told Mackinnon.

The detective sergeant met Elsie and Warren in the doorway and stood back to let them through. He cast a longing glance at the tea trays as he disappeared.

No biscuits, Daisy noticed sadly. She poured a cup and said to Elsie, "Take this to Mr. Mackinnon, at the telephone, please."

"Yes'm." Elsie took the cup and saucer and added with a touch of belligerence, "If you please, madam, Mrs. Dobson wants to know how many for dinner."

"Alec?"

"Just the two of us. Or possibly just Mrs. Fletcher, Elsie. I'll try to get back in time. I'm going to see Jessup and Patrick at the shop after all. Mrs. Jessup pointed out that to keep going in and out of their house will just add grist to the Bennetts' mill. Though there will be enough coming and going if Tom gets those warrants. . . ."

"Couldn't you just have asked her to let you search?" Daisy handed cups of tea to each of the men.

"Not once Irwin turned up. To ask and be refused would just give warning, give them the opportunity to clear everything up thoroughly."

"They had time to do that before the body was even found, sir," said Ardmore.

"True, but in the flurry and scurry of getting Aidan away, they may not have thought of it, and they could hardly do much today, under the eyes of the servants."

"On the contrary," said Daisy, "the absence of both Audrey

and Aidan and the children would give them the opportunity for a grand turnout of their rooms and the nursery. And what more natural than that Mrs. Jessup should take a look around first to make sure any valuables are safe, and to see what needs doing?"

"Dash it, Daisy, you're right. We'll just have to hope they don't get to it till tomorrow. Now. Ross, you'll come with me to Jessup and Sons. Ardmore, it's a late night for you. You'll help Sergeant Tring search next door, and then, if you don't find out where Aidan took a ticket to, you can be off to St. Pancras to see if we can trace him there. Mrs. Jessup gave me a photograph of him." He handed it over. "Mr. Irwin simply couldn't think of a reason why she shouldn't."

"He's about as ordinary-looking as a bloke can get," said Ardmore in dismay.

"Just do your best. I don't want to have to ask every big-city force in the North to make enquiries at every car-hire firm near their main stations. We may get his destination at the shop, but I don't want to wait."

"Can't trust 'em to tell the truth anyways," Warren pointed out.

"What are you going to do about Lambert's disappearance?" Daisy demanded.

"Circulate a description. Why don't you write one out for me?"

"Right-oh." Daisy turned to a fresh page of her notebook, glad that being a journalist meant she always had one available when needed for police business.

It was a pity Lambert had been in England long enough for his very American haircut to have grown out. He still kept his fair hair cropped very short, but in an English way. Horn-rimmed glasses, American-cut clothes, and an American accent were pretty distinctive, though. Unfortunately, the face behind the spectacles was about as ordinary as Aidan's. "Never mole, hare-lip, nor scar, nor mark prodigious" to make him either "despised in nativity" or instantly recognisable.

Concentrating, Daisy missed Alec's instructions to Warren. As she tore off the sheet and slid it across the table to him, Mackinnon came in.

"There's a train I can catch if I leave right away, Chief, but I willna get to Boston till after nine. They're booking a room for me and they'll take me out to the farm. Should I go this evening or wait till tomorrow morning?"

"Farm people generally retire early. Better wait till the morning. It won't make much odds. When you get to Boston, ring up for the latest developments here."

"Right, sir." He turned towards the door, then swung back. "I'll be forgetting my own head next. Mr. Tring rang up while I was looking up the trains. He says he has the warrants and he's on his way here."

"Excellent. I hope he's springing for a taxi, as you may if you need to. Go catch your train." As Mackinnon went out, Alec consulted his wristwatch. "Five o'clock. I want to go and see what visibility is like in the garden."

"The sky's cleared," said Daisy. "It's lighter today than yesterday. By the way, what time did Mr. Whitcomb walk up through the garden yesterday on his way home from work?"

"Who went to the Whitcombs? Number seven."

"Number seven?" Warren thumbed unhappily through his notebook. "DS Mackinnon and me, sir. Mr. Whitcomb wasn't there, and we only asked did he mention seeing anything out of the ordinary. We knew we'd have to try again this evening to talk to all the gentlemen as was off at work."

"I'd forgotten that," Alec said ruefully. "I need more men! You're right, Daisy. Even if Whitcomb saw nothing, the time he didn't see it may help pin things down. Let's see. . . . Tom had better—"

The telephone bell rang in the hall.

"Warren." Alec jerked his thumb towards the door and the eyebrowless detective constable hurried out. "Ardmore, Ross, come outside and we'll check what can be seen from where."

They followed Warren out to the hall. Daisy sat on for a

moment, wondering why Alec was being so obliging about letting her join their conclaves. True, she knew the Jessups better than he did, but such was usually the case when she found herself enmeshed in one of his investigations. In fact, that was almost always why she was involved in the first place. Yet usually he strove to exclude her. Though she felt she had made one or two helpful suggestions, she found it hard to believe he had suddenly realised the inestimable value of her assistance.

There was no understanding it. With a shrug, she went after the men.

She was just in time to hear Warren call Alec back from the front steps. He stood at the rear of the hall, holding the telephone receiver at the full length of the wire and his arm.

"Sir, it's DC Piper. He's talked to three booze sellers, two wholesale, one retail on a large scale. They all recognised Castellano's photo and Lambert's name, though one of 'em tried to deny it. Castellano came to their houses, not their business places, trying to coerce them into shipping to the U.S. Then Lambert came along to the business, claiming to represent the U.S. government and warning them of dire consequences if they did. Half a mo— What's that?" he said, stepping back to the telephone under the stairs.

"So Castellano *was* a bootlegger!" Alec exclaimed. He sent Ross and Ardmore out, shutting the front door after them against an icy draught. As he turned back, Warren reappeared, receiver at arm's length.

"Do you want him to go on, sir? Seems there's a list as long as your arm."

"Not now. Tell him to meet me at Jessup and Sons at quarter past six."

Warren retreated again. After a brief muffled colloquy, he once again reappeared, without the receiver this time.

"Get this, sir: Piper says one of the blokes is already exporting to America. At least, he admits he's sent one smallish shipment. Castellano tried to bully him into selling to a diff'rent gang over there. He says he told Mr. Lambert he didn't want to

get mixed up in a battle between gangs and he was getting out of the transatlantic trade."

"Good heavens," said Daisy, "Lambert won one. If only by default!"

Daisy went off upstairs to visit the twins.

Leaving Warren to man the phone, Alec went out. As Daisy had said, the clouds had cleared. In the west, the sky was still pale blue; a cold wind blustered, already drying out and scattering the neatly raked piles of fallen leaves. He wished he had put on his overcoat. He nearly went back for it, but his men were waiting. It had been a long day and the end was not in sight.

Far from clarifying matters, Ernie Piper's report amounted to confusion worse confounded. It meant Castellano had had a motive for killing Lambert, yet Castellano was the one who had ended up dead.

Self-defence? The bootleggers' emissary had been done in with cool deliberation. Pending the autopsy report, Alec reminded himself. Ridgeway had been pretty certain, though.

Alec was utterly unable to see Lambert as a cold-blooded murderer, or even a hot-blooded one, except by mistake.

And where did the Jessups come into all this?

Time enough to puzzle over that when Tom arrived. For the moment, Alec was glad of something practical to do.

Ross and Ardmore were down by the fountain, in the centre of the garden. He could see them quite clearly from his own front steps. There was a lamp standard opposite the house, at the top of the path, and another at the bottom, but none in the middle. He was pretty sure he wouldn't recognise the men from here if he didn't know who they were. The glow of their cigarettes was not visible, though he could tell from their gestures that both were smoking.

The Bennetts had field glasses, of course. Alec wondered whether they had really seen anything.

He waved. The motion caught the eye of Ross, the taller of the two. He waved back. They went round to the far side of the fountain, nearer to the trail where the body had been dragged across the lawn. There followed an ambiguous melée. Alec had told them to do whatever came to mind, as they didn't know what had really happened. He could make out that they were involved in a struggle, but not exactly what was going on. Then one dropped to the ground. The other followed suit.

The first was supposed to lie on his back, the second to kneel over him, hands to throat. What with the twilight, the marble maiden with her urn, and the eighteen-inch-high rim of the pool, Alec could only assume they were sticking to his orders.

By the time he reached them, both were standing again, Ardmore brushing himself off.

"Get down again. I want to take another look from below."

"Have a heart, sir," protested Ardmore. "It's bloody freezing lying on the flagstones."

"It's Ross's turn. You can just freeze your knees. Wait till I get down to the lamppost."

From the bottom of the slope, though Alec made allowances for the deepening dusk, the scene was even less intelligible. He could see the kneeling figure silhouetted against the pale marble and the paving beyond, but Ross, lying on the flat at just about his eye level, was virtually invisible.

Alec looked back at the Bennetts' house. Their ground floor was only a couple of steps above street level. The view from their first floor, however, would be considerably better than his own from down here.

The best he could do was to take anything they said with a pinch of salt. Perhaps they'd decide they didn't have anything to say after all.

He walked back up.

"Any help, sir?" asked Ross.

"Not really. Certainly not enough to narrow the time frame.

I take it you could see each other well enough to proceed with whatever nefarious business took your respective fancies?"

"Easy," Ardmore averred.

"It'll have to be tried again in full darkness, when the only light comes from the streetlamps. Does either of you know whether there's a moon tonight?"

"Quarter moon," said Ross promptly, "rises after midnight."

"Perfect. How do you know?"

"I'm a sort of amateur astronomer, sir," Ross explained as they walked up the hill. "Very amateur. My great-uncle left me his telescope. Trouble is, you can't see much in London skies, what with smoke and fog and clouds, but I keep a track of the moon's phases, in case there's a good viewing night. You'd be surprised how often knowing comes in handy."

"Good for you. I hope that's Sergeant Tring," Alec said, lengthening his stride as a taxi pulled up in front of number 6.

The cab rose perceptibly on its springs as its passenger climbed out. Definitely Tom.

When they reached the pavement, he had just paid off the cabbie. "Hope that'll go down on expenses, Chief."

"Certainly. I ought to have told you to take a taxi if you were successful."

"Right here in my pocket, Chief." Tom patted the relevant part of his extensive anatomy. "Signed, sealed, and delivered."

They went into the house. Warren's scarlet face peered out from his telephone cubby.

"Any phone calls?"

"Not a whisper, sir."

"Did my wife come down yet?"

"No, sir."

Heavy Teutonic thoughts of *Kinder, Küche, Kirche* crossed Alec's mind. But much as she loved the babies, Daisy could barely boil an egg and was by no means a regular churchgoer. Besides, she was occasionally helpful in his work, and he was a modern husband, content to allow her hers. Still, he didn't send someone up to invite her to join them.

"All right, Warren, you'd better come and listen to this. Leave the door open in case the telephone rings."

They went into the dining room. Tom extricated the search warrants from an inner pocket and spread them on the table. "I managed to get hold of old Fanshawe," he said. "He'd give you a warrant to search Buckingham Palace if you asked him nicely."

Alec looked them over. "Very good. Tom, you'll take Ardmore next door. Ross will go with me, and Piper's meeting us in New Bond Street at six-fifteen. I have to interview the Jessups, *père et fils*. The search there will concentrate on their papers, so Ernie's the best one for that. We have a Yard car, but we'll have to leave in a minute, so let's fill you in quickly on what you've missed. Discussion will have to wait until tomorrow."

He gave a succinct exposition of the results of their enquiries to date. Ross, Ardmore, and Warren also listened closely, he was pleased to see. "Have I missed anything?" he asked them.

Ross spoke up. "About Sergeant Mackinnon going to Lincolnshire after the young lady, sir?"

"Thank you. Yes, he's on his way. It's not to be mentioned to any of the rest of the family. Apparently, there's no telephone at the farm, but I don't want to risk their somehow getting a message to Audrey Jessup. Tom, just run through what you'll be looking for next door."

"Most important, I reckon, Chief, is clues to just what happened last night, though what they might be is anyone's guess. Also, any indication of where Mr. Aidan went. Some sort of weapon Castellano could've been hit with—that'll be difficult till we get a better description from the pathologist."

"And Castellano's gun," put in Ardmore.

"Ah!" said Tom. "That'd put the cat among the pigeons, right enough!"

"Wait till half past six," said Alec, ignoring the ring of the telephone, which Warren dashed to answer. "Ask permission to search before you start waving the warrant. If I'm not back

when you're finished, go round the Circle and see if you can catch those who were out this morning. And have another go at the visibility question—Ardmore, you can explain that to Mr. Tring. Warren's to stick to the telephone. When you get home tonight, Tom, you'll have to present my apologies to Mrs. Tring! Come along, Ross; we'd better get a move on."

They went out to the hall. Daisy was coming down the stairs. She waved and called, "Are you leaving? Toodle-oo, darling. See you—"

"Sir!" Warren popped out of the cubby. "Sir, it's Superintendent Crane, and he doesn't sound too happy!"

NINETEEN

"*Oh Lord!* I can't talk to the Super now," Alec groaned. "Daisy, tell him I've left, will you, and see what he wants now."

"Me!" said Daisy in ungrammatical outrage.

But her outrage was wasted on the closing front door. With a sigh, she went to the telephone.

"Spitting fire!" Warren warned her, disappearing into the safe haven of the dining room.

She picked up the phone, held the receiver at what she hoped was a safe distance from her ear, and raised the transmitter to her mouth. "Mr. Crane?" she said cautiously.

"Who the . . . ?" Even at arm's length, his bellow was deafening. "Mrs. Fletcher?" The voice moderated, and Daisy ventured to move the receiver towards her ear. "This is Crane. I must speak to your husband."

"I'm afraid he isn't here, Superintendent. I believe he's gone to interview some suspects. Can I help you?"

"I'm not sure anyone can," he said bitterly. "But you can transmit a message to Fletcher, if you would be so kind."

"Of course, Mr. Crane. Just let me get something to write on." She had left her notebook in the dining room, but there

was always a pad in the drawer of the telephone table, and usually a sharpened pencil. Yes, here they were. She sat down, so that she could set the daffodil phone on the table and have a hand free to write. "Right-oh, go ahead."

"I have just had an extremely uncomfortable interview with the Assistant Commissioner. He, in turn, had just received an extremely uncomfortable telephone call from the Home Secretary. You are aware, I dare say, Mrs. Fletcher, that the Home Secretary oversees all of this country's police forces?"

"Yes." Daisy might not know much of politics, but she could hardly help knowing that, being married to a fairly senior policeman. She stopped trying to scribble down every word, realising that Crane was blowing off steam as much as trying to convey important information.

"The Home Secretary," he continued, "had just spoken—or perhaps I should say 'been spoken to'—by the Foreign Secretary."

"This is beginning to sound like *The House That Jack Built*," Daisy said unwisely, and went on to compound her error. "It's Oliver's favourite book at the moment."

There was an ominous silence at the other end of the line. Then: "This, Mrs. Fletcher, is *nothing* like *The House That Jack Built*, which, as I recall, has a happy ending. If I may continue . . . The Foreign Secretary had just received a telephone call from His Excellency, the Ambassador of the United States of America."

Daisy managed just in time to stop herself saying brightly, "I expect they talk to each other quite often." For some reason, Superintendent Crane's grimness was making her feel more frivolous than she had felt since Nana found the body that morning. Who, she wondered, had told the ambassador what? No doubt she was about to be informed. "U.S. Amb.," she wrote down.

"The embassy," Crane continued relentlessly, "had received a cable from the State Department, which, I gather, is their equivalent of our Foreign Office. The State Department had

received an enquiry from the Federal Bureau of Investigation—to be precise, from your husband's friends at the Federal Bureau of Investigation—regarding a certain American passport."

"Castellano's. Michele Castellano's."

"Oh, so there's a name attached, is there?" The superintendent's gloom seemed to have lifted a little. At least he had some information to pass back along the chain. "Would you mind spelling that? You see, the FBI had only a number, and it happens to be the number of a passport that was stolen, along with several more blanks."

"It was faked?" said Daisy. "That would explain the ink."

"*Ink!*" exploded from the receiver. "No, don't tell me. I don't want to know. Or rather, Fletcher can explain when he reports at eight o'clock tomorrow morning. On the dot."

"I'll make sure to set the alarm clock. But Mr. Crane, why—"

"The Americans take as serious a view as we do of the sacrosanct nature of passports. Naturally, the State Department wanted to know why Scotland Yard had asked the FBI about a stolen passport. They asked the embassy, and the embassy wanted to know why they had not been notified that the police had found an American passport. How it reached the ambassador's august ears, I have no idea, but he, naturally, approached the Foreign Office and—"

"Please, let's not go back through the whole rigmarole! I'm sure Alec had very good reasons not to get in touch with the embassy right away, which no doubt he'll explain to you tomorrow."

"He'd better! I authorised the damn—dashed cable he sent to the FBI. I could swear he told me the U.S. embassy would have to be notified. Surely he didn't expect *me* to do so, with no information! I ought to have my head examined. I want to know what it's all about."

"He's been rushed off his feet all day, and he's still working," she reminded him. "I'll give him your message."

"Is he getting anywhere?"

"You'll have to ask him, Mr. Crane," Daisy said demurely. "You know he doesn't like me to get involved."

"*Pah!*"

Daisy was sure only the courtesy due to the offspring of a viscount enabled the superintendent to say a choked good-bye before he hung up. She wondered whether she ought to have told him Lambert was missing. But no, it would only mean more fuss if he felt obliged to notify the AC and the AC notified . . . et cetera.

She had scarcely replaced the receiver on its hook when the bell rang again. Sighing, she picked it up again and said, "Hampstead three nine one three."

"This is the Scotland Yard exchange," said an impersonal female voice. "May I speak to DCI Fletcher, please?"

"He's not here, I'm afraid. May I take a message? This is Mrs. Fletcher."

"Mrs. Fletcher!" The change in tone was obvious. Daisy was famous at the Yard—or infamous, depending on how high up the hierarchy one went—as the wife who kept falling over bodies. Sometimes her fame was useful, sometimes the reverse. "I have a cable for the chief inspector, from New York. He left a message to let him know at once. Shall I read it out?"

"Yes, please." Daisy tore the top sheet off the pad. "Not too fast."

" 'Mitcheel'—spelt *M I C H E L E*—'Castellano,' open quotes, 'enforcer,' close quotes, 'for Luckcheese'—spelt *L U C C H E S E*—'family bootlegger gang,' stop, 'delighted news Rosenblatt NYDA.' Got that, Mrs. Fletcher?"

"Got it. Thanks."

District Attorney Rosenblatt. She and Alec had saved him from making a serious mistake a couple of years ago. Now, apparently, he was pleased to learn that they had found a New York gangster dead in London.

What was an "enforcer"? American gangs must be alarmingly well organised if they had rules to be enforced.

Daisy decided she didn't really want to know how they did their enforcing. "Tough guys," she recalled Lambert mentioning when regretting the loss of his gun. "Guys"—plural. Could there be others of Castellano's ilk in England?

Alec ought to have the information as soon as possible. She glanced at the long-case clock. He would still be on the way to New Bond Street. If she waited till he reached the shop to ring up, she'd probably interrupt his interrogation of the Jessups. He hated having interviews interrupted. Too bad, the news would have to wait till he came home.

"What happened to Castellano's gun?" Alec pondered aloud as Ross drove down the hill.

"I don't know, sir. I think maybe I missed a bit, coming in later than the others like I did. He was wearing a shoulder holster?"

"With no gun in it. Suppose Castellano drew the gun, either to threaten his assailant or in self-defence. Why did the murderer not simply put it back in the holster, thus eliminating a link between him and his victim?"

There was silence while Ross negotiated the tricky five-way intersection in Camden Town, competing with four omnibuses and half a dozen taxis. Safely buzzing down Albany Street, he said, "Prob'ly he wasn't thinking too clearly, sir."

"He was thinking very clearly when he pressed his thumbs on exactly the right spots in Castellano's throat. He knew what he was doing all right. Let's say the gun got lost in a struggle and the darkness prevented his finding the damn thing. Why didn't we find it next morning in broad daylight, in the course of an intensive search?"

Again, Ross had the excuse of traffic and the even more complicated multiple intersection of streets at the southeast corner of Regent's Park. Having made it safely into Great Portland Street, he ventured, "I s'pose they looked in that pond thing?"

"Raked it out thoroughly. Can you think of any conceivable reason why Castellano might have gone out wearing the holster, an uncomfortable contraption, without his gun?"

"No, sir."

Nor could Alec. Customs might have confiscated Castellano's gun when he entered the country—did Customs keep records of such things?—but unless he'd managed to acquire another, he'd have packed away the holster. And if he'd managed to acquire a gun, the question remained: Where was it?

Customs had confiscated Lambert's gun, to that young idiot's disgust. Lambert had disappeared. Castellano's gun had disappeared. Had Alec completely misread Lambert's character?

He shook his head. Lambert was a young idiot, but no cold-blooded killer. Which left the Jessups.

Oxford Street, left into New Bond Street, and then Ross pulled alongside the kerb just beyond Jessup & Sons, Purveyors of Fine Wines and Spirits. The fashionable shops were still open, though most of their clientele would be people of leisure, able to shop earlier in the day. The biting wind whistling down the street was icy enough to deter pedestrians, and passersby were few.

The nearest plate-glass shop window, next door to the Jessups', displayed five skeletally thin celluloid mannequins elegantly posed in jewel-toned, elaborately beaded silk with jagged hemlines. They looked to Alec as if sharks had been at them. Not for the first time, he thanked heaven that Daisy didn't care two hoots about the latest modes.

In the Jessups' window stood a rustic pergola with artificial vines climbing it. The bunches of purple grapes peeping coyly from among the vine leaves looked like trimmings for an Edwardian hat. Under the pergola stood an equally rustic wooden table and three chairs, and on the table were three wineglasses and two bottles. It was a most inviting scene, though probably the bottles were empty, with the corks forced back in. A shop window was not exactly an ideal storage place for wine, and

Alec felt sure the Jessups' vintage wines were stored under ideal conditions.

He wondered what their markup was. Pretty hefty, certainly. New Bond Street leases must cost a fortune, and the sort of people who shopped there didn't cavil at high prices. Pity it was quite impossible to accept Jessup's offer of wholesale prices, especially now he was investigating the family for murder!

Still, since inheriting his great-uncle's fortune, he could afford a bottle of good wine now and then. The difficulty was finding time to sit down and enjoy it.

"There's Piper, sir," said Ross, nodding towards a 125 bus just coming to a halt nearby.

Ernie Piper swung down and came hurrying over to them. "Hope I'm not late, Chief. I was in the City."

"Did you notify the City force? You know how touchy they are."

"Had a word with a mate of mine. All I did was ask a few questions. It's not like I was looking to arrest someone on their patch. They'll prob'ly never know, and if they find out, he'll cover for me."

"I hope so. Right, you're going to be doing the search."

"Single-handed!"

"I want you to start with their papers."

Piper was extraordinarily good at noting and remembering details and picking up discrepancies, though it wouldn't do to tell him so too often. Alec was guiltily aware that he didn't give the young detective as much credit in that line as he deserved, because he didn't want to lose him to Fraud. He justified himself with the certainty that Ernie would hate working in Fraud.

He made sure Ernie knew what he was looking for, adding, "Of course, if you happen to notice a gun among the files, you can abandon them temporarily to let me know. Discreetly."

"You think they'd be that careless, Chief? Knowing we're coming?"

"They don't know about the search warrant. If you're still at it when we're finished asking questions, we'll lend a hand."

Alec saw a sarcastic "Cor, ta, Chief!" on Piper's lips. He'd say it aloud if Ross were not there, but Ross, though they had often worked together, was not one of Alec's usual team.

The glass shop door displayed a CLOSED sign, but it opened to Alec's push. The clock on the tower of St. George's, Hanover Square, struck the half hour as the three detectives stepped over the threshold. Alec noted an inner security door, standing open.

It was immediately obvious that this was no ordinary off-licence. The floor was paved with flagstones. The long narrow room had brick arches along each wall, framing trompe l'oeil vistas of more arches and rack after rack of bottles, row after row of wine tuns stretching into the illusory distance. A few real racks of bottles added to the illusion.

"Blimey!" said Piper. "Reminds you of that mirror room at the house, don't it, Chief?"

"Mr. Jessup certainly has an exotic taste in interior decor." Alec could imagine the younger Jessups at once embarrassed and proud of their father's exuberant imagination.

Spaced along the walls were several desks disguised as rustic tables, like the one in the window, each with a bottle and a couple of glasses. No one was there, but opening the door must have rung a bell in the back premises. Beneath a pergola against the rear wall, the twin of the one in the window, a door opened. Mr. Jessup came through, and with him his long-absent younger son.

Patrick was taller than his father, and very much slimmer, his leanness not willowy, but fit and athletic. He looked as Irish as his name, with black hair, blue eyes, and a scatter of freckles. He had not, however, inherited his mother's acting talent: His face was troubled and wary.

So was his father's, the expression sitting uneasily on Jessup's genial features.

"Thank you for agreeing to see me here," said Alec. "I'm sorry you had to close early. Your wife—"

"Moira rang up to explain. It's we who should thank you.

The Bennetts . . ." He grimaced. "Let me introduce my son Patrick. Our next-door neighbour, Detective Chief Inspector Fletcher."

"How do you do, sir?" Patrick didn't hold out his hand, relieving Alec of the eternal quandary of whether shaking hands with a suspect was appropriate.

"I'm sorry to make your acquaintance in such circumstances."

"Believe me, so am I. It's not exactly the homecoming I was looking forward to."

"These are my assistants, DCs Piper and Ross. Mr. Jessup, I'd like to have a word with you first. Is there somewhere we can go—"

"Can't you 'have a word' with both of us at once, and save time?" Jessup asked, the first sign of annoyance or impatience he had shown.

"I'd prefer to see you one at a time," Alec said firmly.

"Oh, very well. We'll go upstairs. We each have an office up there. Patrick, lock the street door before you come up. This way."

He led the way through the door at the back. It opened into a room furnished like a gentleman's den, with comfortable leather chairs and an antique writing table, but with wine racks where one might expect bookcases. On the desk, the usual blotter and a brass inkstand were supplemented with a tantalus and a tray of gleaming glasses of various shapes and sizes. On the right-hand wall hung a Cézanne still life featuring a bottle, a glass, and a bunch of grapes. Straight ahead, a solid-looking door with bar and bolt as well as a lock probably led to a yard or alley. The left wall had stairs going up and a door that, no doubt, opened on steps down to the cellar.

This must be where favoured customers were invited to consult the Jessups about the replenishment of their cellars, or the provision of drinks for wedding breakfasts and other parties.

"This will do very well," Alec said, stepping behind the desk, to Mr. Jessup's obvious displeasure. He turned to Patrick. "Would you be so kind as to take DC Piper up to the offices? Do you have keys to any locked desks, cabinets, or cupboards?"

"Yes, but . . ." The young man looked to his father.

"And the safe?" Alec cut in before Jessup could respond. "I assume you have a safe?"

"What the deuce is this?" Jessup demanded. "What business do you have going through our papers? This is a private partnership!"

"Have you something to hide?"

"Of course not, but—"

"Then I may assure you that anything DC Piper may see will remain entirely confidential. Your son may stay with him and make sure everything not pertaining to our enquiries is left just as it was found. Until he comes down to see me, at which point you can go up."

"Oh, very well!" Exasperation changed to gloom as Jessup added to Patrick, "Your mother's already told Mr. Fletcher about our sales to America."

"Which, as you need not remind me," Alec said tartly, "are not against English law." In one way, it was a relief not to have to serve the warrant. It would undoubtedly have engendered ill feeling—*more* ill feeling. On the other hand, Jessup's acquiescence to the search after a brief and natural protest suggested they would find nothing useful here.

Alec nodded to Piper, who preceded Patrick up the stairs.

Alec sat down behind the desk. Jessup hesitated, then reluctantly subsided into one of the armchairs facing him. Ross had unobtrusively brought in a straight chair from the main shop. He set it near the door, behind Jessup, where he could take notes without being observed.

"Tell me about Castellano," Alec invited.

"Castellano? That's the man you say has been murdered?"

"Mrs. Jessup didn't tell you his name?"

"She didn't catch it when you mentioned it to her. She told

me she recognised the photograph you showed her as an American who came to the house and was extremely unpleasant to her. He didn't give his name at that time, or subsequently."

"He returned, then. To the house, or here?"

"To the house. In view of his rudeness, I had given orders that he was not to be admitted. If he wanted to do business with the firm, he went the wrong way about it. Had he been an emissary of my American customer, I'd have been notified in advance of his intention to visit us. As it was, I did not meet him, nor had I any intention of doing so."

"Tell me about your transactions with America, and why you sent your son there."

"There's really nothing in it. The firm has been dealing for many years with a chap in Boston, the owner of a drinking establishment. Not our usual sort of customer, admittedly, but we simply continued the relationship with his son. The fact that it's now against the laws of his country is his lookout. I see no harm in supplying superior products to the wealthy elite of America when their alternative, I gather, is what they call 'moonshine.' I'm sure you're aware that improperly distilled alcohol can be deadly."

"Yes, indeed. I can see that, regarded in the proper light, you're a public benefactor," Alec said with only the merest hint of irony.

Unexpectedly, Jessup grinned. "That's a good line. I must remember it."

"You're welcome to it. So, everything was running along smoothly, I take it. Why Patrick's travels?"

"Everything ran smoothly because the American government wasn't putting enough money into enforcement. It stands to reason, as half of them probably enjoy a good whisky as much as anyone. Then last year, President Coolidge talked them into voting more money for the Prohibition people and more ships for the Coast Guard. Perhaps you've heard of the Anglo-American Liquor Treaty?"

"Yes."

"That made things more difficult, too, especially as they'll impound British ships outside the new twelve-mile limit. Even before the change, when it was three miles, they took the *Tomoka* five miles offshore. Well, to cut a long story short, they started intercepting our ship-to-shore messages. I approached a certain brilliant cryptographer of my acquaintance—being very familiar with certain parts of the Continent, I was able to be of some assistance to our government during the War—and he provided me with a suitable code—"

"Not Dr. Popkin, by any chance?"

Jessup looked at him suspiciously. "What my friend did was not against the law, even in America, I believe."

"No, no, it's just that I've had cause in the past to ask for his help."

"As a matter of fact, it was Dr. Popkin. He gave me what I needed. My customer didn't want the information sent in the post, for fear of its being intercepted. My son, having missed the War, was eager for adventure. *Et voilà.*"

"Patrick went ashore in America to deliver the code in person?"

"Since that was the point of the whole exercise . . . He met an agent of our customer, not the man himself. He's a banker with political ambitions and steers clear of personal involvement."

"Will you give me his name?"

"I will not."

Alec nodded. "Or that of his agent?"

"No. In any case, Patrick is fairly sure all the names he was given while in America were aliases, so they would be useless to you."

For the moment, Alec let the question lie. He doubted the principal's name would be helpful, but any others, real or aliases, though meaningless to him, would be worth trying on the New York police.

"I assume the business is profitable."

"Very. Enough to risk losing a cargo now and then, though we've been lucky in that respect."

"Yet you were not interested in hearing whatever business proposition Castellano had to set before you," Alec said sceptically.

Jessup was clearly perturbed by the return to the subject of the murder, but he quickly recovered. "After his behaviour to Moira, it was out of the question. But if you want a more businesslike reason, we are a small family firm. Taking on more American business would seriously stretch our resources."

"I'd have thought with such an unpleasant character hanging about, you'd at least want to know what he was after. You could have arranged to meet him in the garden, so that there was no chance of his encountering your wife again."

"I dare say I could have. I didn't."

"Or perhaps you sent Aidan in your place."

"Certainly not."

"Why did Aidan leave so suddenly last night?"

Shaken, Jessup said, "He . . . It wasn't sudden. He'd been planning the trip for some time. He always goes about this time of year."

"And it was so urgent, he left within an hour of his brother's return?"

"He . . . I don't know. I wasn't watching the clock."

Alec let a moment's silence point out the irrelevance of this statement. Then he snapped out, "Where did he go?"

"North!" Jessup took out a silk handkerchief and wiped his forehead. "To see customers in the North."

"Which city? Where did he take the train to?"

"What does it matter? He wasn't going to stay there. He has to travel all over the place."

"Which city?"

"I don't know. York, I think. I'm not sure."

Anywhere but York, then, Alec thought. He had been hoping he wouldn't have to arrest any of his next-door neighbours,

but if he didn't, after this interrogation, he'd never be able to face them again. Momentarily, his mind wandered. How long did he have to live in his great-uncle Walsall's house to satisfy the terms of the will? He couldn't remember Pearson specifying a term.

Alarmed by his silence, Jessup said, "Perhaps it was Newcastle."

Alec wondered whether, if he maintained a ominous silence, Jessup would gradually run through all the major northern cities he could think of except Aidan's destination. It wouldn't do to underestimate him, though. He wasn't so rattled that he wouldn't catch on quickly and throw the actual place into the list.

"Give me the names of customers he has to visit."

"Aidan took the records of their names and addresses with him."

"Mr. Jessup, I find it quite impossible to believe that you don't remember the names, at least, of customers sufficiently valuable to warrant one of the firm's principals travelling hundreds of miles to call on them at their homes."

"That's Aidan's side of the business. I deal mostly with our suppliers. I dare say I can remember one or two names if I put my mind to it."

"Please do so."

He came up with four surnames, all of such banality that they probably encompassed several thousand families in the northern counties alone. Besides the Dalton already mentioned by Mrs. Jessup, there were a Fisher, a Richardson, and a Parsons. Alec thought he was telling the truth, if not the whole truth, but it wasn't much help. He could only hope Ernie Piper's search of the files would be more fruitful.

"Why are you so anxious to keep Aidan's whereabouts from me?"

"I'm not!" Jessup blustered defensively. "Why should I?"

"That's what I'd like to know. Anyone would think you didn't care whether we caught a vicious murderer who killed as close to your home and family as to mine."

"Aidan is not a vicious murderer!"

"In that case, he may have vital information that will lead us to the right man—if we get it in time."

"I don't know where he is."

"All right, you don't know where he is. Let's see if he mentioned where he was going to his brother as they passed in the doorway. Ross, escort Mr. Jessup upstairs, please, and bring Mr. Patrick down."

TWENTY

Ten minutes after Tom Tring and DC Ardmore left the house, Elsie came into the office and told Daisy that Mrs. Jessup was asking for her, "and in such a state she is, madam, she don't seem to know whether she's coming or going. She's waiting in the hall. . . . I wasn't sure . . . considering . . ."

"Oh dear! I'll come right away. Show her into the sitting room, please, Elsie. You'd better bring in the sherry. And brandy, perhaps."

She rolled the paper out of the typewriter. It was a nuisance stopping in the middle of a page. Either one left the paper in and afterwards it curled up and never quite flattened or one took it out and could never put it back in exactly the right spot. Fortunately, this wasn't part of an article, just her notes on Alec's investigation, so there were no messy carbons to cope with and it didn't matter if the lines didn't match up properly.

Before she went to join her unexpected visitor, she powdered her nose. Mrs. Jessup was always so immaculately made up.

Considering . . . ? she thought as she crossed the passage to

the sitting room. What exactly had Elsie meant by that? Had her sister told her the Jessups were under siege, or were the abominable Bennetts already at work with the rumour mill? Their binoculars had probably been trained on the Fletcher and Jessup front doors for hours. Daisy wondered whether Miss Bennett had come home by now, and whether they had decided on their story.

In the sitting room, Elsie was lighting the fire. Mrs. Jessup stood at the window, the curtains parted slightly with one hand, staring out, though she surely could see only her own reflection.

"Mrs. Jessup?"

Moira Jessup turned. She looked quite composed. Either she had pulled herself together or the parlour maid had been wildly exaggerating. "Good evening," she said. Was there a tremor in her voice?

The fire flared up. Elsie departed. Mrs. Jessup came over to the fireplace and held out her hands to the flames.

"It's a chilly night," she said. "I'm so sorry to intrude at such an awkward hour."

"Not at all. Is there something I can do to help?"

The smile was definitely shaky. "I'm seeking sanctuary. I find it quite intolerable to stand by while those policemen rummage through all our belongings."

"I'm not exactly the best person—"

"On the contrary. You make me feel there must be some sanity in all this. You remind me that it's not a whim, not sheer persecution, that the police have some reason, however inscrutable, for what they're doing to my family. I don't know what they're looking for, or why, but if *your* husband is in charge, it must make sense, somehow."

Daisy was at a loss for words. All she could say, weakly, was, "Won't you sit down?"

Elsie came in with a tray of drinks. Mrs. Jessup gratefully accepted a b and s. Daisy, who didn't like sherry and didn't feel the need of brandy, was impressed that Elsie—she really was a

jewel of a parlour maid—had thought to bring her own favourite aperitif, Cinzano. She poured herself a drop of vermouth with lots of soda water and then sat down opposite Mrs. Jessup.

"The police can't just search wherever they feel like it," she said tentatively. "It's against Magna Carta or something. They have to persuade a magistrate that they have enough evidence to justify a warrant."

"But what evidence can they possibly have against my boys? What makes your husband so sure it was . . . murder?"

"He won't tell me. Did they show you the warrant?"

"Oh yes."

"Knowing Sergeant Tring, I'm sure he was perfectly polite."

"Yes, he asked my permission first. I'd have given it for my own room, and perhaps Patrick's, but I couldn't let them poke around in Aidan and Audrey's, when they aren't even in town."

"I do understand." Daisy sipped her drink, wishing she had made it stronger. What on earth could she say to bring comfort when everything she knew confirmed Alec's belief that the Jessups were involved in Castellano's death?

"I'm sorry, I shouldn't have come." Mrs. Jessup put her brandy down, almost untasted. "It was thoughtless of me. I'd better—"

"No, don't go. You're very welcome to stay here until . . . until they're finished in your house. Just think, the Bennetts are bound to be glued to their field glasses, and if they saw you leave so soon, they'd be convinced I'd thrown you out. You can't want to give me such a reputation for inhospitability!"

Mrs. Jessup summoned up a smile. "No, it's bad enough that they'll be shredding our reputation." She leant back wearily in her chair.

"Do you think anyone credits anything they say? Among people who know them, I mean."

"Those who want to. And there are those who wouldn't dream of inventing nasty stories about people but can't resist passing them on. At least, so far, I haven't had neighbours dropping in to ask nosy questions."

"What about reporters? They haven't discovered you yet?"

"No." She looked aghast. "I hadn't thought of that possibility. I suppose they're bound to come?"

"We had one earlier, but Elsie got rid of him very quickly. She's simply marvellous. I dare say he told the rest there was nothing doing. I'll tell her to explain the technique to your Enid. I'm so glad Enid mentioned her sister needing a position when we first came here."

"I'm glad you're happy with her. So many people never stop complaining about their servants. We're very lucky in ours."

"Luck's a big part of it, but in my opinion, how you treat them makes a huge difference." Daisy had started simply ages ago doing research for a serious article on domestic service, concentrating on the contrasts between the way servants were regarded by the middle class and by the aristocracy. Though she hadn't made much progress, having been diverted by other matters, she was still interested in the subject. Discussing it with Mrs. Jessup not only gave her further material but distracted Mrs. Jessup from her woes for quite forty minutes.

When they started to run down, Daisy said with a laugh, "I told Belinda she'd better prepare for a day when there are no more nannies."

"How is Belinda doing at school?" Mrs. Jessup asked.

"Very well. She's learning science, and Latin, and all sorts of things girls weren't supposed to be capable of in my day."

And there was another fruitful topic, that lasted another quarter of an hour. Unfortunately, in the end it reminded Mrs. Jessup that her grandchildren were far away.

"I hope they arrived safely," she fretted.

"Haven't you heard from Audrey?"

"They have no telephone. It's . . . not primitive, but very *rural*. The village is several miles away. I'm sure she'll write as soon as they get settled."

"I'd like to write to her. I know Alec has the address—"

"That fool Jonathan Irwin!"

"But I'd rather get it from you than from him." *Pour la politesse*, and because he might refuse to give it to her.

Listlessly, Mrs. Jessup told her. "You won't mention that the police are looking for Aidan, will you? In her condition . . . That's why we didn't want to tell your husband where she is, of course."

"Of course," Daisy agreed, but hadn't the refusal—or rather, claim of ignorance—come before the hunt was apparent?

"Though I suppose she'll find out soon enough from the police."

"I'm afraid so. You haven't heard from Aidan since he left?"

"No." She frowned. "No, not a word. I hope . . . But he'll have been on the road all day. Sometimes the people he calls on offer him a bed for the night, but usually he just stops at the nearest inn. Even in this day and age, not all wayside inns have telephones."

"Does he usually ring up when he stops for the night, if there's a phone nearby?"

"If Audrey were at home, he would. As she's not . . . I can see it looks odd, both of them leaving at such a moment, but they honestly had been planning their trips for ages. How could they guess there had been a murder, let alone that the victim was someone I'd met? I didn't know myself until they showed me the photograph, didn't even know his name until they told me. Neither Aidan nor Patrick had ever seen him before. I suppose Enid had to say she recognised the man in the photo." She sighed.

"She really had no choice, and no reason not to. She couldn't have guessed it would cause so much trouble for you," Daisy assured her.

"Nor could I, or I might have insisted she was mistaken. I'd

better be getting home. I only hope the servants don't all depart when they see the mess the police leave behind."

"Tom Tring—Sergeant Tring—won't leave a mess. You'll find everything just as it should be."

Mrs. Jessup looked sceptical. "Thank you for lending a sympathetic ear," she said. "And for the brandy. I didn't notice it going, but I see I've finished it! Good night, Mrs. Fletcher."

Daisy saw her out. The wind had died and the sky was clear, as bright with stars as ever a London night could be. There would be a frost tonight.

No reluctance to face the police was apparent in Patrick's jaunty step as he came down the stairs. He sat down opposite Alec without waiting for an invitation, and started talking before Ross was ready with notebook and pencil.

"To think I was afraid I'd be bored coming home to the business! No fear of that with a 'tec moving in next door in my absence."

"You had an exciting time in America?"

Patrick considered. "Not so much once I was ashore. The voyage had its moments."

"You seem to have brought a spot of excitement home with you. A curious coincidence, don't you think?"

"Oh, I don't know. The world is full of coincidences."

"But it was no coincidence that your brother left within an hour of your return. Did you quarrel with him?"

"With Aidan? Lord no! None of that prodigal son stuff, with the disgruntled older brother. I was on business, remember, even if it involved a spot of fun. Besides, old Aidan and I get on quite happily together. He's a bit of a stodgy sort of chap. I tease him about it, and he reads me the odd lecture when I'm not stodgy enough, but that's about it."

"Then why did he leave in such a hurry?"

"Aren't you bored with the story, Mr. Fletcher? I'm sure my parents have both told you, and likely the servants, as well."

"Detective work is often boring, believe it or not. I'd like to hear your version."

"Duty called! It's not a call Aidan is capable of disregarding. Some old geezers up north have to have their hands held when it comes to choosing their booze, and Aidan's elected. He's very good at it, I understand."

"Tell me whose hands he's gone to hold."

"Their names? You forget, I've been out of things for a couple of months. I haven't the foggiest."

"And did he happen to mention, in the brief hour you had together after a two-month parting, where he intended to begin his peregrination of the northern reaches of the kingdom?"

"He did not. We had other things to talk about."

"Such as?"

"Why, the success of my mission, of course."

"Of course. And was it successful?"

"It was indeed. Sold all the goods, brought home the shekels, and paved the way for the next venture. If this chappy getting done in doesn't put paid to the whole thing."

"Why should it?"

"Well, if you were an American . . . let us say 'businessman,' and you heard that an American had been murdered just outside the house of the people you were doing business with, how keen would you be to continue the association? Especially as he happened to be an Italian American. I don't know if you're aware that the Italians are rapidly taking over the bootlegging business? At any rate, it's certainly not going to help the firm, so it hardly makes sense to suspect us of having a hand in his death."

"I'll bear it in mind. Did you ever hear the name Michele Castellano while you were in America?"

"Not that I recall. I don't think so. I wasn't actually there very long, you know. That kind of voyage is apt to be a lengthy affair. As a matter of fact, the people I was with didn't go in for introductions on the whole, and those names I did get, I'm not at all sure they were their real ones."

"Fair enough. Come to that, we can't be sure Castellano is the real name of the deceased. Tell me about coming home. Where did you land?"

"Liverpool. We ran into a squall in the Irish Sea that slowed us down, so I was glad I'd sent a wireless cable telling the parents not to try to meet the boat train. And as they weren't expecting me at any particular time, I simply couldn't resist popping into the Flask—"

"The pub just off the High Street?"

"That's the place. Not that I'd been deprived of alcohol for two months. I came home on a British ship, and over there, there was no shortage of 'hooch,' as they call it. But speakeasies and ships' bars just don't measure up to the local pub."

"I suppose they know you there?"

"Oh yes. Ask the proprietor or any of the regulars. I was there from—oh, I don't know—about six till half past or thereabouts. Just time enough for a pint and a chat. Then I went on home."

"You walked up through the garden?"

"Well, yes. It doesn't make sense to go round by the street, does it? Not to our house, or yours. I didn't see any bodies, nor anyone hanging about."

"Was it raining?"

"Coming down cats and dogs."

Alec nodded. He thought he heard the merest breath of a sigh of relief. He was pretty sure nine-tenths of what Patrick had said was true. The other tenth was hogwash. He suppressed a sigh of his own. No hope of getting home for dinner.

In the offices above, a telephone bell rang. Piper would answer it.

Alec took out his fountain pen and wrote down reminders to himself: The pub must be checked, and the time it had started raining, and the time of arrival of the delayed boat train.

"What ship did you sail back on?"

"The—"

"Chief!" Piper came running down the stairs. "Sorry to interrupt. It's the Manchester Royal Infirmary on the line, the head almoner. Aidan Jessup was taken ill at his hotel and he's in hospital."

TWENTY-ONE

After showing Mrs. Jessup out, Daisy decided not to change for dinner. If Alec came home in time, which she rather doubted, he wouldn't want to change, and a man should be allowed to be comfortable in his own home, when there are no guests.

She went back to the sitting room, kicked off her shoes, and curled up in a chair, sipping the remaining half of her vermouth and soda. She had a feeling Mrs. Jessup had said something important, but she simply could not pin it down. She went back over their conversation. As far as she could recall, no new information had emerged.

The doorbell rang.

"Again!" she groaned aloud. "Who now, for pity's sake?" It was too early for dinner guests, even if she had expected any, and much too late for anyone else.

She heard Elsie come through the baize door and tap-tap along the hall. The fire flickered in the draught under the sitting room door as the front door was opened.

Elsie's voice came to her loud and clear, and firm. "Madam is not receiving."

A murmur of voices. Reporters?

"No, there's not a policeman in the house, neither. Not at the moment, there isn't."

Although the voices were slightly raised, Daisy couldn't quite make out the words, nor recognise the voices.

"Well, really!" Elsie sounded thoroughly put out. "You can just wait right here and we'll see what madam has to say about this!" The front door closed with a thud.

What on earth had ruffled the polite, well-trained parlour maid to the point of being rude? As Elsie's footsteps approached, Daisy stood up and started to go to meet her. Then she changed her mind: Discretion was the better part of knowledge—or rather, vice versa. Better to wait and find out what she was going to face before she went to face it.

"Oh, madam!" Elsie closed the door behind her. "It's them Bennetts. I said you're not at home, but they up and pushed right past me. Worse than that reporter they are, and that's saying something. They want to see the master. I told 'em he's not here, but they won't take no for an answer. I'm that sorry, madam."

"Oh, BH! if you'll pardon my language. I'll go."

"I left 'em in the hall, madam, but I wouldn't put it past them to go into the drawing room without an invitation."

This measure of the Bennetts' iniquity proved all too accurate. Daisy found them in the drawing room. They had turned on the electric light. Miss Bennett was sitting by the unlit fire, and her brother stood with his back to it. As Daisy entered, Miss Bennett said in a voice meant to be overheard, "Too penny-pinching for a fire in every room, I dare say."

Since the room had not been in use—and, in any case, the radiators made it quite warm enough for comfort—the remark was quite uncalled-for. Daisy ignored it.

"I understand you hoped to see my husband," she said. "I'm afraid he is not here and I don't know when he'll return."

"Some men are so inconsiderate about letting their households know when they're going to be late."

That was a bit of cheek, in view of Mr. Bennett's claim that she hadn't told him when, or even whether, she'd be home tonight! Daisy nearly pointed out that it was inevitable in Alec's job, but once again she decided not to rise to the bait.

"I presume you wish to see him in his professional capacity," she said sweetly—was there such a word as *saccharinely*? "If you have a statement to make, may I suggest you either ring up the local police or go directly to Scotland Yard?"

"It's not the local bobbies we want," snapped Mr. Bennett, "and I should have thought you could see I can't possibly be dragging myself down to Whitehall with my arthritis. We'll tell you what we saw and you can pass it on to your husband."

It dawned on Daisy that this was exactly what they had intended all along. Doubtless they had watched through their binoculars until they were sure she was alone before they came. Quite a few people found it more comfortable to avoid the official commitment of reporting to the police, by telling Daisy what they wanted the police to know. Usually she was in sympathy with their concerns, but not this time.

Warren was still on duty by the telephone. She could call him in, but a mere detective constable, and one, moreover, without eyebrows, would neither appease the Bennetts nor be able to cope with them.

What would Alec want her to do? It was all very well thinking she ought to put the Bennetts off until he could talk to them, but suppose they refused to see him? On the other hand, did she really want to hear whatever slander they chose to promulgate?

Daisy decided she had better hear them out. She didn't have to pass on to Alec anything she considered gratuitous twaddle.

"You won't mind if I write down what you tell me," she said, with an inward smile at their obvious dismay. "It wouldn't do to get it wrong when I report to Alec."

Without waiting for a response, she went off—not hurrying—to fetch her notebook from the office.

Returning through the hall, she met Elsie, breathless and

chilled. "Oh madam, I hope as I haven't done wrong. I dashed over to my sister and told her to go right away and tell that Sergeant Tring the Bennetts are here pestering you. I know he's a friend of yours, 'sides being a policeman."

Bother! thought Daisy. If she didn't get a move on, there would be an official witness to their mischief making, if Tom Tring's arrival didn't shut them up altogether.

"That was very thoughtful of you, Elsie. If he comes, show him right in, won't you?"

"I'm sure he'll come, madam," said the parlour maid, shocked. "He wouldn't leave you alone with the likes of them. Why, it wouldn't surprise me a bit if it was them as done that American in. Nasty, they are. Me and Enid don't believe it was the Jessups, not if it was ever so. I'll wait right here to let Mr. Tring in quick as can be, madam, so if you need me, just call out."

"Thank you, Elsie." Daisy was touched by the Bristow sisters' loyalty.

She hurried into the drawing room. Mr. Bennett had taken his seat opposite his sister. He made no attempt to rise when Daisy came in, tapping his knee as if to remind her of his rheumatics. She was not impressed. She knew plenty of elderly gentlemen far more rickety who would die rather than not stand up when a lady entered the room.

She sat down, notebook and pencil at the ready. "All right, let's have your statement. Then I'll type it up and you can sign it."

They exchanged a glance. "We're not signing anything," said Miss Bennett belligerently.

"That's for you to decide. Of course, the police won't take anything you say very seriously if you're not willing to put your names to it." Daisy hoped to make them think twice before letting their unpleasant imaginations run riot. "Go ahead."

"We saw him!" Miss Bennett was eager now.

"Who? When? Where?"

"Patrick Jessup, of course."

"Everyone knows he came home yesterday," Daisy said dampeningly.

"We were the first to see him," Mr. Bennett claimed. "He came out of the passage, right beside our house, a few minutes after half past five."

"That's right!"

That's torn it! Daisy thought. "How can you be sure it was Patrick? It was dusk on a gloomy evening. He must have been wearing a hat, and very likely a muffler."

"No muffler. Patrick Jessup has always claimed he doesn't feel the cold. He goes around without an overcoat in midwinter. Just wait till he starts getting arthritis; that'll put a stop to him."

"He had a hat on, one of those newfangled soft felts, a trilby or a homburg, or whatever they're called. What's wrong with a bowler, I say. But he always wears his hat on the back of his head."

"Makes him look like a racecourse tout."

"Lowers the tone of the neighbourhood."

"But one can see his face."

"And he turned his head towards us, speaking to the man with him. It looked as if he was pointing out the Jessups' house."

"There was someone with him?" Daisy asked sharply. Did Alec know Patrick had a companion?

"*He* was wearing an overcoat, and had his hat pulled down over his ears. One of those soft felts, like Patrick's. If he'd been wearing a nice hard bowler, it wouldn't have been so easy to knock him out, would it?"

"You saw Patrick hit him over the head?"

"Well, not to say 'saw.' I had to go and pack for a night away from home, to be ready to meet my friend Emmeline Lagerquist for the theatre. My brother's eyesight is not as keen as mine."

"I had the glasses. I watched them walk up the path. They stopped near the fountain. Aidan—" He stopped, glancing

resentfully at Daisy's pencil and pad. She allowed herself a smug feeling that she had stymied the worst of his venom—if that was what one did to venom. "There ought to be a lamp-post by the fountain. It's much too dark for safety in the middle of the garden. Someone else came down the slope to meet them. I can't be sure who it was."

"Fortunately, I hadn't quite got around to writing down any name," Daisy said in that saccharine tone. Then a dismaying memory struck her: Mrs. Jessup saying that neither Patrick nor Aidan had seen Castellano *before*. Before what? She couldn't think about it now. She had the Bennetts to be put in their place. Firmly, she went on: "I believe juries are awarding quite tremendous damages for slander these days."

Mr. Bennett blenched and repeated hurriedly, "I can't be sure who it was."

Miss Bennett gave him a scornful look but didn't actually contradict him. "You saw what happened next, though."

"Not clearly, not clearly at all. It's shockingly dark in the middle of the garden, and then, my eyes are not what they were. That vulgar statue—"

"Barely half-clothed!"

"It complicates things, too. One can't be sure how many people one is seeing, when they're moving about in front of it, and one keeps catching glimpses—"

"You should have called me! I would have gone upstairs and had a much better view."

"It was over very quickly."

"What was?" Daisy demanded.

"I saw . . . what appeared to be . . . what might have been a struggle. Someone fell down. I'm fairly certain someone fell down. Then suddenly there was no one standing, no one at all."

"What!" Daisy frowned at him. She couldn't begin to guess what the police, let alone a coroner, prosecutor, or jury, would make of this farrago. It didn't make sense.

"It started to rain," Mr. Bennett said querulously. "I really couldn't see much at all after that."

"That's not what you told me!" his sister snapped.

"You weren't writing down every word to throw up against me in a court of law. Besides, with you badgering him, how is a man to think straight? What I saw isn't necessarily what you'd have liked me to see."

What he had seen was bad enough, Daisy thought. She was glad she had taken notes, and not only because of the dampening effect. If she could quote to Alec their exact words, then any tall story Miss Bennett might persuade her brother to tell, or come up with on her own account, would be belied before uttered.

"Detective Sergeant Tring, madam."

The Bennetts' quarrel had covered the sound of Tom's arrival. Daisy jumped up and went to meet him. Brown eyes twinkling, he raised his eyebrows questioningly at her, with an effect like a pair of woolly bear caterpillars crawling up an egg.

"Mr. Tring! How lucky that you happened to drop in." She waved her notebook at him and turned back towards the couple by the fireplace. "I believe you haven't met Mr. and Miss Bennett?"

"I have not had the pleasure."

Daisy wished she were not far too well brought up to inform him that it was no pleasure. "They came looking for the police. Since you'd all left, they've been telling me how the disgracefully bad lighting in the garden prevented their seeing anything much last night. You'll be glad to hear I wrote down their statements verbatim, so there can't be any disagreement about what they've said."

His moustache twitched. "Very good, Mrs. Fletcher," he said gravely. "If you would be so good as to type your notes, the lady and gentleman can sign them immediately and we shan't have to trouble them again this evening."

Miss Bennett gave him an affronted glare. "We cannot possibly wait."

"It won't take me more than a few minutes."

"We dine precisely at eight. It is now twelve minutes before the hour."

235

"We have to go round by the street," Mr. Bennett explained, levering himself out of his seat, "what with the steps and my arthritis, and the lighting so poor in the garden."

"We wouldn't have come out at all, but unpleasant as it is to have anything to do with the police, we know our duty as citizens, I hope."

"Very obliging of you," said Tom as Daisy rang for Elsie, who must have been listening at the door, since she arrived instantly to show the Bennetts out.

They departed, noses in the air.

"Paint themselves into a corner, did they?" Tom enquired.

"Not at all. I painted them into a corner."

"You didn't go putting words into their mouths, Mrs. Fletcher."

"Of course not! I just made pointed remarks about slander and *huge* damages, and made sure they realised I was taking down every word they said. Oh Tom, aren't they awful? And the worst is, the one unshakable thing they agree on is that they both saw Patrick Jessup coming into the Circle at half past five with a companion who sounds just like Castellano."

TWENTY-TWO

Alec's first call was to Superintendent Crane.

"You again!" moaned the Super. "What the devil is it now? We're just sitting down to dinner. I trust your wife has passed on my message?"

"No, sir," Alec said cautiously. "I'm still at the wine shop. I haven't spoken to Daisy since I left to come here. Is it urgent?"

"I suppose not, unless you consider a complaint from the Home Secretary urgent. Nothing to be done tonight, at any rate. I haven't my notes with me, so ask her when you get home."

"I'm not going home, sir."

"What! Here, I say, Fletcher, don't go off the deep end! She means well, you know. She can't help falling into these scrapes, and you have to admit she's pulled your irons out of the fire once or—"

"I mean, sir, I'm asking your permission to go to Manchester."

"Manchester! Filthy dump. What the devil do you want to go there for, eh?"

"The man we've been looking for has turned up there—in hospital."

"He has, has he?" The policeman alter ego took over from the diner interrupted in the middle of his soup. "Don't suppose you could send that sergeant of yours? No," he answered his own question, "touchy business questioning a sick man."

"I really think I should do it myself, sir."

"Right-oh. Leaving at once, are you?"

"Yes, I'll just stop by my office to pick up the autopsy report—it should have come in by now—and my bag, and catch the same train Aidan Jessup presumably caught last night. I may find out something from the train staff on the way."

"You'll telephone Mrs. Fletcher to tell her you're off," Crane said severely.

"Of course, sir. And ask her for your message about the Home Secretary."

"Don't worry about him. I'll deal with him," the Super promised. "I'll ring up the Manchester force for you, too. And now, if you have no objection, I'm going to finish my soup before it's stone-cold." He hung up.

Alec rang home. Warren answered.

"How is your face?" Alec asked.

"It feels sort of tight, sir, like I was wearing a rubber mask. And hot. But Miss Bristow brought me some more ointment from Mrs. Dobson, and that helps, so could be worse."

"Good. Anything to report?"

"Mrs. Jessup came round, sir, and had a long talk with Mrs. Fletcher. And then those Bennetts—Miss Bristow fetched DS Tring to give Mrs. Fletcher a hand with them. I dunno what they said. Mr. Tring's still here."

"All right, put Mr. Tring on the line, and then you can go home. There's not likely to be anything else this evening. You can go to your own station tomorrow morning, and you needn't turn up till noon, unless you're called in earlier. I'll make that all right with— Oh, your sergeant's on his way to the wilds of Lincolnshire."

238

"Yes, sir. He was going to ring up when he gets there to find out what's up here."

"That's right. My wife can tell him." Which meant telling her more than Alec had intended to, but she seemed to know a good deal more than he did of some matters, so he supposed it all came out even. "Off you go, Warren. I suggest you see a doctor in the morning if your face is still uncomfortable."

A moment later, he heard Tom Tring's deep rumble. "Chief?"

"Tom, I have to catch a train to Manchester, so let's keep this as brief as possible. Have you found anything in the Jessups' house?"

"Nowt, like they say in Manchester. We were nearly done, me and Ardmore, when I was called over here to repel boarders."

"The Bennetts. Warren told me."

"Not that Mrs. Fletcher needed help. She'd routed 'em, foot, horse, and artillery, before I got here."

"She didn't—"

"Not to worry, Chief. She got their story out of 'em first, and wrote it all down. She's typing it up now. The bit you need to know is, they're ready to swear Patrick Jessup reached the Circle at half five."

Alec whistled. "Did he, now! Six-thirty, he says."

"And there was a bloke with him, with his hat pulled low."

"Indeed! The Bennetts are sure they were together?"

"I don't know about that, Chief. I haven't read their statement, and you know how Mrs. Fletcher does her best to avoid leading questions."

"Insofar as she understands the term," Alec said dryly. "If you have nothing more to report, put her on, would you, please?"

"Have a heart, Chief! At least tell me why you're off to Manchester."

"Aidan's there. In hospital."

Tom whistled. Alec could imagine his moustache puffing out. "Right, Chief, I won't ask any more. For now. What do you want me to do tomorrow?"

"Let's see ... The Bennetts first; Whitcomb— We still haven't much to go on in the way of times, but maybe the post-mortem report will help—you'd better have a look at it. And see if you can get any news of Lambert. That should keep you busy for a bit."

"Right, Chief."

"Ardmore can help you. He won't need to catch up on his beauty sleep, as he needn't bother with St. Pancras tonight after all."

"Right, Chief. Here's Mrs. Fletcher."

"Darling! Manchester?"

" 'Fraid so. I'm going to have to rush to catch the train, so tell me the absolute minimum. I'll ring from Manchester tomorrow to get the rest."

"Right-oh, darling. The Home Sec—"

"Crane's dealing with him."

"Thank heaven! Did he tell you Castellano's passport was stolen and faked?"

"No, he didn't go into detail. That would explain the ink."

"That's exactly what I said, at which point Mr. Crane exploded. Did you get the telegram from Rosenblatt in New York?"

"Rosenblatt? The district attorney?"

"That's the man. He says Castellano was an 'enforcer' for a crime gang."

"Great Scott!"

"Rosenblatt's pleased as punch to hear he's dead. I think that's all the essentials, darling. I hope you get something decent to eat on the train."

" 'Bye, love. I'll talk to you tomorrow."

"Toodle-oo."

Alec hung up. Too pressed for time to consider the implications of what Tom and Daisy had told him, he strode to the

door of the office where he had taken the call. Opening it, he found himself looking at DC Ross's back. Beyond this solid and effective barrier, Mr. Jessup confronted him, with Patrick at his shoulder. Both looked more distressed than belligerent.

Hearing the click of the latch opening, Ross spoke without turning. "Mr. Jessup wants a word with you, sir."

"Thank you, Ross, that's all right now. I'm finished on the telephone." As Ross moved aside, Alec said, "I can spare you two minutes, Mr. Jessup." Not "sir," not yet. There was still a possibility, though it seemed more and more remote, that one day they would once again be amicable neighbours.

"Patrick says Aidan is in hospital in Manchester. Do you know what's wrong with him?"

"It appears to be the aftereffects of a severe concussion."

Aidan's father and brother looked worried but not surprised, Alec noted.

"I'm sending Patrick up there to make sure he gets the best possible care." Jessup sounded determined not to take an expected no for an answer.

But nothing could have suited Alec better. "He can travel with me. I have to stop in at the Yard on the way to the station. Ross will drive you both back to Hampstead and then bring Patrick to St. Pancras to meet me. Pack lightly," he told Patrick, "and quickly. We'll catch the express your brother took last night"

"I'll go to Scotland Yard with you," Patrick said eagerly, apparently regarding a visit to the headquarters of the Metropolitan Police as a thrill, not a possible prelude to arrest. "I don't need any bags. I was travelling pretty rough for weeks, remember?"

"Nonsense," said his father. "If you're to organise Aidan's care, you'll need to look your best. Come along. You'll make sure the place is locked when you leave, won't you, Fletcher?"

"Of course."

As Ross and the Jessups hurried down the stairs, Ernie

Piper came out of the next office, switching off the electric light. "I'm done here, Chief. Could've told you Manchester. There's a note to their secretary to send a cable booking him into the London Road Station Hotel."

"So the trip really was planned in advance, as they claim," Alec said in a low voice, following the others down, Piper at his heels.

"For tonight."

"He intended to travel today! Anything else of interest?"

"Not a thing. You talked to Mr. Tring? Did he find the gun?"

"No."

"Aidan probably took it and threw it out of the window of the train."

"Why? Why the devil should he do anything so stupid? The gun must have been Castellano's." Alec checked that the inner shop door had latched securely behind him. The lock was one of Chubb's best, set in a door that had the heft of steel. The outer glass door had no lock. "If he, or they, hadn't moved the body and had left the gun beside it, they'd have had a good chance of getting off with self-defence."

"If it was just a bash over the head." Piper waved down a taxi. "Not if Dr. Ridgeway's right about the way he was killed."

"No." Alec sighed. "That's the sticking point."

The taxi whirled them to Scotland Yard. Alec found the autopsy report on his desk. Amid a great deal of obscure medical verbiage, the plain fact stood out: Castellano had first been knocked out by the impact of an unidentifiable blunt instrument on the skull. Subsequently, he had been murdered by compression of the carotid arteries. It would have taken no more than a couple of minutes.

Alec sent Piper home and took a taxi to St. Pancras Station. Ross and Patrick were waiting for him, anxiously scanning the arriving cabs. Not until he saw them did Alec realise he had been metaphorically holding his breath, worrying that Patrick might give Ross the slip and run for cover.

Though nothing like it was during rush hour, the station was still busy. Passengers and porters streamed in and out of the brick archways. Alec had cut it fine, so he was relieved when Patrick said, "I've got your ticket. Platform seven. We'd better hurry."

"Thanks. Ross, you'll be giving DS Tring a hand tomorrow."

He and Patrick joined the swarms beneath the cavernous iron-vaulted glass roof. The cries of boys hawking food baskets augmented the voices of anxious travellers, the rumble of luggage trolleys, and the din of steam engines.

"I'm ravenous," said Patrick as they made haste towards Platform 7, dodging old ladies with umbrellas and lapdogs and young ladies wielding careless cigarette holders. "I don't know whether the dining car will serve supper this late, so I bought us a couple of baskets. Rather infra dig in first class, but it can't be helped. A porter's taken them and my bag to nab seats for us."

First class! Alec had intended to travel third, as was appropriate to a lowly policeman who had to explain his expenses to a clerk intent on saving the taxpayers money. However, the scion of a wealthy wine merchant would be accustomed to better things. Thanks to his great-uncle Walsall, Alec could reimburse him without wincing.

"Over here, guv!" A porter waved vigorously from an open door. "Gotcha two window seats." His waiting hand was appropriately filled by Patrick. He took Alec's bag, led them a little way down the corridor, and ushered them into a compartment. Chucking the bag up onto the rack, he wished them "Bong voyidge," and departed.

Both the corner seats by the corridor were occupied. Dismayed, Alec recognised the gentleman facing forward as a distinguished King's Counsel with whom he had more than once clashed in court.

The KC frowned at Alec, as if he felt he ought to know him but couldn't quite place him. One thing was certain: He would

not have chosen to travel in this compartment if he could have found an empty one. He was not going to approve of his unwanted companions' impromptu meal.

Alec had hoped for privacy on the journey in order to continue his interview with Patrick in light of what he had learnt. It was not to be.

With the usual whistle, clanging and clashing, and the hiss of escaping steam, the train pulled out of the station.

TWENTY-THREE

Daisy dined alone, an occurrence too frequent to be bothersome. It allowed her to read while she ate, though, naturally, she'd rather have been talking to Alec. After a delicious apple snow, light and frothy and sweetened just enough, she took her demitasse of coffee up to the nursery.

Miranda was fast asleep in her crib, but Oliver was teething yet again and inclined to be fretful. Daisy rocked him in her arms, crooning a lullaby, while Nurse Gilpin and Bertha went down to the kitchen to have supper with Mrs. Dobson and Elsie.

Oliver soon settled down, sucking his thumb. Mrs. Gilpin would have strongly disapproved. Daisy let him suck. Pulling it out of his mouth would only get him upset again. She debated whether to lay him down in his crib, but she was very comfortable in the rocking chair by the fire, and it was difficult to get out of it holding a large baby, so she stayed put. It was a cosy comfort, not at all conducive to thoughts of murder, yet she couldn't help her mind turning that way.

Aidan was in hospital in Manchester, suffering from the effects of a concussion. Perhaps he had fallen getting in or out of

the train. Perhaps something had fallen on his head from the overhead rack.

Unfortunately, it seemed more likely that he was feeling the delayed aftermath of a fight with Castellano. Had he attacked because Castellano had threatened him or Patrick? What had become of the mysterious vanishing gun, or had Castellano not carried one? And why—the question always recurred—*why* was Alec convinced Castellano's death was cold-blooded murder? Not knowing made it very difficult to see either Aidan or Patrick as a cold-blooded murderer. And she must not forget Lambert, though he seemed still more unlikely.

Elsie came in. "Oh madam," she said in a hushed voice, "Enid just brought a note from them next door."

"Whatever can they want now?"

"I'm sure I don't know, madam. It's sealed. Not that me or Enid would stoop to reading someone else's letter!" She came over, holding out a blue envelope. "Ooh, who's a sweetie pie, then!"

"Do you think you could take him and lay him down in his crib without waking him?"

"Sure enough, madam. I've got little brothers and sisters, I have." She picked up Oliver and bore him away.

The envelope was addressed to "Mrs. A. Fletcher" in a hand she didn't recognise. Opening it, she glanced first at the signature—"Maurice Jessup." What on earth . . . ?

He apologised for troubling her. Moira was greatly distressed by the latest development in this horrible business and begged for Mrs. Fletcher's advice. Would she be so very kind as to call at her earliest convenience, tonight if possible?

"Little lamb," cooed Elsie, leaning over Oliver's crib. She turned to the other crib. "And I haven't forgot you, Miss Miranda. Such a good quiet mite." She tucked a blanket in more securely.

Daisy hardly noticed. Her advice? About what? Did Mrs. Jessup still, after Daisy's denials, believe she knew everything in Alec's mind and would be willing to share it?

Alec would undoubtedly say she shouldn't go. Luckily, he wasn't here to say it. She knew she'd never sleep tonight with curiosity gnawing at her. If she could satisfy it while bringing some comfort to Mrs. Jessup . . .

"Elsie, I'm going to pop next door for a few minutes. Did you finish your supper?"

"All but the pudding, madam. Mrs. Dobson will save me some if you want me to stay with the babies."

"Would you, please, until Nurse comes back? I'd hate her to find Oliver crying and no one here. I shan't be long."

Daisy dispensed with hat and gloves, but she did don a coat for the brief venture out into the frosty air, down the steps and up the steps. Enid opened the Jessups' front door promptly.

"I'm ever so glad you've come, madam," she said. "We're all that worried about poor Mr. Aidan in the hospital."

Hospitals were still regarded by many as a place where you were taken to die. "It's the best place for him," said Daisy. "He'll get proper care there."

"I'm sure I hope so. If you'll please to come this way, madam." She showed Daisy into the drawing room.

Mrs. Jessup, as immaculate as ever, came to meet her and took both her hands. "How kind you are!"

"I don't know if I can help." Daisy's voice was full of doubt.

"Come and sit down and let us explain our quandary."

Daisy had expected to see Mr. Jessup, but somewhat to her surprise, Mr. Irwin was still there, as well. As Aidan's father-in-law, she wondered, or as a lawyer, or a bit of each? He had freely given Alec the address of Audrey's sister. Daisy wouldn't give much for his legal advice in a criminal matter.

He was the first of the two men to speak. "Good evening, Mrs. Fletcher. We are approaching you as a friend of my daughter, the only friend we feel able to bring into this shocking affair, as you are already conversant with its details."

"Yes?" Daisy said cautiously.

"Audrey *must* be told that Aidan is in hospital," said Mrs. Jessup. "I simply can't countenance keeping it from her."

"She ought to know," Daisy agreed, reflexively accepting a tiny liqueur glass Mr. Jessup pressed into her hand. She tasted—Drambuie.

"The trouble is, Vivien isn't on the telephone. Jonathan—Mr. Irwin—was going to send a telegram, but I can't help thinking how I'd hate to get such news in a wire, not knowing what to do or—"

"I've *said* I'll go to her." Irwin sounded goaded.

"And take her to Manchester."

"*And* take her to Manchester, if that's what she wants. I'll hire a motor, leave at once, and drive through the night. But it's my opinion that the police will consider our arrival unwarranted interference. I repeat," he added doggedly, "I am not conversant with criminal law."

"Mrs. Fletcher," Mrs. Jessup appealed to her, "do you think your husband would consider it—what's the phrase?—'obstructing the police in the execution of their duties' if Jonathan took Audrey to Manchester? Heaven knows, Aidan and Patrick seem to be in trouble enough already. The last thing they need is any further complications."

Daisy's sympathies were entirely with Audrey. How much comfort her father would be to her was uncertain, but he was indubitably better than a telegram announcing her husband's having been rushed into hospital. On the other hand, Alec might reasonably be annoyed if Mr. Irwin reached Audrey and whisked her away before Mackinnon had spoken to her.

"I can't see that Alec can possibly object to a wife hurrying to her husband's sickbed," she said, thinking fast. "And I don't believe he's allowed to object to the presence of a lawyer, at least in certain circumstances. Couldn't you go with them, Mrs. Jessup? A worried mother as well as a worried wife would be awfully hard to take exception to."

Mrs. Jessup shuddered. "There's nothing I'd like better, but I simply can't travel by motor-car. I'd be no use to either Aidan or Audrey if they had to tuck me up in the bed next to his."

"*Mal de voiture*," said Daisy understandingly, "or it ought to

be. I don't know if the French have a word for it. You ought to learn to drive, you know. A friend of mine gets frightfully sick when she's driven, but she's perfectly all right driving herself."

"Oh, I'm much too old to learn."

"Rubbish! But that's beside the point. The more I think about it, the more I think Audrey needs a woman to go with her to hold her hand. Wouldn't you agree?"

"Oh yes!"

"We can't bring anyone else into this," Jessup said grimly.

All three looked at Daisy.

"Well . . ."

"My dear Mrs. Fletcher," said Irwin, "I'd be exceedingly grateful if you could see your way to coming with me. I'm certain your support would mean a great deal to my daughter. Women are so much better on such occasions—'When pain and anguish wring the brow, a ministering angel thou!'"

The solicitor's lapse into poetry startled Daisy. She didn't mind that couplet, but she took serious issue with the first part of the verse. "Uncertain, coy, and hard to please" was not a description any modern young woman would put up with. Not that she couldn't think of a few to whom it applied neatly, but in her opinion, not a one of them would ever turn into a ministering angel under any foreseeable circs.

"It's a lot to ask," said Jessup, refilling Daisy's glass.

His wife just projected hopefulness that would have easily reached the balcony in a theatre.

"I think it's quite a good idea, actually," said Daisy. "If Alec's furious, it'll be with me, not with you, and I'm used to it. However, I can't possibly be ready to leave before the morning. Reasonably early in the morning, but not tonight."

Mrs. Jessup agreed that the support Daisy could offer her daughter-in-law was more important than speed in announcing the bad news. Mr. Irwin agreed to have his hired car pick her up at eight o'clock the next morning.

Returning home, Daisy breathed a sigh of relief. They might think they had persuaded her into going, but it was just

what she wanted. By the time she and Irwin arrived at the farm, Mackinnon would have had his talk with Audrey. When she explained that to Alec, he'd have to agree she'd acted for the best. On top of that, she would not only be a comfort to Audrey; she'd be back in the thick of things, instead of languishing in London while the action was in Manchester.

As she entered the house, the telephone bell was ringing. She reached the instrument just as Elsie pushed through the baize door. "You get it," she requested, stepping back. "I'm not sure I can cope with any more excitement this evening."

"It's that Mr. Mackinnon," Elsie announced a moment later. "The Scotch detective. It's a trunk call."

"Oh dear! Right-oh, I'll talk to him." Daisy took the receiver and put her hand over the transmitter. "Elsie, I have to go out of town for a couple of days. Would you get started on packing? I'll wear country clothes tomorrow—the heather tweed costume and a motoring coat—and then— Whatever do you suppose one wears in Manchester?"

"A dirty place, by what I've heard, madam. You'll want something dark."

"Right-oh. I'll be up in a minute." She uncovered the transmitter. "Hello, Mr. Mackinnon, this is Mrs. Fletcher. What can I do for you?"

The line was terrible, with a crackling noise interrupted by periodic pops.

"Mrs. Fletcher?" Mackinnon shouted.

"Yes!" Daisy shouted back.

"I'm in Lincolnshire, at the Boston police station. The Chief told me to ring up to find out whit's going on, but they told me at the Yard he's on his way to Manchester, and Mr. Tring's gone hame." He always sounded more Scottish than ever when harassed. "Can ye no gie me an inkling whit's happened sin' I left?"

Using initials for those involved, in case the exchange girl was listening in—country operators usually having more time to spare than those in town—Daisy passed on all she knew.

Her exposition was punctuated at regular intervals by the operator's "Your time is up, caller. Would you like another three minutes?" The really irritating thing was that the line always cleared miraculously for these announcements, then reverted to hissing and spitting like an angry cat for Mackinnon's reply.

"So you don't have to try to find out from Mrs. A.J. where her husband is. And that's about the lot," Daisy said at last, "or at least all I can remember. Alec doesn't tell me everything, of course. But if I may venture a suggestion, I wouldn't mention Mr. A.J. being in hospital, if I were you. It'd only upset Mrs. A.J. and make it more difficult for you to get answers out of her. She'll find out soon enough."

"Yon's no the Chief's notion, Mrs. Fletcher?"

"No, just my opinion."

"I s'll have to consider—"

"Your time is up, caller. Would you like another three minutes?"

"No, thank you, operator. Thank you, Mrs. Fletch—"

The line went silent.

Oh well, Daisy thought, she had done her best for Audrey. She could only hope Mackinnon would see the sense in her suggestion. She went upstairs to pack.

TWENTY-FOUR

Alec and Patrick arrived in Manchester in the small hours of the morning. It was raining. Patrick wanted to go at once to the Royal Infirmary. Alec, not entirely disingenuously, persuaded him that his brother would be sleeping and ought not to be disturbed. Indeed, the hospital would certainly not allow a visit to the ward, and moving Aidan to a private room—let alone to a nursing home—in the middle of the night was not a good idea, was, in fact, a rotten idea. Rest and peace were what a concussion victim needed most.

He felt only slightly guilty. The truth of his words was not altered by his own intention of disturbing the patient at the earliest feasible hour of the morning. He was not about to permit the brothers to meet before he had taken Aidan's statement.

They went to the London Road Station Hotel. Patrick went straight to his room. Alec's day was by no means yet ended.

First, he rang up the Manchester police headquarters. True to his word, Superintendent Crane had paved the way. The duty sergeant promised him a car and a detective constable to pick him up at the hotel at quarter past six. Hospitals were no-

torious for starting their day ridiculously early. Alec reckoned that by the time he had worked his way through the bureaucracy and spoken to the almoner and the doctor, Aidan Jessup should be washed, shaved, fed, and as ready for interrogation as he was likely to be. Assuming he was not inconveniently still unconscious.

This arranged, Alec returned to the reception desk. No one was there, but a sleepy-eyed porter limped over from his post by the door and advised him to ring the bell.

"Thank you, in a minute. Were you on duty last night?"

"Oh aye, that I were."

"You saw the man who was taken away to hospital?"

"Oh aye. Coom in here lookin' like death, he did, 'bout this time last night. Cou'n't stand up straight and wobbling abaht like a one-legged parrot. I thought he were drunk as an oyster, but he were dressed like a gent, an' 'e gave the porter what brought his bags from the station an 'alf crown. Gave me another when I lent him a hand. He'd wired ahead to book a room, so Mr. Greaves didn't—"

"What I did or didn't do cannot possibly interest this gentleman, Wetherby." The voice of authority emanated from a very small man, not much more than a midget, slim and dapper, with only crow's-feet and greying temples to distinguish him from a boy. He had appeared through the door behind the reception counter, which hid all but his head until he stepped up onto a stool.

"But it *does* interest me," said Alec, producing his warrant card. "Detective Chief Inspector Fletcher of Scotland Yard. You're the night manager, I take it, Mr. Greaves? May I have a word with you?"

Greaves raised his eyebrows. "A police matter, is it? You'd better come back into the office."

"Thanks, Mr. Wetherby," Alec said to the porter, and followed the manager through the door.

An electric fire, occupying a stingy Victorian grate, made the office considerably cosier than the lobby outside. There

was a utilitarian desk, a safe, and a filing cabinet, but two armchairs flanked the fireplace and the fragrance of coffee filled the air. A pot steamed gently over a spirit lamp on a small table.

"Take a seat. Coffee?"

"That would be very welcome. It's been a long day."

As he poured, Greaves said, "The man who was taken ill was a Jessup. The man who arrived with you was a Jessup. I hope the family hasn't called in Scotland Yard because of any suspicion of skulduggery in this hotel having caused Mr. Jessup's collapse."

"Scotland Yard is not so easily called in, I assure you. Does your recollection of his arrival agree with the porter's?"

"I didn't hear everything he said, but I'd be surprised if it differed by much. As you can imagine, there's been a good deal of talk among the staff."

"Well, then, tell me how you saw it."

Greaves shrugged. "I'm always at the desk at that time, as when you arrived, because of the express from London. Mostly businessmen take that train. It's not unknown for one or two to arrive slightly squiffy, and I can tell you, it's a delicate balancing act whether to give them a room or not. We've the reputation of the hotel to consider, both the reputation for hospitality and as being a quiet, respectable place. If they're not at a noisy stage of inebriation, and if they've booked in advance, we let 'em stay, especially if we know them."

"You know Aidan Jessup?"

"He's stayed here for a few days every autumn since I've worked here. Nice gentleman, sober and steady as they come, I'd've said, but . . ."

"But last night?"

"Last night, he couldn't walk or talk straight, seemed sort of dazed, looked alarmingly as if he might be sick at any moment. You know that greenish look? He complained of a splitting headache. I did ask if he was ill, but he denied it. Said he just needed a few hours in bed. He had a hired car and driver or-

ganised for nine the next—that's *this* morning. That's as far as my personal knowledge goes."

"Thank you. You'll be asked to sign a statement later. Now, off the record, will you tell me what you were told about subsequent events when you came to work this evening? As far as we're concerned, this is hearsay, which cannot be used in evidence, but it may help me decide whom else I need to interview."

"Can't you tell me what this is all about? If the hotel is going to be mentioned in the papers in the context of a police enquiry, I'll probably be blamed for letting him stay, and jobs are few and far between. Forewarned is forearmed."

Alec wondered if the poor devil, intelligent and well-spoken as he was, had trouble finding jobs because of his diminutive stature. "It's highly unlikely the hotel will play much of a part, if any," he assured him. "It's a London affair I'm investigating. I can't tell you more, I'm afraid. Go on, please."

"There's not much to tell. I gather the motor-car and chauffeur turned up as expected. Mr. Jessup had got himself down to the lobby somehow and was sitting huddled up in a chair in his coat and hat, still looking deathly ill. The driver took one look at him and said he wouldn't be responsible. He was afraid he'd find himself out in the country somewhere with a corpse in the backseat. And the poor gentleman wasn't even well enough to sit up straight and argue. So Mr. Hatcher, the day manager, called a doctor and Mr. Jessup was whisked off to hospital, a hotel being no place to care for a sick man."

"You didn't hear what the doctor said was wrong with him?"

"No. Oh, I believe he had a bandaged head. A sticking plaster or some such. No one had seen him without his hat before the doctor examined him."

Though Alec was no medical man, he'd dealt with the aftermath of enough assault and batteries and grievous bodily harms to know that the worst effects of a blow to the head are often delayed. The symptoms sounded appropriate. But what on

earth had happened the previous afternoon in Constable Circle? Castellano and Aidan Jessup had hit each other over the head with one or more blunt instruments? It sounded ridiculous.

Had Aidan, at the time, remained sufficiently compos mentis to murder his assailant? Or had he been knocked out, leaving vengeance to his brother?

There was still the remote possibility that Aidan had been injured after leaving home, or, even less likely, after reaching Manchester. Tracing him among the hordes at St. Pancras was a long shot, but Manchester's London Road Station after midnight was a brighter prospect. Aidan's railway porter must be found and questioned, Alec decided. Sipping his coffee, he wished it could be postponed till the morning, but the night staff would go off duty and memories would fade.

He swallowed the last drop of coffee, regretfully declined another cup, thanked Greaves, and went to see if the hotel porter happened to know the name of the railway porter.

"Fred Banks," said Wetherby promptly. "We was in the Manchester Regiment together."

Alec trudged back into the station. Knowing the name, finding the porter was easy, and he was as willing to talk as his regimental mate.

"Course I remember the gent," he said, his Manchester accent thick as the industrial city's soot-laden air. "When the train pulled in, I seen him standing at a door. Waved me over and pointed out his luggage."

"Was he talking normally?"

"Yes, sir, normal as any Londoner do. Didn't seem nowt the matter with him, barring he looked tired, which all the passengers do comin' orf that train. He stepped down to the platform as I went over to him, and he missed his footing seemingly. He didn't fall acos I caught him, but he landed on his feet with a bit of a jar. He were a mite shook-up, like, that's all. It's only a few inches. Then when I come down with his bags, he were leaning against my barrow, looking sick as a dog."

"Did you suspect he might be drunk?"

"No, sir, acos he were all right before. I did wonder was it shell shock. It takes some people funny, and a jar like that might bring it on. Any road, I arst was he all right, and he said, sort of slurred, like, yes, he just wanted to get on to the hotel. So I took him, and I can tell you, I didn't think he'd make it, for all it's hardly a step. But I got him there and turned him over to Jim Wetherby, as is porter at the hotel. He give me half a crown. A nice gent, and I'm sure I hope he'll be all right. It's a funny thing, shell shock."

Alec did not need another complication such as shell shock. He wondered what Aidan had done during the War. He'd have to find out, but he didn't seriously consider the porter's theory. A jarring of the spine such as he had described would be quite enough to set off the aftereffects of a concussion.

That, however, brought him no nearer to understanding the crime.

After scarcely three hours' sleep, Alec was picked up at the hotel by the police car and the detective constable he had requested. In a wet, grey dawn, they drove to the Royal Infirmary.

The hospital smelt of disinfectant. Alec supposed it was better than the other smells it undoubtedly disguised. He tried to breathe shallowly.

A long wait ensued before Alec was at last permitted to speak to a doctor. The young man who then appeared looked as somnolent as Alec felt, and nowhere near old enough to have earned his white coat and stethoscope. Dr. Gibson was old enough and awake enough, however, to be adamant that on no account was Aidan Jessup to be disturbed.

"Not even by the police."

"His brother?"

"No one will be allowed to visit him." After many hours of two eminent consultants disagreeing as to whether the patient needed an operation to relieve pressure on the brain, he had at

last fallen into natural sleep. "Left to sleep until he rouses naturally, he has an excellent chance of waking as his normal self. He's even been given a private room to reduce the risk of premature awakening. And," said Dr. Gibson with a tired grimace, "his clothes and his hotel suggested he'd be able to pay for it."

"He can. Excellent," said Alec. "I'll be able to leave DC Peters in his room without exciting undue interest or inviting questions."

"Can he sit still and silent for as long as need be?" the doctor asked sceptically.

From the corner of his eye, Alec saw Peters about to burst a blood vessel. Smoothly, he forestalled an outburst that would have seriously undermined their credibility. "It's a skill every detective has to master. He can sit outside the door if you insist, but you must see that people will wonder what's going on."

Not to mention that he wanted Aidan's very first words captured, and wanted to be informed at once when he came round. He hated to badger a sick man, but it would be best to catch him before he had time to come up with an explanation of his plight, and, with luck, before Patrick tried to see him. The story the brothers had agreed upon had very likely been wiped out by Aidan's concussion, always supposing he had taken it in in the first place.

Dr. Gibson capitulated. "Oh, very well."

DC Peters had already been given his instructions. He melted away unobtrusively to take up his post.

"Thank you. I have one more question. Is it possible to tell when the patient received the injury to his head?"

"You'll have to ask the consultant."

"You didn't hear him offer an opinion? I'm not asking you to give evidence, just to give me an indication."

"I wasn't on duty yesterday morning. According to the patient's chart, at the time when Mr. Jessup was brought in, Dr. Penstone considered the degree of healing of the external injury suggested that twelve to eighteen hours had passed since it

was inflicted. Now, if you can possibly spare me, I *do* have other patients to take care of."

Alec thanked him absently. Here was unwelcome, though anticipated, confirmation of his guess. Aidan Jessup had been injured the very evening that Castellano had died; another strand in the rope that might hang his next-door neighbour's son.

He went to find a telephone. No doubt he ought to report to Superintendent Crane, but three hours' sleep was not sufficient to enable him to tackle his irascible superior. Whatever the Home Secretary's complaint involved, he'd rather not know.

He asked the operator for Whitehall 1212 all the same. It was still early and Tom Tring might have gone in to the Yard before setting about the various enquiries left for him—the Bennetts' tale, Lambert's whereabouts, Whitcomb's evidence. One might suppose that Whitcomb would have come forward already if he had seen anything. In Alec's experience, however, businessmen were prone to negligence in matters where no profit was to be made. At the very least, finding out the time he had walked through the garden might be helpful.

The connection to London took forever, and when at last Alec got through to the Yard, he was told DS Tring had not come in. Quickly, before the operator lost the London connection, he asked for his own home number. Daisy might have news of Tom. If not, there was a good chance she would see him at some point during the day, and she could pass on the doctor's report on Aidan Jessup. Besides, as always when he was out of town, he just wanted to hear her voice.

Elsie answered the phone. "Oh dear, sir, I'm ever so sorry. She's already gone."

"Gone where?"

"To Lincolnshire, sir. Mr. Irwin picked her up in a motor-car. I think they went to see Mrs. Aidan."

So he just wanted to hear her voice, did he? Now he realised that what he had really wanted was to make sure she wasn't meddling in the investigation.

And he didn't like the answer.

TWENTY-FIVE

By the time they left the Great North Road at Norman Cross, Daisy was heartily wishing she hadn't come. A couple of hours confined with Mr. Irwin, even in the luxurious comfort of a chauffeured Lanchester, was enough to convince her that her first impressions, gained when he showed her around Alec's great-uncle Walsall's house, were accurate. He was a fussbox, and an incredibly boring one.

After she had assured him four or five times that she was perfectly comfortable and quite warm enough, he started fretting about the unfortunate state of affairs that was taking them to Lincolnshire. His concern was natural. Daisy had no quarrel with that. But she felt he should be more worried about his daughter and grandchildren than about the effect on his standing with the Law Society of having a son-in-law arrested for murder.

Nor did she see why she should be forced to listen to a lengthy diatribe on his advice to Maurice Jessup not to engage in shipping alcoholic beverages to America. He went into great detail about the laws and treaties involved, all of which passed over Daisy's head.

She had been trying for some time to shut out his droning voice when it dawned on her that his words were addressed not to her but to Alec, through her. Though she was accustomed to people giving her information they wanted to convey to the police without actually having to speak to the police, she considered it most improper in a lawyer.

He didn't even have the excuse of being a suspect. She listened with increasing indignation as he explained how he couldn't possibly be held to blame for the consequences if his clients chose to disregard his advice.

"I'm sorry, I must have missed something," she said. "Are you saying you advised the Jessups not to bump off Castellano? Because if so, surely it was your duty, not just as a lawyer but as a citizen, to warn the police that they were contemplating murder?"

Irwin stared at her aghast. "Oh, no, no, no!" He took out a linen handkerchief and mopped his forehead. "Oh no, my dear Mrs. Fletcher, you misunderstand me entirely! I knew nothing of their plans in advance, I assure you."

"They didn't tell you till afterwards?"

"No, no, they never breathed a word to me, neither before nor after."

"Then why do you think you could be held responsible?"

"Well, I did know about the . . . er . . . the 'bootlegging,' and since that led to the murder—"

"So you believe they did it, do you? Aidan or Patrick, or the two together?"

"Not Aidan! No!" he said violently. "Aidan is a very steady and responsible young man, or I should never have let Audrey marry him. But who knows what sort of criminals Patrick consorted with in America? The . . . victim was American, I gather."

"Did you know Patrick had gone to America?"

"I was not told. I guessed. Had I been consulted, I should have advised very strongly against it, and with reason. Look what has come of it!"

Mr. Irwin had clearly persuaded himself that Patrick was guilty. Daisy could only be glad he was not her solicitor.

Did he have a reason for that belief, beyond his determination not to suspect Aidan? Did he know something Daisy did not? And if Patrick was the murderer, why had Aidan fled?

As an afterthought, what had happened to Lambert?

Beyond Peterborough, the land was dead flat, crisscrossed by ditches draining the fens. There were pastures dotted with cattle, but much of it was rich arable land. Here and there, a windmill loomed, great sails slowly turning. Daisy's thoughts turned to Audrey's sister's farm.

Audrey had talked about her sister occasionally, saying Vivien had married a farmer. Daisy had no idea what to expect—it could be anything from a cottage to a mansion. The inhabitant of either might be described as a farmer, from a cowman to a gentleman who never went nearer the fields than his bailiff's office. On the other hand, she couldn't imagine Mr. Irwin permitting a daughter of his to meet a cowman, let alone marry one; and if she had married into the aristocracy, or even the gentry, the family wouldn't refer to him as a farmer.

No doubt he was something in between. Daisy realised she didn't know his name, either, but she decided not to ask Mr. Irwin, who had mercifully fallen silent at last. She didn't want to incite another peroration. Sooner or later, she would find out.

The driver stopped in Boston to ask the way to Butterwick, and in Butterwick to ask the way to West Dyke Farm. The end of the long trek was in sight.

Farm turned out to be a modest term for a substantial house. Architecture was not Daisy's strong point, but she thought the original brick farmhouse must have been enlarged as long ago as the eighteenth century to make a pleasant manor. The green-and-brown-striped fields extended right up to the gardens, with no extravagant park intervening. Perhaps a park had been ploughed under during the War. Or perhaps the family— what was their name?—that continued to call their home "Farm"

when it might have aspired to a grander title, had seen no sense in wasting valuable cropland.

As the chauffeur pulled up the Lanchester in front of the house, Daisy realised that for all his talk, Irwin had said nothing constructive about the purpose of their trip.

"Are you going to tell Audrey about Aidan privately?" she asked him. "I mean, are you going to try to keep it from her sister?"

"I?" he exclaimed. "But that's what you came for, Mrs. Fletcher, to break the news to Audrey."

"No, I most certainly did not," Daisy said crossly. "I came to support her, to hold her hand, and to accompany her to Manchester if she decides to go."

"But *I* can't tell her. She'll very likely cry!"

"It wouldn't surprise me. That's why I'll be there to hold her hand and make soothing noises."

"You know much more than I do about what's happened. You'll be far better able to reassure her."

"Nothing I know is in the least likely to be reassuring," said Daisy, her tone uncompromising.

"Oh dear! I thought I'd keep Vivien occupied while you—"

"So you don't want her and her husband to be told?"

"That is entirely up to Audrey," Irwin said with some dignity. "But even if she's willing for her sister to hear the whole, she may well not want Bessemer in the picture."

Bessemer—at least Daisy had a name now. She recognised that she was losing the argument, though. What chance had she against a lawyer, trained to keep a dispute running for years? Just look at *Bleak House!*

"All right," she said crossly, "but you'll have to explain why I want to speak to Audrey privately. You can't expect me to barge into the house of people I've never met and drag their guest away from whatever she's doing."

Even a lawyer could scarcely argue with that.

Daisy hadn't realised how stiff she was till she stepped out of the car, nor how cold and hungry she was until she stepped into

the warm house and smelled lunch. The Bessemers and Audrey were, in fact, in the middle of their midday meal. The newcomers were welcomed without overt curiosity, and places were quickly set for them.

Vivien Bessemer and her husband indeed seemed genuinely incurious about the reason for the unexpected arrival of her father and her sister's friend. Audrey, however, was very much on edge, and she pushed her food around her plate without, as far as Daisy could see, eating more than the odd morsel. Daisy ate well, not so much to postpone the distasteful task she'd landed herself with as to fortify herself for it.

At last, she and Audrey were settled in a small parlour with their coffee.

"What's wrong?" Audrey asked at once, leaning forward, her hands clasped in her lap. "What's happened?"

At least Daisy didn't have to announce the fact of bad news. Audrey was obviously expecting it.

"I'm afraid Aidan has been injured—"

"I know that much. I thought he was all right, though, just a bit of a headache. The policeman who came this morning, that Scotsman, didn't mention anything else."

"There have been some aftereffects," Daisy said vaguely. "He's being properly taken care of. Don't worry. Why don't you tell me about that evening, the evening before you left, so that I don't go repeating what you already know."

"I already told the policeman."

"It's not for the police I want to know, Audrey. I came as your friend, to try to help. It'll be easier if I have a better idea of what happened, and DS Mackinnon's not likely to tell me."

"Oh, right-oh. Everyone was excited about Patrick coming home. They're a very close family, you see. Usually, I feel very much a part of it. I wouldn't want you to think they shut me out in any way. No one could have a dearer mother-in-law than Mama Moira. But . . . I suppose—I'm afraid, looking back, I was a little jealous. I didn't tell Mr. Mackinnon that. I'm so ashamed of it."

"It seems to me perfectly understandable, and none of the police's business."

"It's not that I don't like Patrick, but they were making such a fuss about his return."

"Mrs. Jessup had been pretty worried about him, hadn't she?"

"Yes. It was stupid of me to feel that way. Anyway, Aidan and his father came home early the day Patrick was expected. Aidan said he was going to go out to walk about and get a spot of fresh air and see if he could spot Patrick's taxi arriving. It wasn't even a pleasant evening! I went up to the nursery. I don't know how long I was there—you know how time passes when you're playing with the children."

"Like a flash," Daisy agreed.

"Then Mama Moira came in—all the servants would have been busy with preparations for dinner—and she asked me to go down. She didn't say why. I assumed Patrick must have come in, but I didn't ask because she seemed . . . well, rather upset. We didn't go down to the drawing room as I expected. She took me to our bedroom—Aidan's and mine—and there was Aidan with a plaster on his head, right on top. He said he'd had an accident and bumped it."

"Didn't you ask how?"

"He just said he'd been careless and slipped. I didn't ask for details because then he told me he'd decided he couldn't put off his trip to the North any longer and he was going to wait to welcome Patrick home and then catch a train. And Mama Moira said she was sure I'd want to make the best of my time and leave in the morning to come here, to stay with Vivien. I felt as if I was being rushed, but they both seemed a bit peculiar, so I didn't like to make a fuss. It was all . . . strange. I did wonder if perhaps Aidan had met Patrick and they'd quarrelled . . . ?"

Her voice rose in a question. Daisy said, "I'm pretty sure you needn't worry about that."

"I didn't really believe it. They've always been such good friends. Anyway, Mama Moira helped me pack for Aidan and

start to organise my own packing. Nurse wasn't to be told till after the children were asleep, for fear of them getting over-excited."

"Miranda and Oliver aren't old enough yet to be excited about things that haven't happened yet."

Audrey smiled at that. "They will be, all too soon!"

"No doubt. You started to pack. . . ."

"Then Patrick arrived and we all had Champagne to celebrate, in the mirror room. But it was all frightfully artificial somehow. It's hard to explain. You know Mama Moira was an actress. It was as if everyone was acting, including me. I was desperate to know what was wrong, but I just didn't quite dare to ask. Then it was time to change for dinner. That's when Aidan left. He kissed me, just as if he was going off to work on an ordinary day, and he told me not to worry, but how can I help it? And now my father's come all this way, and you . . ." Her voice failed.

"Only because Mrs. Jessup decided a telegram would be too upsetting. She'd have come herself—"

"Thank heaven she didn't! Travelling in a car makes her frightfully sick. She'd have been half dead and in need of nursing. You said Aidan's getting proper care. What's wrong, and where is he?"

"I don't know very much. We tried to ring up the hospital—"

"Hospital!"

"He was taken ill at his hotel, and they couldn't keep him there. You know what hotel people are like, always worrying about what the other guests might think. Aidan just needs rest and absolute quiet and someone to keep an eye on him. It was too early to speak to anyone at the hospital when we rang up this morning, but I dare say he's perfectly all right after a good night's sleep."

"I must go to him, of course. Vivien won't mind keeping the children."

"Your father intends to take you."

"You'll come, too, won't you, Daisy? I love Father dearly, but . . ."

"If you really want me," said Daisy, but what she thought was, *Try to stop me!* For one thing, she had no desire to attempt what sounded like a wretched train journey back to London. Luckily, Audrey didn't seem interested in why she had come in the first place. It would be hard to explain that she'd let herself be dragooned into doing something she really wanted to do.

"Oh, I do!" Audrey hesitated. "Daisy, is all this something to do with . . . all those policemen in the garden?"

"You saw them?"

"They were hard to miss! The morning after Aidan was hurt—but Aidan couldn't have anything to do with that. It's just a coincidence. It must be."

"The most extraordinary coincidences do happen."

Audrey took a deep breath and visibly braced herself. "Daisy, I don't know what they were looking for, and I don't think I want to know, but your husband isn't going to arrest my husband as soon as he's well enough, is he?"

"As far as I'm aware," Daisy said with careful precision, "Alec hasn't yet worked out exactly what happened in the garden. He's hoping Aidan may have some information that will help him find out."

Which was the truth, as far as it went. Daisy had no desire whatsoever to be the one to enlighten Audrey about the murder in the garden and the indisputable connections between the Jessups and the murdered man.

TWENTY-SIX

Before going to Aidan Jessup's room, Alec had a word with the matron herself. That formidable figure, once convinced of the necessity, assured him that Patrick would not be allowed access to his brother until Alec had finished with him. Hospital visiting hours, though stringent for ordinary patients, were usually relaxed for private patients, but it would be easy to delay the young man. Fortunately, he had slept late and was still breakfasting when Alec received word that Aidan was awake and coherent.

As an added precaution, Alec beckoned the Manchester DC out of the room and posted him outside the door.

"How is he?" he asked in a low voice.

"Fair addled," said Peters succinctly.

Alec raised an eyebrow.

"In his right mind," the young man elaborated, "but no lawyer worth his salt 'd agree he's fit to make a statement."

"Thank you. I won't take a statement, then, just try to get enough out of him to know what questions to put to his brother. Who is not on any account to be allowed to interrupt."

"Got it, sir."

"I take it he hasn't said anything of interest?"

"Nowt but asking for a drink o' water, sir, which I gave him. He seemed to think I were a hospital orderly, and I didn't set him straight."

With a nod of approval, Alec went on into the room. It was Spartan but very clean and neat, a haven from the public wards for those who could pay a little for privacy but could not afford a private nursing home. Aidan lay flat on his back, his arms at his sides on top of the tightly tucked-in covers, a model patient. A nurse must have tidied him back to hospital standards since Peters gave him a drink, Alec assumed.

Aidan turned his head on the pillow as Alec entered. His eyes appeared to focus with difficulty, but he recognised his visitor.

"Mr. Fletcher." His voice was slightly slurred. He didn't seem surprised to see Alec, whether because he was as yet incapable of experiencing surprise or because he had half-expected him.

"Good morning, Mr. Jessup. How are you feeling?"

"*Much* better. My God, it was awful! I've had a concussion before—playing rugger, you know—but nothing like this. It was like being drunk as a lord and having a frightful hangover at the same time."

Alec moved the room's one chair to the bedside and set it so that he could see Aidan's face. "I'm afraid I have to ask you some questions."

"I know. I can't remember much, though."

If he pleaded amnesia, no one would be able to prove otherwise. It was a common symptom of severe concussion. He might be tricked, though, if he were lying about it.

"I'm not taking a formal statement at this time," Alec said, "but if you want a lawyer—"

"My father-in-law? No thanks!"

"Or someone else."

"No, thank you."

"All right, then, tell me what you remember of the evening you left London."

"I've been lying here thinking about it—I'd sit up, but my head still gets a bit swimmy. As I say, I've been thinking about it, and I still don't see what else I could have done. We were expecting Patrick home, as I'm sure you know by now. We weren't sure exactly when he'd arrive, but Father and I left work early so as to be there when he came. I got fed up sitting there waiting, and it had stopped raining, so I decided to stroll down to the corner. If I didn't meet him, at least I'd have had a breath of fresh air and stretched my legs."

"You were very keen to see him."

"Well, he'd been away a long time, and on his own for the first time. And there were business reasons why we were eager to hear his news."

Also, thought Alec, there was a good deal of brotherly affection between them. Though Aidan was no public school boy, he had absorbed enough of the ethos not to mention it, but Alec had a hunch that their mutual fondness played a considerable part in the whole affair.

"You went out of the house. . . ."

"And crossed the street. I expected Pat to come by taxi. The quickest way from our house to the street exit from the Circle is across the garden—though, come to think of it, he could have been driving round the Circle while I cut across. Anyway, it was getting dark and I was nearly at the fountain before I realised that the chap coming up towards me was Pat. And a moment later, that damn Yankee popped out of nowhere—"

"Out of nowhere?"

"I don't know if he'd been hiding behind a tree or if he just happened to come around the Circle and see me walking down, and followed me. He suddenly appeared beside me and started the same old jabber. He had a business proposition for the firm, it would be worth our while, we'd regret it if we didn't listen to him, and so on. Father wasn't interested. I brushed the fellow off, as per usual. Next thing I knew, he was pointing a gun at Patrick!"

"You're sure of that?" Alec snapped.

"Sure as you're a copper," Aidan said wryly. "I didn't get into

combat during the War—they put me to running an officers' mess, because of my experience in the trade—but I saw plenty of firearms. Well, I reacted without thinking. I'm still a pretty useful rugger wing forward, you know, or was until this." He touched the top of his head. "I tackled him, as if it were the ball he was holding. I hit him pretty hard and we both went down. The paving was wet, slick, so we started to slide. I don't remember the next bit. I was out. Pat says we both hit the rim of the fountain head-on."

"The missing weapon!" The *other* missing weapon. What the hell had become of the gun? The Jessups would have had no conceivable reason to dispose of it.

Aidan smiled crookedly. "Were you looking for the traditional blunt instrument? It's there, in plain sight, though I presume any blood Pat failed to clean up has been washed away by the rain. I was out for nearly five minutes, Pat reckoned. He was beginning to get really worried. He started splashing water from the fountain in my face—ugh!—to try to bring me round. Maybe it worked, who knows. At any rate, I started to show signs of life. Then it dawned on Pat that he'd better check on the other chap. He turned—"

"Could you explain your relative positions?"

"It's all a bit vague. . . ." Aidan frowned in concentration. "Pat was kneeling between us, so somehow the American and I got separated. Perhaps we rolled apart when we hit the fountain. I suppose I let go of him when I was knocked out."

"More than likely."

"Pat turned away from me to— What's his name? I can't go on calling him 'the American.'"

"He never introduced himself?"

"Neither Father nor I ever let him get that far. We have a long-standing and satisfactory arrangement with our American customer and we just weren't interested in changing."

"Castellano. Michele Castellano. Though there's some question about whether that's his real name, as his passport was faked."

"He looked Italian. He was a thoroughly objectionable type, but I didn't mean to kill him. I couldn't let him shoot my brother in cold blood, could I?"

Silently, Alec cursed. A confession, and he couldn't use it! But having spoken the words, Aidan would find them difficult to retract in circumstances more useful from a police point of view. He was no hardened criminal.

"Tell me exactly what happened," Alec urged.

"Pat said something like 'Oh hell, he's still out. He can't have as thick a skull as yours.' And then he said—he sounded a bit panicky—'He's not breathing. I don't think he's breathing!' I said, 'Feel his pulse,' or perhaps Pat said, 'I'll feel his pulse'— I'm not awfully clear which. I was still a bit groggy. Does it matter? What it comes down to is that there was no pulse. Castellano was dead."

So much for the confession. If Aidan was telling the truth, he was implicating his brother, unaware that the blow to the victim's head was not the cause of death. While Aidan lay unconscious, or semiconscious, Patrick had compressed Castellano's arteries until, starved of oxygen, the brain stopped sending signals to the lungs to breathe, the heart to beat.

"I still don't see what I could have done differently," Aidan said dully, "except not to let the others hustle me away. I wasn't thinking straight. I should have stayed to take my medicine. It wasn't exactly *self*-defence, but I was defending my brother."

"What reasons did they give for your leaving in such a hurry? You're speaking of your parents and your brother? Your wife?"

"Not Audrey! She was in the nursery, thank heaven, when I came in bloody-headed. Before she came down, Mother had patched me up and we'd decided I should go. Why? It's all a bit of a blur, but there seemed to be a dozen reasons. Patrick swore he'd hidden the body so that it wouldn't be found for days."

"When did he do that?"

"While I was sitting holding my head, wondering whether I could make it back to the house. If I'd been able to think, I

wouldn't have let him, but he always was impetuous, and once it was done, it was done. He said if I stayed away until my head healed, there be no reason for anyone to suppose I had anything to do with it. Then he buzzed off to create an alibi for himself."

"At the Flask."

"Yes, he really did go there. Luckily, the servants hadn't seen him arrive. If it was luck."

"That remains to be seen. So far, your only reason for having left is that your brother hoped to get away with it."

"He was, naturally, grateful that I'd prevented Castellano's shooting him," Aidan said vehemently, "and he didn't see why I should suffer for protecting him."

"What other reasons?"

"Mother was terrified that I'd go to prison. You've got to remember that she's Irish and an actress, and she has enough temperament for both, though she hides it well most of the time. Father, naturally, was concerned about the effect on the business. And there were Audrey and the children to consider. I suppose I'm bound to go to prison now? It's going to be a terrible shock for Audrey, and awfully hard on all of them."

Alec wondered how much Daisy would reveal to Audrey. She was perfectly capable of being discreet if it suited her ideas of what was right. However, he had never quite fathomed how her mind worked in that regard. In fact, he wasn't at all sure she'd be able to explain it if she tried.

"My job is to find out what happened," he said. "What the public prosecutor and the courts decide to do about it is not for me to decide."

"No." Aidan closed his eyes, looking exhausted and defenceless. "Go easy on Pat, Fletcher, if you can. He's just a boy still. I wish Audrey were here."

She might well be at her husband's bedside soon, if Daisy had her way. Irwin might dissuade her, though. He wouldn't be too happy about having a gaolbird in the family.

As for Patrick, Alec had more than enough to pull him in on a charge of interfering with a corpse, if nothing worse.

Before he sent DC Peters to find Patrick, Alec arranged for the use of a room where they could be undisturbed. It was little more than a cupboard, badly lit, but adequate for his purpose, with a small table and three hard wooden chairs.

While Peters went to fetch Patrick, he moved the chairs into his preferred arrangement, himself facing the suspect across the table, with the DC to sit against the wall, slightly behind Patrick, to take notes. On the whole, people were more willing to talk if they didn't actually watch their words being written down. On the other hand, some found it easier to lie if they forgot their lies could be quoted back to them word for word.

Patrick burst into the room. "He's not . . . Aidan . . . He hasn't died?"

"Great Scott no! He's very much improved."

He slumped onto the chair. "Thank God," he said fervently. "I was afraid . . . I was afraid you were going to break it to me gently. . . . But you're being a detective here, aren't you? Not a friend of the family, I mean."

"Yes. Your brother has been telling me what actually happened the night Castellano died. I'm now going to ask you if you'd like to revise your previous statement. You do not have to say anything, but anything you choose to say will be taken down and may be used in evidence in a court of law. You're entitled to have a lawyer present—"

"A lawyer? I don't need a law— Oh hell, I suppose I shouldn't have hidden the body."

"Why did you?"

"I hoped it wouldn't be found for a while. That Aidan could go away until his head healed and no one would connect him with it. It seemed like a good idea at the time. There wasn't time to discuss it, and Aidan was still pretty woozy anyway. You can't blame him for that."

"All right. Now, suppose we start at the beginning. You took the boat train from Liverpool?"

"Yes, and the tube from the station."

"At what time?"

"The Flask was just opening, so it must have been half past five."

"But you didn't go in." Alec hadn't read the report of who-ever had questioned the people at the Flask, but if Aidan's story was true, his brother hadn't had time for a drink on his way home.

He flushed. "No, not then."

"You walked on to Constable Circle." That was for the record. "You took the path up through the garden in the centre."

"Yes."

"Tell me what happened."

"I saw Aidan coming down the hill. He told you about the man with the gun?"

"You tell me."

"I know now it was this fellow Castellano, but I wouldn't have recognised him even if it hadn't been getting dark. I'd never seen him before in my life."

"You hadn't come across him in America?"

"No. I gather he'd been in England for ages, long before I actually reached America. I was at sea for most of the time I was away, as I told you."

"Castellano was with your brother? He introduced him to you?"

"Lord no! The man was pestering Aidan. Aidan was trying to ignore him. My father told me he'd been making a nuisance of himself on and off for weeks. Nothing serious, just irritating. I mean, nothing that would give anyone a reason to . . . to kill him, let alone Aidan, who's the most peaceable man on the planet. He doesn't even have a temper, far less lose it! And why Castellano should want to shoot me— Well, it's beyond the bounds of credibility." Patrick shook his head in disbelief.

"Describe the sequence of events, please."

"Aidan saw me and waved. I think he started walking a bit faster, though it's hard to be sure. Castellano kept up with him, anyway. They came on down the slope until they reached the

fountain. As they came round it, Castellano took one look at me and pulled out a gun!"

"Did he say anything?"

"Say anything? He could have sung the 'Hallelujah Chorus' and I wouldn't have noticed. I was too stunned to move. He was pointing the damn thing at me! If it had happened on the other side of the Atlantic, I might have been halfway prepared, but I'd just come home safe. I tell you, I froze. This can't be happening, I thought, not here! But big brother came to the rescue once again."

"Again?"

"He's eight years older than me, you see, and he's always considered it sort of his mission in life to keep me out of trouble. He tackled the brute round the knees, brought him to the ground. Only the ground wasn't a nice muddy rugger field; it was slippery paving surrounding a fountain. They slid into the rim of the pool and both got knocked out."

"*What happened to the gun?*" Alec couldn't keep the urgency from his voice. Without the gun as evidence of a threat from Castellano, the Jessups hadn't a leg to stand on. Not that one of them did anyway, he reminded himself, considering the pathologist's damning evidence.

Patrick looked surprised. "Gosh, I'd forgotten. It flew out of Castellano's hand when Aidan hit him, and I caught it. Aidan may be the rugger star, but I'm a fair hand with a cricket ball."

"And?"

" 'And'?"

"What did you do with it?"

"I can't rem— Yes, I can!" he said triumphantly. "I chucked it away. When you get your hands on a ball in cricket, you hardly ever hang on to it unless you've caught the batsman out. You bung it to the wicket-keeper or the bowler. Besides, I didn't know when I caught it that Castellano was unconscious, and I didn't want him getting hold of it again. I don't know much about guns, but I reckoned if it landed in the pool, it wouldn't be much use to him if he did find it."

"You threw it towards the pool?"

"Yes, and on the whole I'm a pretty accurate shot. With a cricket ball, that is. The shape and weight and balance of a pistol are quite different, of course, so I might have missed."

"It has not been found in the pool, nor anywhere near it."

"You mean you haven't found it at all? Damn it, I couldn't have tossed it out of the garden!"

"Never mind that, for the moment. Go on. Your brother and Castellano were lying unconscious by the pool."

"Well, naturally, I went to make sure Aidan was all right. Only he wasn't. When someone gets hit on the head and knocked out, you expect them to open their eyes in a minute or so, don't you? He just wouldn't come round. He seemed to be breathing all right, though. I tried dipping my handkerchief in the pool and bathing his face."

"How long do you estimate he was unconscious?"

"Gosh, I don't know. It seemed like forever. I suppose it can't have been more than about five minutes. It can't have been that much darker when he blinked at me at last, or I wouldn't have seen him blink. I'm telling you, I nearly sang the 'Hallelujah Chorus' myself."

"Explain to me, please, your relative positions while you were trying to bring him round."

Patrick gave him an odd look. "Right-oh. They'd rolled apart, Aidan and Castellano, when they hit. There was just room to kneel between them. Oh! I suppose it was pretty stupid to turn my back on him like that. I never gave it a thought at the time. I was too worried about Aidan to worry about anything else. And then, when I did remember him, it turned out the crack on the head had killed him." He was silent for a long moment. "It was an accident. Or at least pure chance. Aidan attacked him, but he didn't intend to hurt him, just to stop him shooting me. You must see that!"

If it weren't for those two telltale bruises on either side of his throat, and the internal evidence that confirmed their meaning . . .

The rest of Patrick's tale matched Aidan's closely. After hiding the body, he had helped his brother home, quickly explained to his parents what had happened, and then gone to the pub to establish an alibi. When he returned home, Aidan was ready to leave. He seemed perfectly all right except for a bit of a headache.

Alec found the brothers' story damnably convincing. He couldn't see either of them as a cold-blooded killer, yet everything suggested one of them, probably Patrick, was just that.

Could the pathologist be wrong? Or had they both inherited their mother's thespian talent?

He wasn't quite ready for an arrest. First, he'd get them both to Scotland Yard and see whether they had a different song to sing in those austere premises.

One thing was certain, it wouldn't be the "Hallelujah Chorus."

TWENTY-SEVEN

By the time Daisy, Audrey, and Mr. Irwin reached the Manchester Royal Infirmary, Aidan had been pronounced out of danger. He would have to forswear Rugby football for at least a year, preferably forever. But if, after another night in hospital, there was no relapse, he might go home.

The consultant was not happy to learn that home was two hundred miles away. A train journey was out of the question. But he conceded that a private automobile driven with the greatest care at a moderate rate of speed could do his patient no harm.

Mr. Irwin's hired car could not accommodate everyone in comfort if Aidan was to have room to lie down on one of the seats. Alec announced very firmly that he and Patrick would take the train. Daisy expected to go with them, but Audrey announced equally firmly that she wanted Daisy to travel with her and Aidan. She knew, she said, her father wouldn't mind going by train, so as not to crowd the invalid.

Her father did mind, but he gave in after a little grumbling. Audrey explained to Daisy later that Aidan would go mad shut up hour after hour with his father-in-law, unable to escape his homilies.

In the meanwhile, the only time Daisy saw Alec alone was back in their bedroom at the Station Hotel. By then he was so exhausted, he hadn't the energy to rag her for going to Lincolnshire and then proceeding to Manchester. He did ask whether she had learnt anything useful from Audrey or Irwin, but when she said, "No, nothing," he promptly fell fast asleep.

She was glad to be able to tell the truth. She didn't know what she'd have done if Audrey had told her, as a friend, something she really ought to pass on to the police. But Audrey *did* know she was married to a policeman, she reminded herself drowsily. She wasn't—wouldn't have been—hearing confidences under false pretences. . . . She, too, fell asleep.

The next day was a different matter. As the Lanchester purred southward, the strictly admonished chauffeur doing an excellent job of avoiding bumps, swerves, and sudden stops, Aidan told his wife what had happened on that fatal night.

Daisy couldn't help but hear. When he started talking, she pointed out that she was, to some degree at least, the ear of the Law. Aidan said it didn't matter.

"I've already told your husband everything," he said wearily.

Audrey listened in increasing distress, Daisy with interest that turned to puzzlement. Something was missing, though she couldn't quite put her finger on it. She didn't mention it. Audrey would only assume she was accusing Aidan of deliberately concealing the worst.

The story was bad enough. Aidan expected to be prosecuted for involuntary manslaughter, or something of the sort, and Patrick was in trouble for moving the body and concealing a crime.

"But they won't send you to prison, darling?" Audrey asked in anguish. "You didn't mean to kill him! And he would have shot Patrick."

"They can't find the gun," Aidan told her sombrely. "I don't know whether they believe Castellano really threatened Patrick's life. If they can persuade a jury I attacked him without immediate cause, even not meaning to kill him . . ."

Audrey got a bit weepy. Daisy pretended not to notice Aidan comforting her and not to hear her promising to wait for him forever.

The missing gun—was that what was bothering her? More crucial was Alec's certainty that Castellano had been murdered with cool deliberation. Was Aidan protecting Patrick still, with lies now, rather than with action? Was Patrick protecting Aidan, similarly, by lying about the cause of death, as he had previously hidden the body and rushed his brother out of town? Did neither of them know the police had evidence of purposeful murder?

Would Alec have let her travel with Aidan and Audrey if he believed Aidan to be a cold-blooded murderer?

With a brave attempt at normalcy, Audrey started to talk about how much the children were enjoying her sister's farm. They had helped feed chickens and collect eggs, watched the milking from a safe distance, and even taken brief rides on the broad backs of the cart horses. Her description of the last, with Marilyn hanging on like grim death and Percy blithely waving with both arms, made Aidan smile. But his eyelids soon drooped and he slipped into sleep.

Daisy and Audrey stared silently out of the windows at the endless drab industrial towns of the Midlands. At least it wasn't raining. Daisy was still plagued with a feeling that she had forgotten some vital fact. As so often happened, the harder she tried to pin it down, the less certain she was that she hadn't imagined the whole thing.

It was late when they reached Hampstead. They were all exhausted. Brief good nights were said on the pavement, then Daisy plodded up the steps to her front door, followed by the driver with her suitcase. At the top, he set it down. She tipped him, and as he ran back down to help the others, she rang the bell rather than dig for the key in her bag.

Elsie opened the door. "Oh madam, I'm ever so glad you're back."

"So am I," said Daisy fervently, hurrying into the warmth of the hall.

"There's messages," announced the parlour maid, lugging the suitcase in and closing the door. "The master rang up, and he may be very late tonight. And that Mr. Lambert called twice, and I know it was him, even if he did have his collar up and his hat down and wouldn't give his name."

"Oh no!"

"Yes'm, it was him for sure."

"What did he want?"

"He wouldn't tell me, 'm. Said he needed to speak to you or the master, so I told him you was in the North and if he wanted the master, he'd better go to Scotland Yard, and he said he wasn't going there, thank you very much, the way they treated him last time. He said to tell you it was urgent, but he wouldn't leave an address or telephone number."

"Oh dear, I wonder what's wrong!"

"Not to worry, madam. He said he'd keep coming back till he got hold of you. And there's one more."

"One more what?" Daisy asked blankly, her mind on Lambert's gyrations.

"Message, 'm." She went to the hall table. "My sister brought round this note. They're in a terrible state over there, she said, but she wouldn't tell me what about, and I reckon she don't really know."

Daisy's heart sank. On the whole, she would have preferred to remain in ignorance. Trying to hide a sigh, she said, "Thank you, Elsie. Take my suitcase up, would you, please."

She opened the note. It was from Mrs. Jessup. Patrick had been asked to go to Scotland Yard to "assist the police with their enquiries." What did it mean? Mr. Irwin was no help at all, since all he did was reiterate that he "took the gravest view" of the situation, which she and her husband were quite capable of doing for themselves. Would Daisy please come—when she had recovered from the journey, of course—and explain the significance of those ominous words.

There was a blotch that looked alarmingly like a tearstain. Daisy couldn't imagine Mrs. Jessup crying. Had the note sounded

even remotely accusatory, she would have sent a refusal, wrapped decently in mentions of fatigue and the lateness of the hour. But nothing suggested Daisy or her policeman husband was responsible for the Jessups' plight.

She decided she'd better go right away. If she took off her coat and sat down, or went to see the babies, she might never get moving again. With a sigh she made no effort to conceal, she called up the stairs to Elsie. "I'm going next door!"

"The only question I want you to ask him," Alec said to Tom Tring, "is, 'And then?' I want you to hear his story just as he chooses to tell it. With any luck, we might learn something from comparing it with what he told me in Manchester. I want it word for word, Ernie."

"Don't I always, Chief?" Piper asked, injured.

Alec grinned. "On the whole, unless my wife is present." Ernie Piper was expert at omitting from his notes the bits of Daisy's interventions that were best omitted.

On this occasion, close similarity of wording would suggest Patrick was reciting a tale he had learnt by heart. On the other hand, if minor details varied, odds and ends he'd surely remember if they'd actually happened, the presumption would be that he was making it up and had forgotten exactly what he had said before.

Tom and Ernie went out. Alec turned to the pile of reports on his desk. On top were those compiled during his absence.

Mackinnon had returned from Lincolnshire. According to his official typed report, Mrs. Aidan Jessup appeared to have been kept in ignorance of her husband's and brother-in-law's activities. A paper clip appended a single pencilled sheet: He had not tried to find out from her the whereabouts of her husband because Mrs. Fletcher had assured him that was already known.

Alec crumpled the paper into a ball and chucked it in the wastepaper basket. Mackinnon was getting as good as Ernie Piper at covering up Daisy's meddling.

Tom had talked to Whitcomb, who had returned home from the City at about twenty to seven, by taxi because of the rain. He had seen nothing and no one in the garden. It had been dark and wet and he had not been looking.

No one knew where Lambert was, but his landlady, going into his room to dust (so she claimed), thought he had come back while she was out shopping and taken his razor, toothbrush and hairbrush, and some clothes. Alec was relieved that he had shown signs of life. The man was an incompetent, frequently irritating idiot, but one wouldn't want any harm to come to him, not least because of repercussions from the Americans. Daisy would be glad.

And speaking—or rather, thinking—of the Americans, next in Alec's pile was a lengthy tirade from Superintendent Crane explaining exactly what the U.S. State Department had said to the U.S. embassy had said to the Foreign Secretary had said to the Home Secretary had said to the Assistant Commissioner (Crime). . . . Alec skimmed through it. They were all unhappy.

He sent for a cup of tea.

The last of the new reports was Tom's interview with the Bennetts. They had not changed their story in any material way. They had seen Patrick Jessup, accompanied by—

"Bloody hell!" Alec swore aloud. The constable just entering with his tea slopped it in the saucer. "How could I have forgotten?"

TWENTY-EIGHT

Daisy had done her best to convince the Jessups that, though probably more conversant with police procedure than the average law-abiding citizen, she was not an expert on the subject. Nonetheless, they hung on her words.

She didn't want to give false hope, nor to crush all hope. It was very difficult.

"It's true that the police don't usually ask a person to go to the Yard, or the nearest police station, to answer questions unless they have strong grounds for suspicion," she said. "But sometimes it's just for convenience' sake or to avoid interruptions, or something like that."

"Then it doesn't mean Patrick has been arrested?" Mrs. Jessup asked, hands clasped in supplication.

"No, though it quite often precedes an arrest," Daisy admitted. "But he did move Castellano's body, didn't he? That's an offence, I believe. I don't know if it's a felony or a misdemeanour, but surely it can't be terribly serious." She looked at Irwin, who sat with lips pursed, saying nothing. No help there. "They can hold him for twenty-four hours without charging him, I think."

"If that's all they're asking Patrick about," said Audrey, clinging to her husband, who looked pretty much all in, "does it mean they still might arrest Aidan for killing him? When he's recovered?"

"I really can't—"

"Please, madam . . ." The parlour maid turned pink as everyone looked at her.

"A message from Mr. Patrick?" Mr. Jessup asked eagerly.

"No, sir. It's my sister, sir, from next door. There's a gentleman come to call and Mrs. Dobson—that's Mrs. Fletcher's housekeeper—said Elsie better come over right away 'cause the gentleman's already come by twice when no one's home and he says it's urgent. If you please, madam," she added with a bob towards Daisy.

"Mr. Lambert?" Daisy asked, resigned, and quite glad of an excuse to escape the unhappy Jessups, if only temporarily.

"Yes'm."

"I'd better go, Mrs. Jessup. I'll come back if I can, if you'd like me to."

As she rose, Mr. Jessup followed suit, saying, "We mustn't trespass on your kindness any longer this evening, Mrs. Fletcher. We all greatly appreciate your willingness to give us the benefit of your experience in . . . in such matters."

To a general murmur of thanks, he escorted her to the door of the room. The whole debacle was essentially his fault, Daisy thought. He might have nothing to do with Castellano's death, but he was responsible for the illegal trade with America that had brought his family into the orbit of the bootleggers.

Enid showed her out. In spite of a biting wind, she paused on the Jessups' porch, gazing down across the garden. Where could Castellano's gun be, if a thorough search had not discovered it? Finding it was vital to the Jessup brothers' defence. She had to persuade Alec to search again.

The Greek maiden in the fountain was silhouetted against a light in the Bennetts' front room, a light not obscured by a

curtain. They must be watching through their binoculars, gloating over their neighbours' misfortune.

They couldn't spend all their time spying. What rotten luck that they happened to see Patrick coming home. . . . Patrick and . . . That's what she'd been forgetting! Patrick and a man with his hat pulled down . . .

Oh Lord, she thought, not Lambert!

Had Lambert somehow found out Patrick was on his way home, from a trip involving precisely the business it was *his* business to prevent? Had he accosted him, or simply followed him? Had he recognised Castellano as a bootlegger, even as a thug belonging to the "Luckcheese" gang? Could he have . . . ?

No, Lambert was no more capable of cold-blooded murder than Patrick was, or Aidan. He wouldn't know how to set about it, in the first place, and if he did, he couldn't carry it out effectively. The pathologist had to be mistaken!

Daisy hurried down the Jessups' steps and up her own.

Alec strode into the room, leant with both fists on the desk, and loomed threateningly over Patrick Jessup. "You blazing fool!" he snarled. "Why the devil didn't you tell me there was someone with you?"

Patrick blinked up at him. "What . . . ? Oh, Callaghan. D'you know, I'd almost forgotten about him."

Alec dropped into the chair behind the desk, hastily vacated— without comment—by Tom Tring, who in turn dispossessed Ernie Piper. Ernie leant against the wall and selected a fresh, well-sharpened pencil from his endless supply.

"Callaghan," Alec said sarcastically. "We progress. Why did you not tell me about your friend Callaghan?"

"He's no friend of mine," Patrick protested. Alec just looked at him. He wriggled under that hard, cold gaze. "Actually, there were several reasons." Alec let him wriggle. "Well, he wasn't a

friend, but he looked after me in America. Sort of like a guide, but he called himself my 'protector.' He worked for the man I was dealing with."

"Name?"

"I'm not supposed to . . . Well, all right, he calls himself Frank Costello, but I think he's Italian, not Irish. He's not our customer. He runs the bootlegging for him. Callaghan—Mickie Callaghan, but that may not be his real name—he is Irish, though—he came to England with me. I don't think Michael Callaghan was the name in his passport, actually. Customs took away his gun. I didn't know he'd brought it, or I'd have told him they wouldn't allow it into the country."

In which case, Alec thought, forewarned he'd have taken precautions and smuggled it in. One must thank heaven for small mercies. He waited.

"It didn't seem fair to get him mixed up in our troubles when . . . when Aidan accidentally killed that man."

"Lord preserve me from chivalrous fools!"

Patrick flushed. "Anyway, he skedaddled pretty quick."

"You saw him go?" Alec asked sharply.

"Well, no. But when I looked for him to ask him to help me get Aidan into the house, he wasn't there."

Alec exchanged a glance with Tom, who nodded with a look of enlightenment.

"I was quite glad, as a matter of fact," Patrick went on. "I didn't really want to take him home."

"Not the sort you'd want to introduce to your mother?"

"No. That was another reason for not mentioning him, keeping him out of things altogether."

"And? You had other reasons?"

"Well, once I'd not told you about him, it seemed best not to complicate matters. There didn't seem to be any point, and I thought you probably wouldn't believe me anyway."

"It didn't cross your mind . . . No, why should it? You believed your brother had killed Castellano."

"Accidentally!"

"Accidentally. As it happens, Castellano did not die from the crack on the head. He was murdered, deliberately, probably while he lay unconscious."

"And you think . . . You thought . . . No wonder . . ." Patrick's mouth dropped open as realisation dawned. "Oh Lord, you think Callaghan did it? While I was taking care of Aidan?"

"And then scarpered. You're not off the hook yet, but it seems likely. If you had informed us right away of his existence, we might have had a chance to catch him. Still, however long the odds, we'll have to give it a shot. Let's have all the details."

Elsie had left Lambert standing in the hall, a mark of disapprobation with which Daisy heartily concurred. It was quite the wrong time to drop in without an invitation.

Lambert seemed uncharacteristically pleased with himself, as Daisy could see, because he had hung his hat on the coat tree and his coat collar was for once turned down. Nana fawned adoringly about his ankles, obviously remembering all those wonderful walks she had taken him on.

"Good evening, Mrs. Fletcher. I thought I'd never catch you home."

"Good evening." She hoped he hadn't had his wallet pinched again and come looking for a bed. Then she remembered that he had rescued her from a sticky wicket next door, albeit inadvertently. "Do come in, Mr. Lambert, and tell me what I can do for you."

She led the way to the small sitting room and waved him to a chair. "May I get you a . . . Oh, no, of course, you don't drink. I'll ring for coffee."

"Never mind that." He was too excited to sit down. "I've collared him!" he announced triumphantly, striding back and forth.

Daisy was not too excited to sit down. She slumped into a chair and enquired, "Collared whom?"

He looked at her in surprise. "The murderer, of course."

Daisy sat up. "The murderer?" she asked incredulously. "You mean the man who killed Castellano?"

"The guy in the park out there. That's his name?" His eyes gleamed behind the horn-rimmed glasses. Daisy noticed a bruise on his cheek. "Oh wowee! That's one of the guys I was sent to find. I've seen him about, but I never could discover his name. Oh wowee!"

"Mr. Lambert, you didn't kill him yourself, did you?"

"Gosh, no, Mrs. Fletcher." He gave her a look of reproach. "I wouldn't do a thing like that, not even for the Government. I saw Callaghan strangle him and I've been tailing him ever since. Didn't you wonder where I was the last couple of days?"

"No. Who the blazes is Callaghan?"

"He's a heavy for the Luciano family."

Daisy thought of the Lucchese family. "Is that the same as an enforcer?"

"More or less."

"You *saw* him kill Castellano? Why on earth didn't you come straight to Alec? What do you mean, you 'collared' him?"

Lambert went for the first question first. "I saw Castellano pull a gat and the Jessup guy tackled him—boy, that was some neat tackle—and both of them went down."

"What happened to the gat? The gun?"

"Geeze, I don't know. It flew up in the air, but I didn't see where it landed. Does it matter?"

"Yes, but never mind now. Go on."

"The other two, Callaghan and the guy with him, they knelt down. I didn't know what was going on, and I couldn't properly see what they were doing, so I worked my way around. When I got to where I had a better view, Callaghan had his hands around Castellano's neck. I was trying to figure out what to do, when up he jumped and ran off, so I followed. Geez, Mrs. Fletcher, d'you think I should've stayed?"

"Yes. No. *I* don't know. No, I suppose you did the right thing. Especially if you've really caught him."

"I have!" Lambert sat down at last. "See, I tailed him for two days. He never stopped moving except to get a meal in cheap cafés. I couldn't collar him in public, so—"

"You could have stopped a policeman."

Lambert looked sulky. "These British bobbies, they didn't take me seriously when I got here. I know Mr. Fletcher doesn't have much of an opinion of me. I wanted to show them I could do the job."

Daisy had been brushed off by police officers—American as well as English—often enough to sympathise, to a degree. "Right-oh. But now you've caught him, you should have gone to Scotland Yard. Where is he?"

"And get sent home with a pat on the head and a dime for bus fare? Sure!"

"Where is he?" Daisy repeated.

"He took a room at a hotel in a lousy part of town, the sort of place where you pay up front and they don't ask too many questions. I slipped the porter a pound to give me his room number and I went up there and knocked on the door. I put on a limey accent and I said I was the manager and he'd been overcharged. Told him I had some change for him."

"Brilliant! Who wouldn't open the door for that?"

"I thought it was kind of cute," Lambert said modestly. "We had a bit of a roughhouse. He got in a lick or two." He touched his cheekbone and winced.

"So I see."

"But I floored him and tied him up with an electrical cord and a ripped-up towel. It had a tear in it already," he assured her. "I know I'm not allowed to arrest anyone here, so I locked him in the closet. Wardrobe. I stuck a sign on the door saying 'Do Not Disturb.' I've been back a couple of times to check and tighten the knots, and he was still there, quiet as a mouse. I don't figure he'll be making a lot of noise that might make the hotel people call in the cops."

"Well done!" said Daisy warmly. "And now it's time *we* called in the cops."

Piper answered the knock on the door. There was a murmur of voices; then he turned back. "It's Mrs. Fletcher on the telephone, Chief."

"I said *no* interruptions!"

"Seems it's about the case and it's desp'rately urgent. I bet she's worked out who did it, Chief."

Alec gave in and went to the phone.

"Darling," said Daisy, "you'll never in a million years guess what . . ."

The Jessups' dinner party in honour of Lambert was a small affair. They didn't want to broadcast their troubles to their friends and acquaintances, even now Patrick and Aidan were cleared of all but minor offences. The Fletchers were invited, of course, and, at Daisy's request, Mrs. Jessup kindly included the Pearsons.

"They're frightfully discreet," Daisy promised. "He's a lawyer, after all. As they saw poor Lambert's disastrous arrival, it's only fair that they should witness his triumph."

Over the meal, Patrick, Aidan, and Lambert told their stories. Alec finished up with the extrication of Callaghan from the wardrobe and his arrest.

Madge was thrilled. "What an adventure!" she exclaimed. "What a terrible time you had, Mrs. Jessup, and Audrey."

"I know you don't need to specify motive in court, Fletcher," Tommy Pearson objected, "but what I don't see is why Callaghan killed Castellano. And come to that, why Castellano aimed the gun at Patrick in the first place."

"He didn't, sir," Lambert blurted out. He blushed as everyone looked at him, but he continued gamely, "He was aiming at Callaghan."

"You may remember, Pearson," said Alec, "when Mr. Lambert appeared among us, we were talking about the bootleggers organising themselves into gangs? It would appear to have come to open warfare among them."

"Castellano belonged to the Lucchese family," said Lambert, "and Callaghan to the Luciano mob."

"Castellano was poaching—or attempting to poach—on Luciano territory," Alec explained. To Mr. Jessup, he added, "That's you, sir. Callaghan was actually sent here to rectify the situation—that is, to deal with Castellano. He nearly got potted first, but thanks to Aidan's tackle, he was presented with the opportunity to turn the tables."

"I have a question, too," said Madge. "What happened to the gun?"

"Oh, I forgot," said Daisy. "I think I've guessed—"

"Great Scott, Daisy!" Alec exploded.

"Well, Mr. Lambert says it flew up into the air. No one's been able to find it. Don't you think it might have landed in the fountain's urn?"

Patrick stared at her. "Gosh, Mrs. Fletcher, what a pity I wasn't aiming at it. That would have been the throw of a lifetime!"

Alec said repressively that he'd send a man to check in the morning.

Champagne came out with dessert. At the head of the table, Mr. Jessup rose to propose a toast to Lambert. After an effusive expression of gratitude, he continued: "And I may add that I've come to a decision. Jessup and Sons will no longer be shipping to America. There's just too much risk involved. Mind you, we shan't refuse to deal with any customers who come along, no matter their country of origin, but what they do with their purchases is up to them. So there's another success for you, Mr. Lambert."

He raised his glass and everyone drank to the blushing American.

"Speech!" cried Tommy Pearson.

"Speech!" Patrick seconded him.

"Who, me?" Lambert spluttered.

"Yes, do please say a word, Mr. Lambert," said Mrs. Jessup.

Lambert stood up. His mouth opened, and closed again. Then he leant forward and picked up the unused Champagne glass that Enid had set at his place.

"The heck with seltzer!" he said recklessly. "Pour me Champagne!"